PIMLICO

311

RULES OF THE GAME
BEYOND THE PALE

Nicholas Mosley, born in 1923, is the author of a dozen novels, most recently *Hopeful Monsters* (winner of the 1990 Whitbread Award) and *Children of Darkness and Light*. Films have been made of two of his novels, *Accident* (using a screenplay by Harold Pinter and directed by Joseph Losey) and *Impossible Object*. He has also written non-fiction books on politics and religion, and most recently, his autobiography, *Efforts at Truth*.

Mosley, a major Channel 4 television series, has been based on *Rules of the Game* and *Beyond the Pale*.

RULES OF THE GAME
BEYOND THE PALE

Memoirs of Sir Oswald Mosley and Family

———————

NICHOLAS MOSLEY

PIMLICO

Published by Pimlico 1998

2 4 6 8 10 9 7 5 3 1

First published by Martin Secker & Warburg 1982, 1983
Pimlico edition 1998

Pimlico
Random House, 20 Vauxhall Bridge Road,
London SW1V 2SA

Random House Australia (Pty) Limited
20 Alfred Street, Milsons Point, Sydney,
New South Wales 2061, Australia

Random House New Zealand Limited
18 Poland Road, Glenfield,
Auckland 10, New Zealand

Random House South Africa (Pty) Limited
Endulini, 5A Jubilee Road, Parktown 2193, South Africa

Random House UK Limited Reg. No. 954009

A CIP catalogue record for this book
is available from the British Library

ISBN 0 7126 6536 6

Papers used by Random House UK Limited are natural,
recyclable products made from wood grown in sustainable forests.
The manufacturing processes conform to the environmental
regulations of the country of origin

Printed and bound in Great Britain by
Mackays of Chatham PLC

Contents

VOLUME TWO: *Beyond the Pale*

Preface

The two volumes of these memoirs were originally published separately with an interval of a year. There is thus some slight overlapping in the present one-volume edition, unavoidable if threads in the story are not to have loose ends.

On page 432 I say 'The story behind my father's detention in May 1940 and his imprisonment for the next three and a half years has remained obscure because of the refusal of the authorities to release their papers about it'. Since this was written (1983) some of the relevant papers have been released, but in them there has been nothing that does not support and even confirm conjectures I made in this part of the book.—N.M., 1994

Foreword

On May 11th 1979 a remark was reported in the *New Statesman* that my father, Oswald Mosley, 'must be the only Englishman today who is beyond the pale'. This statement was made about a man of eighty-two who had not been active in politics for thirteen years: who when he had been active – a period of world-wide violence and crime – had been convicted of no offence (he had been acquitted of one charge of assault and one of riotous assembly) and whose policies had for the most part been ignored and had come to nothing. The remark seemed ridiculous but in one sense apt – as being representative of what undoubtedly were many people's feelings about him. The phrase 'beyond the pale' gives an impression of something taboo: of a person not just whose attitudes had once been strongly disagreed with (he had been leader of the British Union of Fascists in the 1930s) but in contact with whom even now there might be danger. The commentator in the *New Statesman* continued – 'Nobody would flinch if you'd come back from Moscow and said you'd lunched with Kim Philby'. This implied that the news that someone had lunched with Oswald Mosley, in contrast to the news that one had met a notorious traitor, might cause almost physical alarm.

My purpose in writing this book is not to provide a biography of my father nor to give a comprehensive account of his politics: these tasks have been done admirably by his biographer Robert Skidelsky. I have tried to write a personal story of him and of my efforts to understand him: his child had to make these efforts to make sense of himself. The story might be of interest to others because in so far as it is true that there was something akin to a taboo about my father, then an understanding of this might give an insight into the nature of human beings and society.

My father was adored and hated, respected and feared, pitied and reviled. But both those who abominated him from a distance and those who were charmed by his presence (most people were) had the impression of something awesome about him that could not quite be put into words. It was as if he were a Greek tragic hero to whom disaster had occurred (or which he had caused to occur) which had set him apart: the power of the taboo in this tradition resides in the paradoxical impression that the disaster both is, and is not, the person's fault. The history of the twentieth century has revolved around men who through overweening pride and force of circumstance have felt themselves set apart: who have both ridden on, and felt themselves driven by, the slavish adorations and hatreds that others have felt towards them.

It is difficult for an academic biographer or a political historian to write about such paradoxes: it is their tradition to deal with what is seen as a world of facts. It has been the job of dramatists and novelists, traditionally, to try to relate facts to what might be seen as patterns and recurring predicaments of mind: to try to write of human experience as if what human beings were was not separate from it.

I myself am by vocation a novelist. My father did not read novels: he thought it was the task of an individual to try to order reasonably the world of facts. But his relationship with me, his eldest son, was often paradoxical. From my side at least there was loyalty and some hostility, anger and bewilderment, nearly always love. Towards the end of his life he left me out of his will on the grounds that I was 'not his sort of person': yet the very last time I saw him, ten days before his death, he announced that he wanted me to inherit all his papers. I had told him that I hoped to write this book. It was as if when death approached he did not retract anything he felt about power (money, to him, was a form of power) but he knew as part of him had always known that if anything was to survive of what he had cared about it would be to do with efforts at truth.

VOLUME ONE

Rules of the Game / 1896-1933

CHAPTER 1

Tom

My father Oswald Mosley was born on November 16th 1896; he was in line to be the heir to a Staffordshire baronetcy and estate. His mother, Maud Mosley, had three sons in quick succession and then she left her husband – on account (this was the family legend) of his insatiable and promiscuous sexual habits. Maud Mosley was a woman of piety and rectitude; she moved to Shropshire to be near her own family. There, without the sort of money she might have expected, she brought up her three sons of whom her favourite was the eldest Oswald. She called him her 'man-child': he became the man-about-the-house. He wrote years later of how he had always been 'passionately devoted' to his mother: how even as a child he had repaid her devotion to him by 'gratuitous advice and virile assertion on every subject under the sun'. Apart from members of her family there were no further male influences in her life, he said, 'other than an occasional preacher of exceptional gifts'.

The chief male influence in Oswald's early life was his paternal grandfather, also called Oswald: he too had quarrelled with his son and did not see much of him. There was thus an alliance between the grandfather and the grandson Oswald, and the latter's childhood alternated between his mother's comparatively small house in Shropshire and the stateliness of his grandfather's house Rolleston Hall in Staffordshire. Grandfather Oswald was an imposing, paternalistic figure nicknamed John Bull: he too, like his son, lived apart from his wife. Rolleston Hall was a Victorian mansion with a full complement of grooms, gardeners, coachmen, indoor servants and so on. Life in both Shropshire and Staffordshire revolved mainly around horses and dogs, as it was apt to do in upper-class county families. There was hunting, steeplechasing, shooting and fishing. It was held to be much easier in those days, my father wrote later, to show emotions towards animals than to human beings.

The exception to this in some ways seemed to be his father, the ne'er-do-well, also called Oswald. This Oswald was a rake, a gambler; one of his bets had been to do with a game of golf down Pall Mall; another with shooting out all the street lights in Piccadilly with a pistol from a hansom cab. He had for a time set himself up in an inn in a village next to Rolleston in opposition to his father: there he had entertained women: it was said he was trying to emulate one of his ancestors who had been known as The Tutbury Tup (Tutbury was the name of the village; 'tup' the local name for a ram). Another story was that the last straw that drove his wife Maud to leave him was not just the sum of his infidelities, but her finding a bundle of letters to his mistresses which showed that he was saying just the same things to them, and even giving them the same presents, as he was to her.

What grandfather Oswald objected to was not so much the fact of his son's relationships with women but that these should be flaunted publicly. Grandfather Oswald was not averse to 'recompense' (his grandson wrote) so long as it was conducted 'with the utmost discretion and dignity'. However there was a tradition amongst the three Oswalds – grandfather, father and son – that their quarrels should be aired publicly. Each father challenged his son to a boxing match in front of assembled servants: grandfather Oswald once fought his son with one of his (the grandfather's) hands tied behind his back: the son was knocked out. Years later this Oswald, the rake, challenged his son, my father, to a match: he was again apparently on the point of being knocked out when the bout ended. This Oswald (his son wrote) had on the mantelpiece of his bachelor apartment a contemporary drawing of an ample lady in a very tight skirt with a monocled dandy walking behind her: it bore the caption 'Life is just one damned thing after another'.

My father used to claim that he had made a study of psychoanalysis in later life and had decided that the violent complexities of his childhood had had no effect on him whatever. He would explain – the healthy psyche can throw off an injury which in the weak becomes a complex. But also – 'It is possible to go even further, and to say that additional strength can come from an early injury'. This assertion seems somewhat to contradict the former: also, additional strength can take the form of numbness or armour plating.

There was a story my father told in his autobiography of how his mother had been hurled out of a pony-cart which was being driven recklessly by his father just before the birth of one of his brothers: from her diaries, however, it appears that the child about to be born was himself.

His mother kept a daily diary from the time of her marriage for over fifty years. When she died she left these to her youngest son; whom my father persuaded to hand them over, and then he burned them – all except those to do with the first four years of his life, and one of a slightly later date which survived half scorched. My father also tore out, and preserved, the entry for the day of his mother's birthday (January 2nd) from each of the diaries that he burned. But what was it that he wanted to eliminate by this *auto-da-fé*?

In his autobiography my father wrote movingly of his childhood: of the orderliness, the hierarchical but somehow classless patterns of life in his mother's house and in the semi-feudal grandeur of the estate at Rolleston. His grandfather ran a champion herd of shorthorn cattle: he was a passionate advocate and producer of unadulterated wholemeal bread. In the pursuance of good stockbreeding and correct land-management everyone on the estate seemed to work willingly and to accept his allotted place: there were few incitements and few opportunities to change. All his life my father retained a love of the English countryside and of its seasonal pursuits. But there were also things in him that seemed to rage against this tradition, and to demand change.

What he did not remember perhaps or indeed tried to cauterise memories of in the burning of his mother's diaries was that running parallel to the orderliness of country life was also a tendency ferocious and dismal which haunted people with too many servants and not enough to do: there were the quarrels, the separations, the lawsuits, the punch-ups; much of the emotions seemed to be taken out on horses as things to spur on or be spurred by. But even in the pages that remain of his mother's diaries before he was four she tells of an instance of my father being bullied by his father: 'Had a miserable time W teasing Tom and I trying to defend him; and finally W caught hold of my wrist hurting it badly'. (W is for 'Waldie' – the name by which the middle Oswald was known: and Tom is the name by which my father, the youngest Oswald, was known and will be known here).

And then in the diary that survived the flames, Tom's mother wrote of a fortnight's visit that he and his younger brother Ted had to pay to their father: the year was 1909; Tom was twelve and Ted nine.

During their stay their father repeatedly urged them to kiss the Parlourmaid (before her) and the Cook. He went into the children's bedroom with nothing on but a nightshirt and talked to the P.maid who was there calling them. Told Tommy how he had a box at the Gaiety each night for a month and took the actresses out to supper and he would do the same . . . they would go to the Metropolitan and sit in the front and yell the choruses. Had rats down from London in a box (3 doz) and let the dogs worry them. No bath, hat on in house, altogether low.

Compared to this, life in Tom's mother's house must indeed have seemed lofty: nothing much seemed to happen to her other than tea-parties, shopping, going to church, and bad weather. Tom in the holidays hunted and went ferreting. But perhaps the very lack of impositions of such a life – and freedom for the most part from his father – gave him confidence. From his young boys' school in Shropshire he wrote to his mother in the only surviving letter of his childhood – 'We had a preliminary debate last night, and I made a speech which came off tremendously'.

He was sent to a preparatory boarding school at the age of nine, and to his public school, Winchester, at the age of twelve. He hated both schools unashamedly and with an intensity that went on into old age. He made few friends: he wrote in his autobiography – 'the dreary waste of public school existence was only relieved by learning and homo-sexuality; at that time I had no capacity for the former and I never had any taste for the latter'. His escape was into the gymnasium where he became a boxer and a prize-winning fencer. He won the public schools championships in both foil and sabre at the age of fifteen: both the double victory and the early age were records. His mentors at Winchester were his boxing and fencing instructors Sergeant Major Adam and Sergeant Ryan: he wrote about these in later years with something like love.

At home he had been able to go his own way: at school, he was forced to be a subordinate member of a group. His dislike of this situation, and his determination to be trapped within it for as short a time as possible, seemed to stay with him for the rest of his life. He persuaded his family to let him leave Winchester when he was just seventeen: he went to Sandhurst to train to be a regular soldier.

At Sandhurst he had to submit to strict and almost brutal discipline while on duty and on the parade ground; but there was toleration of quite anarchic behaviour out of hours. What the cadets liked to do in the evenings was to pile into cars (this was 1913) and go up to London and there provoke fights with the chuckers-out at places like the Empire

Music Hall (might Tom have bumped into his father?): the point of
these expeditions were the fights, more than the pursuit of women.
Then when the cadets arrived back at the barracks somewhat battered
and drunk they would be helped to bed as if by nannies by the same
sergeants who, the next day, would revile them for any indecorum on
the parade ground. My father used to call this 'the corinthian tradition':
and it seemed to represent, as if in some echo from childhood, a
condition by which group-life might be possible for him. He described
how on his arrival at Sandhurst he had noticed 'some fifty to a hundred
boys who seemed to me particularly objectionable' and these later
became his friends. Team spirit was made palatable so long as there was
at the back of it the chance of swashbuckling, or revolt.

The gangs of toughs, however, were apt to fight amongst themselves.
In one dispute about a polo pony there were insults, threats of horse-
whippings, violence; and in the subsequent fracas my father, while
attempting to evade pursuers, fell from the ledge of an upstairs window
and injured his leg. The details of this story are confused: such goings-
on were common at Sandhurst: what is indubitable is that my father
accepted even if he did not originally provoke a fight, which for a
time he seemed to be winning, and then he ended up a victim.

By the time the war came in August 1914 he had recovered from his
injury and he was commissioned into a smart cavalry regiment, the 16th
Lancers. He spent some time in Ireland and then, because there did not
seem to be much chance of the cavalry being used in the war, he
volunteered to join the newly formed Royal Flying Corps who were in
need of observers. These did not need much training. Like many young
men at the time he was afraid that the war might be over by Christmas
and that he would have missed it. By Christmas he was in fact in France
flying in one of the flimsy aeroplanes that were used mainly for purposes
of observation. He and his pilot were shot at from the ground and they
could not retaliate; though pilots and observers occasionally shot
at enemy planes with rifles and pistols. There were not more than about
sixty men in the RFC actually flying at the time; this was war in an élitist
tradition even more than it might have been with the cavalry. In Tom's
words he and his fellow airmen were 'like men having dinner together
in a country-house-party knowing that some must soon leave for ever;
in the end, nearly all'. They were heroes: but, suspended in the air in
their flimsy machines, very much in the tradition of being in some sense
sacrificial. There was a song popular among the men of the RFC at the
time which was called *The Dying Aviator*, in which there was described,
with the lugubrious humour that the English traditionally make use of

in times of stress, how a crashed airman's mutilated body had become inextricably intermingled with parts of his machine. ·

One incident in the war which stayed in Tom's mind came during the second battle of Ypres in April 1915 when he had been detailed to take a message by car from the RFC to some Canadians in the front line; he had stayed drinking with the Canadians longer than had been intended; he had to make his way back on foot. Then he saw, from the vantage point of a hill, massed German infantry regiments moving with parade-ground precision to the attack – to what might be either success or annihilation by machine-gun fire. He seems to have been half enthralled, half repelled, by this spectacle. He wondered about such dedication: was it necessary for it to be involved with such a prospect of death?

In the spring of 1915 he went to train for his pilot's certificate at Shoreham in Sussex. He wrote in his autobiography 'My flying was not bad though I was weak on the mechanical side ... my argument was that once in the air you could do nothing about it if anything went wrong, and on the ground the machine was looked after by our friends the mechanics and riggers'. This attitude was a forerunner of his attitudes in later life – his belief that mundane day-to-day jobs could safely be left to what he called 'professionals'.

He got his pilot's certificate. But soon after, when he was being watched from the ground by his admiring mother who had come specially to see him, he decided to show off, did not notice that the wind had changed, came in too fast to land; then – 'the machine hit the ground with a bang and was thrown high into the air'. Still flying, he realised that the plane's undercarriage was damaged: he had to circle and make a pancake landing which involved stalling just above the ground. He managed to do this, but from too great a height: the floor of the cockpit was driven up against his legs. The leg which he had injured a year ago was crushed again but this time more severely. Once more, what had begun as an act of bravado had ended with his being a victim.

His leg was patched up. Then he was called back to his cavalry regiment who were now fighting as infantry and needed their officers. During the winter of 1915–16 he was on and off in the trenches or marching to and fro; much of the time he was in deep mud and water. The bones of his leg had not properly healed: they became infected: he was sent home, and there was talk of his leg having to be amputated. He persuaded the surgeon to try to save it; and this the surgeon did, replacing the infected parts with other bits of bone from the leg. Tom finished his active service in the war with his right leg an inch and a half shorter than the other.

There is something unfulfilled about Tom in the war: this is one of the areas his mother's diaries might have shed light on. He had flown bravely in the RFC: but it is evident that when in the trenches he was involved in no attack, and it seems unlikely that he had to undergo a large-scale enemy attack or he would have mentioned this. In his auto-biography he tells as one of the highlights of his time in the front line a story of how when an attack was expected his colonel came round and told the junior officers that they would be recommended for the Military Cross if they held their ground: then the attack did not materialise. The way Tom told such a story (it would seem to have been unusual for a commanding officer to have held out the bait of an MC to anyone for doing something so ordinary as resisting an attack) suggests that he wanted to establish as much as possible that he had been close to direct fighting. He certainly suffered under bombardments: he endured the nerve-breaking business of tunnelling for the placing of mines. But having set out with courage to be something of a hero, he found that he was to survive the war through a series of misfortunes.

The war's last two years he spent working in London in the Ministry of Munitions and in the Foreign Office. He read a lot, and entered into what used to be called London society. This was for him a time of transformation. He himself described how before this he had been intellectually dim: he had loved boxing, fencing, and horses. He had also been much on his own and usually at odds with the people around him. Now, having done his duty, and as a wounded soldier returned from war, he made up for lost opportunities. He read 'voraciously' – about history and politics; often, the speeches of famous politicians in history. He wanted to train himself for what he wanted to become. He thought of going to a university; but it seemed to him that other require-ments were more pressing.

The war had affected him deeply: he was appalled by human stupidity – by what seemed to be the wilful waste of human life and resources. He had also observed, and tried to emulate himself, a sort of dashingness which seemed to surmount the waste: which might be a way to prevent it, if only it could be harnessed to reason instead of to destruction. He determined himself to try to do this.

It was during these years at the end of the war that he first got his reputation as a seducer of women. Up till now he had wanted to be a hero among men: but in London during 1917 and 1918 it would have been difficult to avoid the challenges, and opportunities, provided by women. Women like wounded soldiers – who can be mothered, as well as admired. And Tom must have felt himself ready to try a new form of conquest. He was taken up, at first, by somewhat older married women: it was the convention of course in the society in which he moved that young men should have affairs only with married women: unmarried girls were to be worshipped from afar. Tom became a lover of Margaret Montagu, who was a hostess in Leicestershire; of Catherine D'Erlanger, of Maxine Elliott, who entertained on the outskirts of London. Through the latter he met for the first time eminent politicians – Lloyd George, Winston Churchill, F. E. Smith. His successes with women gave him confidence with older men: confidence with politicians of course added to his successes with women. It cannot be known what sparked the whole process off: there was something sudden about his reputation for brilliance and wit. When, years later, people used to ask him how it was that someone like himself had emerged from such a family background he would say – as if it were a quotation and poking fun at himself – 'when fire meets oil, then springs the spark divine' – fire being his father and oil his mother – and then he would laugh; especially if this was said in the presence of his mother.

The older politicians whom Tom met and liked at this time he admired for their toughness, their cleverness: it is unlikely he much admired them for their politics. They, having won the war, seemed to be not so much resting on their laurels as selling off bits of them to bidders. There was little will amongst older politicians to re-order the world with burning enthusiasm and in the light of reason. The old political games went on in the old way played by the 'hard-faced men who had done well out of the war'. The difference between Tom and other idealists of his generation was that he, in addition to his idealism, felt that he had the skill to take on the older generation at their own machinations.

The reputation for brilliance he had won in social and political salons meant that he was soon approached by Conservative and Liberal whips to see if he would stand for Parliament: both parties wanted young candidates who might seem some leaven to the hard-faced lump. Tom was asked if he would stand as a Conservative for the Stone division of Staffordshire; also for the Harrow division of Middlesex. He chose the latter, ostensibly on the grounds that he did not want to seem to be taking advantage of family connections, but also because thus it would be easier to maintain his social connections in London. He made it plain he did not care about political party labels; he was going into Parliament to represent the war generation – or himself.

The war ended on November 11th 1918; a general election was set
for December 14th. Tom's election manifesto set the tone for much of
the rest of his political life. What he undertook to fight for were – high
wages, nationalisation of transport and of electricity, ex-soldiers to be
offered smallholdings, grants for housing and educational scholarships
to be provided by the state, fiscal protection for home industries and
trade with the colonies, prevention of immigration by undesirable
aliens, and the promotion by all possible means of the strength and
prestige of the British Empire. These were fine words: he was no
different from other politicans in not elucidating how they were to be
implemented.

Tom was officially the candidate of the coalition government: his
opponent, Mr Chamberlayne, a sixty-five year old solicitor, was standing as an Independent. Tom joked – 'An Independent is someone on
whom no one can depend.' Mr Chamberlayne attacked his opponent
for his youth, his wealth, and what he said was his inflated war record.
Tom won the argument about this (the dispute had been about the date
of his commission): and retaliated by saying he would not follow 'into
the political gutter' such 'aborigines of the political world'. He was not
yet good at making set speeches; but he had from the beginning a talent
for fighting back; for vituperation. He was duly elected the member for
Harrow with a majority of 10,000. He became the youngest MP. He
was just twenty two.

His successes had been sudden and startling but his talents were still
those of the individual fighter; on unaccustomed ground he could be
awkward and shy: he still had little aptitude for the business of working
in a group. One cause he did take up was the promotion of the
embryonic League of Nations. But a contemporary remembered him
in his early days in the House of Commons as being 'a lonely, detached
figure wandering unhappily about the lobbies of the House, uncertain
of his mind'. The war, he would say, had planted the seeds of doubt;
parties were changing, new political creeds running molten from the
crucible of old faiths; and he did not know which way to make his own.

He had got into Parliament by his individual skills: it perhaps seemed
to him that he would not make his way far in Parliament unless he could
find some sort of status, some vantage-point, which would balance his
solitariness and haughtiness and enable him to work with other people
or from which to impose on them his personality. He needed to turn
people's view of him from that of a somewhat louring if elegant lone-
wolf into someone more approachable. He needed, in fact, something
personal. He was very good looking. He was practised at love.

At the end of 1919 he went down to Plymouth to help Nancy Astor in the by-election in which she was campaigning to become the first woman MP. There he met a fellow helper, a girl whom he had come across once or twice during the last year. She was Cynthia, second daughter of Earl Curzon of Kedleston, the Foreign Secretary in Lloyd George's coalition government. He fell in love with Cynthia: he had not fallen in love before. He asked her to marry him. At first she refused. She had, it seemed, heard something of his reputation. He pursued her with letters. He tried to make legible his strange, angular handwriting.

My mother Cynthia was always known as Cim or Cimmie, just as my father was known as Tom.

> Betton House
> Market Drayton
> Shropshire

Cim darling.

Do not forget dinner Tuesday 7 pm. Really that is only an excuse to write to you – and I do so hate writing letters! I could write such wonderful letters if I could only dictate them like a speech or a newspaper article; but with a hand like this how can any sentiment or expression be other than ridiculous. An authority on these matters told me once that my writing could only mean genius or lunacy: in my youthful arrogance I welcomed the former conclusion, but since the present obsession I am driven to believe that the latter alternative is true. Not very complimentary to you! but a consuming disease of this intensity can be nothing short of lunacy. I remember Disraeli said somewhere that it was better to doubt of the creed in which you have been nurtured than of the personal powers on which you have staked your life. I now so agree with him. I have always believed, and so far found it to be true, that the will of men could conquer all emotion or pain whether spiritual or physical and mould the world to be just a reflection of its own personality. And now I have discovered an emotion, or is it a disease of the mind, which is more powerful than even the human spirit. What nonsense I write!

I have come down here after a strenuous League of Nations trip; staying alone with my mother until Monday, return London *mutatis mutandis*. A good meeting on Friday at Leamington. I became embroiled with some Roman Catholic priests – Canon Berry and others – who are opposing the League. Sir Ernest Pollock's ministerial dismay at the prospects of a brawl between the clericals and myself

in his constituency was very comic! However after a slightly acri-
monious debate we got a nearly unanimous resolution in the League's
favour. They have now asked me to take over the League of Nations
campaign throughout the country as the chairman of Campaign
Committee at Headquarters. It entails several hours of work a day at
their London office in addition to everything else, but I think I must
do it as it is in the greatest of all causes, and really the more I am
smothered in work the better.

I have thought so much of things down here in the lull after the
storm. As you too have heard of these dead things from my short but
weary past – as it now appears to me – I wonder whether you set out
in some strange idea of avenging anything your sex has suffered from
me? If so I must congratulate you, for few mortals have attained so
complete a measure of success in even their most facile aspirations! I
do not believe it to be true; for – worst of all – I think you were not
even sufficiently interested for that! I would surrender the present
with the ages to come and those past, just once to make you cry as
I have made others cry; and then instead of leaving as I have always
left tears, to kiss those tears away. Whatever you feel for me whether
nothing or everything will never affect my love for you. I do want
to marry you and always shall: but until you also feel as I do, if indeed
you ever do, I am so happy just to be with you in a way I never
thought possible between men and women. I shall have been a whole
week on Tuesday without seeing you and I do want to be with you
so often and will not make love to you (yet awhile!)

Tom

CHAPTER 2

Cimmie

Cynthia or Cimmie Curzon was from a background odder than Tom's, and was thought by her friends to be herself unconventional.

Her father George Curzon was the eldest son of an aristocratic Derbyshire family, the Scarsdales, who had been from time to time on visiting terms with the Mosleys. George Curzon had emerged from an upbringing by neglectful parents and a sadistic nanny, had flourished at Eton and Balliol, had travelled across Persia on horseback, had been a founder member of the social élite called The Souls, had entered Parliament at the age of twenty seven, and had seemed set for a remarkable political career. His only hindrance was that as heir to a not very rich estate and with his father Viscount Scarsdale still alive, he did not have much money.

Cimmie's mother was Mary Leiter, the daughter of Levi Zebidee Leiter, a Chicago millionaire. It would seem from the names that the Leiters were Jewish; but apparently in origins they were Mennonites, an obscure protestant sect in Switzerland. The Leiters had emigrated to America in the eighteenth century. Levi Leiter made his fortune in Chicago real estate in the 1860s: then, at the insistence of his wife, he moved to Washington, in order that the family might exercise its fortune at one of the centres of American social life. That the Leiters successfully managed to do this was largely due to the charms of the eldest daughter Mary. Before her eighteenth birthday she was being hailed as the belle of innumerable balls, and was on socially intimate terms with members of the political and literary intelligentsia. Having 'conquered' Washington and New York (girls in the 1880s were talked about in those terms) she moved on, with her mother, to Paris and London. There, in 1890, she met George Curzon.

George proposed marriage in 1893: Mary accepted: they professed undying love. George said he wanted to keep the engagement secret in order to consolidate his political career by travelling in India and Afghanistan: they were with each other for only two days in the next two years. When they were finally married in 1895 Levi Leiter settled £140,000 on his daughter and an additional income of £6,000 a year. George had hoped for £9,000 but had 'no doubt that we can perfectly well get on with less'. There is a legend in the Leiter family that on the eve of the wedding George asked for more money from Levi Leiter. Whatever the truth of this, there seems to have been little liking between the two families.

The couple settled in England in London and then at Reigate Priory in Surrey. George was appointed Under Secretary of State at the Foreign Office. Mary was unhappy; after the social successes of her youth she now found herself often alone. George's old friends seemed to ignore her: perhaps she did not want to play the game by which English upper-class married women made themselves sexually available. George was much of the time in London.

George's family was not much help. When visiting Kedleston, the Scarsdale home in Derbyshire, Mary noted that George's father was:

> very fond of examining his tongue in a mirror. When he sits reading or writing he makes the most fiendish grimaces. He sleeps with his feet 2ft higher than his head with no blanket over him in the midst of winter, he has 18 thermometers in his sitting room and the tables are covered with magazines and railway almanacs of 1839.

A first child, Irene, was born in 1896. By the time my mother Cimmie was born on August 23rd 1898 things were looking better. George had just been appointed Viceroy of India at the extraordinarily young age of thirty nine. Mary (she wrote to her mother) was about to fill 'the greatest place ever held by an American abroad'. There were interviews with Queen Victoria: enormous expenditures on clothes and jewels. It was accepted that Viceroys had to find huge sums out of their own fortunes. Mary asked her father for more money. But all this happened just at the time when Mary's brother Joe Leiter, in Chicago, had attempted to 'corner the wheat market', which meant borrowing huge sums of money to buy up, literally, all the wheat in America with a view to pushing the price up before selling. In the end he had been outwitted by a rival who imported wheat from Canada across the frozen Great Lakes by means of ice-breakers: so now Joe was in debt to the extent of nine million dollars. There was a conflict of interests – and indeed of styles – within the family, that came to a crisis now and lasted for generations. Joe Leiter, Levi's only son, was an outlandish character: once when there was a strike at one of his coal mines he hired an armoured train with machine guns on it to carry blackleg labour through the pickets; in the last coach was a travelling brothel.

Levi Leiter managed to raise two million dollars for his son, and another million for his daughter. The Curzons departed in state for India.

A nanny and a wet-nurse had been engaged for the new baby Cimmie: George Curzon had insisted on interviewing the applicants himself. The wet-nurse was sick most of the way across the Bay of Biscay.

Children have imprinted on them patterns they observe from their parents: George and Mary's relationship was enigmatic. They were often professing their love; yet in fact they seem to have been curiously removed from one another. The most telling description of George Curzon has been given by Elinor Glyn, who became his mistress for a number of years after Mary's death. Much of this description might also have applied to Tom at the time he met Cimmie.

> He has always been loved by women, but he has never allowed any individual woman to have the slightest influence on his life . . . He likes their society for entirely leisure moments . . . He likes them in the spirit in which other men like fine horses or good wine . . . They are on a different plane altogether.
>
> He is the most passionate physical lover, but so fastidious that no woman of the lower classes had ever been able to attract him. Since his habit is never to study the real woman, but only to accept the superficial presentation of herself which she wishes him to receive, he is naturally attracted to Americans.
>
> He never gives a woman a single command, and yet each one must be perfectly conscious that she must obey his slighest inclinations. He rules entirely: and when a woman belongs to him he seems to prefer to give her even the raiment which touches her skin, and in every tangible way show absolute possession, while in words avoiding all suggestion of ownership, all ties, all obligations, upon either side. It is extremely curious.

When the Curzons arrived in India they found themselves in a world in which they were almost always on show, almost always surrounded by obsequiousness, almost totally dependent on each other for companionship. They were like royalty but even more solitary, not being members of what are usually large royal families. Mary wrote to her mother that she felt as if she were on a stage; she did not seem to mind this, perhaps because in recent years she had been neglected. George, as was his custom, threw himself into work: he became obsessed with details: he did not delegate responsibility. Mary was still, except when acting like a queen, very much on her own. She and George showed their devotion to each other by writing passionate but hurried notes from opposite ends of Government House. The children were in the hands of nannies, nurserymaids, wet nurses. My aunt Irene remembered of the time when she was three or four:

> we used to drive in a landau with three nurses, two red-liveried men on the box, and two standing up behind. When we were out in the morning in our rickshaws there was an army of attendants including the Viceroy's policeman who usually carried one or two of our broken dolls . . .
>
> According to my mother I was a very hard child to handle, whereas Cynthia was a saint. I was often naughty to 'saintly Cim': I kicked her savagely one day and this ended in a fight. I recall my father smacking me and locking me in the bathroom.

There is a mystery about the reign of the Curzons in India. They were in most ways immensely successful: George Curzon pushed most of his administrative reforms through: he embarked on a programme for the restoration of historical monuments which makes him still (1982) the best-loved viceroy in Indian memory. He was not always popular amongst his compatriots: when two Indian servants were murdered by some drunken 9th Lancers and the regiment found itself unable to find the culprits, he stopped the leave of the entire regiment, and for this was booed by the fashionable crowd on Calcutta racecourse. But Mary was always popular in her role of Vicereine; she backed up her husband and made people warm towards him; and his practical achievements were undeniable.

Then after seven years, half way through a second term of office which against precedent had been given to him, George Curzon began to antagonise everyone around him. He wrote letters home which infuriated even his oldest friends in government; at work, he became increasingly intransigent and appeared to be heading for some sort of breakdown. The point at issue was an important technicality of army administration – about how far the army should remain under the direct orders of the Viceroy. George Curzon was probably correct in his insistence that it should; but his methods of attacking head-on the commander-in-chief, Kitchener, resulted in his own defeat. He resigned; and came home to some sort of ostracism at the hands of his old friends.

Mary found herself in an odd position in all this: as was her custom she manoeuvred ostensibly in support of her husband; but in doing so she seems to have carried on a more or less serious social flirtation with two of his arch enemies – Balfour, the Prime Minister in 1905, and Kitchener himself. She herself became ill: she wrote 'the bell will go, and India will kill me as one of the humble inconsequent lives that go into the foundations of all great works': and it did become the legend that the Indian climate killed her. But in fact she had flourished in India; and she had been for the first time seriously ill when she was on leave in England in 1904. George had then wanted her to remain in England, but she had insisted on rejoining him in India, and there she had again flourished while he had begun to crack up. Then after he had resigned and they were back in England she took to her bed again; and while she and George were once more writing love-notes to each other from the opposite ends of a not-so-enormous house, half way through 1906 and without much explicit cause, she died. The newspapers called it a heart-attack. She was only thirty four. In her last note delivered to her husband by a footman she had apologised for her 'devilish ills' and had said that she feared she was going out of her mind: George had replied that 'nothing else matters except to make my darling well again'; but then he had gone 'crying to bed' without seeing her. As she was dying he had sat beside her and had made notes of the tragedy. Then he set about constructing an elaborate monument to her in the church at Kedleston.

Cimmie was seven when her mother died. George Curzon and his three young daughters (a third, Alexandra, had been born in 1904) settled in their large and now somewhat lifeless houses at 1 Carlton House Terrace in London, and Hackwood Park in Hampshire. These houses were paid for largely by Leiter money which was now in trust to the children – Levi Leiter had died in 1904 and this had been one of the terms of his will – but George Curzon had the use of the income.

Life for the children continued to circulate around nannies, nursery-maids, other servants, horses and dogs. They saw their father at weekends when they would help him with the tasks that he still insisted on performing himself around the house – holding the ladder for him while he hung pictures; carrying a basket of old bread with which he rubbed out finger-marks on doors. He continued to interview the children's maids and governesses, questioning them during meals on obscure historical subjects and then appearing appalled when they did not know the answers. He would also turn this sort of teasing against himself: many of the pompous sayings for which he later became notorious ('I didn't know the lower classes had such white skins' when he saw soldiers bathing) were acted out partly as a parody of himself, by which it seems he felt he might protect himself.

As time went on his old friends returned and there were Saturday to Monday parties at Hackwood at which once again were played the games of The Souls that were erudite and childish – charades, clumps; paper-games in which it was required that one wrote verses in a certain style, or composed witty telegrams from given initial letters. The children were brought up on the edge of all this: there were the more straightforward games they themselves played with their father: he would describe a historical scene to them and they had to recognise what it was; there was one particularly lugubrious game which consisted of just writing down the names of all the famous people one could think of beginning with a certain letter.

At the outbreak of war in 1914 Cimmie was nearly sixteen. The Belgian Royal Family came to stay at Hackwood as refugees: Cimmie corresponded with the young prince Leopold in a schoolroom code fashionable at the time. She corresponded with young men at the front, and during the next four years they replied to her in hundreds of letters in the tiny, meticulously pencilled scrawls on lined or squared paper that are the memorials of men hunched up in mud or dug-outs. These letters are brave, flirtatious, cheerful, correct: they give off the smell as it were of huge and terrible events and yet say almost nothing. Cimmie had four or five correspondents who seem to have been servants at Hackwood or Carlton House Terrace: there is some sort of straightforwardness about their letters that is missing from the usual upper-class style: 'I think it would take all my strength to bear another winter': also – 'I have never been so happy as I have been during this war: I sometimes think it may be because I at last find that I am of some use in the world. If it were possible to make a wish and have that wish granted, I should just wish for health and strength to continue the fight and to become a billet for the last bullet fired, don't you think that would be a glorious end?'

These men sent her presents ('It is a genuine Sennussi earings and necklace presented to me by one of those ladies in return for a small kindness I was able to render') and she sent to them cigarettes, cakes, clothes, a mouth-organ. Like most young girls (and indeed almost everyone at the time) she found it difficult to get a hold in her mind of what was going on: people wrote so passively and laconically about horror: no one seemed much interested in stopping it. Cimmie kept a diary on and off during the war: much of it was concerned with the trivia of everyday life. She was still having trouble from the naggings of her sister Irene; she was ashamed of not being more 'constructive' herself. She made her good resolutions: but she felt there was little use in these unless there was:

> a Big Solemn Comprehensive idea that holds you and me and all the world together in one great grand universal scheme . . . Religion is the perpetual discovery of that Great Thing Out There . . . Marriage has got to be a religious marriage or else it is a splitting up of life; religion and love are most of life, and all the power there is in it; therefore they can't afford to be harnessed in different directions . . . I love people loving me more than anything in the world. I am going to try to make people love me more. No one knows how it hurts when someone I adore doesn't adore me. I must say very gratefully it has never happened for long.

Cimmie went to a boarding school at Eastbourne in 1916. There she became the centre of a rather tomboyish, dashing circle of girls. In the winter of 1917–18 she worked as a clerk in the War Office: in 1918 she was on a farm as a landgirl. She liked this because it gave her freedom – far more than would have been allowed to a girl such as her before the war, or indeed after it. Then she did a short welfare course at the London School of Economics including social work in the East End. She maintained her reputation for being somewhat wild, anarchic: a rebel with a conscience.

In 1916 George Curzon had become a member of the War Cabinet: also President of the Anti-Suffrage League. In 1917 he married again, a Mrs Duggan, the widow of a South American millionaire. Cimmie's rebelliousness coincided with her father increasingly being seen as a pillar of the conservative establishment. Cimmie found her relations with him difficult; but she continued to respect much of what he stood for in the way of dedication to duty and hard work. She wrote concerning her confusions about all this to Elinor Glyn, her father's ex-mistress, who had earlier been to her some sort of mother-substitute. Elinor Glyn had had to make her own way in the world: she had been a romantic novelist, a business woman, and a courtesan. She replied:

Get to the real meaning of things and the *real values*. True socialism should be to help conditions so that every child has a chance till it comes to fifteen say, and then sift the chaff from the corn. But lawlessness can never accomplish this, only reason and self-control. Therefore when you say you have 'Bolshevick' feelings examine them. They are probably only the unrest of overstored energy and the evolution of sex, which unconsciously works in every normal and healthy human being. If I were you dear child I would pull right up and examine where I was going and what I *really* wanted to *become*. I *fully* understand that spirit you have and sympathise with it, only it must be turned to fine ends, not disastrous ones. Just think of the *wonderful* power you could have if you wanted to! No hampering poverty or small position: you could be a leader of splendid things if you liked. I would set myself a model to rise to and *nothing* of personal weakness or foolish desires should be allowed to stand in the way of it; make myself into the most beautiful and cultivated and *attractive* young woman in England, so that when the right man came along he would not have to *blink* at certain aspects of me but would worship me as a queen; not take me as a 'jolly girl' or 'good old sport' or because he could not obtain me for his mistress in any other way, as is the attitude that most modern young men approach their choices with. You should *reign* – not be commiserated with as 'Poor dear Cim, what a mess she has made of it!'

There was something in Cimmie, evidently, that might accept being taken as a 'good old sport': perhaps her tomboyishness covered a vulnerability. Many of her boyfriends from childhood and to whom she had written in the war had been killed; it was not unusual for people to protect their feelings by an armour of gaiety. This was what young men in the trenches had done. Cimmie wrote to Lady Desborough whose *Family Journal* had just been published in praise of her two sons Julian and Billy Grenfell who had been killed – 'Words cannot express how I wish I had known those boys: always I have longed to be friends with people like that: I feel I have missed something that perhaps I may never find again.'

Tom Mosley remembered that one of the first times he saw Cimmie was on armistice night when she was at the Ritz Hotel draped in a Union Jack and singing patriotic songs: later that night (in her sister Irene's description) 'she tore round Trafalgar Square with the great crowd setting light to old cars and trucks to the horror of my father'. Tom himself was filled with sadness at the memory of his dead friends. However, a year later when he met Cimmie at Plymouth what he loved about her perhaps was her exuberant energy. He asked her to marry him. But when he wrote to her of his lunacy, his sufferings, the phantasms attendant on his unrequited love, she did not see, at first, what she might love in him. Perhaps she wished for a less histrionic attack. To his letter quoted at the end of the last chapter she replied:

> Hackwood
> Basingstoke
>
> I was carried off tonight and didn't have a chance of saying good-night and thanking you for giving me dinner and wangling me such a wonderfully good seat – so this is just to thank you now very much indeed. I do think it splendid the League making you Chairman of the Campaign Committee, I am glad and shall love to be roped in if there is any mortal thing I could do. Also remember the clubs in Hanwell, and that Phyllis and I are only awaiting further instructions.
>
> And now Dear about your lunacy, don't let it be a disease, don't let it obsess you, don't *please* go on wanting to make me cry or thinking me avengeful – I am really terribly compassionate, and having to hurt you hurts me dreadfully though you mayn't think it. I am not so hard as you imagine or even I make out; I just, well, I can't love you as you love me. Don't think I am merely callous saying that, it seems to me the only thing. I love being with you, I love talking to you, I should adore to be the really glorious friends we could be: please be satisfied with that, I know it's a rotten poor return for all you meant to give me, I am so intensely aware of all you would like to give me, I know how you love me, I am wonder- even awe-struck by it: but Tom, I can't give you anything like that back. Forgive me for saying that my dear ... only I would like to be of comfort to you instead of a disease. But I send love and blessings and again if only you could be devoted to me just as I am to you and not any other way – Goodnight Tom dear. Cim (I am not a humbug and don't think I am asking the impossible).

Tom was not much abashed by this; there has to be a fight if one is to be conqueror. He pursued her by letter to Switzerland, where she had gone to ski.

105 Mount St
21/12/19   W.1.

Cimmie darling,

I expect by now you are with the snow and sun and all beautiful things forgetful of this land of mist and sorrows. I rather love it tho', despite its sadness, perhaps on account of it, especially down here in my beloved Leicestershire where I should always be so happy with horses and hounds if it was not for the other people! I have buried myself for the weekend in the midst of that community which poor Wilde in his arrogant days prescribed as 'the unspeakable in pursuit of the uneatable'. Middle-aged survivors of the 'unseemly brawl' [the war] which interrupted their activities still carry on melancholy intrigues with the strenuous married women of the Melton district. The famous charms and antics of the latter now appear to me in a more garish light even than of yore. I suppose everything in life is comparative! ...

No politics or clamour for a little while. In detached moments such as these the struggle seems rather distasteful, tho' we revel in it while the fight is on. The incentive of mere personal ambition, except as a means of achieving our conceptions, seems more ludicrous than usual, and the ideas behind it all stand alone as the force that drags us back and will do so until the end.

The House starts again on February 10th but I fear I shall be forced to do a weeks speaking tour in the country about January 20th. I return tomorrow to hear L.G. evade the Irish issue and to compare notes with fellow Bolsheviks. Next session promises embittered controversies as of old ...

Come back soon but not before you want to. I do hope you are very happy out there and that life is wonderful. I am sure it always will be for you because life only gives us but a reflection of ourselves. I think this is the longest letter I have ever written in my ridiculous handwriting. It may carry to you a little of the dull things and a little of the joyous things that occupy me in this interval of existence if nothing of the things to which I look beyond it.

Tom

So long as Tom talked of 'the dull things' Cimmie could reply in kind:

So dreadfully sorry not to have answered your letter before really very very apologetic as I loved getting it and have meant to write and say so for days but always there seems something to be done ...

And so on. But then, a week or so later, Tom returned to the attack.

I do so want you to marry me you see as I tried to explain that last wonderful night at the fancy party. I am tired of next session and all its dull things and duller people and only want to love you – perhaps this bores you – I cannot tell – it is for you to settle but please do so *quickly*! My life has been such a hustle that I seem to have acquired the habit and people in a hurry are usually unpleasant to others ... Write and tell me what you feel about it all and I only pray that this and every other decision in your life will bring you happiness which is all that matters to me ...

But then, Cimmie was immediately on the defensive again.

Darling child, don't be tired about next Session, please, and don't be unhappy, but I am very very sorry, I don't want to marry you. I hate just putting it like that, it seems so horrid, but you said you were an impatient person and I must let you know. Don't think the idea of you loving me bores me (as you say) you never would bore me and I loved getting to know you and talking to you. But I am sad that I should make you sad now whereas I only so much wanted to help and make you happy. *Please* be happy and full of interest in your job and let me know that my being unable to love you in the way you want isn't going to spoil things for you between us ...

'Being unable to love you in the way you want' probably included a reluctance on Cimmie's part to risk herself in the area in which she knew Tom was renowned. She was safe so long as she remained in Switzer- land. But when she was back in England, Tom seems to have brought the style of his pursuit as it were down to earth. He arranged for Cimmie to stay in Leicestershire and go hunting with him. After this he wrote:

Funny Baby, Please do not be cross or distressed with me for tonight's few moments or above all frightened ever of me, because I would rather anything than ever hurt you for a single instant. I fear that side of me is very vital and strong and indeed if it was not I should not be much use in this life of struggle! But I do love you with all the strength of the other side, which is the only side that matters and which I have never given to any other woman.

My real love for you will always prevent the original wild animal hurting or distressing you because in me the spirit always wins when it is interested or affected. How crudely expressed: but you will understand, and I am so anxious that you shall never be alarmed or weary with me. I adored being with you in the places that I love – and I adore you – all of me does!!

Tom

Cimmie was a practical, sensuous person and once her sensuality was aroused she seems to have adored Tom and never to have ceased from adoring him. Soon he was writing to her – from his bachelor apartment, and in a note now torn down the middle but still as it were carefully legible –

His own darling Cim . . .
It occurred to me that Molyneux might possibly let me his flat for us to go there in the day time while he is away. If you know him well enough will you ask him, as this place is alright for Tom but not very con｡enial for his one. He feels so lonely tonight! It is all wrong!

Bless her. X.

By March 26th 1920 they were engaged.

CHAPTER 3

Marriage and Politics

Tom and Cimmie were married on May 11th 1920 in the Chapel Royal, St James's. Cimmie had wanted a quiet wedding: the Chapel Royal, in the words of a contemporary newspaper, was 'so small that the guests scarcely have room even to study one another's gowns – but the privilege of being married in this building is a highly prized favour'. King George and Queen Mary were present, as were the King and Queen of the Belgians, who had been flown across the channel in two two-seater aeroplanes specially for the occasion. Outside the Chapel there was such a crowd that it had to be held back by police. Cimmie's wedding dress had a design of green leaves in it, in defiance of a superstition that green at a wedding was unlucky: there was also a superstition that it was unlucky to be married in May. Cimmie herself chose the music: during the handing-over of the ring the *Liebestod* from Wagner's *Tristan and Isolde* was played; though the organist, a newspaper reported, did his best to make it inaudible. Another newspaper commented that 'Mr Oswald Mosley, the bridegroom, was in the happy position of arousing little attention'. Photographs of him at the wedding show him, almost without exception, like an actor acknowledging the applause of a crowd. Cimmie's younger sister wrote to her 'You must tell Tom for the sake of his political career to put on a less footling expression when photographed'.

Before the wedding there had been one or two voices advising Cimmie not to rush in too quickly. A war-time boyfriend wrote 'There is a reason for knowing your Tom very thoroughly, but this is best discussed with a married woman'. But Tom himself, it seems, had already discussed this sort of thing with Cimmie. Cimmie had wondered what her father would make of the engagement; in the event he was relieved at her choice of Tom, since he knew of what were only half jokingly called her 'bolshevick' tendencies. He wrote to his wife Grace 'It turns out he is quite independent – he has practically severed himself from his father who is a spendthrift ... He did not even know that Cim was an heiress'. For the rest there were just hundreds of letters saying how perfect everything was. Nancy Astor wrote 'This is just a line of real love and I do love Tom too. You will be *just* the kind of wife he needs and wants. I feel he must have a great soul, or he would never have asked you to share it.' Elinor Glyn wrote to Cimmie 'One day you will rule England.'

They went for their honeymoon to Portofino, in Italy. There Cimmie taught Tom how to swim; before, he had had a terror of putting his head under water. (He wrote in his autobiography that he considered this due to his having been nearly smothered at birth, which was not in line with his view that early traumas had had no effect on him). About the house where he and Cimmie stayed he wrote – 'Both Dante and Napoleon had slept in the mediaeval fortress; across the lovely bay you could see at Spezia the tragic water wine-dark with Shelley's drowning; along the heights which linked Portofino with Rapallo strode Nietzsche in the ecstasy of writing Zarathustra; Cimmie and I followed the same route more prosaically riding donkeys'.

Cimmie's two sisters Irene (sometimes called Nina) and Alexandra (always called Baba) felt, in their different styles, an almost personal involvement in the wedding and with the honeymoon couple. Irene, aged twenty-four and unmarried, wrote immediately after Cimmie and Tom had left the reception at Carlton House Terrace:

My 2 'tweets' Tim and Tom
    This is a tiny little breath of a lonely house left behind: thinking of you so hard: my thoughts will fly to you both tonight with all the prayers and wonder and sacredness that surround that little wedding-ring – my sweet Cim. May all the stars twinkle and bless you tonight and all the divine fresh green trees and flowers whisper spring – spring – spring – with your two hearts.

Your Nina

And Baba, a schoolgirl of sixteen, wrote after she had heard from Cimmie at Portofino:

My most pessus darling Tim,
I am *so so* happy that it has turned out so wonderful as I have thought about you such a lot and longed for it to be like a perfect dream. I am just living for the time for you to come back ...

For Tom his honeymoon was the beginning of the twelve years of his life during which, he wrote later, 'the summits of private happiness were balanced by the heights of public acclaim'. He not only loved Cimmie: he had seen her as someone with whom in partnership he might set out to alter the world. Cimmie had felt him as her child when she had been reluctant to marry him: she now also felt him as her conqueror. And she too had been brought up to think that in such a partnership she might alter the world.

What is striking about Tom's early years in Parliament is that he was on the 'liberal' or progressive side in almost every issue of any importance. From the first he saw that the coalition government under Lloyd George which had been elected to 'make a land fit for heroes to live in' had little intention of trying to do so: elderly men who had not been in the war were making a country profitable to themselves. Tom saw himself as the champion of the young versus the old: he became President of a body called The League of Youth and Social Progress: but even this, he found, was in fact run by 'a smooth and smug little Liberal . . . typical of the middle-aged politicians who in each generation exploit youth.' He could use his talent for vituperation however as a speaker on its platforms: in his inaugural address as chairman he declaimed – 'Beware lest old age steal back and rob you of the reward . . . lest the old dead men with their old dead minds embalmed in the tombs of the past creep back to dominate your new age, cleansed of their mistakes in the blood of your generation.' Such violence of phraseology got him publicity: he was still not at this time an impressive speaker when controlled.

His more serious efforts were to do with his championing of the new League of Nations: he cared above all about means for preserving peace. He had already been made Chairman of the Campaign Committee in England to publicise the League: he made speeches up and down the country. His mentor in this work was Lord Robert Cecil, the British representative at the League; of whom Tom later wrote (probably his highest recorded compliment about any living politician) 'he was nearly a great man and he was certainly a good man; possibly as great a man as so good a man can be'. Together in Parliament they condemned the British annexation of a former German island in the Pacific for the sake of its phosphate deposits: Tom declared this represented 'the worst days of predatory imperialism'. He described General Dyer's slaughter of Indian civilians at Amritsar as an example of 'Prussian frightfulness inspired by racism'. When British troops were used against the Bolsheviks in Russia he protested – 'It went to my heart to think of

£100,000,000 being spent in Russia supporting a mere adventure while the unemployed are trying to keep a family on 15s a week.' Then in 1923 when Mussolini's troops occupied the Greek island of Corfu he called for the League of Nations to impose sanctions against Italy. His whole political life, he wrote later, was 'predetermined by this almost religious conviction – to prevent a recurrence of war'. He felt that this might be done by the refusal by Britain to become involved in any aggression or even adventures; and by Britain's backing all internationally controlled efforts to prevent aggression by others. About the means necessary to do this he did have a different view from Robert Cecil: the latter had an almost mystical trust in the triumph of human reason so long as conflicts of opinion could be aired. Tom at this time had no illusions that even if a majority of nations agreed on some solution to a conflict, this might not have to be imposed on a minority by at least a show of force. In later years he himself came to have an almost mystical belief in his own powers of reasoning: but by then there were fewer illusions about the efficacy of the use of force.

The issue however with which Tom became most notoriously embroiled during his early years in Parliament was that of Ireland. After the 1918 election the Irish MPs elected to Westminster had unilaterally declared Ireland to be a republic: the Irish Republican Army was formed to gain independence from Britain by force. By 1920 the IRA were in control of much of the country: Lloyd George chose not to fight back openly – this might have alarmed public opinion – but rather to organise, or allow to be organised, gangs of mercenaries who would take on the IRA in their own style. These toughs became known as the Black and Tans from the colour of their uniforms: they found themselves engaged in a prototype of modern guerrilla warfare in which there were atrocities on both sides – especially the use of torture to extract information. Tom, in Parliament, railed against the government both for its responsibility for the Black and Tans and its denial of responsibility: the government was engaged in activities like 'the pogroms of the barbarous slav': it had 'denials on its lips and blood on its hands'. He was booed and jeered by Conservative MPs: he replied that he was 'unperturbed by the monosyllabic interjections of the otherwise inarticulate'. On November 3rd 1920 he left the Conservative benches and sat with the Independents: he had lasted as even a nominal member of the Tory establishment for less than two years.

The Irish nationalist leader T. P. O'Connor wrote later to Cimmie – 'I regard him as the man who really began the break-up of the Black and Tan savagery'.

Tom had made his mark in Parliament as someone who would fight
for the rights of the oppressed and underprivileged: but he was in a
position of being able to object to government callousness and to
government duplicity because he himself was only a critic and he was
not in a position of power. He was outraged at the methods of the Black
and Tans not only because they were wicked (he approved of the
controlled use of force to prevent aggression elsewhere) but because they
were stupid: in the event, they aroused support for the IRA. But still,
what else was to be done? He suggested when not in a vituperative mood
that the Government should take personal responsibility for the fight
against the IRA by means of a properly organised Intelligence Service:
thus it 'should' be possible to round up the 'murder gangs' without
recourse to one's own terrorism. But within the word 'should' there lies
all the difference between those who have power and those who do not.
Tom, in later life, when faced with a form of violence against himself,
felt it right to reply in some sort of kind – even to become involved in
inevitable duplicity.

Tom's sitting on the opposition benches in the House of Commons
meant that he fell out with most of the old men who had earlier
befriended him. He seemed to relish attacking the men at the top: he
accused Winston Churchill, whom he saw as being responsible for the
attack on Russia, of 'borrowing his principles from Prussia ... but my
complaint is that he is an ineffectual Prussian ... it is no good keeping
a private Napoleon if he is always defeated'. He said of the editor of the
Observer, James Garvin, that he was a 'musical doormat which plays
"See The Conquering Hero Comes" whenever Mr Lloyd George wipes
his boots upon it.'

He became involved in attempts to form a Centre Party which
would stand against the corruption and inefficiency of Lloyd George's
Coalition and might draw support from both Tory and Liberal
malcontents and even Labour. He wrote to Robert Cecil in April
1921 –

A real opportunity presents itself for a confederation of reasonable
men to advance with a definite proposal for the reorganisation of our
industrial system upon a durable basis and a concurrent revision of
the financial chaos ... The trouble is we are so immersed in the detail
of everyday existence that we lose the *a priori* mind – the only
attribute in the world that matters ... One loses entirely the vision
splendid of politics within the four walls of the H of C. It was so much
easier in the past with such long intervals for dreams!

Lord Cowdray, the industrialist, was approached, and gave an under-taking that in certain circumstances he would provide money for a Centre Party. Lord Grey, the Liberal Foreign Secretary at the outbreak of war, was asked if he would emerge from his retirement and be its leader. Cimmie and a dozen other wives of interested politicians wrote to him – 'We see in your return to public life the best hope of an effective rallying together . . . of all the stable progressive elements in the country'. But Tom found, as he found in later life repeatedly, that however much men might like to talk about new alignments of forces in the play-grounds of the political arena, their attitudes usually changed when anything more than talk was proposed. Lord Grey replied:

> Even if I were not under the disabilities of bad sight and of being in the House of Lords I should feel that the possible results of my taking an active part in public affairs are being greatly overestimated by my friends. I do not believe that any remedy for the present discontent is to be found in politics, but I will not enter upon a discussion of that large question now . . .

And then Robert Cecil himself, when Tom approached him to be leader ('I am convinced it lies within your power to change the whole course of the history of the decade') replied:

> I think we should go on as heretofore saying as little as we can about our personal position and continuing to hammer the Govt and set up our alternative policy. Believe me it is facts that count in politics and they seem more and more going against the Govt . . . It is no use chopping and changing, and until I see a very clear advantage in moving again I think it would be better to stick where I am. I have practically dropped the word 'conservative' . . .

Years later Tom wrote of Robert Cecil that he 'embodied the mature, experienced and traditional wisdom of statesmanship not only in mind, but in the physical presence of an age-old eagle whose hooded eyes brooded on the follies of men while they still held the light of a further and beneficent vision.' Of Lord Grey he wrote – 'I always found him a singularly tedious and ineffective figure.' But whatever his personal predilections, he was learning, for the first of many times, that if one wants to pursue 'the vision splendid of politics', it is likely that one finds oneself at the head of the field alone.

The fact that Tom was breaking away more and more from his conservative and establishment background meant that he and Cimmie found their relations increasingly strained with her father George Curzon. Curzon had become Foreign Secretary in 1919; but such was Lloyd George's insistence on keeping most of the strings of foreign policy in his own hands (Curzon took responsibility for Asian affairs) that on the issues about which Tom at first was outspoken he and his father-in-law seldom found it necessary to clash. However Curzon's tentative approval of Tom as a son-in-law became, over the Irish question, tinged with alarm. His wife Grace wrote to him 'What a fool Tom Mosley is making of himself! If he goes on you should talk to him.' But then when George Curzon tried to be fatherly to his daughter and his son-in-law he ran into further difficulties. To one invitation to a very grand dinner at Carlton House Terrace Tom's secretary replied – 'Dear Lord Curzon, Mr Mosley asks me to say that he and the wife will be glad to dine with you and the King and Queen on the 15th prox.' Lord Curzon replied to his daughter in his own handwriting in a letter which began 'In the first place your secretary should address me, if he must address me at all, as My Lord . . .' and continued with pages of detailed instructions about correct modes of address and the answering of invitations. Tom remarked that this information was 'most useful'.

But the chief matter of contention between father and daughter and son-in-law was about money. After Mary Curzon's death in 1906 her Leiter money was held in trust for her children. George Curzon was able to get hold of the income from this on the grounds of his providing suitable homes for the children; but then, under the terms of Levi Leiter's will, when the children came of age the income was supposed to go direct to them. Irene, at twenty one, had demanded that she should have her money: her father had protested. Cimmie, even after her marriage, had for a time left part of her income with her father because it seemed to her unfortunate that he still had comparatively little money of his own to spare (his father Lord Scarsdale had died in 1916 but most of the Scarsdale family money went into the upkeep of the estate at Kedleston). But now, in 1921, Cimmie claimed the whole of her income; probably because Tom had got into financial difficulties in Harrow. When local newspapers had given up printing his speeches about Ireland he had himself bought one of the papers in order to air his views: later the paper had failed, and there were debts. George Curzon protested about Cim's proposal to claim her money: Cimmie wrote him a letter in which (he reported to his wife) she called his attitude 'mean, petty, unwarrantable, unaccountable and incomprehensible'. George Curzon replied that he was 'unwilling to continue any controversy on the matter'. Relations remained broken off. When in 1925 George Curzon was dying, he was still not on speaking terms with his two elder daughters. Irene, when she went to make her peace with him, was turned away at the door by a footman (she would tell this story in later years with much distress: she professed an undying love and respect for her father). There is no record of Cimmie having got as far as the door.

Tom was also engaged in cutting himself off from his own past and his family. His grandfather whom he had loved had died in 1915: his father had nominally inherited the Rolleston estate, but his grandfather had arranged that much of the money bypassed his son and went straight to Tom. In 1919 Tom persuaded his father to put Rolleston up for sale 'foreseeing the ruin of agriculture which politics were bringing, and feeling that I could best serve the country in a political life at Westminster'. Tom claimed that this was 'a terrible uprooting causing me much sorrow at the time': but it was a deliberate decision to sell what had been built up by past generations and with an eye to the future, for the sake of Tom's short-term political advantage. Rolleston was bought by a developer and pulled down. By the time Tom died in 1980 there were very few family heirlooms left from what had once been the admittedly rather hollow magnificence of Rolleston.

Cimmie and Tom were acting instinctively, emotionally, in this cutting-off from their pasts. Tom even sold his hunters and his polo ponies: he wrote 'politics had become for me the overriding interest and required singlemindedness'. He wrote of Cimmie that she 'reacted strongly against the splendours of Conservatism so faithfully reflected in her early surroundings, and this led her to seek close contact with the mass of the people and to prefer simplicity in her own home'. But at no stage of their life did this claim make much sense: it was not that from now on they hob-nobbed single-mindedly with the working class, but that they substituted one smart social set that they found boring for an even smarter one that they did not. This was a time when they began to go abroad for many of their social amusements to France and to Italy.

The social life by which Tom and Cimmie were taken up at this time was what nowadays might be called international jet-set. Tom wrote in his autobiography – 'What was the purpose of it all, this going into society? Apart from fun, which is always worthwhile so long as you have the time, meeting people is clearly valuable, particularly people with influence in divers spheres ... There was too the "open sesame" into the world of culture, literature, music and art ... It was a university

of charm, where a young man could encounter a refinement of sophistication whose acquisition could be some permanent passport in a varied
and variable world.'

Tom described the style of this 'university of charm'. The hostesses
in the cities of Europe during the nineteen twenties were mostly
American: they had the money. In Paris there was Elsie de Wolfe, who
had 'made a considerable fortune in New York as an interior decorator'.
On Sundays she usually had 'twenty or thirty people of all nationalities
and professions to luncheon or dinner ... Miss de Wolfe's conversation
was distinguished by immense vivacity rather than intellectual content
... When nearly ninety she was still doing what she called her morning
exercises which consisted of being flung about by two powerful men
of ballet dancer physique. Her gentler entourage included two well-
known characters of the period called Johnny and Tony who were
always at festive board and had a more delicate appreciation of haute
couture than of high politics.' Then in Rome and Venice there was
Princess Jane di San Faustino, another American, who 'regaled the
fashion world with the extremities of scandal floodlit by her unfailing
and eccentric humour'. She would sit at the beach at Venice and
'unnerve' newcomers with some 'searing comment' or her 'basilisk
stare'. She would tell the story of her husband who, when he left her,
had 'signalled the coachman to stop, teed up on the kerbstone as if for
a golfshot, and hit her as hard as he could over the head with his
umbrella'.

Compared to these, the leading London hostesses of the time – Lady
Cunard, Lady Colefax, Mrs Ronnie Greville – might indeed have
seemed rather tame.

Tom would explain that he saw social life as some sort of antidote,
or balance, to what might have otherwise become the grim and over-
riding obsessions of politics. What was required, he used to say, was a
'Ganzheit' (wholeness) for the attainment of 'the complete man'. But
the style of people in Tom's and Cimmie's social world does not seem
to have been very different from that of politicians: there was more wit,
perhaps: but this was still the Proustian world of Paris or Venice in
which personal relationships, even love, were matters of intrigue,
conquest, possession, power; everyone was in the business of becoming
one up on everyone else. Certainly there seems to have been little in it
of music, literature, art: not much of that austere standing back by which
Proust transmuted what was tawdry into beauty.

What these *salons* were useful for, of course, was the business of men
picking up women. Tom had a phrase for this – 'flushing the covers'

– a reference to partridge or pheasant shooting, in which birds are put up by beaters. There are different opinions about how long Tom was faithful to Cimmie after their marriage: her sisters imagined possibly a few years: Tom's second wife, Diana, suggested a few months. He would not have remained faithful for long while moving in this café-society world: what would have been the point? Talk of art and literature was known as being a cover under which lurked the avail-ability of young married women. Another form of camouflage was that provided by the life of an MP. As one of the wits in Tom's entourage put it – What other job gives one such a valid excuse to be away from home night after night till 1 am?

Tom had embarked on his social and political life as a conqueror: it seems to have been agreed by both he and Cimmie that their marriage should in some sense spur him on – she as well as he wanted him to do 'great things'. But then what is this style of 'greatness'? And what is the style of a wife who has pledged herself to support her husband thus faithfully?

CHAPTER 4

Love Letters

Cimmie's first child, a girl, was born on February 25th 1921. She was christened Vivien Elisabeth. The nanny that came to look after her had been Cimmie's nurserymaid in India. Nanny Hyslop stayed with the family in one capacity or another for over fifty years.

Cimmie and Tom had settled into a house in London – 8 Smith Square – within easy reach of the Houses of Parliament. For weekends and holidays they rented houses in the country or abroad. In the summer of 1921 Nanny and Vivien were in Devon while Tom and Cimmie were in Scotland: in 1922 they were on the Norfolk coast while Tom and Cimmie were in Venice. In the winter of 1922-23 the family were together in a house, Lou Mas, in the south of France, on Cap Ferrat near Nice. Tom had to leave early to go home to speak in Parliament about a crisis in Mesopotamia: Cimmie stayed behind with Nanny and Vivien and her sister Baba who had come to stay. Cimmie was five months pregnant again and had been told to rest. This was the first time that Tom and Cimmie had been away from each other for more than two nights since their marriage. During the ten days that they were apart they each wrote to the other almost every day: Cimmie's first letter to Tom had been written even before he had left: Tom's first letter to Cimmie was written in the train so that he could post it at his first stop at Cannes. The letters talk of their love; their dependence on each other. Tom told the story much later to his second wife Diana that during this time when Cimmie was pregnant he was having an affair with a mutual friend with whom they had been in Venice the previous summer: Cimmie had learned about this and it had caused her upset; also upset (this was Tom's theory) to the child. This perhaps happened after the time of the letters. The child Cimmie was pregnant with, was myself.

I have cut some of the repetitions: but these letters show, as nothing else can, the peculiarities of the relationship between Tom and Cimmie; also something of the style of social life at the time.

> Monday 12 February am. Lou Mas.

My beloved precious beloved

You haven't gone yet but my heart is aching so I write now so as for you to get a lett from me soon soon after you get back.

Be happy, be happy I do love you so frightfully I want you to miss me but to be happy too. Will be back soon and till then kiss you every morning every night, think of you every moment.

Bless you my precious I do love you so.

Kisses and love and love and kisses from

> Your own Tim

> Monday 12th February. Cannes

My own darling

I am so terribly unhappy at leaving you – nothing would have made me go if I had realised what it meant and nothing will again. Please, please do not be too sad and look after your wonderful darling self for your T who adores you. I never understood before I left you on the platform quite how much I loved you. You have brought all the beauty and holiness and wonder with you that my life has ever known or ever will know – something apart from – higher – and yet wonderfully interwoven with my stormy existence – all that has rendered it possible. Come back to me soon my beloved.

> Tom.

> Monday 12th February pm. Lou Mas.

My sweetheart, I hope I didn't make you too unhappy when you went off. It just suddenly seemed too awful and my heart nearly broke. I don't know really how I shall get through the next week. I am so utterly dependent on you, you don't know how my every thought is of you, I really have no 'me' to speak of, only *you you you*: a *you* to adore, a *you* to look after, a *you* I admire, a *you* that fills my entire horizon. You have made such a difference to my life – filling it completely – making it *so* happy, blissfully happy and content – content in having found someone really big, really worthwhile, a life and a person worthy of one's whole endeavours and furthest effort. I do hope I give you back a little of the ... [rest of the letter missing].

Tuesday February 13th Calais.

My own darling,

Afraid missed Paris letter as train did not get there until 10 and went on eleven – Tommy still in bed and by time he had dressed was going on. Now only short let as feeling very sick – train rocking terribly – if it is rough on channel disaster may ensue. Already his insistent and plaintive cries of woe have evoked the compassion of fellow voyagers. Truly so terribly wretched and depressed without my one – such lonely little meals and sad feeling bring home to me every moment how much you have become to me in all the little as well as the big things in life. I nearly jumped off the train when she milked out and would have done so if others had not been there to think was too foolish. Shall be so mis without you but terribly realise how much you mean. Please do not be too unhappy but go on loving your adoring Tom and get well and strong to have a lovely time in a few days when you get back.

Tom   X for Mum   x for baby.

Train very good for Odie [Nanny] and baby: she would be very comfortable at other end of single compartment, they are much better than double.

Tuesday February 13th Lou Mas.

Blessed heart of mine, I can't tell you what your beloved letter has just given to me such a joy, such a love and such aching tears – Oh Bill I do miss you so. Perhaps it's a good thing you went away tho' you must not ever ever again – coz without you here I am overwhelmed by how much you mean to me: but my sweet, I am also sadly conscious of how little I let you know how *infinitely* much you *do* mean.

Dear heart I am so sorry for the way I harry and worry you – have made too high a mountain out of the molehills of your faults and let them so much exclude the sweet shining light of your love and darlingness. No one has ever had a sweeter man and I do appreciate everything, all you give me. I have been silly and overwrought and I am sure awfully difficult – no doubt thoughtless things you never dreamt I'd notice or mind well I have minded and have been mis and hurt and hopelessly grumpy. I have let you get the capacity to hurt me more easily than the capacity to please – No – that is too far, but anyway I have been a bit upside down tho' never for one instant loving you less. All the time the only great integral vital thing in the whole world that matters to me is You, my loving You, You loving me – it's so wonderful and beautiful and from now on I am going to make so much better use of it. Help me will you my sweet. I am now feeling awfully well, awfully resolute, intensely sorry for my shortcomings and failures – aching to be back with you to do anything I can. I wish I could explain better. I feel we have a good bit been box and cox – very often when you have been sweet and charming to me, or when you have wanted gaiety from me, or when you have wanted to talk serious matters with me, I have still been grieving over some row or trouble we've had and which you have already completely forgotten. I have resented you forgetting what seemed to me so easily – not realising that maybe I oughtn't to have, as it were, wallowed in being hurt. I have been too sensitive and have lost elasticity in recovering.

I really have been abnormal about everything connected with you – too proud too intricate too naked too introspective too violent. The beauty the peace the greatness the real sympathy between us so far and away miles and miles transcends the pettifogging puerile unnecessary squabbles. Let's have no more of them. You do your part will you as sometimes my pet it is your own sweet fault. And I swear I will do mine. I look forward so much to coming back to you and the time to come, peaceful happy unclouded. I wonder however the seven days will pass that are left here.

It is too bad, weather perfection and just when you have gone. I am out of doors in the deck chair writing this on my knee – we go Nice this afternoon shopping. It's really broiling. Tomorrow we start at 10 the Colefax expedition to go to St Paul and Grasse. Thurs I take Baba to Cannes and leave her with the Coates – Lady Rock has just written to Bab asking her and us to dine one night. We are going to ring up and ask if she will give us lunch Thurs instead. Nothing more so far except going with Connie to see her house. I have got all the necessaries for our journey Tuesday.

My beloved one I think of your sweet woolly head and the corner of your eye where I love to kiss – and how sweet you look in your new smart shirts, in your chic black 'smoking'. Dicks has just been up. She had two very exciting new engagements, at least one dullish, Mary Pease to a Mr Lubbock: the other thrilling to me, I wish you were here to guess – about the only girl friend I have left – one you like very much – can you guess –

Darling I wonder whether you will ever ever wade through all this. Oh I am so lucky to be married to you my precious fellow – you are

so miles and away above and beyond all others – I am so privileged
to be sharing in that wonderful star of yours –
Never doubt yourself. Never doubt me for one second.
You will never fail you. I will never fail you.
How I long to touch you and hear your voice.
Infinite love and a kiss on your dear wicked mouth
                                                    from you own Tim

                                 Tuesday night 11pm. Smithers [8 Smith Sq]
My own darling fellow,
    Back in Turtle land after many adventures – Dined at the House
with M. Wood who has been made Liberal whip under Phillipps chief
whip in place of Hogge sacked for intruging with L.G. – great
uproar in Lib circles. Oh he is so lonely in Sweet Smithers without
his one and does long for her return. I have become so accustomed
to having you with me that I am so lost and foolish without you in
addition to such ache in heart. My crossing was perfect and who
should be on the boat but old Bob [Cecil] with P. Baker [Philip Noel-
Baker] from Lausanne – great political talks – he asked me what I was
going to do and I replied with truth I did not know. Feels a lost mut
[drawing of an animal like a sheep with the tail crossed out] tail should
not be there as he left it behind at Cap Ferrat. Please soon take up her
little crook.
    I have talked to Whitly and expect to speak tomorrow or Monday
– terrible lot of requests for me to speak etc – not much for you, and
those I am refusing. Bless you my own beautiful treasure. I do so miss
my wonder one and her baby. X for Mum x for baby. So tired and
lonely in bye [another drawing of an animal] Tiny mut in big
pen all alone. Does love her.

                                              Wednesday   Lou Mas.
My darling one I am so bitterly disappointed – no lett from you
today. I so badly wanted one on my return from Cannes. I felt so
dreadfully lonely and was so sure one would be waiting on the hall
table. Naughty puss you can't have posted one in either Paris or Calais
or it surely would have been here by now. Write me all you can
belovedest -- it's all I have of you to carry me on and altho' I promise
you I am feeling very well and quite serene-ish still, I am a bit desolate.
Now *all* alone. I think and think of you and us 2 and have remembered so many little funny sweet episodes in our life together that I

had quite forgotten for the while. Now I'll tell you about yesterday and today.

Well yesterday Colefax and a nice little old man (55 to 60-ish) called Johnson started off in one car Baba and I in another, and went to St Paul (right behind Cagnes) where a large grey Rolls Royce was already drawn up belonging to Kennard; he then joined on to us we saw a church and town and then went on to Grasse stopping on the road for a picnic lunch. Lovely lovely day, magnificent scenery. At Grasse we went over the scent factory – Oh, I never knew before how scent was made it's revolting and interesting. We emerged after ½ an hour smelling like civet cats. Then we went to see the Croisset villa (daughter just married Charles de Noailles) its supposed to be wonderful. I have never contemplated any such atrocity.

We came back a splendid road through divine little old towns and gorgeous scenery. Had tea in Nice then home. Box left today for Florence.

Now I am writing in bed and wondering how ever I shall get through the days that remain. I am bored and longing to have you here oh my sweetheart if only you could just walk in now and start going to bed I could put my arms around your neck and kiss you. I want to touch you so, and have you up against me. Blessed heart I wonder if you acutely miss me as I do you, if you have an ache all the time.

8 Smith Square. S.W.1
Wednesday

My own Darling,

He has just got the sweetest letter of all his life – thank you so much – it nearly broke my heart when she milked out – do hope now a little bet – only a week more today and five days only when you get it.

Just been to the House – fine bout between Lady M.P. [Lady Astor] and J. Jones [Labour member]. Opening rounds with references to J.J.'s inveterate consumption of spirits, and counters re her making money through illicit whisky selling. N.A. finally takes the count with peach of a punch as follows – The Speaker: Millionaires are useful people – N.A.: Hear hear! – J.J.: They have been some use to you! The worst day we've had for weeks, fog and cold terrible. Tiny T very depressed and longing for the return of his precious fellow. All love in world for his beloved.

Thursday 15th February. Lou Mas.
My own sweetheart, it's already 24 hours longer than I have ever been away from you before. I do wish you hadn't had to go but I am longing to hear from you whether or not you really think you were right in leaving: are you going to speak or take any part? I hope you will be able to, but my sweet remember if you can't be good be careful: *no* nasty personal allusions to Pa.

Am dreadfully disappointed no lett *all* yesterday and none this morning's post. Now we are just off to Cannes where I leave Baba after lunching with Rocks.

Hope so much there will be one waiting when I get back.

Will tell you about yesterday and today when I write tonight. Poor Tinkie *all* alone at Lou Mas.

My belovedest I love you so.

Blessings from your own Tim

Friday 16th February. House of Commons.
My own darling,

Just got the let which she wrote prior to his departure – delayed owing inadequate stamping & 6d to pay!! Rather glad he came back – speech apparently *immense success*. Scores of fervent congratulations and cheers. R. MacDonald came up and said he so wanted to talk to me in his room. So look out for bolshie boy in red tie when you return. Just a few quips at Marquis [Curzon] which were greatly appreciated. Please not too cross – not too bad! Great hurry for post. Elsa Maxwell in London. Very bored with everything except his Tim. Only thing in world that matters to him.

My own darling. X.

Friday AM. Lou Mas.
My sweetheart pet, so happy and glad to have your lets at last. Was wanting them so badly nearly burst all Wed: all Thurs no line: then Fri morning 2 at once the Calais one and the Smithers. Precious one they have make me so happy tho' have made me ache ache ache for you. I do miss you *too* terribly and wish with all my heart you had jumped out of the train. She couldn't help her milk out.

His letts are so *sweet* she does treasure them so. She'll look after his tail so carefully and bring it home. Poor lonely fellow in the big bed. Darling one can't help saying she is glad he is missing her, is glad he finds a gap instead of her fussing around.

How nice for you meeting Bob, was he very Tory. Sidney Greville has just been up to say goodbye he leaves Maryland tomorrow for Monte and goes home Wed. I am just going to Rosemary now to see Dicks before she goes off to Genoa to join Con and to get Evelyn's address to write to her. Having lunch early going into Nice for 'grand shopping'. Joan coming to tea then lonely evening doing bills and accounts.

This is just before I go to sleep. Have just read all your letts over again my Billy boy you are too darling for words I am so lucky to have such a sweet one for a husband. So many of the little things you write, the little divine things, the drawings, every single sweet thought, every touch, is treasured so passionately – by me. The little 'you and I' touches, the 'muts', and the 'tiny fellow in the big bye': I am so glad we are like we are and not just ordinary hus and wife. I *do* appreciate you so – your tenderness and un-ordinariness about things that matter so much to me.

Saturday 17th Febuary. White's.

My own darling,
I expect this will be the last let you get before you jump on to the Blue Train and are wafted away from flowers and sun to the dingy little retreat where adoring Tomby awaits his beloved fellow. Just had a lovely lunch all by himself and is settling down for a *lonely* weekend – won't see a soul until Monday – poor lamb. Last night Oggie [Olga Lynn] had a very amusing dinner party of about 20 – usual people with additions of Maxine Elliott, Gladys Cooper type, wonderful shouts: Viola Tree funnier than you would believe. A new stunt – 'learning to skate'. Napier Alington and Lois did some dances and everyone was at very zenith of form. Did so long to see his round-eyed one honking out her pleasure or looking in pawky disapproval like a shocked baby as occasion might arise. A new and enchanting lyric has taken our more esoteric circles by storm – as follows, to the tune of the Old Pink Lady Valse –

> A wonderful bird is the pell-i-can
> His beak holds as much as his belly can
> Some say that he can pass
> This beak right up his ass
> But I'm damned if I see how the hell-he-can!

The evening was appropriately concluded by Mr W Rummel rendering the 'Entry of the Gods into Valhalla' and the rest of his concert programme in Nice. Such fun; but I did so want his pretty one to enjoy it too. Oggie says we will have another when you come back *if you like*. Tomby thinks he ought to be rather political for a bit as things are developing. Has enjoyed this little bit of gaiety; as having spoken, could do no more. Lots more multi-congratulations. But *he* thought he was bad: what does *she* think?

Saturday evening. Lou Mas.

Belovedest, isn't it thrilling this will be almost the last letter I will be able to write to you. It won't go till tomorrow Sunday and you will get it the very day before I at long long last get back to you. I will write just one more Monday for you to get Wed morning as really I couldn't bear to let a day go by without writing to you. I wonder if you have been bored by my endless screeds – I have *had* to write tho' it has appeased a little my loneliness. I have loved sort of getting into contact with you as it seems. Fancy I have written practically twice a day every day since you left. I wonder if you got them all? Did you get the one I wrote even before you had left? You cannot imagine my loneliness and want of you – I literally have felt all these days that there has been 'no spirit left in me' no resilience, no capacity for enjoyment; only aching void, the French word 'lasse'. I don't mean physical health at all, as I really am feeling awfully well, awfully rested and keen to get back, I know I am quite collected and serene and more vital than I have been for months – it's just YOU YOU YOU I must have – I must have. Quite honestly if you died (as I don't contemplate anything else on heaven or earth ever ever separating us) I should never never be the same again. Something would go out of me for ever – everything mortal and immortal that one human being can give another I have given you – All the good and bad and little and big – You are everything in life to me – I really mean it. The sort of affection one gives parents children brothers sisters friends the comrade element of life you have *all* of that, I rejoice utterly in you as a perfect gay heart free companion. No Mum has ever passionately loved a baby boy or a splendid grown up son as I do you. No brother or sister have ever felt the complete accord I feel to you. No two men, no 2 women, no child ever looked up to a parent as I do to you. And then above and beyond all that I can't write at all of what I feel about you as my husband and lover. No words in the world could ever tell you that, only if you could look with my eyes and heart how would you know. Don't think me stupid but I must tell you.

I wish I knew what you were doing tonight just so as to picture and visualise you. I wonder apropos of what I said awhile back of your meaning every thing and person in the world to me whether I am too wrapped up in you (can one be) expect too much from you, ask for *nothing* from *any one else*, only *all* the time things from you. Poor you. And then when as is only human you sometimes can't give, then I think you are bored with me – I think you ought not to ask anything from anyone in the world but me – I am afraid I am narrow and stupid but the excuse is that I am dotty potty about you almost (I believe this to be very nearly true) to insanity. I must steady myself. I think this week has done a great deal towards steadying and will you help when I get back to you – help by being not too moody, not too fierce, not too getting into rages and finding fault. I really am looking forward with the utmost confidence to a time of great peace and enjoyment of each other and no worries, anyway in our real inner lives.

My heart I love you so, trust you so, respect you so, and yet again love and adore you so. Goodnight.

Saturday night. 8 Smith Square.
My own most beloved darling,

Just a very last line in hopes you may just get it before you go – I have missed you so terribly – I do adore you more every day I live and I realise so terribly through this parting how tragically dependent I am on you – My own treasure darling I long to see your wonderful face again (kisses its pic every night) Only 4 more days and I shall on Wednesday be waiting on the station for my adored wife.

X.

Sunday evening. Lou Mas.
My sweet one, I believe I have it in me to find fault with you this evening – you are a worse correspondent than ever I had anticipated or else the posts have been bad. Another 2 days without letters at all. I got one Tuesday, none on Wed, none Thurs, then 3 on Friday almost *too* good, then none Sat, none Sun – I wonder how all mine to you have arrived, have you received them every day? I hope so, you ought to have. I have had so little to do, so many long hours alone, I have had much more time at my disposal than you. I find myself awfully bad about going out without you, I really have been the week I have been alone alone here an absolute hermit, all my meals alone, I have refused practically every invitation to go out and am terrified and shy and woefully haughty and *un*selfconfident. Went to lunch at Maryland today, arrived 20 minutes late because of our damn fool clocks, found Princess Louise, Lady Londesburgh, Jack Wilson,

Muriel Ward, husband, Harry Stoner etc: got on pretty well with Muriel found her easy and charming went up with them to Rosemary this afternoon the same party as the other night with Eric Mackenzie and Lady Maidstone extra.

I am very ill at ease with those sort of people they talked of nothing but bridge and smoking how could I join in – I tried desperately hard to be friendly and gay – I think I was all right . . .

I wonder what it will feel like seeing you, having you, touching you again. Your actually going away was so *far* worse than I had anticipated I hope perhaps actually meeting may be better: though it would be hard, my anticipation is *so* running riot . . .

My last goodnight to you in writing, I wonder if you'll get this before me – you ought to – I put my arms around you tight tight and kiss your dear eyes and mouth I love and worship you and send everything I can across the land and water, between every line is my love for you, filling every corner of the envelope even as it fills every corner of my life – I keep back just a tiny bit extra for Wed – no – I needn't as I shall have such a lot over and to spare all Monday Tues and till Wed evening I shall be bursting.

My precious heart

Your fellow

Our baby has been so sweet and an unbelievable joy and comfort.

CHAPTER 5

Politics and Society

I was born on June 25th 1923; almost immediately I became very ill. My mother did not feed me: it was not the custom at the time for upper class mothers to feed their children: my nanny however told me later my mother had tried to, but could not. A wet-nurse was hired – a Mrs Green – and while my mother and father went off in August for their summer holiday to Venice (it was also not the custom for such wives to become socially unavailable to their husbands who it was thought needed them more than babies) myself, my sister Vivien, Nanny, Stella the nursery-maid, Mrs Green and Mrs Green's own baby, all went off to a rented house at Birchington, in Kent.

Nanny wrote every other day to my mother at the Excelsior Hotel on the Lido at Venice and at the Palazzo Priuli in the town. She reported on how I was getting on with Mrs Green. I was vomiting, I could not swallow, I cried most of the time, and my motions (as Nanny called them) had become, aptly, green. Doctors were called and recommended that I be 'put on' first bismuth, then castor-oil and barley water, then something called peptonised milk: but all this was only in preparation for being 'put back' to Mrs Green. Nanny became alarmed ('I am sure the 3 oz he lost last week was all from his face'); on her own initiative she took me up to London and got a specialist to see me in a sitting room at the Grosvenor Hotel. The specialist recommended that I should be fed with nothing but 'sherry whey'. Nanny wrote 'He has had nearly a whole bottle of sherry this week, little tippler, he loves it'. Thus, it seems, my life was saved. Later it was found that Mrs Green (this story is not in the letters to my mother: it was told to me later by Nanny) had all the time had a crate of gin bottles under her bed. Surprisingly or other-wise, I am not yet (1982) an alcoholic.

Nanny continued to rescue the lives of myself, my sister and my brother for many years. She was one of sixteen children of a working class family (her father was a gardener) who, having helped her mother to bring up her younger brothers and sisters, had gone out to work aged fifteen as a nurserymaid to America; then had joined my mother and her two sisters in India after Baba had been born. As the sisters grew up and Nanny had had to leave, she had promised Cimmie that she would come back to her when she, Cimmie, had children; she had done so when Vivien was born. Nanny Hyslop represented everything steadfast, trustworthy, down-to-earth, in our childhood. The world of our parents seemed to do with ambitions and passions like that of gods on Mount Olympus.

My mother seems to have tried, in a way beyond what was usual at the time and for her class, to be a 'good' mother: she was certainly seen as such: but it would have been almost impossible for her to take much of her allegiance away from Tom. Tom himself tried (for the sake of 'Ganzheit'?) to be a good father: but it was his theory that the upbringing of children should be left to 'professionals': this was the same sort of theory that had led him to believe that technical knowledge about aeroplanes should be left to professionals when he had crashed in 1915. The conventions of the time were that upper-class children should visit their mother in her bedroom after breakfast, and that they should go down to be on show in the drawing room after tea; but for the rest of the time their place was in the nursery, which to them was in relation to their parents' world as real life is to a stage.

Cimmie's and Tom's political life was in transition at this time: they were moving from being members if only peripherally of the conservative establishment to something more adventurous and left-wing. This was reflected in their choice of godparents for my christening in the summer of 1923. One was Nancy Astor, the Conservative MP for whom Tom and Cimmie had campaigned in 1919; others were Violet Bonham Carter and Archibald Sinclair, both prominent Liberals. A certain mystery however seems to have hung over my other godfather, or godfathers. Prince George, the youngest son of King George and Queen Mary, had been approached and had accepted; he had become a friend of Cimmie's in the south of France earlier in the year. But now he was a friend of her younger sister Baba and there had been stories about the possibility of their marriage. Prince George wrote to Cimmie from Buckingham Palace 'I hope you don't mind my asking you not to say anything about my being Godfather but there has been such trouble already about Baba that they would be furious if there was anything else seen in the papers'. So it seems that I had an additional godfather – Mr B. A. Campbell, General Secretary of the 'Paddy's Goose Boys' Club' in Shadwell, East London. Mr Campbell wrote to Cimmie 'You know I would love to have the honour and privilege of being godfather to your boy ... there is only one difficulty ... I only have one suit – an ordinary working suit – and if I can attend in that I will'. I myself never knew that Mr Campbell was my godfather until I came across this letter in 1981.

Tom's political disillusionment with his establishment friends came to a head during the summer holiday of 1923 when he and Cimmie were in Venice, I was with Mrs Green at Birchington, and Mussolini invaded Corfu. Tom hoped that sanctions against Italy would be ordered by the League of Nations: he left Venice for Geneva, where Robert Cecil was the British representative. Robert Cecil too favoured sanctions: he went to consult Stanley Baldwin, the Prime Minister (a Conservative government had taken over from Lloyd George's coalition government in 1922): Baldwin was taking the waters at Aix-les-Bains. Baldwin told Robert Cecil that he should do whatever he thought fit: Robert Cecil had hoped for firm orders. He returned to Geneva dejected. Tom was repelled both by Baldwin's inability to give orders and by Robert Cecil's need of them. He wrote 'Will was not available, because in such men it is only aroused by intense emotion': they had remained passive when 'by an act of cold will fortified by the calm calculation they had every prospect of victory and their opponent had none'. (He later compared this attitude to the 'white-hot emotion' with which such men had started what he saw as a profoundly risky war in 1939).

Tom advocated, in theory, the use of calm calculation as a prelude to decisive action: but what he himself often used calculation for, as do nearly all politicians, was skilful prevarication. In the general election of 1922 he had stood again for Harrow, but now as an Independent. The local Conservative Association had tried to pin him down about his opinions before they decided to back him. However the President of the Association reported:

> We found it extraordinarily difficult to bring Mr Mosley to the point. He could never be persuaded to give a direct answer to a direct question, and developed an unrivalled skill in qualifying any written or spoken statement he could be induced to make with some loophole by which, if convenient, he could escape from the obvious meaning of his words. This feature in his conduct became so marked both in private discussions and meetings of the Executive that we were gradually forced to the suspicion that Mr Mosley was merely tem-

porising with us and that he intended at his own time and in his own way to throw over his Party in his constituency as he had already thrown it over in the House of Commons.

But the reason for his prevarication, Tom stated, was:

I cannot enter Parliament unless I am free to take any action of opposition or association, irrespective of labels, that is compatible with my principles and is conducive to their success. My first consideration must always be the triumph of the causes for which I stand; and in the present condition of politics, or in any situation that is likely to arise in the near future, such freedom of action is necessary to that end.

One of the charges that could be laid against Tom perhaps throughout his political career was that he claimed for himself the rights of manipulation and prevarication that were part of the normal game of politics, while he seemed genuinely outraged by the use of such methods by others. This was a self-deception that created an impression of honesty; though in the end, as with all self-deceptions, it worked to his disadvantage.

The Harrow Conservative Association decided not to back him, and to put up an official candidate against him. Tom, as an Independent, appealed to the electorate:

The war destroyed the old party issues and with them the old parties. The party system must, of course, return in the very near future, but it will be a new Party system ... My intention not to wear a label which at present, may be confused with past controversies, does not mean that I adopt the empty independence of men who can agree with no one. I am not a freelance incapable of such cooperation, and am prepared to work immediately with men who hold similar opinions in the face of the great new issues of our day.

At the election Tom had got in with a majority somewhat reduced but still over 7,000. This was a personal triumph. His oratory, his dashing style, his ability to arouse devotion irrespective of party loyalties – all this had maddened his opponent who had, as before, been driven to personal abuse; accusing Tom of treachery about Ireland and about India. Tom, it was claimed, had incited Indian students to revolt against British rule. Tom threatened a libel action; his opponent unreservedly withdrew. Tom wrote 'I had very speedily in self-defence to develop a certain ferocity in debating methods ... or I would not have survived'.

This independence meant that he was increasingly isolating himself politically: but he must have known he was unlikely to be effective in British politics if he remained without allegiance. Both the Liberal and Labour parties were in need of young and energetic men: they were out to catch him: it had been significant that neither had put up a candidate against him in 1922. It seemed natural at first that he might turn to the Liberals. As early as 1920 Margot Asquith, the wife of the Liberal ex-Prime Minister, had written to Cimmie about how highly her husband regarded Tom: now Violet Bonham Carter, Asquith's daughter, wrote:

Father came into my bedroom last night on his return from the House to tell me that your Tom (may I call him Tom?) had made the most brilliant speech he had almost ever heard: I have never seen him more completely swept away.

Tom and Cimmie went to stay with the Asquiths at their country house The Wharf: the Liberals began to talk of them as 'one of us'. But Tom was probably doing some of the 'calm calculation' that he advocated for men of action. At the 1922 election the Labour Party had been the chief gainers with an increase in the number of MP's from 63 to 142 (the Liberals had 117). When Baldwin called another general election at the end of 1923, on the issue of protectionism versus free trade, Labour became the strongest Party in the House of Commons with 191 seats and the Liberals, although their fortunes had improved at the expense of the Conservatives, were even further behind Labour with 159. A Labour Government was formed. It seemed obvious that if Tom was going to put an end to his isolation by joining a party – and with an eye to being part of a government in the near future – it made sense if one's feelings were more for Labour than for Liberals.

Another impetus to join a party was the fact that in the 1923 election his majority at Harrow was down to 4,600: his old conservative supporters were leaving him. It had been, as, usual, a vituperative campaign. His old friend F. E. Smith, now Lord Birkenhead, had come down to speak for Tom's official conservative opponent and had referred to Tom as 'the perfumed popinjay of scented boudoirs'. Tom took umbrage. He did not mind, he said, the reference to boudoirs; but he seemed to think that 'popinjay' was a slur on his performance there.

There is little record of Cimmie in politics during Tom's years at

Harrow. At the time of her wedding she had received a letter from
Tom's mother handing over to her the position of 'political leading
lady': she had made a speech of thanks to the constituency for their
wedding present after which a local newspaper reported that 'her
victory was greater than her husband's at the polls 18 months ago': she
had helped, together with his mother, in Tom's electioneering cam-
paigns. But she never seemed to have had much time for the Harrow
style of politics. Most of the first four years of her marriage was spent
in settling into the house in London, giving birth to two of her children,
and making the complicated arrangements for holidays, servants, dinner
parties, and so on, for Tom's cosmopolitan entertainment. There is no
evidence that she ever indulged in the game of upper class married
women being available for love affairs: she was always available to use
her social charms for the advancement of Tom. But as Tom moved
closer to Labour her involvement became more political. As early as
May 1923 she was entertaining the Labour leader, Ramsay MacDonald,
to lunch: she struck up some sort of flirtatious relationship with him.
Later that summer she invited him to join her and Tom on holiday. He
replied:

> Thank you very much for your letter inviting me to stay with you
> in Venice when I am passing through. Sidney Arnold is with me and
> the two of us would I am sure be too big a handful for you. But in
> any event let us have a feast together.
> I hope the little person who I saw had come to smile on you both
> gives you much happiness ...

When the first Labour government was formed in January 1924 with
Ramsay MacDonald as Prime Minister Tom made a strong speech in
Parliament abusing the Tory record ('drift buoyed up by drivel') and
wishing the Labour well ('tonight the army of progress has struck its
tents and is on the move.') It now seemed only a matter of time before
Tom joined the Labour Party. His Liberal friends were annoyed. On
January 19th Margot Asquith wrote:

> Dear Tom, You and Cimmie are very dear to me. I am old and you
> are young. I have watched politics closely since I was 15, having 3
> great friends – Gladstone, Morley, and A. Balfour – 3 very different
> men. Clear conviction and patience, courage and ambition and not
> too much self-love with perfect self-control go to make leaders of
> men. I have watched men of great ability – 1. Rosebery 2. Balfour,

Winston and Birkenhead, all ruin themselves in turn. I am not persuading you to be a Liberal and you can change from Tory to Liberal or vice versa: I am writing to warn you to take *long* views. Your future might be a great one in the Liberal Party; possibly, Cim says, in the Labour Party. But I myself see little difference between the extremes of left and right; I have never seen anything more selfish, jealous and petty – apart from gross and pathetic ignorance – than Labour; and every word you say of Tory is true. Class consciousness devours both. I have not seen you lately but before joining Thomas – a liar: Ramsay – a coward: I should think twice.

Tom made a joke about this letter saying that Margot Asquith had abused his best friends. But in fact it was his old acquaintances who were, as usual, abusing him. The main criticism of the prospect that he might join Labour was that he would be pandering cynically to a desire for power: that he saw his own future brighter in the Labour Party in that he wanted to be a 'big fish in a little pond'. But these accusations made little sense. Tom could have done as well as he wished in the Conservative Party if he had not been outraged about matters of principle; there was little enough talent among young Conservatives for him to have felt much danger of being outshone. And although there might be an initial glamour about himself as an aristocrat joining Labour he was clever enough to know that there would also be reactions and repercussions. He felt drawn to Labour because of what he felt as the sluggishness and corruption of the establishment parties: and in so far as it was true that he could do something about this only as a member of a group, then the Labour Party was the one most likely to act in the way that he desired.

There is some truth, however, in the charge that he saw politics largely in terms of what might be a platform for himself: he was always, and he thought justifiably, something of a one man party band. Even at this time (he was twenty seven) he was imagining that it was the democratic tradition of a government being harried by an opposition that prevented things being done: this was the 'drift buoyed up by drivel'. If words were to be turned into action, this would be through unencumbered power being given, albeit democratically, to a single group led by a single responsible man. He seldom prevaricated about this. In every attitude he had taken (and was to take) in politics he stood on some principle: and he said to other people in effect that they could either follow him or not as they chose. This was something unusual in

English politics – where the tradition has been to manipulate and manoeuvre possibilities. The one charge it was difficult to bring against Tom was that he manipulated what he saw as his principles for the sake of success: if he had, he might have succeeded.

At the time when he was attracted to Labour and Labour was wooing him his mother wrote to him:

> I must pen a line to try and tell you how enormously I admire your amazing courage and self-sacrifice of most things that appeal to men of your age and up-bringing; and how I pray with all my heart that your dreams for the benefit of struggling humanity may come true, and that I may live to see your present attitude justified by results and the world appreciate that far from being a pushing self-seeking politician you were in fact willing to be a martyr for your Religion – for it seems to me that is what your Politics are.
>
> And oh darling how I wish with all my heart and soul I could honourably back you up ... I do honestly believe that if the 'Labour Party' meant what you and some of those in the party are striving to make it every one of us would back you. But to my mind the tragedy of it all is that the vast mass of your often very ignorant supporters do not mean what you mean by Socialism ... It is an old story – as old as the Bible. When the Jews found following Christ meant the cross and not an earthly sovereignty and defeat of the Romans they turned on him and crucified their Lord ...

Tom's mother, a pious Christian, seems to have been the first person to see – and almost to welcome – that there might be something self-immolating in Tom's heroic stands. In the meantime there was the formal business of his application to join the Labour Party. To this, on March 27th 1924, Ramsay MacDonald replied –

> My dear Mosley,
>
> Although I have welcomed you into the Party by word of mouth, I would like to tell you in writing how pleased I am that you have seen your way to join us and to express the hope that you will find comfort in our ranks and a wide field in which you can show your usefulness.
>
> I am very sorry to observe in some newspapers that you are being subjected to the kind of personal attack with which we are all very familiar. I know it will not disturb you in the least, and I assure you

it will only make your welcome all the more hearty so far as we are concerned.

With kind regards
I am yours very sincerely,
J. Ramsay MacDonald

CHAPTER 6

Rebels

In the spring of 1924 a young German newspaperman, Egon Wertheimer, attended a meeting of the Labour Party in the Empire Hall in south-east London. He wrote:

Suddenly there was a movement in the crowd and a young man with the face of the ruling class of Great Britain but with the gait of a Douglas Fairbanks thrust himself forward through the throng to the platform followed by a lady in heavy, costly furs. There stood Oswald Mosley, whose later ascent was to be one of the strangest phenomena of the working class movement of the world . . .

The new man spoke . . . unforgettable was the impression, the visual and oral impression, which the style of the speech made on me. It was a hymn, an emotional appeal directed not to the intellect, but to the Socialist idea, which obviously was still a subject of wonder to the orator, a youthful experience. No speaker at a working class meeting in Germany would have dared to have worked so unrestrainedly on the feelings without running the risk of losing for ever his standing in the party movement . . .

But then came something unexpected; something that, by its spontaneity, shook me; although it was a trifling thing and seemed a matter of course to all those around me. From the audience there came calls; they grew more urgent; and suddenly the elegant lady in furs got up from her seat and said a few sympathetic words . . . She said that she had never before attended a workers' meeting, and how deeply the warmth of this reception touched her. She said this simply and almost shyly, but yet like one who is accustomed to be acclaimed and, without stagefright, to open a bazaar or a meeting for charitable purposes. 'Lady Cynthia Mosley' whispered in my ear one of the armleted stewards who stood near me, excited; and later as though thinking he had not sufficiently impressed me, he added 'Lord Curzon's daughter'. His whole face beamed proudly. All around the audience was still in uproar; as at a boxing match, or a fair.

Another commentator, John Scanlon, viewed this sort of scene with some despair, and said that whatever Tom's entry into the Labour Party had done for him, it was a disaster for the Party.

Stories of his fabulous wealth had spread themselves all over the country, and coupled with that was the fact that his wife was the daughter of Lord Curzon. The press lost no point in this human story, and those of us who had visions of a dignified working class steadily gaining confidence in itself as the future owners of Britain had our first shock of disillusionment. No sooner had Mr Mosley come into the Party than there began the heartbreaking spectacle of Local Labour Parties stumbling over themselves to secure him as their candidate. At that time there was not a particle of evidence to show that he understood one of the problems in their lives ... It was truly an amazing and saddening spectacle to see these working men, inheritors of a party formed by Keir Hardie in the belief that a dignified Democracy could, and should, run its own party, literally prostrate in their worship of the Golden Calf.

These two commentators were Marxists: Marxists are often amazed and disappointed at the ways of the working class. The British Labour Movement had been little influenced by international Marxism: its loyalties had been given to trade unions; or beyond them to the nation. Also in Britain, Tom used to say, there had always been an instinctive and emotional sympathy between the aristocracy and the working class who (in Lord Randolph Churchill's phrase) were 'united in the indissoluble bonds of a common immorality'. Together they showed disrespect for the puritanism both of left-wing intellectuals and of the bourgeoisie.

But then, in turn, it was natural that Labour intellectuals should distrust Tom after having been tempted to be charmed by him. Beatrice Webb wrote in her diary:

We have made the acquaintance of the most brilliant man in the House of Commons – Oswald Mosley. 'Here is the perfect politician who is also the perfect gentleman' I said to myself as he entered the room . . . So much perfection argues rottenness somewhere . . . Is there some weak spot which will be revealed in a time of stress – exactly at the very time when you need support – by letting you or your cause down or sweeping it out of the way?

This was the feeling also of such Labour Party stalwarts as Hugh Dalton and Herbert Morrison, who had worked their way up diligently through the ranks of the Party and resented Tom's sudden jump half way to the top. Almost immediately Tom had more than seventy invitations from constituencies to stand as their candidate for Parliament.

Tom's power was in his use of words: as a public speaker he could go over the heads of the Labour hierarchy and appeal directly to working class audiences. As soon as he had joined the party he was taken on a speaking tour of the midlands and north: the editor of a Birmingham newspaper wrote – 'His power over his audience was amazing; his eloquence made even hardened pressmen gasp'. He had learned to speak without notes (a trick he had learned, he wrote, by getting someone to read to him a leading article from *The Times* and then speaking in reply to it 'taking each point *seriatim* in the order read'). He had an amazing memory for figures. He liked to be challenged by hecklers, because he felt confident in his powers of repartee. But above all what held his audiences and almost physically lifted them were those mysterious rhythms and cadences which a mob orator uses and which, combined with primitively emotive words, play upon people's minds like music.

This power that Tom had with words did not always, in the long run, work to his advantage. There were times when his audience was being lifted but he himself was being lulled into thinking the reaction more substantial than it was. After the enthusiasm had worn off like the effects of a drug an audience was apt to find itself feeling rather empty. (In the same way Tom's girlfriends, one of them once said, would feel somewhat ashamed after having been seduced.)

Tom never understood the limitations of the power of words. He was apt to think that once a case had been reasonably and passionately stated the cause had been won: that if a difficult question had been parried or skilfully avoided, it had somehow disappeared. He did not see that it was often his very skill in the manipulation of words that made people suspect he might not be quite serious: for what is serious about a person who does such clever tricks with the difference between words and things? People reacted sometimes as the Conservative Association had reacted to him at Harrow: they admired his ability to spellbind, to bluff, to hit, to parry: but what had this got to do with what actually was required?

While he was on his speaking tour he wrote to Cimmie from the Durham and North Yorkshire Public House Trust Co:

His own darling Moo-Moo,
Does so miss her, but lucky she did not come as life is like the Great War – billets – no sheets etc – everyone very kind but a tiresome tour, lots of little 500 meetings, not my form at all, same kind friends also always accompanying, so have to improvise a different speech each time. Longing to return to wiz land and hopes to do so 10 p.m. tomorrow Monday (great excitement). All love in world from adoring
       her fellow.

Cimmie herself had joined Tom as a member of the Labour Party. The jibes which hitherto had been directed at Tom for his anti-Tory activities now also began to be directed at her. There were comments in the newspapers about her money: if she and Tom were socialists why did they not give their property away; why did they live in a house with sixteen rooms; why did Cimmie appear on Labour platforms in jewels and 'costly furs'? To this she and Tom replied that it would not help others in any serious way if they gave away their money and they could be of more use to socialism by themselves using it to finance organisation and propaganda. As for Cimmie's 'jewels' – they had been, in the instance quoted, she explained, bits of glass in a dress bought for a few shillings in India. There was then a peculiar wrangle with the Press on the subject of family titles. Tom was reported as having said he would not use the 'Sir' of his baronetcy when his father died; Cimmie as having remarked, rather irrelevantly, that she wanted to drop the 'Lady' Cynthia and be known as plain Mrs Mosley but that unfortunately there was no legal way of doing this. Tom summed up: 'In any case inside the Labour movement my wife is always known as Comrade Mosley and what she is called outside does not really matter.' But some of the Labour Party rank and file apparently did not want to let the matter rest: about a meeting in London the *Daily Mail* reported:

a series of quarrels were in progress among the audience about whether Mr Mosley is a duke, a knight, or a commoner. The Chairman attempted a compromise by describing him as 'Comrade Mosley' but this found disfavour with a row of very young women in front. Mr Mosley, caressing his miniature moustache with one hand and gaily slapping his razor-like trouser-leg with the other, beamed delightedly at the girls. One of them put his titular dignity beyond all doubt by exclaiming – Oh! Valentino!

Tom had gone on his tour of the midlands and north partly in order to choose a new constituency: he had decided that it would make no sense to stand for Labour at Harrow. The constituency he settled on was Ladywood, in central Birmingham: the sitting member was the conservative Neville Chamberlain. The Chamberlain family enjoyed almost feudal political power in Birmingham: it would be an extraordinary feat if Tom could even get near to dislodging him. Tom had been offered a number of relatively safe seats, but he seemed to sense that the initial euphoria in the Labour Party might, if he took too easy advantage of it, turn against him; and thus it would be most sensible for him to become involved in a serious fight.

The Labour Government of 1924 lasted less than a year. During the run up to the general election in November it appeared that there was such support for Tom in Ladywood that he might even win: then there was the Zinoviev letter – a document published just before the election purporting to come from the Communist International and encouraging British Communists to infiltrate the Labour Party but in fact a Tory forgery – and this had the effect of a number of hopeful Labour candidates just losing. At Ladywood it appeared at the first count that Tom had lost by seven; at the second count he had won by two; then at the third he lost by seventy seven. It was said that a Tory official had been seen 'disappearing towards the lavatory with a pile of votes'; but Tom discounted this, knowing that such stories were apt to crop up in close-run elections.

He did not seem to mind, in fact, the prospect of being out of Paliament for a while. This would give him time, he said, to sort out and to formulate his ideas: and he could probably choose when he liked a by-election by which he might be returned to Parliament.

Tom did in fact use the next two years to take stock of his position and to prepare for the future. He was twenty eight: he had had an extraordinarily crowded and successful career: but he had become known primarily as a critic with a cutting tongue and without much steadfastness or commitment to policy. It was essential, if he was to continue to claim to act on principle rather than on expediency or conventional party loyalties, that he should have a policy which would give substance to his principles.

During 1925 he and Cimmie went on a trip to India. The long journey by boat gave Tom an opportunity to read. He took out with him versions of the Vedas and the Upanishads ('every aspect of Indian religion had to be studied'); but the book that at this time made the most profound impression on him was one he picked up by chance in a bookshop in Port Said – Shaw's *The Perfect Wagnerite*. In the book Shaw takes the story of Wagner's *Ring* and interprets it as a parable about the collapse of capitalism and the emergence of a classless type of man to lead the proletariat: but Shaw cuts his own parable off before the last act of *Siegfried* and claims that from then on Wagner loses his grip on his serious theme and resorts to the histrionics of grand opera. But the point of the final dramas of the *Ring* is to illustrate how even the highest human intentions can be wrecked by human frailty; that the hopes of the most glorious leaders fail if frailty is not recognised. Tom, at this time, seemed to accept Shaw's truncated view of the allegory: drama might properly end with the hero in control. During the second half of his life, however, Tom wrote an essay which showed that he agreed more with Wagner than with Shaw.

One of the highlights of Tom's trip to India was a meeting with Gandhi: the latter was acting as chairman of a stormy meeting between Moslems and Hindus: Tom wrote – 'Throughout the uproar Gandhi sat on his chair on a dais, dissolved in helpless laughter, overwhelmed by the comical absurdity of human nature.' Tom seems to have loved India ('land of ineffable beauty and darkest sorrow') but at the time he did not seem to feel there was much in its paradoxes to be learned by him. He saw that India was being 'lost' by the 'bad manners' of Englishmen: but he did not easily think of politics in terms of what were and what were not good manners.

Another of the books he read on the journey to and from India was Keynes's *Tract on Monetary Reform*. Before this, his interest in politics had been mainly to do with matters of foreign or Irish policy – with the business of keeping the peace. He had made one important speech in 1921 on tariff reform; but for the most part he had felt no passionate concern with economic affairs. But when he joined the Labour Party he had seen, because he had been shown the manifestations of them, the most terrible and urgent problems of post-war England – poverty and unemployment. During his tour of the midlands he had been taken round the slums of Liverpool: he had written – 'The rehousing of the working classes ought in itself to find work for the whole of the unemployed for the next ten years.' This was typical, from now on, of the style of his thinking: if there were both unemployment and poverty, then surely, logically, it was the job of the government to use the unemployed to get rid of the poverty: questions of how, and using what money, should be secondary to the decision. But perhaps he did not have the confidence to expand on such theories until he read Keynes.

Tom's understanding of Keynes happened at a time when few English politicians were paying attention to him and there had been little in Tom's background to have made it likely that he would be the one who did. There were two strands of orthodox economic thinking at the time: one was the liberal laissez-faire attitude which insisted that world trade and the functioning of markets should be left to themselves: government interference not only threatened individual liberties but actually made economic conditions worse: this was a sort of ecological argument like that about the dangers of trying to manipulate the balances of nature. This made sense when the British, as pioneers of the Industrial Revolution, had been at the centre of the manipulation of world manufacture and world trade: it made less sense now, when British exports of machinery had resulted in a situation in which other countries, with cheaper labour, were now manufacturing more cheaply goods which had previously been almost a British monopoly. The second attitude was that of protectionism, which sought to keep out of Britain the products of other countries' cheap labour by imposing tariffs on imports. The trouble with this was that it required a market which would continue to accept, without imposing retaliatory tariffs, British manufactured goods which Britain needed to sell in order to be able to buy raw materials. Such had been the imperialist policy of Joseph Chamberlain and the Conservatives. But imperialist politics presupposed that colonies should be kept as producers of raw materials and buyers rather than producers of manufactured goods, and thus in a state of subjection. This not only seemed immoral but, in the face of world opinion and the threat of war, impractical. Thus British manufacturing industries, with the lack of a clear policy, continued to lose ground. There was poverty and unemployment.

Keynes's *Tract*, published in 1923, suggested that the government, by deliberately controlling and manipulating the supply of money, might affect the economic life of the country in areas which previously had been thought to be at the mercy of almost inexorable forces of nature. Tom became interested both in this new attitude to money and in the idea of government manipulation. In India he had been struck by the self-defeating attitudes of what had been up to now a mixture of laissez-faire and imperialism: he had seen the cotton mills where Indians worked 'for five shillings a week often with modern machinery supplied by

Lancashire for its own suicide: this was no monument either to the humanity or to the intelligence of the British Raj'. By the time he came back from India he had begun to work out his own theory – stimulated by Keynes, but arising from his own powers of reasoning unconfused by the complexities of academic training; also from his faith, now, that there were few human problems that could not be solved by reasoning.

Tom's economic theories became known as the Birmingham Proposals – after his candidature at Ladywood, he had made a political base in Birmingham. The proposals were outlined in speeches that he made to the Independent Labour Party Conference and Summer School in April and August 1925: they were of such importance to Tom's thinking and indeed to his whole political career that they deserve a chapter to themselves. Tom himself used to say in old age that he would like best to be remembered for his economic thinking; and all his subsequent economic thought – with its original vision and practical weaknesses – was for the most part an elaboration and elucidation of the Birmingham Proposals of 1925. Tom presented his theory in a pamphlet called *Revolution by Reason*: and in the very title can be seen something of the optimism and idealism of Tom's ways of thinking.

In 1926 Tom and Cimmie travelled in America. They tried to keep out of conventional smart society, though they were fêted by William Randolph Hearst and had a fine time as usual in esoteric café society. There was a big lawsuit going on at the time between Cimmie's Leiter relations: an English branch of the family, the Suffolks (Mary Curzon's younger sister Daisy had married the Earl of Suffolk in 1904) were suing an American branch, headed by Joe Leiter, who had become senior trustee of the Leiter Estate and whom his sister Daisy Suffolk was accusing of misappropriating funds. The Curzon branch of the family were nominally backing the Suffolks but were trying to keep clear: in Chicago, where the capitalist lawyers were at work, Cimmie and Tom painstakingly ensured that they were entertained by the Socialist Party of America. The chairman of this however telegraphed to them in rather grandiose style: 'It is a rare privilege to join with the good Comrades in Chicago in giving a royal welcome to these notable and high-souled comrades and making them feel they are at home in the hearts of their comrades in the glorious international'.

Tom and Cimmie also went on a fishing trip with Franklin Roosevelt on his yacht: they became friends: Tom thought Roosevelt 'a compassionate man' but with 'scarcely an inkling of the turmoil of creative thinking then beginning in America'. This creative thinking seemed to Tom to give support to his proposals in *Revolution by Reason*: he noted that 'the Ford factory produced the cheapest article and paid the highest wage in the world': was not this evidence that 'mass production for a large and assured home market is the industrial key'? He did not notice, or at least did not mention, that in Chicago for instance in 1926 there was enormous corruption.

When Tom got back to England he found that there was a by-election pending in Smethwick, a neighbouring constituency to Lady-wood in Birmingham. Tom was asked almost automatically if he would stand. He agreed. All the old skeletons were dug by the Tory Press out of their class-obsessed cupboards: Tom and Cimmie were supposed to drive up to Birmingham in a Rolls Royce and change into an Austin Seven in the suburbs: Tom was accused of having bribed the previous member of Parliament to retire (he was ill and died three months later): there were cartoons of Tom as a jewish-looking money-lender bribing the poor with bags of gold. Even Tom's father, the reprobate and by now somewhat alcoholic Sir Oswald, was unearthed by the *Daily Express* and in an interview said that Tom had been 'born with a golden spoon in his mouth... lived on the fat of the land, and had never done a day's work in his life'. Tom replied that he had been 'removed from the care of my father when I was five years of age by a court of law and since that date my father knows nothing of my life'. At the election meetings there was some violence: Tom's conservative opponent was, ironically a coal miner: when he referred to Tom's aristocratic background he was shouted down by Tom's followers singing *The Red Flag*. When this was reported scathingly in the Tory press a group of 'socialist amazons' tried to manhandle reporters in a press box. One of Cimmie's old school friends wrote to her from Scarborough – 'It isn't true, is it, that *you* climbed up on a wall and helped to shout down your opponent... My dear, I simply dare not own up that I know you here!'

But an editor wrote – 'If I were an elector of Smethwick the vicious personal attacks that are being made on him [Tom]... would certainly lead me to vote socialist'. And after Tom had got in, by a largely increased Labour majority of 6,582, the *Birmingham Post*, his chief opponent among the local papers, admitted that it had been unwise with its abuse: 'left to himself he would have fouled his own nest'.

Tom announced to the crowd outside the Town Hall – 'You have met and beaten the Press of reaction... My wonderful friends of Smethwick, by your heroic battle against a whole world in arms I believe you have introduced a new era for British Democracy.'

The Smethwick Labour party asked him whether, now the election

was over, he and Cimmie would at last consent to appear in their Rolls
Royce for the victory parade. Tom had to explain that the car really
was part of a myth.

CHAPTER 7

The Birmingham Proposals

Tom's Birmingham Proposals, which he regarded as central to his political thinking, were an attempt to move beyond both laissez-faire economics which allowed British manufacturing industries to be undermined by the produce of cheap foreign labour, and imperialist-protectionist economics which depended for success on colonial exploitation and the risk of war. Tom called his pamphlet *Revolution by Reason*. 'Revolution' was necessary because of the urgency of the problem: 'time presses in the turmoil of war's aftermath . . . crisis after crisis sends capitalism staggering ever nearer to abysses of inconceivable catastrophe to suffering millions'. A solution by 'reason' was possible because men had not yet taken all peaceful steps available in the matter of control.

With laissez-faire economics there was by definition little government control. With imperialist-protectionist economics there was still the threat of foreign retaliation and the country's vulnerability to it. Tom's 1925 proposals claimed that the problem could be faced in the first place exclusively in terms of the home market – over which, it might reasonably be thought, a government might have control.

The problems at home were poverty and unemployment. A cure for these was available, it was suggested, once a connection was seen between the two. The reason why there was industrial unemployment was because there was no demand for manufactured goods: the reason why there was no demand for manufactured goods was because there was so much poverty that people could not afford them; the reason why there was poverty was because there was unemployment. There was no way out of this vicious but almost ridiculously simple circle so long as laissez-faire dogma ordained that any government interference would only make things worse, and protectionism increased no one's ability to buy manufactured goods. What was required was that the government should make life-giving injections into this otherwise moribund circle – injections of money from State banks, so that the whole process should be reversed.

The injections of money were to take the form of credit being made available to the poorer sections of the community so that their new purchasing power would stimulate a demand for goods. This demand would in turn create employment in industries hitherto moribund, and this increased demand for labour would mean that in a short time the poorer sections of the community would be employed and earning their own keep. The whole scheme seemed rather magical: you just touched with a wand the viciously circular economic pumpkin as it were, and the national economy turned into a golden coach. Tom perhaps felt himself justified in having a certain contempt for people who seemed not to have thought of it before.

The reason why people had not talked much of this sort of thing before was of course a fear of inflation. If the government just pumped more money into the economy then it was likely that the effect would be simply that prices would rise and real purchasing power be lessened. To counteract this Tom proposed that the availability of credit should be commensurate with the production of goods: 'new and greater demand must of course be met by a new and greater supply of goods or all the evils of inflation and price rise will result. Here our socialist planning must enter in . . . the whole of Socialist strategy must be directed to preventing any attempt by Capitalism to avoid meeting the new demand with a greater supply of goods and to play for a rise in prices'.

To safeguard against this, it was essential in the first place that the money made available should get into the right hands: it should go, simply, to the poor and not to the rich. 'Money in the hands of the workers means demand upon the great staple industries in which men and machines are now idle'. In the hands of the rich 'it concentrates in sudden whim upon some unprepared industry or rare commodity: prices soar and an unhealthy boom begins': then the rich man's fancy changes, and there is collapse and unemployment. The traditional means of making credit more easily available was to lower the rate at which money could be borrowed from banks; but this 'encourages the least desirable kind of borrower . . . a rush of speculators follows in order to borrow cheap money from the banks to buy and hold up commodities in expectation of a rise in price . . . little of the new purchasing power percolates through to the working class'.

In order that credit should be made available to the workers, banks would have to be nationalised: also an Economic Council 'vested with statutory powers' of supervision and direction would have to be set up. This Economic Council would give directions about where credit should be made available to consumers and where it should not: moreover it would direct where and how credit should be made available to the producers, the industries. This was the second essential factor in the task of ensuring that the supply of money would not be greater than the supply of goods and cause inflation.

The business of this Council will be to estimate the difference between the actual and the potential production of the country and to plan the stages by which that potential production can be evoked through the instrument of working class demand. The constant care of the Economic Council must be to ensure that demand does not outstrip supply and thus cause a rise in price. It is evident that the new money must be issued gradually and that industry must be given time to respond to the new demand. If the whole working class were suddenly given a £1 rise in wages one Saturday night, an all-round rise in prices would be inevitable... The Council would feel their way gradually to the maximum production. Sometimes they might enforce a wage rise of 3d or 6d a week. Sometimes they might cry a halt until supply had time to catch demand.

The way in which it was suggested that credit would best be extended both to the working class and to industry would be through a method whereby credit was given to certain industries on condition that they paid higher wages: thus money would be made available for both workers and producers at the same time. 'The Economic Council would fix from time to time wages which individual firms or amalgamations were to pay. The State Banks would then grant overdrafts for the payment of these wages until the Economic Council directed that the industry could shoulder its own wage bill by reason of its increased prosperity. No additional overdraft for wage purposes would then be granted.' In this way, increased production of goods would balance an increase in money and inflation would be avoided. All this would not affect the responsibility of the State for 'the proper maintenance of human existence' at a more basic level: suitable sums would continue to be paid to the unemployed through Labour Exchanges. But by the manipulation of credit for wages and the production of goods it was expected that the unemployed would quite rapidly be absorbed.

This method of controlling credit to industries for the payment of higher wages would also ensure:

1 Luxury trades need not receive the accommodation and could be closed down as and when desired. The operatives could then be maintained on unemployment pay while they were trained for absorption in useful industry.

2 The extra profits arising from the new demand created for consumers would be automatically absorbed by wages to whatever extent was decided. The Economic Council would arrange the gradual cessation of overdraft accommodation . . . Special taxation to deal with excess profits would thus be unnecessary.

3 Wages could be forced up in the highly skilled trades as their production increased simultaneously with the rises in the less-skilled and lower-paid occupations.

4 The firm grip of the Socialist State over the whole remaining field of Capitalist activity would be finally established. All industry would owe money to the State banks. The Constitutionall Government would wield the vast powers now exercised by private bankers.

One of the chief aims of the operation, in fact was to take away power, and profit, from the hands of private financiers, and to give power to government and profit to workers and producers. Even if there was a small amount of inflation this would work to the detriment of financiers who obtained their money through fixed rates of interest, and it would be to the benefit of workers whose income was flexible. The whole scheme was one of 'summary socialism': if it worked it might indeed be some 'revolution by reason'.

The area of weakness in this otherwise admirable scheme and one that Tom did not explore – as he had not yet explored the weaknesses of Shaw's interpretation of Wagner's *Ring* – was the fact that it depended on human beings to make it workable. The Economic Council would have almost dictatorial powers: it is the case with human beings who have great powers unrestrained by traditional safeguards that they become corrupt or at best inefficient: even more, schemes that depend for their health on the near-miracle working of human beings usually carry with them the seeds of an almost deliberate self-destruction – as if the imposition of such responsibility sends people mad. Tom's proposals for the overriding powers of an Economic Council were forerunners of what later came to be his views about the necessity of a corporate Fascist state: it was his belief, rational in theory, that only by such powers could something decisive be done about situations of crisis. Tom in fact usually exaggerated the imminence of crises: but even in so far as he did not, he mistook something about human nature: he believed that human beings, when it had been clearly explained to them what were their vital needs and necessities, would not only altruistically but selfishly become honest and reasonable: they would sacrifice what might be short term advantages for long term ends. What he never saw was that in politics as in other forms of human activity human beings are for the most part interested in some sort of struggle, in manoeuvrings for power, in risks and even unpleasantnesses; and that these are often in direct opposition to what might reasonably be seen as long-term ends. Tom always saw himself as the perfectly reasonable man at the head of something like the proposed Economic Council: about other people, he was torn between imagining they were like how he imagined himself, and being dismissive of them when he found that they were not. If he had had talent for introspection or had allowed himself much practice at it, he might have seen that within the area of his own short-term drives and obsessions there were possibly seeds of self-destruction: he had a gambler's love of challenge and risk: the way he showed his contempt for his fellow politicians, for instance, was unlikely to work for his long-term ends. But his refusal to see that a consideration of what human beings are actually like is a vital part in any scheme about what human beings can actually do, is at the heart of the failures of this story.

Perhaps what allowed him to be so impervious to rumination about human nature or himself was the tendency of his critics to be just the same. It had been the tradition of economists to assume without argument that human beings were reasonable: this was a rule of the game: how else could they carry on as though their pronouncements were scientific and not at any moment likely to become nonsensical? It had been the tradition of left-wing politicians to make out that however much capitalists and conservatives had been and always would be corrupted by power, the revolutionary working class would not be: how else could they go on playing the game of protesting that as representatives of the working class they were incorruptibly driving for power? But whereas most of these people for all their lack of facility for introspection did seem to have some unspoken instinct, in England at least, about what human beings were actually like – they usually in fact withdrew before the probable consequences of their words had had much effect – Tom, by reason perhaps of his upbringing or nature, did not: he had the aloofness and perhaps the arrogance to believe that reasonable words, at least his own, might in fact mean what they implied. This was one reason why he could so often make rings round his opponents by reasoning: he believed in it; while they, although they said they did, ultimately did not. Yet what they felt instinctively, and might have answered Tom by, was traditionally unspoken. They could not say to him in effect – Look, in your reasoning you leave out of account something about human nature: you leave out the fact that human beings with part of themselves like turmoil and something to grumble at and perhaps even failures to feel comfortable in: your economic perfect blue-print will not work simply because people will not want it to. They could not say this to him because this sort of language was not in the area prescribed for politicians. But then they could not argue with Tom because he could beat them by his un-trammelled faith in reason. As a result they had to answer him by ostracising him and hardly answering him at all. This had the effect on Tom of making him think that his arguments were unanswerable: and so a new vicious circle was set up – that of Tom having contempt for his opponents for their silence, and they, stung by this, having no reply except a hatred that might indeed sometimes seem contemptible.

Tom might have learned something of the paradoxes of human nature, it might have been thought, from his relationship with Cimmie: but the convention was overwhelming that human beings might be one sort of thing in their private lives, but were something quite different and altogether more straightforward in politics. Every now and then Tom did seem to have an inkling of where the demands he was making on people by his proposals might lead were they ever put into effect – of how there might be failure unless a demand for something more than economic rationality was met. But then – what was a proper attitude to the risk of failure? Towards the end of even such a staid document as *Revolution by Reason* Tom dropped his tone of logic and entered into the rhetoric which was his other special talent, and which he used to try to persuade people when he felt the sands of reason running out; also, perhaps, to cover doubts that he must sometimes have felt yawning beneath himself. The style of the pamphlet suddenly changes: the substance of the rhetoric – and this is characteristic of the perorations of nearly all Tom's speeches – is permeated by a concern that has nothing to do with reason. The final tone of *Revolution by Reason* is a call for sacrifice and a bid for glory:

> We have reached a supreme crisis in the history of humanity. We stand, indeed, at the cross roads of destiny. Once again in the lash of great ordeal stings an historic race to action ...

We must recapture the spirit of rapturous sacrifice. That immortal spirit was evoked by war between men of many common interests for purposes still obscure or frustrated. Why cannot a greater spirit be summoned forth by the war of all mankind against poverty and slavery? In our hands is the awakening trumpet of reality. Labour alone holds the magic of sacrifice. Dissolved are all other creeds of baser metal beneath ordeal by fire.

CHAPTER 8

Nursery World

My own consciousness as it emerged into this setting of strangely mixed reason and rapture was such that very little remains in it of these early years: I remember nothing of the country houses in which we stayed during the summers before I was four: and of the London house in Smith Square – where we lived on and off till I was eight – I remember a few scenes but with myself as a spectator as it were looking down on myself rather than as a participant. 8 Smith Square was a Queen Anne house or more accurately two houses knocked into one: my father used to say it was too small because the family were so much on top of each other: literally on top were the day nursery and night nursery on the third floor. In the night nursery the cots of my sister Vivien and myself were side by side and at night we would tell each other fantastic stories about children who had run away from their families and who lived in jungles or on rafts. When Nanny came to bed we would try to lie awake and watch her in half dark and through half closed eyes as she performed her amazing trick of undressing and putting on her nightdress without appearing at any moment to be wearing anything less than her full complement of clothing. In the day nursery there were cupboards full of toys all along one wall and life there seemed to be mainly a matter of being ready to do battle with my sister about minuscule matters of possession or prestige: however spoilt we were in our vast quantity of toys, there was still the desire for what the other had got and the possibility of a fight almost to death against dispossession. If my father had wanted to learn about human nature, he might have come up more often to the nursery.

From the square below – we were usually in London during winter – there would come from time to time strange noises that did seem to emanate from some jungle: the sound of the muffin man with his bell, who carried his tray on his head; the cries of the any-old-iron man with his horse and cart who seemed to be calling for dead bodies. In the evenings there was the lamplighter with his long pole with a star on the end like the wand of a magician.

Each year there was a great festivity in the streets, which was boat-race day. Two men would appear very early on opposite corners of the square selling pale-blue and dark-blue rosettes. Huge crowds seemed to gather and drift past. The part of the river where the race took place was miles away, as indeed was anything to do with Oxford or Cambridge from most of the people who liked so arbitrarily and passionately to take sides. My sister and I, for no reason, were dedicated to Cambridge.

Most mornings our normal routine was for Nanny, Vivien and myself (at first in a pram) to go up Great Smith Street, past Parliament Square, across Birdcage Walk, and into St James's Park and then on to Hyde Park if Nanny felt energetic. In St James's Park we would feed the ducks or the pelicans: we were dressed very smartly for this: I remember buttons on boots and gaiters which were fastened with a sort of torture-instrument with a hook. One of the points of being immaculate in the parks was so that Nanny should not lose prestige with other nannies. Before she had come to us, Nanny had been for a time with a branch of the Rothschild family: we met, and had to keep up with, their children Rosemary and Eddie.

In the afternoons we would go down to our mother in the drawing room when she and my father were there. I remember nothing of these times. One of my sister's few memories (she was at Smith Square on and off till she was ten) is of our mother reading a story to us in the drawing room and then having to break off and rush away to vote in the House of Commons – a bell which had been installed in the house having gone off like a burglar alarm.

Sometimes my mother and father would come up to the night nursery to say goodnight before they went out to dinner. I have more memories of my father than my mother at these times, perhaps because he tried to be funny. Once he was going to dinner at Buckingham Palace and he was wearing full evening dress with medals: he showed us how he had pinned these medals on his behind. I remember thinking this enormously funny.

My sister Vivien is two and a half years older than I. When I was born, my mother reported that she was 'very gentle and attentive': Nanny reported that she exclaimed 'I'll bite him!' A year later Nanny wrote 'Vivien gets so excited when he walks and usually yells so loudly that it frightens him and down he flops'. By 1925 she was recording – 'Nicko tries so hard to turn cartwheels and somersaults like the clowns but Vivien's one ambition is to hold him high above her head with one hand.' My stepmother Diana used to say that my sister and I were like the characters in the *Peanuts* cartoon, Charlie Brown and Lucy. We were very close, and loved each other, and fought, and doubtless did much to save each other's lives.

Nanny's letters to my mother were beautifully written in a clear unadorned style. They began 'Dearest Lady Cim' and ended 'Love from Odie' – which had been Cimmie's nickname for Nanny when she herself had been a child. Nanny was a brave, strongwilled woman without a trace of subservience: she seemed to look on most of the grown-up world as children. She accepted some conventions of the time about upbringing which would now be thought idiosyncratic: she would keep my sister and me for what seemed hours (and I think sometimes was) on our pots: we became adept at moving about the room on them like hermit crabs: our word for shit became – in the light of Nanny's injunctions – 'try-hard'. I have wondered what Freudians would make of this conjunction of shit with 'try-hard'. It was also about this time that I apparently got an obsession about taking keys out of doors and putting them down lavatories.

The time when I first seemed to become a participant rather than an onlooker in my childhood scene was when my mother and father bought a house near Denham, in Buckinghamshire, at the end of 1926: this was to be our home for the next fourteen years. Denham was only twenty miles from London but in those days it was in farming country: the house when we bought it was called Savoy Farm but my mother changed the name back to its more ancient form of Savehay Farm which was more in keeping with what she liked in the way of rustic simplicity. It was an Elizabethan farmhouse with six bedrooms and four reception rooms and a huge garden surrounded by water. My mother and father added a new wing at the back which contained four more guest rooms and servants rooms and a servants' hall. We moved into Savehay Farm in the spring of 1927 and the best of my childhood seems to have been nurtured by this house: I can remember details of every room in it: I still sometimes dream that I have bought it back, and am living there. I suppose it represents some Garden of Eden.

The river that ran past the end of one of the lawns of the garden was the Colne, a tributary of the Thames. There was a punt and a large canoe on the river and these could, with difficulty, be manoeuvred by my sister and me along a sidestream that ran right round the house – over a waterfall and under bridges – a notable adventure. There were two weirs on the river, one at each end of our land (a hundred and twenty acres of farm-land which went with the house): across one weir there was a bridge that led to an island thick with undergrowth like a jungle; across the other a bridge led to a thatched cottage, empty, like something in a fairy tale. During weekdays my father and mother were usually away: Nanny miraculously (or because she had been brought up in a home of sixteen children) did not take too much notice of what went on out of her sight: my sister and I were thus allowed much freedom. We would devise fantastic explorations and obstacle courses for ourselves: these were known as 'mucks': from branch to branch of trees, along the tops of walls, down over a water-wheel, up through high barn windows. (There were huge high barns unused because of the state of farming at the time in England). The bridge across the weir to the magic island jungle had partly collapsed, but it could still be crossed with legs on either side of the handrail: beyond the island there was a gigantic railway viaduct and beyond this, like an ogre, someone called Sir Robert Vansittart lived, who was an enemy of my father's, being something to do with the Foreign Office. In the thatched cottage at the other end of the river my sister and I were sometimes allowed to camp; like Hansel and Gretel having been freed from their fairy tale.

What meant most to me about Savehay Farm I think was that for the first time I was able to be alone: before this, I had had to go under bed-clothes and pretend to be in a one-man submarine before I felt alone. At Savehay Farm there was space – also room to hide. There was a carved-out hollow in a thicket of bamboos; a passage through brambles and nettles; a disused tank in the rafters of a barn. In such places I could crouch, and listen, and hear the cries of huntsmen and steps of predators going past. The huntsmen and predators were only my good nanny and sister – those denizens of my unconscious. But my main memories of Savehay Farm have become to do with my own five senses: the hot buzzing of flies above nettles; the high ribs of the viaduct from which cold drips dropped down; the soddenness of weeds like bodies against the grating of a weir; the acrid smell of old plaster coming off the walls of the thatched cottage like dead skin.

Even when my parents were at Savehay Farm they usually dallied in their own part of the garden. There was a rose-garden where my father sometimes walked: he would go to and fro, up and down; preparing his speeches, I suppose, by which he might order the world. In summer he would sometimes walk there naked: Nanny would warn us – Do not go near! God walked thus, I suppose, in the Garden of Eden. So by seeing my father, or God, naked, might one know the difference between good and evil? I would creep along the passage on the first floor to where there was a window that looked over the rose-garden: this was risky because the window was in my father's bedroom: but if he was in the rose-garden he could not – or could he? – be in two places at once? However then, after all – how white and gentle and vulnerable he looked! So what was all the fuss about our not being allowed to see him in the rose-garden?

My father was, it was true, sometimes frightening. He had a way of suddenly switching from being the benign joker to someone with his chin up, roaring, as if he were being strangled. He would usually roar when he was not getting what he wanted – from servants; from my mother. Once when he was trying to work in his study and a small dog that belonged to my sister and myself was outside on the lawn barking, he leaned out of his window with his shotgun and fired off both barrels in the general direction of the dog. The dog stopped barking. My sister and Nanny were somewhat outraged at this: but I remember thinking – He would not have missed, would he, if he had been aiming at the dog? And how more efficiently do you stop a dog barking?

Nanny would tell stories of my father's terrible rudeness to servants: but she would add – 'He was only once rude to me.' Then she would wait, looking stern; and we children would understand that she had perhaps just looked thus at my father. She also told a story about Mabel, the parlourmaid, an equally formidable woman who was the friend of May, the gentle housemaid. Once my father had been rude to Mabel and then to her too he had never been rude again: she had answered him back with a very rude word. We knew it was no good pressing Nanny to tell us what was this word: it was something that grown-ups could tell stories about, but not utter.

Life for the children revolved, as usual, around Nanny, Mabel and May, and Andrée, my mother's lady's maid. Andrée had been with my mother before she had married: she stayed with the family, as Nanny did, after my mother's death for more than twenty years. She was a small determined Frenchwoman; indeed it is difficult to imagine my father being rude to her. I think my father must have got his reputation for rudeness from his relationships with manservants; which is probably why they do not seem to have been permanent figures in my childhood. There was for a time a Mr Cox, the butler, who hung about in a striped apron in the pantry and was the guardian of a huge knife-sharpening machine like a butter-churn, and another machine which curiously could sharpen two pencils at once. I have no memories of any cook; they too must have come and gone: my mother had no reputation for caring about good cooking.

There were three staircases in the house – one at my father's and mother's end, one in the middle between the day and the night nursery, and one in the new wing between the guest rooms and the rooms of the servants. The only person who had a room regularly at my mother's and father's end of the house was my Aunty Baba; she was put in a rather grand room with a seventeenth century fresco on the wall of men in striped knickerbockers playing golf. Aunty Nina was always put at the other end of the house. To the children, in the middle, it often seemed as if we owned the house; it was we who remained, and the people looking after us, when everyone else had gone.

My mother's and father's end of the house was somewhat secret; taboo. You went along the passage, up three steps, were on the threshold of mysteries. My mother's bedroom was large and blue and airy and had a mass of small glass ornaments on shelves: they were of animals and birds and of a kind that would now probably be thought rather vulgar: my mother collected these when she went abroad, especially in Venice. My father's bedroom was smaller and brown and looked out on to the rose-garden: there was a scrubbed oak chest in it that was always locked. Of even deeper mystery were my mother's and father's bathrooms – there were two side by side across the passage. My mother's bathroom had the usual array of bottles and bowls and powders and creams; my father's had an enigmatic apparatus that hung on the back of the door and looked like a gutted octopus. I knew it was no use asking Nanny about this: the subject would be unmentionable like the word used by Mabel the parlourmaid. I worked out later that it was an apparatus for giving enemas.

When the children came down in the evenings at Savehay Farm we went not to the formal drawing room which was used only when guests were in the house, but to my mother's sitting room which was known as the Garden Room. This had low beams and a huge open fireplace and glass walking sticks hanging on the walls: there my mother would read to us. Once my father was persuaded to read poetry: he read Swinburne, and I fell asleep, and when I woke was covered with confusion. I wanted to ask – But might not such beautiful noises be supposed to send you to sleep?

There were certain moments of the year when it was the tradition that mothers and fathers should make special efforts with their children; the most striking of these was Christmas. After the usual opening of the stockings at Savehay Farm and the going to church with Nanny (my mother and father never went to church) and after further presents and the christmas lunch, we had our special ritual. My father would say that he had to have a short sleep; we would exhort him not to, because after lunch was the time when Father Christmas arrived and my father might miss him. My father would promise that he would only have a nap, and be there for Father Christmas. But then at about three o'clock we would hear Father Christmas's sleigh-bells outside – this was my mother and Mabel the parlourmaid tinkling away in the garden – and we wanted to wake up my father but it was held to be too late: we were rushed out of the house by Nanny: Father Christmas was said to be already arriving at the top of the chimney. Father Christmas was of course my father, who in his study having dressed up in Father Christmas clothes complete with realistic beard and mask was now climbing up the Garden Room chimney on a stepladder held by May the housemaid while we were hoping to see him coming down from the sky at the top. We were again too late! Father Christmas was already on his way down the chimney – we were rushed back into the house just in time to see him emerge into the Garden Room down the steps held by May. All this was expertly handled by my mother – or else we children were rather thick. But my father was a very good actor: he spoke in a slow exhausted voice: poor Father Christmas! with all the other children in the world to get round to! one should not ask too many questions. And of course he had to wear a mask, to protect his face from soot. Anyway there was not much time: after we had got our presents from his sack we were rushed out of the house to see if we could catch him coming out of the roof: we just missed him again! but couldn't we hear the sleigh bells? And then after a suitable time of chasing bells around the garden there was the business of running back to my father's study and accusing him of being, yet again, so greedy and lazy that he had to go to sleep after lunch and miss Father Christmas! After a time I think I came to believe that Father Christmas must come from Harrods. Neither my sister nor I saw through my father's act while he was doing it.

There was a further ritual on Christmas evening which my father once more dominated and by which he charmed his children as indeed he charmed women. Just as my mother, when he was being loving towards her, was his mutton, his moo-moo; so were his children, as his term of endearment, porkers. When we children were making too much noise in his presence he would intone, as if it were some mystic mantra – 'What is it that makes more noise than one porker stuck under a gate?' – and we would groan, because we had heard the answer so many times before: and then he would give the answer himself – 'Two porkers stuck under a gate!' – and then he would laugh, with a strange clicking sound behind his teeth. On Christmas evenings, then, we would gather round the Christmas tree and we would all hold hands and my father would begin one of his mantra chants and this would go faster and faster as we went faster and faster round the tree until we all fell down and my father's chant would be just – Porker porker porker...

All this was rather magical for children: the gods descended, and played, and put on a tremendous performance. But still, when the excitement was over, what was the world from which the gods came down? It did in fact seem that much of ordinary grown-up life consisted of things like making remarks that did not require answers with a distant look in one's eye; uttering noises which had the effect of everyone's falling about roaring with laughter. My awareness of my mother's and father's friends at Savehay Farm belongs to a slightly later time in this story: but what I remember from an early age about the grown-up world – not the world of Nanny and Mabel and May who stayed around and got things done but the world of god-like figures who came and went – was the way in which people did in fact seem to be making noises that were more like a baying, a trumpeting, than the telling of anything: noises just to let other people know that they were there, perhaps; or to give warning; or possibly to attract new friends. These noises most often came from behind closed doors: grown-ups did not seem to want to perform their most esoteric rituals in front of children. But at Savehay Farm I would creep down from time to time and would listen outside the dining room door which was just at the bottom of the nursery stairs; this was when my mother and father were having what Nanny called a dinner. The uproar seemed to be talk: but what on earth were they talking *about*; and who was listening? It was like the cries of the any-old-iron man; the bell of the man selling muffins. It was the roar of some jungle: not the nice quiet jungle across the broken bridge over the river: it was as if there were a forest fire.

CHAPTER 9

The Legend

When Cimmie arrived back from America in 1926 she gave an interview to an American newspaper in which she explained about what had been thought from her youth to have been her 'bolshevik' views, and why she had become a socialist.

> If you are to understand my position, you must take into account all the facts in my upbringing. You will understand that either I had to give in absolutely to the past – to ignore all that was happening in this country and the rest of the world – or to resist upon every issue. I suppose my father and I were two very typical figures, and that the same drama has been enacted in many homes; only I do not know another man who was so splendidly, so utterly symbolic of the old world, the pre-war world, as was my father. I should like to think that I am as typical of the new world, the post-war world.

When George Curzon was dying in March 1925 and he was already not on speaking terms with Cimmie owing to the quarrel over her money, she and Tom had just returned from their trip round India. George Curzon was told a story about how Tom, when in India, had been present at an official dinner at which the King's health had been drunk and he, Tom, had refused to raise his glass. At first Curzon had not believed this story; then, because he learned that so many other people had heard it, he believed that it 'must be true'. All this was related back to Cimmie by a Curzon aunt. A few days later her father died.

The story of the wine-glass in India is typical not only of the sort of stories that were told about Tom but of his own and other people's reactions to them. It is inconceivable that the incident in the story could have been enacted by Tom deliberately: such a gesture would have seemed to him just silly. But there were of course people who would want to imagine such a story; and Tom did little to persuade them it might not be true. The Curzon aunt who related the story to Cimmie finished her letter with – 'But why does Tom not take steps to deny these stories?' – and her question seems relevant to something that might be true.

Members of the aristocracy in those days had put upon them some of the fantasies that are now put on to pop-singers and film-stars: they were the stuff of newspaper gossip: people queued up in streets to see them. Cimmie had become a somewhat legendary figure at the time of her marriage: there were other upper class girls like this: but there was no one quite like Cimmie after she had become Labour.

In the Labour Party Cimmie and Tom took upon themselves a new form of adulation: it seemed part of the new legend perhaps that they should also suffer calumny. Cimmie's old friends took trouble to write to her about things they had overheard at dinner parties or on the tops of buses – 'It's enough to make 'er father get up out of 'is grave and smash 'er, vulgar little beast'. But if she and Tom started to worry about replying to such remarks, they might not be able to be able to maintain their energy and dignity as pioneers. People who become legendary must have something in them that wants to be like this: they must be impervious to, thrive on even, something of calumny: part of their strength, and their magic, is that they should seem to scorn herd-reactions. This can be a danger, as well as a strength. Tom sometimes went to great trouble legally to take action about libels against him: he almost never, in the light of what people said about him, showed much personal concern or modified his behaviour.

What Tom in his possibly for the most part unconscious heart seems to have wanted to do is to create a legend: this was more fundamental to him than that he should acquire power. Tom's biographer, Robert Skidelsky, has written about him that 'he was a complete professional in everything except the winning of power'. This was not just through mischance: it is an aristocratic attitude that says – Take me or leave me; I am as I am; either follow me or do not. It is this sort of attitude, also, that creates legends. And there is a way perhaps, in which the world in the long run is more affected by legends than by the manipulation of power: legends alter the way people think: this is on a higher level (if they are recorded) than that of power.

This would not have been worked out by Cimmie or Tom; there was something of it inevitably in their natures. They both came from backgrounds in which what mattered was more what you were than what you did: aristocrats are supposed to have star quality – they are not simply actors. Both of them moreover seemed to have had some need of the aura that surrounds legends: as if only by this could they live up to the expectations they had found themselves landed with. They had to have constant reassurance – as if to placate demons.

With Tom there was his compulsion to be so frequently running after, and conquering, women: by this he got reassurance. He also used his seductive powers politically. A Labour colleague remembers being bowled over by Tom's flattery; then seeing Tom's eyes going past him to a waiting crowd.

Tom was good at telling Cimmie how wonderful she was: his letters contain almost endless protestations of love. He and Cimmie were known to quarrel: he had a terrible temper: he sometimes abused her publicly. Yet in all his letters to her there are hardly any words of reproach. It is as if, so far as letters were concerned, what was important to him was the use of gentle and reasoned words to retain her love: this was more important to him than efforts to face facts or get at the truth. He willed that he should retain her love by telling her so often how she had his own.

> My own most precious in the world, take care of her darling self and be strong and well for his return and fun with him. My own beloved – give a kiss to herself from her adoring Tom

With Cimmie, there had always been her recognition that she needed protestations of love: she had written of this as a schoolgirl: her mother had died when she was seven: her father, whom she admired, had fought her: she had needed to put herself at the centre of a group of adored and adoring friends. She would have accepted Tom's protestations simply because she required them.

> I do think it's been a good thing to be apart just for once, it may even be a good thing some time again, but please not for a very very long time. I so adore your letters, but I do so terribly miss you.

Then by joining the Labour Party Cimmie opened herself to a whole new form of adulation: she became like some star actress suddenly offered a stage. She and Tom became the special favourites of Independent Labour Party politicians from Glasgow – James Maxton, Pat Dollan, John Wheatley. Tom was in great demand as an orator: he was loved for his rhetoric, his style. Pat Dollan wrote to Cimmie 'He has leader qualities but he must be prepared to fight every inch. I like him when he is combatant because his combatant temper is what we need'. Glasgow politicians did not much like his pamphlet *Revolution by Reason*, because its reasonable socialist proposals would interfere with the freedom of Trade Union bargaining. But Cimmie began to be almost as much in demand as Tom: this was due not to her power with words, but simply to her ability to get herself loved. Pat Dollan wrote after an Independent Labour Party summer school – 'Yourself were one of the best of sports and everybody was pleased with you for your fun, fellowship, adventure and readiness to help. There is big work for you to do for the ILP and Socialism, and you can do it.'

The Independent Labour Party had been formed at the end of the nineteenth century to keep pure the creed of socialism at a time when many groups which called themselves Labour had not been sure about what alliances might be made. It still in the 1920's saw itself as the power-house of true socialism. It held its summer schools at Easton Lodge, a house belonging to Lady Warwick; where, in Tom's words 'very serious discussions' were rounded off in the evenings by 'charades, songs and dances'; also 'elements of the modern love-in'.

During 1925 Cimmie received many offers herself to stand for Parliament: she accepted one to become the Labour candidate for Stoke-on-Trent. This was not far, but perhaps, far enough, from Tom's constituency at Smethwick.

In London Cimmie had for some time been giving dinner-parties for Labour politicians – Ramsay MacDonald, Arthur Henderson, J. H. Thomas. James Maxton refused – 'I make a point of steering clear of all social functions.' Ramsay MacDonald continued his rather flowery flirtation with Cimmie – 'That disgruntled left-winger, Providence, has given me a nasty knock since we whispered "Easter" to each other and Tom made the scandalous proposal that I should take you to Corsica whilst he went to the ILP conference'. But then – 'I shall do what you like on Tuesday, dine in or out, go to a solemn or gay play (the latter preferred)'. Cimmie sent him a Christmas present for which he thanked her:

One corner of my books shelves says to the other 'I was given by so-and-so' and looks most self-satisfied. Another answers 'Poof! do you know what Lady Cynthia gave *me*?' and puts its nose in the air.

Cimmie became something of a guardian angel to men who were now working with Tom and who might have been somewhat in awe of him but who found Cimmie approachable. Foremost amongst these was Allan Young, the son of a railway worker in Glasgow, who came to Birmingham as Labour agent for Tom and later became his full-time political secretary in London. He wrote to Cimmie after a weekend in the country in 1926 –

> My thanks for a jolly weekend are delayed but sincere. I blush occasionally in fear that my crude behaviour may have irritated you but you will be kind and tolerant I am sure. After all I was 'born to the thong and the rod' and my body and mind are perhaps not yet attuned to sweeter things ...

Then later, when he had been with Tom and Cimmie abroad –

> You gave me beauty – pictures that will live for ever: space – in the sense that I was separated from the vortex of petty problems: privacy – in the sense that your fine culture (which is feeling) enables you to refrain from interference. I shall *dream* no more of France and Italy – I shall enjoy their beauty because I have absorbed it. The sun will stay with me now, and the added width and scope of my life and imagination will enable me to appreciate to the fullest the sweetness and generosity of your friendship.

Another of Tom's Birmingham colleagues that Cimmie took under her wing was John Strachey, five years younger than Tom, son of St Loe Strachey the editor of the *Spectator* and cousin of Lytton Strachey. He had joined the Labour Party before he had met Tom; then Tom helped him to get a constituency at Aston in Birmingham. John Strachey was unlike most of the people who worked in politics with Tom and Cimmie at this time in that he was upper or upper-middle class: he had been to Eton and Oxford. He hero-worshipped Tom. He was some sort of cavalier to Cimmie.

During the summer of 1925 he had spent much time with them and he was their guest in Venice in August. He and Tom there worked together on *Revolution by Reason*; later John Strachey wrote a book with the same title as Tom's pamphlet. Bob Boothby was also a guest of Tom's and Cimmie's in Venice that summer: he wrote years later – 'Every morning Tom Mosley and John Strachey discuss *Revolution by Reason* ... This was the period when Mosley saw himself as Byron rather than Mussolini ... He was certainly a powerful swimmer and used to disappear at intervals into the lagoon to commune with himself.' When

Strachey's book was finished he dedicated it to 'O.M. who may one day do the things of which we dream.'

John Strachey was by far the closest of Tom's Labour associates: he was an intellectual: he was the only friend who without much difficulty straddled, as Tom and Cimmie apparently so effortlessly did, the world of Birmingham socialist politics and international high-life in Venice. In 1925 he wrote a thank-you letter to Cimmie:

Dear, dear Cim
(I can't rise to Bob's beginning).
When one has stayed with someone off and on for about six months there is something rather comically inadequate about writing a Collins. Still I do want, somehow or other, to thank you for Venice. I quite literally can't tell you how much I enjoyed it. But almost more than that it has somehow *meant* a most tremendous lot to me. In some obscure way I feel quite different to before I went – altogether more capable of *coping* with life. Of course it is largely that one feels so marvellously well – with deep reserves of sun-energy in one.
And I do terribly want to tell you how grateful I am to you. I know very well my many imperfections and shortcomings as a guest, so I realise *how* nice of you it has been to bear with me so many months. But Venice was marvellous. I ran through, in that month, as many kinds of emotions and experiences as would last in England for a year. It somehow enlarged and liberated one. (Bob felt it – as he showed in that never sufficiently admired letter of his!) A little more and we shall, as he put it, strike the big notes again.
I am talking nonsense – I only mean that when we were all together we sometimes seemed able to strike points, moments, sparks, of enjoyment, of *fun*, which set the place on fire.
A more incoherent letter than usual. But please, please, take it as a symbol, a token, o something felt very deeply, even though not expressed at all. You were, you are, the centre round which we all radiated. Thank you.

John

Bob Boothby was a young conservative MP. He disagreed with Tom politically: but he believed, and continued to do so during a friendship which lasted for the whole of Tom's life, that there were more important things in life (and indeed in politics) than political agreement. The letter he wrote to Cimmie and which John Strachey mentions in his letter, was:

Darling Lady Cynthia,

(I humbly apologise – all other words are hopelessly inadequate).

How can I thank you as you ought to be thanked? An impossible task! I enjoyed – rapturously – every moment. No, there was one – at Faustino's entertainment – when I had drunk too little and too much – that which produces the 'grumpy' stage – and I was a credit neither to you nor to myself: but I withdrew once more to 'commune alone with the sea' ...

I can truthfully say that never in my life have I experienced such sustained enjoyment at so high a pitch. It was MARVELLOUS (one l or two? one I think). I thank you 1000 times ... If and when I do return I am going to ask you to let me spray myself with your palm oil and sit, at intervals, within hail of your 'cabano' and throw a medicine ball at you and give you dinner at the Luna – if you will. I did a crazy thing the night I left – took the fastest motor boat in Venice and flew to the Lido and looked at the moon, which was farcical, and lay on the sands and got bitten by sand-fleas, and vastly overpaid the motor-boat man, and came back god knows when in a 'vapore' and the slowest gondola in Venice. But it was exquisite and I loved it.

I think your husband (damned Socialist though he is By God) will be Prime Minister for a very very long time, because he has the Divine Spark which is almost lost nowdays, and getting less and less. They had it once – all of them. I've just been reading here a life of Chopin: a medium composer maybe, but a tremendous man. Broken by his own powers of emotional feeling – a hitch in some paltry love affair enough to send him to bed in a decline for months – what reduces us to inane guffaws reduced them to a temperature of 104, consumption, and death. The result being that they produced creative geniuses by the dozen – and what do we produce? The Lido beach. It's a little disheartening.

I'm so sorry about this outburst but I learnt with you what some have tried in vain to teach me – that the only possible thing to do is to steep oneself in the XVIIIth and early XIXth centuries and try to understand (if not try to catch a touch of) the spirit that moved them. For this – for the gondola, for the palatial drawing room, the food, the champagne, the fun both in and out of the water (bar that appalling boat that sank, and a dive I can never quite forget) the arguments (not least the one about Torcello) and the staggering hospitality in every direction – I thank you ...

Yours ever most gratefully and sincerely
Bob Boothby

PS. I am conscious of having been, on the whole, *not* a success. But I think I have *one* conquest to my credit. Mabel (that Great Woman) said 'Goodbye Old Man' — and I *thought* her voice broke.

There were many people who at this time wrote to Cimmie similar (if not so good) letters: they tell of her gaiety; of her ability to give enjoyment; of how under her attention people seemed to expand and feel transformed. This ability to produce warmth and wit in personal life seemed as important to her as was the ability to produce enthusiasm in the world of politics: it seemed important to Tom too, who got pleasure from social life far beyond the taking up of opportunities for flirtation and conquest. Before he had met Cimmie he had of course shone in this area, but perhaps without much ease: throughout his married life Tom depended for naturalness in social relationships largely on his wives. But in 1925 it would have been the problem for both him and Cimmie to try to relate — if they wanted to — the world of Venice and the South of France to that of the Birmingham and Clydeside politicians.

Sometimes Cimmie was warned of such a difficulty by more a serious voice than those of newspapers which continued to ask simply — How could anyone be a socialist and go to Venice and have fun? Tom's and Cimmie's answer to this sort of question continued sensibly to be — their money could be put to better socialist uses by themselves than if it was given away: also class barriers are genuine, and they can better be dealt with by suitably crossing them rather than by pretending they don't exist. But the trouble with this type of answer was that it had traditionally been held by socialists that it was just the possession of unearned money that was the evil in capitalist societies and not the uses to which it was put. (Lenin had remarked that a 'good' capitalist was worse than a bad one because he delayed the revolution.) A Marxist acquaintance wrote to Cimmie to ask — had she faced the serious dangers inherent in what she was trying to do?

You an aristocrat and I a petty bourgeois are equally unreliable in the world situation of today because however good our principles, honest our intentions, and steadfast our will, we cannot be relied on to crush in our own characters those inborn tendencies which carry us back to our own sets in any crisis — we *may* be faithful when the time comes, but we cannot be sure of it until the time. The declassed aristocrat and the declassed artist are individual tragedies which simply don't matter when civilisation is at stake. Within our private lives we may have compensations ...

Cimmie was never a Marxist: nor was Tom: the difference between their sort of socialism and communism was that they believed openly (communists might put their trust secretly) in the role of heroic leaders. But then there was still the business of having to explain to people – those whom they wished to vote for them for instance – how the 'compensations' of their private lives did not interfere with their commitment to the cause of the working class. B. A. Campbell (my putative godfather) wrote to Birmingham newspapers a sort of testimonial for Tom and Cimmie, after there had been renewed attacks on their private life:

> I happen to have had the intimate friendship of Mr Mosley and Lady Cynthia for many years, the last sixteen of which have been spent living in the heart of East London engaged in all forms of social work. Amongst many who have helped me in this work, not merely by giving money but by giving service, which those of us who share the lives of the people have learned to value far more than money, have been those two friends ... I may mention that, as far as they are concerned, the accusation of 'living in large country houses with motor cars and luxurious expenditure and making no kind of personal sacrifice for the poor' is not applicable. At present their town house is a very modest sized one (and by a curious coincidence condemned by the London County Council) ...

This sort of defence made sense on the level of words: it was what Tom and Cimmie themselves were good at. But the problem remained – What is the effect of such justification on reality?

There is a letter from Nancy Astor to Cimmie of this time in which she says – 'Tell Tom not to allow on a platform what he is not willing to do himself.' There had for some time been the feeling amongst Tom's old friends that his very skill with words might result in cutting-off from reality. It seemed that some testing would occur now he was with Labour.

But if Tom and even Cimmie were allowing themselves to be set up as people slightly above the normal run of things – as legendary – then how was it that they were to be tested? Tom made no pretence about the fact that he believed that it was his right, almost duty, to ask to be judged on a rather superhuman level. And Cimmie, in her capacity of being someone who liked to be adored, sometimes found herself for good or ill, stranded on this sort of level too.

Allan Young wrote to her:

> My wish for you is that you should be surrounded by friends who
> do not irritate, who do not criticise, who are never exacting, but who
> interest you and help you to express your real self . . .
>
> It is a great joy to me that in the circle in which I have met you
> you help me to understand the meaninglessness of material things.
> You make life less lonely because of your capacity to '*feel*'. Ideas and
> actions are the playgrounds of life — but to feel is to live greatly.

CHAPTER 10

Rules of the Game: Philandering

When Tom re-entered Parliament in January 1927 as Labour member for Smethwick he had for the first time both a policy and what must have seemed a suitable political base from which to launch it.

He was not popular in Parliament. He had first been Conservative, then an Independent, now he was Labour. He could say with justification that he had put his principles before party loyalties; that he had been right to explore different territories: but this was objectionable to those who felt strongly about party loyalties not only because they might distrust his motives but because they might feel guilty about their own – they might themselves feel more strongly about loyalties, that is, than about principles, because their livelihoods depended on their so doing while Tom's and Cimmie's did not.

There was also still Tom's arrogance, his air of disdain, his cutting tongue. Looking around in Parliament at the chosen representatives of society around him, he would remark 'A dead fish rots from the head down'. When people heckled him he referred to their 'zoological noises striving to attain the heights of human speech'. The Conservative Party was 'sublime mediocrity at the head of inveterate prejudice': Baldwin, its leader, was someone who 'may not be a good companion for a tiger hunt, even for a pig hunt; but every time he runs away he proves afresh the honesty of his convictions'. This was good stuff for the legend: it was of not much help in fostering the personal bonhomie which, apart from the battle, is necessary if there is to be any exercise of power according to the rules of a game.

To most MPs Parliament was a place where issues were raised, passions aired, votes taken: then after these activities had done their job as a safety-valve as it were, the machinery of government could be left to go on its way. Tom never saw Parliament like this: he imagined it as a sort of officers' discussion-group before orders should be given for an attack. This was due to an ingrained habit partly of seeing contemporary circumstances as always on the edge of a crisis – 'Pleasant sleepy people are all very well in pleasant sleepy times, but we live in a dynamic age of great and dangerous events' – partly of assuming that the right methods of dealing with a crisis were those of war. In 1927 there was a certain justification for this attitude. He left his audiences in no doubt about how he saw the enemies at the gates.

> Unemployment, wages, rents, suffering, squalor and starvation, the struggle for existence in our streets; the threat of world catastrophe in another war; these are the realities of our present age. These are the problems which require every exertion of the best brains of our time for a vast constructive effort. These are the problems which should unite the nation in a white heat of crusading zeal for their solution. But these are precisely the problems which send Parliament to sleep. When not realities but words are to be discussed, Parliament wakes up. Then we are back in the comfortable pre-war world of make-believe: politics are safe again; hairs are to be split, not facts to be faced. Hush! do not awaken the dreamers! Facts will waken them in time with a vengeance.

In order to find an audience that would listen to what he had to say in the style which he felt suitable to say it in he went increasingly outside Parliament; he continued to address mass meetings in the midlands and in the north. He had already made his mark as a champion of the miners at the time of the General Strike in 1926: before it, he had in theory opposed the idea of a strike – he had thought both that it would not succeed and that if it did it would have meant revolution by violence. But when the strike was on he had backed it by organising, and paying for, the publication of a strike bulletin in Birmingham, and had given a considerable donation (£500) to the miners when their own strike dragged on into the autumn. From 1927 onwards he was a regular and popular speaker at the annual Durham Miners' Gala: he became a political and personal friend of the miners' leader Arthur Cook: he learned from him some of the rhythmical, hypnotic techniques of mob oratory. Beatrice Webb described Arthur Cook as being 'a mediumistic, magnetic sort of creature ... an inspired idiot, drunk with his own words, dominated by his own slogans'. Tom said that he had 'one of the coolest and best heads among the Labour leaders'. With the help of Arthur Cook and his union Tom was elected to the National Administrative Council of the Independent Labour party; then to the National Executive Council of the Labour Party itself. In Birmingham, where he seemed personally to be winning the city from the grip of the conservative Chamberlain family, Tom's legendary qualities were taking a bizarre hold: newspapers reported that children went through the streets singing 'Oswald is merciful! Oswald will save us!' There were cartoons of him in top hat and tails like a conjuror; then as an anarchist with a cloth cap and huge boots and a small man behind him with a bomb. Tom's characteristic reply to this sort of thing was just to complain that the cartoonist had not given him enough hair. There were also, inevitably, the cartoons about money: a money-bag labelled 'advantages of high birth and wealth' was being put away by Tom for the time being in a cloak room. But in fact of course Tom had no intention of hiding his money: he used some of it to buy an interest in one of the papers that was pursuing him – the *Birmingham Town Crier*.

In 1928 Tom's father died. He had lived apart from his wife and children for nearly thirty years. Recently there had been some rapprochement: his grandchildren (myself and Vivien, with Nanny and Granny) had been to visit him in 1924: there is a photograph of a rather young-looking middle-aged man like a professional cricketer holding me up like a trophy. Tom's mother had written to Tom – 'I'm trying hard to forget things that have made my life bitter for twenty five years.' But then there had been the Smethwick bye-election in 1926 and his father's story about Tom having been born with a golden spoon in his mouth, and Tom had again become bitter. When the news reached him that his father was dying Tom was in the South of France; he was in the middle of one of his long, hot summers; he declined to move in response to a telegram from his brother Ted. Ted, who was with their father who was himself in France, wrote 'I am disgusted to find that on the one occasion I have asked you to help me you have let me down ... I can assure you I should not have asked you to come here if I considered that your presence would disturb my father at this time.'

Tom went to the funeral: there is a photograph of him and his mother and his brothers at the graveside. In the South of France, just before he left, I remember Nanny telling Vivien and me that our grandfather had died, and so our father was now a baronet. I watched out of the window (so many childhood memories are of myself looking down at grown-ups out of windows) and saw my father on the terrace walking up and down, up and down; wondering, perhaps, about how both to be, and appear not to be, a baronet.

Tom was not mentioned in his father's will: it seemed to be becoming a habit in the Mosley family that eldest sons should not be mentioned in their fathers' wills. But much of the family money had gone anyway to Tom from his grandfather over his father's head. His father left what money he had to his 'housekeeper Mary Elisabeth Hipkiss' who had 'served me faithfully and looked after me in various illnesses for over sixteen years'.

The question of family money is of interest because there was so much about it in the papers at the time that it seemed to have gone, like so many things about Tom, into legend. The rumours were that he was a multi-millionaire. It is difficult to give exact figures when so many family assets were in settlements, trusts, and property whose capital value could not be realised: but it seems that Tom, when his father died, came into control of an estate of about £250,000: before this he had had a yearly income from trustees of £8–10,000. Much of the estate however was in the form of land in Manchester which the Mosley family had once owned but which in the last century had been made over to leaseholders on 999-year leases – one less 9, my father used to say, and the family would indeed be multi-millionaires. But the income from this land was fixed: so that with inflation and the threat of further inflation it was difficult to find a buyer for the leases. Thus Tom was rich but not extravagantly so: and not nearly so rich as legend suggested. There was also, of course, Cimmie's income from the Leiter Trust – about £8 or 9,000 a year – but here there was no chance of the capital being touched.

Tom had found the dubieties of his financial position useful during the Smethwick by-election of 1926 when he had been able to say 'I own no lands and neither does my family: I doubt if there are half a dozen acres in the family.' This was after Rolleston had been sold, and just before Tom bought his 120 acres at Denham. But it is doubtful if the electors of Smethwick would have been put off even if Tom had not been able to play down the stories of his wealth. Such concerns were those of the newspapers: there was still little evidence of envy amongst the working class.

John Scanlon wrote in *The Decline and Fall of the Labour Party* with reference to workers' further reactions to Tom and Cimmie:

Instead of believing that salvation for the working class would come from the working class, they still had the superstitious notion prevalent in all simple minds that salvation would come from above ... Heaven to them was a place where only rich people congregated and where was an abundance of rich food, rich drink and rich raiment.

To most of them it was quite unattainable, and therefore when anyone chose to leave this perpetual nightclub in order to mix with the workers, their love and admiration knew no bounds.

The 'perpetual night-club' world which Tom and Cimmie were supposed to frequent and occasionally come down from for the delectation of the workers – this was a fancy that had some slight relevance to facts. But Tom and Cimmie had gone to great lengths to break out of the conventional upper-class night-club world; and it was more that they themselves descended to it only from time to time for their own delight. Upper-class London 'society' at this time consisted of about six hundred people (Tom used to say) who all knew each other and knew much of what was going on between each other but who kept this secret from the outside world: the rules of the game were like those which require honour amongst gangsters, that one should not talk. A view of this world, which is indeed like that of some hellish underworld, is provided by Cimmie's older sister Irene who kept a daily diary from 1926: in this she also provides contemporary glimpses of Tom and Cimmie. Irene had inherited the same income from the Leiter Estate as Cimmie had: on the death of her father in 1925 she had become a peeress in her own right – Baroness Ravensdale. (George Curzon had managed to have this subsidiary title created for himself in 1911 when it seemed certain he would have only daughters and no son: the title could pass for one generation through the female line but then had to revert to male inheritance – to the annoyance of my sister). Irene Ravensdale never married: she was rich, titled, and unencumbered by ties: in later life she did much good work with charities and with East End clubs in London, but mostly during these early years she did what she liked. The life that she lived was the sort of life that Cimmie and Tom might have led if they had not chosen to be socialist politicians.

Each winter she would go to Melton Mowbray for the hunting; there she kept a house with four or five servants, several horses, and a groom. She would hunt four or five days a week – with the Quorn, the Cottesmore or the Belvoir. Having exhausted herself and two or three horses during the day she would spend the evenings almost invariably playing poker or bridge – at which she lost also almost invariably. (Entries in her diary end with a phrase such as 'Lost £15 as usual' with the frequency of Pepys's 'And so to bed.') Often at night there were parties at which people quarrelled, tried to swap husbands and wives, and got drunk. When there was no hunting Irene would stay in bed till lunch time: much of the time she felt ill. She had lovers; but did not find anyone for whom she would give up her freedom or who would take it on. When the hunting season was over she came with her servants to her London house for the summer season of parties and balls: there were special occasions like Derby Day, Ascot, the Eton and Harrow match; there were the Opera and gala matinees and tableaus; the night-clubs The Gargoyle and The Embassy. In the autumn she would travel, sometimes round the world – like a mythical figure in the expiation of some guilt. From time to time she drank too much, and she did a cure. She had hundreds of friends whom she loved and who said they loved her, but she was for the most part lonely. She was a good, warm hearted woman with nothing at this time to commit herself to.

Her relations with Cimmie and Tom were enigmatic. Cimmie had been her loved yet envied little sister when they were young: Cimmie had complained of her domineering ways. Then when Cimmie married and had children Irene seemed to claim a corner of these experiences. (When Vivien had been born she had written 'It is all so sacred, wonderful; it will remain in my mind as one of the great lovely mysteries'.) Tom told a story of how she had been to bed with him during some romp at Melton Mowbray; yet she was heavily censorious of Tom's extra-marital relationships and especially of causing Cimmie pain. She took no interest in Tom's and Cimmie's politics except for a week in 1929 when she went to canvass for Cimmie during her cam-paign at Stoke-on-Trent. In her diaries in their early days at least Tom appears as a rather fragile figure: Cimmie is still the envied sister. But it is likely that Irene saw and noted in her diaries mostly what she wanted to see.

Just after Tom's Labour victory in the 1926 election she was staying for Christmas with Nancy Astor at Cliveden – a powerhouse of con-servatism. Irene observed:

Cim and Tom came down to dinner and everyone was very decent to them tho' Geoffrey Dawson and Bob Brand hate him. They were both very pathetic – Tom even looking lonely and lost for once, tho' she was utterly at her ease. After dinner we played charades. Nancy Astor was inimitable as a rich Jew and a fat girl with that bulging mask, and Bobby as a tango teacher.

Another entry in another diary of this time seems to corroborate this unexpected view of Tom and Cimmie. Zita Jungman, who later became one of Cimmie's greatest friends, first met the Mosleys in August 1927 when she was taken by Bob Boothby to a picnic on the islands off the coast of Cannes. She had not expected, from what she had heard, to like Tom; but in the event she found him gentle and attentive and it was Cimmie who was – 'pretty, rather fat, strong, and ruthlessly direct'.

That Tom appeared vulnerable at this time does not in fact conflict with the other view of him as the dashing, debonair buccaneer. Newspaper reports of him talked of his 'distinguished bearing, singularly handsome face, much charm of manner'; but also that – 'shyness still hides the reckless spirit which is shown by his political career'. Part of his charm and ability to get away with things was that at this time he could appear to be both savagely dominating and yet open to being hurt: like this he had something of the attractiveness of a child. Both in politics and in private life people looked up to him and sometimes wanted to protect him: this is perhaps a characteristic of people who succeed in leadership. It was only later that Tom seemed to be the potentially all-powerful figure whom people thought might do everything himself.

Certainly in front of Cimmie there was something of the child still in him that liked to show off, to be given approbation, as well as to be looked up to. In 1927 Tom and Cimmie began to see more of her younger sister, Baba, who in 1925 had married Major Edward 'Fruity' Metcalfe – who was known as the Prince of Wales's best friend. Tom liked to tease Baba: to be boyish in front of both her and Cimmie. He wrote to Cimmie:

Today lunched with Fruity and Baba – showed them the new Bentley. Babs very envious and says we now 'stink of money'. Bentley is marvellous, but I break into a sweat when I think of the mutton at the wheel. With this light body acceleration is terrific – much more than Merc – you are up to anything in a few yards – must be careful. Body very good but a trifle flash. Silver wheels and red seats!

He liked showing off to Cimmie too, about his harmless social conquests. Once when Cimmie was in Stoke-on-Trent and Tom was in London he was asked to dinner by Sylvia, the wife of his brother Ted. He wrote:

Wednesday night dined with Sylvia. She elected to appear for the occasion in a bright scarlet costume – everything blazing red from her lips to the heels of her shoes. Afterwards she desired to go to the Embassy Club. I advanced rather diffidently across the floor behind this 'People's Banner' but nevertheless our entry appeared to cause a

certain sensation. Even the granite features of Lord Blandford assumed a momentary mobility.

About Tom's more serious flirtations it is difficult to tell just what, at
this time, Cimmie thought. It was a convention of the world in which
she moved and had been brought up that husbands were expected to
take some interest in other people's wives: their own wives seemed to
have evolved a state of mind by which they both did and did not notice
what was going on. There were rules-of-the-game about what was
acceptable; and so long as Tom kept to these – the purpose of which
was to ensure that the whole business remained somewhat childlike –
then Cimmie could perhaps treat him as her naughty boy. For a time
Tom did seem to stick to the rules. He would go over to Paris, which
was a different world; there he had a mistress called Maria. (When he
came across her later in America and sent her flowers and asked when
he could see her she replied 'Darling friend, I prefer not to see you at
all and have very good reasons for that.') Perhaps the reason then was
that Tom was by this time pursuing Blanche Barrymore, the wife of
John Barrymore, the actor: she herself was an actress who used, Tom
remarked in his autobiography, to act Hamlet in competition with her
husband. Perhaps this pursuit was stagey enough to come within the
rules of the game. Also in a manner stagey but not, one would have
thought, within any recognisable rules, was his brief affair with his step-
mother-in-law, Grace Curzon; with whom, at St Moritz, while Cimmie
skied (Tom could not ski because of his injured leg) he would drive
around in a horse-drawn sledge. Tom would usually go after the women
who would be the biggest challenge to him by possessing the greatest
prestige. He never, like his father-in-law George Curzon, saw the point
of pursuing anyone who might not be passed off as upper-class.

Thus when he became Labour and a whole new game might have
opened up because this was the time when to be left-wing and intellectual was to be an advocate of easy free love – Tom did not take very
enthusiastic advantage of this situation. He had a brief walk-out with
one of the wives at the ILP summer school: but soon after this he coined
a witty slogan – Vote Labour: sleep Tory – and reverted to type. He
became involved with the wife of a Conservative MP who managed to
get hold of a photograph of Tom without any clothes on (this was
Tom's own story): the photograph was passed round the Tory benches
while Tom from the Labour front bench was making a speech: Tom,
made aware of what was going on by the resulting laughter, considered
that this was outside the rules of any game and threatened a fight.

For almost the first ten years of her marriage it does not seem from her letters that Cimmie kicked up much of a fuss about all this: she felt that, the rules being what they were, Tom would always return to her: she seemed essential to him, politically and personally. It was essential politically that there should be no public scandal: but it was personally that he still seemed dependent on her in spite of what he admitted were his 'tiresome ways'. He would assure her of this dependence in his adoring, child-like letters full of baby-talk and drawings of animals: he would call her 'My own blessed Moo Moo': 'My own darling baby bleater': 'His own darling soft-nosed wag-tail'. He would sign himself by his own baby-names – porker, mutton: he would dash off his drawings of animals in his wild primitive hand. All this – itself a game – was to show that the other game – that of affairs and flirtations – was the lesser: it could not stand up to the heartfelt, caring, genuine dependence of children-husbands on their mother-wives.

Own Beloved,
   Promise be happy. Don't work too hard. Rest and be strong for lots of fun Friday. Does love her so. If he didn't he wouldn't be tiresome. Life impossible without her.

Or:

Wishes he could make his mutt [drawing of animal] less of a goat [drawing of animal with horns] loves her so.

And Cimmie would reply:

My belovedest,
   It was so wick of me to have wasted that whole long day when I had you and now when you aren't here my heart aches for you. I will really try and be bet, not maddening or cross, but do believe nearly all my stupidity comes from excess of love which makes me often overwrought, not anything else. I so frightfully love you and do above everything in the world want to be a perfect wife to you . . .
   Oh my Bill I do so adore you, my lovely one, so beautiful and so brave, such a clever one and so tender and beloved. Such a hero and yet such a baby boy. Your own Moo moo.

Cimmie and Tom were now approaching the zenith of their political

and social careers. Their progress in the Labour Party was still triumphant: the Tory press campaign against them was wearing off. Tom was
even being asked to write articles by Lord Beaverbrook. People were
beginning to speak of him as a future Prime Minister. The house at
Denham was filling at weekends with people from the more exotic and
enlightened fringes of the 'perpetual night-club world': also with
writers and musicians and painters and designers – Sacheverell Sitwell,
William Walton, Cecil Beaton, Oliver Messel. These mixed in with the
old political friends – John Strachey, Bob Boothby. All these people felt
perhaps closest to Cimmie; but Tom was the attraction. However much
people felt him somewhat removed, awkward, they caught the glow
of his company. This sort of social life at Denham was interspersed with
visits from constituency socialists or representatives from the Durham
Miners Gala. Cimmie had her 'ups and downs': she wrote that her curse
was to be 'either so frightfully hap or so frightfully mis'. Tom came and
went like (as a French journalist put it) 'the young Alcibiades . . . driving
too fast in a big car, trailing after him many entangled hearts, many
sarcasms, and a few confidences'. And somewhere in the middle of all
this were the children telling themselves stories about how to get
somewhere on a raft.

CHAPTER 11

Savehay Farm

Into the peaceful mundane world at Savehay Farm which consisted of myself and Vivien, Nanny, Mabel and May, and Mr Streeter the gardener in his cottage beyond the woodshed, there would erupt from time to time, like Vikings in their long-boats from the east, invaders, who were my mother's and father's weekend guests. Then there would be the business, for myself at least, of being always ready, like some villager, to hide. Savehay Farm was a good house within and around which to observe without being observed: there were the nooks and crannies I had discovered in my explorations with my sister Vivien: there were vantage points from which one could look down, as I liked to look down, upon the behaviour of these sophisticated hordes. There was a way out from the first floor nursery across a sort of roof-patio and then in through another door to a gallery above a loggia. Within this loggia some of the more esoteric rites of the grown-up world took place – the conversation, the badinage, the drinking, the horseplay – and even if a watcher were on the point of being caught, there was a further escape-route at the far end of the gallery which went across a cluttered loft with a ceiling too low to allow for easy pursuit and down into a mysterious area known as the End Room where were stored huge trunks containing bric-a-brac from the time when my mother had been a child in India: and this refuge was almost impregnable, because the key of the door from the outside had nearly always been lost.

Once or twice a year there were seasonal invasions of a type different from usual: enormous trestle tables would be set up on the lawn: tea-urns and trays of sandwiches would be carried from vans: then masses of people wearing thick dark suits and with hats would emerge from buses and would stand about looking cheerful like people do when they think they might be photographed. These were Labour party workers from Smethwick or Stoke: the occasion was known as The Garden Party. This festivity was especially terrifying for children because the impression had been given that it was more than an arbitrary duty for them to appear – it was a moral and political duty – something that might be of importance in their parents' careers. So there we were, my sister and I, amongst the tea and buns and smiling faces like victims being led to sacrificial altars.

At another time of year there would be tents like those of Red Indians suddenly in the field across the river: large boys in long khaki shorts would appear carrying pots and pans: in the evenings they would sit round a camp fire and sing songs. These were the denizens of Mr B. A. Campbell's Paddy's Goose Boys' Club, on their annual holiday outing. With regard to them, too, there seemed to be some sort of moral obligation to go and visit: grown-ups even suggested that one might cheerfully join in their sad songs.

But for the most part the weekend invaders were as unlike constituency party workers or members of the Paddy's Goose club as could be imagined. On Saturday mornings in the summer garden-beds of wood and webbing would be set out in front of the loggia: mattresses and coloured cushions would be arranged; there would be a portable gramophone and perhaps an umbrella; it was as if a stage-set were being prepared for some ballet. Then in twos and threes from the house where they had arrived the night before when the children had been in bed or from the place where cars were parked by Mr Streeter's cottage there would emerge the people who were my mother's and father's special friends: the men perhaps in white trousers and dark blue jackets: the women in short skirts with waists falling down towards their knees. They would gather round the beds in front of the loggia: they would laugh, talk, recline; they would sway in front of each other like reeds. But what on earth were they *doing*? And what were they *saying*? All this was observed with eyes through some slit-hole at the bottom of a window; on hands and knees in the gallery above the loggia. These representatives of the grown-up world always seemed to be *acting*: they would gesture, jerk their hands in their pockets, fiddle with pearls; but who were they acting *to*; and what was it *for*? A man might go down on one knee, a hand on his heart, as if making some passionate declaration: a woman would lean back, kick her legs in the air; but was this in acceptance or disdain? There would be lunges, shrieks, and cumbersome runnings-after. Someone would be caught, and carried, and dumped on a bed: but were all these struggles yes or no? Of course, it was all a game. But did anyone win? And was it fun?

The portable gramophone would be wound up with a handle and play tunes like *Just A Gigolo* or *You're Driving Me Crazy*: people might dance a little in a desultory, am-I-or-am-I-not-being-watched way. They would do this as if in front of cameras: often, in fact, there was a camera – my mother had a primitive box-like cine-Kodak that you held at your waist and looked down into: she was one of the first people to make home movies fashionable. In front of the camera people of course were expected to perform: they would do the Charleston flicking their legs sideways and back; they would put their arms round each other's waists and trip to and fro like Sugar Plum Fairies. They did not seem to be involved so much in dancing as in the business of trying to find out what to do about being watched. A few games would begin: two men would get down on their backs on the lawn; they would face one another and each would put a leg up and hook it round the leg of the other; the object was to force the other person over on to the back of his head. The women would hop about like birds round carrion. Then there was a game in which two people were blindfolded and lay on the lawn and held hands and whacked at each other with rolled-up news-papers: this was called, for some reason, *Are You There Moriarty?* When all this had gone on for some time the women would drift back to the beds and perhaps file their nails and croon snatches to the gramophone.

There were more formal games. Half way down the drive there were two tennis courts side by side: I do not remember anyone playing much serious tennis. The point seemed to be the badinage, usually in mixed doubles. My aunt Irene had a very slow underarm service that her opponents could deal with as they liked, depending on what they felt about my Aunt Irene. When my father served he would flash his eyes at the same time as he flashed his racket and he seemed to be trying to hit his partner on the back of the neck.

There was even a realistic duelling game that the men played on the lawn: they would dress up in fencing jackets and masks; they would march away from each other back to back carrying pistols; then would turn and fire with bullets of uninjurious wax. The women would watch this as if rather at a loss: traditionally, had not women liked men fighting over them with some danger of death?

There was a thing called a pogo-stick with a spring on the bottom on which you jumped up and down like a kangaroo. One day Dick Wyndham slipped and broke his jaw: there was a queer funeral cortege down to the river – to throw in not Dick Wyndham, but the pogo-stick.

In the river there was swimming from a wooden landing-stage or diving-board in an area that was supposed to have been cleared of weeds by Mr Streeter in the punt. We children were allowed to bathe here as soon as we could swim. There were stories of how weeds stretched up like tentacles and dragged you down.

We would fish with nets for tiddlers in the river. Sometimes the movements of grown-ups seemed to be curiously like those of fish; they would seem all to be facing one way; then they would suddenly dash off and face in another.

One summer at Savehay Farm the play-acting did seem to have some practical or rather aesthetic point: my mother and father set out to make, with their box-like camera, a film with a story. What the story was is obscure since only one uncut reel of it survived: the rest was tidied and burned by a house-maid in the South of France who thought that the bits and pieces in the process of being cut and stuck together were rubbish. From the one reel it seems that my mother was a dairy maid who was being pursued by both John Strachey and Dick Wyndham – the former was some sort of rustic, and the latter a dashing man who turned up in the Bentley. These two had a terrible fight on the big bridge over the river: first John Strachey got hurled into the water; then he climbed out and ran back on to the bridge and hurled Dick Wyndham into the water; this scene seemed to be repeated, over and over. Then there was a brothel scene in which Cecil Beaton was the *Madame* made up to look like Margot Asquith: one of the girls in her charge was, again, my mother. Dick Wyndham returned in the Bentley and there was another struggle – with revealing close-ups of legs and thighs. Towards the end of all this Cecil Beaton went off to drown himself in the river; but it was his wig that kept on coming off and floating away like Ophelia. There was an odd blind boy, very beautiful, played by Stephen Tennant; who sat and made daisy chains by the river.

All this was scripted, directed, and filmed by my father. It was shot in a rather German-expressionist style, with reflections in water of poplar trees and clouds moving.

One of the more bizarre activities that grown-ups liked to indulge in at weekends was to play practical jokes on one another. In the downstairs lavatory there was a box which held the paper and when you pulled a snake jumped out: Olga Lynn had hysterics, and the door of the lavatory had to be broken down. Then there was a story of how my father once arranged to have soap on toast served to his dinner guests as a savoury: Oliver Messel was warned by Mabel the parlour maid, and went behind a screen with a pack of cards which he let fall to the floor thus making a sound as if he were being sick. Nanny used to recount to us these stories: it seemed to be accepted that they were about just the sort of things that grown-ups did.

Nanny, in fact, had her own fund of such stories, which we children asked her to recount to us over and over again. When she had been a nurserymaid in the employment of George Curzon she had stayed in the house of his father, Lord Scarsdale, where there was a butler who tyrannised over the other servants. One day Nanny, and her great friend Sarah the still-room maid, put some sherbet in the butler's pot, so that when he peed at night it foamed: he, too, was supposed to have had some sort of fit. Then there was Lord Scarsdale himself who was known to be mean about food: one night Nanny and her friend were having a midnight snack when they heard a scuffling outside their bedroom door and they opened it and found Lord Scarsdale on his hands and knees trying to see underneath. The impression from all these stories was that, of course, the grown-up world was mad: why else, indeed, did they have to have people like nannies to tell us stories about them?

In the evenings after guests had gone my sister and I would come down to the Garden Room where there were the glass walking sticks on the walls and we would pick up bits of family life after the invasion. My mother would read to us or at a slightly later date would play with us one of the upper-middle-brow games that she had played as a child with her father. There was the game called 'I see' in which a famous historical scene was described and the children had to guess (or rather to know) what it was – Julius Caesar on his way to the Senate: Napoleon on St Helena. Sometimes my mother would rope in my father to describe a scene; but after a time he would get bored, and begin – I see a tall dark handsome man – and we would all start groaning, because we knew he was describing himself. Similarly if my father was ever prevailed on to play the enervating game of compiling lists of famous men beginning with a certain letter he would with mysterious quickness finish his list and wait till the end of the allotted time and then when invited to read out his list would announce just – whatever the letter – Mosley! And so there would be more groans: and my father's strange clicking laugh. I continued to think this sort of thing very funny. This was the pattern of my father with his children: he would become the joker: he would be no longer distant, removed: what better could he do?

Then there were more of the strange mantras, or slogans, that he used to declaim in response to what he might feel were unnatural demands on him. On the comparatively rare occasions on which all the family were having a meal together and Vivien and I were being obstreperous and he was appealed to to keep order, he would intone, with the far-away look in his eye:

> Let us see if Nicky can
> Be a little gentleman
> Let us see if Viv is able
> To behave herself at table –

Or if there was some dispute about plans – between our two aunts, for example, who kept up a rivalry sometimes about who should do what with which of the children – he would murmur just:

> Whoever would you rather be –
> Aunty Baa or Aunty Nee –

and then would drift off, laughing again, leaving myself at least thinking that something magical had happened. I did not know why: I think it was something to do with grown-ups being able to laugh at their own pretensions.

There were the other sayings my father would use to discourage earnest personal speculation. When the question came up, as it often did, about the oddity of his emergence from his background, he would declaim, as alternatives to the 'when fire meets oil then springs the spark divine' remark quoted earlier:

> The Lily, its roots dug deep in the dung of the
> earth, yet rears its glorious head to heaven –

Or –

> Nurtured as I was in the rough usages of camp and field –

Or –

> Staffordshire born and Staffordshire bred
> Fat in the bottom and fat in the head –

all these being said as throwaway lines, real or made-up quotations, self-mockery to do away with boredom or embarrassment. Then there was a line that he would intone as he entered the sea to swim in the Mediterranean – And bluer the sea-blue stream of the bay – which meant that he was peeing.

My father was an arch-manipulator of words: it seemed that at these moments he was mocking the pretensions of words. But there were also his rages.

He never directed any violence against us children – except perhaps once, when Vivien and I had been having a fight in the rose-garden and Vivien, accidentally, had kicked me in the balls and I had flopped about like a footballer in the penalty area. My father hauled Vivien up to his room and smacked her. He examined me solicitously. But this incident stands out for its rarity.

The scarcity of memories about my mother has resulted in those scenes that do remain being lit portentously. There was a day in London when my mother and father and Vivien and I were walking along the Mall (this is by far the clearest memory I have of my mother and father in relation to each other): we were turning up by St James's Palace and my mother was asking me why I did not like the child of one of her friends whom she had hoped I would like; I was saying I did not know why (I cannot remember now how much in fact I did not know or how much I was declining to pass on childhood secrets). My mother was saying that of course I must know – that if one had feelings about not liking someone one must be able to describe them – and I was beginning to feel miserable: I was thinking – surely, feelings are sometimes too complicated to be put just into words? My father was walking ahead with my sister Vivien: my mother called out to him – Was it not correct, would he not say, that if one had feelings then these could be put into words? I remember my father turning, at the bottom of St James's Street, and saying no, surely, there were some feelings that could not well be put into words. I think I felt some sort of liberation.

But it was about this time, when I was about seven, that I began quite badly to stammer. My mother had recorded in notes that she made about our early childhood – 'Vivien was inclined to be a bit bossy and Nic was led a good deal of a dance always having to play second string, he was much more highly strung than her, and occasionally used to have stammering fits.' But my own consciousness that I stammered came later when both my mother and my nanny in the night nursery – this scene again is portentously etched – were standing over me and telling me earnestly that I must try to speak carefully: up to that time I had not realised that I did not. There is a lesson to be learned by parents here: if your child stammers, do not remark on this when he or she is young: the stammer may naturally go: but if you remark on it, the child has to struggle and the stammer may get dug in.

There are psychological theories about stammering that have seemed to me to make sense. One is that it is a sort of protection against the verbal aggression of others (it is difficult to be rude or sarcastic towards a stammerer): another and deeper theory is that it is a protection against the stammerer's own potential aggressiveness towards others – an aggressiveness which, without the stammer, would be alarming. But it has seemed to me also that stammering on some level is simply a protest against a too easy flow of words; against one's own and other people's terrible tendency to bury living things under a verbal lava-flow.

In the notes that my mother made in her photograph book of our childhood were sayings attributed to me at an early age: one was 'Isn't it lucky that Mummy didn't marry Mr Strachey?' Another – 'I think we are really dead, and we think all this is a dream.'

In my mother's Garden Room, when she was away, there were certain explorations to be made amongst the piles of glossy magazines that lay on a table behind the sofa. Some of these magazines had been sent from Russia; some from Paris. In the former there were pictures of enormous industrial complexes with pipes and cones and spheres: these seemed like very advanced children's toys. In the magazines from Paris there were reproductions of modern paintings and drawings which took one out of the world of toys towards some secret that might be at the back of the grown-up world. There were women with no clothes on lying on their backs with their knees in the air – Egon Schiele perhaps. But why was this so strange? And what was its power in the grown-up world?

At the not-often-used end of the house on the ground floor beneath my mother's and father's bedroom there was a panelled hall with portraits of Mosley ancestors on the walls: these were almost the only relics (apart from library books) that had been saved from my father's abandonment of Rolleston. Each year after the Christmas Tree had been cleared away (here we had circled to the incantation of porker, porker) for the rest of the winter I was allowed to make this room my own. Here I would set about building or rebuilding – the Mosley ancestors looking primly or benignly down – a whole model village, a landscape, an estate: the basis of this was a beautifully made set of toys called The Belgian Village (given to us children, I think, by my mother's childhood friend the Queen of the Belgians). This consisted of houses, gardens, churches, shops, inns; it could be set out on the floor of the empty hall and extended into parkland, farmyards, animals, railways, cars, buses – these taken from my other sets of toys. Thus a whole new world could be created; which unlike much of the real world was orderly, aesthetic and exact. I would work at this painstakingly through much of the winter holidays: the task, and the result, seemed to be of mysterious significance. I knew it would be cleared away by Nanny and May the housemaid in the spring: but it could always be taken out of its boxes again and made the same and yet slightly different: and perhaps it was this ordering of something beautiful that seemed to make life worth while.

CHAPTER 12

Labour Politics

In 1927 Cimmie, in the train to Dover wrote to Tom, who was at 8 Smith Square:

Sweetie old boy, be a happy one and be a good one – miss his Mum a good deal but don't get plooey. Get Mabel to fix up people to come and see you. Try and make the Docs start doing something in the way of treatment. Anyway suggest a tonic to keep your strength up.

Why not also have the spermy doc to see you as well, his add is on envelope on dressing table, name of Kenneth Walker. Talk to Kirkwood about the French specialist from Bagnolles and get Mabel to ring Eva up and find out when he is coming over.

Darling fellow let's have loveliest happiest time yr 31st year. I will do all I can. As well as our work-y good times let's have fun-y good times. Let's really try and achieve the ideal modus vivendi! *I do so love you* and as well as that I'm frightfully fond of you for yr sake too. Feels like a Mum as well as a Mistress (can one be the Whore as well as the Bore or vice versa?)

I do think we are trying to give better chances and more happiness to people in general and ought to give just our 2 selves a really good chance too – a chance to be a better happier couple than any other – it would help in the long run and I am quite sure we have a duty to ourselves as much as to everyone else. A Frenchman opp has just blown his nose and released by flourishing his hanky such an odious cloying scent I feel sick. H. G. Wells on the train, can't make up my mind whether to speak to him or not.

Let's arrange a party soon after I'm back (if you're well) and go to Greta Garbo.

Love and kisses my belovedest.

Don't leave this about it is stilted and restrained as it is just for that very fear.

Loves him Loves him Loves him Loves him.

Does think him a bloody marvel, really, and as the train rushes her farther and farther away is inclined to reconsider her opinion that he is evil and wick (doubtful tho') and thinks – Oh Hell, I don't know what I think.

But I do know you are often a pet and adorable and are quite without rival in public life and that all the time I love you except when I hate you so much it must come quite near to love and be mixed up with it. God bless your schemes and plans. Don't get fed up with the silly old Labs yet awhile. Give Jimmy my love and fix up some NAC fun for me. Play your new grammy and think lovingly and kindly of your Simple Sincere Suburban Sim!!

It seems that at the time Tom was quite often ill or on the edge of being ill: or he was something of a hypochondriac; he liked to put his trust in glamorous doctors whether or not there was very much for them to cure. But he had genuine recurring trouble with his injured leg. Cimmie wrote to him from Stoke-on-Trent – 'My poor sweetie old fellow I am miserable at your being phlebitic it really does seem that yr troubles are unending and cumulative (is that the right word?) always piling up – oh I am just longing for Tues when we can settle peacefully down to being normal decently idle creatures.' Ramsay MacDonald wrote to Cimmie regretting 'that Tom's illness is to drag', but making a date with her to go to the theatre.

In October 1928 Tom and Cimmie went on a motor trip with Ramsay MacDonald to Vienna, Prague and Berlin. In Berlin MacDonald addressed the Reichstag and made a passionate plea for disarmament: the press seemed more interested in Cimmie's clothes. 'Lady Cynthia, the famous champion of the proletariat, was in an evening frock of grey tissue with a rich grey cloak ... slowly, and with an air which a great actress might envy, she went to the place assigned to her followed by her husband and Mr Ramsay MacDonald ... a shawl of snowy white ermine fell from her gracious shoulders.'

While in Berlin Tom and Cimmie were taken round the night clubs by Harold Nicolson who was Counsellor at the British Embassy. Tom wrote about this in his autobiography – 'Cimmie and I had never seen anything like it ... the sexes had simply changed clothes, make-up and habits of nature ... scenes of decadence and depravity suggested a nation sunk so deep that it could never rise again. Yet within two or three years men in brown shirts were goose-stepping down these same streets round the Kurfurstendamm'. Tom does not seem in this description to have been being ironic.

Ramsay MacDonald did not go with them on the tour of the night clubs: his own raffish behaviour on this trip was to do with becoming involved again with an Austrian lady who had previously been his mistress. Tom too became involved in this affair. In a passage which he dictated for his autobiography but then left out he told the story of this odd incident and its aftermath.

In Vienna we met a woman who as a type seemed to me something of an old Viennese tart: faded blonde, very sophisticated, very agreeable. And being young people, and never thinking that people much older than ourselves could have love affairs, Cimmie and I thought nothing of it. In Vienna the old pair used to go and look at museums.

A month or two later MacDonald suggested that we all go down to Fowey in Cornwall, and named the party which he wanted to take – a gay party and altogether different from MacDonald's colleagues. Just before we went he said to me 'My little Austrian friend whom we met in Vienna is in England. It would be such fun if she could come. Will you explain it to the others?' So we said all right. He used to read poetry to her, and they wandered off together making a strange couple.

Then we went into the election. We fought it and we won, and I found myself sitting in the Treasury as Chancellor of the Duchy. Then one day I was informed that a Mrs so-and-so wanted to speak to me. I said 'I'm delighted to hear you're in London but we're all very busy'. She said 'I'm living in a flat in Horseferry Road,' – at that time almost a slum area – I've got serious news for you. The Government may fall. I must tell you'.

So I went round and there was this old girl. She said 'I rang you up, you're very young, but you're the only man in this government who knows anything of the world at all. So I had better tell you'.

She went on 'I'll come straight to the point. I was once a very rich woman. The Prime Minister, when I used to meet him in Switzerland, was a very poor man and I helped him a lot in those days. Now he's got the whole Treasury of Great Britain behind him.'

So I said 'Dear Lady, you can't have the Prime Minister putting his hand in the public Treasury to support his lady friends.'

Then she got very nasty. She said 'I went to Downing Street, I was admitted, and I told him I had to get some money. He saw me in the Cabinet Room and became completely hysterical and began to bang his head against the wall. Isobel came in in the middle of this performance. Then he took me by the shoulders and pushed me out in front of all the porters in Downing Street.'

I always remember how her story ended – 'I fall down, I break my lorgnettes, my eyes they are blinded with tears. The policeman, he pick me up and put me in a taxi'.

So I told her it was terribly shocking, the Prime Minister was tired and overworked.

She replied 'I've got letters from him. You know, he's a very innocent man and he wrote to me letters which were pornographic. They were written from Lossiemouth in his own handwriting but he's cut off Lossiemouth with a pair of scissors.'

I said to her 'Now look, no newspaper will publish them here, and if you try to blackmail the Prime Minister he will be Mr X in court and you'll go down for 10 or 20 years.'

She knew a trick worth two of that. 'You may be able to stop me here, but I shall go to the Quai d'Orsay and the whole thing will blaze in the French press.'

So then I pulled a real bluff, because you can imagine in a Labour government anything of that kind would wreak havoc. But with her being a central European I thought she might fall for it. I said to her 'Do you really think a British Government is going to be brought down by one lonely woman? You have no friends, you have no helpers at all. You've got to go by train to Dover and on the channel boat to Paris. Do you think you are ever going to get to France?'

It worked. She was in floods of tears. She said 'Please, I want to leave, please don't!' I said 'Of course not, we're friends, everything will be gentle. Take the advice of a good friend, don't go near the Quai d'Orsay, very, very, dangerous. Go back to Vienna as fast as you can get.'

As Tom told the story, there were further repercussions. Years later, when he had founded the British Union of Fascists, he was approached by a man who wanted to join him who had previously been a secret service agent: this man told Tom that the flat in Horseferry Road had in fact been bugged so that the incident, and Tom's part in it, was known to the security people. And the story, the man said, had continued – the

Austrian lady had indeed returned to Vienna but then had reappeared
in 1931 or 1932 and 'Jimmy Thomas was sent with £3,000 of Abe
Bailey's money to buy the letters ... he went to Paris, met her there,
came back without the three thousand and without the letters.'

Then many years later, Tom related, Charles Mendl, who had been
at the British Embassy in Paris, told Tom that he had once seen the
allegedly pornographic letters and that all he remembered of them was
a poem which contained the line –

Porcupine through hairy bowers shall climb to paradise.

Back in 1928 – it seemed that Tom and Cimmie were in various ways
trying to make themselves useful to Ramsay MacDonald. He came
down to Savehay Farm to work: he was photographed writing a draft
of his election manifesto in the loggia. There was even talk that in a
future Labour government Tom might be made Foreign Secretary. But
Ramsay MacDonald's way of going round with the rich and fashionable
had led to hostile comment within the Labour Party: Beatrice Webb
wrote sourly of MacDonald's liking for 'the Mosleys, De la Warrs, and
other lithe and beauteous forms – leaders of fashion or ladies of the stage
attended by 6ft tall and well groomed men'. And it might even have
been true, as Harold Nicolson wrote later, that 'Cimmie Mosley's hold
on Ramsay is one of the things that makes it difficult for Tom to be
specially favoured.' Also Ramsay MacDonald might have sensed a
growing hostility to himself in Tom at this time: it was their Berlin trip,
Tom wrote later, that first opened his eyes to 'the deep element of
hysteria' in Ramsay MacDonald's nature: such men might be 'figures
of infinite worthiness, the models of public virtue and private decorum':
but because they were 'products of the Puritan tradition' they were
'entirely different animals in all things, great and small, to the masters
of action whom history has revealed to our judgement'. This feeling
arose, he would explain, not of course as a result of the discovery that
Ramsay MacDonald had a mistress but because of his failure to deal with
the situation with dispatch. But Tom made his own odd calculations in
this area: and in the coming three or four years he might at times have
reflected back on himself the comment he made on Ramsay MacDonald
– 'It seems to me that men in high office ought to live like athletes ...
statesmen are poor fish if even for the few years at the height of their
responsibilities they cannot be serious'.

There was some confusion at the heart of the Labour Party about
what should be a proper attitude to puritanism. One strand of Labour

thinking, represented by the ILP, was dedicated to socialism as if to some kind of puritan religion: this was in the tradition of Marx, Lenin, Trotsky: socialists had to keep clear of even social contacts with establishment ways of living for fear of almost moral contamination. But this had never been the attitude of the majority of Labour parliamentarians: for them, just as socialism would evolve out of capitalism without a revolution, so new social attitudes might be grafted without too much trouble on to the old. It was Tom, ultimately, who became distrusted by both sides in the confusion – by the puritans for being too much of a rake, and by the compromisers for being too much of a rebel.

From the evidence of Cimmie's 1927 letter there was a danger even then of Tom's becoming disillusioned with Labour: neither the puritans nor the moderates seemed to be much interested in getting things done. The former declaimed passionately about theory without much interest in what was possible: the latter, with their eye on the possible, held to no theory to spur them on. Tom did what he could from his position of not being quite in step with anyone to suggest what might be done.

In 1927 he was made a member of a sub-committee of the Labour Party National Executive to prepare a draft programme for the general election which would come at the latest in 1929. He wrote a personal letter to Ramsay MacDonald in which he expanded on the Birmingham Proposals of two years earlier; in particular he advocated the setting-up of an Economic Council with far-reaching powers to interfere in the economy. MacDonald was sympathetic to some of the ideas about ways in which credit might be provided to stimulate employment: what he objected to (and what most of Tom's critics must have objected to although for the reasons suggested it seemed they could not say this) were the methods that Tom proposed were necessary if the policy was to be put into effect. Tom claimed that there had to be dynamism with authority from the top: MacDonald wrote in his diary 'quiet cautious leadership is what I think is wanted'. But it was under just such cautious leadership that the economy had for years been failing.

The Labour Party programme that was prepared for the 1929 election under the title of *Labour and the Nation* was in fact largely written by MacDonald; it was a compendium of pious hopes that socialism would benefit all sections of the community without much mention of how this miracle might occur. But it served the Labour Party well at the time of the election.

The reason why the men whom the Labour Party and indeed the

country trusted found themselves more and more tending to ignore Tom seems to have been not just that his proposals for political action alarmed them, but also because there was something in his personal style that they felt might justify this alarm. It was about this area that it was difficult to talk – it was the political tradition that politics should be talked about in terms of politics, and questions of what human beings were should be kept to another context. But Tom as a person was such an obvious oddity on the political scene that personal pronouncements by political commentators kept on mysteriously breaking in: there had been Beatrice Webb's view of Tom – that 'with such perfection there must be some rottenness somewhere'. Ellen Wilkinson wrote 'The trouble with Oswald Mosley is that he is too good looking . . . he is not that kind of nice hero who rescues the girl at the point of torture but the one who hisses "at last we meet!" ' The suggestion seemed to be that, with so many talents, the temptation to be out for oneself must be overwhelming. But there were many confusions here: what might have been a serious point about an ambivalence in Tom's moral attitudes became lost in what seemed to be fear or envy of his energy and even his sexual drives. There might have been serious points to be made about these too: but not in the traditional context of judging who was to be listened to on the National Executive.

During the summer of 1928 Tom and Cimmie were visited by her sister Irene at Denham and in the South of France. There was an evening at Savehay Farm in May when, having listened on the wireless to Stravinsky's *Oedipus Rex,* Cimmie (Irene wrote in her diary) 'gave us a long socialist dissertation and was so earnest and heart-whole one could not argue with her'. Then a weekend or two later Cecil Beaton and Stephen Tennant came down: they dressed up in Mary Curzon's old clothes and – 'did the most fantastic dances as passed description for effeteness tho' brilliance was in every line'. Tom seems to have been a bit aloof from all this. Cimmie, Irene reported, 'seemed on the edge of a breakdown'. Then in August at Antibes there was a hugely successful birthday party for Cimmie to which there came 'the whole world and his wife': a few days later – 'I talked for the first time in my life for 2 hours to Cim over the misery of her present life and Tom's insulting behaviour to her: it killed me to hear of her rending loyalty to him saying he had never been unfaithful she only wished he would not make a fool of her in public.' Cimmie herself however seems to have been a ring-leader in the party-going activity: certainly she never seems to have tried to get Tom away from the areas in which he could so easily hurt her.

It was Cimmie's very devotion to Tom, probably, that allowed him to feel free and confident in this world: people from time to time encouraged Cimmie herself to flirt; even to take lovers: she used to say she did not want to. No one advised her to leave him. On the evidence of her own letters there was something self-destructive, almost provocative, about her obsession with Tom; she would say this herself – that her possessiveness was making her nag him and sending her 'mad' without reference to whether he was going after anyone else or not. So, by behaving as he did, what had Tom got to lose? And by his endearments it seemed he could always mollify her. And at this time Cimmie did probably believe that Tom's flirtations could for the most part be explained in terms of the social game which was to do not with love but conquest; that apart from doing what was natural to him, what Tom was looking for was prestige. And she could try to convince herself that it was not unreasonable to want prestige.

Tom tried to justify his behaviour on the grounds that it was to do with 'wholeness', with health, with a necessary refusal to deny what was his nature: such behaviour balanced, and gave him energy for, the rigours of his life in politics. But in fact he seemed quite often to be ill. Cimmie wrote that she wished they could settle down for a time and live like ordinary people: but she did not arrange a time, even a holiday, in which this might be possible. She herself could not pretend that she flourished at the social game: but she, as much as he, seemed trapped by it.

A pattern was emerging of Tom as the swashbuckling, vituperative rebel in public life who in private life became also something of a naughty boy; who, having shown off, could return to its mother for forgiveness. (Tom's mother wrote to him at this time – 'It seems almost incredible to me to realise "The Honourable Gentleman" is my very beloved fat *obstinate* baby of so little while ago, and yet you haven't changed much.') Cimmie was now becoming seen as the angelic martyr mother: but she knew that there was something daemonic in her own attitudes to Tom: she both wanted and did not want him to be as he was: she saw him as both saint and devil. She did not, from the evidence of her letters, seem to be all that much interested now in his day-to-day politics: what he liked to do was to bring her news of them and she liked accepting this: it was as if he were saying to her – Look, what a good boy am I! People who want to be heroes perhaps also have to be somewhat like children: Freud said that anyone who has been the undisputed favourite of his mother keeps for life the feelings of a conqueror. With Tom there had been pushed aside the image of the father – which inculcates the faculty for being discriminatory; self-critical.

Thus the would-be hero has no recognition of the dark side of himself:
he sees the devil only in others. In himself, he feels a power that can be
used. And so he goes out to do battle with a make-believe confidence
and with make-believe attitudes to the world: he cannot distinguish
between reality and what is imposed by childhood patterns. In this he
is cheered on by his mother – or by the mother-figure he has chosen and
who accepts him. All Tom's baby-talk with Cimmie – the porkers, the
mutts, the moo-moos – seem to have been tapping some childhood well;
he needed perhaps to draw strength from this before going out to fight
– with his words, his tongue – the terrible dragons. But heroes continue
not to see the dragons that are in themselves.

> My own beloved moonbeam one
>   Adored his weekend so with all his blessed fellows – big, tiny and
> very tiny [drawing of three trees]. Hated going back so to this
> turmoil.
> Last night a thrilling discussion, but not for paper!
> All love in world my own socialist one. Tom

Tom went on a speaking tour of the country as a run-up to the general
election: Cimmie involved herself with her constituency at Stoke. They
each wrote solicitously about their own and the other's health. Tom –
'Good meeting here but my voice going badly at the end – three
meetings and long motor drives in a night – will return I hope to find
his sweet sausage lying down.' Cimmie – 'Stayed in bed all day and only
had 4 cups of milk and a compôte of apples ... You were quite right
when you said things went wrong when I thought of myself – I will
try not to!' They were both driving themselves hard. They must have
felt this necessary, if they were to take on the world seeing themselves
and others as heroes or demons.
    At the end of 1928 – in reply to a letter from Cimmie reiterating her
sorrow at not always being able to live up to the high hopes she had
for both of them and pleading for further 'special efforts' – Tom wrote:

> My own darling Moo-moo,
>   Yes let us be happy when you come back – life and especially youth
> is so short. In our life it is so difficult to preserve the steel that
> withstands great strain with the sweet gentle things that make life
> happy – so hard to meet an age of turmoil and yet to be fit inhabitants
> of the world we wish to create. Yet to excel in the fulness of life the
> great incompatibles must be combined. Let us make together that

great attempt on which so far all have failed – the attempt to reconcile the epic life with gentle sensitive things. I would inscribe my name on the page of my epoch in letters of flame and of rose – success would be the first shadow of the superman on earth – it will probably fail, but better the empyrean flight and disaster than earthbound crawlings – let us live always with the epic sense. Tom.

But even Tom could not quite let things rest on such a note of hyperbole, and added:

This really means he thinks her the only one in the world for him – is sorry he has been a bit overwrought lately and is feeling a bit up in the air tonight – loves her so very much and does so passionately want her to be happy – sorry he is such a difficult one – she is a bit diff too sometimes but that is his fault for putting her in such a dogfight. Don't mind any *little* things my sweet one – though he will try and be better.

But it was the little things to which they were vulnerable – those dwarves that come up from the underworld and penetrate heroes' armour. In May 1929, just before the general election, Irene was at Denham with her eye again ready to perceive chinks in armour –

A most tragic and painful row took place between Cim and Tom at dinner over the cars for the election and he was vilely rude to her and I tried to argue to both long into the night but they both seem to be at deadlock. I wish at times he could disappear off the face of the earth as he only brings her endless agony. And to make it worse, she thought of all things she was in for a baby.

Cimmie was in fact pregnant. Irene went to help her in her campaign at Stoke. The election there had aroused enormous interest because Cimmie as a rich socialist had drawn on herself all the publicity and abuse that Tom usually attracted, and there was the added appeal of her being a good-looking woman. The old stories about wealth and duplicity were trotted out: Cimmie was supposed to have a penniless brother in America whom the heartless family allowed to live in a workhouse: Tom and Cimmie ran factories where they paid their workers eighteen shillings a week. Irene heard a woman telling such stories on a bus, and remonstrated: the woman called Irene 'a bit of scum'. At a meeting of Cimmie's conservative opponent, Colonel Ward, a group of Cimmie's supporters challenged him about the spreading of such stories: in the resulting confusion Irene:

> had to yell that I was her sister and knew more about the Leiter fortunes than Colonel Ward and my grandfather did not corner wheat. The chairwoman yelled for the police. Ward was white as a sheet. I left the room taking ¾ of the clapping and shrieking women with me and I was cheered all the way down the streets.

Irene and her band of maenads in fact so alarmed Colonel Ward that he announced that as a result of 'organised hooliganism' he had decided to cancel his further meetings on the grounds that 'the socialists have determined to put an end to free speech in this country'.

At her eve-of-poll meeting Cimmie herself received:

> the wildest reception ... We went on to Fenton Town Hall Square where she had another thundering welcome save for a small group of hysterical booers one of whom, a woman, tried to tear everything off Cim. To get away we had to have barriers of strong young men to prevent us from being torn to shreds by the yelling crowd.

Cimmie got a 7,850 majority over Colonel Ward – his majority at the last election had been 4,500. She doubled the Labour vote from 13,000 to 26,000: she recorded one of the biggest swings to Labour in the country. Later that day she was again 'nearly torn to ribbons' when she met Ramsay MacDonald in London: she was rescued 'shaking with emotion'. Four days later, on June 6th, she had a miscarriage.

At his own eve-of-poll meeting at Smethwick Tom had joked with his audience – 'I have got the wind up. I am afraid my wife will get a bigger majority than me.' She did. Tom's majority was 7,340.

After Cimmie had had her miscarriage Irene reported – 'Poor old Tom was pretty hard hit.' But Irene herself seems to have caught something of the fever of heroic politics. With Cimmie and Tom both now in Parliament and with Tom obviously set to enjoy his first taste of practical, ministerial power, she wrote to Cimmie:

> I don't want you to think it was all the election, because I think Bonny found your inside unsatisfactory and you might have had a real tragedy later whereas now if you rest peacefully for 10 days or more and let it get pitched right again then you stand a far better chance of having a real strong baby and being yourself strong too to carry

it. I don't want you to feel the bitterness of this too much, my very dear one. Great things have come to you and Tom in parliament things – this is indeed a heartbreak in the midst of it – but have faith it was for the best.

CHAPTER 13

Rules of the Game:
Ministerial Office

In the General Election of May 1929 Labour won 287 seats, the Conservatives 261, and the Liberals 59. Ramsay MacDonald formed a Labour Government with Liberal backing. The rumours that Tom might be made Foreign Secretary did not materialise. There were too many party stalwarts who had to be satisfied; and in any case Tom's reputation, both political and personal, was probably thought not yet to be sufficiently secure. He was made Chancellor of the Duchy of Lancaster with special responsibility for unemployment – a ministerial post outside the cabinet. His boss within the cabinet was J. H. Thomas, the Lord Privy Seal, ex-secretary of the railwaymen's union.

Tom entered his one year of ministerial power with an enormous task placed somewhat nebulously above his shoulders but with no effective administrative apparatus by which to handle it. He was given a room in the Treasury, and as his private secretary a Treasury official who had been an assistant to Keynes: he personally employed Allan Young, his agent from Birmingham, as his political secretary. But even in government he seemed fated to be very much a lone voice. Winston Churchill described him as being 'a sort of ginger assistant to the Lord Privy Seal; and more ginger than assistant I have no doubt'.

J. H. Thomas was a flamboyant character, a 'card', the inspirer of innumerable comic stories. When he arrived in his minister's office in 1929 he was said to have remarked 'What a bloody awful 'ole, more privy than seal.' Lord Birkenhead found him with a hangover one morning complaining 'I've an 'ell of an 'ead': Lord Birkenhead said 'Why not take a couple of aspirates.' Once at a railwaymen's meeting a heckler called out 'Jimmy you're selling us!' and Thomas replied 'I'm trying but I can't find a buyer!' Tom remarked in his autobiography that it was difficult personally to dislike a man who could make a remark like that. But it was also difficult to work at the huge and largely uncharted problem of unemployment with someone whose talents, however endearing, had been for negotiating, bargaining, disarming people, making them laugh. He had never shown much interest in transforming society.

The other members of the government put on to deal with unemployment were George Lansbury, First Commissioner of Works, a 70-year old party stalwart with (in Beatrice Webb's words) 'certainly no capacity for solving intellectual problems'; and Tom Johnston, Under Secretary of State for Scotland, a man of intelligence but carrying little weight. These four – Thomas, Mosley, Lansbury and Johnston – were supposed to work together; but there was no timetable nor structure by which they regularly met, and they had no control over machinery for implementing their decisions if they did. After some months, Tom Johnston wrote that he was uncertain even whether or not he was in fact on the 'Unemployment Committee'. The only discernible difference in administrative machinery from that used by the previous government was that whereas before responsibility for providing both work and benefits for the unemployed had resided with the Ministry of Labour, now the responsibility for providing work had been taken away and given to J. H. Thomas and his staff in the Treasury – consisting of four civil servants seconded from the Inland Revenue, the Board of Trade, and the War Office – and the responsibility for implementing any recommendations remained invested with the Board of Trade. So that what in words had seemed to be a step in the direction of setting up an economic supreme council with executive powers such as Tom had always advocated, in fact turned out to be a bureaucratic proliferation of functions which made effective action more difficult than ever.

This perhaps in some ways suited J. H. Thomas. His biographer wrote of him that at this time 'the projects that seethed in his mind ranged from a bridge over the Zambesi river to a traffic circus at the Elephant and Castle: he saw civil servants, businessmen, local government authorities, trades unionists, engineers, scientists, post office officials, railway directors'. He was the chairman of an unending succession of committees, thrashing out the feasibility of railway schemes, harbour schemes, road schemes; for drainage, forestry, electricity and slum-clearance. But after all the talk, nothing much happened. Nothing much in fact could happen unless the government provided money; and J. H. Thomas and the other members of the Cabinet knew that it was unlikely that money would be forthcoming. Thomas agreed with

Snowden, the Chancellor of the Exchequer, that above all there should
be no departure from strict free-trade principles: no subsidies to
industry; no danger of inflation. But then, what on earth did a government think it could do about unemployment if it had no money with
which to employ people? All the talk, all the committees, began to seem
as if they were just noises to cover up the silences of nothing being done;
while the government waited helplessly for world trade to pick up on
its own.

Tom for a time tried to work loyally with Thomas. Just before his
first speech in Parliament for the government front bench on 4th July
Thomas told him to announce that between 75 and 100 million pounds
would be spent on the electrification of Liverpool Street Station. Tom
announced these figures: later in the debate Thomas reassured members
anxious about the fact that money might at last be poured out that of
course his colleague must have been referring to 'the total amount of
all possible electrification schemes under consideration'. Tom wrote
later – 'It was the only time in my life I ever gave to the House of
Commons a fact or a figure which was not valid.' To Thomas, all this
was part of the game of making noises that might reassure people in one
way, knowing that noises could be taken back and used to reassure
people in another.

Tom liked to tell a story of how he was going in to a committee room
with Thomas one day and he noticed how Thomas was holding an
object under his coat-tails. The committee was on the subject of Post
Office expenditure; in particular on the cost of a new box for telephones
that was to be put on the walls of houses. Thomas had been told by his
civil servants that the wooden box they recommended would cost
fifteen shillings: in the committee, Thomas produced from beneath his
coat with a flourish a tin box and announced – 'Four bob!' The civil
servants explained that the wooden box itself cost three shillings: it was
what was inside it that cost the other twelve.

During July Tom did manage to pilot through the House of Commons a Colonial Development Bill which contained provisions about
safeguarding native labour. A newspaper commented – 'His name will
live as the minister responsible for the first Act laying down important
principles to protect native labour from exploitation.'

He also – working in his 'semi-dungeon high up in the Treasury'
(Lansbury's phrase) – produced his own plan for creating vacancies for
young people in industry by offering those over sixty-five better
pensions if they retired – increasing the payment to married couples
from 10s to 30s a week. The Treasury said that the cost of this was

prohibitive. Tom then suggested that pensions could be offered to those employed in certain depressed industries – coal mining, iron and steel, ship building. While the Treasury was working out ways in which to discourage this, Tom went off on his summer holidays.

Just before he left, at the Durham miner's Gala at the end of July, he declared – 'I would rather see the Labour Government go down in defeat than shrink from great issues, because from such defeats men rise again with strength redoubled.'

During August 1929 – two months after the Labour Government had taken office with their urgent and primary commitment that of dealing with unemployment – all the four responsible ministers were out of England. Thomas was in Canada, Lansbury and Johnston were on holiday in Scotland. Tom's life in the South of France will be described in the next chapter.

During the summer of 1929 the unemployment figure was just over a million: it had been much the same for six years. Unemployment was held to be a great evil both because it was not seen how the dole could reasonably be raised above a level of barest subsistence, and because wasted potential productivity seemed to be an affront to accepted ideas about progress. On his return from holiday Tom returned to the attack about pensions: 'a man of sixty who has worked all his life will not suffer much demoralisation from living in idleness but a man of 20 may suffer irreparable harm'. He worked out his scheme in even greater detail: all insured workers who reached the age of sixty by a certain date were to be offered a pension of £1 a week for a single man and 30s a week for a married man on condition that they retired from work within six months: the cost of the scheme could be spread over fifteen years. By this, Tom estimated, 'at one stroke we reduce by one third the wholly unemployed'. The scheme was put to the cabinet: the cabinet appointed a sub-committee: the Treasury told the sub-committee that the cost (£22 million) was still prohibitive because they were traditionally committed to annual budgeting and could not think in terms of fifteen years. They put up the further argument – how could it be proved, until it happened, that the young would in such a scheme be absorbed into industry? Tom replied – How could anything, in fact, be proved until it happened? The Treasury's argument was for never doing anything.

Tom started a new line of attack by proposing a national programme for building roads. At the moment there were less than 4,000 men throughout the country employed in road-building: the business was entirely in the hands of local authorities. Tom planned an additional national scheme in which high wages would be offered to those in areas of the worst unemployment to build trunk roads and motorways. This scheme was received with ridicule. Did Tom not see, his critics said, that local governments would simply shelve their own schemes in the hope that the Labour Government would take over their costs? And how would a national organisation fare any better in the lengthy business of going through the formalities of acquiring land and so on than local authorities were already faring? And in any case, how could it be proved, again, that the building of roads would be of long-term assistance to the national economy? But above all – would not providing money for roads involve withdrawing money which might have been used by industries engaged in the export trade: and the encouragement of this, in the Treasury's view, was still the only hope of the country's recovery.

To this Tom replied that it had been the blind faith in the export trade that had led the country to its present moribund predicament: with every country giving priority to exports in a free-trade world, only those would get along which produced the cheapest goods by paying the lowest wages. In fact the Treasury itself had very little to suggest as a cure for unemployment except a reduction in wages – but then other countries could reduce wages more. Tom referred back to his Birmingham proposals of 1925 in which he had advocated that a closed economic area should be created in which a strong central government should have control over investment in industry, the buying of raw materials, and the manipulation of wages and prices. In the face of questions about how a central organisation would effectively control myriad local interests and organisations Tom simply asserted that of course if it was to be effective it would have to be given powers to do just this: that if it was not, then of course this implied that effective action was not wanted. But it was in the face of this sort of argument of Tom's that people found it easiest not to answer him at all: there was no accepted political language by which it might be stated that in certain circumstances, in the face of the danger of greater evils, it might be better perhaps even in such a grave area as that of unemployment if in fact things only got talked about and not much was done.

In the middle of all this argument, or silence, there was the Wall Street crash of October 1929 when the bottom, as it were, seemed to fall out of capitalists' lives in skyscrapers. Tom's prophecies seemed to be being fulfilled – there was indeed something suicidal about a world in which it was imagined that progress could be maintained by everyone competing against others to produce ever cheaper goods. J. H. Thomas had returned from Canada where ostensibly he had been to try to stimulate trade: it became evident that he had stimulated little but an anxiety about himself. By December he was reported by Beatrice Webb to be 'completely rattled and in such a state of panic that he is bordering on lunacy: Henderson reported that the PM feared suicidal mania'. Arthur Henderson suggested that Thomas 'must be sent away for a rest and Oswald Mosley installed under the Council to carry out agreed plans'. But the trouble was there were no agreed plans; and within the existing organisation there was no hope of carrying them out even if there were.

Tom had been on a speaking tour of the country trying to get support for his own plans: 'Every citizen should enrol himself in the great national army that is fighting unemployment.' But what, apart from building roads, was this army actually to do? Tom poured out schemes that were sometimes as bizarre as J. H. Thomas's: he admitted they were 'some hopeful, and some a little fantastic'. He wrote to the Air Minister suggesting – what about a roof over Victoria Station, to make a mid-city aerodrome?

MacDonald himself had for most of this time been occupied with Foreign Affairs: he had been in America successfully discussing naval disarmament. For the first six months of the Labour government he remained popular: he was the sort of Prime Minister that people liked: he was handsome, had a fine speaking voice, and he uttered noises of reassurance. In December 1929 he and Philip Snowden, the Chancellor of the Exchequer, were made freemen of the City of London: Beatrice Webb reported that during his speech to the assembled financiers at the banquet at the Mansion House 'his handsome features literally glowed ... which enhanced his beauty – just as a young girl's beauty glows under the ardent eyes of her lover'. In contrast, there sat 'Jimmy Thomas in the front row gazing at the ceremony, his ugly and rather mean face made meaner and uglier by an altogether exaggerated sense of personal failure'.

It seemed that Thomas was to be the scapegoat for the government's failure to deal with unemployment. But no government since the war had managed to deal with unemployment; and Tom, whatever he felt about Thomas, was not interested in questions of who was to be scapegoat. He went to see MacDonald in December and told him that he, Tom, was preparing a memorandum in which there would be put together all his proposals during the last six months. He would then ask MacDonald to put this before the Cabinet.

MacDonald went to his home at Lossiemouth, in Scotland, for the Christmas holidays. From there on December 30th he wrote in his own handwriting a letter to Tom.

My dear Mosley,

I had no chance of renewing our conversation about unemployment but I have thought much of what you said. Indeed for months I have been concerned with the state of things.

1   I am troubled about the lack of cooperation amongst the Junta to which the problem has been handed over. I was hoping that you would have all pulled together and hammered out from your diversity of view some agreed policy. I must admit the facts. That has not happened, and into whys and wherefores the crowded state of my own work has prevented me from going. I thought I could safely leave it to you all and took on things which I should not have done had I thought that you would not have all pulled together ...

2   The Economic Advisory Committee will be set up soon but there are various things to be provided for which at the last minute have caused delay. I am dealing with them here. That would be helpful but of course its fruits would not ripen in a month.

3   I am disturbed that the main features of our work hitherto has been to give further allowances for distress ... On outsiders it is having a depressing effect and is certainly lowering production. I have seen a good many old supporters and have had rather voluminous letters from others. The general tone is one of warning against those who are sponging and clamouring.

4   I have been looking into the pensions at 60 to relieve the labour market and I am quite certain it will not do that to any appreciable extent ... When one thinks this idea down to its essence, it is that we are overpopulated: that that old ruffian Malthus is right. The condition of the derelict areas is of the same class of problem. The whole thing must really be tackled in a way other than money aids ...

5   As I see the problem (dimly) we must hang on to what we are doing but weed out the spongers all round ... At the same time we should tackle the problem systematically. For instance the Department should present to the Treasury its views upon the financial and taxation policy – the Economic Advisory will soon do this I hope – for a situation has to be handled and not merely theories applied. We ought also to have really sound information as to expenditure upon unemployment, if for no other reason than to assure ourselves and enable us to defend ourselves against the attack which will soon be launched upon us.

But I must stop. My guardians here demand my presence for a walk. Only now am I feeling the work of past months in consequence of which I can tell C [Cimmie] a most bloodcurdling adventure in dreamland – a real good horror.

Unto you both much affection.

Yrs.   JRM

Tom was already preparing his memorandum. He worked on it through the Christmas holidays: he showed a draft to Keynes in the middle of January. Keynes remarked that it was 'a very able document and illuminating'. Tom sent a copy to MacDonald on 23rd January.

What became known as the Mosley Memorandum is a 15-page document in which Tom reiterated his proposals of the previous four years and put them into a form which, if the Cabinet still ignored them, he could use to appeal over the Cabinet's head first to the Parliamentary Labour Party and then to the country. The style of the memorandum is conciliatory and even tentative: it is emphasised that the aim is not to suggest clear-cut answers, but to set out unavoidably the serious questions which had to be discussed with a view to finding answers.

The second and third sections of the memorandum deal with long-term and short-term plans for providing work. It is pointed out that there is a certain conflict of interest here: long-term plans rely on the rationalisation of industry – on the bringing of industry up to date in both matters of technology and uses of manpower – and this may actually increase short-term unemployment. Thus it is all the more necessary that short-term employment should be treated as an urgent and separate issue.

To deal with short-term employment the memorandum concentrates on road construction. There are proposals concerning the technicalities by which movement and employment of labour should be handled sensibly by cooperation between national and local authorities. The whole short term scheme could be financed by 'a loan based upon the revenue from the Road Fund'. The cost to the taxpayer should be little more than the equivalent of 'a sixpenny tax on unearned income'. Such moderate expenditure, Tom suggested, would hardly cause such inflation as would involve a 'flight from the pound'. Then, discussion on long-term plans could begin.

But the success of the whole scheme depended on the proper working of the administrative machinery by which it would be operated: and it was just this area – that dealt with by the first and by far the most important section of the memorandum – that Tom's critics found it difficult not just not to reject, but even to talk about.

It was suggested that at the head of the Executive Committee to be set up should be the Prime Minister himself and under him, as if in a war-time inner Cabinet, the Chancellor of the Exchequer and five or six other ministers of relevant departments. Under this Executive Committee, which would meet once a week, there would be standing committees to implement its decisions headed by the relevant ministers. As part of a permanent executive machinery there would be a secretariat of twelve top civil servants who would also provide the information for the committees on which they themselves would serve. There would also be a research committee of economists and an advisory committee of financiers and businessmen to work with the committees of politicians. Finally, there would be attached to this apparatus an Industrial Bank, which would provide credit for the rationalisation schemes, higher wages and industrial development, as ordered by the Executive Committee or the Standing Committees. The aim of the whole was, simply, that authoritative action should be made possible. 'An attack upon the economic problem can only be effective under the auspices of the Prime Minister himself who should be armed with an adequate staff for such a purpose. He alone possesses the power to secure coordination and the authority to enforce action when decisions are taken.'

But it was just this suggestion that produced the silence amongst Tom's critics. Everyone in government circles knew that the organisation under J. H. Thomas was not working: Thomas himself was breaking down: his lieutenants on their own were powerless: even what committees there were were seldom meeting. And unemployment was growing. But it seemed to be the case that in this situation most people in positions of authority continued to think that they should make noises of lamentation – and do little else. Their fear, of course, was that if Tom's proposals were put into effect, there would be danger of some sort of dictatorship – with its attendant corruptions. But if such methods seemed to be the only way to cure unemployment, how could they say they were not interested? It was the tradition that politicians were supposed to say they wanted to get things done.

Tom sent his memorandum to Ramsay MacDonald on January 23rd 1930. Shortly before this, he had mentioned to J. H. Thomas that he was formulating some opinions about unemployment which he would like Thomas to see in due course. Ramsay MacDonald telephoned to Thomas early in February to ask if he knew of the Memorandum. Thomas said he did not. Then there ensued the sort of game by which politicians effectively evade talking about things that matter, by getting in a state about things that do not.

Thomas wrote to MacDonald complaining that Tom had improperly gone over his, Thomas's, head; and so he, with much regret, had no alternative but to offer MacDonald his resignation. MacDonald wrote to Thomas saying that he quite understood his, Thomas's, hurt feelings; but he had no alternative but to refuse his resignation out of considerations of national interest ('we must endure however hard the road may be'). MacDonald also wrote to Tom saying how very surprised he, MacDonald, was about Tom's behaviour which had been quite properly resented by his boss, Thomas ('I need not explain why that should be so'). But the best thing of course, all round, MacDonald suggested, would be to patch the whole matter up and say no more about it. In the middle of all this John Strachey, who was now Tom's Parliamentary Private Secretary, left a copy of the Memorandum lying around in his house when journalists were present and its contexts were 'leaked' to the press – whether by design or accident, of course, people could hint darkly. This gave Thomas further opportunities to demonstrate hurt feelings. With all this posturing going on the memorandum itself could be, and quietly was, put on the shelf – to be considered in due course by a Cabinet sub-committee consisting of Snowden, Greenwood, Margaret Bondfield, and Tom Shaw – who were all known to be hostile to Tom's ideas. This committee then could, and did, push it even further to the back of the shelf by sending it to the Treasury for a thorough examination. There it would lie, as if in some morgue.

In all the business about the Mosley memorandum – concerning both the contents and the reactions of people to it – there was a confusion, barely conscious, not just about the nature of the political game, but about the nature of language and even about human nature itself. Tom had been brought up outside a political tradition: he believed that, politically, words should mean roughly what they said. He had become a socialist because he thought it vital, amongst other things, that the unemployment problem should be solved: that the socialists, when they got power, should try to fulfil their election pledges and give priority to doing this. But then, when they achieved power largely through holding out hopes by their promises, they seemed to be doing nothing serious about the problem at all. Tom was outraged by this. He thought – If you say you want to solve the unemployment problem then you set up machinery by which the unemployment problem can be solved; if you do not, then this means that you do not want to solve the unemployment problem. You should then admit this: any other attitude is cheating.

Those who had been in the Labour Party or indeed in any political tradition for a long time knew that in some sense all this had to be a game: you had good intentions: you honestly professed them in your manifestos: you hoped by this to get power: none of this was cheating. But when you did get power of course there were often realities which were stronger than the good intentions you had had: you were forced to adapt yourself to realities not because you were betraying your good intentions, but because if you did not you might be betraying other good principles more severely. There was often a choice of evils: you had sometimes, possibly, to do almost nothing. But you could not quite say this. Political language had to be about will, and dynamism, or there would never be hope of improvement.

At the back of this there was a question of how one might see human nature. Tom thought, or believed (or wanted to believe: the words are difficult) that human beings are rational: that if human beings are rational then words should properly mean roughly what they say. There seemed to him no sense in the idea that sometimes a game with words might properly by played in which the point was that they are not quite believed: but such words are none the less valid because this non-belief is recognised by the participants from a higher point of view. In certain areas human beings play games because the demands on them are too paradoxical to make sense if they do not: in the area for instance to do with the necessary exercise of power and the salutary limitation of power it is not in the simplicities of words that there is truth; but in the recognition that there is something that can be honoured beyond words' limitations.

Tom's critics in the Party, however much they said they believed in the rational processes of socialism, yet believed in their bones, most of them (they had been brought up with less opportunities for self-deception than Tom) that human affairs were for the most part irrational and there had to be safeguards against the dangerously over-rationalising tendencies of human beings and of words. When Tom made his proposals for strong central governmental machinery they could not attack him directly because, as socialists, this is what they had always been advocating; how else could they have got as far as they had with evolutionary or revolutionary change? But it was by instinct that they feared the exaggerated implementation of government control: there is nothing more irrational, they knew, than human beings who have been given total power – even to act in such a way as they think is wholly rational. But still, they could not quite say this, or how would they ask for, or be given, any power at all? Both they, and the people who voted for them, had to pretend they could be trusted with power: and it was still in fact by dealing in limited power that people could strive and hope bit by bit for reasonable change. But all this only made sense if it was held together by rules of an instinctively accepted political game – rules that were known, but not stated, on a supra-rational level. So what did such people do when someone came along with rational arguments that did not take into account styles or levels of understanding – who did not see from some metaphysical level what had to be, and what was not, a game? It was safest, presumably, to ignore such a person, if he could not properly be spoken to. One of the rules of the game was that you could not exactly explain what was and what was not a game: if you did, then the someone who did not accept that there was a game could simply make you seem a hypocrite.

Tom might have understood some of the complexities of games-playing if he had pondered more about himself. Of course, he himself played games: his letters to Cimmie were genuine games: how better could he write to her? It was on his perceiving something like this that there might have been truth. He seemed to have to insist that other people were not playing games: it is difficult to imagine how, in his private life, he succeeded in thinking this of himself.

CHAPTER 14

Entertainment

Cimmie had her miscarriage early in June. She took her seat in the House of Commons at the end of the month. In August the family went for their usual summer holiday to Antibes.

Cimmie's sister Irene joined them there. She recorded in her diary in her cloudy, anarchic style what life in the South of France was like. Tom and Cimmie and the children were staying at the Eden Roc hotel; the other *dramatis personae* in Irene's account were in the hotel or in villas round about. The chief attraction of the long hot summer was the film star John Gilbert, who had recently been acting with Greta Garbo, and was with his wife Ina Claire. In supporting roles in Irene's story were – Baba and Fruity Metcalfe, Cimmie's younger sister and her husband; Bobby and Paula Casa Maury (the latter Tom was currently pursuing); John Strachey and his recently-married wife Esther; Dick Wyndham, a painter and Cimmie's confidante; Babe Barnato, a racing motorist; Rupert Belville, a banker; and Americans Ben Finney and Dudley Malone. Irene had been enraged by overhearing Tom at a dinner party speculating in whispers to Paula Casa Maury about which of the three Curzon sisters would succeed in the contest to attract John Gilbert – 'the heavyweight, the lightweight or the middle' (Irene, Baba or Cimmie.) The evening had ended in uproar, with Tom accusing Cimmie of being drunk. The next day:

> Tom was so foul to Cim when she asked him about her birthday plans saying he did not care and was fed up with all of us I lost my temper and called him a cad. So we left him and went with the children to the beach. The weather was too vile for Ben Finney's party by boat to Monte Carlo so a lot of us joined up. Bowls and bowls of punch were made as we flopped about on mattresses in the drawing room

– Dick, Cim and I were sober adjuncts to a very stewed party. Ben suddenly brought in 'Miss America' who had won the world's beauty competition – utterly out of it and left crying in about an hour. It was discussed and discussed what we should do for hours till it resorted to more punch and sandwiches – and a marvellous dish of Ben's, chili and rice and meat. Ina was thoroughly drunk and gay and sweet Fruity was well over the odds with Baba very annoyed. He disappeared and made up like John Gilbert and came in with Gilbert and Cim and proceeded to circle all the ladies as the great lover and was very funny. The fun was entirely ruined at 10 pm by Maurice and Miss Stephenson both dead drunk being pressed together asleep and she gently fondling his hair and we all left the room in disgust and found bed the only solution. Tom emerged when we got back in haughty solitude having been away alone in a huff.

Went to the beach with the children. Cim came very late and I felt from her face and eyes Tom had been tiresome again. Poor Fruity was carried off having nearly cut his foot in 2 with glass from a bottle on the Cannes beach. Fearful arguments with Ben and everyone as to whether we should have his boat party. Ben Finney's dog did the most lovely dives for us and simply loved it.

August 23rd. Cim's birthday.
Gave Cim a black bag for the House of Commons. She got some lovely 'presies' and Tom came up to scratch with a lovely modern Metropolis Cocktail Set and Lamp. Had a family bathe with the children on the Roc, and a family lunch with the children and Baba. Joined up with Babe Barnato's big party at the next table ... tore across the ocean in Barnato's speed boat ... played vile tennis with Barnato and 2 tiresome men with 4 dirty tennis balls getting lost the whole time. Had a swim and gave Cim another bag, an exquisite one, before dinner. She gave the most perfect party down on the rocks: lovely lit tables all round, huge cinema lights making wonderful effects on everything, a marvellous band that did turns walking about and sitting out on the diving boards. Dudley Malone made a speech to Cim after a bad effort by Finney. Diving races went on with Babe Barnato, Rupert Belville and John Gilbert. I had Gilbert and Finney for dinner and had an absorbing talk with Gilbert on his view of women – *his* women – and he told me he was going off alone as things were screw-eyed with him and Ina. The whole trouble is he needs an alsatian dog like Ben's for a wife – absolute obedience. Went to the Beouf about 1.30. Tom deliberately took Ina to see Fruity and

left her there. Gilbert, losing her, went mad, tore back to the hotel thinking she was left behind, came back to find her dancing and savagely dragged her into the street where Cim and Dudley witnessed a fearful scene. A bit later Bobby found him walking into the sea and drove him round Cannes to steady him. Then he came back and Baba and Cim had hour after hour battling and appeasing Ina and him. It was the most fantastic evening I have ever witnessed. Dudley finally took Ina to his villa for the night and exhausted with waiting on other people's rows Knottman drove me home at 5 am. No one knew what happened to Gilbert. I saw him vanish down the road with Baba before I left. Rupert Belville had got very drunk at dinner and said filthy things about the rich socialists – about Esther and John and Cim and Tom – which Esther overheard, and she got up and left the table.

The next day Tom left by train for London – to get back to work on his plans for the unemployed. John Gilbert, it was discovered, had also left at dawn by taxi for Paris. He was said to have told the driver – 'Don't have an accident: my face is my fortune.' Irene stayed on for a few more days with Cimmie and the children: she had a talk with Nanny about how they thought Cimmie was becoming 'awfully callous'. Cimmie wrote a letter to Tom – 'It has been incredibly quiet since you left . . . John G returned late that night after getting to Lyons in his taxi before coming to . . . Dick is getting well away with his countess, and has already had a flog.'

Cimmie returned to London. Tom was working in his semi-dungeon in the Treasury. They both made efforts that autumn to sort out their own problems – or at least to view them rationally. Tom was becoming more impatient and scathing with Cimmie publicly. Cimmie wrote for advice to Dick Wyndham, who had stayed on in the South of France to paint. He replied:

Darling Cimmie, Your letter did rather upset me, and I wish I could give you some advice that would make your life happier. There seems no solution because you have had the misfortune to have been born a naturally happy person. This sounds like a paradox, but it isn't. Nearly all intelligent people are born naturally miserable. I am sure that Tom is just as unhappy and probably more so than you. And if you take all our friends – for instance Sachie, Hutchy, William – if you could see their real thoughts, how dismally sad you would find them! their quite unexpected hopes, regrets, and longings. And even I, who am supposed to lead such an ideal life with my painting, freedom and money, live, in reality, a life of acute misery, worry and loneliness relieved occasionally by moments of great exaltation; but these happen far too seldom to make life worth while. I suppose only the human sheep are able to lead a continuously happy life; they have their 'dope' – religion, the Empire, their hire-purchase furniture; other sheep to look down upon; their aspidistra; and finally a respectable funeral and a very white marble or speckled grey granite tombstone. They have no moments of exaltation: they don't want them. But your natural happiness refuses to admit such an unpleasant state of affairs. You feel that having been born in a world filled with so many beautiful things one should be allowed to enjoy it without hindrance and help others to enjoy it. How right you are! But just because you are filled with such capabilities of enjoyment you are constantly being disillusioned and hurt. You are still like a child who sees an infinite source of fun in every object around him only to find that they are all protected by those words – 'you mustn't touch'.

On reading through this rigmarole I find it hasn't got us very far. The only logical solution seems to be that you must damp your natural happiness in order to be immune from the misery of a miserable world; and that is a remedy I would hate to advise. It comes under the heading of innoculation of which I disapprove.

The only thing I can suggest is to make a list of the things that don't matter so much – such as the mastif,* and even an occasional flit to Paris: they are annoying, but no more so than an occasional attack of flu. Then make a list of all the things you do really mind about like hell. Make up your mind never to say a word about the less important things for fear that in time you might find yourself perpetually nagging. Not only don't mention them, don't think about them, *don't mind them*. About the things that matter make a real *definite stand* – raise hell, throw things, do and say anything you like. But you must make your two lists and stick to them.

You will probably say that it is just the mounting up of the relatively small things that is so unbearable – I know – but if you start by disregarding them they won't mount up, they will never have been born.

I shall be leaving here in a few days now, all my four paintings having come to a bad end; so we soon will be able to have a 'crack'.** I shall devote some of the time to extracting the name of the 'old friend' who has fallen in love with you ...

* *Tom had recently bought a large dog.*
** *talk.*

This letter was posted on October 20th 1929. On October 21st Tom
posted his own long letter to Cimmie. He had come to Denham to rest.
Cimmie was in her constituency.

Savehay Farm
Denham
Bucks

Meanderings of a sick mutt.

My darling fellow,
Lying in bed with this wretched cold I have thought so much of our
relationship and my mind moves to these conclusions – write and tell
me if you agree.

(1)   The thing that matters most is our love and alliance in all
things. That should be our absolutely fixed and unchanging relation
– a basis of life in which we both have complete confidence – sure
that never in any crisis or misfortune will it fail us.

(2)   The next most important thing is the individual happiness and
development of each of us – without that, many of the gifts and
powers we have to give to the world must be damaged and reduced:
without happiness and a sense of all-pervading freedom and power
we cannot be complete people. Yet none but complete people can
succeed in the stupendous task that we have set ourselves

Our problem is how to reconcile and to blend into a perfect life
these 2 premises of our existence: (1) our marriage and alliance in all
things (2) our individual happiness and freedom which are essentials
of the full personality.

To achieve this we must put away all small things. We really deny
ourselves (2) because our confidence in (1) is not enough.

Each of us is afraid that the small incidents of (2) may destroy (1):
each of us consequently is inclined to snatch small bits of (2) for
himself or herself while striving to thwart rather than to assist the
other. That situation is a commonplace in the marriage of all remarkable people – it is small, contemptible and atavistic – in our case it
should be entirely lacking because (1) is so much stronger than in
almost any other example of which one can think. We have not only
love, a great companionship, children, home, etc – we have also a
tremendous alliance in public life which has bound us together against
the whole squalor of things as they are in face of a storm of hatred
and mean lying abuse which no other couple has ever had to face.
That is a great alliance which should be far above every factor in the
sphere of (2). Yet I believe it is really our unexpressed fear that (2)

will affect (1) that leads to trouble in sphere of (2). From my side such apprehension might perhaps reasonably be stronger as you are so much younger and less sophisticated in sphere (2) than me – I know I should not be affected by it – you might be – yet even here I might be more reasonable to you in sphere (2) if I did not feel that in past and even present you had there severely restricted me. Such a feeling of course must arise on both sides and has created a vicious circle.

. The way out I feel is this – we should not only acquiesce in (2) for each of us – we should be as much partners there as we are in (1). We should have such confidence in the permanence and inviolability of (1) (our marriage and alliance in all great things) that we should not only be unafraid of (2) (personal freedom and happiness) affecting (1), but we should actively promote complete confidence in each of us developing in sphere (2) with the assistance of the other – we should have no feeling of fear and regret of any kind if one of us enjoyed things apart from the other – we should realise that the complete development of each individual contributed to the success and greatness of the whole alliance.

We must of course do all things in the light of our position and mission in the world – we must never disarm before the enemy – only before each other. That is what I mean by 'Tenue'.

We are in a sense conspirators together against things as they are and conspirators cannot take the enemy into their confidence. To lead what we believe to be a moral life in our immoral society some concealment and even subterfuge is necessary if we are to retain our power to change that society for the great end we seek. Together we can retain our greatest power in public life to change the miseries of present society to live a full and human life.

We already have a great comfort in (1). Let us also have a great comfort in (2).

Let us have such confidence in the permanence and the superiority of our marriage and love over everything else in life that we can be partners in promoting the freedom and happiness of each of us as well. I believe it is possible – it means an end of all small things – of all small jealousies and fears – it means the triumph of the modern mind. I believe we are capable of it. Let us try to have a great compact – a great alliance in all things. (This reads like a very muddled and badly delivered political speech but it means he loves her very much and wants both of them to be happy fellows).

It was perhaps a saving grace of Tom's that he could write a bracket such as at the end of this letter – at moments he could laugh at himself even when he was being carried away by one of his more extreme flights of self-justifying rationalisation and rhetoric. But, between the rhetoric and the laughter there was not much sign of practicality. The same evening that he posted this letter he played one of his more extravagant practical jokes upon his sister-in-law Irene. She was giving a large after-dinner party in her house at which her guests included Lord Beaverbrook, Ivor Novello, Beatrice Lillie and Arthur Rubinstein. Then (Irene recorded) – 'Some brute (a joke we presumed) rang me up as from Scotland Yard and tried to infer some of my party were thieves and were wanted'. The voice instructed her to keep all her guests with their hands up facing the wall until further notice. Irene paid no attention. When later she discovered the joker was Tom, she refused to speak to him or Cimmie for a week.

Cimmie received Tom's long letter when she was in Stoke: she travelled down to London and handed her reply to Tom.

Darling Darling Darling Darling. I am so glad you wrote that letter – I agree with every word of it and *will* try – all the things you said are true. Now taking your two premises – it always has been because I have never been quite sure of (1) that I have been tricky about (2). You started off with (2)s so very soon after marriage before I had ever got confidence either in myself or you while you were my *whole* horizon literally in every way. I have never been persuaded you really really appreciated me, you were always finding fault, and liking people so utterly different to me, it made me apprehensive and always on the defensive.

I must say I do not agree that you should be more apprehensive of me than I of you. I have only been driven to my small successes in sheer self-defence. In fact till very recently I have had none – and that alongside of your varied assortment has been very bad for me. I always felt you had so much more success (not generally speaking, I know I am all right as a general success, but I mean a 'particular' success) and that gave me an inferiority complex. You don't know the agonies I have gone through time after time when you have got off with lovely ladies and I have been left; it has very often nearly driven me dippy. I am sure you will never realise how even a success with nonentities like Mario Pansa, Ridal or Rochefoucauld restores my confidence, and you take it away again by sneering at the 'quality' of my fellows. You see while we are about it I had better be quite frank: I have always felt that you won on the swings and

roundabouts; that if it came to complete freedom inside category
(2) you would profit by it much more than me; you would have
more successes greater fun – have your cake (i.e. Mum) and eat
it!! While I, well, I would have no cake at all – no fun on swings
or roundabouts. I think maybe I am wrong but you must remember nothing really matters one toss to me except you and the
children. I am terribly frightened on my own, and a good deal
bewildered.

My success with Gilbert and the Frenchies last week was balm and
oil to my 'tortured spirit' but believe me does not go very far. I am
sure my whole trouble is I am small enough to feel that under such
arrangement you would get much more than me and that stops me
risking it. You have it in your power to hurt me so dreadfully – you
have hurt me so dreadfully –

If only my confidence in (1) could be assured but I so often feel
we only stick together because of our public position and not because
we really do love and value each other. Now if we could have a
perfect (1) all else follows. I will try. But do you see my point: if only
I had more confidence, less of an inferiority complex; and you the
one person in the world who could help most always finding fault,
always criticising, always belittling me, making it worse; any efforts
I do make on my own mocked and derided.

I retaliate in the obvious silly way – it *is* a vicious circle as you say.
How are we to get out of it: if you were kinder to me, more
considerate, I know I would 'respond to treatment': but in order for
me to be nicer to you you *must* be nicer to me: I am not capable of
the martyr-like effort, it may be very small and petty but I am not
going to make an effort alone.

Oh dear even writing those few lines I feel resentment rising in me,
and that I must not allow. But I think even you will allow making
a success of living with you is hellish difficult if one also strives to keep
one's own individuality and end up. I do hope this won't appear as
a very one-sided sort of letter as yours was *so* fair – forgive me if it
is – I think this a very good moment to really have a grand try at (1)
and (2) and let us become experts at avoiding all minor exasperations;
they cause endless bother and with skill can be avoided.

Remember this, I do adore you, unless in a mood (generally
engendered by you) when I could kill you. I would die for you. You
and the children are always the only things that really matter. I am
not a bad sort of person neither are you. We both want to be happy
– well here's to it. And bless you my love. Be my sweet Tommy I

fell in love with. Help Mum to be the grandest sort of person she can
be. Kisses and devotion. Timmy
This is not nearly a nice enough letter. I did *love* yours and do thank
you for it and *am* glad you wrote it and do love you.
Is your cold better?
I hope so.

In this letter Cimmie seems to have faced truly something of the
predicament she was in with Tom: Tom had more energy, a more
daemonic quality than she: he had the power to use words apparently
rationally to justify his drives and ambitions: he could claim his own
freedom and feel safe in it, because he could make impossible her own.
Cimmie was a good woman; she loved Tom; she felt she could not
challenge the whole process of their lives without losing him; but then,
she did not seem to want to challenge this for herself. When he hurt her,
she cried out; she tried to answer him back in kind; she did not turn away
from him. Tom did not see that part of his energy and his success might
depend on his having someone who adored him and whom he could
manipulate: whom he could, when his own supremacy was threatened,
mock and deride; and then win back with his endearments. Tom tried
to sort out his problems with Cimmie in terms of reason: he thought
– as he did about politics – that human problems could and should be
solved by the presentation of a case so rational that it was unanswerable.
It is not clear how often he had glimpses into his manipulations: even
his laughter was something of a protection: soon with Cimmie, as in
politics, the grandiose words would take over again – the 'mission to
the world': the 'stupendous task'. But how did he and Cimmie imagine
that with their quarrelling, their baby-talk, they were achieving 'the
triumph of the modern mind'? This mind was to be controlled by will:
but how was there to be any reality of will if there were no observations
of the nature of the self that was wielding it?

Cimmie's innocence (as Dick Wyndham had said) was to believe not
in the efficacy of manipulation, as Tom did, but just that life could be
made beautiful by efforts at being straightforward. She believed this
with regard to Tom: she believed it with regard to her politics. She had
almost as little sense as Tom had of the irony of the contrasts between
private and public life.

Soon after she got back from the summer holiday she made her
maiden speech in the House of Commons. It was on the occasion of the
second reading of the Widows', Orphans', and Old Age Contributory
Pensions Bill, which aimed at providing pensions for the first time for

half a million widows. Cimmie said she welcomed the bill because it 'definitely takes us along the road towards the abolition of poverty and destitution': it was 'an approach towards the full acceptance of the fundamental truth that economic insecurity is socially created and should be provided for by the social services until it can be abolished by socialism'. To the opposition's suggestion that a working man or working woman might possibly be a better citizen if they were not too much looked after by the state she replied:

> I have noticed a word that has been greatly in use since this measure was brought in and that is the word 'demoralisation' – demoralisation of getting something for nothing. That is ground on which I am very much at home. All my life I have got something for nothing. Why? Have I earned it? Have I deserved it? Not a bit. I have just got it through luck. Of course some people might say I showed great intelligence in the choice of my parents, but I put it all down to luck. And not only I, but if I may be allowed to say so, a great many people on the opposite side of the House are in that same position – they also have always got something for nothing. Now the question is: are we demoralised? I could not answer that question for anyone but myself – but, looking at members opposite, may I be allowed to say they don't look too demoralised physically, though their mental and physical condition is beyond me to determine. I stoutly deny however that I am demoralised –

Cimmie got many congratulations for her speech – one from the Prime Minister ('excellent matter and excellent style'); one from Bob Boothby ('It was so good, my dear, that if I said all I want to you you wouldn't believe it'); one from an anonymous 'Mother of Ten' – 'You are splendid, you are magnificent ... those who as you say have all their lives had something for nothing cannot imagine what it is like to be all one's life giving all and getting nothing – their health and strength, their love and sacrifice, their leisure their pleasure, yes even life itself – that is the fate of the working class mother'.

Neither Cimmie nor Tom by instinct or by upbringing were equipped to do what in fact most people do whatever their idealism or protestations – which is to try their best in whatever areas are available to them, and about the rest not too much to worry. This was just what Tom and Cimmie objected to about people like J. H. Thomas and Ramsay MacDonald – who talked of stupendous tasks and then did nothing. Tom and Cimmie were too proud: they had had too many expectations pinned on to them: they could not be satisfied, as so many Labour people seemed to be satisfied, by having simply 'arrived'. They had the curse – whether of a good or a bad angel – to want to alter the world.

Humdrum politicians have almost necessarily to feel that idealism is dangerous: they feel it upsetting their day-to-day plans. Their jobs in administration, it seems, are properly to do with preventing anything disastrous being done by idealists. Tom, an idealist, was correct in thinking that such people were out to thwart him. It was perhaps their tragedy, as well as his, that at this time some idealism was probably necessary if there was not to be a drift towards chaos or war. It was the curse of the humdrum politicians that they had no use for the talents of someone like Tom: it was the curse of Tom to treat what he saw as their lethargy only with contempt. Few people at the time seemed capable of seeing a pattern into which they themselves and others of a different temperament might fit if all this was observed as it were from a higher viewpoint. Tom, certainly, did not see how his energy might be effective if he submitted it to the restraints of its being for a while thwarted. Everyone was accustomed to think in terms of antagonism – in one sort of view, or characteristic, not embracing but cancelling out another.

In war Tom had had little experience of the terrible helplessness of people even with good intentions when in authority: he for the most part had been war's victim. But it is people who have had actual experience of responsibility for life and death who have often learned that there is little good that can be done except in ways of steadfastness, and hope, and painstaking bit-by-bit efforts. And it is those who rage against the fact that there are victims, who want to alter the world; and so are apt to make victims of the people round them.

CHAPTER 15

Resignation

On May 9th 1930 the Cabinet sub-committee headed by Snowden, the Chancellor of the Exchequer, recommended that the Mosley Memorandum be rejected. Their reasons were – the Prime Minister could not take on the added burden of direct responsibility for employment; the proposed Executive Committee would undermine the tradition of the individual responsibilities of ministers; the road-building scheme ignored the rights of individuals and local authorities; the memorandum as a whole paid no attention to the one programme for recovery that in the long run would work – the encouragement of exports. Whatever might be useful in the scheme would have to be done at the expense of other things that might be useful: so it was best to play safe, and carry on just hoping that world trade would get better. What the Labour Cabinet objected to in fact was that the Memorandum was too socialistic: the arguments they put up against it were those of conservatism. But these were the arguments which, as Tom and other socialists had pointed out before the election, were resulting in society's breakdown. It seemed that socialists did not want to govern: they wanted to continue in the role to which they had become accustomed – that of being in opposition to any exercise of power.

The Cabinet set up another committee to consider the report of the Snowden committee – and to confer with Tom, Lansbury and Johnston. Discussions went on for ten days. The point at issue now was mainly about how to initiate some sort of road-building scheme: did you just raise money and get on with the job (Tom): or did you do nothing about money till you had worked out detailed plans with local authorities, (J. H. Thomas and Herbert Morrison, the Minister of Transport) – and then wait for the Treasury almost certainly to say that there was no money anyway. Tom was accused of wanting to

'Russianise' the government: Herbert Morrison said that he spoke 'like a landlord addressing his peasantry'. The issue was becoming simply between someone who wanted to give priority to getting something done over the probable cost, and the others who did not.

On May 19th Tom and Cimmie dined with Sidney and Beatrice Webb. Tom said that he intended to resign his ministerial post: what he found impossible was not so much the disagreement, but the fact that under Ramsay MacDonald there was no desire for serious practical talk at all. Meetings between ministers, he said, were more comic than anything in Bernard Shaw's *The Apple Cart*. Beatrice Webb noted that the Mosleys seemed 'sincere and assiduous in their public aims'.

Tom felt, correctly, that during the year he had been in office his energies had been used as a safety valve but there had never been a serious intention to get anything he recommended done. He had been quite cynically put in a position where his energy could be expended and his ideas ignored. He either had to resign, or to resign himself to the sort of game that during all his years in Parliament he had abominated.

On May 18th Bob Boothby, a conservative, had written to him:

My dear Tom,
From France I have been contemplating the state of politics with a jaundiced but more or less unbiased mind· and I beg of you not to resign. I cannot see that you would achieve anything: and you might well do yourself irreparable damage. It is a God's mercy that the existence of your memorandum is known to the public.

That was essential; but for the moment it is surely enough. I care about your political future far more than about any other single factor in public affairs, because I know that you are the ONLY one of my generation – of the post-war school of thought – who is capable of translating into action any of the ideas in which I genuinely believe. Consequently I can conceive of no greater tragedy than that you should take a step which might wreck your chances, or at any rate postpone the opportunity of carrying through constructive work.

If you stay where you are that opportunity is bound to come soon. Go, and where are you?

The example of Randolph Churchill is significant and appalling. You deliver yourself into the hands of every enemy, and they are not a few. Your own front bench will heave a sigh of relief, consign you to the Mountain, and take no more risks.

They will point to their own life-long services in the Labour cause, and contrast them with yours. They will regret that they are apparently unable to proceed at a pace sufficient to satisfy the desires and ambitions of a wealthy young 'aristocrat' in a hurry.

Picture the parliamentary scene. You will make your case against the government – a formidable one – but nine-tenths of the audience will be hostile. Snowden will reply with all the venom at his command (I am sure his recent outburst against me was an oblique thrust at you.) He will quote from your speeches at Harrow ten years ago. All the pent-up fury which you have deliberately, and I think quite rightly, roused in so many breasts will simultaneously be released.

The Tories will cheer vociferously and savagely.

Your own orthodox back-benchers will be against you because they will feel that you have delivered a fierce blow at the Government which may well involve their defeat at the next election ...

The cumulative effect of so many hostile forces would overwhelm Napoleon himself.

I don't see how you could hope to stand up against them.

You can't return to us.

And however impelled you may feel to work once more with the 'gentry', you would be wretched if you did. I know to my cost the limitations of the existing young conservatives. They are charming and sympathetic and intelligent at dinner.

But there is not one of them who has either the character or the courage to do anything big ...

What is the alternative?

Surely to remain within the official fold and by making yourself increasingly oppressive and uncomfortable to what Ellen Wilkinson so aptly describes as 'The Bright Old Things' consolidate and strengthen your power. The forces economic and political now at work must assist you.

With every increase in the unemployment figures the position which *you are known* to have taken up becomes more impregnable and easier to justify ... Why should you not work with, and ultimately direct, a moderate Government of the Left?

You occupy a key position at the moment. For God's sake don't chuck it away. Incidentally, if you have a moment to spare, you might modify the divorce laws.

My own difficulties do not diminish with the passage of time and the march of events ...

Good luck to you.

Don't think of answering this.

Yrs ever

Bob

But this letter, with its admirable advice, was about how to play the political game: it was about techniques of how to win by appearing for a time to be steadfast in losing. Tom did not want this: the people with whom he had been playing the game had been making such a nonsense of it for so long that he wanted to give it up altogether. His revulsion was personal rather than political. But then, as Bob Boothby had asked, did he really think he could take on the whole accepted political machinery single-handed? If he would not play according to the rules, did he think he could alter the whole tradition of games playing?

On the afternoon of May 19th Tom had been to see Ramsay MacDonald and had told him he thought he should resign: MacDonald had asked him to reconsider. He found Tom (he wrote in his diary) 'on the verge of being offensively vain in himself'. Johnston pleaded with members of the Cabinet that there was still time to use Tom's talents which had been 'trampled on and ignored'. But people wanted to ignore Tom's talents.

On May 20th he handed his letter of resignation to MacDonald. In it he reiterated that his Memorandum 'was not advanced in any dogmatic spirit' but that he found it 'inconsistent with honour', to remain a member of a government that would not even seriously discuss its election pledges. The letter was written in a tone, MacDonald said, of 'graceless pompousness'. MacDonald added (these comments are in his diary) 'Test of a man's personality is his behaviour in disagreement: in every test he failed.' Most of the newspapers the next day however praised Tom for his courage. The *Daily Herald* added a warning – 'What Mosley needs is a break in his success: he has been a wonder child for too long.'

On May 22nd there was a meeting of the Parliamentary Labour Party to which Tom, now out of office, could present his proposals over the heads of the Cabinet. G. R. Strauss, a young MP personally unsympathetic to Tom, recorded that Tom's speech to the Parliamentary Party was a 'magnificent piece of rhetoric' and that most MPs were obviously of the opinion that the Memorandum 'should be carefully considered'. J. R. Thomas in a 'lachrymose and emotional vein', announced that it was 'the most humiliating day of his life': but then Arthur Henderson, an experienced tactician in the party game, played one of the traditional moves: he appealed to Tom 'in very moving language to take the noble line' of withdrawing his censure motion against the government to allow further talks to take place – for the sake of party unity. John Strachey whispered to Tom that he should refuse

– 'What people want is action'. Tom did refuse. In the words of G. R. Strauss – 'instantly all the support and sympathy he had received deserted him'. A junior minister remarked 'Pity he didn't withdraw, he would have done himself a lot of good': whereupon Cimmie, overhearing this, said 'He didn't care for his own good, but only for his party!' Tom lost the vote by 29 to 210. His failure to withdraw was seen as a grave tactical blunder. But it made sense in the light of his determination not to go on playing the parliamentary game: and it added to his already somewhat legendary reputation for courage.

And there were, in fact, outside his own party, people who saw precisely that the real battle was not between this or that party but about whether one should, or should not, continue to play political games. On May 27th Harold Macmillan, a young conservative temporarily out of Parliament, had a letter printed in *The Times* in which he said:

> Faced with a startling and even spectacular calamity [the doubling of unemployment figures since Labour took office] Sir Oswald seems to have conceived a novel, and no doubt according to the accepted political standards of what are called 'responsible statesmen', incredibly naive idea. He drew up, and actually went so far as to present to his chief, a memorandum which suggested an attempt should be made to carry out at least some, if not all, of the pledges and promises by the exploitation of which the Socialist Party obtained power . . .
>
> Is it to be the accepted rule in our politics that a political programme is to be discarded as soon as it has served its electoral purpose? Are we to accept the cynical view that a statesman is to be applauded in inverse ratio to the extent to which he carries out in office what he has promised in opposition? Must a programme always sink to the level of a fraudulent prospectus? Is a course of action, which in business affairs would end in the Old Bailey, in affairs of state to lead to Downing St and Westminster Abbey? . . .
>
> I suspect that this is the real way that the game ought to be played. Only, if the rules are to be permanently enforced, perhaps a good many of us will feel it hardly worth while bothering to play at all. Sir Oswald Mosley thinks that the rules should be altered. I hope some of my friends will have the courage to support and applaud his protest.

The next day R. A. Butler, a conservative MP in his first parliament, had (with three other signatories) a letter in *The Times* which said:

> We have read with interest and some surprise Mr Harold Macmillan's

letter published in your issue of today. When a player starts complaining that it is 'hardly worth while bothering to play' the game
at all, it is surely the player, and not the game, which is at fault. It
is usually advisable for the player to seek a new field for his recreation
and a pastime more suitable to his talents.

On 28th May Tom made his speech in Parliament to justify his resignation: this was his statement of belief that politics should be more than
a 'recreation' or a 'pastime'. He reiterated the points of the Mosley
Memorandum – an effective machinery of government had to be set
up to deal with the unemployment crisis; it was to the home market that
people had to turn for the solution to trading problems; after a short-
term programme of road building power had to be given to an
Executive Committee to control imports, prices, wages, and finance for
industry. He spoke without looking at his notes; there was a dazzling
display of figures; in a passionate peroration he begged that the country
should not be allowed to 'sink to the level of Spain' and exhorted
Parliament to give a lead. The message of the speech was epitomised in
a sentence half way through – 'the first duty of the government is, after
all, to govern'.

When Tom sat down he was cheered. It had been a magnificent
performance. The papers the next day were unanimous – 'A tremendous
personal triumph': 'one of the most notable parliamentary achievements
of modern times': 'the triumph of an artist who has made his genius
perfect by long hours of practice and devotion to his art'. But then, with
all these curtain-calls as it were – might it not be possible that after all
Tom had made a successful move in terms of the game?

He was taking his stand on being the 'honest man' of politics; in the
long run such an 'honest man' might have the best chance of winning
the highest honours. Tom of course felt this: other people after his
resignation began to feel it: Beatrice Webb wrote – 'Has MacDonald
found his superseder in Oswald Mosley? MacDonald owes his pre-
eminence largely to the fact that he is the only artist, the only aristocrat
by temperament and talent in a party of plebeians and plain men ... But
Mosley has all this with the élan of youth, wealth and social position
added to them.' She added however in her usual warning style –
'Whether Mosley has Mac's toughness of texture – whether he will not
break down in health or in character – I have doubts.'

But one of the manoeuvres by which people who stick to the rules
of the game instinctively try to outwit those who do not, is by giving
them extravagant applause just when there is no particular danger to the

Tom in 1918

Cimmie in 1918

Engagement: Tom and Cimmie with the King and Queen of the Belgians at Hackwood, Lord Curzon and Baba in background

Wedding 1920

Harrow constituency   Top: Receiving wedding present
Bottom: Irene and Cimmie canvassing

Vivien's christening 1921; with Nanny Hyslop

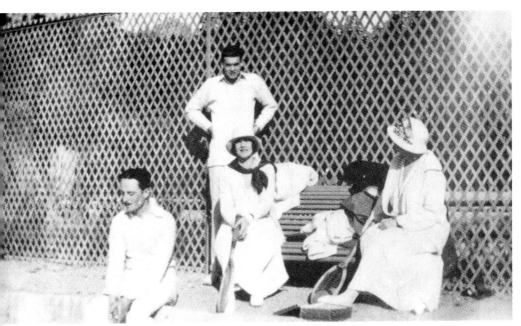

Tennis party 1922

Bathing in Venice 1922: Tom with Hester Astley, Olga Lynn, Lois Sturt, Diana Cooper

"KING OF THE BEACH"

Letter from Tom to Cimmie 1928

Letter from Cimmie to Tom 1923

Letter from Tom to Cimmie 1925

Vivien and Nicholas: Birchington, August 1923

Savehay Farm

Venice 1923: Cimmie, Olga Lynn, Diana Cooper and Tom

Independent Labour Party Summer School 1926: Work and Play
Top: Fenner Brockway (centre) with John Strachey and Tom
Bottom: Fenner Brockway and James Maxton facing camera

Savehay Farm 1927: the Loggia

Dina Erroll, Tom, Nicholas, Cecil Beaton, Ivan Hay, Dick Wyndham, William
Walton, Georgia Sitwell, Cimmie, Vivien, Sacheverell Sitwell

Tom's film.   Left: Cecil Beaton, William Walton, Cimmie
Right: John Strachey climbing out of river

Sir Oswald and Lady Mosley (Tom's father and mother) with Vivien and Nicholas
1924

South of France 1928: Tom, Bob Boothby, Mrs Shaw, John Strachey, Eileen Orde,
George Bernard Shaw, Cimmie

Fowey, Cornwall 1928: Kiki Preston, Ramsay MacDonald, Cimmie, Paul Maze,
Lily Lord

Picnic on the islands off Cannes 1928

Antibes 1929: Paula Casa Maury, Fruity Metcalfe, Baba Metcalfe, Tom, Rudolph
Messel

Tom and Cimmie with Franklin Roosevelt on his yacht 1926

status quo: like this the rebels get carried away and overreach themselves. And would-be heroes anyway have primitive instincts ready to be tapped by applause. After his resignation speech Tom's mother had written to him:

My darling Tom,

So many judges and abler folk must have congratulated you on your masterly performance of last night my congratulations are almost absurd. But oh! my dear lad, I can never tell you what it meant to your old mother. I was so full of pride and joy in my man-child it almost choked me. It was wonderful. People of all shades and opinions were thrilled and staggered by 'the finest speech heard in the House for 20 years' ...

Tom had said "The first duty of a government is to govern': but then, what was he doing resigning from government and putting on magnificent performances? Was he really now going to trust just his own rationality and rhetoric – and other people's rationality in being carried away by his rhetoric – in order to govern? Might this not be the mark of someone with such overweening confidence in himself that it would seem to have sprung from fantasies?

But if he was ever to have a chance of exercising practical power, Tom knew he had to form new loyalties. This was not going to be easy from the ranks of the Parliamentary Labour Party. Jennie Lee, a young Labour MP and one not unsympathetic to Tom at this time, wrote of her own reactions to her colleagues:

What I was totally unprepared for was the behaviour of the solid rows of decent, well-intentioned unpretentious Labour back benchers. In the long run it was they who did the most deadly damage. Again and again an effort was made to rouse them from their inertia. On every occasion they reacted like a load of damp cement. They would see nothing, do nothing, hear nothing, that had not first been given the seal of MacDonald's approval.

When Tom resigned, the only back benchers who he was certain would be loyal to him were Cimmie and John Strachey. He soon got four other young labour MPs to commit themselves to some sort of an alliance – W. J. Brown, Oliver Baldwin, Robert Forgan and Aneurin Bevan. He also got young MPs from the other parties interested in talking about alliance – from the Conservatives Harold Macmillan, Bob Boothby,

Oliver Stanley, Walter Elliott, Henry Mond; from the Liberals Archibald Sinclair and Leslie Hore-Belisha. During the summer the unemployment figures rose to over two million: the battle more than ever seemed to Tom to be not between this party and that, but between anyone who seemed interested in getting something done and those who did not. Tom himself saw it in many respects still as a battle of the young against the old. In June he wrote an article in the *Sunday Express* in which he claimed that the young man of today was:

> a hard, realistic type, hammered into existence on the anvil of great ordeal: in mind and spirit he is much further away from the pre-war man than he is from an ancient Roman or from any other product of ages which were dynamic like his own. For this age is dynamic and the pre-war age was static. The men of the pre-war age are much 'nicer' people than we are, just as their age was much more pleasant than the present time. The practical question is whether their ideas for the solution of the problems of our age are better than the ideas of those whom that age has produced.

This was the language of some sort of heroism – of preparation for future battle; of appeal to the glories of the past. It was this that attracted would-be knights to Tom's banner. 'In those days Mosley's drawing room was an exciting place' Hugh Massingham, a journalist, wrote: 'the gay Bob Boothby flitted in and out: there was John Strachey who could be relied on to give the talk a Marxist twist: C. E. M. Joad, a philosopher of sorts, could be discovered cowering in a corner occasionally letting out a squeak of protest whenever the necessity of violence was mentioned which it usually was'. Harold Nicolson, himself a member of the group, wrote – 'They talk about the decay of democracy and of parliamentarianism. They discuss whether it would be well to have a fascist coup. They are most disrespectful of their various party leaders.'

Two politicians from the older generation were naturally attracted to such ebullience – Lloyd George and Winston Churchill. They occasionally joined in discussions. There were also the press lords Beaverbrook and Rothermere in the background, who by their vocation were interested in matters sensational or dynamic. Beaverbrook wrote to Tom, 'I am ready at any moment to make overtures in your direction in public if you wish me to do so'. Churchill made a speech at Oxford in which he echoed Tom's proposal that an Executive Committee should be set up 'free altogether from party exigencies and composed of persons possessing special qualifications in economic matters'. One reason why Churchill, Beaverbrook and Rothermere were interested in Tom was the fact that in his economic thinking he was coming to the conclusion that the closed economic area over which the government should have tight control should be expanded from the home market to include the Empire and Commonwealth. With all this talk and intrigue going on it could not have worried Tom much that the 'damp cement' of Labour was not following him. Beatrice Webb wrote 'He will be a great success at public meetings; but will he get round the Arthur Hendersons, the Herbert Morrisons, the Alexanders, the Citrines and the Bevins ... the natural leaders of the proletariat?' Tom and even Cimmie were even demonstrably not worrying: they went out a lot during that summer to parties: Tom seems to have felt liberated by the fact that he had staked everything like a gambler on forming his own group.

Bob Boothby wrote to him another of his long, marvellous letters setting out his opinions on gambling and the sort of odds a gambler has to face because there are rules even for adventurers.

My dear Tom,
If ever I signed on the dotted line I would play to the end – and beyond.

I think you know that.

But *in the meantime* I don't think the game is practical politics, and for the following reasons.

(1)   Our chaps won't play, and it's no use your deluding yourself that they will. You saw Oliver [Stanley]'s reactions last night.

Of the whole lot Walter and I would be most useful, because we have a territorial base and between us we could shake up Scotland. But Walter has spent the last twelve months consolidating his position in the Conservative party: he has won for himself a good deal of rank-and-file support: he won't give it up unless he's sure he's going to win. And he doesn't think this will win.

As for Oliver, his influence could, and almost certainly would, be countered by Edward Stanley. And so far as the Conservatives are concerned, Harold would be a definite liability. I know you think I'm prejudiced against him. I'm not. But even on the assumption he decided to play (a large one) how many votes can he sway.

Not one.

Who is left?

George Lloyd, generally regarded as the 'Super Diehard' and rightly or wrongly regarded in many quarters as a shit. And this brings me to the second point about our chaps, which is that they simply aren't good enough for the job (I include myself with becoming modesty).

(2)   Now what about your side? I agree you can sway more votes than any other contemporary politician.

But I don't believe, at present, that you can bring over any substantial section of organised Trades Unionism. And as for the Parliamentary Party, do you really think you can send Aneurin Bevan to the Admiralty to lay down more cruisers, and John Strachey to spank the blacks? I confess I doubt it. Who else is there? The mugwumps who comprise 95% of your party will be solidly arrayed against you. The intelligentsia of the Dalton–Baker school will be actively and venomously hostile.

(3)   We come now to the main source of strength – Beaverbrook, with the dubious support of Rothermere.

Beaverbrook's qualities are sufficiently obvious. I don't know him as well as you do. But I have long since come to the conclusion that he would be very nearly impossible to work with. And, as Oliver pointed out, he is in the impregnable position (which we are not and never can be) of being able to double cross and let down the side at a moment's notice without loss of power or even prestige.

If he were to do that we should be marooned, and ultimately sunk politically.

One other point.

What is going to be the reaction of the great British public to a Beaverbrook-Mosley-Rothermere-Lloyd-Macmillan-Stanley-Boothby combination?

I don't know. But they might conceivably say 'By God, now all the shits have climbed into the same basket, so we know where we are.' Would they be so far out? . . .

(5) · Lastly, don't underestimate the power of the political machines. I believe that in the long run it far exceeds that of the press . . .

On this assumption, the only game worth playing is to try and collar one or other of the machines, and not ruin yourself by beating against them with a tool which will almost certainly break in your hand.

To all this I make one qualification and one only.

If there is a really serious economic crisis this winter, there may be a widespread demand for a national government, new men, and new measures.

It must come from the country and be *interpreted* by the press. If it does come, then the situation will be fundamentally changed, and a game of a kind we cannot yet envisage may open out ...

Well my dear Tom, I've been very frank. I always will be with you, and I hope you don't mind. I happen to think you can do more for us than anyone else now alive – a view I've held, and from which I've never deviated, for six years.

Only for God's sake remember that this country is old, obsolete and tradition-ridden; and no one, not even you, can break all the rules at once. And do take care of the company you keep. Real shits are so apt to trip you up when you aren't looking. And flat-catchers who want to be hauled along are only an encumbrance.

No answer.

Yours ever
Bob

CHAPTER 16

Cimmie in Russia

At the beginning of 1930 Cimmie wrote in her usual style to Tom:

> Sweetie fellow, this is just a line to tell him on New Years' Day of
> all the wishes wished thoughts thought and resolutions resolved by
> her on New Year's Eve. Does hope 1930 will be a happy one for them
> both. Does hope he will go on loving her. *Sure* she will love him. Will
> try try to do everything she can to make it a success.
>   Success politically. Success fun and good times.
>   Success them 2 together . . .

Cimmie was busy in local and national politics during 1930. She opened
nursery schools and art exhibitions in Stoke; spoke at a Labour Party
May Day rally at Alexandra Palace in North London; spoke in Parliament in favour of the Rural Amenities Bill which gave greater governmental powers to safeguard the environment, and in favour of the Bill
which ratified the provisions of the Court of International Justice at The
Hague. Her speaking voice, a reporter said, was 'like that of Cordelia
– soft, gentle and low: "an excellent thing in a woman".' She wrote an
article in the *Sunday Express* which considered whether or not rich
socialists should spend money on their children's education (her sister
Irene called this 'shattering bilge'): she gave an interview on the radio on
the subject of Social Conventions. In this she was eloquently in favour
of breaking conventions: 'I want to bring out the frightful danger latent
in *all* conventions, of their proving an obstacle to living thought and
self-expression, because that for me is the most precious thing in life –
lose that and you lose everything.' She got quite a few letters in response
to this broadcast – one from a 17-year-old girl who wanted to be a dirt-
track rider and asked Cimmie for the loan of £50 to set her up.

She backed Tom publicly in his struggles with J. H. Thomas: privately, in spite of her resolutions and perhaps because Tom was becoming increasingly under strain, their quarrels – and her own part in them – seemed to get worse. In April Irene was recording in her diary – 'That naughty Cim kept having awful gibes at Tom so unnecessarily as he was quite peaceful.' Then in July – 'Cim and Tom had a couple of sparring matches Tom as usual scoring in getting a raging rise out of Cim.' And later – after a dinner party in Irene's house with Cim and Tom and Sacheverell and Georgia Sitwell – Irene found 'Cim and Tom having a row about some stupid bill and he dashed off in the car in a rage and poor dazed Cim still could not see how it had all arisen'.

Two days before this myself, aged seven, had been taken to a nursing home for an operation for appendicitis. On the night of their row Cimmie stayed on in Irene's house and wrote to Tom:

3 Deanery St W.1.

I don't know what you felt like when you got home but I know I have seldom felt worse, it is now 3 o'clock-ish and I am still sitting on my bed not having closed an eye – I cannot make out what it is all about, I am entirely bewildered, I just don't understand – why have you been so horrid to me, not only tonight but ever since I got up from chickenpox. As the sound of my voice and my presence (and you've seen so little of me) seems to drive you demented I resort to poor Irene's method of putting pen to paper ... You leave me *alone* in London for weekend to look after Nicky and go away with another woman for weekend. You never see Nicky from before his op Sat am till Mon evening ...

The woman whom Tom went away with might have been Georgia Sitwell, with whom Tom was carrying on about this time: there is a letter from her to Tom consisting of just one enormous O covering most of the page which seems to have been some symbol of sexuality. (It was Georgia Sitwell who said to Tom's second wife, Diana, later in life – 'Of course we all went to bed with him but afterwards we were rather ashamed'). One of the points of conflict now between Tom and Cimmie concerned a flat that Tom had got at 22 Ebury Street, about a mile from the family home in Smith Square. Ostensibly Tom had rented this flat in order that he should have peace to do his work as a government minister: but the flat consisted of one huge and very elegant room like a stageset for a bachelor's apartment; the bed was in an alcove at the back across which curtains could be drawn and (one of the occupants

remembers) at the press of a switch warm air be wafted in. Cimmie had
felt that the style of this was not aimed at entertaining Ramsay Mac-
Donald or J. H. Thomas.

Cimmie's letter to Tom, written from Irene's house, continued –

> I feel very lonely and unutterably depressed and so puzzled and tired
> it is difficult to think or even see much ... I know you'll make out
> it's all my fault ... I could not think why it went on and then you
> driving off after what you said. Why did you?

Tom was apparently clever at making out things were another person's
fault: also probably at using rows as a means of being able to get away
– and do what he wanted. And then, the next morning, he could think
about making things up again. He wrote to Cimmie:

> Darling Fellow,
> Terribly sorry if I upset you, but you did drive me almost demented
> – and he too was upset all right! It is that aggressive student talking
> about little things which (1) do not matter (2) could be settled in two
> minutes quiet talk – do be your own sweet self – a charming woman
> – and not a lawyer attacking a hostile witness. We are all rather on
> edge after a very tiring session and many worries – do try to make
> the little things of life easy and not more difficult. I do love you so
> and was so looking forward to seeing you again and longing to get
> off to the South of France with you away from all this turmoil – you
> can be the sweetest most feminine one in all the world, or you can
> be a real old nagging harridan which you were last night (but I do
> understand you too are on edge a little after Nick) ... I believe you
> are lunching out but we will dine together and I will ring you up at
> Nina's 7 pm if you are not in the H of C. So much love. Tom

It was true all this was happening at a time when Tom was increasingly
under strain in public life: he knew he might not be able to get back
into conventional party politics: he had chosen his role of gambler. He
probably felt it consistent that he should gamble on getting everything
that he wanted in private life too. He would have the power to ration-
alise to himself that it was not his fault if this sort of thing caused Cimmie
pain: he did his best to leave her free to do as she wanted. He would
probably not consciously have seen that one of the reasons why he had
strength as a gambler was because she, having suffered, was still there
for him to come back to.

People close to Cimmie and Tom were trying to 'get her to see she ought to stand up to him and give him a fright' (Irene): this presumably meant threaten to leave him. But Cimmie could not do this. It remained a mystery however about Tom and Cimmie why she as much as he insisted on their having 'fun' in places like Antibes and Venice – where one of the rules of the social game was simply that husbands should try to get off with other people's wives. But now at the end of the summer of 1930, they did plan, for a while, to go their separate ways. After the usual two or three weeks at Antibes (I myself, after my operation, had followed the main party with Nanny in a bath chair or being carried by porters) Cimmie went off on a trip to Turkey and Russia accompanied by her friend Zita James. Tom went with her as far as Venice, then returned to the South of France.

Cimmie's trip to Russia is of interest because it seems to have been her effort to gain some independence from Tom: for a time she seemed to be succeeding. Zita was one of two sisters (Zita and Theresa Jungman) who were in the social worlds of London and Venice and the South of France: she had recently married: she too was travelling apart from her husband. She kept a diary, which provides glimpses of Cimmie in her efforts to be herself apart from Tom. Cimmie and Zita met in Athens, where –

We went out to see the Acropolis at sunset. Of course it didn't come off again and Cimmie was bitterly mocking – I was rather annoying and kept giving details about blank bits of stone that I'd heard the guide saying days before. I felt rather like a governess but couldn't stop myself. I was annoyed that the sunset was so bad. In the meantime Cimmie had left a message for a Greek young man she knew about, and later as we were lying on our beds in the hotel shouting from one room to another a card came up to say he was waiting below so we hurried and Cimmie went on down. I found her drinking a cocktail with a very good looking Greek and a very American American called Francis Peabody Krane. After a good deal of gay talk and familiar badinage we finally decided to go in Peabody's car to a native restaurant on a hill far away.

They went on the American's yacht, they swam, they had picnics: 'after a huge meal Cimmie and Kartali (the Greek) went and lay down on the moonlit horizon and talked in whispers to each other while Peabody went miles to fetch me a cushion'. They went to see the church at

Daphne; they did not think much of the museum at Athens. They travelled on by boat to Istanbul, where Cimmie wrote to Tom:

Hotel M. Tokatlian. Istanbul.   Sept 5th 1930

Darling Sweetie, you will never guess what I did yesterday. I think something very exciting, but in order to get you all expectant I won't tell you yet. We had hardly arrived before a very insignificant young man called round from the Embassy to say Sir George Clerk [the ambassador] was away in Ankara but he was to put a car at our disposal so we arranged to have it for the next day ... We sight-saw, but really there is nothing much: Mosques awfully ugly and Sophia definitely disapointing. Afterwards heavenly time in lagoon and then a row in caique up to Eyouli and a moonlight picnic in the cemetery and coffee in the cafe where Pierre Loti used to sit. Yesterday morning more sightseeing; lunch at Embassy where we made a great hit with Sir George who is taking us out all day on his yacht today – and then we did the exciting thing. They all said at the Embassy we would never pull it off.

But we did!

We went and saw Trotsky!!

You know he lives on a small island called Prinkipo about hour and $\frac{1}{2}$ away from here by boat. He is allowed nowhere else in the world. So I thought – We'll go off to Prinkipo and try! Wrote a lovely note and set off. Deposited outside iron gate at top of hill, long straggling walk down between vegetables to a fountain small pond court and square peeling white house. By this time a sec: had popped out to ask us our business – he said it was *quite* impossible – never done. I said well anyway could he not take my letter. No. Well could he not read it himself – which he did. He then reconsidered and said he would go and see. In a few moments he was back and said the great man would receive us. So up we went through an absolutely bare hall absolutely bare staircase another absolutely bare room except for thousands of newspapers knocked on a door and there we were. Magnificent head, masses and swirls of the most beautifully cared-for grey hair, the softest most soigné rather sallow skin, *huge* eyes behind prince nez, large thick fleshy mouth, moustache and imperial, immaculate snowy white suit and *beautiful* hands – nails polished and shining. He was courteous and charming and talked for about $\frac{1}{2}$ an hour, absolutely scathing about English Labs. Very funny. And Clynes and Duchess of York got it very hot.

Cimmie's description of her visit to Trotsky ends here abruptly. Her long letter then continues, for pages, to talk about her relationship with Tom. Other accounts of the visit to Trotsky are of interest however both on account of the incident itself (Trotsky had been outlawed from Russia the year before and had few contacts with the outside world) and because they confirm the impression that to Cimmie the visit was at least in part some dare-devil act which she could present as a trophy to Tom.

Zita had written in her diary about lunch at the Embassy the previous day:

> We could see the secretaries and wives sniggering as we told rather exaggerated stories of what up to now we had done, they thought us a little mad, so we piled it on and said the most startling things. Cimmie capped the lot by declaring that she was going that afternoon to see Trotsky. At this suggestion the whole table went off into a guffaw, several bets were placed against us achieving our object, and everyone winked slyly round the table and patronised our idiocy . . . We went back to the hotel where Cimmie composed a letter beginning 'Dear Comrade Trotsky' and ending 'Yours fraternally'. She took his book of memoirs under her arm and off we started for the ferry boat.

Trotsky recorded his own account of the visit in his published diary for 1935. He had made a reference to Tom as 'the aristocratic coxcomb who joined the Labour party as a short cut to a career'; and then reminisced:

> In September 1930 . . . Cynthia Mosley, the wife of the adventurer and daughter of the notorious Lord Curzon, visited me at Prinkipo. At that stage her husband was still attacking MacDonald 'from the left'. After some hesitation I agreed to a meeting which, however, proved banal in the extreme. The 'Lady' arrived with a female travelling companion, referred contemptuously to MacDonald, and spoke of her sympathies towards Soviet Russia. But the enclosed letter from her is an adequate specimen of her attitude at that time. About three years later the young woman suddenly died. I don't know if she lived long enough to cross over into the fascist camp.

But the letter which Cimmie wrote to Trotsky and which Trotsky printed in his diary showed in fact her genuine enthusiasm and courage.

Dear Comrade Trotsky,

I would like above all things to see you for a few moments. There is no good reason why you should see me as (1) I belong to the Labour Party in England who were so ridiculous and refused to allow you in but also I belong to the ILP and we did try our very best to make them change their minds; and (2) I am daughter of Lord Curzon who was Minister of Foreign Affairs in London when you were in Russia!

On the other hand I am an ardent Socialist. I am a member of the House of Commons. I think less than nothing of the present government. I have just finished reading your life which inspired me as no other book has done for ages. I am a great admirer of yours. These days when great men seem so very few and far between it would be a great privilege to meet one of the enduring figures of our age and I do hope with all my heart you will grant me that privilege. I need hardly say I come as a private person, not a journalist nor *anything* but myself – I am on my way to Russia – I leave for Batoum – Tiflis – Rostov – Kharkov and Moscow by boat Monday. I have come to Principo this afternoon especially to try to see you, but if it were not convenient I could come out again any day till Monday. I do hope however you could allow me a few moments this afternoon.

Yours fraternally
Cynthia Mosley

A few days after her exploit with Trotsky, Cimmie performed another feat which seemed aimed at demonstrating her energy and independence and reporting this to Tom. She swam across the straits of the Bosphorus from Asia to Europe – a distance of about a mile. Zita, who accompanied her by boat, reported – 'When she got about half way across it became more difficult as the current was so strong ... large steamers began to pass and their huge wash became very tiring. I kept screaming "Look out!" and Cimmie began to get a little cross. However after one or two desperate moments the heroic deed was accomplished.'

Cimmie went back to her hotel to write immediately of this new deed to Tom. But there she found a telegram from him of which the words, it would seem, did not contain much beyond the usual reassuring and encouraging noises he used to make to her. But it made Cimmie write:

Sunday 7th   Hotel M. Tokatlian
Oh Billo, just to show you what an ass I am your wire has just come and I feel suicidal. Why. It came from Le Lavandou, what on earth

are you doing there unless you have popped off with Paula? I have always longed to go to Le Lavandou, you never would – why now – only to hide. Darling darling you would have been better never to wire me or else to explain why you were there, it has just spoilt everything for me. Even when I am hundreds of miles away your shadow falls on me. How can I ever dare to have holidays away from you – and yet it may be nothing, you may be there with a large party. Then why not all sign the gram. No doubt you'll explain it away. But as the song says – 'How am I to know?' How fed up I am with love. I suppose I ought not to mind but I do so damnably I don't know what to do. Can hardly bear to face dinner and all the rest. Can't wire you as have no address.

Hell Hell Hell. If it's true, I think you and Paula unspeakable cads. If it's not true, then I do apologise, but wish you had not caused the unnecessary anguish – you might have said why you were there – I suppose you thought they wouldn't put where the tel: came from.

So you see all my talk about self sufficiency serenity peace etc – Balls Balls Balls

– goes in 1 second at the bare hint of an idea from you.

Ought (1) to trust you not to do such a thing, or –

      (2) not to mind if you did.

The first impossible, as I fear I have *never really* in my heart of hearts trusted you in that way. The second however much as I try I cannot help such a flame of misery jealousy resentment I can't cope.

Please forgive me if it is all nothing, perhaps I shouldn't even write and keep all my doubts to myself; but somehow I can't do that, it seems clearer to get it off my chest. And darling when I came in I was so gay and full of myself and elated and just sitting down to write you that I had just swum the Bosphorus from Asia to Europe against a strong current in 40 minutes – thought you'd be thrilled – I thought it so terribly in the Grand Style and Byronic and even rather Mosley – and now – those stupid names of tunes – they are so apposite –

          What is this thing called love

          How am I to know?

I don't, either.

I will wire an address from Batoum for you to write. Don't be angry if I am all wrong it's because I love you so awfully. Even if I am not wrong I suppose you'll pretend I am. What a farce it all is.

I wish you were here with me.

We are off to Russia tomorrow.
I'll try to forget about all this. Poor Tom
                                   Poor Tim
My sweetie one.
                Blessings.
                     Mum

Cimmie never spoke to Zita about any of this. The next day they got
on an Italian boat bound for Batum, in Russia, at the eastern end of the
Black Sea. They 'settled down into a sort of routine ... we both adored
reading and hardly spoke to each other: we invented games and ate
rather a lot in view of the future' (Zita). They had a vague certainty that
in Russia 'we should be starved and imprisoned and probably shot and
at any rate never come out of the country the same as we went into it.
The Captain was horrified at the idea of our going to Russia and said
we ought to be at home with our husbands.'

While she was on the boat Cimmie probably dwelt on the things
that seemed never to be far from her mind about Tom. The letter she
had written to him directly after her visit to Trotsky had continued, after
she had told him the news of her exploit:

About our life. I will try, but also remember I *do* try all the time, it's
when I am so tired of trying I get so difficult. I never seem to be able
to let up trying. As to not having complexes about you oh how
difficult – only because I care for you so much – that is what makes
it difficult; and all the side of me you hate, the hard defiant knock-
me-down, curiously enough is created by you – an attempt by me
to clap on some pieces of armour – a sort of sanctuary inside where
I was inviolate and you could not get at me – I might behave
outwardly more sensibly but up to now I have not been able to
preserve one solitary atom or portion of me that you could not get
at and hurt almost beyond endurance ...

I fear so awfully all my efforts to adjust myself to you so as not
to be hurt result in the very symptoms that make you hurt me more
– If I appear to 'don't care' by being 'don't care', you just get fiercer
and fiercer and destroy me more and more: and to just submit to
being hurt without putting up some show seems to me almost
unendurable. So far I have only achieved not being hurt by you (and
rarely enough at that) by thinking you a cad and a swine – by
despising your methods – oh dear how difficult it all is! – as quite
beyond question you matter more to me than anything in the world.

With the children when you are sweet to me I could die of joy. But as you say: in term-time you have to work so very hard – with other people: in hols you play hard – with other people. Where does Mum come in?

It's all very well to talk of the great life we could build up together but we never are together – and don't go off and say we are more together than any other married couple as that is bosh – in the sense I mean *together* we are very little. This may seem an ungenerous answer to you but these letters are no good unless they face facts – after all we have written them before, and the real life we can have – and I agree with you we can have it – must and can only come if we really take trouble about it. You must take some trouble about me. You will say I must about you – my answer is I never seem to cease bothering about you, tho' you may find that hard to believe . . .

Always remember I adore YOU – tho' loathing the thing that masquerades as you every so often and is cruel and unkind and often despicable . . . It's the same about me, the real ME is a dear, but the horrid student creature that I become is awful – but I only become it to fight the masquerading you. Let's both be YOU and ME. I swear I'll try.

But you MUST. I can't do it alone.

There is no way of knowing the words by which Tom 'destroyed' Cimmie more and more, since this was always done face to face with his cutting tongue and not by letter. In later life, when Tom wanted to be rude to people he was just rude; with his chin up, barking at people to 'get out', or stabbing at them with his heavy, relentless sarcasm. But Cimmie in her letter did seem able for the first time to stand back and see that a proper way of describing what was happening to her and Tom might be that there was in each of them something that took them over and made them helpless in their efforts to deal with themselves or each other by will. There was something in Tom that needed to protect himself by having her entrapped: there was something in her that, in pain, still could not escape from entrapment. Tom could not stand back from himself enough to talk to Cimmie in these terms; he was too successful with his manipulations.

Cimmie and Zita landed at Batum; they travelled by train and bus into the Caucasus; they got a boat from Batum to Yalta and from there went by train to Kharkov and Kiev. Their impressions of Russia were much the same as impressions of tourists have been for fifty years: they noted the delays, the inefficiency, the subjects that could not be talked about; at the same time there was 'that queer intangible new spirit, everyone equal, no classes' (Cimmie in a letter to Tom). Also – 'all the nonsense talked about only wearing old clothes so as not to be conspicuous, typhoid, the frightful food shortages, no soap – bunk from beginning to end'. From the Caucasus, Zita had written of 'The Children of the Night – the children who, directly after the revolution, without parents or guardians, infested the whole of Russia especially the south: they were the essence of vice, disease, crime and terror: there are supposed to be few left now, but this little band had the most terrifying faces I have ever imagined'. Cimmie on the coast of the Black Sea had admired the 'thrilling modern white blocks of sanatoria'. They both were rather impressed by the public nude bathing of both sexes. And they wondered why Stalin had thought it profitable to get rid of so many intellectuals.

In Kharkov they discovered from the Intourist office that Cimmie's sister Irene, in the company of John Strachey, had passed through the day before on their way down from Moscow. This rather dampened their feeling of being pioneers. They went on to Moscow where they found in a 'spotlessly clean hotel which 'looked almost normal' other Labour MPs, including G. R. Strauss and Jennie Lee. Cimmie found also a letter from Tom, in answer to the one she had posted in Istanbul.

Darling Baby Mutton,   22 b Ebury Street. S.W.1.
    What a mutt she is! What a let to write him – What an upset to give herself – and him because he felt she was upset! Toured the coast from Cannes to Toulon – *alone or with parties* – got Daisy's speedboat Fish (without owner included let me hasten to add) (and further only 300 francs a day) and had glorious time – shot to and fro just the king of every beach [drawing of pig or sheep] – met many people knew at various spots but much Byronic solitude (which is growing on him a lot in her absence – great feature! St Maxim's and more especially St Tropez proved enormous fun on revisits. Marvellous man with concertina and all Cannes dancing in Marie Antoinette humours at your little restaurant. Found ever so many small cheap but charming places with lovely sand beaches for the children (needless to say the real object of his pilgrimage!) Thinks he hears a porker sizzling.
    Silly fellow, if he had been on such an expedition would he have telegraphed you from the rendez-vous? He may be wicked but he is not such a mutt as that. That place was lovely but I think better still Cavalaire which is nearer to St Tropez and has the same sand beach. Of course would never do it before, as had never had his fill of rest,

immobility and fun – a few days after return to Cannes however had more than enough – very hectic and most of nice people went – further in-solitude-Byron feature plus a speedboat.

What a clever mutt to swim the Hellespont – big and proud Byron mutton! [drawing of sheep swimming]. Sorry, good resolution, never make jokes. Kiss nose. Or pat bottom [drawing of a bottom with a caption 'verboten']. And he is lapsing already (but he loves her so much). Thought her letter did not go very far to meet his sweet and sympathetic gestures. So glad however she is having a lovely time and do hope it will last to the end.

Just been alone to see a flying film *The Dawn Patrol* – best yet – overdrawn in personal things but wonderful flying pictures – very reminiscent – moved and depressed. Seen only serious people in London and been mostly alone – rang up no one of friends – but expect have little tiny bit of various fun in Paris – where he wishes his Mutt was because he misses and loves her so. Resolved to be the perfect husband. She is not to be such a Porker and roarer because she can be sweetest one in world whom he loves. [Drawing of rather wild-looking sheep or pig with the caption 'The Corsair between Cannes and Toulon!!!!']

In Moscow Cimmie and Zita were taken to some show-piece prison in the company of other political tourists. Zita reported – 'The Head of the Reformatory was more than charming and seemed to be an angel of goodness with an immense paternal love and kindness for all his prisoners ... he explained Russia's theories about prison and punishment. He said that their idea was that crime was due almost entirely to environment, and that therefore all they needed was to remove the criminal and place him in another position.' However she did add 'Really I suppose they were completely under control.'

Cimmie, worrying about Tom, must have wondered, having received his letter, about the ways in which politicians use words with little regard for truth. But then, with politicians, what does one do for truth? There was no way of Cimmie knowing with whom, if anyone, Tom had been in the South of France: he had almost certainly been with someone. But then, there were his usual protestations of love. Cimmie seemed to be stuck – as perhaps some Russians might have been feeling stuck – with this endless, vaguely persuasive, duplicity of words. Cimmie had written to Tom from Kharkov – 'Oh I wonder when I will become any better about you: you have me tied up in one of those knots well nigh impossible to undo.'

Back in London Tom was preparing for the Labour Party Conference; which was to be his last conventional platform of appeal to
people to listen to the logic of his words.

CHAPTER 17

The Mosley Manifesto

In one of his letters of the summer Bob Boothby had set out what he believed to be the alternatives facing Tom – '(1) Staying where you are, consolidating and strengthening your hold on the Labour movement in the country and persuading the workers that they will not always be betrayed; or (2) making another speech or two along recent lines and crossing the floor in the autumn. You would be amazed at the welcome you would get.' He had added – 'The former is the long term policy and involves a further bleak period in the wilderness: (2) assures power at an early date, but power limited by the Tory machine, and the knowledge that you can't change again.'

Bob Boothby believed that the Labour government was coming to an end because of its failure to deal with unemployment; that the Tories would soon get in with a huge majority. Liberals would be of no account. 'Two machines, and two only, right and left, will wield political power in this country in the years that lie ahead.' He assured Tom that, if he stayed within the fold of either of the party machines, 'I have not the slightest doubt that you would win through in the end'.

Tom's chance to get a hold on the Labour Party machine occurred at the party conference at Llandudno in October 1930. During the summer his prestige amongst party workers does not seem to have weakened: his stand appearing as the 'honest man' was bearing fruit. He had had copies of his Memorandum printed and sent to local Labour parties with the request that they should consider it and give their opinions on it at the Party Conference: this of course did not make him popular with party leaders. Professional Labour politicians have the gang-solidarity of people accustomed to fight as underdogs; they are particularly susceptible to feelings of betrayal.

At the conference Ramsay MacDonald 'made a wonderful speech: he said nothing whatever, but he said it so eloquently that the delegates were deeply moved' (John Scanlon). Then Tom spoke: he could match MacDonald for eloquence: he also had a policy which delegates could think they might fight for – or die for. In his peroration Tom told those who might follow him – 'at best they would have their majority; at worst they would go down fighting for the things they believed in: they would not die like an old woman in bed: they would die like men on the field – a better fate and, in politics, one with a more certain hope of resurrection.'

A journalist in the *Sunday Graphic* wrote – 'There was stillness save for Mosley's voice gathering in power. Boldly, challengingly, he gave his own plan to restore stability ... The throng was hypnotised by the man, by his audacity, as bang! bang! bang! he thundered directions. The thing that got hold of the conference was that here was a man with a straight-cut policy. It leapt at him.'

Fenner Brockway reported that Tom got 'the greatest ovation he had ever heard at a party conference'. Tom was compared by one commentator to Hitler; by another to Moses. There was a vote taken on a resolution that the Memorandum should be submitted again for consideration by the National Executive Committee. Tom's supporters lost the vote by the narrow margin of 1,046,000 to 1,251,000 – the miners having at the last minute transferred their block vote away from Tom against the advice of their leader A. J. Cook. (There was a story that Cook himself had got held up in a taxi or he might have swayed the vote: there seems no hard evidence for this). But it did not seem to people in the hall that the vote much mattered anyway. The vote had been to do with a technical matter of loyalties: in emotion, party workers were overwhelmingly behind Tom. He was elected to the National Executive of the party: J. H. Thomas lost his seat on it. John Scanlon wrote:

In the Press and the Labour Movement itself the discussion now centred round the question of how long it would be before Sir Oswald became the party leader. Even without a crash in the Party's fortunes it was easy to see that changes must come soon. The controllers of the Labour Party, mostly old men, could not stay the inexorable march of time any more than ordinary mortals. No other leader was in sight. Mr Wheatley was gone. Mr Maxton had none of the pushful qualities which carry a man to leadership in Labour politics, and nobody in the trade unions showed the slightest sign of being able to take charge. Therefore every prophet fixed on Sir

Oswald as the next party leader. Even Socialists, who had no particular love for Sir Oswald, were saying nothing could stop it. All the prophets, however, had overlooked the one man who could stop it – Sir Oswald himself.

Tom himself used to say he might soon have become *de facto* party leader under the nominal leadership of Arthur Henderson. But in order to do this he would have had to work in with the party machine; to humour it, tinker with it, play the political game. His refusal to do this was made partly on an intellectual assessment – he believed that it was the mechanisms of bureaucratic party politics that prevented anything decisive being done – but it was also an emotional decision: he had no natural taste, nor aptitude, for the painstaking and boring manoeuvrings of committees. What he liked, and was good at, was the manipulation of crowds by his oratory and of individuals by his reasoning and charm. After the Llandudno conference it was these talents that he wanted to exercise: he probably had little clear idea, at first, of where the results might lead.

He was perfecting his style as a mob orator – that strange music by which crowds are swayed like snakes. He would declaim – 'We are a party with our eyes on the stars, but let us also remember that our feet are planted firmly in the earth, on muddy soil, where men are suffering and looking at us with eyes of questioning and anguish saying "Lift us up from the mud! give us practical remedies here and now!" ' For practical remedies he was returning with renewed vigour to the matter of trying to form political alliances in London. In his thinking he was putting more and more emphasis on a policy of protecting and controlling trade with empire countries: this was indeed ensuring the interest of the Tories: Stanley Baldwin remarked that Tom was 'now producing ideas which I remember giving voice to in 1903'. But Tom's feelings did not change that if ever he was to do anything decisive in politics he would himself have to lead an alliance. And in fact there seemed to be more potential rebels in the Labour than in the Conservative Party.

In December 1930 a short four-page manifesto appeared entitled *A National Policy for National Emergency*. It was signed by seventeen Labour MPs: amongst them Aneurin Bevan, John Strachey, W. J. Brown, and the two Mosleys – and A. J. Cook, the miners' leader. It became known as *The Mosley Manifesto* (as distinct from the Mosley Memorandum of earlier in the year): it was obviously dedicated to Tom's ideas, though it was written mainly by Strachey and Brown and Bevan. Its main recommendation was that 'an Emergency Cabinet of not more than five ministers without portfolios' should be set up and 'invested with power to carry through the emergency policy'. The emergency was that the unemployed had now increased to two and a half million: the policy was that 'we should aim at building within the Commonwealth a civilisation high enough to absorb the production of modern machinery which for the purpose must be insulated from wrecking forces in the rest of the world'. This policy was necessary, it was claimed, because there was no other way that either conservatism or socialism would not be at the mercy of the whims of what Tom later called 'international finance'. Nearly all the signatories were young labour MP's in their first Parliament: they had not had time to feel themselves dependent on Parliamentary institutions. It was difficult for older MPs to be sympathetic towards the Manifesto because it was contemptuous of existing institutions. Also for orthodox conservatives it was too socialistic and for orthodox socialists too imperialistic. The manifesto got much publicity: but discussion was apt to descend to the level of jokes about who would be the five 'dictators'. All this confirmed Tom in his belief that if anything was to be done he would have to lead some new political alignment.

All this was according to reason: there remained the practical politics. Tom saw that if he was to make anything of his 'New Labour Group' (as those who agreed with the Manifesto had come to be called) then he would have to equip it with a specific organisation and with funds: this would require publicity: at the same time too much publicity might alarm people, before the funds and embryonic organisation were there. Tom was on a political tight-rope. Allan Young, Tom's political secretary, wrote to Cimmie – 'I am more content now to accept Tom's leadership than ever before. He is made for the job that has to be done ... He has displayed all the qualities of intellectual courage and ability, combined with the caution great actions demand.'

Tom had for some time been making soundings about whether it might be possible to gain backing for his proposals from industrialists or from financiers in the City – and for any organisation committed to putting the proposals into effect. He had had one or two meetings with William Morris, later Lord Nuffield, who had become interested in the *Mosley Manifesto*. In January 1931 Morris sent for Tom and handed him a cheque for £50,000 with the remark 'Don't think, my boy, that money like this grows on gooseberry bushes.' This was a fateful moment for Tom. He thought that other money would follow. He felt that it not only made possible, but was a portent for now putting into effect, his plans for starting his own movement.

Bob Boothby uttered his last precise cry of warning and lament.

Jan 30th 1931   Carlton Club

Pall Mall SW1

Dear Tom,

... Since you wrote and told me that you proposed to play your hand in your own way I never sought to enquire what you were doing. But I imagined you were devoting yourself to the task of building up and consolidating your position in the Labour movement.

If it be true that you are trying to raise money in the City then I feel I must say once more – and for the last time – that I believe this to be madness from your own point of view; and leave it at that.

I became uneasy from the first moment the word 'cash' was mentioned, because I never thought it could be raised except under more or less false pretences: and I don't believe that money, even in large quantities, can ever start a new political movement in this country (witness the fate of L.G., the Empire Crusade, and your own effort years ago with Cowdray).

You will remember that I left the dinner party given by Col. Portal at the Garrick Club because I so heartily disapproved of it.

You are, of course, right to pursue the course you think best.

But I too am entitled to my opinions which in this case are very decided.

Last night I turned up some notes that I made of the letters which I wrote to you during the course of last year.

I find that you have persistently disregarded every single piece of advice or suggestion that I have ever ventured to offer.

And so, my dear Tom, I cannot feel that you will greatly miss the benefit of a judgement which you obviously do not value highly. What I most sincerely hope is that neither you nor Cimmie will allow our political differences to interfere with a friendship which I think we all do value a good deal and which has survived sterner tests than this.

Yours ever

Bob

Events now happened fast. 1931 was the year which Arnold Toynbee called 'annus terribilis' in which 'men and women all over the world were seriously contemplating and seriously discussing the possibility that the Western system of society might break down and cease to work'. In January there were five million unemployed in Germany, between six and seven million in the USA, and two and a half million in Great Britain. Old political alignments were in any event cracking up. It so happened that the height of Tom's reputation and belief in himself as an almost magically potent political figure coincided exactly with the moment of twentieth-century history at which it was felt that in the face of almost certain chaos new and indeed almost magical leadership was called for. For once, Tom's natural impatience seemed undeniably suited to events. On February 4th Cimmie told Harold Nicolson that 'Tom is about to form a New Party'. On 20th February six members of the 'New Labour Group' who had signed the *Mosley Manifesto* decided to resign from the labour Party: these were Tom and Cimmie, John Strachey, W. J. Brown, Oliver Baldwin and Robert Forgan. This was the decisive moment in Tom's political life. All his political manoeuvrings up till now had been, however arrogantly or recklessly, still within the terms of some recognised political game: even his resignation from the government, his narrow defeat at the Party Conference, had in fact seemed to enhance his prestige. But if he resigned from the Labour Party itself (he had already resigned from the Conservatives) and formed his own party, he would be putting himself outside any known game.

It was agreed that the six MPs who were to resign should do so on different days to ensure the maximum publicity. Strachey and Baldwin resigned; and then Cimmie, on March 3rd. Ramsay MacDonald replied to her letter:

5th March 1931   10 Downing Street.
Whitehall.

My dear Lady Cynthia,
    I have to acknowledge the receipt of your letter of the 3rd instant, resigning your membership of the Labour Party. Had it not been announced days ago in the newspapers, I should have been surprised, but I am interested to be put in possession of your considered reasons for the step which you have taken. Needless to say I am very sorry.
    When you came in a year or two ago we gave you a very hearty welcome and assumed that you knew what was the policy of the predominant Socialist Party in this country, and that, with that knowledge, you asked us to accept you as a candidate and to go to your constituency and assist you in your fight. You are disappointed with us; you have been mistaken in your choice of political companions, and you are re-selecting them so as to surround yourself with a sturdier, more courageous and more intelligent Socialism for your

encouragement and strength. You remain true, while all the rest of us are false. Whoever examines manifestos and schemes and rejects them, partly because they are not the sort of Socialism that any Socialist has ever devised, or because they amount to nothing but words, is regarded by you as inept or incompetent. We must just tolerate your censure and even contempt; and, in the spare moments we have, cast occasional glances at you pursuing your heroic role with exemplary rectitude and stiff straightness to a disastrous futility and an empty sound. We have experienced so much of this in the building up of the Party that we must not become too cynical when the experience is repeated in the new phase of its existence. Perhaps before the end, roads may cross again and we shall wonder why we ever diverged.

Yours very sincerely,

J. Ramsay MacDonald

P.S. This is not an official reply, as I am waiting for all the resignations to be in before I decide whether to publish anything, so I mark it as a purely personal communication which is not to be published.

Cimmie also received a letter from the chairman of her constituency committee, who told her – 'Whilst I have always felt you were sincere in your desire to improve the lot of the people, I think your secession from the Labour Party is a bad let-down for all those who worked so wholeheartedly for you in your contest.'

Tom, in the middle of all this, suddenly became ill: he retired to bed in his flat in Ebury Street with pleurisy and double pneumonia. W. J. Brown was also stricken: just before it was his turn to resign, the trades-union that employed him, the Civil Service Clerical Association, threatened to sack him; he got cold feet. Tom got himself driven to Brown's house in an ambulance and was carried in on a stretcher. There, Tom wrote later of Brown – 'his face seemed to be pulled down on one side like a man suffering a stroke and he burst into tears ... The very few men in whom previously I had observed this phenomenon had likewise usually rather emphasised their determination and courage before they found themselves averse to getting out of a trench when the time came.' Tom had himself carried back to his ambulance. He himself never resigned from the Labour Party: on March 10th when the news of the New Party had become official, he was expelled for 'gross disloyalty'.

Tom's illness lasted four weeks. He lay in bed in his flat in Ebury Street – where the warm air at the press of a switch might waft over him – and he ruminated, presumably, on what he had done. He had in his mind accused W. J. Brown of cowardice: he himself had seemed brave to a point of recklessness. But still, it was now Cimmie and John Strachey who were left to launch the New Party in the planned programme of speeches round the country. Tom had had faith in his rôle as hero: but there was evidence, as there had been before, that accidents happen to heroes at decisive moments of their histories; that it is more than will-power that decides who, and in what way, in fact gets out of a trench when the time comes.

CHAPTER 18

The Riddle of the Sphinx

The word 'hero' may seem ambiguous in relation to Tom. In common use it refers to someone of slightly superhuman qualities: it also has the suggestion of tragedy or death, or of someone who never quite grows up.

Tom had probably not set out to put himself beyond the rules of the political game, but there seems to have been something in him that would inevitably have done this. Heroes are fought or followed because of an air of inevitability about them: they achieve what is set out for them not by will, but by becoming legendary.

The next two years were the central ones in Tom's life and the last in Cimmie's. Tom did almost seem to be (as other 'heroes' have said of themselves) sleepwalking. He is remembered at this time as someone whom people 'fawned on': he continued to be attacked with violence: he also was increasingly ignored. People did not seem quite to know what attitude to take to him. It was as if a guerrilla fighter had appeared on a football field.

At the end of his life Tom was like Oedipus at Colonus – 'beyond the pale' in the sense of his seeming to have broken some fundamental rule which had rendered him taboo. The taboo was not on account of his having made a mistake or chosen evil: it was the penalty for some falseness attendant on possible success. Oedipus, in the myth, becomes an outcast not just because he has murdered his father and married his mother: he has assumed a false mantle of omnipotence, having solved the riddle of the Sphinx.

In the legend, after having unknowingly killed his father on the road to Thebes, Oedipus is challenged by the mythical monster the Sphinx. The Sphinx is part woman and part lion and part bird: she is that which devours people who travel hopefully: she is laying siege to the city of

Thebes, whose citizens are starving. The Sphinx will not let anyone pass unless they answer a riddle. The riddle is childish: it seems that anyone might answer it, but they do not.

The riddle is — What has four legs in the morning, two in the afternoon, and three in the evening. Oedipus answers the riddle – a man. Whereupon the Sphinx, instead of devouring him, throws herself over a cliff. Oedipus goes on his way and becomes the saviour of the city of Thebes.

What Oedipus saw in the solving of the riddle was that the Sphinx was playing a game with words: in two instances the word 'legs' is a metaphor; in one it is not: the words referring to time are all metaphors. The riddle was a riddle because in it metaphors and direct reference are mixed. To solve it, someone had to have the power to discriminate between the two.

The people who had not been able to solve the riddle had not been accustomed to see what is a metaphor and what is not: they used words in such a way that they did not question how they used them. So they were trapped by words: they could not break out. And Thebes was starving.

Oedipus had the power of discrimination: he could stand back from words: he could see some words are metaphors and others are not. He lifted the curse from the city of Thebes. But he was left with a false impression of omnipotence.

In the myth, he was crowned King of Thebes: he married Queen Jocasta. But then another curse came down — perhaps even worse than the first. There was a plague attendant on the city being ruled by someone who seemed to have magical powers; who had also, although unwittingly, and although people did not see this at the time, murdered his father and married his mother. Oedipus had solved the riddle of the Sphinx: what he had not solved – in fact what he had landed himself with – was the problem of someone who, when he has power over words, thinks he has power over himself and over reality.

Oedipus learned that he had overreached himself: he had solved a riddle about what were and were not games: he had thought that thus he could control reality. But in fact he had become trapped unconsciously at a deeper level: people cannot get away, ultimately, from the power of the rules of games. He had murdered his father and married his mother: this was a curse within himself; he might have had the wit to see it, if he had not been so carried away by his feelings of omnipotence.

A power to see what is games-playing and what is not is only a first step in coming to terms with reality. There is the further step, perhaps made possible by the first, which is to do not with the illusion that one is above the rules of games but with seeing the new patterns and even rules that are opened up by the fact that one can see patterns.

There are superficial parallels between the stories of Oedipus and of Tom: these are not the most interesting. Tom was the son of a bullying father whom he hardly saw and by whom he was rejected and of an adored and adoring mother who called him her 'man-child'. All this indeed when he was a child might have given him feelings of omnipotence: he could play upon his mother who seemed to be his world; there was no father to instil in him knowledge of limits imposed by morals and tradition. With such a background, a child might well have contempt for the rules of games.

What is of deeper interest is the way in which Tom seems to have come mythically towards his city of Thebes in which people were starving. In England, the plague was unemployment: there was some riddle that could not be solved not because a solution was too difficult, but because it was outside the usual terms of people's minds. Of course unemployment could be solved: a leader could say – You will be employed in this way or that because you will be made to. Most people did not think of this solution because it did not seem relevant: it might work, but they assumed it would be worse than the curse. But they could not quite say this, because it would seem they were not interested in solving unemployment – which they were. And so they said nothing. And they were devoured. And the city starved. The riddle was not solved not because it was too difficult, but because it was too undesirably easy. But what was also unpalatable was the fact that in that case perhaps the only solution was that there was no solution – one had to learn how to live with the curse.

Tom came along with his impressions of omnipotence and said – Of course you cannot solve the riddle if you stick to your customary attitudes of mind; but outside these, the solution is quite simple. The fact that you do not want to consider it means that not solving the riddle is in fact your game: you talk and do nothing about it. If you did, your game would be over: but this is your plague. If you want to cure unemployment then you have to pay the price: if you do not want to pay the price then you do not want to cure unemployment. This is a matter of logic: words refer to reality. If you really want to cure unemployment, then follow me. But you must step out of the rules of the game.

But then, Tom was trapped by the forces of a game on a deeper level, of which he was unconscious. He felt that he could order the world as he ordered words. But he could not step back from himself, as he had stepped back from words, and see what was the nature of human beings – in what ways they might need games-playing, even if there were ways they might not. He could not do this because he could not see what were needs, and helplessnesses, as opposed to powers, within himself.

Oedipus is forced to see that however clever he has been with his power and with his words, he has not been clever with himself – he has not been clever enough to see the riddles that he has been landed with by his own nature and his own history – not to solve them, because perhaps they are insoluble – but just to see them and learn to live with them. He has simply been clever enough, in fact, to think he can ignore all this; and so his power turns to ashes. At the illuminating crisis of his life he blinds himself; as if in some recognition of his failure to see. This does not mean that he is not a legendary hero. People are legends just because they can give light to others: they can still alter the way people think.

Tom, as he lay on his bed in Ebury Street plagued with fever, must have had some archetypal dreams and visions about this. He had seen how much of what politicians said was rubbish: how everyone knew it was rubbish but carried on as if they did not know this: thus they suffered from plague. If you pointed this out to them their minds seemed to go blank: it was as if they were at home in the plague. Tom thought he could free them by discrimination, by reason; but then what was he freeing them into? On some level Tom must have known (or when people faced him with this did his mind go blank?) that you cannot have politics without paradoxes, riddles: there are always enigmas about authority and freedom: this is just what the business of power is like. It cannot be helped if it is like a plague from time to time: if you think you can do away with paradoxes, you bring down a worse curse. In the activities of power you are dealing with other people: if other people are to be respected then there have to be rules of games: if there are not, then other people are not respected. If you do want to respect people the highest emphasis cannot be on 'losing' or 'winning': losing is a lesser disaster than that of destroying the game. You only want to destroy the game if your feelings of omnipotence give you disrespect for other people.

Tom claimed that he was involved in no game: that he could order reality. With this confidence he both did and did not deceive other people: he made them feel at moments it might be true. A more interesting question is, how much he deceived himself.

In his relationship with Cimmie he had always been ruthless with words: he used them without much relevance to what they might mean. He manipulated tenderness in order to keep her: he used rages in order to get away. But also, the tenderness and the rages happened naturally: his manipulations were efforts to make the best of what was there. All this involved some ability to stand back from the forces that were driving him: if he could use them, he was not quite at their mercy. What he lacked perhaps was an ability consciously to see himself doing this – and to see where his ability to manipulate might lead him. In fact, he was involved in some circle in that the more he succeeded the more he failed – his endearments placated Cimmie but made her not trust him: in the end he did not keep her and was desolate when he failed. He might have learned something of all this if he had not himself been so involved in the game of saying that in public life he was not games-playing.

Once or twice during the next two years Tom does seem to have thought about giving up politics – at least for a time. He said he wanted to relax; to think. If he had, what he might have learned was that the most successful way of dealing with riddles and paradoxes is perhaps to enjoy them; to savour them; not to dream that they are not there or can be eliminated. Then, perhaps, one can accept what is possible and what is not. Tom had an instinct about this in his private life: but people are victims of their talents – and circumstances. In public life he had enormous talent for histrionics; and this was a time when people were seizing on people like Tom and offering them power – or at least acclaim. It was in public life that he became a victim.

Cimmie was the one person who might have influenced him in all this – to learn something about himself. But Cimmie, in spite of glimpses every now and then of their both being taken over by forces stronger than themselves, herself was trapped by circumstances and her nature – not so much by the usual traps of class or money, as by the additional facets of her background which had made her believe that she was someone exceptional and thus too proud to believe for long in forces stronger than herself. Cimmie had realised she was apt to see Tom as a saint or a devil: a hero or a baby: that so long as she saw him thus he could make use of her: perhaps she wanted to be so used. But neither Tom nor Cimmie seemed to want to learn to treat the other as an ordinary human being. With Tom there was the baby-talk: with Cimmie the appreciation of this because thus she might feel he was her baby. If she challenged him he might become raging and dash off: but then in need, he might return to her. In a marriage a husband and wife either hold a mirror up to each other so that they can see themselves (this is rare) or each provide food for the other's fantasies. Tom perhaps felt safe through his power to hurt Cimmie: Cimmie in turn could say, almost cheerfully, 'I could die for you' or 'I could kill you'. She sometimes saw the irony of this and could say – 'What a farce!' But for all her life-giving qualities she had less and less enjoyment from the farce. She did not so often see things as she said she wanted to see them – as 'fun'.

Tom, with part of him, always did manage to see things as 'fun': he had an enormous zest for life; a talent for enjoyment. This is what made him personally, in spite of the distaste often engendered by his politics, so attractive to people – and a survivor. People loved to be with him: it was on this level that his life succeeded: he did become a happy old man; a legend. He could not of course easily accept this as his fate: part of his legend was, that politics were the whole of life to him. In some way it was probably his zest for life – even his sexual drives – that helped to render him politically ineffectual: politics are a boring game, requiring that other people should feel safe in one's presence. Tom, with the cutting-edge of his personality, seemed often to be almost knowingly self-destructive. But then – might he not in truth have wanted to become a legend – thus embracing the paradoxes he said he wanted to deny?

When Tom talked about wholeness or 'Ganzheit' this was for him not a matter of conscious integration but of balancing bits of his life at opposite ends of a pole as it were, while he stayed on a tightrope. Much of his contempt, his vituperation, was channelled into his politics: here he had no patience, no forbearance: he loved a fight. But then in private life there was room for open-mindedness, wit, laughing at himself, hilarity. People used to feel what marvellous company he was. He also, of course – again perhaps because of his sexual drives – hurt them.

One of his favourite quotations were the lines from Goethe's *Faust* where Faust makes his bargain with the devil – if the devil can show him a moment of such delight that he, Faust, will cry out for time to stop, then he, the devil, can claim Faust for his own. Tom would roll out this quotation at the dinner table like someone making a strike at skittles. He loved the sound of this; though he felt perhaps that he himself would be too hard-headed to utter Faust's cry: he might have hoped both to get the moment, and to trick the devil.

Cimmie did not want trickery: did not want balancing acts: she wanted wholeness in the sense of being all-of-a-piece and without guile. At least, she thought this was what she wanted. She made resolutions: she struggled: but then, when the resolutions failed, she did not learn:

she just made them, and the same mistakes, again. This wore away her faith in Tom: but why did she have this faith? From the first, she seems to have known what he was like. It was just his complexity, perhaps, that she had come to feel might contain her; that would give her simplicity something grand that she might attach herself to. She had written as a schoolgirl of her feeling of the necessity of a 'Big Solemn Comprehensive Idea'. And perhaps Tom had needed her simplicity to give him a thread through the maze of life. But then, he also now used her like some of his skittles to be knocked down. And then he could come for forgiveness and be comforted again. And she would feel reassured. This was their game. By staying in it, Cimmie in some sense colluded. But she got tired. Perhaps it is always a matter of luck how people do, or do not, get out.

In politics, Tom went on thinking that if you put a rational case to people you had done your job: they either followed or they did not. There was a real sense in which Tom was not interested in power – 'he was a complete professional in everything except the winning of power' (Robert Skidelsky). It was this that rendered him powerless, but also established the legend: in the circumstances this was actually a virtue. Beatrice Webb wrote of him 'He lacks genuine fanaticism: I doubt whether he has the tenacity of a Hitler'. At a slightly later date than the time to do with this book Tom wrote a letter to Lord Beaverbrook in which he himself said, in effect, that Britain was fortunate in having a fascist leader such as himself because another leader might have been more ruthlessly and successfully interested in power. Tom was capable of such irony: though not often, it is true, in politics. Trotsky, in his diary-entry about Cimmie, had called Tom a coxcomb; but there is something in Trotsky's history and character that is similar to Tom's: both men turned away, at crucial moments, from their chance to exercise power; they did this because they had some instinct about their ideals – or about their legends. Trotsky in his autobiography said the reason why he did not make a serious bid for power in Russia after Lenin's death was because he could not face the boring and squalid day-to-day procedures necessary for power: he too became ill (he got cold feet, literally, while duck shooting).

If Tom could not laugh at himself in public it was because he had put himself up on a stage and you cannot laugh at yourself on a stage or you destroy the illusion. Laughter is a sort of safety-valve which stops energy running away with itself: there is inevitably something self-destructive about people who cannot laugh. But legends are often to do with people who risk being self-destructive. Tom had a chance of power at a time when ideas and policies such as his were succeeding extravagantly in other parts of the world: these policies, and ideas, later destroyed themselves at an enormous cost of human suffering. Tom never got off the ground as it were in the matter of causing much political human suffering: he had the private wit to see that his destructiveness remained largely symbolic.

Cimmie, like Tom, imagined she wanted outward life to be orderly: she did not have his sense of curiosity when it was not. She felt passionately; but she feared a lack within her: she blamed it on her relationship with Tom. She said that she could not change unless he changed: but it was not he who felt there had to be change to survive.

Neither Cimmie nor Tom had religion: Tom had faith in himself; Cimmie had faith in Tom. Then when she lost it, she seemed to have nothing. They both, in the way they saw things, thought that life should respond to their will: they both saw death as some sort of let-out. But Tom, knowing the complexities of things, was using a metaphor when he talked about 'going down fighting'. Cimmie did not see life as a metaphor: perhaps, if she could not find faith in herself, she felt death as a condition in which humans might at last be all all-of-a-piece.

CHAPTER 19

The New Party

The New Party, which Tom started in March 1931, lasted for less than a year. It did not attract the number of people Tom had hoped for, and it failed dramatically and almost ridiculously: but the people most concerned did not seem to mind its failure, they appeared to see it as some sort of clearing-ground from which they could move on.

While Tom lay ill with pleurisy it was left to Cimmie and John Strachey and Oliver Baldwin (who in fact called himself an Independent) to launch the New Party: they undertook the speaking tour round the country which had been arranged for Tom. The *Manchester Guardian* commented 'Lady Cynthia contributes intensity, Mr Strachey states the case, and Mr Oliver Baldwin provides comic relief'. The 'case' was that set out in the *Mosley Manifesto* of a few months earlier: it was elaborated in yet another pamphlet under the signatures of Allan Young, John Strachey, W. J. Brown and Aneurin Bevan. The latter allowed his name to remain on the pamphlet although he had not resigned from the Labour Party. The pamphlet, entitled 'A National Policy', went into greater detail about the administrative machinery it advocated for putting its policy (or indeed any policy) into effect.

In general Parliament must be relieved of detail. Its essential function must be to place in power an Executive Government of the character to be decided upon by the nation at the last election; to maintain it in power until and unless it commits some action which in the opinion of Parliament is deserving of censure; in that event to turn it out by way of direct Vote of Censure and appeal to the Electorate...

It is essential that a small inner Cabinet Committee consisting of five or six men should be formed... This proposal has been described as an attempt to set up five Dictators. No accusation could be more

inept. There is nothing either more or less democratic about entrust-
ing the ultimate responsibility for the decision of the Government to
a Cabinet of five men who are free from all other work than entrust-
ing them as at present to a Cabinet of twenty men who are too busy
to give real consideration to their most vitally important decisions...

　　Broadly we say to the Electorate: Choose whatever Government
you like. But when you have chosen it, for heavens sake let it get on
with the job without being frustrated and baffled at every turn by
a legislative and administrative procedure designed for the express
purpose of preventing things being done...

Cimmie and John Strachey and Oliver Baldwin delivered this message
round the country: they attracted audiences of several thousands: but
they found that they were increasingly heckled, and that sometimes
their meetings were broken up by what appeared to be organised gangs
of Labour militants and Communists. The communist paper *The Daily
Worker* was in fact already referring to the New Party as 'fascist': the
militants were behaving with the special fury of people who feel they
have been betrayed by their old heroes. But the New Party, if it was
to get anywhere, depended on public meetings: it had little time to build
up an organisation that would be accepted to deal with the crisis.

　　Tom lay in bed with a temperature of a hundred and five. He wrote
to Harold Nicolson 'The illness has been a strange blow of fate – the
first serious collapse of my life, and what a moment!' At the end of
March he went with Cimmie to recuperate at Lord Beaverbrook's villa
in the South of France. Also with them was his sister-in-law Baba, who
herself had been seriously ill after the birth of twins and had been
recuperating with Tom and Cimmie at Savehay Farm.

　　Up till now Tom had had the naive and presumably Marxist idea that
an appeal to reason could always if necessary be made over the heads
of a stupid Cabinet, a cowardly Parliamentary Labour Party and even
a hysterical Party Conference, to an enlightened proletariat who in some
way would be a fair judge. Marxists had to think this because if they
did not – knowing as they did their non-proletarian colleagues – what
hope was there for reason? But now if this belief was to go or be
rendered ineffectual – if really it was members of the proletariat who
were shouting down or allowing to be shouted down the reasonable
exposition of New Party policy – what was there left?

　　Tom had, perhaps, been preparing for something like this. He had
for long been perfecting his techniques as a mob orator: he seems
consciously to have faced questions about the limitations of rationality

and the fact that the exercise of power is perhaps always to do with manipulations of emotion. Rationality puts a burden on people by asking them to think for themselves; it is apt to make them feel inadequate. The manipulation of emotion achieves some sort of power by making people feel that they belong.

It was remarked that Tom was different when he emerged from his sick bed: he was less patient; it was as if he had personally come to terms with having stepped outside the rules of games. The first big test of the New Party was to be at a by-election at Ashton-under-Lyne in Lancashire on April 30th 1930. Allan Young was standing as the New Party candidate. Tom had played no part in the run-up to the election: the brunt of the day-to-day electioneering had been borne by Cimmie. Jack Jones, a left-wing orator hired by the New Party at five pounds a week, wrote of Cimmie at the time:

> Cynthia Mosley was both able and willing. With me she must have addressed at least a score of very big outdoor crowds during the campaign, and also scores of 'in our street' talks to women. Whilst others in the first flight were looking important in the presence of reporters, or talking about the holding of the floating Liberal vote, the cornering of the Catholic vote, and preparing their speeches for the well-stewarded big meetings indoors each evening, Cynthia Mosley was out getting the few votes that were got.

Tom appeared on the scene six days before the election. His presence had an electrifying effect. He addressed an indoor meeting of six or seven thousand. Harold Nicolson reported:

> Tom then gets up to make his speech and profits enormously by a few interruptions from Labour supporters. He challenges Arthur Henderson to meet him tomorrow in open debate and this stirs the audience to enthusiasm and excitement. Having thus broken the ice, he launches on an emotional oration on the lines that England is not yet dead and that it is for the New Party to save her. He is certainly an impassioned revivalist speaker, striding up and down the rather frail platform with great panther steps and gesticulating with a pointing, and occasionally a stabbing, index; with the result that there was a real enthusiasm towards the end and one had the feeling that 90% of the audience were certainly convinced at the moment.

Harold Nicolson was a newcomer to politics. He had just resigned from the diplomatic service and was working as a journalist on the *Evening Standard*. He had been attracted to the New Party, he said, out of '(1) Personal affection and belief in Tom: (2) A conviction that a serious crisis was impending and that our economic and parliamentary system must be transformed if collapse were to be avoided.' He got carried along by the sense that Tom engendered of being in touch with great events; also by the sense of fun.

Another leading figure in the New Party was Peter Howard, captain of the England Rugby Football team. Harold Nicolson wrote to Cimmie 'Peter Howard I have a feeling is bowled over by your charms – but so are we all'. Peter Howard had organised a group of young men from Oxford to protect New Party meetings: these were referred to in the press as 'Mosley's Biff Boys' or 'strapping young men in plus fours'. The emphasis of the New Party was on youth: a journalist wrote of the party headquarters at Ashton-under-Lyne – 'Young men with fine foreheads and an expression of faith dash from room to room carrying proof-sheets and manifestos: I have seldom seen so many young people so excited and so pleased'.

When the election results were announced the Conservatives had got 12,420 votes, Labour 11,005, and Allan Young of the New Party 4,472 – just saving his deposit. This result was not discreditable to a party only two months old but it was not as good as Tom had hoped: he found, as he was so often to find later, that the enthusiasm he engendered as a one-man-band did not effectively last until his audience went to the poll. But it had lasted long enough, Labour supporters imagined, for the intervention of the New Party to have ensured that the Conservatives won what had previously been held to be a safe Labour seat. In fact, the New Party's intervention had probably somewhat lessened what was a general swing against Labour throughout the country. But political crowds want scapegoats, not analysis.

The crowd of Labour militants outside the Town Hall shouted for vengeance. Tom, standing on the steps, turned to John Strachey and said 'That is the crowd that has prevented anyone doing anything in England since the war'. John Strachey commented – 'At that moment British Fascism was born: at that moment of passion, and of some personal danger, Mosley found himself almost symbolically aligned against the workers.' Tom himself commented later that what he had meant was that 'dedicated agents and warriors of communism always play on the anarchy inherent on the Left of Labour to secure confusion, disillusion and ultimately the violence which is essential to their long term plan'.

In the Town Hall, Tom arranged for Cimmie to be smuggled out of a back door; then, in the face of the crowd which in Jack Jones's words 'had all the appearances of an American lynching crowd', Tom – 'white with rage, not fear' – led his small party through the mob 'howling at him and calling him names'. He 'smiled contemptuously' at them. Jack Jones added – 'An exciting experience it was.' Tom, to Jack Jones's apparent surprise, seemed 'almost cheerful'.

Through the summer discussions went on amongst the New Party leaders – there was an Executive Committee that met almost daily in offices in Great George Street – not so much about policy, as about what was to be done about the difficulty of getting the policy heard. Labóur militants did not deny the attacks were organised: the hostility was not discouraged by Tom's old parliamentary colleagues: A. V. Alexander referred to the 'traitorous Mosley'; Emmanuel Shinwell to 'Brutus ... responsible for "the stiletto in the back".' Young men who had come fresh into the New Party wanted to build up a Youth Movement into a force that would be trained to defend the speakers against physical attack: John Strachey and others continued to be alarmed at this. They agreed that it was right that meetings should be protected from organised disruption, but they feared that a group of young men trained in judo and boxing for this purpose would grow into a proto-fascist defence force. Also they seemed to feel that demonstrations by workers, however suspect, were in some way sacrosanct. But it was difficult to see how one could have the protection without the discipline. The activists seemed to have logic on their side: the intellectuals an instinct.

Everything depended of course on what sort of balance was struck between the two; or rather what sort of skill Tom had in appearing to control or to embrace the two. He announced that in the light of the violence directed against Cimmie during her speaking tour earlier in the year a body of young men would indeed be trained; but they would 'rely on the good old English fist.'

During summer there were weekends at which the intellectuals exercised their conundrums. In Hampstead, John Strachey, Harold Nicolson and Cyril Joad debated – What happens to the New Party, which is dedicated to dealing with a crisis, if the crisis does not come? Harold Nicolson suggested that the party should continue with a pro- gramme advocating 'Sacrifice, Discipline, Service, Courage and Energy of Thought'. Cyril Joad asked – 'But how can *we* put over such a programme?' At Savehay Farm there was a congress at which John Strachey delivered his 'good old Marxian speech' (Jack Jones); Tom spoke 'soulfully of the Corporate State of the future' and 'a young man called Winckworth called for a revival of the Attic Spirit' which would involve the New Party in attracting people with 'the heads of thinkers on the bodies of athletes'. Cyril Joad riposted 'Be careful you don't attract people with the heads of athletes on the bodies of thinkers'. Tom appreciated the wit: but he would have wished, as usual, to cut through the riddles. During the Congress at Savehay Farm, Harold Nicolson recorded – 'The Youth Movement swam'.

In a speech at the Cannon Street Hotel, in London, on June 30th 1931, Tom announced that his movement was trying to create 'a new political psychology, a conception of national renaissance, of new mankind and of vigour'. John Strachey and Allan Young were in the audience: they decided to make a positive show of their alarm. The next day Strachey addressed a meeting of the Youth Movement and spoke against the idea of any disciplined use of violence to counteract violence: a version of his statement appeared in the *Daily Herald*. At the next meeting of the New Party Executive Tom (according to Harold Nicolson) 'reprimands Strachey in terms which, if addressed to me, would have caused the most acute embarrassment'. But Harold Nicolson went on – 'I do not deny that I was impressed by the force of discipline in Tom's speech. It is quite evident that he will allow no independence to any member of the party and that he claims an almost autocratic position. I do not myself object to this, since if we are to be the thin end of the wedge we must have an extremely sharp point and no splinters. I wonder, however, how long other members of the Council will tolerate such domination.' And later – 'I think that Tom at the bottom of his heart really wants a fascist movement'.

One of the hopes that Tom was playing with at this time was that he, and some of his party, might be able to join Churchill and Lloyd George in making up a 'National Opposition' if, in the face of the continuing economic crisis, a National Government was formed by MacDonald and Baldwin. Tom drove to Archibald Sinclair's house to have talks with Lloyd George: on the way he told Harold Nicolson that he thought that Allan Young and John Strachey would be soon leaving the New Party: he said this with little regret. He called them the 'pathological element' – apparently because of their timidity in the face of violence. (Tom used to tease John Strachey by telling him he was 'governed by Marx from the waist up and Freud from the waist down.') Nothing much came of the talks with Lloyd George. Everyone on the fringes of power seemed to be trying to charm everyone else, and to be waiting to see what would happen. Perhaps no one, in the face of the frightening prospects of 1931, really wanted power.

John Strachey then produced a memorandum in which he advocated

making 'a progressive break with that group of powers of which France
and the USA are leaders' and entering into 'close economic relations
with the Russian government'. This was a direct challenge to Tom, to
test his left-wing or right-wing commitment. There was also a dispute
in the New Party Executive about unemployment benefit: it seemed to
John Strachey and Allan Young that Tom was not taking a strong
enough stand against proposed government cuts. Tom made concessions here: but he rejected Strachey's pro-Russian proposals since
they 'contradicted directly the whole basis of the policy we have long
agreed together'. Then John Strachey and Allan Young resigned.

They prepared a joint letter to be made public: but each wrote
privately to Tom.

July 22nd 1931   7 North Street.
Westminster.

Dear Tom,

I think you will agree that the differences between us which have
become apparent during recent meetings are too serious to be left
where they are. In fact they are really so wide as to make argument
impossible. It is quite clear to me that your whole outlook is becoming more and more Conservative: already you regard any other
outlook as 'pathological'.

In these circumstances further collaboration between us would be
nothing but a handicap to both of us. So I send you my resignation
from the New Party and its Council.

I intend making this resignation public tomorrow unless you want
to talk about it first. If you do ring me up tomorrow morning at
North St (Vic 3681) But I don't see what purpose will be served by
such a talk – and frankly I dread it. One can't have worked as closely
with and for anyone as I have tried to work with and for you ever
since I came into politics, and not feel pretty smashed up by such a
separation.

We have obviously quite different conceptions of what the New
Party ought to be and of how it could succeed. Naturally it seems to
me that it is you who have changed. No doubt you feel that it is I who
have changed. What more is there to say? – except for me to thank
you very genuinely for all the kindness and I believe affection you
have shown me.

Yours
John

22nd July 1931   as from – 10 Brookland Rise
N.W. 11

Dear Tom,

... Since your illness and the Ashton bye-election there has been
a change in your whole attitude of mind which has disturbed me
more than I can say. Your semi-public and private statements with
regard to the Youth Movement, India, Unemployment Insurance,
Russia, and the general function and purpose of the New Party has
made me ashamed of my own association with it. Our difficulties in
launching the party were due to the doubts and suspicions of our
friends that you would succumb to the pressure and attraction of
right-wing views. I contested this strongly at the time – placing
reliance on your strength and judgement. Your attitude in the last two
months seems to have proved me wrong and the critics right. From
the beginning I have been aware of the dangers implicit in a movement such as ours. These dangers could only have been avoided by
a leadership above suspicion as far as working-class interests were
concerned. You have not given us that leadership but rather have
provided grounds for the suspicion that the party would become
Hitlerist, Fascist, and ultimately anti-working class. I cannot be
associated with a party which is even open to that suspicion, and I now
tender you my resignation.

I will always remember with gratitude your kindness to me. But
I must pursue the course which my conscience and intelligence
dictates.

Yours,
Allan Young

Tom got in touch with Harold Nicolson who was working at the
Evening Standard and asked him to go round to see John Strachey and
Allan Young and to try to get them at least to postpone the public
announcement of their resignation which was to be made at six o'clock
that evening. Harold Nicolson did not manage to get in touch with
them till 5.30 – they were apparently in hiding – then he found them
in John Strachey's house, where:

Allan Young descends to the dining room looking pale and on the
verge of a nervous breakdown. I say that Tom suggests that they
should not openly resign at the moment but 'suspend' their resignation till 1st December by which date they will be able to see whether
their suspicions of our fascism are in fact justified. Allan might have

accepted this, but at that moment John Strachey enters. Tremulous and uncouth he sits down and I repeat my piece. He says that it would be impossible for him to retain his name on a Party while taking no part in that Party's affairs . . . He then begins, quivering with emotion, to indicate some of the directions in which Tom has of late abandoned the sacred cause of the workers. He says that ever since his illness he has been a different man. His faith has left him. He is acquiring a Tory mind. It is a reversion to type. He considers socialism a 'pathological condition'. John much dislikes being pathological. His great hirsute hands twitch neurotically as he explained to us, with trembling voice, how unpathological he really is.

Harold Nicolson failed to get them to withdraw or to postpone their resignations. He commented -- 'Undoubtedly the defection of John and his statement that we were turning fascist will do enormous electoral harm to the party. Politically however it will place Tom in a position where with greater ease he can adhere to Lloyd George and Winston.'

Tom, however, was now only going through the motions of playing at party politics; he was dreaming more and more of the time when he, as an effective leader, might be in direct relationship to the masses which he was sure was the only way of getting anything done. Harold Nicolson recorded – 'Tom conceives of great mass meetings with loud speakers – 50,000 people at a time'. For the organisation of them, the Youth Movement would of course be vitally important. Tom drafted a farewell note to Allan Young: 'I want just to tell you how sorry I am our association has ended. It has meant more to me than most things in my life. As we go on the sorrow of things deepens'.

Harold Nicolson told Cyril Joad that he was staying on in the New Party because 'I felt it was the only party which gave to intelligence a position above possessions or the thoughts of Karl Marx'. Cyril Joad said he was leaving the party because it was about to 'subordinate intelligence to muscular bands of young men'.

At the end of July the government received the report of a committee it had set up to advise on the economic situation: the main recommendation was that unemployment benefit, already pitiful, should be cut by twenty per cent. The New Party held a rally at Renishaw Park, in Derbyshire, the home of the Sitwells, at which 40,000 people were present. Tom declared 'We invite you to something new, something dangerous'. Then politicians went on holiday.

Tom and Cimmie went, as usual, to the South of France. They left Harold Nicolson virtually in charge of the office at home. He was making preparations for the New Party weekly newspaper, *Action*, which was to be launched in the autumn and of which he was to be editor. The New Party had based its appeal on being the party that would be ready to deal with the crisis when it came: everyone agreed it was coming and it would be the worst economic crisis for a hundred years. Tom was all his life contemptuous of people who 'even for the few years at the height of their responsibilities cannot be serious'. But the trouble was that however accurate had been his forecast of the crisis, he had succeeded in putting himself in a position in which he had no responsibility for dealing with it. Harold Nicolson wrote to him:

I recognise that people may say that at the gravest crisis in present political history you prefer to remain upon the Mediterranean. On the other hand, I do not see what you would do were you here at this moment; and I feel that it is more dignified to be absent and aloof than to be present and not consulted.

CHAPTER 20

Politics as Farce

The extraordinary position that Tom had got himself into – that of preparing for a crisis by finding himself unable to do anything about it when it came – was the result of two major assumptions: the first, that the old parties would disintegrate in the face of the crisis so that it would be better not to be tainted by their failures of responsibility; the second, that he himself would be in charge of a party so patently free of the farcical aspects of the old parties that people would soon turn to him and give him responsibility.

The nature of the crisis had seemed to him to be simple: if the welfare of every country in the world depended on its selling more than it bought on an open world market, then in fact only those countries would succeed which could sell the cheapest goods by paying the lowest wages. It was out of the question for British workers to accept ever lower wages: so there would be crisis. This might take the form of bankruptcy or even of war – by which other countries' economic competitiveness might be broken. But for this sort of crisis too the old parties were not equipped to deal: and in any case, any party led by Tom would be dedicated to preventing war.

The success of a party run by Tom in dealing with a crisis would hinge on a body of dedicated men who would run, without the supervision of Parliament, the 'closed' economic area of Great Britain-and-Empire by means of statutory powers to control wages and prices, industrial investment, a floating exchange rate and the bulk buying of raw materials. Everything would depend on the efficient, incorruptible nature of these 'new' men: without such characteristics they would just have more power to make more muddles and to act more deviously than the old. Tom for some time had recognised this: in his *Sunday Express* article of 1930 he had suggested that no political programme such as his

could work without men of 'a hard, realistic type, hammered into
existence on the anvil of great ordeal'. Now, a year later, the ordeal was
here.

Half way through August an Austrian bank went bankrupt; foreign
depositors called in their money from London; there was what is called
'a run on the pound'; gold reserves (Britain was still on the gold
standard) were depleted; it was believed – this was contemporary
economic dogma – that international 'confidence' could only be
restored if there were cuts in public spending at home. This in effect
meant the immediate implementation of the recommendations of the
report which had advocated the cutting of unemployment benefit. A
large proportion of the Labour Cabinet would not agree to this: they
had however no practical alternative suggestions. Ramsay MacDonald
suggested to the King that a National Government might be formed
consisting of members of all parties: this would obviate everyone's
tendency to wish to pass responsibility on to others. Also it might
prevent Britain being forced off the gold standard; which eventuality
would be, according to dogma again, a disaster. The King agreed. A
general election could follow later.

The formation of a National Government under MacDonald cut
from under the New Party much of the ground on which its appeal had
been based – that of aiming to put in control of the country men who
were above the customary game of party politics and in theory at least
dedicated to the business of getting a job done. The only serious appeal
that the New Party might now have against the National Government
would be if it could be seen to be composed of the type of people more
likely to do a job well.

Harold Nicolson had been to Manchester to interview prospective
New Party candidates. He recorded in his diary:

> They vary from an old lunatic called Holden to a boy of 21 called
> Branstead who scarcely knows what the House of Commons is. Only
> one of the many we interview – a wild-eyed nymphomaniac called
> Miss —— is at all a possible candidate . . . The party has quite clearly
> not as yet attracted the better class of manual worker.

Slightly later Harold Nicolson reported to Tom in the South of France.
His letter is dated August 14th – three days after Ramsay MacDonald
had been recalled to London to face the 'run on the pound' and ten days
before the public announcement of the formation of the National
Government. Of the people mentioned in Harold Nicolson's letter

Sellick Davies was the New Party Treasurer, F. K. Box was the Chief Party Agent, and Dr Robert Forgan was, together with Tom and Cimmie and a recruit from the Conservatives W. E. D. Allen, one of the four remaining New Party MPs.

4 King's Bench Walk.

August 14th 1931　　　　Temple W.C.2.

My dear Tom,

This is going to be a long letter and illegible in parts. It will also, at least at first, be a painful letter. The reason why it will be illegible is that I am using the typewriter of Mr Hamlyn, the Genera Manager of *Action*. To which I am not attuned. The reason why it will be painful is Sellick Davies. I begin with the bloody part. The rest will be cheery enough.

First the iniquities (so I am assured) of Sellick. Box rang me up today in a state of perturbation. Box was perturbed. It seems that he had received a request from Sellick who is now with the admirable Forgan at Berneval sur mer (that obscure Dieppoise resort where the unfortunate Mr Wilde retired after endurances of Reading Gaol). Sellick asked for £25 from the till. Box sent for the books. The books disclosed that Sellick had been withdrawing from from the said till sums which even to me appeared excessive. And for these sums he had provided vouchers which, although proof of his hospitable instincts, were by no means proof of his capacity as Treasurer. Box was shocked. So also, to a lesser degree, was I. I managed to convince Box that a chartered accountant such as Sellick was could scarcelz behave in such a manner unless there was some explanation. We must go careful like. Box was all for calling in other and less Welsh accountants at once. I urged him to consult you. And by this post you will receive a letter which will cause you much distress.

Anyhow we have refused to advance Sellick money for his amusements at the Dieppe Casino. And have done so in a manner which will cause him a certain uneasiness if guilty but no acute displeasure if innocent. The sums involved are not enormous. I think he has been a muddle head. But the fact remains that he is not competent to control our finances, and that som more chartered and less Welsh accountant will have to take his place..

This is unpleasant not only because we cannot face more resignations but also because Sellick has his points. Financial sensibility is obviously a rare quality and one possessed only by those who know nothing of finance...

So much for the bloody part. Now for other more cheering news. (1) The party. I find that the present crisis has enormously increased your prestige. People who treated us as a painful joke five weeks ago are now regarding us with a wild surmise. Men like Keynes are saying you were right all along. I find that 'West End Clubmen' (it is not for nothing that I spent eighteen months at the *Evening Standard*) have adopted quite a different angle towards your movement. People like Middleton Murray in this month's *Adelphi* speak openly in your favour. H. G. Wells today spoke with serious interest about the policy, and Leonard Woolf has written to me asking for full information and pamphlets. These may be straws – but they are straws in an important wind . . . (4) *Action*: otherwise the paper which fills all mz thoughts and most of my time. I shall not bother you with details. It is going ahead like a speed-boat. I have engaged the staff and feel they are good. Mr Hamlyn the Manager is a Jew. Mr Joseph the assistant editor may also be a Jew but his point is that he will corrct my tendency to quote Aristotle. A clever young man . . .

(the bore about this typewriter is that when I want to say 'Y' it sazs 'z'. The result is ungainly. 'Bz' is not a pretty rendering of the word 'by').

One more point. Would you wish to start off the paper with an article by yourself? 'HAVE I FIZZLED OUT?' seems the right note. It is not essential, but I think we should face that question and I think you can do it best. My God, Tom, if that paper is a dud then I am a dud. It WON'T BE A DUD . . .

I think that for once events have moved to help you. Of course the Socialists have cornered Baldwin and are taking your programme leaf by leaf like an artichoke. But that merely increases your opportunity. I find that many people are saying that you will be tempted to join any coalition that is formed. I hope you will if you consider it right to do so and if you are assured of the necessary authority. People always accuse you of being out for yourself. I reply 'Yes, thank God¾ (it is very rude to write God¾ one ought to write God just like that) – I reply 'Yes, thank God, he is one of those people who feel a we should all feel – 'l'etat c'est moïr' I mean 'moi'.

Tom – it is fun being with you since you understand where my nonsense begins and where my my sense begins.

But really everying is gling very well, and if we keep faith in ur own intelligence nothing can to wrong

Yours ever.
Harold.

P.S. Did you get my memorandum on Foreign Policy? I sent it by registered post but have just discovered that I wrote Villa Uzes or rods to that effect beine memerised by the memory of little bo-peep alis Miss Gordon alias Duchesse D'Uzes. But I hope it turned up all right.

To this letter, surely unique in the annals of letters from editors to newspaper proprietors, Tom, from Antibes, replied – 'It is a joy to have you on the job: do not kill yourself'.

The centre of attraction at Antibes this year (apart from Tom and Cimmie themselves: it was true that they appeared ever more glamorous politicians the further they got from the drab corridors of power) was Michael Arlen, the author of *The Green Hat*, whom Tom, according to Irene, so inspired with New Party propaganda over dinner at Monte Carlo that he, Michael Arlen, considered becoming a party member. Life at Antibes went its usual way: Tom was pursuing someone called Lotsie: I, aged eight, was bitten on the head by a pet monkey: people 'massed again, booted and spurred, and in a relay of cars departed to the dirty pictures at Nice and on to Monte' (Irene).

The history of the New Party is crucial to an understanding of Tom: he stayed in the South of France because he had announced that party politics were absurd: he was acting logically according to his convictions. Even if he had had anything to do with the crisis he would have felt it better to wait, probably, until people turned to him; only then would he feel he had a mandate to put what was required into effect. And was it not the case, as people told him, that his legendary prestige was increasing so long as he remained aloof? But the question remained – what use, in the end, could he make of this prestige?

The affairs of the New Party went their own bizarre way. Dr Robert Forgan wrote from Berneval-sur-Mer:

Dear Tom.

Recent public events in England have more than justified the cry of 'crisis' that we raised so long before anyone else . . . unfortunately I have a crisis of my own. Ever since – imprudently or at least improvidently – I entered Parliament two years ago (and gave up moderately lucrative medical work) I have been in financial difficulties . . . I took to borrowing at ruinous rates of interest until now I find myself in such a mess that I must get the ground cleared somehow . . . Just at the moment the New Party can ill afford to lose another Member of Parliament . . .

There followed the request for a loan of £500. The letter ended somewhat disarmingly – 'Superintending the earth is, for me, far more interesting than keeping one's affairs in order!'

Tom arrived back from Antibes on 26 August, two days after the formation of the National Government. Harold Nicolson met him at Dover, and found him cheerful. Tom said that of course he would be pressing on with New Party plans: he hoped to get six members into the House of Commons so long as a general election did not come before February. But he recognized that it was possible the New Party might fail completely, in which case he would retire from public life for ten years. He explained – 'I have never led a civilised life at all since I entered politics as a boy. I can well afford to wait ten years, to study economics, and even then when I return I shall be no older than Bonar Law was when he first entered politics'.

In later life Tom used to say that he sometimes wished he had taken this advice to himself more literally: he knew that he was no longer interested in conventional manoeuvrings for power; he was interested in the presentation of the embodiment of an idea. For this, it was not clear how much there was urgency: what was important was the effort to formulate and give substance to the idea.

For the next four months the New Party end-game was played out to what must have been the bewilderment of a dwindling band of spectators. The first number of *Action*, edited by Harold Nicolson, came out on October 8th: it was a tabloid-sized paper of 32 pages and cost 2d. The tone was set by the first editorial: 'We have adopted certain watchwords – the first is truth: the second courage: the third intelligence: the fourth vigour.' Tom on the front page wrote 'We must create a movement which grips and transforms every phase and aspect of national life.' On the inside pages there was an article by Dr Forgan on old age ('The Commonest Disease in the Wide World') a science article by Gerald Heard ('From Faraday to Kapitza – Great Cambridge Dynamo') a gardening page by Vita Sackville West ('How To Plant And Design Beds') and book reviews of *The Waves* and *Sanctuary* by Harold Nicolson. The next few numbers contained 'Did the Werewolf Exist?' by Gerald Heard and 'Vagabond Camp – Tales of Great Journeys' by Eric Muspratt. Tom continued to emphasise the need to 'imbue the nation with a new idea and a new faith' and to insist that a 'virile group' should be returned to the House of Commons. The editor however announced as the general election approached – 'If, as is far more likely, the New Party has done extremely badly . . . the note will be one of quiet manliness; of resigned British pluck'.

Tom himself carried on powerfully as his one-man-band. On September 8th he made his last major speech in Parliament: he attacked Labour for having followed conservative policies of deflation: he advocated following Keynes's advice to borrow money to finance work for the unemployed: he perorated 'the way out is not the way of the monk but the way of the athlete...the simple question before the house...is whether Great Britain is to meet its crisis lying down or standing up.' On September 20th he was addressing a meeting of an estimated 20,000 people at Glasgow: he referred to the Labour Party as 'a Salvation Army that took to its heels on the day of Judgement': he was attacked by a communist group with razors. His bodyguard, including Peter Howard and the ex-welter-weight boxing champion Kid Lewis, fought off the attack, but a stone hit Tom on the head. (Tom used to tell the story how he had asked Kid Lewis why he had not punched more ruthlessly, and Kid Lewis had said he was afraid of killing someone). Tom's speech however had been heard through the use of loudspeakers: the meeting, Peter Howard reported, was 'really rather a success'. Afterwards Harold Nicolson noted – 'Tom says this forces us to be fascist and that we no longer need hesitate to create our trained and disciplined force. We discuss their uniforms: I suggest grey flannel trousers and shirts.' He also suggested the emblem of a marigold in the buttonhole.

Tom agreed with Harold Nicolson that it was important that the Youth Movement should not appear too military: on the other hand – 'the working class have practically no sense of being ridiculous in the way that we have, and their very drab lives gives them a thirst for colour and for drama'.

On the whole, however, I think that Peter Howard is just the man to hold the right balance. He must see that Mr Kid Lewis is invariably accompanied on his tours by Mr Sacheverell Sitwell – in a Siamese connection they might well form the symbol of our Youth Movement!

Through Harold Nicolson and *Action* Tom was in touch with the Sitwells, the Leonard Woolfs, with other writers and artists: he was also through the Youth Movement in touch with a growing band of toughs. But the true Siamese connection existed within himself. After a wildly enthusiastic and peaceful meeting at the Free Trade Hall the *Manchester Guardian* reported –

In his 35th year Oswald Mosley is already thickly encrusted with legend. His disposition and his face are those of a raider, a corsair ... We speak metaphorically; but who could doubt ... that here was one of those root-and-branch men who have been thrown up from time to time in the religious, political and business story of England.

Then after a meeting at the Rag Market at Birmingham, the *Birmingham Post* reported that it was the presence of the Youth Movement that 'immediately set up a militant feeling in the few who were out for trouble' with the result that there was such a fight that Tom and his bodyguard were afterwards charged with assault. They were acquitted: the magistrate agreeing with Tom's counsel's opinion about the unlikelihood of a speaker hiring a large hall for the purpose of beating up his own audience. Also prosecution witnesses were made to look ridiculous by saying that Tom's 'provocative attitude' was due to the 'smile on his face'. But the two sides of the legend were becoming established in people's minds – that of the hero and the thug.

The general election took place on October 27th. Six months previously the New Party had talked about putting up four hundred candidates: in the event it put up twenty four. All but two lost their deposits. Tom saved his, but came bottom of the poll with 10,834 votes at Cimmie's old constituency of Stoke. Harold Nicolson lost his deposit standing for the Combined Universities: Kid Lewis polled 154 votes at Whitechapel. Cimmie herself had not stood: she was said to be suffering from 'overstrain': she was also pregnant.

The New Party had been in a hopeless position in terms of practical politics at the election. It had campaigned on a programme of 'mobilising national forces to revive trade; linking up with the Dominions to help the export trade; scientific protection of the home market and a General Powers Bill to give the government powers of rapid action.' All these points with the exception of the last had been covered by the manifestos of the National Government; and there had been promises of decisive action of course too. The New Party could not even campaign as the party of opposition, because the Labour Party had broken away from Ramsay MacDonald and was itself in opposition to the MacDonald-Conservative-Liberal government. The New Party had nothing of substance to say to the electorate except that it had been the party which had foretold the crisis and that it was unlikely that the crisis would be solved by the people who had failed to prevent it.

Tom believed that the government of 'the old men who have laid waste the power and the glory of our land' would collapse within a short time and that then politicians would be faced by more strenuous problems than those of collecting votes. This conviction was not unreasonable. Shortly before, there had been the naval mutiny at Invergordon when sailors, faced with the proposal to cut their pay by ten per cent, had refused to turn out for duty. Already the Government had had to take Britain off the gold standard – which action it had ostensibly come into existence to prevent. People other than Tom felt that ordinary structures of society were cracking up; that battles for power would soon have to be won not at elections, but in the streets.

Against this background *Action* continued on its haphazard way. After the debacle of the election (there were no details printed in it of the election results) the editor wrote 'Are we downhearted? Yes we are!' and Gerald Heard's science article was on 'Will Eels Show Us Where Lost Continents Lay?' However in the next number there was a new feature by Peter Cheyney, the crime writer, whom Harold Nicolson had described in his diary as 'a Jew fascist – a most voluble, violent and unpleasant type'. This feature was entitled 'Cutting out the Bunk in Great Britain' and it referred to the 'Nupa Youth Movement' and the 'Nupa Shock Movement' – 'Nupa' being toughened-up jargon for 'New Party'. Peter Cheyney wrote:

> In both these movements he [the young man of today] will learn realism as opposed to bunk, vibrant nationalism as opposed to sloppy internationalism, discipline as opposed to the post-war ideal of sloth, and a comradeship unknown to the Red 'comrades' of the sickly sickle ... You will meet Nupa. It will find you in its own way. Its programme ... aims at the establishment of a country-wide system of Nupa-Shock-Propaganda Controls by June 1933 and the completely organised Political-Shock-Youth Movement by June 1935.

Harold Nicolson's friends wrote amongst themselves in horror at this style (Raymond Mortimer to Edward Sackville West: 'When I walk in the streets and see posters – *Action* edited by Harold Nicolson – *The Prime Minister Needs Kicking* by Oswald Mosley – I desire to vomit'). But Raymond Mortimer himself still wrote an article for *Action* ('The Reasons Why I Prefer The Present'); and so did Osbert Sitwell, Peter Quennell, Christopher Isherwood, and Alan Pryce-Jones ('The World Is Neither Large Nor Remarkable'). The circulation had dropped from an initial 160,000 to 50,000 at the time of the election: by December it was under 20,000 and was losing £340 a week. There did not seem to be much point in its going on.

The last number appeared on December 31st. Harold Nicolson wrote – 'We recognise with cold calm that our failure is for the moment complete . . . we were too highbrow for the general public and too popular for the highbrow . . . The first number was a dud. We were thereafter not quick enough to reduce our printing order . . . (People) accused the paper of lacking punch. Perhaps they were right. Yet it is difficult to punch fairly.'

Tom on the front page wrote:

We were never fools enough to delude ourselves into the belief that we could build a new political party of a normal character in normal conditions. We shall be a movement born of crisis and ordeal or we shall be nothing. If that crisis does not mature we shall be nothing, for the country for perfectly good reasons will not require us . . . In that case we can all retire more happily to more congenial occupations, satisfied that at least we have done our best to meet a menace which might have overwhelmed this country but which fortunately did not mature.

However at the end – and printed in italics as if it were being pointed out to his readers that they were being involved in some sort of change of gear – Tom launched into one of his perorations. Under the headline 'We Are Pierced and Broken – We Advance', he wrote:

Better the great adventure, better the great attempt for England's sake, better defeat, disaster, better far the end of that trivial thing called a Political Career than stifling in a uniform of Blue and Gold, strutting and posturing on the stage of Little England, amid the scenery of decadence, until history, in turning over an heroic page of the human story, writes of us the contemptuous postscript: 'These were the men to whom was entrusted the Empire of Great Britain, and whose idleness, ignorance and cowardice left it a Spain.' We shall win; or at least we shall return upon our shields.

Tom's perorations were demonstrations of the style of his heart, of his dedication, in a more profound way perhaps than was his logic. The style was that of one who gets glory from battle: it had none of the vulgarity of Peter Cheyney's call for a NUPA Political-Shock-Youth-Movement; but the chords it touched were inevitably, and tragically, sometimes the same.

During the autumn in spite of (or because of) Tom's increasingly apparent failure with the New Party there had been continuing moves to try to get him back into the conventional political fold. For a time the New Party MPs had sat on the Conservative benches. Then Randolph Churchill had come to see Tom on a mission from his father Winston to ask him whether he would still consider joining a band of 'Tory toughs' in opposition to the National Government. Tom had asked Randolph why Winston wanted him: Randolph had replied 'Because without you he will not be able to get hold of the young men.' (Harold Nicolson, who recorded this story, added 'Tom is very pleased with that'.) Tom also had had talks with Neville Chamberlain to see whether the New Party could make some electoral deal with the National Government. But it was still obvious that Tom wanted seriously to be involved with none of these moves. Harold Nicolson wrote 'He says that it would be impossible for him to enter the "machine" of one of the older parties: that by so doing he would again have to place himself in a strait waist-coat: that he has no desire for power on those terms'. But by the end of the year the New Party had virtually ceased to exist: the office in Great George Street was closed down. One of the last manifestations of the party was, typically, the completion of a propaganda film exhorting people to join it. In the film there were shots of MPs asleep and then crowds rushing forwards shouting 'England wants Action!' The film was banned in cinemas on the grounds that it might bring Parliament into disrepute.

With part of himself Tom might well have been happy, as he had said he would be, to 'retire to more congenial occupations' while the crisis did not come to a head in the way he had expected it to. He and Cimmie were seen at a great many parties and night clubs that winter: he created excitement and interest wherever he went. He had the style of the temporarily defeated but still potentially justified hero. At the very end of 1931, after cataloguing the disasters of the year and of his association with Tom, Harold Nicolson could still write – 'yet in spite of all this, what fun life is!'

Out of all Tom's political involvement for the past thirteen years there remained only one practical manifestation – the embryonic NUPA Youth Movement. This with its 'Rugger, Cricket, Boxing, Fencing and Billiards' and 'Talks By Famous People Every Tuesday' at 122a King's Road, was the embodiment of that other part of Tom which, whatever the circumstances, would always be concerned with the thought of returning, or not, upon its shield.

CHAPTER 21

Steps to Fascism

Cimmie's practical involvement in politics virtually ceased after her efforts to launch the New Party during the spring and summer of 1931. After this she seems to have lost heart. She had written an article in the *Daily Sketch* in May – 'There is something in the very air of the House [of Commons], something indefinable, which daunts me. I think it is the thought that it does not really matter what you say, that it will have no effect on anyone at all, and that you might as well not say it.' In a letter to Tom she had written of 'the horrible dreary list of engagements and meetings at Stoke which seem 10 times worse as I am so absolutely wretched and miserable.' Almost her last public speech was at a Women's Peace Conference in June: she said 'There is only one way that people could stop war – by refusing to fight'. Harold Nicolson remarked 'Poor Cimmie cannot understand his [Tom's] repudiation of all the things he has taught her to say previously. She was not made for politics. She was made for society and the home.'

At the time of the split in the New Party John Strachey had written to Cimmie – 'To think of the inevitable separation from you is to me *by far* the worst part'. Some months later Allan Young wrote 'I want to meet you, and talk, and touch you, and feel everything is all right again'. She seemed to play a rather distant motherly role to people in the New Party. But in private life, too, there seemed to be something in her that was beginning to give up.

At Antibes in 1931 two days after Tom's return to England, Irene recorded – 'Cim drove herself home at 5.30 am and to my horror fell asleep at the wheel and hit the rocks on the hairpin bend mercifully not on the sea side'. In England, Harold Nicolson noted about Tom and Cimmie – 'They bicker as usual . . . she nags at him . . . but they are really fond of each other in spite of their infidelities'.

Cimmie wrote to Tom – 'I won't repeat any of the things I have said scores and scores of times – please remember them yourself – and I on my part will do everything I can try and think of your point of view . . . I am tired of talking. All I want is something doing, something happening.'

This was about Tom's private affairs. In public life, what Cimmie was at the moment objecting to was Tom's involvement with fascism. In December Lord Rothermere, owner of the *Daily Mail*, approached Tom and said that he was prepared to put the Harmsworth press at Tom's disposal if he, Tom, succeeded in organising a disciplined movement from the remnants of the New Party. Harold Nicolson recorded – 'Cimmie, who is profoundly working-class at heart, does not at all like this Harmsworth connection. Tom pretends he was only pulling her leg. Cimmie wants to put a notice in the *Times* to the effect that she disassociates herself from Tom's fascist tendencies. We pass it off as a joke.' Also – when Tom and Harold Nicolson were talking of the approaches made by Winston Churchill and Harold Nicolson had suggested that Tom was 'destined to lead the Tory Party' – Cimmie 'who is violently anti-Tory, screams loudly'.

Cimmie was by this time five months pregnant. She had not stood again for Stoke in the general election partly out of disenchantment with politics but mainly out of fear of another miscarriage. She was not well: she was having trouble with her kidneys. But she went out a lot with Tom to parties during that autumn. They were both now out of Parliament, and there was not much else for them to do. In this area, she could still try to keep up with Tom.

She talked to Harold Nicolson about Tom – 'about his incurable boyishness and *joie de vivre*. She welcomes his fencing as it serves as a safety valve for his physical energy. That in fact is what is wrong with Tom: his energy is more physical than mental.'

Cimmie also told Harold Nicolson that as a result of the Leiter Estate lawsuit which had gone against the Curzon and Suffolk branches of the family in America, and the huge expenses incurred by the New Party, she and Tom were now 'broke'. 'Tom has lost all his money and there are huge overdrafts': they had to live now 'at a rate of £1,000 a year.' During 1932 both Savehay Farm and the house at Smith Square were let; Cimmie and the children went to live in a mews flat behind Tom's flat at Ebury Street, which had previously been occupied by their chauffeur. Reports of their losses, however, were exaggerated.

Tom had taken up fencing again: this was indeed a means of exercising his exuberant energy. It was also probably an excuse, now the House of Commons was not available to him, to be away from home at all hours practising. At fencing he very quickly again became amazingly good. In 1932, at the age of thirty five, and with his injured leg, he was runner-up in the British épée championships. While in training for this he wrote to Cimmie:

Tiger Boy! Clever lad!
Army List team turned out with Epée won 2 matches drew one double hit. They asked fight foil after not having one in hand for six months. Among those he defeated 5pts to 2 Army champion and 4th in last world's championship.
Won 2 matches with foil and lost one.
Result 6 matches – won 4 lost 1 drew 1.
Proud Porker. [drawing of a pig with its tail up]
Hope after her meeting not [drawing of a downcast sheep].

Cimmie seemed to become more at ease with Tom as she advanced with her pregnancy. She had been told to rest, and she stayed at home, or sometimes went with Tom to parties. There was a fashionable craze that winter for watching all-in wrestling at the Gargoyle Club. She did not involve herself in Tom's preparations for fascism.

Harold Nicolson spelt out to Tom the dangers of fascism with a calm, warning voice like that of Bob Boothby the year before.

I beg Tom not to get mixed up with the fascist crowd. I say that fascism is not suitable to England. In Italy there was a long history of secret societies. In Germany there was a long tradition of militarism. Neither had a sense of humour. In England anything on these lines is doomed to failure and ridicule.

He answers that he will concentrate on clubs and cells within clubs; that a new movement cannot be made within the frame of a political party. I beg him to examine himself carefully and to make certain that his feelings are in no sense governed by anger, disappointment or a desire to get back on those who have let him down. I admit that disasters such as he has experienced in last year are sufficient to upset the strongest character, but I contend that the strength of his own character is to be tested by the patience and balance with which he takes the present eclipse. He says he feels no resentment: that he had expected that the effect of his defeat would be to throw him into a life of pleasure: on the contrary, he feels now bored with night clubs and more interested than ever in serious things. I say that he must now obtain a reputation for seriousness at any cost.

Before 1931 Tom does not seem to have thought much about fascism: he had been outspoken against Mussolini at the time of the invasion of Corfu: he had been in the neighbourhood of an English yacht in Venice which had been blown up by some 'festive young blackshirts'. But by 1932 Mussolini was emerging not only as someone who was giving the word 'fascism' a recognisable meaning, but as the leader of a nationalist revival about some aspects of which it was difficult for even the most sceptical politicians not to be admiring.

In the last number of *Action* it had been announced that Tom and other members of the New Party were going to visit Italy and Germany and 'probably at a later date Russia' to 'study the modern movement in all countries'. By modern movement was meant – 'new political forces born of crisis, conducted by youth and inspired by completely new ideas of economic and political organisation'. In January 1932 Tom set off for Rome: he left Cimmie behind staying with friends in the country and guarding her pregnancy. On his way he stopped off in Paris where he 'spent *reveillon* at the Fabre-Luces' and was 'kept up doing *jeux de société* till 8 am.' (Harold Nicolson). Concerning this, Tom wrote to Cimmie:

> Last night was just her party: wished she was trumpeting her instruction for the games and attendant swains . . . Much dancing in the dark: young Tommy coyly against the wall of course. Then a lovely romp at supper with little puff balls iced in champagne buckets and thrust down ladies' backs (in his mind's ear he could hear her bellows indignant if she had suffered!) Perhaps he better confess that he invented this game, which went with a real swing!

In Rome he was joined by Harold Nicolson and Christopher Hobhouse, a young recruit to the New Party. Tom and Cimmie continued to correspond while he was in Rome. In the background to their letters is the struggle between Tom's interest in fascism (what he called 'fascio') and Cimmie's continuing wariness about it (what he called 'fatio'). In the foreground is what Cimmie had called his increasing 'boyishness'.

January 6th 1932.

Darling Baby Squasher,
   Completed 2 days in Rome and what days – yesterday dark and gloomy – today radiant sunshine – lay nudo in his room – flooding in – real sun bath – so wished she was here – nose squashed sideways – turtle on a rock – feel much better after sun.

Royally received and ushered into palatial apartments – thought at first was spontaneous tribute by regime to the British hopeful – learnt later that Quag [Quaglino] of London had written to Quag in Rome saying tiny T was a swell guy who always paid up – rather dashed.

In things that would interest you (roar!!) saw Jane [Princess Jane di San Faustino] last night – same as ever – same people – in same positions – backgammon substituted for bridge . . . Jane addressed me as 'beautiful boy' which delighted me (a great Italian doctor next to me at lunch refused to believe I had been in the war and said I could not be more than 25) perfect country! Lunch tomorrow with Jane and a Hesse Prince who was there last night – said he was on Hitler's staff . . .

Saw today the newly appointed secretary of the Party – they are arranging for us a resumé of the whole story and methods (trumpet crash!) Poor Tomby is so nervous – everywhere he goes hands go up; but as his tiny paw creeps upward in return he hears in his mind's ear [drawing of an ear] an indignant trumpet which pulls it down again – roar roar. I am seeing everyone and very interested – no panache or mum-indignant – but quiet interest. They all know about us. Except in Jane's drawing room, where I was asked if I was still Bolshevik!!

Thursday we go to the Pontine marshes to see the great reclamation scheme. When I asked why they did not publish their doings like the Russians they said 'We are more interested in achievement than in propaganda.' *One for squashland.* Another on the squasher – The Russians last year took 100 to 150,000 children to holiday camps – the Fascists 250,000. Roads rebuilt, land reclaimed, systems of child welfare and youth training – wa wa wa – (piling it on a bit, but a good show!!)

When Fatio and Fascio resume the stout debate he will be better armed. The most interesting thing is the new psychology – 'Opposition? we do not understand! we believe in "solidarita!" Political career is then not only career in one's profession' etc. There are some trumpety reasons, but on the whole with stout prejudice she would yet be interested.

I am thinking of slipping up to Milan for fencing for a day or 2 and then back when Nach returns – unfortunately he goes tonight – I watched him training the Olympic foilists and sabreurs tonight – he is marvellous – I fight with them tomorrow – the épéeists are all at Milan. If I come back here to work with Nach I will go straight to Berlin on 21st via Munich (another little interruption trumpet

trumpet suspicious eye). We really learning a tremendous amount, and will be equipped more on return. [drawing of an outraged bird or turtle].

After Cimmie had got Tom's letter about the Fabre-Luces' party in Paris, she had written:

Darling old boy you are a scream –

I do wonder how Rome is going. Longing to hear that. Remember Fatio a bit, and not too Fascio. And do find out about 'the workers' and their conditions and what about wives and children.

Precious mutty you are the only one in the world for me. Bless you and bless you and love and love and love and happiness in abundance and fun and for old Mummy that soon too . . .

On 8th January Tom wrote from Rome:

Sweet Fatio [drawing of figure with arm raised in the fascist salute] Such a fascinating day. Started early to see great reclamation scheme in Pontine marshes where first time since days of Rome the Pontine waters rush to the sea (Hola Fatio!) escorted by Gelasio Gaetani younger brother of Sermoneta – qualified and worked in America as mining engineer – best type of aristo Fascist – great charmer – would undoubtedly be listed – accompanied by old McClure, G. Jebb, Murray of Embassy, Harold and Hobhouse – had lunch at one of Gaetani's houses – ruined town of Ninpha reclaimed after 5 centuries – 13th century castle of honey-coloured stone where a pope was crowned – complete ruined city of the middle ages – limpid stream with 9lb trout of type imported by Romans from Africa – lunch in castle – wonderful cakes and honey – saw reclamation scheme – fascinating country – buffaloes imported by Hannibal [drawing of a buffalo]: if they had been a little more bellowsome, would have made him quite homesick.

Gaetanis originally owned nearly all land from Rome to Naples and 200 castles – now going in with State in great consortium – the powers of the State are enormous – corporative system interferes immediately with inefficient ownership and management. Everywhere en route *Dopolavoro*, the state assisted club houses of the workers after work (come on fatio, just a sideline that).

Harold who was originally a little shaken by 'Solidarita' is visibly more and more impressed by constructive elements. Young Tom of course maintains a balanced view –

Hurried back just in time for an interview with Mussolini – who was charming and asked a lot of very good questions. He speaks English well. Tomorrow interview minister of Corporatives and later in day fence with crack Italians of Olympic sabre team. Yesterday fought one of the Olympic épéeists and was not at all overwhelmed. May go up to Milan for a day or two as the Olympic épée team train there.

Yesterday lunched with Jane and Prince Philip of Hesse (married Princess Matilda of Italy) was intelligent and is a great Hitler man . . .

Rome very dead – backgammon and gambling – nothing else – we have no frivolity – work and read the whole time – all very interesting – WISHES HIS SQUASH WAS HERE – . . . They all miss her and send love and happy sniffs XXXX.

Cimmie wrote from Sussex:

Darling Mutty boy,

You really are sweet the lovely letts you write me and I can promise you I simply adore them and look forward to them ever so. The first Rome one arrived this morning and cheered me up no end as I was feeling low-ish – very sick and faint – slightly coldy – and these cursed signs again . . .

I had a long letter from Peter [Howard] from Birmingham and he said there was a good nucleus of keen serious young men to form a Youth Section . . .

Do stay as long as you want my sweet, I am quite hap-chap and will have lots of people to see me in London and still one or 2 country visits I can arrange . . .

Not on the warpath, loving him velly much, full of resolutions which she does hope will stand his return!! and weather 1932 triumphantly . . .

One of the joys of getting Tom's letters, Cimmie added, was that although he took immense pains to write clearly she had to 'read each page again and again before I get it all quite clear and even then there are some words I never get at all!' She did not think 'old Fascio' [Mussolini] sounded too bad: but she still worried about the 'WORKERS'. Tom said – 'All the great men here look like undergraduates – they are so young and mostly listable'. 'Listable' meant they might go on Cimmie's 'list' of attractive men.

Christopher Hobhouse had come to Rome from Munich where he had talked with Nazis: this was a year before Hitler came to power. Hobhouse reported 'The Nazis think that we of the New Party have tried to do things too much on the grand: we should have begun in the alleys, not in Gordon Square.' Also – 'They think the fact that Tom is not a working class man will be a disadvantage to us.' Christopher Hobhouse said he saw the NUPA Youth Movement turning into something like the Nazi SS.

Argument went on in the Hotel Excelsior. Harold Nicolson insisted 'the party should be constitutional and Tom should enter Parliament'. He read fascist propaganda pamphlets: 'I agree that with this system you can attain a certain degree of energy and efficiency not reached in our own island. And yet, and yet . . .'

He and Tom went to dine in 'a lovely flat with a view one way to the Villa Medici and the other way all over Rome' Harold Nicolson wrote in his diary:

Signora Sarfatti is there. She is the friend of Mussolini's whom we met at the Embassy yesterday. A blonde questing woman, the daughter of a Venetian Jew who married a Jew in Milan. It was there that she helped Mussolini on the *Popolo d'Italia* right back in 1914. She is at present his confidante and must be used by him to bring the gossip of Rome to the Villa Torlonia. She says Mussolini is the greatest worker ever known: he rides in the morning, then a little fencing, then work, and then after dinner he plays the violin to himself. Tom asks how much sleep he gets. She answers 'Always nine hours'. I can see Tom doing sums in his head and concluding that on such a time-table Musso cannot be hard-worked at all.

When Tom returned to England the New Party was formally disbanded and his association with Harold Nicolson came to an end. Harold Nicolson wrote 'He is prepared to run the risk of further failure, ridicule and assault, rather than to allow the active forces in this country to fall into other hands.' Also – 'If Tom would follow my example – retire into private life for a bit and then emerge fortified and purged – he will still be Prime Minister of England. But if he gets entangled with the boys' brigade he will be edged gradually into becoming a revolutionary, and into that waste land I cannot follow him.' Harold Nicolson, but not Tom, had been to Berlin after they had left Rome: he had recorded – 'Hitlerism, as a doctrine, is a doctrine of despair.'

This was the last time that Tom was talked about as a probable future Prime Minister. His 'last-chances' in conventional politics had been as numerous as the farewell performances of the most magnificent prima donna; but now this style of things was over. Tom knew he would have to start from the beginning again; building up from cells; parading in the streets. He wanted to do this because old forms of growth seemed degrading to him.

Mussolini sent him two messages from Italy: one was 'not to try the military stunt in England'; the other was to go ahead and call himself fascist. These injunctions seemed somewhat contradictory.

Fascism is a form of activity where what is usually contained in games becomes reality; where what is logic is forced into flesh; where rules are broken and are not replaced. It is a state of mind that does not see that words are different from things; that suggests that what in abstract argument might be desirable can be put into effect with people. Fascism denies that there is anything above decision and justification for decision that can judge their worth; it is a style by which activity seems to be a justification for itself. The drive is towards order: but in so far as there is glimpsed almost from the beginning the fact that orderliness may not be achieved, there are the safeguards of the rhetoric of returning upon one's shield. If the drive to orderliness is towards death, it is still the drive that matters.

There has for the most part evolved in human beings a feeling that however much words are used in justification for drives there is always something slightly different, and more important, at stake: this is a more subtle feeling than that of transcendence: it is a feeling of oneself being part of a whole; of the whole being something other than the sum of the parts of the whole; it is a feeling for the significance of something aesthetic. Fascism denies this sort of aestheticism; it feels no governing shape of the whole. Fascism is an immediacy, a sorting out, a tidying-up; the elimination of some things for the ostensible sake of others. Of course, the whole structure may fall down. The point of aestheticism is that it tells what will not fall down: the shape of the whole is more important than the expansion of some of the parts. With fascism, the feeling of some 'greatness' is an end in itself.

Tom knew that by embracing fascism he was making some move like a gambler staking all his fortune on one number at roulette: that whether he won or lost, he would never get back to the ordinary political game. The luck he required was that the sort of crisis he had envisaged would turn up: but in his acceptance of this he did not behave like a fascist, for he made few moves to try to bend the rules of the game. He took on all the trappings of fascism; he waited for the number, or the crisis, to turn up; but he did not, curiously, try to fix, as it were, the wheel. In this respect he was politically self-defeating; but he stayed alive.

The story of Tom's fascism is the story of the next volume. He was seen by orthodox fascists as a rather unsatisfactory fascist: it was to non-fascists that he sometimes seemed almost the most outlandish fascist of all. For how could someone get all dressed up for fascism and then not quite play the ruthless fascist game? Did not this put someone almost beyond belief?

Fascism is to do with ferment, with war, with the challenge of great events. But Tom was a fascist dedicated to stopping war. When he first became a fascist the established fascists called him a 'kosher fascist'. What was frightening about him was that he seemed to be playing some super-game with himself. He seemed to care not about becoming violent nor even ultimately victorious; but about seeing which way an ideal or a legend might develop.

By the summer of 1932 few people in England were still thinking in terms of the immediate crack-up of the western world. The crisis had come and not of course gone, but was not so much talked about. Newspapers do not bother to report the end of a crisis. It suddenly is boring.

In Tom's private life too things suddenly seemed to be orderly. Cimmie had been ill, but was now ready to have her baby. On April 25th it was born by Caesarian operation – a boy, to be called Michael. Tom was being attentive to Cimmie: on the 11th May, their twelfth wedding anniversary, she wrote to him her most optimistic letter for some time.

> My darling darling – Have a happy time –
> I only want to send you a line at the end of *such* a happy anniversary to say how much I want the next year to be a happy one for us 2 as private people and a successful one for you publicly. How I long for it to be better than beastly 1931 and how much I want above all else for loveliness and understanding and sympathy to be with us and between us . . .

But some time earlier that spring, in his stalk like some knight-errant through the coverts of dinner parties and balls, Tom had come across – as if indeed she were a legendary maiden – a young married girl called

Diana Guinness. Their hostess had told them they would get on well together: they did not in fact get on too well at first (Diana was apt to say at this time 'I'm just an old fashioned liberal'). But then, Diana was a great prize – at the age of twenty-one she had already gained a reputation for intelligence and beauty not only in the fashionable world but in the literary and artistic worlds of London and Paris – and it would not have seemed to Tom, since Diana appeared unique, that it mattered very much if they did not get on well at first.

CHAPTER 22

The Greater Britain

People suggested in later life that Diana might have influenced Tom in his turning to fascism; but there is no evidence for this: Tom was virtually committed to fascism before he met Diana: Diana at twenty-one had not come across fascism and would have had little power to influence Tom if she had. What she did give him however was a chance to exercise his need and talent for risk and conquest: and so perhaps just by her arrival on the scene she created something of the atmosphere as it were of fascism.

Tom's pursuit of Diana was contemporaneous with his work on his book *The Greater Britain* which was to be his public statement about British fascism. The story of himself and Diana ran parallel to what he was trying to do in politics: he was trying to become responsibly committed both to Cimmie and to Diana: he was trying to start a fascist street-movement that would be respectable. It was not his ruthlessness or singlemindedness that made him at this time seem to be doing things that were taboo: it was the way in which he seemed to be both breaking the rules of games and at the same time trying to demonstrate he was keeping them. This seemed to involve a confusion of rules as it were on a higher level.

Diana was the third daughter of Lord and Lady Redesdale: she was a Mitford: the Mitfords were not then the legendary figures they have now become (1982). But Diana was in fact at twenty-one already something of a legend – with her beauty, her cleverness, her ability to seem both conventional and unconventional at the same time. When she was eighteen she had married Bryan Guinness, the eldest son of Walter Guinness, soon to become Lord Moyne. She had gone from her eccentric but somewhat restricted schoolroom straight into a world of freedom and riches: all this has become part of the Mitford legend chronicled

by her sister Nancy, her sister Jessica, by Diana herself. It was conventional of course in the world in which both she and Tom moved for
married men to take out young married girls to lunch and even to
dinner; it was conventional (though this was not spelt out) for them to
have affairs. But the smooth running of all this – as in the world of conventional politics – depended on the participants observing rules – not
even really questioning them. The rules of the social game were to do
with there being no public scandal. There was little chance of scandal
(newspapers kept to the rules in those days and people within the game
did not talk) unless there was a question of divorce. This was the
equivalent of, in politics, gangs taking to the streets.

At first in his pursuit of Diana Tom appeared to be doing no more
than what he had been doing for years: he took her out; he talked; they
went to his flat in Ebury Street. Then in June 1932 the Guinnesses gave
a party in their house at 96 Cheyne Walk to celebrate Diana's twenty-
second birthday. Diana recorded in her autobiography:

> A few things about this party dwell in my memory: myself managing
> to propel Augustus John, rather the worse for wear, out of the house
> and into a taxi: Winston Churchill inveighing against a large picture
> by Stanley Spencer of Cookham War Memorial which hung on the
> staircase and Eddie Marsh defending it against his onslaught. I wore a
> pale grey dress of chiffon and tulle and all the diamonds I could lay
> my hands on. We danced until day broke, a pink and orange sunrise
> which gilded the river.

What also happened at this party was that Tom made some formal
proposal to Diana that their relationship should be of a more committed
kind than could normally be covered by the terms of the game. He told
her that he did not intend to leave Cimmie, but he was in love with her,
Diana. Diana said she was in love too. She also said she wanted to be
committed to him because he had convinced her about the importance
of his ideas for altering the world. What would be the precise nature
of the commitment could be worked out through the rest of the
summer.

There is a home movie in existence of this time taken by Cimmie at
the christening-party of Dick Wyndham's daughter Ingrid to whom
Tom was godfather. There are the usual shots of people posturing, or
performing, in front of a camera – Tom coming down a staircase and
pausing with a hand on his heart; Dick Wyndham shaking a bottle of
champagne so violently that it foams like a fire extinguisher. Then the

camera moves to, and rests on, Diana: she is smiling and quite still; like some statue come across in a jungle.

There had always been something awkward, enthusiastic, school-girlish about Cimmie. She had grown rather fat and heavy: she seemed not to take much trouble now about her clothes or her appearance. People remember her at this time still with the exuberance that could light people up when she came into a room. But she was perhaps no longer elegant.

Diana wrote of this time that her life had seemed 'absolutely useless and empty' before she met Tom. Her great friends Lytton Strachey and Dora Carrington had just died. She had enjoyed her brief reign as one of the princesses of the smart social world: she had had two children, Jonathan and Desmond, within two years. But she wanted something more. When Tom came along he was not only 'handsome, generous, intelligent and full of a wondrous gaiety' but also 'completely sure of himself and his ideas: he knew what to do to solve the economic disaster we were living through'.

Tom and Diana made plans about what they should do in the summer holidays. Diana was going to motor down through France with friends; Tom and Cimmie were due to go this year to Venice. Cimmie was still not well enough to travel by car: it was agreed that Tom should drive, and Cimmie should follow by train with the children. Tom made a plan with Diana to run into her as if by chance at Arles or Avignon.

Cimmie does not seem to have realised yet that there was anything out of the ordinary about Diana. Tom had always gone after the socially most glamorous women: two years ago he had seriously upset her with Paula Casa Maury. But she had learned to believe he would always come back to her; probably to trust that what he said about the triviality of his affairs was true. Also now he was being particularly attentive to her. As late as August 3rd Cimmie was telling Irene that Tom 'had been exquisite to her since the baby and she had not been so happy for years'. But it is an ironic fact that when people are in love they are apt to make happy for a time the other people around them.

At Avignon Diana became ill suddenly with diphtheria and had to go to bed in a hotel. A doctor from the Institut Pasteur came and gave her 'enormous injections'. She was frightened lest a letter from Tom might arrive at the hotel desk and have to be opened. She got her friends Barbara Hutchinson and Victor Rothschild enrolled in the plot and a message was got through to Tom. New arrangements were made that they should all meet in Venice when Diana got well. Tom got Diana's message in Arles. He drove to Cannes, where he wrote to Cimmie:

His own darling soft-nosed wag-tail

. . . Rather slacked up last two days. From Lyons Thursday went to Valence – tremendous lunch – bottle of beautiful Rosé – afterwards began to write you very witty letter but remembering both you and Lady D W [Lady de la Warre with whom Cimmie was staying in England] were a little literal minded tore it up, in case produced as evidence of insanity. Waddled on via Avignon to Arles – 'Tomby you stand where Caesar stood: twenty centuries gaze down on you and acclaim you'. [drawing of man doing fascist salute and saying 'wee wee'.] . . . Got to Cannes 6 pm . . . quickly landed by Lotsy and a merry thing who pressed him to come to a grand gala at Monte Carlo: he *refused* and had vegetable soup *alone* in *room*. Since striking attitudes on moonlit balcony alternating between Missolonghi and St Helena – very spacious apartment – asked very diffidently price – they said loftily they would make him a special arrangement – must be distinction of his appearance – always given much better rooms when she isn't there (I feel my indignation rising within me, better stop). THIS IS ALL A JOKE. Lots of love my sweet fellow misses her so much. Love to all [drawing of four pigs of decreasing size].

From England Cimmie replied –

My sweet darling heart. Does wish you hadn't torn up that witty lett, not *soooo* literal minded as all that, still absolutely loved the one she did get. I am sitting in the sun and the gram is playing 'Goodnight Sweetheart' which reminds me irresistibly of Lotsy and last year oh dear oh dear I wonder if she's keeping you up all night, still really I don't think I mind, as I do love you so and am pretty happy and serene about you loving me at the moment, it makes me more happy than anything in the world . . .

You know, given good weather England now is a knockout – the lushness, the quiet, the colour . . . I'm not sure we shouldn't try a summer or just a fortnight in Aug at Savehay once. There is some-thing southern climates utterly lack; it's much softer and the birds sing. I really don't envy the hurry and bustle of the Croisette one bit and even the Excelsior seems garish and ugly when I think of it. I'd like to have you and the children in a quiet place where it's green and peaceful sometime . . .

Darling Darling Darling You are my heart's delight . . . I don't know why I love you like I do, I don't know why but I do. I do I do I do I do I do I do I do.

Love and kisses from the Porkers united and loving Wag Tail. I really am looking forward to Venice terribly. Let's have a beautiful time. 'I want to be featured by you' – words for new song by one of Tomki's girls!!

A week or two later, on the Lido at Venice, where Tom and Cimmie were staying, and the Guinnesses, and many of their mutual friends, for the first time what Tom and Diana felt about each other became apparent. They would go sightseeing in a group round the town; then they would disappear round corners, down alleyways, and would not be seen between lunch and dinner. Diana in her autobiography remembered this summer as one in which 'our countrymen were not on their best behaviour: at one party, a picnic on Torcello, there was a fight': at another Randolph Churchill called Brendan Bracken 'my brother' and there would have been another fight if Randolph Churchill had not 'snatched off' Brendan Bracken's spectacles and thrown them into the sea. Bob Boothby remembered a dinner party on the Lido at which all *dramatis personae* were present: Tom leaned across the table and said 'Bob, I shall need your room tonight between midnight and 4 am'. Bob Boothby said 'But Tom, where shall I sleep?' Tom said 'On the beach'. Bob Boothby, recalling this story fifty years later, added with a great smile – 'And I did!'

Cimmie's children did not notice anything very unusual going on: were not grown-ups always jumping about and exclaiming and shouting? During this holiday Vivien and I were nominally under the care of Cimmie's lady's maid, Andrée: Nanny had stayed behind with Michael. An incident that stuck in our minds was when Randolph Churchill, on the beach, referred to us as 'the brats': nothing else seems to have pierced us so much during a fortnight in Venice.

During the summer, and concurrent with his pursuit of Diana, Tom had been engaged in writing *The Greater Britain* – a 40,000 word book in which he sorted out for himself, and presented to the public, his ideas about the nature of British fascism. In the second half of the book there were recommendations for Britain's economic recovery which were not different from those which he had put forward in his New Party and Labour days – the necessity for centrally controlled economic planning within a protected home-and-imperial market. But the important part of the book was its first forty pages, in which Tom outlined what he saw as the attitude and spirit of fascism.

The argument of *The Greater Britain* was that the crisis facing the world was of a more fundamental kind than that talked about in the terms of the current economic breakdown. The inventions of science and the products of modern technology had created a new type of world during the last hundred years: yet the political institutions to deal with it had scarcely changed at all. The machinery of life was once such that it could be handled by a leisurely system of balances: now complexities and pressures and the possibilities of destruction were so great, that mankind had to fashion stronger and tighter methods of control or else there would be catastrophe.

The problem was how to organise for this control while allowing for freedom: 'to harmonise individual initiative with the wider interest of the nation.' There was not much difficulty in doing this with words. The word 'fascist', Tom said, implied 'a high conception of citizenship': it 'recognises the necessity for the authoritative state' in which 'there is no room for interests which are not the State's interests'. But somehow at the same time 'wise laws' would allow human activity 'full play'. The desire of men 'to work for themselves' would be guided into 'channels which serve the nation's ends'.

In practical terms – '*Government must have power to legislate by Order subject to the power of Parliament to dismiss it by vote of censure*' (the italics are in the original). Fascism 'seeks to achieve its aim legally and constitutionally by methods of law and order, *but in objective it is revolutionary or it is nothing*'. So long as the power of an elected Parliament to dismiss a Government was retained, then 'the charge of Dictatorship has no reality'.

The naiveties of *The Greater Britain* were deliberate: the paradoxes concerning the use and abuse of power were commonplace: it was from their recognition that had grown the delicate system of democratic checks and balances. But it was specifically these that fascism was now claiming were dangerously out of date: fascism stated the paradoxes, and then ignored them. It said that there just *will* be freedom for individual energies within complete state control. It was using words in such a way that the things they referred to seemed equally malleable – and thus words became almost meaningless.

Fascism 'combines the dynamic urge to change and progress with the authority, the discipline and the order without which nothing great can be achieved'. The word which cuts through the paradoxes is 'greatness': it is in following this device held aloft like a sword that questions of individual freedom, of state authority fall away. 'Our hope is centred in vital and determined youth, dedicated to the resurrection of a nation's greatness and shrinking from no effort and from no sacrifice to secure that mighty end.' 'In every town and village, in every institution of daily

life, the will of the organised and determined minority must be struggling for sustained effort.' Every now and then it is as if Tom remembered he must recognise he was dealing with paradoxes: 'Voluntary
discipline is the essence of the Modern Movement': 'the beginning of
liberty is the end of economic chaos': even – 'in a superficial paradox,
it will be necessary for a modern movement which does not believe in
Parliament as at present constituted to seek to capture Parliament'. But
then the tone of voice goes back to that of the warrior who has broken
through; who when he finds one side of a paradox being obstructive,
throws it away.

Into the measured prose of *The Greater Britain* there comes from time
to time – like fighting breaking out in the hall of a political meeting –
the rhetoric of contempt. The favourite words of scorn are 'children'
and 'old women'. Politicians of the old parties are 'like children in the
dark . . . [they] put their heads under the bedclothes rather than get up
like men and grapple with the danger'. Orthodox economics are the
remedy of the 'eternal old woman'. One of the most scathing words is
'Spain' – 'alive in a sense, but dead to all sense of greatness and to her
mission in the world'. (This is odd in the light of the fact that it was Spain
that was shortly to provide the one and only relatively successful fascist
government.) Another contemptuous phrase for conventional politicians was 'united muttons' – odd, again, in the light of the fact that
'mutton' was one of his favourite words for Cimmie.

As well as the words there were the promises of activities attendant
on contempt. 'So soon as anybody, whether an individual or an organised
interest, steps outside those limits [of the national interest] so that his
activity becomes sectional and anti-social, the mechanism of the
Corporate system descends upon him . . . The State has no room for the
drone and the decadent, who use their leisure to destroy their capacity
for public usefulness. In our morality it is necessary to "live like
athletes".'

In the last pages of the book, which return to the themes of the
beginning in the style of one of Tom's perorations, his struggle to try
to appear once more reasonably to embrace paradoxes results in his
language becoming almost openly without content: 'We appeal to our
countrymen to take action while there is still time and to carry the
changes which are necessary by the legal and constitutional methods
which are available. If on the other hand every appeal to reason is futile
in the future, as it has been in the immediate past, and the Empire is
allowed to drift until collapse and anarchy supervene, we shall not shrink
from that final conclusion, and will organise to stand between the State

and ruin ... In no case shall we resort to violence against the forces of the crown but only against the forces of anarchy if and when the machinery of state has been allowed to drift into powerlessness.'

What would have given such a statement meaning was, of course, a consideration of who was to be the arbiter of when such a moment of decision had come, and what would be the extent of the moves to deal with the crisis. It was Tom's total ignoring of such questions (or the assumption that of course the arbiter of everything would be himself) that rendered the reasonableness of much of his argument irrelevant.

In the eyes of most people in 1932 the worst of the economic crisis had already gone; it was only Tom, and his incipient band of dedicated followers, who were insisting that it was still coming. But whoever might, or might not, be proved right by history, to ignore questions about how the crisis would be judged was not just to trivialise the discussion but to make the whole form of it suspect. Tom made no secret of the fact that his whole movement was a preparation for (and in fact depended on) crisis: 'in a crisis the British are at their best: when the necessity for action is not clear they are at their worst ... a complete breakdown would be a stronger incentive to action than the movement, however cumbrous, of a crippled machine.' After breakdown it might be true that 'in the highly technical struggle for the modern state in crisis only the technical organisations of Fascism or Communism have ever prevailed, or, in the nature of things, can prevail'. But then, people might reasonably ask – might not Tom, with his 'organised and deter- mined minority', if the crisis he insisted he foresaw did not in a time that suited him materialise, be tempted reasonably (since it would come anyway) to spur on the crisis himself? The irony of Tom's political career was that he deliberately put himself into a position in which reasonable men could hardly fail to ask such a question and be alarmed at the lack of a coherent answer: while Tom himself, without giving the question any publicity or apparently even much thought, probably gave to himself an answer that reasonable men might not have had all that much cause to fear.

What Tom did publicly go on stressing was 'the ferocity of struggle and danger' and the fact that the inevitable catastrophe would only be able to be dealt with by 'new men who come from nowhere'. It was only after these ferocious men had sorted out the crisis that once more (this was one of the paradoxes Tom most naively cut through and just left) 'rational discussion of the world's economic problems would super- vene'.

Throughout *The Greater Britain* there is not one reference to Jews. In

Hitler's *Mein Kampf,* written ten years previously, it is explicit that Jews are the enemy. In *The Greater Britain* the enemy is decadence. This decadence is in society; in oneself.

There is a curious impression as one reads *The Greater Britain* that the problems it presents are philosophical and psychological and have not much to do with practical politics. In politics anyone can have high-sounding ideals: anyone can slice with words through paradoxes about authority and freedom. Practicalities depend on responses to events: upon the style in which is discovered what is not possible and is practised what is. The appeal of fascism was to a 'greatness' that would march through human affairs like a column of ants: but this has not much to do with what human beings are actually like; it is to do with a longing of the psyche. Once the idea of 'greatness' is projected outside as a way of cutting through paradoxes then there is in fact no control of them but rather a helplessness – a runaway situation towards death. There is no 'greater' challenge that a man can pit himself against than one with the likelihood of death: this is a way in which life can in fact be cut through.

A way in which it might conceivably have struck Tom and those closest to him that what was being talked about were paradoxes concerning themselves was Tom's curious insistence on the need to eschew and even destroy everything 'decadent' and to 'live like athletes'. For years Tom and Cimmie had enjoyed during their leisure moments the company of people who in any normal understanding of words 'use their leisure moments to destroy their capacity for public usefulness'. Tom had perhaps reasonably justified himself in this – on the grounds that it was necessary for personal equilibrium that portentous human attitudes should be balanced by some such relaxations at the other end of the scale. But then why did not he, or those closest to him, see that such balances or at least tolerances might be necessary for the equilibrium of society – and that there was a likelihood of disaster if they were treated with contempt? Diana might have seen this: before she had met Tom she had been involved in some of the more bizarre incidents of the 'decadent' age: she and her brother had put on an exhibition of paintings by Brian Howard said to be by a German artist called 'Bruno Hat' and critics had enjoyed the joke: Evelyn Waugh's *Vile Bodies* was dedicated to Bryan and Diana Guinness. Throughout her life Diana has always seemed personally to embody a balance between the passionately serious and an enjoyment of the absurd. But she, at the time, seemed to insist on some simple commitment: it seemed not to be fashionable anywhere to think about balances in politics.

The result of this sort of failure – to see that all life depends on balances; that a definition of life is in fact that which has feed-back and response; that the simplicity, the drive to the doing away of balances, results in a runaway situation towards death – the result of this sort of failure is that it can affect the mind and heart as well as the outside world. Cimmie was the person who now suffered; who perhaps wanted at last to get out of the whole arena; who had her dreams of being with Tom and the children 'in a quiet place where it's green and peaceful sometime'. She was not getting well after the birth of her baby Michael; she was still suffering from her kidney disease and she had pains in her back. Then there had been the holiday in Venice when she had discovered the seriousness of the threat of Diana and had cried much of the time. In September she went to a spa called Contrexeville in eastern France. She was trying to get her health back. She took with her her two older children.

CHAPTER 23

The British Union of Fascists

Contrexeville is a place I remember quite well, perhaps because it was one of the few times Vivien and I were on our own with our mother – in the sense of there being no other grown-ups around by whom her attention would inevitably be taken away. In practical matters (we were aged eleven and nine) we were still 'looked after' by our mother's lady's maid Andrée. We were in a big hotel called Hotel des Etablissements, which was next door to a building called the Pump Room, where people drank water out of little metal mugs. After doing this they would walk about, or sit down, until it was time to go back to the hotel or to have another drink of water. There was a park where children went round and round on paths between flowerbeds on bicycles. Our mother would sit in a wicker chair with a writing pad on her knee and write to Tom, who was in London.

> My dear darling,
>   I wonder what your plans are. I am afraid this place would bore you unbelievably, it is just BOREDOM personified – bourgeouis dreary self-satisfied – mediocre hotel, fairly good cooking, hideous revolting people, nothing to do. I drink a glass of water from 8 am every 25 mins for 2 hours, then am massaged for an hour, then go across the way and have Diatherm treatment then ionisation – then am finished except for more and more water and a diet.
>   In the pm we go out in the car – lovely country road. Today went to Domremy where Joan of Arc was born. I have no breakfast, no tea, lunch at 12.15, dinner 7.30. It is now 9, and after this letter I shall go to bed. There is a Casino but I have not been in, and a Cinny. I hope it really will do me good, and I will come home well and hearty . . .

Cimmie in these letters makes few references to her children. She makes no direct reference to what Tom might be doing in London. It was as if she were going more and more into her private world in which nothing much mattered except the dream in which she and Tom would somehow, some day, be all right together. It was this that signified to her the recovery from her illness.

> I really feel we will have a good winter – you building up your organisation, coping with the sales of your book, having a happy time *with* your family – and some stolen moments with lovely sillies but not *too* many – mum seeing to household, coping with children, getting together nice intelligent Circle, arranging *fun* – does it seem a nice proposition. I hope so.

Children find it difficult to be aware of their parents' sicknesses: parents are like the natural course of events: what happens when a course of events gets out of joint? I remember getting on badly with my sister at this time: we had ferocious fights: after one which went up and down the corridors of the huge hotel like one of our father's street-fights my mother came out of her room and admonished both of us equally. I was outraged at this: I thought I was in the right: but anyway, where was justice in a world that did not even enquire into rights? I rushed into our bedroom and I locked myself in the lavatory. I thought I would stay there until I died; then the grown-ups would be sorry. My mother and sister did come to the door from time to time and ask me to come out: they even pushed food under the door for me: I pushed this back. It seemed that I was in there for a vast stretch of time: I suppose in fact it was no more than most of a day. I became aware after a time that although I seemed to be winning there was in fact no such thing as winning: I would lose face if I came out but if I stayed in I would die: this might be some sort of victory, but I would not be there to see it. This perhaps is a common romantic predicament. Eventually I emerged tentatively at night and my mother appeared at the bedroom door and held out her arms to me and I ran into them and cried. I remember this well: it is almost the only time I remember my mother holding me.

Tom wrote to Cimmie from London:

> His own darling soft-nosed wag-tail
> Glad to hear that Flexyville is not so bad – working very hard – organising sale of book and many statements on current politics etc.

Fencing every night and morning at RAC – seeing no one – practically! Might turn up at Flexyville at any time but do not wait as in a great turmoil. Rather enjoying it all. Directly I am satisfied organisation can run without me will go off on another trip. Forgot to tell you – an idea that B. Bracken (listed CM) and I should meet Winston and Lindemann on Como. Lots of love and happy squashes. [drawing of a gondola; then of a pig with its nose against a wheel]. Back at the grindstone – far, far away from Venice *pleasure* and *temptations*.

One of the expeditions that Cimmie took the children on was to the trenches and dug-outs of the first world war which had been preserved near Verdun. We were taken round the sand-bagged passages like sewers and the holes in the ground like those of rats: these were the memorials of man's urges to get rid of himself. We were aware that our father had been somewhere near here some sixteen years ago: that he cared passionately that there should be no more war. He was in London, we understood, doing something about an organisation which would prevent war; which would appeal to reason over the heads of mad politicians.

At times Cimmie seemed to be dealing with her own predicaments quite well. She wrote:

Bless you my darling right deep down I *have* confidence, my most secret soul knows we are all right, I love you and you love me till Death do us part; but various surface selves need encouraging now and then, need a little bolstering up, want a little public demonstration, want to show off a bit, and it is that part that gets hurt and upset. All the sweetness in the world isn't quite the same as a demonstration of affection and choice in public and my bowels yearn for the latter as well as appreciating the former.

Shan't expect you here more than 1 or at most 2 nights, would *love* that, but *at pinch* would understand none at all. Remember always how I love you.

But then again – as if she were indeed under some attack in war, or plagued by the illness she had come to Contrexeville to cure – the other part of her would come out on top.

My heart is not yet quite right about you, it hurts when I think of you, it misses you dreadfully, and is as jealous as hell. All the time I try to reason with it, with my head. Theories could hardly be improved on: practice not so good I fear. Still, Tom, doing some thinking and philosophising – how much it will stand any strain of events remains to be seen ... I hug you. I love you. What am I? I forget. Is it your soft-nosed squash-tail?

There are medical reports on what was wrong with Cimmie at the time it was decided she should go to Contrexeville: they were written in July 1932, just before the summer holiday in Venice.

Very briefly the history is that she had spinal curvature from child-hood and in recent years this has been getting worse. Has had six attacks of lumbago in her life. For the past two years she has been stiff in the back.

In September last she fell out of a wagon loft and soon after had acute pyelitis with high temperature etc. The exact date of onset of the increase in the back is indefinite, but the pain definitely became worse at her last pregnancy, so that she even had to have morphia to relieve it. She was in bed three months in all. She was better after the child was born but the pain increased again as soon as she got up and she is now unable to take any form of active exercise ... Sneezing is agony. For history of kidney infection see (enclosed) note.

Lady Cynthia Mosley has a bacillus coli infection of her urinary tract which appears to date from Sept 1931 ... On several occasions the question of terminating the pregnancy arose. Since the Caesarian section the kidney has settled down; the urine still contains colon bacilli ...

It was to get rid of these, ostensibly, that she had come to Contrexeville. After a fortnight a report read 'Colon bacilli nearly disappeared'.

Tom announced his intention of coming out. 'Here is the plan of squash world – say if it is not porker – he will cross Saturday 10th, stay night in Paris, and come on to Flexyville next day. Porkers united!' There is a photograph of Tom at Contrexeville standing by his Bentley, and looking rather sad.

In London, he had been seeing to the publication of *The Greater Britain* which was to be put out by his own publishing company and was to coincide with the launching of the British Union of Fascists in October. Representatives were sent out all over the country with the book: this was to provide information for the cells of the 'organised and determined minority'.

The story of the British Union of Fascists will be told in the next volume: but the beginnings of it belong here, because they overlap with the story of Cimmie's life and death. Harold Nicolson had recorded in April that Tom did not want 'to allow the active forces of this country to fall into other hands': it was because of this he was prepared to 'run the risk of further failure, ridicule and assault'. By 'active forces' was meant, presumably, the fascist-type bodies already in existence.

The two main home-grown fascist groups were – the British Fascists, founded by Miss Lintorn Orman who (it was often explained) was the grand-daughter of a Field Marshal, and to whom in 1923 the idea of saving the country from communism had come while she was weeding her kitchen garden; and the Imperial Fascist League, founded by Arnold Leese, who had been a vet specialising in the diseases of camels and whose anti-semitism had arisen (so the story went) from his objection to kosher methods of slaughtering animals. Throughout the nineteen-twenties there had been numerous schisms and splinter-groups from these bodies: for a time Brigadier Blakeney, previously an administrator of the Egyptian State Railways, took over the British Fascists; then he joined Arnold Leese, and both of them disassociated themselves from Italian fascism on the grounds that it was too favourable to Jews. There were splinter-groups called the British Empire Fascists, the Fascist League, the Fascist Movement, the National Fascisti, and the British National Fascists: it seemed that the number of bodies was limited only by the availability of names. None of the groups had much of a policy: they felt they existed to protect old fashioned virtues to do with patriotism and law and order against the world-wide conspiracies of people like Communists and Jews. They marched to and fro, and cared about uniforms and flags and badges.

When Tom came along and proposed a merger of all these groups into the British Union of Fascists he was objected to violently by Arnold Leese on the grounds that he was being manipulated by Jews – to divert attention from Leese's true anti-semitism. And in fact in March 1933 the *Jewish Chronicle* declared – 'The Mosley Fascists themselves are our best supporters in the fight against The Imperial Fascists League.' It was the latter who called the British Union 'Kosher Fascists'; and claimed that Cimmie was Jewish. In a fight between Mosley fascists and Leese's Imperial Fascist Guard in 1933 Leese was beaten up and Brigadier Blakeney got a black eye: this was the only fight, Tom said later, in which his stewards got out of control. At the time he was soon claiming that the only fascists left outside his organisation were 'three old ladies

and a couple of office boys'. But then – what kind of people were the
fascists within his organisation?

It is easy to write slightly mockingly about early fascists: such an
attitude is in reaction to Tom's own idealistic claim that he was dis-
covering a 'new' type of man. They were mostly sincere idealists. The
British Union of Fascists officially came into existence on October 1st
1932 when there was a flag-unfurling ceremony in the old New Party
offices in Great George Street. Tom said 'We ask those who join us . . .
to be prepared to sacrifice all, but to do so for no small and unworthy
ends. We ask them to dedicate their lives to building in the country a
movement of the modern age . . . In return we can only offer them the
deep belief that they are fighting that a great land may live.' But the
question of interest, as usual, was how successful Tom would be in
putting his fine sentiments into effect.

The first public meeting of the BUF was on October 15th in Trafalgar
Square. There was not much of a crowd. Photographs show Tom
making his speech on the plinth at the bottom of the column: he is
wearing a dark suit and tie and a white shirt: eight men with black shirts
and grey flannel trousers are around him. Newspapers reported that
Cimmie and her two older children were there. I have no memory of
this.

A week or so later there was an indoor meeting in the Memorial Hall
at Farringdon Street in the City. Here Tom, answering rather obstreperous questions from a group in the gallery, referred to 'three
warriors of class war all from Jerusalem'. Fighting broke out: two of the
questioners were ejected. Afterwards Tom was reported by *The Times*
as saying 'Fascist hostility to Jews was directed against those who
financed communists or who were pursuing an anti-British policy.' This
was the first public reference by Tom as a fascist to Jews.

After the meeting there were further scuffles in the street. The scene
was the prototype of what was to become an archetypal pattern of fascist
and anti-fascist behaviour. *The Times* reported:

Sir Oswald marched in the midst of about 60 or 70 of his supporters
along Fleet Street, the Strand, and Whitehall, to the headquarters of
the British Union of Fascists at 1, Great George St, S.W. Of this party,
all young men, many wore either grey or black shirts, without
jackets, and nearly all were hatless. They roared patriotic songs and
the rallying cries of their organisation in turn, and behind them
walked a smaller party of men and women roaring revolutionary
songs and slogans.

The sort of slogans that the fascists and anti-fascists used to sling to and fro at each other like tennis-balls were:

> Two, four, six, eight,
> Whom do we appreciate?
> M.O.S.L.E.Y. – Mosley!

and:

> Hitler and Mosley, what are they for?
> Thuggery, buggery, hunger and war!

As a result of Tom's reference to Jerusalem in his Farringdon Street speech (Irene recorded in her diary) Israel Sieff, a prominent Jewish businessman, withdrew a tentative offer of support for Tom.

The British Union of Fascists was not in its origins a working class movement; it was composed mainly of lower-middle-class men who resented the inequalities and lack of opportunities under capitalism; they also feared the prospect of repression of individualism under socialism. They were mostly young: those who were not, looked back to a spirit of youthfulness such as they had found in the war. They joined the movement not so much because they cared about any policy but because they wanted order; and they felt the disorderly paradoxes of life might be solved if they handed responsibilities to a leader whose words seemed to cut through difficulties like a knife.

In the first edition of *The Greater Britain* (5,000 copies had sold out quickly) Tom had written 'Leadership may be individual or, preferably in the case of the British character, a team'. In the second edition the sentences were added 'But undoutedly single leadership in practice proves the more efficient instrument. The Leader must be prepared to shoulder absolute responsibility.' This was undoubtedly what he found his followers wanted. A black shirt uniform for the BUF was designed which was copied from Tom's fencing jacket: Tom was reported as saying that the shirt was 'the outward and visible sign of an inward and spiritual grace'. A uniform was useful for control if there was to be fighting at meetings: also it did seem to be some sacrament (did Tom realise the significance of his words?) by which his followers might feel they were absolved from responsibility themselves.

Tom's activities in the streets brought forth comments from friends and associates in his other world. Harold Nicolson wrote that he was saddened by the thought of 'young Bermondsey boys with *gummiknüppel* (rubber truncheons). Irene complained – 'I wish everyone would not come in and say Tom was a musical comedy fool with his blackshirt group'. Both Irene and Baba had been at the Farringdon Street meeting: afterwards they discussed it with 'rather broken hearts'.

> Baba said his speech had been so fine, why descend to the Jerusalem inanity, and really the little man in the balcony was quite inoffensive. She waited for Tom for hours at Smith Square and finally he swaggered in like a silly schoolboy only proud of some silly scuffles and rows whilst marching home and glorying over his menials throwing two lads down the stairs at Farringdon Street and possibly injuring them and all this swagger and vanity to Mrs Bryan Guinness and Doris Castelrosse – muck muck muck. When he is such a magnificent orator, and if he had vision, he could have carried the entire hall with him without descending to these blackshirt rows he seems to revel in, and none of his friends will tell him what a ludicrous figure he makes of himself.

But on the path that Tom had chosen for himself it was not ludicrous that he should chuck hecklers out of his meetings, nor that he should not be too concerned if there were scrimmages on his marches. He had a policy that he wanted to be heard: it was a fact that in his pre-fascist days people had defeated him by ignoring him. He believed that his economic policies might save the country: if he was to make himself heard, not only had he to ensure that he was not shouted down but he needed publicity. The sort of public image he wanted to project was that of someone who would guard law and order in the face of those who were out to cause disruption. Logically, all this made sense. And in Italy, fascists had in fact got power by presenting a tough, theatrical image. There was still the question of tactics – if all this in political terms was not to be turned against him.

Cimmie, now back in Smith Square, made designs for a fascist flag; she discussed with Tom the prospect of turning Sousa's 'Stars and Stripes' into a fascist anthem with words by Osbert Sitwell. (William Walton was later asked if he would write music). Cimmie went to Tom's meetings, but she did not appear on platforms nor take part in the marches. It was as if she still could not quite make up her mind about what was happening.

Diana, for all her seriousness and sophistication, might have found it easier to accept in the BUF what Irene called 'the musical comedy element': there was something in all Mitfords, as was later said about

Diana's sister Nancy, that saw the world as something of a 'tease', and that they might tease.

In his private life Tom seems to have been managing his juggling act quite well; he was keeping all his plates, or whatever, fairly harmoniously up in the air at the same time. On October 8th, a week before the BUF's inaugural meeting in Trafalgar Square, Cimmie, in a plane between Paris and London, wrote to Tom, who was staying (according to the address on the envelope) with the Guinnesses at their home at Biddesden, in Hampshire.

> Just want to send him love. Don't know yet of course whether she is to go on [this refers probably to the Trafalgar Square meeting] but if so will do best gladly and proudly for him: if not will come home determined to really try and both be happy and helpmeet to him. Bless your heart, if I do try and see your point of view, please be sweetie and see my p. of v. Be kind. Moo moo.

But Tom, involved in his public life with 'the ferocity of struggle and of danger', would not have had time for much kindness. The style of the task he had set himself was that you had to fight to stay alive: you attracted people to you by your ability to show off ruthlessly and win. A month after the Farringdon Street meeting newspapers reported one at St Pancras where 'some of the fascists had the shirts torn from their backs and received razor slashes': the battle with left-wing militants was once more under way. Each side said that they were fighting for what they believed in: but what they believed in was the struggle against the other: this was the nature of their power, and the chance of their extending it. Fascists and communists needed one another as enemies: if each did not have the other, then indeed they were ludicrous because they were punching at empty air. No one was talking much about Tom's economic proposals now: but then, not many people had wanted to talk about them before.

At the time of the launching of the New Party a year and a half ago it had been Tom who had become ill: he had perhaps glimpsed the nature of the path from which he would not be able to turn back. He was now on that path: he had gambled on gaining political power on his own terms, or nothing. In private life he was gambling too against almost impossible odds - for the perfect arrangements by which he could have Cimmie as wife and Diana as mistress and everyone be happy as he himself strode in and out of protecting rings of fire.

CHAPTER 24

Diana Guinness

In the autumn of 1932, when I was nine, I was sent to boarding school. My mother had taken trouble to find a suitable school: the one chosen was Abinger Hill, near Dorking in Surrey. It was known as being 'progressive': the sort of school rich socialists or ex-socialists might send their children to. What was progressive about it was that boys were allowed to do a lot of their work in their own time and in their own way, and a good deal of freedom was allowed to them in the surrounding countryside.

My father used to say he was haunted up to the end of his life by memories of how he had hated boarding schools; he was bitter against his mother for sending him away.

I look back on Abinger Hill with some gratitude. There were the usual squalors and miseries, but it gave a child a chance to learn, and to make, what adjustments were possible; and thus it did what all schools should do, which is to teach a child what are the terms of the grown-up world by which later he might feel free. What I remember about my first year at Abinger Hill was the way in which life on the mundane level seemed to be dominated by schoolboy gangs: the masters floated almost in another dimension like gods. It was comparatively easy to learn to come to terms with the gods: apart from a few compulsory lessons the work that boys did could be arranged by the boys themselves: when they had done a piece of work they were supposed to present it to a master who would judge it and then according to its quantity and quality would mark up a line on a graph in this or that coloured pencil. Each boy carried his graph around with him as the frontispiece of a loose-leaf notebook. It struck me almost at once that the most sensible way of dealing with this situation would be to lay in a store of pencils oneself – particularly those of the colours denoting 'good' or even 'excellent' – and to mark up, from time to time, one's own graph; thus doing away with the need for a lot of boring work and leaving time free for reading interesting things like *The Modern Boy* and *The Wizard* in the lavatory. (How much of childhood seems to have been spent locked for safety in lavatories!) When the time came for end-of-term examinations one could always mug up quickly all the work one was supposed to have done, and this was the only way work could be made interesting anyway; because it would be for a purpose and in response to a challenge.

The problem of the older-boy gangs of bullies was much more difficult. When I arrived at the school there was a ritual known (I have changed the name) as 'Brown's Daily Blub'. Brown was I suppose a rather unprepossessing boy, and each day after breakfast a column would form and would follow Brown through the passages and round the changing rooms chanting, as if it were one of the political slogans used at my father's marches, 'Brown's Daily Blub!': until, in the course of time, it became a self-validating statement in that Brown did, in fact, blub; after which the column would disperse. I remember being amazed at this: at first because I could not see the point of it; then because I could not understand the odd pleasures of joining in.

Even more alarming rituals were apt to take place in the woods on Sunday afternoons. One Sunday shortly after I had arrived the new boys were rounded up by the senior boys and were marched off into the woods and there we were split into two groups and one group was ordered to dig the graves of the other group and to bury them up to their necks. If anyone in the digging group demurred, it was explained, he would be put into the other group – or worse. This was indeed a sort of predicament about to become common in the grown-up world. I was, by luck, in the digging group. We dug rather shallow graves. Then one or two of the other group were told to lie in the graves and we were told to pee on them. I remember there was a bit of a remonstrance about this: I don't remember, perhaps mercifully, exactly the outcome. What I do remember is that some days later the whole school was assembled and the headmaster announced that it had come to his notice via a letter written by one of the new boys to his mother that certain of the new boys had been out in the woods burying others up to their necks and then – but the sequel was not mentionable. And so – for this, certain new boys were going to be beaten if not expelled. Nothing was said about any older boys. What I remember about all this was a feeling of the inexorability of it: there was nothing one could do: this was what life was like. Older boys took you into the woods and told you to do these things: of course it was against the rules to tell about the older boys: even the boy who had written to his mother had not told about them. He had broken a rule by writing to his mother; but then, at least he had been buried up to his neck. And so myself, and other boys, were beaten. One had to learn about the ways people behaved.

Boarding school was a place in which one learned that the world away from home was cold and damp and smelt of ink and herrings; in which one had to be cunning in order to survive; one of the ways of being cunning was to accept somewhat arbitrary injustices but if one did this there were magical moments of laughter at the awful ways of bullies and of gods. I do not know what the masters made of all this: perhaps, like wise gods, they thought it best to pretend not to know what was really going on and to let their children learn in their own ways. But at boarding school one learned one could not fight the system; the danger of this was, one might believe it of later life.

One of the agonising matters for boarding-school children is the appearance or almost existence of their parents: parents are required to be conventionally prosperous yet completely unremarkable. My first term at Abinger Hill coincided with my father's launching of The British Union of Fascists: this was such a profound embarrassment that it placed me as it were beyond usual categories of alarm. I was nick-named by a friendly master 'Baby Blackshirt': I had to make some virtue of this, or die. This was not impossible. I had loyalty and admiration towards my father: were not he and my mother outstanding after all: how lucky to be the son of someone so unique as a rich titled ex-socialist fascist! And how boring to be a child of unremarkable, conventionally prosperous parents! Somewhere floating around in the background, I suppose, was the gratefully accepted respectability conferred ' y the memory of grandfather Curzon. I built up a good deal of armou   bout all this: but was still vulnerable as it were to torpedoes below the consciousness line. My stammer, not bad when talking to friends, in any sort of school activity got worse.

A week or so after the incident of gravedigging in the woods I wrote home – 'Darling Mummy and Daddy, I am very happy here. Thank you very much for all your letters. I am not at all homesick. Yesterday 7 of us went blackberrying but we did not get much. We have very nice meals. Love from Nick.

Neither Tom nor Cimmie had much talent for noticing what life in fact was like around them: their talent was for ideas, for resolutions, for insisting that life should be what it ought to be; for making passionate gestures when it was not. Tom's very determination that a new type of society had to be built by a new type of man prevented him from looking and seeing what men actually were: Cimmie's faith that in the end she and Tom would be all right stopped her perhaps observing cunningly how to make them so. She endured: she complained. Tom was cunning: but there was danger of catastrophe in his use of cunning for his own ends.

After the somewhat public imbroglio about his private life at Venice Tom seems to have managed in his usual way to placate Cimmie while he continued with his amazing juggling act. But sometimes things went wrong; manipulations flew out of control.

Darling Tom, As I don't want to spare any time we may have together by nags and reproaches I write to explain about Sunday. If only you would be frank with me, that is what I beg. If when you refused Mereworth you had said it was because you thought you would like to take Diana out for the day Sunday I would have known where I was. I started by thinking it odd but as you said nothing about another plan I began to think it must be that you wanted to stay at home and just be with us and I was so pleased. Then you tell me about Sunday as if it was vague and only planned last night – and then I realise the whole thing was arranged before and you had been putting off telling me and letting me go on thinking we were going to have a lovely Sunday together and then jump it on me after the party last night. Even then you first say 'Go a drive for an hour or two' and I get adjusted to that; then this morning it's lunch and I rearrange my point of view but you say anyway back for evening; then you ring up and say whole bally day and night – well it's pure funking, why not tell me days ago, why not be truthful and honest. That is honestly and truly what I want – beloved Tom do believe that – but the feeling that you are not telling me, that you do things behind my back, that you are only sweet to me when you want to get away with something, gives me such a feeling of insecurity and anxiety and worry I am more nervy and upset than I ought or need to be.

The book I am reading says this: 'If John were extra sweet to you then he had something to hide' – very Tomki.

Oh darling darling don't let it be like that, I will truly understand if you give me a chance, but I am so kept in the dark. That bloody damnable cursed Ebury – how often does she come there? Do you think that I just forget all about her between the Fortnum and Mason party and last night? I schooled myself the whole week never to even mention her in case I should nag or say something I should regret.

And then I have the horrid feeling this morning you've let me down
– don't do that my angel please, I'm complicated because I feel
insecure and afraid. Don't be secretive and hidey – I love you so much
I'd cope if you were open with me.   Mutton

But human beings do not on the whole succeed in coping openly with
this sort of situation: openness succeeds with simplicity: when complexity is at stake what is demanded is self-sufficiency, or some style.
Cimmie wrote to a woman friend (Mary Pearson) to ask for advice. She
got the reply:

> It is natural and essential to mind unfaithfulness. It should always be
> done a la Victorian without the knowledge of the other party. We
> place an intolerable and mad psychological strain on ourselves with
> all this so-called frankness. If Tom wishes to have affairs he is welcome
> – but you shouldn't know ... It's 'contrary to nature' as the old
> women used to say ...

This was the old aristocratic attitude. But it was just this that Cimmie
had spent her life trying to break away from. And she did not seem to
have the resources, now, to re-build a life on her own.

During the autumn Tom went again to Rome for a fascist anniversary: he wanted to keep the visit secret. From Rome he wrote the last
letters that are in existence from him to Cimmie: after this, when he was
not with her, he seemed to think it better to keep quiet.

> His own darling fellow
> What a roarer – no harm in a few pictures!
> Rome very interesting. Celebration and illuminations – the reception
> of M tremendous – a great tribute to the system – very interesting
> accounts of the 10 years work in the papers which I will bring home.
> Have not seen any friends yet but have heard from some of them.
>   [series of squiggles as if ending the letter]
> Was rather cross, but opened this again to say he loves her very much
> – not to be a goat because he adores her and she is his own sweet one
> he loves. Darling fellow, they could have such a lovely life together
> if his little frolicsome ways did not upset her. She does mean so much
> to him and he does so appreciate her. She is such a great fellow. He
> loves her so.   [drawing of a piglet]   X

Enclosed in this letter were two advertisements cut out of newspapers.

The first was headlined *The Wolsey People Have Got At Poor Matilda* and went on 'No self-respecting sheep is safe. Let it once be observed that her fleece is really first rate, and away it may go at any moment to the Wolsey mills ...' Above this Tom had drawn two illustrations – one of a sheep with its wool on beside which he had written 'But he prefers –': and the other of a shorn sheep beside which Tom had written 'Sad effects of getting in a stew about nothing.'

The other advertisement was of a charging rhinoceros with the headline *Nature In The Raw Is Seldom Mild*: and beside which Tom had written 'Fatty finding out after a few peeps.' (It is not known what were the 'pictures' referred to at the beginning of the letter).

Tom's second letter to Cimmie from Rome was:

His own darling fellow [drawing of piglet]
Has a really great regret did not bring her with him. Suppose could not have foreseen. But does really regret it awfully. Might have had a *lovely honey squash*. Seeing some of friends tomorrow – may have to wait longer for others – everyone so terribly busy over anniversary ...

One great regret I did not bring her – how one wastes life and yet so difficult to foresee – should really have settled definitely stay a week – always see you amid such turmoil of work or if a holiday of other things. Would have liked this to be a sweetly sweetly lovely time – misses her so much wiffling and sniffing about! Really loves her very much indeed, sure she is the one for him, glad she still loves him, sorry he is such a Porker. Feeling very calm and rested now, my life is so strenuous and hectic, I must recapture a little calm. Very ill and wretched on arrival – caught chill on boat – but all gone now. First lovely sunshine. I hope anyhow return before end of week but will wire you. Would be ever so happy if she were here. As it is rather sad and down. But hopes see her soon. Loves my darling fellow. Think sweetly of him who loves her!
[huge drawing of a piglet]

Tom meant this when he wrote it: no one who knew him ever denied that he meant it when he said he loved Cimmie: what people questioned was how he could both mean this and behave as he did. This was the peculiarity about Tom – how he did not seem restricted by other people's inability to hold opposites at the same time; and he did not feel guilt. It is probable that he had stopped feeling sexually attracted to Cimmie: she had often been ill in the last two years and had grown heavy. But even if he had continued to be sexually attracted to her he had shown often enough he could be involved in this way with more than one person at once. What was happening now was that he loved two people at once.

That Tom felt little guilt can be seen by the calmness with which he justified himself all round: to Cimmie he referred to Diana as part of his 'little frolicsome ways': he would not have told Diana of the re-assuring things he said to Cimmie. This was, in the circumstances, reasonable. But Diana would not have known how Cimmie suffered. What other people could not forgive Tom for was his lack of guilt.

Cimmie was helpless because she was lulled by his sweet reasonable-ness, by what seemed his simplicity, by his baby-drawings hung out like bait on the end of a line. Then when she found he also loved someone else the bottom fell out of her life. She did not have the capacity – as many people do not have – to accept the terrible complexities of love; that in such areas things can both be and not be at the same time.

What was destructive about Tom was that in spite of his manifest complexities he still, in the matter of words, insisted on doing his simple baby-talk with Cimmie: he hardly ever helped her to attain her own complexities of mind. He had probably learned that this was the best way of preventing her protesting too strongly about his 'frolicsome ways': but in so doing he was allowing some outrage to fester inside her.

Cimmie kept on trying to make her calm, serious decisions about learning to accept Diana as she had accepted other women in Tom's life. She kept on being defeated because the extent seemed never ending of what she had to accept.

At the end of 1932 Tom and Cimmie rented a house at Yarlington, in Somerset – Savehay Farm was still let. There we had a family Christmas with Cimmie's sister Irene and her sister Baba with her three children: for some reason Uncle Fruity Metcalfe was Father Christmas this year and the children at last all guessed who he was because of his unmistakable Irish brogue. Tom and Cimmie planned a New Year's fancy-dress party with many of their old friends. Irene reported 'a lot of talk about how to conceal it from those foul gossip writers who had already written it up and asked to come down and photograph the guests'. Friends who lived in the neighbourhood such as Cecil Beaton were to bring their house parties. The last time that Tom had been pursued by newspapers had been after the razor attack on him at St Pancras. It was odd that he should have wanted to give such a party now – when he was in the business of building up the image of the hard, 'new' man. But then – might not in fact a 'new' man be someone who took pride in being all things to all people? Among Tom and Cimmie's own house party guests was Diana Guinness.

The party was rather wild – Tom got over-excited and threw an éclair which hit Syrie Maugham on the head. She had hysterics: the newspapers duly reported the scene. The *Daily Worker* commented – 'The above picture of fascists at play should remove once and for all any lingering doubt as to the superman nature of Mosleyini self-cast for the role of the future dictator of Britain.' This was a muddled conclusion to be drawn from the evidence of a thrown éclair: it does not always suit Marxists to link fascism to images of effeteness. But it was probably true that Tom was at the height of his superman feelings just then – thinking he might get away with everything.

Some time before the new year it had been agreed between Tom and Diana that she would leave her husband and set up house on her own so that she and Tom could see each other more easily. People's jealousies were making it difficult to abide by any rules of the game. And in fact Diana anyway wanted to 'nail her colours to the mast'; to 'throw in her lot' with Tom (the phrases are hers): it was one of her characteristics, as it was one of Tom's, that when emotions and beliefs became serious she would want to throw over the boards of games. Tom himself probably wanted publicly to be seen to carry off some great prize: this would be a compensation for other disappointments. But above all, Tom and Diana were involved in a grand passion: they thought they were made for each other, and continued to think this for fifty years.

Diana's sister Nancy Mitford wrote to her in November – 'You know, I feel convinced that you won't be able to take this step . . . everybody that you know will band together and somehow stop you . . . I believe you have a much worse time in store than you imagine.' However – 'Whatever happens *I* shall always be on your side.'

In January Diana moved with her two small children and a nanny into 2 Eaton Square – a house made available to her rent free by the Grosvenor Estate on condition that she repaired it and redecorated it – she was even given a grant for this purpose. This does not seem to have been done as a special favour to Diana: with economic conditions such as they were in January 1933 (the unemployed had reached nearly three million) it was just that it was difficult to find suitable tenants for empty houses in Eaton Square.

Diana's friends continued to predict nothing but disaster for her in her relationship with Tom. Her three younger sisters were forbidden to visit her house. The taboo that she had broken was to have set herself up openly as Tom's mistress: Tom had broken the taboo of accepting this while remaining openly married to Cimmie. Tom seemed to be claiming simply that he had the right to have two wives – a state of affairs traditionally indeed held to be taboo. Moreover one of the wives had been for years a favourite of society because of her enthusiasm and charm, and the other was the currently most sought-after young beauty of the tribe. Tom could not have been surprised that there were strong feelings against them.

Irene recorded in her diary:

My heart was in my boots over the hell incarnate beloved Cim is going through over Diana Guinness bitching her life wanting to bolt with Tom and marry him and the whole of London getting at me and Baba with the story he had gone with her and needless to say every Redesdale up in arms and Walter Guinness only wanting to 'crash' him and this blithering cow-faced fool insanely ditheringly recklessly trying to ruin Cim's life for her 19-year-old crush on that vain insensate ass Tom.

In fact Lord Redesdale and Walter Guinness (Diana's father-in-law) did try to scare Tom off: they went in a deputation together to his flat in Ebury Street. Tom was with Randolph Churchill before they arrived; he said 'Those two old men are coming to see me': Randolph Churchill said 'What are you going to do?' Tom said 'I suppose wear a balls' protector'.

It was not true that Diana expected to marry Tom: he had made it clear that he would not break his marriage to Cimmie: he had made this clear to Cimmie herself. It was just that 'the whole of London' (Irene's phrase) could not believe that Diana would have left her husband on those terms. But this was, of course, one of the great attractions of Diana: that she would stake her life, as Tom was doing, on something she believed in but which was unlikely to go all her own way. In fact she expected to see Tom only 'when he could spare time from his all all-absorbing political work and the family to which he was devoted' (this was Diana's description in her autobiography). And Tom's engagement diary for 1933 does bear out that this is roughly what happened: he would see Diana for lunch or dinner two or three times a week; he would also enter his dates for lunch or dinner with Cimmie. He also entered the dates he had with Cimmie's sister Baba. Sometimes he would see all three on the same day – 'January 6th: Lunch Cim; Baba 4.15; Dine D.'

Cimmie, in her few remaining letters, seems to have alternated between faith that in the end Tom would be left more hers than anyone else's as had happened before – 'My darling one, my own sweet love, just a line to say I am happy and all is well and I am looking forward to all being back at Smith Square' – and the old schoolgirlish rage which, God knows, Tom could hardly now think he could placate with baby-talk. 'What an idiot you are, really, Tom, going through the fencing prints to stick up in Ebury this p.m. . . .' (this is the only letter from Cimmie that seems to have been censored: the page is torn off below this point.) But then Cimmie would be making her resolutions and requests again (Tom in letters was now silent); and in one case Cimmie wrote as if she were forming an inscription on a tombstone:

I herby make a
Solemn Vow &
Covenant
not to again what you call nag
I will really
TRY & TRY & TRY
& can only ask in return a certain measure
of kindness and decency as to *Provocation*
Herby sealed and signed the 26th March
by
Cynthia Mosley
Do let's start off by having a lovely happy day
today so sunny and birds twittering. Help me
my darling.

CHAPTER 25

The Death of Cimmie

It became fashionable in later life for people to say that my father was responsible for my mother's death. I remember the scene when this was first suggested to me: I was in the nightnursery at Savehay Farm: I was twelve or thirteen: I had been trying to get Nanny to explain why she would never speak to my father's friend Mrs Guinness who was staying in the house. Nanny said – Well, if it had not been for – whatever it was – she did not think my mother would have died. Nanny had her back to me by the washbasin: there were blue and white striped curtains in front of a cupboard. I remember thinking even then – But you can't say something like that is a *cause* of why people die: I mean, there is that sort of thing, isn't there, and people don't die? I suppose I was quite a clever little boy. I had also, for years, thought that much of the grown-up world was mad: that they liked not liking one another. It seemed to me the most striking thing about this bit of news was that it showed how people must hate my father: I was glad that he seemed so impervious to this. And anyway – if people thought that my mother had died because of whatever my father was up to with Mrs Guinness, what about her children, did people think she had cared more about that sort of thing than about them?

Tom was a fool, I suppose, to imagine he could go on juggling with people as if they had no hearts to fall and break: he could not have foreseen such a bitter nemesis. Many people get into the same sort of situation as Tom and Cimmie and Diana: not many, in fact, die. Cimmie became ill; she had an operation: there could be conjectures about what weaknesses were in her to make her not equipped to get well. But weaknesses are not a cause of death. If Cimmie had not died, Diana did not believe that Tom would ever have left her. In time she, Diana, might have got tired and left. Or Cimmie and she might eventually have made friends.

The reason why people felt so bitter about Tom was not rational but symbolic: if Tom had put himself outside the rules of the social game it was inevitable that he should be blamed for any nemesis. He himself was always curiously unaware of such bitterness: for the most part he thought life so wonderful himself, that he could not believe others might need bitterness.

It was suggested also that Cimmie had been losing heart because of Tom's fascism: but here again there is little evidence. She liked Mussolini: she called him 'that big booming man': she would have been content, probably, to wait and see what would happen to Tom's politics. It is true that she seemed to have become increasingly distrustful of Tom's power with words – his belief that he could manipulate people, and the world, just by his skill with words – but she might have learned to live with her distrust. There was however some joint inability with her and Tom to face the reality of the forces of darkness or helplessness within themselves; and thus in the other, and in the outside world. Cimmie perhaps began to lose heart because she could not get away from her innocence: if she began to, she did not know where she was: 'What am I? I forget: am I your squash-nosed wag tail?'

Tom wanted to alter the world; it is such wilful dreamers who do sometimes alter the world: but the whole perilous edifice of fascism was some demonstration of how things are not, rather than how they are. Before the demonstration people did not know this: they believed that human society and even human nature could be altered by reason and will: that if it could not, then at least people might die splendidly in the attempt. One demonstration of fascism was of the style in which people do in fact die in this attempt. Tom was an odd exponent of fascism because in spite of his talk about returning on his shield he did not in fact do so: there was always a part of him that was not taken in by his own romantic rhetoric. This did not prevent his being taken, by others, symbolically to be responsible for deaths.

In January 1933 Hitler came to power in Germany. There was an immediate outcrop of public brutality in which people who it was thought would not fit into the regime were sorted out as if they were dirt. Other people could have learned from this, then, if they had wanted to. Once the power of the party in Germany had been thus established public violence for a time calmed down. Perhaps it had been too sudden, and too arbitrary, for some people to have taken in what it meant.

Harold Nicolson in his diary never suggests anything except that Cimmie was opposed to fascism (he wrote to her jokingly about his godson Michael 'Does Mikki have a swastika on his crib? that would

be the worst crib of all'). But Tom maintained she had come round to
the idea before she died: she was certainly accepted as Tom's wife as part
of the early fascist scene. There is a letter to her of January 1933 from
the Battersea Branch of the BUF beginning 'Hail! Lady Cynthia' and
asking for the loan of furniture and crockery to help set up the Area
Office. But then at the same time came a letter from Russia from one
of her friends of two years ago – 'Have you studied Marx yet? You
would find it a tremendous help in clearing up doubts which continue
to arise.'

In February there was a debate at the Friend's House in Euston Road
in which Tom and James Maxton of the Independent Labour Party
argued against each other with Lloyd George as chairman. There was
a large audience containing many of Tom's and Cimmie's social friends.
Fascism was still on the edge of being respectable. It was thought that
Tom won the argument; but then, when people went away, there was
still the question of what the winning of an argument meant.

In the middle of April Cimmie at last went to Rome with Tom, to
take part in the celebrations around an International Fascist Exhibition.
Starace, the Secretary of the Italian Fascist Party, presented a banner to
the British Union of Fascists delegation: the banner was black with a
Union Jack in the top corner and in the centre the fasces symbol (a
bundle of bound sticks and an axe) around which were the words – *The
British Union of Fascists For King-Empire and International Justice*. It was
intended that the British delegation should be given the honour of
sharing with Mussolini the saluting platform at a march past of contin-
gents from all over Italy; but at the last moment it rained, and Mussolini
retired to a covered balcony some distance away. Tom and his seven
men stood to attention in front of the platform holding their banner
while behind them in a stand – there are photographs of this – Cimmie
looked down on them as if from a great height, rather bewildered and
amused. She wore a raincoat and a sort of schoolmistress's brown felt
hat. The other occasion during this trip to Rome of which a photograph
has survived was of an official visit to the Roman Royal Academy. Tom
and Cimmie are surrounded by frock-coated dignitaries and they both
look absurdly young. Tom was thirty six. Cimmie was thirty four.

While she was in Rome Cimmie received a letter from a young
admirer she had met at the Embassy:

... Unemployment being the big problem and the British Fascist's
opportunity, surely the job is to strike the English imagination. What
about voluntary labour battalions? I don't know anything about the

finance and organisation side, but it seems to me that if the fascists were to form battalions of unemployed (all classes) headed by determined young men who would march on the places where a job needs doing – building sports' grounds, clearing slums – and work scientifically and like hell, they'd capture the imagination of the public by a manifestation of ENERGY ...

I'm not going to chop words – the English are afraid Mosley is out for himself: they don't see that belief in oneself and belief in oneself as an instrument are different things. When they see a man who has actually got hold so to speak of a spade and is digging away with his pals it'll change the attitude a lot ... Mosley probably talks excellent sense on unemployment, but so many people are talking: let him form these labour battalions and choose definite and if possible spectacular jobs which can be done in record time ... It's the man who *does* something that is going to capture the imagination ...

No *physical* offensive. Defensive and if necessary *passive* in suffering. An example of *doing* in the physical sense and enduring in the spiritual.

This was the sort of good advice that Tom took at no time in his life: to him politics were a matter of oration, of argument: the matter of doing, though he talked about it so much, seldom seemed to get past the stage of making sure that his words could be heard. He was from now on never in a position of power from which he could put his words into direct effect: he did not see the strength of an action as a symbol. He never recognised for instance the harm that the activities, however logically justifiable, of the stewards at his meetings were doing him: he would not have seen the good that the rather absurd but symbolic use of voluntary labour battalions might do him. It would certainly have been some sort of anathema to him to have had to consider the idea of victory through suffering.

When Tom and Cimmie got home from Rome at the end of April Tom continued to visit Diana at 2 Eaton Square: Cimmie continued to fail to keep for long her 'solemn vow and covenant' not to show how much she suffered. She was encouraged by friends to have an affair of her own: she said she did not want to. Tom himself (so he told the story) encouraged her to have an affair: the lover he suggested for her was Dick Wyndham.

There is a story of this time that once when Tom was talking to Diana she asked him why Cimmie was so upset about her, Diana, when he had been involved with so many other women; Tom replied that Cimmie had probably not known about most of the other women. Then the thought struck him (after all, rationally) – might it not help Cimmie to know about the other women because then it would help to take her mind off Diana? So he went home and told Cimmie a list of his women: and Cimmie said 'But they are all my best friends!'

The follow-up to this story was told by Bob Boothby. He and Tom were both at the same dinner party that night and Tom asked him, as one of Cimmie's greatest friends, if he would go to Smith Square after dinner and comfort her, because she was upset. Bob Boothby said 'What have you done to her now, Tom?' and Tom said 'I've told her all the women I've been to bed with since we've been married.' Bob Boothby said 'All, Tom?' and Tom said 'Well, all except her stepmother and her sister.'

In the spring holidays my sister and I were home from school and we were back again at Savehay Farm. My mother, for something to do, began to clear a two-acre wood at the end of the garden on the banks of the river. I helped her with this work: we dragged brushwood and fallen logs, and made bonfires. We did not often talk. Perhaps this was my mother's attempt to be 'doing in the physical sense and enduring in the spiritual'. I liked the work: it seemed more sensible than most things I had been part of in the grown-up world.

In early May there was school again and my mother drove me there in my father's dashing Bentley. After she had said goodbye and was going back past the rhododendrons she turned to wave – in her brown felt hat like the cup of an acorn – that figure which I suppose meant much of the world to me. I went off into the world of changing-rooms where boys were lethargically bashing one another up. Cimmie went to spend the weekend with Tom at Savehay Farm. At least, they had intended to spend the weekend together; but they had a terrible row on Sunday night – so Nanny later told Irene – and Tom walked out. Nanny heard Cimmie crying during the night.

On the morning of Monday 8th Cimmie wrote her last letter to Tom.

Darling heart, I want to apologise for last night but I was feeling already pretty rotten and that made me I suppose silly. Anyhow I had a star bad night of feeling wretched and this morning was all in with sickness and crashing back and tummy ache I can't think what it is. The Dr says my 'wee' shows slight recrudescence of coli bacilli but he thinks it must be a chill. No temp, so it's nothing to worry about, but it's just as painful and ill-making a feeling as if I were 106. Enough of myself.

My darling precious if you can remember that it's a sort of crazed for-the-moment-off-her-balance and all-her-good-resolutions-gone Cim who 'nags' and just be kind to it – not fight back – I always regret so bitterly after, I could kill myself. I wouldn't have married anyone else for the world, I am ever so proud of being your wife, I do love and adore you so – that's the trouble – as much as 13 years ago and in a way more frightenedly as then I had confidence and was happy and now I cannot figure anything quite out any more. But I love you, love you, love you, want to look after you, help *you*, be with you: be a joy and assistance – an 'ever present help in trouble' instead of which half the time I am the exact opposite. I am feeling too done in to cope more now. Don't, I beg of you, say unkind things to me, and however much I drive you to it don't compare me unfavourably with the other one. You have no idea how desperately I mind and I am trying and fighting every min: of the day. I never have a 'let-off' to speak of.

My beloved darling darling Tom I love you so wholly as a wife and a mum, but also I want you as a lover and sweet companion and want to be 'gay bird' with you as well as 'stress and strain of public life'. I want the sun and the stars and the moon and they are all called Tomki. I still thought I had them right up to last Xmas in spite of everything. Perhaps I still have, who knows.
I wonder how the ancients acquired wisdom.
How tired you'll be with this my mutti-one.
Lotsie is coming for this weekend and I am getting ahead with the party.
Let's have a radiant day Thurs: without one cloud.
X O X O X O X O X O

that is a hug and these are loving thoughts
//////////////////////

Thursday May 11th was the thirteenth anniversary of Tom's and Cimmie's wedding. On the evening of May 8th, the day on which she had written the above letter, Cimmie was rushed to a nursing home in London with acute appendicitis; the appendix had perforated; she was operated on that night. There was a danger of peritonitis. (This was before the days of penicillin). For a few days the danger did not seem too great. Then it did.

The story of Cimmie's death is taken from Irene's diary. Irene was not an impartial witness; she wrote in her usual emotional, anarchic style. But this was the sort of style that must have surrounded Cimmie from childhood; that she had hoped to get away from in marrying Tom. It is perhaps not inappropriate that Cimmie's death should be recorded in a manner in which it might seem that childhood was reclaiming her.

Irene was abroad in Switzerland when Cimmie became ill: she had just become engaged to be married at the age of thirty seven. She wrote a letter to Cimmie telling her of her engagement; and saying that she longed for her, Cimmie, to come to the wedding which was to be quietly in Switzerland but she did not want her other sister Baba to come; so could Cimmie please not tell Baba.

Irene learned of Cimmie's illness when she read about it in the *Continental Daily Mail* of May 11th. She sent a telegram to Tom, who replied that there was no need for her to come home as all was well. Then three days latter – 'A wire from Tom bombshelled me with utter horror: it said that Cim very seriously ill . . . peritonitis has set in.' Irene and her fiancé, Miles Graham, caught an aeroplane from Zurich and arrived in London on May 15th. They were met at the airport by Baba, but were too late to see Cimmie that day. The next day Cimmie was worse – she was having saline injections because she was too weak for blood transfusions. Irene went to the nursing home but she still did not get into Cimmie's room: 'Baba held the fort and sat outside Cim's door'. Then – 'Tom came in and said I must decide whether or not to see my Cim: it might kill her, and whilst there was life there was hope: and was it not better to remember her always as lovely, not now, ill and drawn.' And so – 'I refrained from going into that tragic bedroom.' Irene waited outside with Tom's mother, 'Ma'. She spoke to the doctors about Cimmie.

Oh that afternoon of horror! Dr Kirkwood then divulged – she had never fought from the start, and her gaiety on the second day was a bad sign: both mentally and physically she had never lifted a finger to live. Ma, Andrée and I crouched outside that door whilst my angel breathed out her last few hours. Poor Tom came out once or twice and said he could get nothing through to her: if only the doctor had warned him she was going he has so much to tell her, and now he was trying to get through to her how magnificent her life had been in its splendour and fulfillment. She had said to him that morning 'I am going, goodbye, my Buffy' – what she always said when he walked away through the garden at Denham. Baba sat in broken solitude in the bathroom and try as I would to hold on to her hand she turned away from every advance. Ma told me alas! alas! Cim had got her to read my last letter to her and so of course she read – 'I only want you not Baba at my wedding'!!

My precious got weaker and weaker and oh! her stertorous breathing in the last ½ hour was torture to hear through the crack in the door where I could just see the mirror: Tom murmuring to her his last words of love. I shall *never never* forget the pure ruthlessness of the pretty young nurse attendant on her all day: she stood outside that door going in and out and never even shed a tear though another little nurse by me was weeping sadly. I knew my love's spirit had fled by the sudden quiet and I saw Tom laying her beloved hands out. Baba went in and I ran to tell the men to get on to poor Nanny. I made plans for her to tell Viv and go at once and fetch Nick and I would be at Denham by the time they got back from Abinger. Tom came out after a bit, he hugged Baba pathetically, and thanked her for being there, and if I had not kissed him on the stairs he would have passed me by. But I saw so clearly Baba had been in the picture, I came in late, I could only stand and wait till needed. I went round to Dr Kirkwood's and waited there whilst he went to get luggage for Denham. Dr Kirkie said he had purposely written up all the slush of Tom's love at Cim's bedside because of so much Guinness scandal talk going about. I then sobbed and sobbed on the floor till Miles came back for me. I would not be able to get into my house because I had lent it to Elsie Fenwick for a debutante cocktail party party for Una!! Miles took me in his car to Denham. Oh! how the beauty of the place hurt me ... Her bedroom I went to pray in to help her children for always. But oh! she was everywhere – everywhere – and yet gone: the place was crying out for her. I met the children about 8.30 and took them up to their suppers. Nanny had told them and they had cried all the way back. I chattered over their ovaltines and God sustained me not to break down; and Micky Mouse awake in his bed got over sweet Nick getting into his. I then knelt by sweet Viv and explained to her Mummy was tired and would have been an invalid and God had given her perfect rest by taking her away but she was always so near us and around us. I then lay on the bed and the housemaid sustained me with sal volatile. Tom then appeared alone to walk hopelessly in the garden. Miles did such a good thing, he got the revolver out of Tom's room as I told him I felt Tom might do something dreadful. Ma then phoned would Tom go back as Cim was looking so lovely.

At Abinger Hill, in my dormitory, I remember the headmaster coming in and saying Nanny was downstairs and would I go to her; and I was so pleased, so pleased; I had been back at school for about a week; I had been told my mother was ill, but children do not quite believe their parents' illnesses. (I had written to her two days before. 'How are you feeling? And is your tummy still aching?') I ran down to the head-master's drawing-room and there was Nanny on the sofa and she told me my mother was dead and there was the feeling of the bottom falling out of the world, space and time going, and a terrible fear that this might not be bearable. I cried. Perhaps it is true that I remember so little about my mother because of what was not bearable.

I do not remember my Aunt Irene at Denham when we got back: my Aunt Irene was very good to us, but I suppose children have an instinct about what is required when things are falling. Nanny and my sister Vivien and I sat in a little heap by the nursery fire. Then our father came in and held out his arms to us. I don't think he could have done better.

Nanny told Irene about the last weekend at Savehay Farm before Cimmie went to the nursing home: it was presumed that Tom had gone to Diana when he had walked out on Saturday night. Irene wrote – 'Oh God what a terrible doom for Tom! and to think that Cim is gone and that Guinness is free and alive and oh! where is any balance or justice!'

Diana remembered the day when Cimmie died as being one of the worst of her life: many of her friends realised this, and wrote to her, and sent her flowers. Tom came round to see her briefly that night: he said that they would not be able to see each other for some time. She wondered if she would ever see him again. But he told her – It will be all right.

The 'slush' that Dr Kirkwood said he had 'written up' about Tom because of the 'Guinness scandal' came out in the papers the next day. The *Daily Telegraph* reported the doctor saying about Tom:

> Through the days and nights he never left her. He kept a ceaseless vigil by her side, and his devotion to his dying wife was the one bright spot in a losing fight. There was something perfect and beautiful about it . . . how Sir Oswald stood the anxious strain I do not know . . . Before Lady Cynthia lost consciousness it was wonderful to see them whisper encouragement to each other. She must have meant far more to her husband than the world knows. It may seem a rather strange thing to say, but they had a very beautiful time together during their last few days.

This was not the feeling amongst those who had once been Cimmie's and Tom's friends. Irene recorded that Nancy Astor was 'defiant and adamant in her opinion of Tom ... all this theatrical grief would pass like a mirage ... it was unbelievable the hatred against him and Cim's death in the House of Commons.' Irene herself 'tried to see it was best she had gone to suffer no more at Tom's hands'. Baba however explained (in Irene's words) 'Cim would rather have lived for her children and all the hell he put her through for one of the short elysian heights he and she definitely attained now and again.'

It was planned that Tom would build a tomb in a memorial garden for Cimmie in the wood by the river at Savehay Farm which she and her children had been clearing during the easter holidays. Until this was ready the coffin would lie in the chapel of the Astors' house at Cliveden a few miles away. There was a funeral service around the coffin at Smith Square for just Tom and his mother and Irene and Baba: at the same time there was a memorial service at St Margaret's Westminster for her friends. These had been told that Cimmie had wished that no one should wear mourning; so almost the only people who turned up in black were members of the BUF in their new shirts. Tom had asked that the organist should play the *Liebestod* from *Tristan and Isolde*, which had been played at their wedding thirteen years ago. The children were not taken to either of these ceremonies: it was thought that 'the sight of the coffin might shock them and mummy locked inside it'. Irene recorded that we were kept at Savehay Farm doing basket-work with her secretary: but I remember going out with my fishing net to the river and wondering about the damned grown-up world that did not teach you to know when your mother was dying and made it so difficult to say good-bye when she was dead.

After the service in Smith Square, in a room full of flowers, Tom sat for hours 'gazing and gazing at her coffin'. No one close to Tom at this time thought his grief was not genuine. Baba was called round to Ebury Street by a mutual friend that night because he was 'frightened for Tom'.

Tom made up bunches of flowers, and photographs, and messages, to lie on Cimmie's coffin while it remained at Cliveden. The messages were written on tiny bits of paper like confetti. After Tom's death I found them in an envelope with Tom's writing on it – *Not to be touched*. On these scraps that are like petals fallen from trees there is written – My love's last present to me on the anniversary of our wedding last Thursday May 11th – Tiny Pres for my darling love I love you so always and for ever – Happy kippers my own darling one with love for ever misses her so – Come over Denham my darling where you are with me always and I love you for ever. And at the bottom of each note there is one of the tiny drawings in Tom's wild, child-like hand that were the talismans of his and Cimmie's life together – the sheep, the turtle, the piglet.

CHAPTER 26

Beyond the Game

Whatever was destructive about Tom's and Cimmie's life together was the result of their trying for too much, not a failure to do enough. Tom had the crazy belief that he could get away with almost anything – adoring wife, passionate mistress, goodness knows what else – keep everyone happy when he wanted them to be happy and avoid them when he wanted to get away. He wanted to create and run a revolutionary political movement that when he chose might seem conventional: that would both break and not break the rules. He evolved some sort of philosophy about all this – in later life he tried to write it – that it sprang from a genuine conviction that old forms of life, social and personal, were dying, and that some new type of society and of human being had to emerge if there was to be hope for humanity. He took his pessimism about the old world from Spengler and his optimism about what might be new from Nietzsche: but he thought he could 'go beyond' Spengler and he misread Nietzsche (or did not read him enough): he imagined that Nietzsche was talking about politics when he was talking about states of mind. Nietzsche had found that to talk about a new type of man required a new style of language: this language was often ironic: it half mocked the so desperately serious things it was trying to say. Nietzsche thought that some such style was necessary if one was to face truth about human affairs and not get carried away or overwhelmed by the vision. This style, possibly, might be the mark of a new type of man. But there would still be rules, on a higher level, of a new type of game.

Tom with part of himself picked up this style: he was unusually witty: he was sometimes humorous about himself. But then some sort of curtain would go up and he became like a ham actor on a stage; he became roaring, runaway, all-of-a-piece, savage; he was like a bus with no brakes going down a hill. It was always a bit of a mystery why he let himself go like this. Rudeness was perhaps some sort of relief when the pain of looking at the truth of things became too much.

The image that Tom built up for himself was that of Faust: of someone always striving, always searching, because that was what a human being was for. This was his justification for his arrogance and his energy: it was not just for himself, but was part of a training by which 'great' things could be achieved. But the only justification for this justification is that he should have been ready to face, to examine, everything: he should not have picked what results of his experiments he should pay attention to and what he would not. When he went roaring off on his hobby horses it was as if he were turning his back on pursuers. Protection is an activity natural to politicians: it has nothing to do with Faust.

Cimmie could not free herself from Tom whatever he did or did not do to her: this had given him security to go roaring off. The more he went his own way the more Cimmie heroically put up with it: by increasing his confidence, she increased her pain. This circle went on running away with itself until, suddenly, there was a death. It is difficult to see, perhaps, another outcome. Cimmie does not seem to have been able seriously to consider the possibility of her leaving him: until she could do this Tom would always have been able to hurt her. And so she would nag at him, and so he would have an excuse to get away from her: and so it would go on; but it was to herself the nagging caused too much pain.

After Cimmie's death Tom's great grief was genuine; but he used his grief, as he had once used her love of him, to spur himself on. Tragedy was not something that might make him change his ways. He built his memorial to her in the garden at Savehay Farm: he told Harold Nicolson that he 'now regards his [fascist] movement as a memorial to Cimmie and is prepared willingly to die for it'. There was nothing in fascism that could not assimilate images of death.

Another memorial was planned for Cimmie: there was to be a children's Day Nursery in south London named after her, and subscribed to by her friends. This was organised by Irene and Baba. An appeal went out over the signatures of Ramsay MacDonald, Stanley Baldwin, George Lansbury and Lloyd George.

Tom became involved in attempts to 'get through' to Cimmie by spiritualist mediums: these were organised by one of his mother's sisters. There was one quite striking result when a medium came up with the word engraved on the inside of Cimmie's wedding ring which was thought to be known only by Cimmie and Tom. Most of the messages that came through however were, as usual, strangely impersonal; though they did often have a peculiarly political content – 'Tom pursues a good course by going to Manchester: he should try to fight Salford and a better spirit will prevail'. One such message, passed on in a letter from his aunt to Tom, had even a weirdly prophetic ring: 'I feel he will never be able now to manage to move near another new policy while he gives stiffs all the more important posts'. The medium was asked twice if 'stiffs' was the right word: the reply each time was 'Yes'.

Tom took up again the reins of his fascist movement: his mother 'Ma' emerged from the shadows and became leader of the woman's section of the British Union of Fascists. She announced 'When my son married Lady Cynthia, she took her place by his side. Now she is dead there must be someone to help him in his work and I am going to do my best to fill the gap.' In July Tom and his mother led a big fascist march round London which began, whether by chance or design, close to Diana's house in Eaton Square. Irene reported:

> Saw Tom amassing his fascists in Eaton Square and Ma the women: then from Colin Davidson's window in Grosvenor Place we watched the March Past along with Zita, Beatrice Guinness, Patrick Hepburn, and Hitler's jester lover 'bugger' Hanfstaengl – a magnificent type of man who plays the piano beautifully, is anxious and oily and utterly evasive on any real question. At first with Colin and Zita and then alone I followed on foot, car and taxi Tom's march all round London to see no harm came to him: it was a splendid show and no trouble and I greeted him when he came back to H.Q. and he made a short speech from the top of a car.

Tom's ex-sisters-in-law were being very solicitous about him at this time: they stopped talking about his 'musical comedy' blackshirts. With Cimmie dead, they were trying to comfort him: they saw that he was doing his best to be a good father to his children. 'Nanny said Tom was very sad yesterday and his sweetness with the children hour after hour Sunday was wonderful.' But above all what Baba and Irene and 'Ma' seemed to be getting together about was a determination to try to prevent him seeing Diana.

> Baba and I were scared stiff when we learned Tom had gone up for dinner Sunday night and was back by 1 a.m. and was doing the same tonight. Who could it be but Diana Guinness. Baba and I, I know, were both sick with terror.

The reason ostensibly given for this attitude was that any further association between Tom and Diana would in some way be hurtful to Cimmie: Baba 'could not make him see the cruelty of it to Cim first and foremost'. But even Irene, with her haphazardness of mind and style, must have found it difficult to continue to convince herself that hers and Baba's feelings were as grandiose as this. A plan was made that later on in the summer, while Irene took the older children on a holiday, Baba should go on a motoring trip in France with Tom to give him further comfort – having 'asked for a fortnight's leave' from her husband Fruity. Irene consulted Tom about this: 'I definitely sensed he wanted Baba alone or no one, and I saw his point about this'. Fruity, however, seems to have seen a less blinkered point: to Irene he 'muttered about all this Tom hysteria and Baba's sacrifice to him watching and guarding him – he saw it as all bunk and false' – here Fruity even got out a bit of resentful rage '– when Tom had killed sweet Cim in cruelty and mental torture'. People were becoming involved in the sort of manipulations, conscious or unconscious, that they blamed Tom so bitterly for.

In early May Diana had asked for a divorce: this had been agreed: moreover it had been arranged that her husband would, according to the gentlemanly conventions of the time, appear to be the guilty party so that Diana need not be accused.

Tom went to see Diana again in June: Eaton Square was only three minutes walk from Ebury Street. He came after dark. He said – referring to her proceedings for divorce – 'Have you jumped your little hurdle yet?' Diana replied 'It's my whole life!' They had a terrible row; and Tom went away.

Irene and Baba and Ma were all on the telephone about this.

When Baba rang him up he had gone to London – there could only be one – and we were scared stiff. I had a talk with Ma over the phone and she told me she was worried – that the horror had sent for Tom after her divorce coming up ... It puts Baba in a fearful fix about motoring in France with Tom as if he is seeing Diana none of us could have the heart to deal with him: the idea is utterly unthinkable. Zita could give us no gossip on her; she had seen her at 2 dinners doing the grim-wan-dead-white-face line ...

But Tom, as was his way, seems to have used the row with Diana to give his ex-sister-in-law and his mother the assurances they required:

He had asked Ma to tell Baba and me he never contemplated meeting Diana after his trip with Baba. Ma had told him what gossip she had heard about the girl saying she was going to get him now and that those who knew her said she was the most determined minx and that she talked to everyone. Tom refused to believe the tales and said she was dignified and sweet and would never gabble. Ma cried and said Tom was so marvellous to his children and that perhaps Cim had died to save his soul: I wondered!

Tom's assurance to Diana – they soon made up their quarrel – was that it would be useful to themselves if it became known that he was seeing a lot of Baba: during the long period before Diana's divorce became final he and Diana had to be careful! about their being seen together and so a 'cover' would be useful: these were the days when any hint of adultery on the part of the petitioner or so-called 'not-guilty' party could, if it was brought to the attention of an official called the King's Proctor, render a divorce invalid.

Tom told Baba (Irene reported) that he had to see Diana occasionally because he could not 'shirk his obligations'. All this intrigue was representative of something which Cimmie by her good nature previously within the family at least had rendered almost innocent. This was now the conscious style of life around Tom: the permutations of passion and deception and self-deception seemed endless:

When I saw Baba later although she could not tell me details as she has been sworn to secrecy by Tom I knew he had killed something in her after all these months of devotion and sacrifice to him as she could not reconcile and told him so this frenzied love for Cim trying now to get mediums and the horror of seeing Diana on and off – dining with her as he says platonically – and she still could not make him see the cruelty of it to Cim . . . I knew she felt she could hardly start on the motor trip now if at all . . .

Baba had had lunch with Tom and had fairly let fly about Diana whom she loathes and she tried to make Tom see that if he went on like this he would be utterly killed and his future smashed as people would not stand for it but he seemed more smashed over having hurt Baba and was asking her to tell him what to do – anything to restore that confidence . . .

I cannot get over Tom's consideration towards Babs . . . I pray this obsession with her will utterly oust Diana Guinness . . .

Such was Irene's view of events. What was happening, of course, was that Tom was once more managing to do his juggling act of keeping people and passions in the air at the same time. There was even a curious incursion from his private world into his public world, which people apart from Tom seemed to view with the deepest suspicion:

> Ma was harrassed by Unity Mitford now joining the Fascist cause, and she was sure she was doing it to spy on Tom in the office as she had asked such curious questions of Lady Makgill . . . This wretch is wanting to sell blackshirts and walk in parades and attend all meetings – for what reason?

Tom and Baba went off on their motoring trip through France: Irene and Vivien and Nicholas and Andrée, Cimmie's ex-lady's-maid, set out on a cruise to the Canary Isles: Nanny and Michael went to the Isle of Wight. Diana and her sister Unity went on a journey to Germany which, Diane said later, changed Unity's life. In Munich they met Putzi Hanfstaengl – he whom Irene had just previously described (in words not literally but perhaps metaphorically apt) as 'Hitler's jester lover bugger'. Putzi Hanfstaengl – 'a huge man with an exaggerated manner' (Diana's description) – took them to the Nuremberg Parteitag, the first huge Nazi rally after Hitler had come to power. Diana wrote – 'A feeling of excited triumph was in the air, and when Hitler appeared an almost electric shock passed through the multitude.'

This is the moment to end this volume; with the characters abroad and getting ready for their new parts and re-alignments. The story of the next thirteen years is the story of Tom's fascism; of his attempt to prevent war; of his new and extraordinary private juggling acts; of the passions and duplicities surrounding these, but also of the bright, violent feeling that followed my father wherever he went; as he made stands about crucial events; as he occasionally dallied on the Mediterranean; as he marched his blackshirt army against the blank wall of war. His children had to learn to come to terms with all this: not only with a world in which their mother had died and people suggested their father had killed her (and their father told them how wonderful his marriage had been) but with a world in which now their father was apt to march down Oxford Street at the head of people who if you looked at them in one way were magnificent and if you looked at them in another were like soldiers from Selfridge's toy shop. Also – why was the world going towards war? And why were people so angry at my father for trying to stop this? As an adolescent, one built up one's own defence works;

came up against one's own brick walls. There were not so many refuges now in the hidey-holes of childhood. Some sort of acceptance, or technique, had to be worked out in the mind.

Tom's energy seemed to carry him over difficulties like someone on a flying carpet. He went on perfecting his marvellous powers with words: he lifted people off their chairs with them. Part of his appeal as a fascist was that he seemed to be a single, lonely figure taking on all the challenges of the world. But then, he was too powerful for people to think they might really help him. He did perform some service by getting what he had called the extremist forces of the country in his hands: violence in England, unlike that on the continent, was for the most part symbolic.

His children learned something from Tom about how to trust themselves: but how might they explain this? Part of what they learned was that the power of words was both wonderful and terrible.

There is a photograph of myself and my sister Vivien and my Aunty Irene at this time: we are on our cruise ship between the Canary Isles and Southampton: we are at one of those fancy dress balls so beloved by people with nothing to do. Aunty is dressed in what she referred to in her diary as her 'white lace veil as a mantilla'. Vivien is in 'her mummy's turkish harem dress'. Nicky is just 'in his burnous'. We do seem to be involved in some journey through purgatory: I at least am dressed for the part. When we got back from our cruise we went to join Nanny and Micky in the Isle of Wight: then Daddy and Aunty Baba came down and told us of their wonderful motoring trip through France: and everything was much as before, except that 'Tom was getting up and handing the vegetables round' and it was now Tom and Viv who 'went bang bang at each other with the coltish smacking and chaffing which I hate' (Irene). But what about Uncle Fruity? This however was the sort of question one did not ask grown-ups: they were apt to shoot at each other hurt glances, like that time for instance when I had told Nanny an amusing limerick I had picked up at school. It was better, I had learned, if one wanted to find out about life, to wait to talk with people of one's own age; who seemed to have the gift to laugh and be serious and be curious without deluding themselves or dying because they were hurt.

VOLUME TWO

Beyond the Pale / 1933-1980

Prologue

In the autumn of 1932, when my father, Oswald Mosley, was approaching his thirty-sixth birthday, an article was published in the *Evening Standard* which summarised his career up to that date. It referred to him as both an 'astonishing man' and an 'astonishing failure': it suggested that he had 'thrown away a succession of wonderful opportunities' and was now destined for 'an ultimate and tragic retirement into obscurity'. The occasion for this article was the founding by my father of the British Union of Fascists, and thus the ending of his involvement with conventional politics.

My father wrote a long reply to this article: in it he echoed and mocked the way in which the *Evening Standard* had summarised his career. By this style – which was typical of a certain side of him – he seemed both to be trying to justify himself and to show his contempt for the conventional attitudes of those against him. The *Evening Standard* had described, he said, how he had begun as 'an obscure member of the disappearing and politically impotent landowning class' yet by the age of twenty-two he had become a Conservative member of Parliament; then, at the age of twenty-four, he had taken 'some crankish exception to the Versailles Treaty which pushed Europe back into the cauldron of war which had already swallowed up the great majority of his friends in an old man's holocaust' and had also manifested 'some squeamish feelings about the shooting of women and children in Ireland'. It was true that these 'callow sentiments' had resulted in his having to face 'some social ostracism'; and it was this sort of thing that the *Evening Standard* must be referring to as the throwing away of 'wonderful opportunities'. My father commented – still as if it were the *Evening Standard's* comment on himself – 'What an impossible fellow! He never knew which side his bread was buttered!' After he had left the Conservative Party, and after 'a long and painful period of transition', he had 'adhered to the Labour Party which, with all its faults, was the only party presenting any hope of any action of any kind'. It was indeed the case – this was now my father talking more passionately and directly about himself – 'that he had a curious predilection for dynamic things; he cherished the strange belief that after the war something had to be done by someone to clear up the mess'. He wrote:

> For two winters running he spoke every night for three months without a break and often two or three times a night at large meetings. He was employed by Labour Headquarters to wind up their campaign on the eve of the poll at almost every by-election. At all these great meetings, in which he addressed hundreds and thousands of his fellow countrymen, he persuaded men and women to vote Labour on the plea that they would 'tackle unemployment'.
>
> The election came, and Labour won. He was given the job of tackling unemployment in the company of Mr J. H. Thomas. The dreary farce of those efforts has become one of the stale jokes of politics. Every proposal he made to implement the Labour pledges by a policy of action was rejected. No alternative was forthcoming from those who rejected these proposals, although they were equally pledged to keep faith with the unemployed: he decided to keep faith with those whom he had asked to vote Labour, and whom Labour had betrayed. This time he had a really serious seizure: he actually resigned from the government and gave up a safe job. Notwithstanding this fresh aberration or 'tactical blunder', the *Evening Standard* says that at this stage 'massed behind him was the whole rank and file of Labour'. This was largely true, as at the Party Conference at which I challenged the government the overwhelming majority of constituency representatives voted with me.....
>
> So then followed another strange aberration. Our curious case had worked within the Old Parties for a period of twelve years in a great variety of attempts to secure some policy of action in post-war Britain. In a fit of petulant impatience at his inability to remedy at all conditions which left him very comfortable but which left the majority of his fellow countrymen very uncomfortable, he decided to fight for a policy of action outside the Old Parties. This time the seizure was fatal. He 'turned again' and for the second time left an established Party. He waded through all the classic and inevitable failure which in every country in post-war Europe has

preceded the arrival in power of a new and modern movement, until he had laid the foundations of a Fascist organisation.

My father continued in this vein. The *Evening Standard* was 'generous enough to admit' that he changed each time his party rather than his principles: it admonished him with Disraeli's words: 'Damn your principles; stick to your party!' This was 'certainly the way to get on in England in 1932: yet even the young among us remember days in England – and not the least days in her history – when principles were not "scraps of paper". But those days were when England had muscle instead of fat around the heart'.

He summarised the conventional attitudes towards him:

He could not have done these things because he believed in them! Away with that absurd idea! Are we really being driven to the conclusion that a public man actually did something because he thought it was right?

In the first volume of these memoirs I told the story of my father up to the time of the *Evening Standard* article and just beyond. During this period he demonstrated something common to both the *Evening Standard's* view of him and the view that he had of himself. During the twenties and the first two years of the thirties it had indeed been possible to see him as someone who, for all his passion for politics, had never found a style by which he could appear wholly committed: his open contempt for the two political parties with which he had hitherto had to work must have given him at least a temporary impatience with himself. Everything depended on the future. He was only thirty-five. Either he would be able to create for himself a political movement which would have a chance of putting into effect his passionately held principles, or he would not.

In his reply to the *Evening Standard* it is as if his sarcastic view of the conventional attitudes towards him and his serious view of himself suddenly coincided:

The fellow is clearly a great gambler, who prefers backing a horse at 5 to 1 with a prospect of winning great stakes, to backing an even-money favourite with the prospect of winning stakes too small to attract him. He is not interested to play for the small stakes of normal politics; he is only interested to play for the great stakes of abnormal politics. To his peculiar mind, the blue and gold prizes of democratic statesmanship – the pomp and decoration without power of achievement – are not worth the having or the buying. He prefers a great gamble on abnormal events; on the winning of a position which might enable him to re-write the pages of history in terms of achievement for the British Race.

At the end of my first volume the founding of the British Union of Fascists was followed shortly by my mother's death. This was an end, for my father, of a time not only of political confusion but of disruption and confusion in his private life. Now he announced that his total commitment to his fascist movement would be a fitting memorial to his late wife: he told his followers at their headquarters – 'From now on this will be my home.' He did in fact give up nearly all the social life that he had once shared with his wife Cimmie – that had run parallel to the life he had with her in politics and which indeed, colouring both areas, had given him something of the reputation of a playboy. Now his dedication to politics was to be manifest. But this meant also that he was to meet fewer people who might give him criticism – even the nagging sort of criticism that had, from time to time, come from my mother.

All this was happening at a time when throughout Europe men of my father's age were feeling that there was a compulsion to commit themselves personally to some extreme in politics: old forms of civilisation were seen to be cracking up: systems of balances, and a feeling for transcendency upon which these systems depended, appeared to have collapsed. It was felt that some rebuilding process had to be undertaken in which old moderating influences should be sacrificed for the sake of the task in hand. In 1930 my mother had travelled in communist Russia and had observed, as well as the obvious inefficiency and the signs of oppression, an atmosphere of what she had felt was hope: my father had been to Italy in 1931 and had been excited by what seemed to him to be the dedicated energy of fascist young men. Repressions and even certain brutalities might be taken, it seemed, as the growing pains of any youthful revolutionary movement: they might be dealt with, in time, with the movement's coming of age. It would have been impossible for my father to have become a communist: he came from a tradition in which there was no sense in the idea of an autocratic organisation pretending to be anything other than what it was.

The founder-members of the British Union of Fascists saw themselves as being on a crusade: their aim was to wipe out the sins of an older generation and to lay the foundations for a new society in which there would be no more prevarication and no more war. Mussolini's fascism was pragmatic: it had been to him in the first place a way of obtaining and wielding power. The way in which such power might be used in 1932 still seemed open to choice. It was not then part of even conventional thinking to dwell on theories about the corruptions inherent in all power. Hitler was not in power in 1932.

When Hitler became Chancellor of Germany in January 1933 he brought with him a whole paraphernalia of theories about racialism and the necessity for conquest which were accepted by his nation of national socialists: fascists soon seemed to feel they had little choice except to follow him. The question of whether fascism could have moved in a different direction without Hitler is hypothetical; no fascist leader ever felt strong or secure enough to stand out clearly against Hitler.

My father was unique amongst fascist leaders in that with regard to his own country he was dedicatedly against war: he was even, at least with the formal side of him that gave orders, against his followers being responsible for violence. But his attitude was permissive of Hitler's attitudes to war; and he seemed content to allow himself and his followers to put themselves in situations conducive to violence and thus to become identified with it in the public mind. When Mussolini had struggled for power in 1919–1922, between one and two thousand people had been killed in street fighting; during Hitler's years on either side of gaining power his men killed hundreds, not only of his opponents, but of his potentially troublesome friends. Throughout all my father's fascist years in England no one, whether friend or enemy, was killed in a street fight; and at the time of the height of his reputation for violence – that surrounding the Olympia meeting in 1934 – there were, according to the records, only three victims kept in hospital overnight. This evidence is not a condonation of such violence as there was; but it is evidence that there was something quite different happening in England from that which was happening on the Continent. Nevertheless, my father allowed himself to be seen as representative of things going on on the Continent.

When Hitler, with Mussolini as his camp follower, went to war and conquered most of Europe, my father, protesting against war, went to jail. The course on which Hitler and Mussolini set themselves resulted in their self-destruction: my father used to say that in jail he had had a chance to learn. How much he did learn, and what, are questions opened, if not precisely answered, by this book. The book begins with a slight overlap with the previous volume: there was both an end and a beginning with the founding of the British Union of Fascists. At the end of this second volume my father seems to set out again in 1948 to repeat many of the political mistakes that he had made in the 1930s — but on an even less realistic level, as if he felt constrained to follow some echo. But on another level there was perhaps something he had learned. The questions at stake were: are politics best seen as belonging to an area in which precise plans can be made and ruthlessly fought for, or are they more to do with plainly demonstrating one's attitudes and then not caring too much about whether people follow one or not? My father, towards the end of his long life, seemed able to embrace both attitudes. He still thought that he had the answers to most questions about politics; yet how genial he remained when so few people listened! Perhaps it was because of this (it is unnerving for others if a failed revolutionary seems to be happy) as well as because of his reputation, that people continued to see him as somehow beyond the pale.

CHAPTER 1

British Fascism

Fascism had emerged on to the British political scene when the idea came to Miss Lintorn Orman that Britain was being invaded by alien influences just as her vegetables were being overrun by weeds; she advertised for volunteers to join a movement which would be called the British Fascisti, and which would fight the forces of disruption.

By the summer of 1924 her organisation claimed (the figure was exaggerated) a membership of 100,000 which was distributed, on paper at least, in military-style units throughout the country. The movement had no policy; it saw itself simply as a force to defend King and Parliament. It had come into existence specifically in reaction to what was felt as an enemy threat: the enemy was an amalgam of communists, socialists, anarchists, freemasons and Jews. The British Fascisti were not particularly anti-semitic: Jews were seen as no more than likely members, because uprooted, of a much wider alien conspiracy.

The British Fascisti had no uniform: they wore a badge with the words 'For King and Country' encircling the initials B.F. As more public-school and military-type men entered the movement, they persuaded Miss Lintorn Orman to change these initials to simply F. After a time Miss Lintorn Orman increasingly withdrew to her Somerset background and the headquarters in London were taken over by Brigadier Blakeney, who changed the wording of the title from 'Fascisti' to 'Fascists' and found other ex-service officers to take over local leadership: there was a General Tyndal-Biscoe in Bournemouth and an Admiral Tupper at Liss. The chief activity of the British Fascists was to act as stewards at right-wing meetings when these were in danger of being broken up. When the editor of the movement's newspaper *The British Fascist Bulletin* had to print some sort of policy in order to fill up space, he suggested that, as a means of reducing unemployment, income tax should be lowered so that rich people could employ more servants.

During 1924 when there was a Labour Government, and during 1925 and 1926 when there was the threat of strikes paralysing a Conservative Government, the British Fascists to a certain extent flourished; there was talk of, and some training in, motor-cycle squads which could be rushed to the aid of government forces in an emergency. But even during these years there was the tendency for individuals dedicated to discipline to choose, somewhat anarchically, their own style of commitment: it was during 1925 that there broke away from the British Fascists the numerous splinter groups; these included the British National Fascists whose speciality was the attempt to break up Labour Party meetings; one of their victims in 1927 was the young up-and-coming Labour MP Oswald Mosley, addressing a meeting at Cambridge.

During the general strike of 1926 the British Fascists offered their services to the Home Secretary but were told that these would be acceptable only if they dropped the word 'Fascist'. They achieved their first martyr when one of their members, acting unofficially as a fireman on a train, leaned too far out of his cab window and hit his head on a bridge.

British Fascists were mostly middle-class men who had no experience of, nor indeed taste for, serious revolutionary nor counter-revolutionary violence: they never went in for the intimidation of civilians by street fighting as their counterparts on the Continent did. The violence of the British middle class had for years and for the most part been absorbed somewhat formally in the business of controlling outlandish parts of the Empire. At home, such violence as existed was mostly of the student-ragging, de-bagging type which might be perpetrated after a rugger match or on Boat Race night. It was to these sort of people that, in 1932, Oswald Mosley sent Robert Forgan, his henchman from Labour and New Party days, to take soundings about whether the members of the various fascist groups would come together under his leadership. He felt it sensible, before he launched a wider appeal, to try to get control of such forces as seemed readily available.

The more strident fascist group was the Imperial Fascist League run by Arnold Leese, who was specifically and strongly anti-semitic. It was he who, when in 1932 Robert Forgan approached him with a proposal that he should accept Oswald Mosley's leadership, had replied that he considered that Oswald Mosley himself was in the pay of Jews. Miss Lintorn Orman refused on the grounds that, from his record, Mosley must be a near-communist. Many other fascists however agreed to the proposal.

When my father launched the British Union of Fascists on 1st October 1932 at a flag-unfurling ceremony in the old New Party offices in Great George Street there were thirty-two founder members present – new recruits from the fascist splinter-groups and remnants from the New Party. The New Party had contained too many disparate elements for even such a magnetic figure as Oswald Mosley to hold together; in particular, there had been a conflict between those who did not wish to be responsible for organised force even when it was used in defence against left-wing militants who were trying to break up New Party meetings, and those who did. The intellectuals and the aesthetes had for the most part gone; those who lingered on in the New Party through the summer of 1932 were mainly those who had been involved with the NUPA Youth Movement and who were trained to defend meetings: it was men of this kind who were present at the launching ceremony of the BUF. Oswald Mosley told them that he had 'finished with those who think: henceforth I shall go to those who feel'.

Thus at the beginning the nucleus of the British Union of Fascists was composed of people who were concerned not so much with the elaboration of a message as with the business of allowing to be heard whatever message might be felt to suit the occasion: the NUPA Youth Movement was transformed without difficulty into the Fascist Defence Force. Fascism is a mechanism by which an individual can commit himself dramatically to the service of a society: it does not presuppose what a society shall necessarily be committed to. My father was, again, unusual as a fascist leader in that he did in fact promulgate a message at the same time as he unfurled the banners which were the symbols of commitment: the message was contained in his book *The Greater Britain,* published on the same day as the ceremony in Great George Street. In *The Greater Britain* he reiterated much of the economic policies of his New Party and indeed of his Labour Party days: but there was now a new emphasis on how this, rather than what, should be done. There was the specific call to service and to dedication to a leader: 'the Leader must be prepared to shoulder absolute responsibility'. There was the impression that once this handing over of responsibility had been done, there need be few doubts about the availability of solutions. Looking back in 1935 my father wrote of this time* –

> The origin of the British Union of Fascists was the formation of
> an emergency group of men and women to advocate a practical
> policy capable of being put into immediate operation in order to
> meet a specific plan for the crisis in Britain. There was no dogma,
> no theory, no principle.

In the conditions of 1932, this attitude was not naive. There was
indeed a crisis in Britain: it seemed likely to get worse. Financiers
had panicked; unemployment was at nearly three million; there had
recently been the mutiny of the fleet at Invergordon. Mussolini had
come to power in Italy by leaving himself free to make multifarious
changes of policy according to whatever crisis presented itself. Hitler
was now playing down the explicit dogmas of *Mein Kampf* in order to
appeal to different sorts of people in different ways. What fascists
offered to people in the early nineteen thirties was order: it seemed that
for them to gain support what was required was not so much doctrine,
as evidence of strength. It was still reasonable to think that the crisis
in England over the moribund body of democratic politics would
resolve itself into a battle between communists and fascists; and it
seemed incumbent on fascists to make it seem likely that they would
win.

The first public meeting of the BUF had been in Trafalgar Square
on 15th October 1932; there were some interruptions and a few
scuffles; on the whole the scene was peaceful. Then on 24th October
at the indoor meeting at the Memorial Hall in Farringdon Street
three hecklers, after due warning, had been thrown out by members
of the Fascist Defence Force with what was seen, according to the
predilections of the viewer, as either unavoidable or undue violence.
This set the tone for many fascist meetings in the future. After the
Farringdon Street meeting the columns of fascists and left-wing
militants had marched through the streets singing *The Red Flag* and
Rule Britannia in counterpoint; they had hurled abuse and slogans to
and fro; not yet bricks and stones. But then, by December, Mosley
was complaining to the press that he was being followed from meeting
to meeting 'by an organised band of communists whose object was
to interrupt all my speeches' and at Battersea Town Hall there was
a fight in which bottles and chairs were used by a group of fifty

★ *The Fascist Quarterly.*

hecklers during which time nothing of Mosley's speech could be heard. The Fascist Defence Force quietened the hall in five minutes. After this the speech continued. But what the audience remembered, of course, was the violence.

All this made sense if what was being demonstrated was the ability of fascists to keep order when threatened by disruption – if the paramount fear in the country was the likelihood of anarchy. But the danger to fascists here was that it could be suggested by their opponents (who had their own techniques for fighting battles) that it was the fascists who were themselves provoking the crisis which they claimed they would be so good at dealing with when it came: was it not indeed reasonable to suppose that people who claimed to be so dynamic would not wait for their expected crisis to materialise in its own time, but would help it on its way?

In February 1933 there was the public debate between Oswald Mosley and his old friend from Independent Labour Party days James Maxton; many of the Mosleys' old social friends were present – fascism was still potentially fashionable. In the course of the debate Maxton challenged Mosley about what exactly his Fascist Defence Force would do in the face of what he might judge to be a threatened left-wing take-over. Mosley replied that when the Labour Party had 'led us more rapidly to the situation which comes anyhow but which they precipitate, behind them will emerge the real man, the organised communist, the man who knows what he wants; and if and when he ever comes out we will be there in the streets with Fascist machine guns to meet him'. The next day the evening newspaper the *Star* reported that 'Sir Oswald Mosley warnèd Mr Maxton that he and his Fascists would be ready to take over the government with the aid of machine guns when the moment arrived'. Mosley brought a case for libel against the *Star* which eventually came to court a year later. Then the fear of a communist take-over – and the distinction between combatting this and instigating a take-over oneself – were still sufficiently clear in people's minds for a jury to award Mosley £5,000 damages. But from the beginning it was difficult for him to walk the tightrope between impressing people with the resoluteness of his followers in their ability to maintain order, and exposing himself to the charge of being responsible for violence.

At Stoke there was a meeting at which a heckler advanced to the platform and challenged Mosley personally to a fight; Mosley jumped down from the platform to face him and a general fracas ensued. Then in March 1933 – perhaps as a result of the sort of reputation the fascists were getting – there was a meeting at the Free Trade Hall in Manchester at which Mosley tried to restrain his stewards from being obviously rough to a heckler; the police intervened to restore order and told the Defence Force to leave the building. Mosley instructed his followers to obey, and 'stood with folded arms' (according to press reports) while the police tried, and failed, to produce conditions in which his speech could be heard. Afterwards he pointed out that his Defence Force, if left to itself, could always restore order; it was only the police who could not ensure free speech. But anxieties concerning the cost of the successes of his Defence Force remained. At the Manchester meeting the press reported – 'Lady Cynthia sat in a box in the hall watching'. This was one of the last meetings of my father's at which my mother was an observer.

It was disputed by neither side at the time that it was the communists who set out to break up fascist meetings: fascists did not break up communist meetings possibly because communists did not possess speakers of sufficient quality to attract large audiences, but also, and mainly, because it was fascists' policy to demonstrate orderliness. Oswald Mosley wanted to run a movement that could use to advantage the disruptive tendency that fascists said they would show themselves ready to combat; but at the same time he wished to appear sensible, rational, humane. These were qualities that no other fascist or national socialist leaders bothered even to claim to make much use of. But then, what was Mosley doing so unequivocally putting himself forward as a fascist? This was a question that his old friends continued to ask perhaps more often than his enemies – who assumed for the most part that his appeal to decency and rationality was hypocritical. To those who had once been close to him it must have seemed that there was something wildly foolhardy about this gamble of his with history: either the crisis in the Western world would occur exactly in the style he said it would, or what hope had he of straightforward political power when he was the purveyor of so many opposites? He was the leader of an embryonic private army dedicated to preventing war; he was a revolutionary leader issuing orders to obey the police; he was appealing to men of feeling but was ruling out – at least with the conscious part of him – the sort of hatred and fears by which men's urges towards power have traditionally been canalised. His experiment, certainly, seemed likely to be one of the oddest in political history. He never made any secret of the fact that to him it was the gamble of winning everything – power and decency and orderliness – that drove him on: of secondary consideration was the knowledge, or at least the suspicion, that the odds were quite high that he would fail.

CHAPTER 2

Family Life

So long as my mother had been alive my father's tendency to gamble on the chances of winning everything had extended over his private as well as his political life: he had tried to be adoring husband, sexual conqueror, searcher after truth; someone both ruthlessly manipulative and yet known for humanitarian concerns; at home equally in Independent Labour Party Summer Schools and in the palazzos and villas of Venice and Antibes. For a time he seemed to succeed. It was his achievements in so many diverse fields that perhaps caused people who felt envious of him to call him a dilettante beyond normal pales.

My mother Cimmie had tried to keep up with him; she had encouraged him in his going for high stakes; her letters expressed the determination that jointly they not only should succeed in work but should have 'fun'. She used to tell him how sad she was when he went his own way; but she did not put up a serious case against him, nor did she manage to find much of a life on her own. After a time it was as if his complexities became too much for her. It was coincidentally that she became ill and died.

There is a sense in which my mother's death affected my father in the way that Gretchen's death affected Faust (I do not know if my father had yet read Goethe's *Faust*; in later years both the play and the character became something of a paradigm for him). Faust, too, had wanted to have a taste of everything: he had made a bargain with Mephistopheles that he should be shown all manner of interests and delights: if ever he should find a vision for the sake of which he would cry Stop! – then Mephistopheles might claim Faust's soul for his own. The death of Gretchen – a girl whom he had loved and seduced – made Faust suffer; but it did not seem an occasion at which he should cry Stop! It was rather one from which he felt he might drive himself more fiercely on. In the second part of the tragedy Faust gives up such simple pleasures as revelry and seduction, and throws himself into efforts at understanding and re-ordering the world.

After Cimmie's death my father gave up almost all his old social pleasures in London and on the Mediterranean and occupied himself with work at his headquarters and in speaking tours round the country. He maintained some formal complexity in personal affairs: but this was nothing like the restless drive which had previously characterised his relationships with women. One way in which it did not seem, however, that he made much of an effort to emulate Faust at this time was that in which Faust struggled to understand and perhaps to transform himself by means symbolised by alchemy.

Diana Guinness, aged twenty-two, had left her husband and had set up house with her two small children in Eaton Square; her intention was, she said, to be available for my father whenever he had time to give to her after the demands of his work and his family. While Cimmie had been alive there had been no question of his leaving Cimmie; the matter had been, for my father, simply that he had wanted to have as it were two wives. It was this that, even in the somewhat raffish society in which he lived, had been considered the breaking of some taboo. So when Cimmie unexpectedly died people could say – We told you so!

My father was left with three children the eldest of whom was twelve and the youngest one year old. He had a house in the country with a retinue of four or five servants and a house and a flat in London, the former of which he sold. He also found himself with a mother and two sisters-in-law – Baroness Ravensdale (Irene) and Lady Alexandra Metcalfe (Baba) – who seemed eager in their different ways to fill some of the spaces that Cimmie had left. They wished to be involved in looking after his work, his children and himself: above all, it seemed, they were intent on trying to discourage him from seeing Diana Guinness.

They would explain that it was their duty to do this in memory of Cimmie: my father would explain that he had certain responsibilities towards Diana. But he would come down to the family home at Denham and be (in our Nanny's words) 'wonderfully attentive to the children': he could also then be in the company of people trying to be attentive to him – especially his ex-sister-in-law Baba. On to her he now seemed to have transferred (she used to say) something of his feelings for Cimmie. Then he would return to London and to Diana's house in Eaton Square, walking from his flat in Ebury Street at night and tapping on her ground floor window with his walking stick. He still had to be careful about his meetings with Diana: she was in the process of divorce and this was the time when there had to be no suspicion of adultery on the part of the so-called innocent party. There was once in fact a threat of blackmail by a maid: my father countered this by a technique which he found effective in politics – that of categorical denial, with a demand that the accuser should produce cast-iron evidence. There were many people of course in my father's and Diana's social world who knew of their relationship and who were hostile to them; but to have caused trouble in this area would have been outside the rules of their particular social game.

Few people doubted the genuineness of my father's great grief after Cimmie's death: people who knew him at all knew that he was a person capable of containing truly different sorts of emotion at once. An elaborate tomb was constructed for Cimmie at the family home of Savehay Farm near Denham: it was of pink marble, somewhat like Napoleon's tomb, and was designed by Sir Edwin Lutyens and his son Robert. It was placed in a sunken garden in the two-acre wood by the river which Cimmie had been clearing with her children just before she died. Around the top of the marble were carved the words *A little space was allowed her to show at least a heroic purpose and to attest a high design.* At the side of the tomb was just a circle with the inscription – *Cynthia Mosley My Beloved.*

Cimmie's body had lain for a time in the chapel of the Astors' house at Cliveden a few miles away. When it was placed in its tomb we children were at last (we had been taken neither to the funeral nor to the chapel) allowed to come near it. I remember a wooden bridge across a ditch and then the gate into the wood and the stillness and the insects buzzing; and then – what do you do with a tomb, what is it that is happening, you walk round and round it: it seems to be a landfall blocking enormous events elsewhere.

For the summer holidays of 1933 – three months after my mother's death – my grandmother 'Ma' Mosley went with Nanny and my brother Micky, aged one, to a seaside resort in the Isle of Wight; my Aunt Irene took myself, aged ten, and my sister Vivien, aged twelve, with my mother's ex-lady's-maid Andrée on a cruise to the Canary Isles; my Aunt Baba went off with my father on a motoring trip through France. Diana Guinness went with her sister Unity Mitford to the first big Nazi rally at Nuremberg. This was where the previous volume ended.

During the next year there were repetitions and variations on these themes. Ma Mosley became the leader of the Women's Section of the British Union of Fascists; Irene, who was unmarried (she had been engaged at the time of Cimmie's death but the engagement was broken off) continued with her supervisory role of the children; Baba played her part in the restoring of my father's confidence and affections. Andrée became housekeeper at Savehay Farm; Nanny, as usual, performed all the mundane tasks for the children.

There was not much noticeable change in our finances. Of my mother's money, under the terms of her grandfather Levi Leiter's will, the capital had to remain within the Leiter trust in America; the income (some £8,000 or £9,000 a year) was divided between her three children. So long as we were under age this money was under the surveillance of the Chancery Court and the Official Solicitor, but my father, in theory at least, could call on it to pay for schools and the upkeep of the family house at Denham. Later there was difficulty about this money; a judge withheld some of it on the grounds that its distribution would enable my father to spend more of his own money on fascism.

In the winter of 1933-34 my father and Diana Guinness went on a holiday together to the South of France: my father had been ill with a recurrence of phlebitis, and his doctor ordered him to rest. Diana wrote of this time that they were very happy: 'We sat out in the sun by day and dined in front of a wood fire: I went for long walks in the hills, coming upon washer-women beating their linen on oaken boards in the bright streams and chatting together as they worked, like Joyce's washer-women in *Anna Livia Plurabel*.'*

The watchfulness that his mother and ex-sisters-in-law had kept upon my father in his dealings with Diana seemed to have abated; there is no mention in my Aunt Irene's diaries for instance of this holiday, whereas only a few months earlier she had been recording with 'horror' any likelihood of his meeting Diana in London. Irene seems in fact to have transferred her interest to encouraging my father's growing relationship with her sister Baba; she recorded with approval an afternoon at Savehay Farm when 'Tom and Baba walked the lawn, Tom's arm round her waist, speaking his speech to her'. Irene even told Baba's husband 'Fruity' Metcalfe that he must learn to put up with this sort of thing, and enrolled Fruity's sister to give him 'a good stern talking to about his jealousy'. Irene's idea apparently was that not only was Baba giving comfort to Tom after Cimmie's death, but also he was being good for Baba; Baba had been 'intellectually starved' (so Irene wrote in

* *A Life of Contrasts.*

her diary) for years and it was 'no wonder she blossomed with Tom'. At the same time and on the same grounds Irene seems to have encouraged another relationship of Baba's; this was with Count Dino Grandi, Mussolini's Ambassador in London, whom Irene described as being in love with Baba. There was a weekend at Cliveden at which Nancy Astor wished to interrupt a tête-à-tête between Grandi and Baba but Irene said (according to her diary) 'Leave them alone, it is the first time she has talked to a good brain for years.' Irene also recorded – 'Fruity's retaliation took the form of reading aloud to Mrs Packenham.'

In May 1934 there was a big 'Blackshirt Dinner' at the Savoy with everyone in full evening dress and my father and grandmother, Aunt Irene and Fruity Metcalfe photographed for the *Tatler*. Then in the summer of 1934 it was Baba who was planning to have a look at the Nazi rally at Nuremberg; and she sent to my father a picture postcard of Hitler's house at Obersalzberg with the question – 'Is Mrs G still at Denham?' I do not remember anything directly of Diana Guinness herself at Denham during these years just after my mother's death; what I remember is Nanny's strange persistence in refusing to talk to her.

Granny Mosley wrote to my father after a weekend at Savehay Farm – 'Those children really adore you: I think you mean more to them than you can possibly believe.'

Irene recorded in her diary how my father's attentiveness to his children included what seemed to her unnecessary badinage with thirteen-year-old Viv: she called this 'his insensate silly slapping chaffing "boppy" chaff that makes Viv rude and on the defensive'. My father had this way of teasing children: it was a means of making contact with them: they defended themselves as best they could. References to myself in Irene's diaries at this time are to do with my stammer; it was becoming so bad that I 'could not answer questions in lessons'; yet there was something in my temperament that would apparently 'permit no teaching'. Irene recorded that I said to her – ' "I wish Daddy would tell me about fascism, I know nothing about it." ' Also – ' "I would like to see Daddy a dictator." '

Vivien wrote for her school a report on one of her father's speeches:

> I think Daddy wants to make the Modern World better
> than the old one.
> He said Stability and Progress were the main things.
> He said Progress had been confused with talk.
> In Chemistry, if you put two colours together they make
> another colour.
> You have to have belief in change.

My memories of life at Savehay Farm during these years are awakened chiefly by mentions in my Aunt Irene's diaries. I would wander alone with my .410 shot-gun round woods and streams uselessly slaughtering water-rats and moorhens; I fashioned from the garden a golf-course on which I played with my father's walking-sticks and tennis balls. There were games of cricket on the lawn into which friends, servants, sisters and aunts were dragged. Irene recorded how she was once 'severely bruised' by the 'fearfully fast bowling of Nicky's boy-friend Stubbs'. A few days later however she 'made 31 and got Viv and Nick and Florence [the nurserymaid] all out in 9 balls'.

Occasionally my father brought down friends from London for only slightly more formal sport. Irene recorded a Boxing Day shoot on Savehay Farm's hundred somewhat suburban acres –

An incredible Italian Swordsman from the London Sporting Club arrived with a wild demented galloping setter at 10.30. At last Daddy, Bill Allen, the Swordsman, Nick and Paula [ex-Casa Maury, now married to Bill Allen] made the guns. Granny, Viv, Cox and James [butler and footman] and I beat every field, river, copse and bog till our backs broke. Coveys of partridges flew in every direction and not one was shot; and only Nick got a poor moorhen.

What I remember about these shoots was the mixture of formality and sudden irreverence; once one of the visiting guns – I think some Italian Contessa – was going for a high pheasant and managed to hit the signal-box on the embankment of the main London-to-Oxford line; my father had difficulty in placating the signalman for laughter.

As the summer holidays of 1934 approached there were the jockey-ings as there had been the previous year about who should do what for the sake of which grown-ups and which children. Baba and Irene and grandmother 'Ma' all had a hand in renting a house in France near Toulon in order that my father should re-establish the tradition observed by him and Cimmie of spending the summer holidays by the Mediterranean with the children. It had been decided that Baba should spend at least half the holidays with us, but it had been made evident that Irene was not invited ('Ma and I are left looking like waiting housemaids') – she was to go to some English resort with Nanny and my brother Micky. In the event Baba came to Toulon for the last two weeks of the holidays, and for the first two there was Diana Guinness. My memory begins to come back about this holiday: I remember a white house with a huge terrace above a rocky sea: my father would stride up and down – 'communing with the muses', as he would say jokingly, or 'contemplating the eternal verities'. There was a gardener's son with whom I played until he introduced me to his sport of snipping off the eyes of snails with a pair of scissors. My father would throw empty wine-bottles into the sea and practise shooting at them with an automatic pistol. He let me fire this pistol once or twice; I remember the way it jumped up in my hand. I did not want to hide away and sulk on this holiday as I had done on previous ones: I suppose that to have done this as some sort of challenge to my father would have seemed absurd.

It must have been about this time that something began to sink in about what people felt about my father and Mrs Guinness. There was Nanny who would not speak – who, when Mrs Guinness was mentioned, looked like Medusa. There was the scene in the night nursery when I had pursued Nanny to try to make her tell me her reasons for this (I was a crafty little boy: I would say – I know why you won't talk to me, it's because of my stammer); and eventually Nanny had said – Well, if it hadn't been for Mrs Guinness, I think perhaps your mother – and so on. And I had thought (such are the compensations perhaps of being a crafty little boy) – But life isn't like that, is it? It's not because of that sort of thing that people die?

It was after this summer holiday of 1934 that I was first taken to one of my father's huge political meetings: for the most part, he kept his public life separate from his life with his children. We read about him in the papers of course: there seemed to be something grand as well as embarrassing about his one-man drive to alter the world. The impression we got of his politics from overhearing aunts and other grown-ups talk was that he had what was often referred to as one of the most brilliant 'brains' in England; that this brain was for some reason not being properly used; that this was both his fault, but also in some way England's. When I was taken for the first time to this big political meeting in Hyde Park I had no idea what I would see. My sister and my Aunt Irene were with friends in the country. I went with other members of my father's family to the roof of the Cumberland Hotel.

It was a Sunday afternoon, about tea-time, and there was an enormous crowd in the Park: people were eddying like particles of sand in gentle waves. There was what seemed to be a rather small formation of Blackshirts on the stretch of grass to the south of Marble Arch: this was separated from the crowd by a narrow line of police. Then after a time – our party on the roof of the Cumberland Hotel were like onlookers at some tournament – there was the sound of a drum-and-fife band from the direction of Bayswater Road; a rather straggling procession came in through a gate; this was not the fascists, it was explained to me on the roof, but the anti-fascists coming to make their counter-demonstration. The crowd flowed towards the anti-fascists; they were held back by police; the anti-fascists assembled round a nucleus of what looked like a cart. It was all rather like the sort of thing that went on underneath microscopes at school – forms of life jostled and re-jostled for shape and identity. Then from the other direction, from Park Lane, there was another line of people marching briskly and firmly in a column of threes: these were the fascists; they were rather frail-looking men with stern faces and close-cut hair; they were wearing their black shirts and black or grey trousers. At the head of them was my father, thin and upright and somehow vulnerable; he was striding along so purposefully; but as if to – what? – some platform, scaffold, on which courage could be displayed? By the side of the column were hundreds of police; they wandered along sometimes smiling at the crowd. As they all entered the Park – there had been discussion on the roof about how well my father's leg would stand the march; had he not been warned by doctors about his phlebitis? – the fascists already in the Park formed up in two lines as if making a tube; my father marched up inside them at the head of his men; the fascists on either side of him had their arms up, reaching. The column arrived at an area within which there were four or five vans with ladders up to the roof. The anti-fascists were in a further part of the Park and there was a man speaking from the top of the cart with the crowd held back; fascist speakers climbed to the tops of their vans and began to speak with the crowd held back; we on the roof of the Cumberland Hotel could not hear what anyone was saying. It did not seem possible that anyone in the Park could hear what anyone was saying: it was explained to me that the police had forbidden the use of loud-speakers. A police helicopter, or autogyro, went slowly overhead; it made a great noise; it was a novelty. In the Park the speakers on the tops of vans were waving their arms and opening and shutting their mouths; my father had his hands on his hips and was striking some attitude at the sky; a few people in the crowd were shaking their fists and making faces. It appeared from the papers the next day that the most popular anti-fascist slogans were – 'Where's the old school tie?', and 'You look like kippers sideways'. The discussion on the roof of the Cumberland Hotel had turned to the question of what had happened to Ma Mosley: had she or had she not been marching at the head of her Women's Section? She was fifty-nine now, or was it sixty? There was a big white tent at the edge of the crowd like the buffet at a race meeting: ambulance men stood around with their stretchers like furled flags. Someone spotted Ma

Mosley: there she was on the bonnet of a van, at the feet of my father who was above her, orating. It was getting cold now; bits of paper blew about like confetti. On the roof of the Cumberland Hotel someone pulled out a hip-flask; was it six o'clock yet? or wasn't it Sunday anyway? After a time my father and the other speakers climbed down from their vans and formed up in their columns to go home. The tournament was over. But what had happened? Or had nothing happened – was it not this that the police had been there for? Everything had been kept separate: cells had just formed, broken up; there had been no connections. In the papers the next day it was said that there had been six thousand police; there had been five thousand fascists; no one seemed to have tried to enumerate the anti-fascists separately from the crowd which was estimated at anything from fifty thousand to a hundred and fifty thousand. In the Cumberland Hotel there was a discussion as we descended – had the demonstration been a success or a failure? But what might be meant by this – was it a success that the demonstration had just taken place and no violence had occurred, or was it a failure for almost the same reason that nothing much had happened? No one seemed to know. No one seemed able to formulate quite the right question. What was it that my father had been trying to do? It had been important, yes, that his meeting should be peaceable; but still, what was the point of a meeting if nothing had been heard? My father had been involved with his movement now for nearly two years: he was giving up his life to it. What was it that was happening?

CHAPTER 3

Italian Connections

During the first ten months of its existence the British Union of Fascists had expanded so rapidly that it had had to move to larger headquarters – first to 12 Grosvenor Place and then, in August 1933, to a building in the King's Road which had previously been Whitelands Teacher Training College. This was a large, barrack-like structure (now pulled down) in which, the BUF claimed, there could, if required, be housed 5,000 London members. It was known by its inmates as the 'Black House' and by their opponents as the 'Fascist Fort'. In 1933 (in the words of one of its inmates) 'it was filled with students eager to learn everything about this new, exciting crusade; its club rooms rang with the laughter and song of men who felt that the advent of Fascism had made life again worth living'.

There was at this time enough money coming in for the organisation to be able to pay its regular workers. The first Director of Organisation – a post second only to that of the 'Leader' as Oswald Mosley was always called – was Dr Robert Forgan, who had been a Labour MP in 1929–30 and then had left the Labour Party with the Mosleys and John Strachey to form the New Party. Robert Forgan was a kindly, painstaking man whose task in the BUF was mainly to deal with outside contacts; within the movement he was known as someone who could usually be influenced by a hard-luck story. His Chief of Staff was Ian Dundas, the son of an Admiral, who at the age of twenty-four had just relinquished a commission in the navy: he was in charge of headquarters personnel and would go about his duties at the Black House accompanied by a bugler. The Commander of the Fascist Defence Force was Eric Piercy, a former insurance agent and still an inspector in the Special Constabulary of the police: his passion was for physical fitness and for drill. His adjutant, responsible for detailed planning of the defence of fascist meetings, was Neil Francis-Hawkins, a recruit from the British Fascists. He had been a salesman of surgical instruments, and was renowned for his insistence on things being neat and tidy.

When recruits joined the BUF they undertook to pay a monthly subscription of a shilling if employed and fourpence if unemployed; they were expected to buy their own black shirts from headquarters for seven shillings and sixpence – quite a large sum for an unemployed man drawing the dole which in those days was eighteen shillings a week. In the conditions of 1932 and 1933 it was inevitable that many of the recruits were from the unemployed; when they were given jobs at the Black House they had free accommodation and a pound or two a week pocket money. Membership of the BUF was open to all British subjects irrespective of race or colour: a candidate had to state just that he or she was loyal to King and Empire, and would obey the rules imposed by the leadership. Recruits were given a badge which was a representation of the fasces – a bundle of sticks bound together round a central axe – symbolising that a single stick might be broken but a bunch could not be: this had been the symbol of the lictors (magistrates' officers) in ancient Rome, and was now the emblem of Mussolini's fascist Italy. It was obligatory for members of the BUF when on duty to wear their black shirts: this was a means not only of making them feel separate from the crowd, but of encouraging a lack of class distinction amongst themselves. On the back of the membership card that was given to each newly enrolled member were printed the aims and objects of the BUF. These were –

To win power for Fascism and thereby establish in Great Britain the Corporate State which shall ensure that –

All shall serve the State and none the Faction;
All shall work and thus enrich their country and themselves;
Opportunity shall be open to all but privilege to none;
Great position shall be conceded only to those of great talent;
Reward shall be accorded only to service;
Poverty shall be abolished by the power of modern science released within the organised state;
The barriers of class shall be destroyed and the energies of every citizen devoted to the service of the British Nation which, by the efforts and sacrifices of our fathers, has existed gloriously for centuries before this transient generation, and which by our exertions shall be raised to its higher destiny – the Greater Britain of Fascism.

Those who worked at Headquarters, apart from the Defence Force, were secretaries, typists, printers, messengers, drivers, paper-sellers and so on: they led a semi-military life with meal-times and reveille and lights-out regulated by the calls of Ian Dundas's bugle. In the evenings the inmates would box and fence and play billiards; or they could attend lectures on current politics and economic theory. In the provinces – it was planned that there should be a BUF organisation for each parliamentary division – there was at each headquarters an unpaid District Officer appointed by National Headquarters; he had under him a staff of volunteer officers responsible for propaganda, finance and transport. There were County and District Inspectors moving between the provinces and London. At all levels there were Women's Sections headed by Women Officers: the BUF prided itself on its emphasis on the equality of the sexes. A District Inspector wrote of the Women's Section at National Headquarters –

Lady Mosley, Oswald Mosley's mother, had her office at NHQ: she entered fully into the life of the Movement and was popular with the girls; she kept a motherly eye on some of the less staid and prettier ones and warned them of the hungry looks being cast in their direction by appreciative blackshirts and by one high-ranking officer in particular who was both an experienced politician and an experienced womaniser.

But at the centre of life at the Black House in London was the Fascist Defence Force, or 'I' Squad – the self-professed élite for whose sake much of the rest of the organisation existed. The 'I' Squad were the people involved in action, and action was what the BUF was dedicated to. The Squad had the privilege of wearing breeches and leather boots in place of the ordinary trousers and shoes; they were trained in boxing and judo in order to deal with interrupters at meetings – to be able to handle without weapons opponents who might be armed with weapons themselves. Eric Piercy on one occasion equipped his force with sticks like rubber truncheons: this was at the Free Trade Hall at Manchester in March 1933, but this was the meeting at which the Defence Force had been ordered out of the hall by the police with the result that the speech could not be heard. After this, the instructions that the Defence Force should not carry weapons was made explicit: the printed description of the required behaviour of a member of the 'I' Squad was –

He stands, together with his fellow stewards, smartly to attention with hands down. When the hecklers start, the speaker at first tries to calm them; but if this fails, and potatoes studded with razor-blades come sailing over, it is the steward's duty to stop the disturbance.

Often he finds that these missiles are being thrown by women while their menfolk stand well out of harm's way singing. He is not allowed to harm any woman. If he is hit by a man he is entitled to hit back – not otherwise.

If the police come upon the scene, any disorder is at once left to them. Fascists immediately drop their hands, even if they are in the act of being struck, and leave retaliation to the police.

The pattern of the meeting that had gone so badly at Manchester was not repeated; in October 1933, when Mosley returned to Manchester, there was a quiet meeting controlled by an orderly Defence Force and it was only after the meeting, when the fascists were marching away, that they were 'ambushed by a band of young men who came suddenly down a side street and attacked with a volley of stones. . . . three fascists received head injuries. . . . the blackshirts broke their ranks and made a counter attack. . . . then the fascists were recalled by bugle and reached the railway station without further disturbance'. This was from a report in a local newspaper: the provincial press was often impressed at this time by the fascists' discipline in the face of provocation.

The speakers whom the 'I' Squad were there to protect were themselves subject to training and discipline by headquarters: but it was not always easy (as indeed it became difficult with the Defence Force) to ensure that instructions were complied with. In the early days of the BUF when recruits were joining in large numbers there were more than a few who liked the idea of being given a platform from which they could pour forth their favourite streams of words. Officials at headquarters tried to regulate these; but what are politicians without their favourite streams of words? Speakers were classified according to what sort of audience a particular speaker might be suited to: there was one called Ramsbottom (our ex-District Inspector remembers) who was apt to use phrases like 'the parturition of Palestine' but who was held to be a good rabble-rouser outside a dock gate; there was another called Dalgleish who was of 'such painful refinement' that he was earmarked for 'suburban cultural associations'. By far the most effective speaker after the Leader himself was a small passionate American of Irish extraction called William Joyce. Joyce had joined the BUF in 1933 and by 1934 was playing such a large part in the movement that he began to be talked about as a possible successor to the Leader – if the Leader became seriously ill with his phlebitis.

Joyce had been born in America and brought up in Ireland: as a young man he had an obsessive patriotism for Great Britain and the British Empire. In 1924 while he was still a student (he took a first class honours degree in English at London University) he had been acting as a steward for the British Fascists at a Conservative meeting at Lambeth and after the meeting he had been caught by left-wing militants and had been held down in the street while a razor had been put in his mouth and his cheek had been cut up towards his ear. This was unusually venomous violence for the time; it left Joyce with a long scar at the side of the mouth from which he would pour, as if in some further vindictiveness, long and bitter tirades against aliens and Jews. Joyce thought that his injury had been done to him by Jews. During his early months with the BUF he seemed to accept the restraints on his anti-semitism imposed by the leadership; later, he seemed to feel himself more free to indulge it and he did the movement much harm.

There were the strict orders from the Leader that nothing should be said in speeches that could be taken as anti-semitic: 'racial and religious persecution are alien to the British character'. However – 'We do not attack Jews because they are Jews, we only attack them if we find them pursuing an anti-British policy: any Jew who is not anti-British will always get a square deal with us'. This was said by Oswald Mosley in January 1933. But such a statement of course left open to individual interpretation what might or might not be taken to be 'anti-British policy'; and in the long run such ambiguity seemed a connivance in whatever tendencies there were for anti-semitic phrases or behaviour to emerge. Without doubt many of the people who enrolled in the BUF were instinctively anti-semitic because anti-semitism was the sort of emotion that drew such would-be patriots to band together; on the other hand, Jews themselves were among the early members of the BUF. At first the BUF's anti-semitism was in fact less overt than was the hostility of Jews towards the BUF: the strength of this latter tendency was in the first place, it seems, largely due to what was going on in Hitler's Germany.

Hitler had come to power in January 1933: he had never made any pretence about his anti-semitic convictions. The British Union of Fascists was seen to be similar to the Nazis in certain obvious respects – they used the same salute, they sang their anthem to the same tune (that of the *Horst Wessel Lied*), they had the same style of dress and discipline. It would have been almost impossible for the Jews in the early 1930s not to have seen the BUF as setting itself up as anti-semitic (there is always a chance, of course, that Jews can defend themselves against any form of criticism by bringing charges of anti-semitism). During 1933 Oswald Mosley went out of his way to try to disassociate himself from Hitler's anti-semitism; he told the *Yorkshire Post* that he thought 'Hitler has made his greatest mistake in his attitude to the Jews': he even prophesied that their 'attacks on German Jews would very shortly cease'. (This was not wholly fanciful: in March 1933 Goering himself was reported as saying 'Germany does not intend to discriminate against Jews'.) But what had already been done to Jews in Germany (as soon as Hitler had come to power there had been outbreaks of anti-semitic brutality: it is a fact that for a time these abated) was sufficient to make many British Jews feel themselves justified in launching protests or even attacks on members of the British Union of Fascists; these were in retaliation for what was happening in Germany, and were aimed at preventing the same things happening here.

During 1933 there were several cases of individual and small groups of fascist paper-sellers being set upon by Jews: the *Daily Telegraph* reported that 'about eleven' fascists were giving away pamphlets in Coventry Street one evening when there was a shout of 'Come on Jews' and 'a mob swept round them and punched them and kicked'; a week later two Jews out of a mob of 'about a hundred' were sent to prison for five weeks for assaulting a Blackshirt in Shaftesbury Avenue. According to the police there was no evidence that Blackshirts at this time were indulging in such attacks. Jews, in their defence, claimed that in the current political circumstances just by wearing a black shirt the fascists were causing provocation. But the *Jewish World* gave its opinion at this time that attacks on Blackshirts were 'wicked and stupid, and condemned outright by all decent men of our faith'.

The songs that the Blackshirts sang and which, together with their dress and their salute and their badge and so on, seemed to many members of the public to justify their seeing the BUF as in alliance with German Nazis and Italian Fascists were, chiefly, their 'Marching Song' which was sung to the tune of the *Horst Wessel Lied* and the words of which went –

Comrades: the voices of the dead battalions
Of those who fell that Britain might be great
Join in our song, for they still march in spirit with us
And urge us on to win the People's State!

We're of their blood, and spirit of their spirit,
Sprung from the soil for whose dear sake they bled;
'Gainst vested powers, Red Front, and massed ranks of Reaction
We lead the fight for freedom and for bread!

The streets are still: the final struggle's ended;
Flushed with the fight we proudly hail the dawn!
See, over all the streets the Mosley banners waving –
Triumphant standards of a race reborn!

– and the song 'Onward Blackshirts', which was sung to the tune of
the Italian anthem *Giovinezza* –

> Hark! the sound of many voices
> Echoes through the vale of ages.
> Britain listens and rejoices
> Gazing on tradition's pages.
> Patriots: your cry is heeded!
> Heroes: your death was not in vain!
> We to your place have succeeded!
> Britain shall be great again!
>
> *Chorus*
> Onward Blackshirts! form your legions,
> Keep the flag for ever high.
> For a free and greater Britain
> Stand we fast to fight or die!

The *Horst Wessel Lied* was sung to one of the best and saddest tunes
that a revolutionary movement has ever produced: *Giovinezza* was a
fine rousing marching song. What is striking is that the words of each
are concerned with the image of the revolutionary spirit arising only
over the martyred bodies of the dead.

With its connections with Continental fascism being paraded so
openly it was inevitable that there would be speculation about where
the BUF was getting its money from. The money provided by Sir
William Morris (later Lord Nuffield) for the New Party had run out;
during 1933 there were few signs of large-scale backing from other
industrialists or financiers; yet by the autumn the BUF had moved
into its huge new headquarters in the Kings Road. It was true that
a lot of new recruits were coming in (the *News Chronicle* reported in
February 1934 that it 'understood from an official fascist source that

the membership of the Union up to last Wednesday was 17,707') and it was evident that Oswald Mosley was putting in his own money. He insisted that his movement was financed through the subscriptions and donations of British sympathisers. But there were persistent rumours that the BUF was being financed by Mussolini. These rumours continued, as did my father's denials of them, until the day of his death.

There is evidence now that the BUF was in fact being financed by Mussolini from the middle of 1933 to, probably, the summer of 1935. During the war all the BUF papers were in the hands of the authorities and although they found (according to a Home Office memorandum of 14 April 1943) that the 'income in the two years from February 1934 to February 1936 was £160,500' and the largest part of this was 'moneys which were paid into a secret account by two of its members' in the form of bundles of foreign currency and remittances 'which were further concealed by being passed from a Swiss bank into the account of an individual in this country before they reached the secret account' – in spite of all this, because of 'the elaborate steps taken to shroud the financial arrangements of British Union in mystery', there was still no definite evidence, the authorities reported, that the movement had been subsidised from abroad. Then after the war, on 6th June 1946, the then Home Secretary, Chuter Ede, announced in the House of Commons that there had come to light letters which had passed between Rome and Count Grandi, the Italian Ambassador in London, which showed that between 1933 and 1935 the BUF had received 'about £60,000 a year' from the Italian Government in monthly instalments of £5,000. This statement was 'categorically denied' by my father at the time: he wrote that 'evidence on any subject could now be available at a penny a packet in alleged Italian archives if any ill-disposed person sought to damage me or deceive authority'; and he challenged the government to produce any concrete evidence about the payments in the form of bank statements. But of course, care had been taken that there would be no evidence in bank statements; and in my father's denial he was careful to use the phrase – 'I have before me a Chartered Accountant's certificate concerning the origin of our funds for a considerable period before the war which shows each subscriber to be British'. Critics however could point to the phrase 'for a considerable period before the war' and ask – was it not significant that he had not used a phrase such as 'from the beginning'?

However letters to and from Count Grandi have now been found in Italian archives by the historian David Irving and details of these

have been published in David Irving's broadsheet *Focal Point* of October
1981. (See the appendix to this chapter.) It seems unlikely that a forger
fabricated these letters – what would have been the point? – and in
any case those who were closest to my father at the time no longer deny
the existence of the payments. There was enough evidence even for it
to be possible to guess the identity of the 'individual' at the British
end of the transactions into whose bank account remittances were
passed from the Swiss bank: this was W.E.D. (Bill) Allen, the old friend
of my father's who had been a Conservative MP until he had joined
the New Party in 1931 and was at the time (1933) married to my father's
old friend Paula Casa Maury. Bill Allen was the managing director of
a Northern Ireland printing and advertising firm which had financial
contacts abroad; it would not have been difficult for him to have
received payments and passed them on to the BUF in such ways as
would not have aroused comment – though ex-BUF members did in
fact remember bundles of foreign banknotes being carried here and
there. My Aunt Baba, who was in the extraordinary position of being
a confidante of both my father and Count Grandi, also felt she had
reason to suspect that payments were coming from Italy; though she
never discussed this with Grandi. It has been suggested by Diana that
when in 1935 the payments were said to have stopped (it was stated
by the Home Secretary in 1946 that a letter from Grandi to Mussolini
had been found which said – 'with a tenth of what you give Mosley . . .
I feel that I could produce a result ten times better') one reason for
this now apparently hostile attitude of Grandi's might have been a
personal feeling of rivalry with my father.

In any event there seems little reason now to doubt the authenticity
of the communications which appear to have passed between Grandi
and Rome. The earliest document found is dated 25th August 1933
and is from the Italian Foreign Office to the Embassy in London: it
is headed 'most secret and personal' and tells of a 'second payment'
of £5,000 for Oswald Mosley made up of bundles of small denomina-
tions of Swiss and French francs, Reichsmarks, dollars and pounds; these
will be in packets 'without any identification and secured by seals of
no significance'; they will be sent by a special courier who has been
instructed 'to carry out the consignment with the greatest caution'.
The third and fourth payments, in October and December 1933, were
also of £5,000 each in bundles of small currency; there were instructions
to Grandi that he was to get them 'into Mosley's hands in whatever
form Your Excellency considers best and in such a way that the consignment is made secretly'. Then on 24th January 1934 there was notification

of a payment of £20,000: this was a result of a personal meeting between Oswald Mosley and Mussolini in Rome on January 9th during which the considerably larger sum had been agreed. Grandi reported that on January 30th this payment was handed personally to Mosley 'closed and sealed exactly as it arrived at the Embassy from the Ministry – the Embassy not having wished to open it'. On the same day Grandi wrote a personal letter to Mussolini –

> Dear President,
> Mosley has entrusted me with expressing his gratitude to you for sending the large sum which I have today arranged to have paid to him. As soon as he got back from Rome he came to see me. I have never seen him so sure of himself and so confident. He told me that the talk he had with you 'recharged' and enlightened him, and that he left Palazzo Venezia more determined than ever to fight on. He also spoke gratefully to me of the simple generosity with which you treated his requests for material help in the future, and spoke at length, quoting figures, on how much this help should come to, thinking I had already been told about arrangements he had made in Rome.

No record of any consignment later than this one of January 1934 has come to light: those payments of which records survive amount to £40,000. From the Home Secretary's statement about the March 1935 letter from Grandi to Mussolini it would seem that some payments were being made until then; such a supposition would not be in conflict (though there is no hard evidence beyond the £40,000) with the Home Secretary's suggestion that aid from Italy amounted to some £60,000 a year for two years. The fact that the expensive Black House had to be given up and other economies made in the summer of 1935 would also suggest that it was then that the payments stopped. What seems certain is that during this period large sums passed; and my father felt it vital to conceal this.

One of my father's techniques with his denials was to say, as lawyers do, that of course this or that was not true, but then to ask – what did it matter if it was? When denying the charge of having received money from Mussolini he used at the same time to say – But the *Daily Herald*, the semi-official organ of the Labour Party, received £75,000 from Russian funds during the nineteen twenties; and what is illegal or wrong in a political movement receiving money from a friendly foreign country? All this is a traditional legal style of argument to win a case; but nevertheless it sets up doubts about truth, and even at the time it must have created an atmosphere at variance with the open, straightforward image that the British Union of Fascists was trying to create. There was another peculiarity about my father's lines of defence at this time: he said that he thought it proper to wash his hands of any control or indeed of any knowledge of his movement's finances on the grounds that he wished to be aloof from any suspicion of being influenced by anyone's money; but then, how could he reconcile this with his claim to be absolute and authoritative leader? He was fairly obviously, in fact, playing the game that nearly all politicians play – that of using words for self-protection or attack, since he believed these to be of more importance than truth. But the peculiarity of his position was that he had passionately to deny that this was what he was doing on account of the contempt that he had shown for the untruths of traditional political games. It would have been difficult for him of course in any circumstances to have admitted the payments from Mussolini: he would have known it would have exposed him damagingly to the charge of being in the pay of a foreign government – when so much of his appeal was to economic self-sufficiency, and so much of his attack was directed against interference in British politics by foreign finance.

But he needed the money; and in fact it was true that there was nothing illegal about the transactions; so what was there to stop him from behaving like an ordinary politician? – except, of course, that he was saying so vehemently that he was not. In August 1933 J. R. Clynes, who had been Home Secretary in the Labour Government at the time when my father had been Chancellor of the Duchy of Lancaster, wrote that Oswald Mosley was becoming 'the Greta Garbo of British politics': he was 'surrounding himself with a fog of mystery so dense that even his own followers must be finding it difficult to penetrate it'. This was a reference not only to the question of finances, but to the fact of so many foreign influences being evident in a movement which prided itself on being so patriotic. It also probably referred to my father's dramatic claims to straightforwardness which he defended with such skills in cunning rationalisation. But then – was not Greta Garbo the most adored actress in the Western world? And was not one reason why so many people adored her just her air of impenetrable mystery?

Appendix

The following is a facsimile of the communication of 25th August 1933
from the Italian Foreign Office in Rome to Count Grandi in London –

TELESPRESSO N. 6971

Ministero degli Affari Esteri

Gabinetto

SEGRETISSIMO-PERSONALE

Indirizzato a

A S.E. l'On. Dino GRANDI

R. Ambasciatore d'Italia

L O N D R A

Posizione   *Roma, addì*   2 5 AGO. 1933 Anno XI   *Anno*

(Oggetto)   Missione riservata

(Riferimento)

(Testo)   In relazione a precedente corrispondenza e da ultimo al te-
legramma ~~personale~~ personale n.669 del 22 corrente, si ha il pregi
di far noto all'E.V. che con il corriere in partenza da Roma sabato 26
corrente, viene trasmessa la 2ª rata di sterline 5.000 per Sir Oswald
Mosley. Tale somma viene trasmessa nelle seguenti valute, al cambio del
7 agosto corr. :

Franchi francesi	169.850
sterline	1.000
dollari	7.000
marchi	1.900
franchi svizzeri	5.200

corrispondenti rispettivamente ai pacchi n.1, n.2, n.3 (composto di due
buste), n.4 e n.5. E' stato curato, nei limiti del possibile, di poter
ottenere biglietti di piccolo taglio, specialmente nelle sterline.

     Nella giornata di martedì partirà da Roma il nipote del
Dott. Enderle, Signor Arturo Resio, persona del Dott. Enderle garantita
sotto ogni rispetto, che conosce già l'Inghilterra e la lingua inglese,
incaricato di mettersi a disposizione di codesta R. Ambasciata per ef-
fettuare con la massima cautela la consegna della detta somma.

     Non è stato questa volta inviato a Londra il Dott. Enderle
perchè non è da escludere che egli possa più facilmente essere indivi-
duato, avendo in passato già adempiuto simile incarico. D'altra parte
il Signor Enderle è persona di cui questo Ministero pensa di potersi
servire anche in altre circostanze e pertanto conviene che egli
non offra occasione di poter essere segnalato o sospettato.

     Le buste contenenti le dette valute sono senza intesta-
zione, i sigilli che le chiudono contengono una sigla che non
ha nessun significato.

     L'E.V. disporrà nella forma che riterrà più opportuna
perchè la delicata operazione della consegna avvenga nel modo
più segreto.

     Accluso al presente dispaccio si trasmette una lettera
che il Dott. Enderle indirizza al Signor John Hope con preghiera
di farla pervenire a destinazione a mezzo posta.

CHAPTER 4

The Philosophy of Fascism

Shortly after his launching of the BUF my father gave a lecture to the English Speaking Union entitled *The Philosophy of Fascism*.* This was his attempt to give an account of his beliefs and aims that would give them an intellectual background: that would be on a different level of seriousness from Hitler's threatening rhetoric or indeed from Mussolini's insistence that he had no philosophy at all.

Early in the lecture my father spoke of Oswald Spengler as 'the great German philosopher' who had 'probably done more than any other to paint in the broad background of Fascist thought'. My father did not feel it necessary to go into detail about what this 'broad background' might be; Spengler's book *The Decline of the West* had recently been published in English and he would have assumed that the gist of it would have been sufficiently known to his audience for them to understand to what he referred. Spengler's main thesis was that each separate civilisation – Western, Classical, Indian and so on – had a life-span analogous to that of any living organism – a spring and a summer and an autumn and a winter – and that these patterns of growth and decay were inexorable, making absurd the idea that one civilisation could be said to be more 'advanced' than any other in the sense that it was indefinitely developing and expanding. The fact that at a stage in a civilisation's history such an illusion might be held was in fact evidence of that civilisation being in decline: a naive faith in 'progress' was a symptom of ossification. In the light of what became known as Spengler's 'pessimism' it is one of the mysteries of fascism – a creed dedicated ostensibly to the dynamic re-structuring of the world – how fascists took Spengler as their intellectual hero.

* Published in *The Fascist Quarterly*.

In his speech to the English Speaking Union my father suggested that Spengler's pessimism about Western civilisation was vitiated by 'his entire ignorance of modern scientific and mechanical development: if you look through the Spenglerian spectacles you are bound to come to a conclusion of extreme pessimism because they obscure the factor which for the first time places in the hands of man the ability entirely to eliminate the poverty problem'. In addition to modern science, what my father suggested Spengler had failed to take into account was the ability of Western man to learn from what indeed might be potentially stultifying conflicts of ideas – and to make from these a synthesis which could counteract the forces of decay. 'Where, in an age of culture, of thought, of abstract speculation, you find two great cultures in sharp antithesis, you usually find, in the following age of action, some synthesis in practice between those two sharp antitheses which leads to a practical creed of action.' In this way Spengler's conclusions about present civilisation might be refuted while his analysis of the patterns of earlier civilisations could be accepted: all this might indeed provide fascists with the sort of 'challenge' that they liked. But still – this could be seen by an outsider either as a 'going-beyond' Spengler which was my father's description of his own ideas, or as one more symptom of the delusions of 'Caesarism' which was how Spengler described the characteristics of a civilisation on the decline.

The antithetical forces which, in contemporary culture, my father thought could be put into some practical synthesis were Christianity and Nietzscheanism: 'I would suggest to you that in the last century the major intellectual struggle arose from the tremendous impact of Nietzschean thought on the Christian civilisation of two thousand years ago.... its full implications are only today working themselves out'.

My father's interpretation of what Nietzsche had been saying about Christianity was – 'This is the religion of the slaves and the weakling. This is the faith of the people who are in flight from life, who will not face reality, who look for salvation in some dreamy hereafter – the salvation which they have not the vitality nor the manhood to seize for themselves here on earth'. My father explained that this was not his own view of Christianity because – 'I am going to show you how I believe the Nietzschean and the Christian doctrines are capable of synthesis'.

What he saw as the Nietzschean doctrine was his (my father's) interpretation of Nietzsche's idea of the superman – 'the man who faces difficulty, danger, goes forward through material things and through the difficulties of environment to achieve, to win and create, here on earth, a world of his own'. It was not the fascist doctrine directly to advocate the implementation of this interpretation of Nietzsche, but to combine it with Christianity to form a synthesis.

In the Fascist doctrine today you find a complete welding of the great characteristics of both creeds. On the one hand you find in Fascism, taken from Christianity, taken directly from the Christian conception, the immense vision of service, of self-abnegation, of self-sacrifice in the cause of others, in the cause of the world, in the cause of your country; not the elimination of the individual so much as the fusion of the individual in something far greater than himself . . . On the other hand you find taken from Nietzschean thought the virility, the challenge to all existing things which impede the march of mankind, the absolute abnegation of the doctrine of surrender: the firm ability to grapple with and to overcome all obstructions. You have, in fact, the creation of a doctrine of men of vigour and of a self-help which is the other outstanding characteristic of Fascism.

From the belief that such a synthesis might be possible – that by such an effort of will and by scientific understanding a going-against-the-grain of Spenglerian pessimism might take place – arose the beliefs about the possibilities of the practical workings of the fascist state. If men were rational and dynamic enough to be able to 'go beyond' Spengler and harmoniously to synthesise Nietzschean and Christian thought, then indeed they might be vigorous and self-sacrificing enough to choose and fashion a form of authoritative government that they could reasonably trust and obey – that might do its job without the safeguards traditionally imposed upon democratic governments just because of fears about the stupidities and corruptions of ordinary people wielding power. But such beliefs and hopes were still in the form of words: it was up to my father – as he himself would have admitted – to prove the worth of his words in action. In the meantime, as a result of fascists having taken Spengler and Nietzsche as their intellectual heroes, there was the odd impression that the challenge they had chosen to involve themselves with was one in which they must see that there was a strong chance of their defeat; either this, or they would have to have an ironic vision of the nature of success.

Spengler had specified that during the decay of a civilisation there would be times when the 'private and family policies of individual leaders' would hold sway; this would coincide with 'the inward decline of the nations into a formless population and constitution thereof as an Imperium of gradually-increasing crudity of despotism'. A symptom of this time would be the 'immense optical illusion' that 'everyone can demand something of the rest: we say "thou shalt" in the conviction that so-and-so in fact will, can and must be changed or fashioned or arranged conformably to the order; and our belief both in the efficacy of, and in our title to give, such orders is unshakeable'. Such a tendency to think that people can be ordered and arranged as if they were words was, Spengler continued to insist, a symptom of that which was self-defeating.

With regard to my father's interpretation of Nietzsche's idea of the superman there seemed also to be a confusion between facts and words. My father assumed that Nietzsche was using words as recommendations about how in practice things should be arranged: whereas Nietzsche for the most part himself seemed to say he was talking ironically: he was using words to describe people's hopes and illusions about how things should be arranged and just by this – the recognition of people's capacities for illusion – perhaps not to be trapped by them. Nietzsche's superman is someone who hopes by seeing people's struggles for power and their capacities to delude themselves about these, to have some power over himself; not, in any way except this, to have power over others.

There is in fact something of this ironic sort of optimism even in Spengler – though it is an optimism that neither his admirers nor his critics seemed to see. Spengler did not relent from his vision of the life-and-death cycle of all civilisations; what he did say might be unique about Western civilisation was its ability in some sense to be free of this not in practical terms but in terms of being aware of what the facts of its situation were: 'No culture is at liberty to choose the path and conduct of its thought; but here for the first time a culture can foresee the way that destiny has chosen for it'. It is by the use of this vision that we might yet 'set to work upon the formation of our own future' – not in the way of vainly willing to alter what is inexorable, but in the way of understanding what occurs and thus perhaps altering its style. There is some human freedom here – even power – but on a different level.

Both Spengler and especially Nietzsche were concerned with the fact that if words are used as orders or recommendations they often seem to bring about the opposite of what they set out to recommend; that if anything is positively to be altered it has to come about in its own way – influenced at the best by human efforts at understanding. Nietzsche dealt specifically with these ideas: he, and his superman,

would laugh at themselves holding even such elusive hopes of power –
or words might still run away with them. The way to deal with the
'inexorability of history' was to say to it – All right, go your own
way. Then, because you were watching it, it might not.

When my father talked about Nietzsche he seemed both to see this
and yet often not to see it: one of his favourite themes at the dinner
table was to criticise what he saw as Nietzsche's idea of the 'Will to
Power'. He took it that by this phrase Nietzsche was recommending
as proper human behaviour something like the ordering of human
beings as if they were monkeys in cages: but Nietzsche used the phrase
(or so it seems to me) in the hope that by recognising such primitive
tendencies a human might overcome them. My father would suggest
that one could 'go beyond' what he saw as Nietzsche's 'Will to Power'
by his, my father's, own recommendation of a 'Will to Achievement'
– not the ordering of monkeys for the sake of exercising power, but
the ordering of human beings for the sake of the enjoyment of a full
and harmonious life – but still with the presupposition (seen as so
disastrous by Spengler) that what was required of humans was the
business of imposing order by will. But then – almost as part of the
same oration at the dinner-table – my father's voice would move into
a different key; his eyes would become distant, gentle; he would produce
one of his favourite quotations from Nietzsche – the lines near the
beginning of *Thus Spoke Zarathustra* which refer to the three stages
in the development of humanity – that of the camel, of the lion, and
of the child. My father would say – perhaps now even with something
indeed of the quiet irony commended by Nietzsche – Ah the camel,
we know the camel! that which only moves as a result of the carrot
or the stick! and the lion, we know the lion do we not, that which
wishes to impose order on monkeys in cages: but the child – what is
the child? And then he would do his trick of flashing his eyes on and
off as if they were a lighthouse. And those watching him and listening
to him might think that they had a glimpse, somewhere in the mist,
of what might be the child.

The word used by Spengler to describe modern Western civilisation
was 'Faustian': this was the symbol of someone always searching,
striving, looking towards the infinite and the unknown. What Faust
was looking for, but never found, was some state that might be
embraced with the simplicity perhaps of a child. My father came increasingly and almost self-consciously to see himself as Faustian. Some
fifteen years after the beginning of his incursion into fascism he wrote
an introduction to Goethe's *Faust* in which he saw clearly that the

problem for Faust was one of the loss of the simplicity of innocence: Faust learned that evil could produce good; but he learned also that the knowledge did not absolve a man from the ethical distinction he had made between evil and good; so, with this paradoxical knowledge, how should he act then? It might be that there was nothing much to be 'acted' at this level; there was the need primarily for acceptance and understanding; this was the area of Nietzsche's 'beyond good and evil'. What might be required, indeed, was something of the spontaneity of a child. And was not this also a Christian concept; and so – a synthesis! My father would then smile, with his lighthouse eyes. However – and this was a problem too for Faust – my father was dedicated to action, was he not? How could he become like a child? The effort that might produce effortlessness – were not such paradoxes anathema to men of action? After a while my father would let the vision of the child go. It seemed a grace that he sometimes had it.

It was Mephistopheles in Goethe's *Faust* who saw that the spur of evil often engenders good; that without this spur life in the form we know it might not go on. In *Faust* this matter of good and evil is split: it is Mephistopheles who consciously works the evil and Faust who hopes for the outcome of good; the two are a decadence from the child, whose innocence is that he is one. If men allow this split, their evil inevitably becomes planned like that of Mephistopheles; then guilt entraps them like that of Faust. This is perhaps an inevitable result of the demand for dynamic 'action' – the belief that a person can manipulate ends and means as if they were words.

C. J. Jung, whom during the war my father came to admire, wrote:*

In Faust we see the 'hungering for the infinite' born of inner contradiction and dichotomy, the eschatological expectation of the Great Fulfilment. In him we experience the loftiest flight of the mind, and the descent into the depths of guilt and darkness; and still worse, a fall so low that Faust sinks to the level of a mountebank and a wholesale murderer as a result of his pact with the devil. Faust is split, and sets up an 'evil' outside himself in the shape of Mephistopheles to serve as an alibi in case of need. He knows nothing of what has happened ... we never get the impression that he has real insight or suffers genuine remorse. His avowed and unavowed worship of success stands in the way of any moral reflection throughout, obscuring the ethical conflict so that Faust's moral personality remains misty.

Collected Works, Volume 10.

My father did not personally allow himself to end up like this: there was always something that constrained him like the vision of the child. He could see himself, that is, sometimes in the style of what Goethe called 'sweet self-irony'; he had little 'avowed worship of success'. But then often enough publicly, like some actor, he would be off careering down his slopes again – like some runaway tram, roaring – on his double rails of manipulator and, eventually, victim. Every actor, I suppose, likes to play the part of Mephistopheles; some like to play the striving but tormented Faust. No one – because it is to do with what acting is not – can quite act the child.

CHAPTER 5

Lord Rothermere

In January 1934 the British Union of Fascists was given a boost by Lord Rothermere who wrote an article in the *Daily Mail* headlined 'Hurrah for the Blackshirts!'. This announced that from now on the BUF would have the backing of his entire Rothermere Press – which as well as the *Daily Mail* included the *Evening News* and the *Sunday Dispatch*. Lord Rothermere declared – 'The Blackshirt movement is the organised effort of the younger generation to break this stranglehold which senile politicians have so long maintained on our public affairs'. As if in support of this attitude he admitted – 'Being myself in the middle sixties, I know how stealthily and steadily that seventh decade saps one's powers and stiffens one's prejudices.'

He praised Italy and Germany: 'These are beyond all doubt the best ruled nations in Europe today. From repeated visits to both under their present regimes I can vouch for it that in no other land does the overwhelming majority of the people feel such confidence and pride in its rulers'. He denied that the BUF was under foreign influence: 'the socialists who jeer at the principles and uniform of the Blackshirt being of foreign origin forget that the founder and High Priest of their own creed was the German Jew Karl Marx'. He insisted that the BUF was 'the only force in Britain' working for 'national discipline and organisation'.

However in the letter of January 30th 1934 from Count Grandi to Mussolini quoted in Chapter 3 Grandi wrote of Mussolini's influence over Rothermere: 'Mosley also told me, with what seemed like special gratitude, that he owed the definitive conversion of Lord Rothermere entirely to you ... a word from you was enough to put Rothermere quite suddenly beside Mosley'. Grandi went on to tell Mussolini of his, Grandi's, part in persuading Mosley to accept the backing of Rothermere –

In the conversations I had with Mosley before Christmas I managed to overcome his doubts by pointing out the immediate and practical advantages that would accrue to his movement by suddenly gaining, without effort or expense, the group of newspapers which, because of its circulation and its influence on the masses in Great Britain (above all in the provinces) is by far the strongest of them all. The fact that Rothermere is only a second rate figure in politics (in spite of his claim to be the *deus ex machina* of English politics) is just another reason for not taking too seriously any harm that may later come out of being associated with him.

The 'harm' that might come from an association with Lord Rothermere, and my father's 'doubts', were, it seemed, due to the fact that Rothermere was known as a difficult and obstinate man to work with; also he saw the blackshirts not as a revolutionary force but rather as guardians of some extreme and imperialist right wing. Lord Rothermere was a shy, ponderous man who had pioneered modern tabloid newspaper techniques; he had been launched into politics by Lloyd George as Air Minister from 1916 to 1918; he had joined with Lord Beaverbrook in a crusade for Empire Free Trade in 1929. But it was a fact that the BUF agreed with him in advocating a closed home-and-empire free trade area; and Lord Rothermere was also attracted to the BUF's call for deeds rather than words. A *Daily Mail* leader-writer had the line, perhaps picked up dubiously from my father – 'As Goethe has said, action is the first and most important of worldly things.'

There were several people in the public eye taking the BUF seriously at this time. Lloyd George announced – 'Sir Oswald Mosley is a very able man and he is making considerable headway.' Bernard Shaw lectured to the Fabian Society – 'Sir Oswald Mosley is a very interesting man to read just now: one of the few people who is thinking and writing about real things and not about figments and phrases . . . I know you dislike him, because he looks like a man who has some physical courage and is going to do something and that is a terrible thing . . . you instinctively hate him because you do not know where he will land you, and he evidently means to uproot some of you.' The press reported that in the month following the announcement of Lord Rothermere's backing enrolments into the BUF at the London headquarters alone went up to over 1,000 in a week; and there were by now established over 300 branches throughout the country. However Aneurin Bevan was reported in the press as echoing the possibility that

Grandi had been at pains to dismiss – 'Nothing could do more damage to Sir Oswald Mosley's little movement than the sudden adherence of the Rothermere press.'

The part of Grandi's letter about Rothermere is of additional interest in that it shows how Grandi saw himself concerned in the BUF's affairs:

It is in the provinces they must begin and from where they must move to the siege and to the assault of the city: our own now proven revolutionary experience has taught us this. In fact, what happened in our own revolution will happen with Rothermere: the reactionaries believed they could use us to defeat socialism and democracy and then be in charge themselves; when they realised that the threat of socialism was a joke compared to the revolution that you [Mussolini] were preparing, they were alarmed and tried to withdraw, but it was too late.

Grandi at this time (January 1934) was of course showing considerable admiration for my father –

From the very first day I arrived here Mosley appeared to me to be the expression of something absolutely new and unexpected in England, where no one – I don't say 'dares' – even imagines he could fall short of the standards of traditional Victorian patriotism ... Mosley doesn't give a damn for Queen Victoria, he says this and prints it to the scandal of everyone, and says he wants to bring back Tudor England, the England of Henry VIII and Elizabeth, the England that wasn't 'natural' but sectarian, that ate oxen roasted on the spit, chopped off people's heads, tilled the soil and committed piracy on the high seas. I remember the historian Cesare Balbo's definition of strong peoples – 'peoples possessed by civilised barbarism'.

During the month of January 1934 there were further articles by Lord Rothermere in the *Daily Mail* on 'Give the Blackshirts a Helping Hand' and 'The Blackshirts Will Stop War'. There were articles by Oswald Mosley not so much on policy, as on his resolution to get things done. By February he was writing –

The Blackshirts have only been organised in Britain for the last 16 months: in these early days they have advanced far more rapidly than any fascist movement in the world. Not only in mere numbers,

Ramsay MacDonald at Savehay Farm 1929
Top: Writing Labour Party Manifesto in the loggia
Bottom: Addressing constituency party workers from the nursery roof-garden

Cimmie's victory at Stoke 1929

Tom going to Windsor as Chancellor of
the Duchy of Lancaster

Cimmie with the other women Labour MPs outside the
House of Commons

Antibes 1929

Antibes 1931

Doris Castlerosse, Cecil Beaton, Oliver Messel, Cimmie, Zita James, Michael Arlen,
Tom

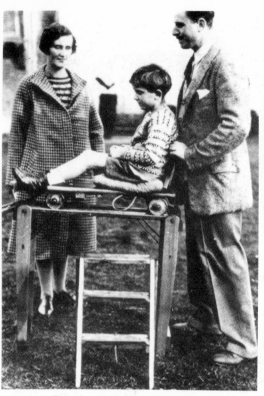

Cimmie and Tom with Nicholas on
switchback

Nicholas, Tom, Vivien

Tom and Nicholas

Tom fencing

Venice 1932: Cimmie, Tom Mitford, Doris Castlerosse, Diana Guinness, Tom

Michael's christening 1932: Harold Nicolson, Zita James, Irene Ravensdale, Robert
Forgan

Cimmie with children

Tom and Cimmie in Rome, April 1933
Top: at the March Past; Cimmie top right corner
Bottom: At Roman Royal Academy

Tom

Tom and Cimmie

Last picture of Cimmie with her children; in the Rose Garden, May 1933

Irene Ravensdale with Vivien and Nicholas at sea, August 1933

The family bathing at Savehay Farm

Savehay Farm 1930
Top: Tom with Harold Macmillan
Bottom: Nicholas, Vivien, W. E. D. Allen and child, W. J. Brown, Countess Karoli,
Aneurin Bevan

The New Party
Top: W. E. D. Allen, Robert Forgan, Cimmie, Tom, John Strachey
Bottom: Congress at Savehay Farm. C. E. M. Joad in foreground

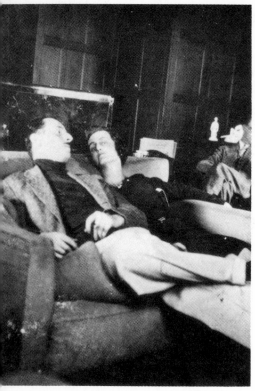

Tom and Cimmie in the drawing room

Nicholas catching tiddlers

Cimmie in her garden room

but in organisation, in spirit and in discipline we have reached a point which our predecessors had not reached until a relatively short space before they came to power.

The mood in the Black House was that the BUF would probably be in power within twelve months: people were called pessimists who forecast a time-lag of two or three years. The ex-District Inspector whose memoirs have been quoted before remembers –

Day and night it [the Black House] buzzed with activity. Typewriters rattled in administrative offices, printing presses clattered out the *Blackshirt* – the first BUF weekly paper. In one lecture room a lesson on election law would be in progress; in another aspiring speakers would be put through their hesitant paces; elsewhere the young tough men of 'I' Squad were being taught their boxing and judo. Cars roared in and out of the transport yard, and all the time there was a constant stream of callers and enquirers, some of whom were well known figures in the literary, professional, business and sporting worlds.

One of these figures from the literary world was Wyndham Lewis, who would come 'hurrying in with his hat pulled down and his coat collar up around his ears': another was Ezra Pound, who somewhat later wrote a pamphlet for the BUF entitled *What is Money for*. This is as difficult to understand, and as full of odd capital letters, as are some of his *Cantos*.

Amongst the cars that roared in and out of the transport yard were five large vans with protective plating at the sides and wire mesh over the windows which had been acquired early in 1934 and were used by the 'I' Squad to ferry them between headquarters and stormy meetings. They were described by the press variously as being 'bottle-proof, capable of holding thirty people and having a top speed of 55 mph'; and as being 'bullet proof, capable of holding twenty people and having a top speed of 65 mph'. In answer to questions about whether or not they resembled the cars used by American gangsters, a BUF spokesman explained – 'In principle they are the same, but the design is different'.

Lord Rothermere put money into the BUF: he also proposed to my father a scheme for manufacturing and marketing BUF cigarettes – he would produce the cigarettes and members of the movement would distribute them. He thought this would be enormously profitable both for himself and for the movement.

As enrolments into the BUF increased (at the height of its popularity in 1934 there were estimated to be between 30,000 and 40,000 members) there was an increasing problem of indiscipline. When Aneurin Bevan had said that nothing could do the BUF more damage than the backing of the Rothermere press he had probably meant that it was Lord Rothermere's personality that would cause confusion; but more important was the fact that the publicity was bringing in so many recruits of all kinds that it was difficult to sift and to control them – and this, in a movement whose *raison d'être* was that it should be able to demonstrate order, was serious. Our District Inspector remembers that as a result of the *Daily Mail* articles the BUF seemed to have 'drawn to itself almost every unstable person and adventurer of either sex ... genuine people who had been attracted by the programme and policy felt that they could not afford to be associated with the types congregated at the local district headquarters, and either refrained from enrolling or, having joined, soon faded out'. This was written by someone who remained a devoted follower of Mosley all his life. He added – 'In these spots nothing remained but a bad odour, still lingering three or four years later.'

It seems to have been one of the peculiarities of fascists and national socialists that for all their emphasis on discipline and obedience to a leader they depended for their *élan* very much on the freedom of lieutenants to go their own way. This was perhaps an inevitable outcome of the appeal to dynamism and heroism. In Italian Fascism and German National Socialism these tendencies were to a certain extent harnessed and unified because there was a common advocacy of warfare and a common view of enemies and scapegoats. But with the BUF's insistence that what it was striving for was peace and that enemies should only be fought in self-defence, there was the chance for every would-be gang-leader to impose his own interpretations. There was the continuing problem about the BUF speakers who disobeyed the orders to say nothing that could be taken as anti-semitic: this problem often now centred on William Joyce. In January 1934 in a speech at Chiswick he said in reply to a question about 'class war' – 'I don't regard Jews as a class, I regard them as a privileged misfortune'. He perorated, 'the flower or weed of Israel shall never grow in ground fertilised by British blood!'. The *Jewish World* called on Mosley to issue 'an uncompromising official repudiation' of Joyce in the light of his, Mosley's, own stated policy: it argued (in perhaps tellingly ambiguous phrasing) – 'either his or Mr Joyce's scurrilous claptrap is the authentic revelation'. But if the would-be toughs of the BUF were not going to be allowed

to find enemies against whom to exercise even their verbal aggressions –
in what spirit was their aggressive energy to be kept going?

With the indiscriminate flood of recruits there were more haphazard
stresses at headquarters. A man called George Crellin, or Captain
Thornton, joined the movement and announced that he was a 'Director
of Finance'; on the strength of this he hired a large car, and a horse
on which to ride in Hyde Park: when it was discovered that he was
a notorious con-man he was thrown out of the BUF and joined the
British Fascists under the name of Captain Latch. There was a man called
Jones who on enrolment persuaded the senior BUF officer in Sussex
to appoint him a District Officer; he then ran off with not only the
senior officer's wife but her child's nanny; when Jones was apprehended
the BUF officer told the police that he thought Jones was acting 'either
for the Labour Party at Brighton or the Co-op or both'. There was
a certain Richardson who had got into the Black House (on his
own admission) to sell to newspapers inside stories of what went on
there; when he was exposed and expelled he sold a story to the papers
of how he had been beaten up by fascist officials and made to drink
castor oil. The officials charged with these assaults were acquitted
through lack of evidence; but of course what stayed in the public's
mind were headlines in newspapers such as – 'Flogging alleged' or
'Castor oil punishment denied'. This was unfair: but the leadership of
the BUF did seem in some respects to be hedging its bets. It protested
its innocence in matters of violence, but it still was at pains to project
the sort of image of ruthlessness that was the hallmark of Mussolini.

There was a balancing act required here that called for a fine degree
of judgment: the Leader himself could spell out his instructions in words
– no force to be used unless provoked, a revolution to be won by
the example of men standing with their hands by their sides – and
if every predicament could have been referred to him and his decision
obeyed, then perhaps the spirit of a balancing act might have been
maintained. But as the movement grew and the expected crisis of chaos
did not materialise – then where was all the canalisation of energy to
go? Except for the spasmodic violence used in defence or retaliation
at meetings the energy had to be turned inwards: and as with most
hierarchical organisations dedicated to discipline there were thus favour-
itisms, jealousies, jockeyings for position – above all concerning
questions about who should have the ear of the Leader. Oswald Mosley
would turn up in his office: in theory he would be available for anyone
who had information to give to him; in practice, power depended on
who was in a position to let their own information through and to

get the information of other people blocked. A system designed to allow everyone dynamically to perform his own function became a matter of court intrigue.

In an increasingly powerful position at headquarters was Neil Francis-Hawkins, who moved from being Adjutant of the Defence Force to the Director General's office and was soon to become Director General himself – a position (after Robert Forgan had gone) second only to the Leader. In the words of our District Inspector, Francis-Hawkins was –

> entirely devoted to the movement. He spent between ten and twelve hours daily at his office while most weekends were given to participation in the outside activities. He expected his subordinates to give an almost equal amount of time to their duties; those who went home after a mere eight or nine hours at their desks were labelled 'clock-watchers' and denounced as unworthy of the cause they served. As many of them had wives or young families, domestic unhappiness too frequently arose. 'Wife-trouble' became one of the recognised occupational hazards of British Fascism.

Francis-Hawkins was a bachelor who lived in a flat in Hampstead with his sister; he was thought to be homosexual: in evidence for this was the hostility he showed to married men and the favouritism he seemed to grant to the unmarried men who formed a group around him known as his 'Mafia'. Francis-Hawkins' aim was to produce a loyal and obedient fascist force; it does not seem likely that he was struck by subtleties such as that solidarity can sometimes produce a deadening constellation of lies; that shows of strength are sometimes counter-productive since they awaken people's resentments and fears. But then these were the sort of subtleties which, when he was talking of politics rather than of literature, were apt to by-pass the Leader.

There was one area early in 1934 in which the BUF did try to be active in a more constructive way than that of the ejection of its opponents from its meetings: members became involved in what was known as the 'Tithe War'. There had been a spontaneous protest by East Anglian farmers against the payment of tithes – levies raised in mediaeval times in the form of produce for the upkeep of the church and which were now payable to the Church Commission in the form of a cash tax. In the impoverished circumstances of farming in England at this time farmers were objecting to the fact that only one section of the community should be called on for this tax; they were refusing to pay, and police and bailiffs were moving in to 'distrain' their property. It had been a particular aspect of BUF policy that British agriculture should be protected; local District Officers thus saw the chance of a form of action which would be constructive and charitable. They were given legal advice that if members of the Fascist Defence Force went to farms at the invitation of farmers and just 'by their passive presence' prevented bailiffs from doing their job, they would be within the law.

Members went to farms and dug ditches and built barricades to make it difficult for bailiffs to carry away equipment and livestock; then they waited, in tents, while bailiffs and onlookers leaned on fences and watched. All this was photographed by the local press; small crowds turned out; there was genuine interest in what might be the outcome of such a challenge to authority. Then government lawyers dug up an ancient statue under which fascists, just by their presence on the farm, could be charged with 'conspiring together to effect a public mischief': nineteen of them were arrested and carried away by police. They made no resistance. At the Old Bailey they pleaded guilty and were conditionally discharged by a Judge who said, 'I am told you are good fellows, and I hope you will remain good fellows, realising how badly advised you were in this matter.' The blackshirts had abided by their policy of doing nothing against the law; but as a result, a self-proclaimed dynamic movement had been made to look somewhat ridiculous.

The faith and hope of the fascists was always with their Leader. When he returned from his illness in the spring of 1934 he held his largest indoor meeting yet – on April 22nd in London at the Albert Hall. There was an audience of 10,000; both those within and those without the movement felt that if anything positive and effective was to be created, it would depend on the will and the talents of the Leader.

It is difficult nowadays to recall the style of a large blackshirt meeting: it had something of the atmosphere of a pop concert. There were the warm-up bands; the waiting; the dramatic entrance of the star. At the Albert Hall a blackshirt orchestra played the songs to the tunes of *Giovinezza* and the *Horst Wessel Lied*: also a new song that had been specially written for the occasion by members of the BUF – the words by E. D. Randall and the music by Selwyn Watson. This was entitled simply 'Mosley!' and began –

> Mosley: Leader of thousands!
> Hope of our manhood, we proudly hail thee!
> Raise we this song of allegiance
> For we are sworn and shall not fail thee.

Lead us! We fearlessly follow
To conquest and freedom – or else to death!
From coast to coast throughout the Motherland
Rings out the summons of the chosen band.

After the singing of this, the *Manchester Guardian* reported –

Just before eight the spotlights were turned on to the long gangway
leading through the arena to the platform and a procession of twelve
standard bearers marched in carrying alternately Union Jacks and
Fascist banners. The standard bearers grouped themselves round the
organ, the spotlights swung back to the main entrance, and there
stood the Man of Destiny.... Slowly he paced across the hall, chest
out, handsome head flung back, while his followers, every man on
his feet, cheered and cried 'Hail Mosley! Mosley! Mosley!'

From the platform beneath the organ he spoke, without notes, for
an hour and a half; there were no interruptions and no violent incidents;
for much of the time his voice was calm, quiet, almost intoning. He
spoke of his movement's being not racialist nor anti-semitic; of its commitment to seek only by constitutional means to come to power. When
it had achieved power, it would alter the present Parliamentary system
in that the government would give itself power to govern by order;
Parliament would only be summoned if there was public demand for
a vote to see whether or not the government should continue. With
such a safeguard (no details of its operation were given) a government
could not be called dictatorial. After a time, it was true, the present
Parliamentary structure would be abolished and a corporate state would
be set up on a basis of occupational franchise. This would –

place every industry in the country under the direct control of a
self-governing corporation on which will sit representatives of
employers, workers and consumers. These will fix by negotiation
the rates of wages, hours of work and prices and terms of competition which will be legally binding for an industry as a whole.
These corporations will send representatives to a national council
of corporations which will function as an industrial parliament. Here
matters of general financial policy will be settled, and the operations
of the various industries controlled and regulated in the interests of
the nation as a whole.

There was always a large part of a speech by my father that was calmly and rationally presented: sometimes his critics said that this was too large a part – that he overestimated his audience by assuming it could follow the technicalities of his arguments. But the flow of fact and argument gave an impression of great control and authority. And then there would be a change; he would stand back from the microphone as if he were a boxer sizing up an opponent before a knock-out attack: he was coming to his peroration. There is still in existence a gramophone record of the end of this Albert Hall speech; my father's voice comes out lashing like some great sea: it is pulverising: it is also, from a human being, like something carried far away beyond sense. It sends shivers up and down the spine – of both wonder and alarm – what is it all for, this yell for immolation? People at the end of such a speech of my father's were on their feet and cheering: it was as if they had been lifted high on a wave; what did it matter if they were hurled against, or over the top of, a cliff?

Let us take this vast Empire of ours, this heritage of our race won by our fathers and forefathers, and let us build up a civilisation far greater than the world has ever known.

Again and again in the long story of the human race, races have struggled up to nations and nations up to mighty empires; have scaled the heights of history and have thought they were safe: and now lit by the flame of such high inspiration this movement rises from the very soul of England to give all, to dare all, that England may live in greatness and in glory.

CHAPTER 6

Schoolboy Patterns 1

The private school I had been sent to shortly before my mother's death was Abinger Hill, near Dorking in Surrey. It was a pleasantly anarchic place run on progressive lines: boys were allowed to do much of their work in their own time; masters played an aloof and somewhat formal role like that of gods. This left mundane matters largely in the hands of boys: we ourselves were free to exercise, and observe, some of the strange patterns of impulses that are at the back of humans' dramatic and grandiose pretensions.

We formed groups, or gangs, for self-identification and self-protection: for this each needed a style, and apparently some mode of aggression. We roamed in the corridors and woods like mediaeval actors or bandits: I was a member of a small gang that affected sophistication. We hoped by this to boost ourselves and ward off enemies; we were like the lizards that puff up their throats to make themselves seem more formidable than they are. We saw ourselves as aesthetes: I think our idea of an aesthete was the sort of young man who might whizz between roadhouses in his sports car on the Dorking by-pass. In my gang was a boy called Plaister and a boy called Mellor and someone called Titus, with whom much of the school was in love. It seemed in keeping with sophistication to be in love. I have an image now of our small group wandering through the Surrey landscape like some illustration to *Don Quixote* or *Winnie the Pooh*. Plaister was tall and rather languid; Mellor was short like Sancho Panza. Titus was like the drawing of the boy going up to bed dragging his faithful animal behind him.

We had our private language; which was of the throw-away, self-deprecating type probably gleaned from P. G. Wodehouse. Gangs need some private language – to make them feel separate from the crowd, and amongst themselves to discourage class distinctions.

We did not pay much attention to games (the school magazine reported 'Plaister often bowled well in the nets but not otherwise': 'Mosley – another bowler who did not come up to scratch') and we pretended to pay no attention at all to work, though at least two of us showed we were quite clever. Our aim was to get as far away and as often as we could from the purlieus of the school; to establish our little kingdom, like that of characters in *As You Like It*, in the forest.

One of my memories of prep-school is of an almost perpetual hunger. The shop in the village was out of bounds: we were conspicuous in our brown corduroy shorts and brown-and-orange jerseys. We tried out various disguises: Plaister got hold of a pork-pie hat; we affected drawling Dorking-by-pass voices. But for the most part we relied on bringing back food from home; we would store it in tin boxes in the woods; here we would gather and munch, like badgers. I remember ham, and butter, and bits of bread that were called baps. One day when we were gnawing away under the trees we were come upon by Mr Tunnard Moore, the cricket master, who had followed us under the impression perhaps that we might be up to more nefarious practices. When he saw that what we were up to was food, he went on his way – informing us briefly of the dangers of ptomaine poisoning. We learned – it is a fact, is it not, that gods do not seem very interested in the needs of people for food?

With regard to sex, which gods as well as humans did seem interested in, we picked up and swapped bits of technical information as if they were conkers or sweets. The would-be sophistication of my own small gang meant that we were somewhat la-di-da about the dirty stories; but the limericks! I still remember the limericks: our sexual education was imbued with such legendary figures as the Plumber of Dee; the Young Girl of Pitlochry. We hoped to find out more details about their strange experiences: our practical interest in this respect became concentrated on Miss Hedge, the Art Mistress. It seemed to be sophisticated to have curiosity about Miss Hedge; but how on earth were we to satisfy this? There was a time I think in my third year when part of the school buildings burned down (it was rumoured that the fire had started after my future brother-in-law, aged ten, had been smoking in an attic; in later life, according to mood, he used either indignantly to deny this or to confirm it) and many of the staff had to be accommodated in pre-fabricated huts on the cricket field. This gave our gang the idea that a positive attitude might be adopted towards Miss Hedge – we would get up at dawn one day and try to get a glimpse of her through her bedroom window. Was not this the sort of thing, we imagined, that young men might be up to on the Dorking by-pass?

What was odd about this incident was that we made no effort at concealment: bravado seemed to be part of the required experience: perhaps this is why I have such a clear memory of it. We awoke with an alarm-clock; set off into the dawn; how wonderful to be so heroic and so alive! As we approached the cricket field we became overcome by fits of giggles. In the event I think we got the wrong window and looked in not upon Miss Hedge, the Art Mistress, but on Miss Someone-else the Under-Matron. And of course we were seen; but we wandered back to our dormitory happy. Had we not completed our mission? And was not this what life was about? Later, when the headmaster questioned us, we said we had gone birds' nesting. We were duly beaten.

The business of being beaten played not a large part in fact in the school routine: it loomed larger in our imaginations. It seemed to be to do with drama, with challenge, with the involvement in great events. To be beaten meant going up to the door of the headmaster's study and waiting outside; others went in first; through the closed door one heard an almost interminable rumbling; this turned out to be the furniture being moved. Then there were six fearsome cracks like pistol shots. Then someone would stagger out clutching himself like people do through saloon doors in western films. When one went into the headmaster's study he seemed as nervous as oneself: and so in the end, what a weird, scruffy shoot-out! But afterwards, there was the rallying round some boy who claimed to have sure legal knowledge that, if it could be shown that skin had been broken, the headmaster could be prosecuted for assault: in which case what an amazing turning of the tables! There was much happy and legalistic discussion and in-spection about this – quite like politics.

An even more bizarre way in which impulses and fascinations ex-pressed themselves was in a school craze known as womb-fighting. Two boys would come across each other in a passageway or changing room (how much of school life seemed to take place in changing rooms!) and one boy would crouch, placing a forearm across his stomach, and with the other would grope outwards as if it were the claw of a crab: this was a challenge for the other boy to do the same. The fight would be, symbolically, to see who could tear out the other's 'womb': in practice, I suppose, it was a means of giving and sustaining a massive tickling. (A later vulgarisation of this craze was ball-fighting, an altogether more hostile and destructive ritual). Perhaps in its origins all masculine brawling is a desire to get back to (to get one's own back on?) the lovely but terrible tweaks and tickles of the mother: it is the impossibility of this, that leads to virulence.

As time went on the formation of gangs and alliances which is the style of any society took on at school a more formally grown-up air. The fact that my father was Leader of the British Union of Fascists had, of course, been noted; I had for a while been called by one of the masters (fairly affectionately) 'Baby Blackshirt'. Boys were not instinctively interested in such things: what mattered to us about our parents was that their appearance should not be embarrassing, and what sort of car they turned up in at weekends. I scored quite well in this respect when my father's chauffeur Mr Perrett came to pick me up in the dashing Bentley: also my Aunt Irene's huge Packard, which was like a hearse, stood me in quite good stead. But then there came a time when grown-up politics did impinge on what was anyway boys' liking for rivalry; this was in 1935 when Italy invaded Abyssinia. The war of course was the subject of newspaper headlines: it caught the school's imagination, like any craze. I wrote to my father –

Darling Daddy,   Sunday 6th October
Two parties have sprung up here, one for the Abbysinians and the other for the Italians. I am the leader of the Italians, and this afternoon we are having a huge fight in the woods. The Abbysinians are the bigger, but we have some good people and are hoping to win. The Abbysinians started their party first, so I thought it would be fun to start an Italian one.

I had taken it for granted, of course, that I should be 'Italian': my loyalty to my father was unquestionable. But I was over-optimistic (as indeed my father often was) about the strength of the forces on my side: Abinger Hill School, being 'progressive', consisted of boys whose parents were predominantly left-wing. I think my 'some good people' consisted of scarcely more than my loyal friend Titus and our mutual friend Frank, who happened to be the son of the Government Chief Whip. Surrounding our small colonial outpost in the woods the Abyssinians were legion: they came down on us in the evening, I remember, as we sat in our small tent; I like to think we went down bravely, like Gordon at Khartoum.

This was the first time I remember having any opinion about politics. I had, I think, been sent weekly copies of my father's paper *Blackshirt*: now I would explain to the benighted left-wing natives in the school – Do you not see that Mussolini is bringing culture and civilisation to a backward Africa? Is it not this that the British have done for hundreds of years with their glorious Empire?

The sort of books I read at this time were those by Sapper and Leslie Charteris and (perhaps this was somewhat later) Dornford Yates. These told of cool, relentless men who made sardonic quips as they dealt with anti-imperialist villains; there were killings but no pain; the enemy were members of an evil world-wide conspiracy of 'aliens' who could be thwarted only by small bands of self-professed 'saints'. All this fitted in with what I had gleaned from the world – both from the arbitrariness of the school world in which one's sanity was preserved by one's gang; also from the grown-up world where there were, were there not, the dark forces of which my father spoke that were spreading and preventing the introduction of order. However, towards the end of my time at Abinger Hill I remember being introduced to and reading Aldous Huxley's *Antic Hay*: this was a revelation. It told of a world of people who were indeed humorous and detached; but whose virtues were concerned not with the thwarting of gigantic machinations but with ways in which pretensions of machinations might, with artistry, be seen as funny – and thus might even best be thwarted?

What I remember most about Abinger Hill is the laughter: there was the impression sometimes that one might take off with suppressed laughter: laughter of course often had to be suppressed, this was the style of the world one lived in. There was a boy called Fawcett who, in the middle of daily prayers, once farted; this was no ordinary fart, it was the most drawn-out, painstaking, trumpet-cry one had ever heard – Roland's call at Roncesvalles; Siegfried's horn in his wood. This burst in upon the Prayer of St Chrysostom or whatever; the headmaster told Fawcett quietly to leave the room. For the rest of us it was as if the pressures were too great; we were lifted like rockets to some beatific vision; several others had to leave the room. I think Abinger Hill was a good school in that it allowed us to see things as slightly ridiculous: that this was not incompatible with a beatific vision.

I remember almost nothing of the classroom work at Abinger Hill: such information seemed to be taken in like stores on to an ocean liner at night. Latin verbs and geometrical theorems appeared to have nothing to do with anything real outside: still, they were perhaps representative of what was fantastical in the interests of the grown-up world. These continued to break into school life from time to time. I remember once talking to my friend Titus about our parents and the parents of some of our friends: he said – But you and I, we're different, aren't we? I did not know what he meant. I wondered – We are more clever? In love? Then I realised – he was referring to something about what the grown-up world called 'class'. I was not able to make much of this – neither of the fact that the grown-up world seemed to think so often in terms of class, nor of my own blankness towards my friend's suggestion. Perhaps I liked to think that my family was unique, incomparable – nothing to do with anything so vulgar as being upper-class. Was not my father after all a rich, ex-socialist, would-be dictator fascist baronet?

One of the activities I remember enjoying at this time was the founding of a school film society which I ran in collaboration with my friend Julian Mond: we hired films from a library in London and showed them on my mother's old projector to audiences who paid a penny or two entrance fee. Then one summer the school put on an ambitious performance of *Twelfth Night* and press-men came down to take photographs of the scene; for a reason I did not at first understand they insisted on my friend Julian Mond and me being photographed together. Later I read the caption to the photograph in the *News Review* – 'Jewish peer Lord Melchett's son Julian assists his schoolfellow Nicholas son of the Fascist Leader Sir Oswald Mosley'.

Quite often at this time I had recurring nightmares. There was one in which I was drinking water from a tumbler and the tumbler suddenly fastened itself over my mouth thus making it impossible for me to breathe: this had, I suppose, something to do with my stammer. In another I was by an ornamental pond upon which brightly-painted toy boats were floating to and fro; looking down, I became filled with terror.

The most lasting image of myself that I remember from Abinger Hill is of me as a machine within which I lived and which I controlled by moving levers as if I were like men in white coats facing dials; I had to tread carefully, as if I was walking through minefields; what was important, was to ensure the efficient working of my machine. I was something inside myself keeping a solicitous eye on myself; what went on outside was another matter. Occasionally there were miraculous moments in the woods for instance with friends when my machinery and that of the whole world seemed suddenly to click into gear: oneself became oneself in relation to everything. But for the most part one was one's own search for some holy grail. There were nights when one walked up a dark lane from the school to an outside dormitory building; there were all these little bits and pieces whirling about inside; there were also the distant stars. And there were connections: was not the network still oneself? Of course, one could not talk much about this: one could laugh – make a joke or pun or something. What was it, this grid, this riddle, this holy grail?

CHAPTER 7

Olympia

The success of the Albert Hall meeting in April 1934 and the continued backing of the Rothermere Press with the resulting influx of recruits had made members of the BUF imagine they were being carried forwards on a wave that might bring them to power within a few years. This enthusiasm made their opponents also feel there might be cause to think this.

The Albert Hall meeting had been orderly: Mosley had got his message across to an audience of 10,000. It was still believed at this time that promulgation of the spoken word was the way to be effective in politics: there was evidence for this from the careers of Mussolini and Hitler. There was one auditorium in London bigger than the Albert Hall – that of Olympia. The BUF arranged to hold a meeting there on 7th June 1934, to which they hoped to attract members of the uncommitted public and especially the establishment intelligentsia who might be ready in the contemporary political climate to take a serious look at fascism.

The communists saw that the fascists had scored heavily at the Albert Hall by their demonstration of good order and discipline: it mattered less what had been said than that the fascist claim had seemed to be justified that it was a movement which could act cleanly and efficiently. Both sides therefore saw the meeting at Olympia as crucial. For the fascists it was a chance to demonstrate their disciplined strength to an audience more than usually sophisticated: for communists it was vital to try to expose the fascists as desperadoes and thugs.

There is little dispute about what actually occurred at Olympia. Contention about interpretation has continued.

The fascists planned, as they always planned, for the sort of orderly meeting which was necessary if the Leader was to be heard: the Defence

Force was given the same instructions as it was always given – not to use force to get rid of hecklers until they had been given due warning; not to strike first, and even then not to use unnecessary violence. It might have been a fault that no special instructions were given in the light of the style of the communist propaganda about this particular meeting: it might have been seen that attitudes more subtle than usual might be required if the image of discipline was to be maintained.

The communists made no attempt to conceal their intention to break up the meeting. On 26th May an announcement appeared in the *Daily Worker*:

In connection with the great anti-Fascist counter-demonstration which is being organised by the London District Committee of the Communist Party on June 7th when Mosley's Blackshirts are holding a Fascist Rally at Olympia, the following are the arrangements:

Marches will be organised from five different parts of London in the late afternoon to arrive in Hammersmith Road in the vicinity of Olympia at 6.30 p.m. Workers who cannot participate in the marches are asked to rally to Hammersmith Road from 6.30 p.m. onwards after leaving work. Arrangements should be made in the localities for parties of workers to travel on the underground and to obtain cheap facilities for parties.

The District Committee of the Communist Party have sent letters to the London Labour Party, London Trades Union Council, the I.L.P., and District Committees of Trades Unions, inviting their cooperation in the counter-demonstration.

There were further notices in the *Daily Worker* during the coming days: on 7th June it published a map illustrating the routes to Olympia and announced –

Inside the large hall and outside the challenge of Mosley will be met by the determined workers ... The workers' counteraction will cause them to tremble. All roads lead to Olympia tonight!

After the event there were accusations by each side that the other had armed itself with weapons – truncheons, knuckledusters, iron bars, and so on. The fascists denied that they used weapons and there is no hard evidence to the contrary. Communists made no secret about their carrying of weapons. Philip Toynbee described in his book *Friends Apart* how before Olympia he and Esmond Romilly 'bought knuckledusters at a Drury Lane ironmonger and I well remember the exaltation of trying them on'. Toynbee and Romilly were teenage schoolboys: they took it for granted that communists thus armed themselves before such a confrontation. Claud Cockburn wrote of these days when he was a communist demonstrator: 'It is fashionable to allege that we were starry-eyed idealists, but we certainly knew where to put the razor-blades in the potato when it came to a fight.'

Outside the hall when members of the audience arrived they had to push their way through a crowd of two or three thousand anti-fascists who were held back by police. There were the usual chants of – 'One two three four, What are the Fascists for, lechery treachery hunger and war'; 'Two three four five, we want Mosley dead or alive.' Most of the audience managed to get through; individual Blackshirts who were caught on the edge of the crowd were punched and kicked.

Inside, there were 13,000 seats costing between a shilling and seven-and-sixpence: communists had bought or forged tickets (some, it was said, had been won in a *Daily Mail* competition) but it would have been impossible in any event to try to stop agitators getting in because there were 2,000 seats available free on the day. Communist demon-strators seated themselves round the hall strategically in groups; some were said to be wearing blackshirts to add to the planned confusion.

There were the usual warm-up procedures of fanfares and songs: the start of the meeting was delayed owing to the trouble people outside were having in getting through. Then, in Philip Toynbee's words –

The Leader strode into the arc lights. He was flanked by four blond young men, and a platoon of flag-waving blackshirts followed in their wake. The procession moved very slowly down the aisle, amid shouts, screams, and bellows of admiration; amid two forests of phallic, upraised arms. Sir Oswald held one arm at his side, thumb in leather belt: the other flapped nonchalantly from time to time as he turned a high chin to inspect us.

As soon as Mosley started speaking the interruptions began: indi-viduals or groups chanted 'Fascism means murder!' or just 'Down with Mosley!' It had been learned from previous meetings that even with a battery of loudspeakers a speech in such conditions could not be heard. The speaker gave the usual warning – If the interrupters did not stop, they would be thrown out. They did not stop. Blackshirt stewards moved towards them.

There is little dispute even in detail about the sort of thing that now

took place. It was obviously in the fascists' interests to eject the interrupters quickly and efficiently or, at the worst, after what could be
seen by the uncommitted part of the audience as a fair fight: it was
in the interests of the interrupters to make the fascist stewards appear
to be incompetent and brutal. It was in this contest concerning the
fascists' image – as opposed to that of who simply won the fight –
that the communists came out on top.

The interrupters were spaced out in the hall so that when one lot
was being dealt with by stewards another lot would start: what seemed
to be a single interrupter was suddenly backed by a large number when
one or two stewards moved in to deal with him. There was what seemed
to be the use of women interrupters to taunt the stewards, who were
then fought by men. The result was that after an initial attempt to
stick to discipline the stewards, under provocation, manifestly got out
of control. Eye-witnesses who professed to have begun as neutral reported – 'Again and again as five or six fascists carried out an interrupter
by arms and legs several other fascists were engaged in hitting and
kicking his helpless body' (Geoffrey Lloyd MP): 'In the corridor a
young man.... was being chased by a horde of Blackshirts: some
collared him by the legs, some by the arms, and held in this way he
was beaten on the head by any fascist who could get near him' (Rev.
Dick Sheppard). While this sort of thing was going on in the auditorium
Mosley had stopped even trying to speak; he waited, hands on his hips,
while spotlights from the roof played on the violence below. This made
it seem as if the whole point of the show might be violence. Mosley
explained later that the working of the spotlights had had nothing to
do with him; they had been under the control of the Newsreel camera-
men who had come to film the occasion. Also, he said he sometimes
could not see what was happening because the spotlights were in his
eyes. But the impression given was of some sort of Roman circus.
Two demonstrators got amongst the girders of the roof and were
pursued there by Neil Francis-Hawkins. It took a long time for the
speech to get going, and then too much had happened for many people
to be interested in listening. Members of the audience had begun to
walk out 'in a steady trickle' because of what they felt as 'boredom'
(Vera Brittain).

Before the end three Conservative MPs – W. J. Anstruther-Gray,
J. Scrymgeour-Wedderburn and T. J. O'Connor – had left and were
making a dash to Printing House Square to get a letter into *The Times*
of the next day. 'We were involuntary witnesses of wholly unnecessary
violence inflicted by uniformed Blackshirts on interrupters. Men and

women were knocked down and were still assaulted and kicked on the floor. It will be a matter of surprise to us if there were no fatal injuries.' There was, in fact, nothing like a fatal injury: after the meeting a number of people from both sides were treated in nearby hospitals for cuts, broken teeth, broken noses and kicks in the stomach; but from the records only one anti-fascist – a student from Sheffield – was kept in hospital for more than a day. He claimed that he had been bludgeoned on the head till he was 'half dead'; he turned up three weeks later however to make this allegation at a meeting addressed by Mosley. Two fascist stewards were kept in hospital overnight. In all, it was the sort of fight that nowadays (1983) would be taken as not all that unusual at a crucial football match.

But the important battle was the one of propaganda: there were other members of the audience hurrying to get their statements to the press. On the side of the blackshirts were M. W. Beaumont MP, who wrote to *The Times* – 'While the forces of law and order make no effort to safeguard the rights of free speech in this country, the use of some such methods [by the stewards] is the only way in which those putting forward an unknown and controversial case can obtain a hearing' and Patrick Donner MP, who wrote to the *National Review* – 'The fact is that many of the Communists were armed with razors, stockings filled with broken glass, knuckledusters and iron bars; that they marched from the East End, the police kindly escorting, with the avowed purpose of wrecking the meeting.... Can it in equity be argued that the stewards used their fists, when provoked in this manner, with more vigour than perhaps the situation required?' And Lloyd George, who had not been at the meeting, wrote in the *Sunday Pictorial* – 'It is difficult to explain why the fury of the champions of free speech should be concentrated so exclusively not on those who deliberately and resolutely attempted to prevent the public expression of opinions of which they disapproved, but against those who fought, however roughly, for freedom of speech.' Participants on each side spoke of the 'unenglishness' of the other: to one it was the fascists in their black shirts who were the 'alien' force; to the other, it was those yelling with their 'hebraic features'.

The fascists won physically the battle of Olympia: the hecklers were, for the most part, thrown out. That the communists won the propaganda war was due partly to the fact that they had a preponderance of influential and literary eye-witnesses who supported their version of what happened – they published a pamphlet called *Fascists at Olympia* in which accounts of the violence, in addition to those mentioned above, were given by Aldous Huxley, Storm Jameson, Naomi Mitchison, Ritchie Calder – but above all (and this probably influenced the way in which the eye-witnesses interpreted what they saw) the communist propaganda victory was due to the fact that the image of fascists as thugs was being imprinted in people's minds anyway – and this was to a certain extent irrespective of particular instances of behaviour of the BUF. Oswald Mosley could, as usual, win some sort of war with words – he gave interviews after the meeting on the lines of: the communists started the trouble, so what did they expect? – but none of this outweighed the public vision of fascism that was growing as a result of the example of Hitler's Germany. Hitler's SA and SS were seen as almost self-admitted thugs. The British Union of Fascists, people reasoned, must know Hitler's men were thugs; since the fascists seemed to emulate them – or at least made no effort to dissuade people from thinking they were emulating them – thus they must want to take the responsibility of appearing to be like thugs.

Shortly before the Olympia meeting the United Front Committee which had been summoned to co-ordinate the various plans for the anti-fascist demonstrations had written to the management of Olympia to try to get the meeting cancelled. They had said:

> Realising the torture undergone by the thousands of individuals of all classes and the thousands at present suffering in concentration camps and the persecution of the Jews at the instance of Hitler and his Fascist regime, we demand that the letting of Olympia be cancelled to the British Union of Fascists and that on no future occasions will they be allowed to hold a meeting in your building.

Shortly after the Olympia meeting, on 30th June 1934, Hitler murdered Roehm, the SA leader, and at least eighty of his colleagues (the figure has been put as high as a thousand) in the purge that came to be known as the Night of the Long Knives. Roehm had been one of Hitler's closest friends: the SA had been the gang of loyal toughs to a large extent responsible for bringing Hitler to power. But now Hitler wanted to appear respectable: above all, he needed to get the support of the army to whom the SA were a threat. So he had his old friends the SA leaders killed by his new friends the SS – there was a whiff here of a new sort of terror – were fascists then people liable to kill not only their enemies but their friends? Norman Angell wrote in the *Foreign Affairs Digest* – 'One cannot imagine that Oswald Mosley was altogether happy at the news from Berlin on Saturday night.' Images that were floating around in the public mind must have seemed to constellate – those of Olympia, of the black uniforms of both the BUF and the SS, of attacks on Jews and of nights with long knives. Almost without anyone knowing, a pattern of mind had been set up that would be almost impossible to break – that of fascists being identified with thugs.

One of the first casualties on the fascist side in the propaganda war was Lord Rothermere: in July he withdrew his support from the BUF. It had lasted for no more than six months: there had been some mystery about why, apart from the encouragement of Mussolini, he had ever given it. He had met and admired Hitler, but he had always said he would not be associated with anti-semitism. After Olympia the chairmen of certain Jewish firms let Lord Rothermere know that if he continued to support fascism they would not advertise in his papers. It seemed to them evident that if the blackshirts got power, British Jews would be persecuted in the way that German Jews were being persecuted under Hitler. Rothermere asked Mosley to come and see him: Mosley later told the story:*

> I went to see him in a hotel he frequented and found him in a relatively modest apartment, an imposing figure of monumental form lying flat on his back on a narrow brass bedstead.... Lord Rothermere explained that he was in trouble with certain advertisers who had not liked his support for the blackshirts.... The long struggle fluctuated, but I lost. He felt that I was asking him to risk too much, not only for himself but for others who depended on him.

The threat of Jewish advertisers however was probably not the decisive influence in the story. On 20th July a correspondence between Mosley and Rothermere was published in *Blackshirt* –

Dear Lord Rothermere,
.... At present some doubt has arisen in the public mind as to our relationship. That doubt arises from the basic fact that you are a Conservative and we Blackshirts are Fascists. We hold the new creed of the modern world which we are striving to bring to Britain by British methods and in accordance with the British character.... You, on the other hand, are a Conservative and would like to see a revived Conservative Party.... You have stated your doubts as

* *My Life.*

to certain aspects of our policy, and have expressed your desire that
we should abandon or modify them.

There followed a list of the areas in which Mosley suggested Lord
Rothermere wanted modifications – The Corporate State, Reform of
Parliament, the use of the word 'Fascist'. Mosley wrote – 'You would
like us to abandon the creed of Fascism and the word "Fascist": we
cannot do this because it is the creed which means everything in the
world to us'. Then there was the question of Jews. Mosley continued:

We have given our pledge that no racial or religious persecution
will occur under Fascism in Britain; but we shall require the Jews,
like everyone else, to put the interests of 'Britain First'. We no longer
admit Jews to membership of our movement because (a) they have
bitterly attacked us; (b) they have organised as an international movement setting their racial interests above the national interests and
are, therefore, unacceptable as members of a national movement
which aims at national organisation and revival. We certainly are
not prepared to relax our attitude towards the Jews in view of the
fact that in the last year 80% of the convictions for physical attacks
on Fascists were pronounced on Jews while the Jewish community
represents only .6% of the population....

To this Lord Rothermere replied:

My dear Mosley,
...... As you know, I have never thought that a movement calling
itself 'Fascist' could be successful in this country, and I have also
made it clear in my conversation with you that I never could support
any movement with an anti-semitic bias, any movement that had
dictatorship as one of its objectives, nor any movement which would
substitute a 'corporate state' for Parliamentary institutions in this
country ... The assistance which I have rendered you was given
in the hope that you would be prepared to ally yourself with the
Conservative forces to defeat Socialism at the next and succeeding
elections.
..... I have never thought that the political situation here bears any
relation to the political situation in Italy or Germany. In each of
these countries parliamentary institutions were largely of exotic
growth, whereas in England they have, since the time of Queen
Elizabeth, exercised the real decisive influence.

Lord Rothermere's support had landed the BUF with a crisis to do with the influx of unsuitable personnel; his withdrawal landed it with a crisis about money – the scheme to market BUF cigarettes fell through, and he made no more personal payments. The money crisis could, with courage and hard work, be surmounted; the problem of the BUF Defence Force being linked with Hitlerism was much more serious. There was the continuing dilemma – if the BUF turned back now from its aim of establishing itself in the public mind as a force able to deal promptly with the sort of crisis that it had always said was to be expected – what would it have left? On the other hand – if both the BUF and Hitler continued as they were, how could they not be linked in the patriotic public mind to the grave detriment of British fascism?

There is a sense in which Hitler made impossible the success of other fascist or national socialist movements in Europe: there was nothing in the philosophy of fascism ostensibly to do with racialism or the desire for conquest which were the drives which pushed Hitler to destruction and eventually to self-destruction. On the other hand some archetypal drives (even excesses?) seem to be necessary if groups are to be welded dynamically into a single force. But Mussolini was not anti-semitic until he came under the influence of Hitler; and Franco in Spain, after his success in the Civil War, showed great skill in keeping out of warfare. In July 1934 it might have been possible for my father to have repudiated Hitler: he had already called Hitler 'mistaken' in his persecution of Jews: the public reaction to the Roehm purge must have struck him forcibly. (The magazine *John Bull* threw in its comment – 'Hitler killed fascism in this country on that night!') But my father chose to make no strong moral comment on all this: he did not try to find a different form of impetus. He probably felt it was too late to turn back now: movements such as his wither and die if their impetus is changed. And besides – in fact, did not Hitler seem to be winning?

Coincidences occur both in the public and in the personal world through which – and through a person's responses to which – life seems to be fashioned. Such coincidences are not matters of cause and effect: they are yet perhaps instances whereby a person's character can be decisive. It was perhaps never in my father's character to be someone who could turn back: with his passionate belief about how the world had swiftly to be altered, how could he? But being the sort of person he was – who gambled on everything – coincidences now seemed to turn against him. Coincidences perhaps work for those who watch and listen. He was like a ship moving into an area of icebergs.

CHAPTER 8

Hitler

When in the summer holidays of 1933 myself and my sister Vivien and Aunt Irene had gone on our cruise to the Canary Isles and my father and my Aunt Baba had gone on a motoring trip through France, Diana Guinness and her sister Unity Mitford had set off on their motoring trip through Germany: in Munich they were taken up by Hitler's friend Putzi Hanfstaengl and went with him to the first huge Nazi Rally or Parteitag at Nuremberg. There they attended the parades and were present at Hitler's speeches: Diana wrote years later of how 'a feeling of excited triumph was in the air, and when Hitler appeared an almost electric shock went through the multitude'. Diana and Unity asked Hanfstaengl if they could meet Hitler, but he put them off with excuses that Hitler was too busy for personal matters – and anyway he did not like women who wore lipstick. Unity became obsessed by the idea of meeting Hitler: she said however that even for him she would not remove her lipstick.

The following summer, after the holiday in which Diana spent two weeks with my father and Vivien and myself in the house near Toulon, Diana and Unity went again to Nuremberg. Hanfstaengl was still not helpful about an introduction to Hitler, so Diana and Unity went to Munich and Unity stayed there at a finishing school to learn German (she was just twenty) and Diana, after having returned home briefly and consulted my father, went back to Munich and took a flat there with her maid. Unity had discovered that when Hitler was in Munich (where the headquarters of the Nazi Party still were) he sometimes went for lunch to a restaurant called the Osteria Bavaria: Diana and Unity took to going there to catch a glimpse of him. He would come in from time to time with one or two adjutants and friends – Hoffman, his photographer; Dietrich, his press chief; Wagner, the Gauleiter of

Bavaria. There would be a table in the corner reserved for him: the
waitresses would flutter; there would be an atmosphere both glamorous
and informal like that surrounding a pop star. Unity recorded that
Hitler had come in one day in his 'sweet' mackintosh and asked a
waitress who she and Diana were; then he had stared at them in silence
for a long time so that 'one couldn't think or move or anything'.

Diana returned to England before Christmas: Unity stayed on in
Munich going hopefully to the Osteria Bavaria. Then in February 1935
she wrote to Diana –

Yesterday was the most wonderful and beautiful day of my life.
I will try and describe it to you, though I can yet hardly write.

I went alone to lunch at the Osteria and sat at the little table by
the stove where we sat you know last time you were there. At about
3, when I had finished my lunch, the Fuhrer came in and sat down
at his usual table with two other men. I read the *Vogue* you sent
me. About ten minutes after he arrived he spoke to the Manager
and the Manager came over to me and said 'The Fuhrer would like
to speak to you'. I got up and went over to him and he stood up
and saluted and shook hands and introduced me to the others and
asked me to sit next to him.

I sat and talked to him for about half an hour, at least of course
I don't really know how long, but I think it was about that. Mona
(the fat waitress) came and whispered to me 'Shall I bring you a
postcard?' so I said Yes, really to please her. She brought it and I
was rather embarrassed to ask him to sign it but in the end I did,
and I said I hoped he wouldn't think it very American of me.

He made me write my name on a piece of paper which I did
as you may believe very shakily and then he wrote on the card –
Frl Unity Mitford, Zur freundlichen Erinnerung an Deutschland und
Adolf Hitler. Tom [Unity's and Diana's brother] will tell you what
it means. I can't tell you all the things we talked about as it would
take too long. I told him he ought to come to England and he said
he would love to but he was afraid there would be a revolution
if he did. He asked me if I had ever been to Bayreuth and I said
No, but I should like to, and he said to one of the other men that
they must remember that the next time there was a Festspiel there.
He said he felt he knew London well from his architectural studies,
and that from what he had heard and read about it he thought it
to be the best town, as a town, in the world. He thinks 'Cavalcade'
is the best film he ever saw.

He talked about the war. He said it was like the Niebelungskampf, and that international Jews must never again be allowed to make two Nordic races fight against one another.

He told me all about the great road and halls and stadium they are building in Nuremberg for the Parteitags which are costing 8,000,000 marks and will be ready in 8 years. He says that then the Parteitags will be really tremendous.

Well, I can't remember more of our conversation but we talked of a lot of things. In the end he had to go. He kept the bit of paper with my name on. Mona told me it was the first time he had ever invited someone he didn't know to sit at his table like that. He had also apparently made sure my lunch was put on his bill.

So after all that you can imagine what I feel like. I am so happy that I wouldn't mind a bit dying. I suppose I am the luckiest girl in the world. I certainly never did anything to deserve such an honour.

In March Diana drove to Munich in a Voisin car that my father had bought for her: she got stuck in a snow-drift in the Black Forest and had to be pulled out by a team of farm-horses. In Munich she and Unity went to the Osteria Bavaria and Unity introduced Diana to Hitler. Diana's description of Hitler at the time of this her first meeting with him was* –

Hitler, at this time aged forty five, was about 5 feet 9 inches in height and neither fat nor thin. His eyes were dark blue, his skin fair, and his brown hair exceptionally fine. It was neatly brushed: I never saw him with a lock of hair over his forehead. His hands were white and well shaped. He was extremely neat and clean looking, so much so that beside him almost everyone looked coarse. His teeth had been mended with gold, as one saw when he laughed. At the Osteria he was generally in civilian clothes; he wore a grey suit and a white shirt and a rather furry soft hat which he called 'mein Shako'. His most unusual feature was his forehead. He had a high forehead which almost jutted forward above the eyes. I have seen this on one or two other people: generally they have been musicians. At this little bistro he was in a relaxed mood; if he had not been so he would have lunched at his flat.

* *A Life of Contrasts.*

Diana described how he was extremely polite to women; he would bow, and kiss their hand, and would not sit down till they did. He invariably ate 'eggs and mayonnaise and vegetables and pasta': his guests could order what they liked – even to having food sent from a renowned restaurant next door. Hitler listened to what his guests had to say and did not indulge in monologues – except occasionally one on the subject of motor cars, which Diana and Unity 'rather dreaded'.

During the next four and a half years Diana saw Hitler 'fairly often, though not nearly as often as Unity did'. Very many years later she said to me, the author, that she thought her meeting with Hitler had ruined her life. She added – 'And I think it ruined your father's.'

My father went to see Hitler for the first time in April 1935; he was received in his flat in Munich and the two of them talked through an interpreter for an hour before lunch. My father described the scene:*

At first Hitler was almost inert in his chair, pale, seemingly exhausted. He came suddenly to life when I said that war between Britain and Germany would be a terrible disaster, and used the simile of two splendid young men fighting each other until they both fall exhausted and bleeding to the ground, when the jackals of the world would mount triumphant on their bodies. His face flushed and he launched with much vigour into some of his main themes, but in the normal manner of any politician moved by strong convictions. The hypnotic manner was entirely absent; perhaps I was an unsuitable subject; in any case he made no attempt whatever to produce any effect of that kind. He was simple, and treated me throughout the occasion with a gentle, almost feminine charm.

My father said that this first interview with Hitler was 'exactly the opposite of a first encounter with Mussolini: there was no element of posture'. My father had got on well with Mussolini: he felt they had had things in common. He used to say that my mother, for instance, had liked Mussolini: she had called him 'that big booming man'. My father never, it seemed, much liked Hitler: in old age he used to refer to him as a 'terrible little man'. One of the sayings he liked to bring out over the dinner table was that Italy, being a feminine country, had fallen in love with Mussolini, a man; whereas Germany, being a masculine country, had fallen in love with Hitler, a woman. At the other end of the table my stepmother Diana would smile patiently

* *My Life.*

with closed eyes. There is some evidence that Hitler and his Nazis never much liked my father: in 1935 a member of the BUF called Dr Pfister was in Germany and brought back information that 'a certain high Nazi official who visited this country some time ago had not been favourably impressed of a meeting he had had with the Leader'; also that there was some displeasure over 'Ma' Mosley having given an interview to the press in which she stated that 'Hitler was the greatest enemy to the BUF since people in this country would not join on account of the brutal methods in Germany'. Dr Pfister also reported that 'the Nazi Party were very disappointed that the leader had shown so little appreciation of their victory in the Saar'.

In later years I once asked my stepmother why it was that Hitler seemed to have such hypnotic power over so many different kinds of people – storm-troopers, financiers, fashionable women, generals, peasants – whereas my father, however much he impressed people when they met him, had not evoked the same obsessed loyalty by which people even when they had not wanted to might seem ready to give up their lives. I had thought this would be a difficult question, but my stepmother said – I will tell you exactly: when people met your father they thought: Here is this wonderful man who has an answer to everything himself so what is there for us to do? When people met Hitler they thought: Here is this wonderful but unfortunate man who seems to have all the cares of the world on his shoulders, so we must do all we can to help him.

Unity was only twenty-one when she met Hitler: Diana was twenty-four. Germany was a place which had been transformed in two years from a country of hopelessness, cynicism and mass unemployment into a nation in which a large majority of people were observably purposeful and cheerful, and almost everyone and everything worked.

There was something in Hitler that evoked adoration; something in the people around him that wished to give it. Hitler's power of attraction resided in paradoxes: he was enormously confident yet awkwardly alone; people were awe-struck by him, yet felt he was so fragile they had to treat him gently. They rushed to gather what they needed of his confidence; in order to maintain this, they gave their confidence to him. Goebbels wrote of Hitler – 'He is like a child; kind, good, merciful: like a cat; cunning, clever, agile: like a lion; roaring, great, gigantic'. Goering put this in more ponderous terms: having likened what he saw as Hitler's infallibility to that of the pope –*

---

* In *Germany Reborn*.

Wherein lies the secret of the enormous influence he has on followers? Does it lie in his goodness as a man, in his strength of character, or in his unique modesty? Does it lie in his political genius, his gift of seeing what direction things are going to take, in his great bravery, or in his unbending loyalty to his followers? I think that, whatever qualities one may have in mind, one must nevertheless come to the conclusion that it is not the sum of all these virtues: it is something mystical, inexpressible, almost incomprehensible, which this unique man possesses; and he who cannot feel it instinctively will not be able to grasp it at all. For we love Adolf Hitler because we believe deeply and unswervingly that God has sent him to us to save Germany.

The needs of people to have an unswerving belief arise from a desire for salvation and yet an inability to hope for it from oneself. Albert Speer, one of the closest to Hitler in his entourage, wrote, 'The whole structure of the [Nazi] system was aimed at preventing conflicts of conscience from even arising.' By referring all questions to Hitler, and by Hitler's accepting this transference, people had no doubts.

C. J. Jung wrote of Hitler and of the Germans:*

He represented the shadow, the inferior part of everybody's personality, in an overwhelming degree, and this was another reason why they fell for him. But what could they have done? In Hitler, every German should have seen his own shadow, his own worst danger. It is everybody's allotted fate to become conscious of and learn to deal with the shadow. But how could the Germans be expected to understand this, when no one in the world can understand such a simple truth?

In Munich, Unity Mitford wrote of her second meeting with Hitler – 'When one sits beside him it's like sitting beside the sun, he gives out rays or something.' Then in June 1935 – 'Today he was so kind and so divine I suddenly thought I would not only like to *kill* all who say and do things against him, but also *torture* them. It is wonderful to think that someone like him can ever have been thought of.'

There were projections, transpositions here, of a child who has grabbed at an imagined heaven and is in terror of its being taken away.

* *Collected Works*, Volume 10.

It is possible to understand the desire to protect an imaginary perfection: but then, how does one distinguish between what is imaginary and what is real?

Unity wrote a letter to Streicher's Jew-baiting magazine *Der Stürmer* –

The English have no notion of the Jewish danger ... Our worst Jews work only behind the scenes. They never come out into the open, and so we cannot show them to the British Public in their true dreadfulness... I want everyone to know that I am a Jew hater.

One of the themes of this book is that politicians use grandiose words without believing the reality of what they say: it is also possible for people to say squalid things without being much in contact with what they say. Words are often expressions of primitive forces; the reality that results from them can still take one form or another.

What Unity in fact did was to accept an invitation from Streicher to attend a pagan festival in the country on midsummer night at which young Nazis rolled burning wheels down a hill. Unity was asked to 'say a few words' into a microphone. She said to the assembled company that there should be lasting peace between England and Germany. The young men cheered and shouted 'Heil England!'

This was a time (mid-1935) when in Germany not much openly was being done against Jews: the original violence had died down: the Nuremberg laws and the public displaying of anti-semitic posters came at the end of the summer. There was at this time even the beginning of talks between Nazis and Zionists by which both sides hoped to stimulate the peaceable movement of German Jews to Palestine: Eichmann was in Cairo two years later talking to Zionists.

Albert Speer has described the atmosphere of life amongst Hitler's closest entourage at the time when Unity and Diana met him. Hitler's personal style is of interest here because it shows the vacuum into which people were sucked which was the German National Socialist way of operating power; my father's style was never dominated by this – but then, of course, he never wielded that sort of power.

Speer wrote:*

During these days in Munich Hitler paid little attention to government and party business, even less than at Obersalzberg. Usually

* *Inside the Third Reich.*

only an hour or two a day remained available for conferences. Most of his time he spent marching about building sites, relaxing in studios, cafés and restaurants; or hurling long monologues at his associates who were already amply familiar with the unchanging themes and painfully tried to conceal their boredom.

And about life at Obersalzberg:*

> The day actually began with a prolonged afternoon dinner... questions of fashion, of raising dogs, of the theatre and movies, of operettas and their stars were discussed, along with endless trivialities about the family lives of others. Hitler hardly ever said anything about the Jews, about his domestic opponents, let alone about the necessity of setting up of concentration camps.... Shortly after dinner the walk to the teahouse began... Hitler was addicted to this particular walk, which took about half an hour...
>
> The second part of the evening began with a movie, as was also the custom when Hitler was in Berlin... Hitler preferred light entertainment, love and society films: revues with lots of leg display were sure to please him... Afterwards the company gathered around the huge fireplace... Occasionally the movies were discussed – Hitler commenting mainly on the female actors and Eva Braun on the males. No one bothered to raise the conversation above the level of trivialities... In the early hours of the morning we went home dead tired, exhausted from doing nothing. After a few days of this I was seized by what I called at the time 'the mountain disease'. That is, I felt exhausted and vacant from the constant waste of time.

Speer wrote of Hitler's relationship to himself as being like that of Mephistopheles to Faust: the attraction of Mephistopheles is that he has positive and energetic opinions about everyone and everything; he can have these because he is always contemptuous; he believes in nothing and in nobody, and so he has free rein to show any certainty he likes. And if others choose to trust him, he can impart such certainty to them, they are liberated into dreams – just because of the nothingness in reality.

Diana's descriptions of life with Hitler are in style the opposite of those of Speer; she writes of Hitler's jokes, his frankness, his cleverness, his charm; but the substance of her memories is not so very different.

---

* *Inside the Third Reich.*

Speer was hypnotically charmed at the time by life around Hitler, it was only in looking back that he saw that there had been emptiness. Hitler's power over people seems to have been due less to his persuasiveness about politics than to his conviction that by will he could put into effect any idea that he chose; it was this that ran away with people, as it ran away with himself, as it if were some cancer. Trust in will overreaches itself to self-destruction because there is no recognition of the balancing requirements of reality; without these, there can be no maintenance of life.

Unity, and later Diana, seem to have been liked and respected by Hitler perhaps because they themselves were too exuberant to be swallowed in his vacuum; they would have posed no great threat to him, coming from a different world. Hitler's adjutant Schaub wrote of Unity – 'With all her admiration for Hitler the young Lady Mitford is quite clearly of the opinion that she is more or less his equal.' Speer himself wrote that the 'sole exception' to the tacit agreement amongst Hitler's personal entourage that politics should not be mentioned was 'Lady Mitford, who even in the later years of international tension persistently spoke up for her country and often actually pleaded with Hitler to make a deal with England'.*

Unity died when she felt her hopes had ended; Diana lived; and gave up her life to, and succeeded in creating a life around, my father. My father put up with some of the vacuums of political life – he sat on platforms, he charmed people, he talked – but then he would get fed up, and go his own way. He failed in politics; but he succeeded in that he ultimately did not let himself be sucked into the black hole of willed self-destruction. Perhaps he simply enjoyed himself and life too much. But it was probably because he was too serious that he did not let himself be trapped.

From Hitler's house at Obersalzberg Unity wrote as if from an English country-house weekend: 'I cannot tell you how wonderful the Führer was today copying a woman buying a hat! We all nearly died of laughing.'

* *Inside the Third Reich.*

CHAPTER 9

William Joyce

The financial difficulties which came upon the BUF as a result of the withdrawal of the support of Lord Rothermere coincided with the hostile publicity resulting from Olympia. After a momentary upsurge in recruiting due to stories of violence, members, seeing more soberly the way things were going, began to fall away. Our District Inspector wrote:

> Public opinion was fomented against the blackshirts and physical assaults became more frequent and more dangerous. Open air meetings often ended in trouble, affrays and minor riots; public halls in areas controlled by Councils with Labour majorities were refused to the Movement on trivial pretexts. Now scrambled to safety all those erstwhile members who had been pleased to be identified with Mosley when the climate had been mild. Those worthy of the cause stuck it out, and found that the almost universal hostility put more iron into their souls.

Many who left were those who had joined on the Rothermere bandwagon and who were of the type of 'unmitigated nuisances to all new political movements – those crooks and adventurers who come in for what they can extract in the way of spoil'. But there was a number of those who had been with Mosley since New Party days who also left – amongst them Robert Forgan the Deputy Leader and F. M. Box the old New Party Agent. The inner circle of the movement became increasingly dominated by those who were by temperament idealistic fascists, whether propagandists or organisation men – William Joyce, Neil Francis-Hawkins. A new recruit during 1934 was John Beckett who came in as an admirer of William Joyce: he was a histrionic, pugnacious man who had been a left-wing MP from 1924 to 1931 and had gained notoriety by seizing the Speaker's mace and threatening to carry it out of the House of Commons. He was an anti-semite, but not so much in a doctrinaire way as in the way of someone who needed an enemy to fight. A good public speaker, in the hierarchy of BUF speakers he soon gained a position second only to Mosley and Joyce.

The falling-off in income was not noticed for a time: money from Mussolini was still coming in; Mosley himself was putting in more of his money (he estimated later that he spent in all £100,000 on the movement). There were a few other rich backers – Wyndham Portal and Sir Alliott Verdon Roe. There was a story that the eccentric Lady Houston once wrote out a cheque for £100,000 to give to the movement and then read in *Blackshirt* an article calling her a silly and vain old woman, whereupon she tore the cheque up. My father commented later – 'These things were liable to happen when I was constantly away touring the country and speaking at least four or five times a week, because often I did not see a line of what was written in our weekly press.'

The 30,000 to 40,000 members at the height of the movement's success had paid a shilling a month if employed and fourpence if unemployed: this probably brought in some £12,000 a year. The two weekly papers *Blackshirt* and the somewhat more highbrow *Fascist Week* roughly paid their own way: they cost a penny and twopence respectively and each had a circulation of around 25,000. Expenses at the Black House in London consisted largely of salaries: the top one or two executives were paid £750 a year; John Beckett as Director of Publicity was paid £600, the editors of the two papers – Rex Tremlett and W. J. Leaper – £400, and William Joyce as one of the chief speakers £300. There were the usual expenses of running a large headquarters, and the hire of halls throughout the country. In London the Albert Hall cost 150 guineas for a night and Olympia 250. Local branches were expected to pay their own way.

Mosley had, he said, been so busy making speeches that he had kept himself clear of financial arrangements and also from day-to-day supervision of the papers; this had resulted in the somewhat anarchic style in which the BUF had developed. But in the wake of the hostile publicity about the Olympia meeting and of the withdrawal of Lord Rothermere some fundamental reappraisal of the way in which the movement was going was unavoidable; in particular, some decision had to be made about the BUF's attitude to anti-semitism. The old claim that fascists attacked only individual Jews for what they did and not for what they were was simply not believed. The chief culprit responsible for the fact that it was now being taken for granted by the public that the BUF was anti-semitic, was William Joyce.

Joyce was liable to slip into his speeches or articles in *Blackshirt* references to 'aliens imported from Palestine' or 'hairy troglodytes who crept out of the ghettos of Germany to seek sanctuary in the British Museum'. It was the style of these remarks, rather than that they expressed any deliberate policy, that seemed obviously to exhibit an obsessive anti-semitism; and the fact that Joyce apparently was not restrained nor even reprimanded seemed also fairly obviously to indicate that this was the sort of style that the leadership – despite its protestations – required. Joyce in fact had a hatred of almost any form of intellectual ('fascism is not a creed for the smug mice who choose to emerge from under Bloomsbury tea-cosies to have a nibble at it') but it was easiest to canalise this feeling into hostility to Jews. The question was now pressing: what was in fact the attitude of the leadership? There were enough responsible and moderate members in the BUF to insist that the predicament should no longer be ignored.

In the aftermath of Olympia G. S. Gerault wrote a report for the Leader:

> The Movement has become identified in the public mind with the Hitler movement chiefly through the fault of our own speakers, and the tone adopted in the *Blackshirt*.
>
> The original attitude of the Leader on the Jewish question was very sound and appealed much to the public mind; but of late it has been felt that the movement is going definitely in for the persecution of Jews on German lines, and that has produced very grave repercussions.
>
> In this connection it should be realised that the country as a whole is 95% against Hitler and all that he has done; and all the protests and explanations which may be made fall on deaf ears. We are definitely wasting time in any attempt to defend the Hitler regime, and we should have contented ourselves with saying that it is far too early for any intelligent man to form any sort of conclusion.
>
> There is an undoubted feeling throughout the movement that the leader is being jockeyed either knowingly or unknowingly into an impossible position by A.A.O. [Assistant Administrative Officer] Joyce; and there are those who say that he is now, to all intents and purposes, the Movement.
>
> This feeling is intensified when members see pamphlet after

pamphlet on policy appearing over this officer's signature; when they should either be anonymous or signed by the Leader.

Furthermore, older members can see quite clearly how issues upon which the leader spoke with perfect clarity in the early days of the Movement now appear to be modified in directions known to suit the personal predilections of this officer.

Intelligence and real thinking are definitely at a discount. Either the movement does not possess them, or no effort is made to find contributors who use them.

Far too many lies are cheerfully printed with a disastrous result. When a local branch reads a highly coloured account of what it knows was only a trifling business the immediate reaction is that the ordinary member considers the whole paper to be composed of similar lies and values it accordingly.

The only terms on which it is safe to lie in propaganda is when you cannot be found out, least of all by your own people; but this elementary truth appears to be beyond the understanding of some of the contributors to the *Blackshirt*.

Confronted by this, Oswald Mosley could hardly continue to claim that he was too busy to be able to know what was going on.

Amongst the numerous pamphlets by Joyce referred to in this report was one on India: this in draft form was seen by two BUF members who had personal knowledge of India – B. S. James and Leigh Vaughan-Henry. James sent a marked copy of the draft pamphlet to Mosley with the comment –

In my opinion should any of the portions I have marked come into the hands of knowledgeable Anglo-Indians, not to mention Indians, all sympathy for the BUF in India will be killed. In addition I consider that as India is such an important question, the distribution of the pamphlet in this country even will do us grave harm. The mind of the writer appears throughout to be superficial, pretentious and priggish – without real power. The pamphlet is a deplorable manifestation of a lack of even elementary insight into psychology (especially Asiatic).

The comments of Vaughan-Henry were –

Its tone from start to finish is wholly wrong. It is couched in a cheap, windy demagogic style which might go over as Hyde Park Corner

oratory.... there are transparently rhetorical touches of cheap lurid-
ness and journalistic sensationalism of the least convincing kind...
a continual touch of insufferable condescension. It it likely to irritate
the very kind of Indian who can be useful – the type who wishes
to support Britain because of its literacy and its care for Indian culture.

I know positively that it has alienated five potential Indian ad-
herents; I know equally that it has either infuriated or caused derision
among seven equally initially–sympathetic Anglo-Indians of some
experience and standing.

I respectfully submit that this pamphlet should be suppressed
immediately: I ask this urgently, with the interest of the movement
at heart.

About BUF policy in general Vaughan-Henry continued:

I feel that we need to take more care now than ever, not only in
all literature issued, but in the *Blackshirt* itself, to eliminate the kind
of dull, cheap clap-trap which has occasionally disfigured that paper.
The Movement has passed into a new phase. We can have the support
of fresh types from those initially supporting it. I am not for inclination to the Right; I am rather for a judicious incline to the Left
if the Corporate State is to work efficiently; and now it is our business
to be working to cement its fabric, for immediate operation of its
machinery when power is attained. I sincerely trust that you will
give your attention to this and find yourself able to carry out a sound
purge and reform.

The style and content of Joyce's pamphlet on India was indeed the
sort of stuff with which *Blackshirt* readers had often been regaled: it
began: 'True imperialism knows nothing of disintegration; true imperialism knows nothing of surrender; true imperialism knows nothing
of injustice, and Fascism is true imperialism.' It described Lord Irwin
as 'the phenomenal freak whom it would be indecent to describe as
Viceroy' and Stanley Baldwin as 'the steel merchant metamorphosed
into a squire by casual experiments in pig breeding'. It suggested that
'Indian education affords no source of justifiable pride' and that 'British
law and order had repressed and replaced chaos, violence, rapine and
habitual atrocity'. When Joyce was informed of the criticisms of him
and his pamphlet he reacted in a way which seems to have become
increasingly typical of those with influence at headquarters; he went to
the Deputy Leader and complained that there was a 'plot' against him.

There were two courses open to Mosley as a result of the crisis, particular but symbolic, aroused by this pamphlet. On the one hand he could suppress the pamphlet and demote Joyce and try to redirect blackshirt propaganda to appeal to a more sophisticated and responsible audience: the danger in this was that he might lose some of his most energetic and dedicated supporters and be left with nothing of the spirit that might make a revolutionary party work. On the other hand he could ignore the critics and back Joyce on the grounds that he, Mosley, had always said he was appealing to people who feel rather than to those who think: the danger in this was that he would be increasingly and inevitably seen as allying himself with the style of extremism that was becoming commonplace on the Continent. In the event, my father tried to pursue something of both courses: this was what he might have called a synthesis, but it was also a falling between stools. Announcements were made about reforms and the strengthening of discipline; but what the public saw was mainly the style of Joyce taking over.

The pamphlet on India was published; and in fact within a few months Joyce was promoted to be Director of Propaganda. As if in celebration of this, on 24th May 1935 Joyce published on the front page of *Blackshirt* an article on India which contained sentences which seemed to be epitomes of his style. Referring to the India Bill which would transfer powers to Indians, he wrote of the Tories who had backed it that they were 'one loathsome, fetid, purulent, tumid mass of hypocrisy'; behind them was 'the mean, narrow-souled, pig-eyed, comfortable employer of labour ... to this little beast all other issues are irrelevant ... [he is] unable to open his mouth lest the Jewish dictators of "Society" should foreclose'.

My father's backing and indeed promotion of Joyce can only be understood in terms of the situation that he had got himself into in which it was necessary, if he was to carry on at all, for him to believe that in some way he was hand in hand with destiny: that in spite of (or almost because of) the size of the odds against him, it did not matter much with whom he travelled because in the end his spirit and will could not fail. With this sort of vision and against the evident sort of odds what he needed was loyalty; since he was a gambler, he would not turn back but had to double up as it were on all his stakes. There were two occasions in the second half of 1934 which might have influenced him to support Joyce. The first was the rally in Hyde Park in September which I had watched from the roof of the Cumberland Hotel; this had been kept in order by the huge attendance of police but nothing of the BUF's message had been heard; the attempt to conform to respectability had resulted in the movement's being made to appear faint-hearted. The second incident was at Worthing a month later when there was a fight after a meeting at the Pier Pavilion: Mosley, Joyce and local organisers were confronted by a crowd shouting 'We want Mosley dead or alive' and 'Felix keeps on walking'; and singing 'Poor old Mosley's got the wind up' to the tune of *John Brown's Body*. As the fascists made their way through the crowd they had 'struck out with their fists' (the police alleged) and 'bodies had thudded against shop windows as people had been thrown aside by powerful rushes'. As a result Mosley, Joyce and others were charged with riotous assembly. When the case came up at Lewes Assizes there was the following exchange between Mosley and the prosecuting counsel:

Counsel: The whole idea of your movement on the streets is to hang together is it not?
Mosley: I trust not to hang together...
Counsel: Did you make any complaints to a policeman?
Mosley: It is not my habit to complain.
Counsel: Will you answer yes or no –
Mosley: I will give evidence in my own way, and I do not require any instruction from you.
Counsel: Don't be offensive.
Mosley: To be offensive is not the prerogative of a King's Counsel.

Members of the BUF were feeling both persecuted and belligerent: they were comrades-in-arms in a tough struggle: if they were to survive, they needed solidarity and courage. It must have seemed that now was not the time to think of casting out – of too severely reprimanding even – party stalwarts such as Joyce of whom there could be no doubts about their almost reckless courage.

Mosley was due to make his second large speech at the Albert Hall on 28th October 1934: before this it seemed imperative there should be decisions about policy. A report on the movement's attitude to Jews had been requested from A. K. Chesterton – a journalist and ex-public-relations-officer who had become a member of the BUF at the same time as John Beckett. Of this report, and of this time, Chesterton later wrote:*

* *The Tragedy of Antisemitism.*

Genuinely puzzled (I have the clearest mental picture of him at the time) Mosley ordered a thorough research into the Jewish question, especially into the financial and political activities which the movement attacked; and it was found that there was a very close identification between those activities and specific jewish interests. Rightly or wrongly, Mosley imagined that he had stumbled on the secret of Jewry's bitter attack on the movement.

What the report suggested was that the BUF was not in essence anti-semitic, but that when it had attacked as a matter of policy financial and political interests – such as those to do with banking, with advertising and with what is nowadays called the media – it had discovered almost as an afterthought that these happened to be run by Jews; and it was because of this that Jews were attacking the BUF; so was the BUF not now justified in more openly retaliating against Jews?

It was sometimes suggested (by John Strachey and Irene Ravensdale among others) that my father came to embrace anti-semitism openly for wholly cynical reasons – to maintain impetus in a party which for all the success of its first two years was by the end of 1934 running down: the expected economic crisis had not come and in fact the country was beginning to enjoy a small boom. But there was more at the back of BUF anti-semitism than simply a need to find a spurious crisis as a substitute for the expected real one to deal with which the BUF had come into existence: there was more to the BUF's anti-semitism, certainly, than what could be explained away by its Leader's skills in rationalisation. It was true that British Jews associated the BUF with German Nazism; it was true that Jews thus wanted to attack the BUF and could claim as justifiable the use of weapons such as those to do with publicity, banking and trade. But all this made it inevitable that there would be brought into the open what was anyway an intrinsic anti-semitism in the BUF, which up to now had only been partly restrained. The state of mind of people such as fascists who believe that they can and should set the world to rights requires scapegoats so that things may seem bearable when plans and hopes go wrong: this is a necessity if dynamism is to continue.

In 1934, Mosley seemed to accept A. K. Chesterton's report on the prevalence of a Jewish conspiracy in the attacks on the BUF: it was only years later that he wrote scathingly of people who –*

* *My Life.*

believe in a world conspiracy run by the Jews, which always seems
to me the most complete nonsense. The basic reason for my disbelief
in any such possibility is simply that from long experience I know
men are not clever or determined enough to organise anything of
the kind. Anyone who knows how difficult it is to keep a secret
among three men – particularly if they are married – knows how
absurd is the idea of a world-wide conspiracy consciously controlling
all mankind by its financial power: in real, clear analysis these deep-
rooted plots are seldom anything more sinister than the usual vast
muddle.

People who hold the conspiracy theory of history are those whose
minds work practically and logically: they cannot accept that there
are coincidences and occurrences simply by chance – that what appears
as a 'conspiracy' is just the fact that a great many people's minds happen
to work in common patterns, and thus patterns, if this is what is desired,
can be imposed on what is fortuitous. Not only bankers and Jews but
in fact most people like power: so (reason being the tool of what is
required) must there not be a vast conspiracy for power involving
powerful bankers and Jews? (Modern conspiracy theory sees a secret
alliance between Russian Communists and American Capitalists; both
sides, certainly, are united in their love of power). Conspiracy theory
depends for its devotees on those who feel themselves both to be rational
and to possess the power to effect things by will: marching with destiny,
they required scapegoats to explain the collision with reality.

The reason why Jews are so often picked as the heroes or victims
of conspiracy theory is because they have from the beginning seen themselves as involved as it were in conspiracy – even one with so grandiose
an aim as that of saving the world – and thus it is not difficult for
others to see them in some caricature of their own style. Also would-be
anti-semites can see that within the self-recognised Jewish conspiracy-
group there are both the enormously powerful and the apparently
abject: and so – how useful this is for those who wish for scapegoats!
They can explain their own failures as being caused by the enemy that
is all-dominating and threatening, and they can take out their envies
and rages on that which is helpless and abject.

At the Albert Hall meeting of 28th October 1934 it had become
known that there was to be some statement of policy about the BUF's
attitude to Jews; great care was taken by the police to keep fascists
and anti-fascists apart. Blackshirt stewards were detailed to see that only
ticket holders got in; as a result the hall was only two thirds full, and

Mosley spoke to an audience of blackshirt supporters. It was to them that he made what was expected, and what was taken to be, his declaration of open warfare against Jews. In fact (but who would see this and who would not?) this was still resolutely, almost absurdly enigmatic.

> I have encountered things in this country which I did not dream existed in Britain. One of them is the power of organised Jewry which is today mobilised against Fascism. They have thrown down their challenge to fascism, and I am not in the habit of ignoring challenges. Now they seek to howl over the length and breadth of the land that we are bent on racial and religious persecution. That charge is utterly untrue.
>
> Today we do not attack the Jews on racial or religious grounds; we take up the challenge that they have thrown down because they fight against Fascism and against Britain. They have declared in their great folly to challenge the conquering force of the modern age. Tonight we take up that challenge: they will it: let them have it!

CHAPTER 10

The Party

The other and apparently contrary steps that my father took to deal with the sudden aimlessness of the BUF in the second half of 1934 were to do with trying to re-establish discipline and decency. Although the movement had defended itself energetically with words after the fracas at Olympia, it was evident to anyone who cared to look beyond propaganda that things got out of hand amongst the stewards and the headquarters personnel who were supposed to control them. The District Inspector quoted earlier wrote:

> It must be admitted here that there were denizens of the Black House who would not have been welcome additions to any decent lads' club... They hoped to cash in in a big way eventually out of victory, but meanwhile were content with chicken-feed from petty theft and mean little rackets. Plain clothes officers from time to time showed interest in some of the individuals accommodated in the Black House. It took time to comb out these undesirable characters, but eventually the movement shook itself free of them.

Oswald Mosley set great store by the image of purity that he believed should be characteristic of his movement. It should be composed of men who were austere and incorruptible because it was only through such men – 'new men who come from nowhere' – that a fascist-type government could properly work; that power could safely be vested in the centrally dominated corporate state without traditional democratic safeguards. Years later he wrote of his vision of a fascist party: *

* Europe: Faith and Plan.

The party can be the greatest influence in the modern world for good or evil... the party must be a party of men and women dedicated to an idea... its character should be more that of a church than of a political party... the old axiom that 'all power corrupts' has doubtful validity, because it derives from our neglect of Plato's advice to find men carefully and train them by methods which make them fit for heroes.

In 1934 it must have become unavoidably apparent that Plato's advice was not being attended to; that now was the time to repair this. Mosley wrote of this time: 'The supreme merit of defeat to a great party is that it purges the worst and preserves the best: not sweet, but vital, are the uses of political adversity.'

He called in to advise him Major General J. F. C. Fuller, a recent convert to the BUF. Fuller had been Chief of Staff to the British Tank Corps in 1917; he had then been Chief Instructor at the Camberley Staff College, and Military Assistant to the Chief of the Imperial General Staff. He had retired from the army in 1933 in order to devote himself to writing. He was a methodical and articulate man with a mind of his own; he could be trusted to be aloof from the in-fighting and accusations of 'plotting' that bedevilled the regular staff at BUF head-quarters. Fuller wrote to Mosley in the summer of 1934:

> ... I am glad the position between you and Rothermere has been cleared up. The press is valuable, but as an instrument only; its danger is that it always aims at mastership, and that its principles are regulated by dividends. As it can only create great emotions and not great movements it cannot destroy a great movement. In fact its hostility is, I believe, as powerful an advertisement as its friendship; because, anyhow in the early days of a movement, it puts enthusiasts on their mettle and keeps out the jelly-fish. In fact hostility gives quality while praise, at its best, is of 24 hours duration in this age of ball-bangers and squeeze-and-kiss-me girls. Considering that the press is supposed to be almighty, which it isn't, it is strange that no press has ever created or even assisted any great national movement – e.g. the Salvation Army or even the Boy Scouts. Every great movement starts off in a minority of *one*. The strength of a new movement is in indirect proportion to the resistance offered to it.

This, in the circumstances, must have been just the sort of thing that the Leader wanted to hear. He asked Fuller to carry out research and to produce a report on the way in which he considered the BUF should be reorganised. Fuller produced his report on October 8th, some three weeks before the Albert Hall meeting.

After two months close study at N.H.Q. I am of the opinion that the Movement cannot fail to succeed if certain radical changes are made in its organisation and discipline. It is obvious that the Movement has grown up on enthusiasm rather than to plan; that it is lacking in authority, requires pulling together, and needs to be guided towards a clear-cut and attainable object. Unless this is done, I am of the opinion that either the movement will decline or it will break up into hostile factions. The time has come when quantity should definitely give way to quality. This is very largely a question of organisation.

Object

As the ultimate object of the Movement is to establish constitutionally a new form of government, the immediate object is to win a number of seats in the next General Elections. Consequently all means should be directed towards this end.

Propaganda

Of the little I have seen of propaganda it appears to me to be somewhat crude. It lacks art and common sense. In place of being persuasive it is aggressive. I agree that to start with a challenging spirit is necessary in order to wake people up: but now that the Movement is on its feet, and seeing that there are at most but eighteen months to work in, tactics must be fitted to circumstances. It should be remembered that for every one man and woman who applaud the words 'revolution' and 'dictatorship' there are ten who actively dislike them.

The BUF

I consider it imperative that what may be called 'Blackshirtism' is modified. It may appeal to the young and inexperienced, but if it is unchecked, it will lose more votes in the next elections than anything else. I consider this question a perturbing one. 'Blackshirtism' leads to coattrailing and gasconading, and if unchecked may develop into a Frankenstein monster. Though the wearing of the blackshirt appeals to young people, it must not be overlooked that this is an old country, very solid, stable and matter of fact. It is still instinctively a feudal country. The masses of the people will always listen to men and women of experience and importance, but they will seldom listen to boys and girls. They know that things must change, but their instincts are against violent change.

Most of the Blackshirts are too young to realise this. They are out for a game rather than to foster a Movement and consider that those who do not agree with them are old fashioned or lacking in energy. In a revolutionary country they would be right, but in a conservative country they are wrong. They do not see that attack, attack, attack, is a poor policy and a somewhat ridiculous one to assume in this country. It is not the Communists, Jews, etc., who are going to prevent the B U F winning seats in the next election, it is they themselves – not because they lack enthusiasm, but because they do not understand the conditions which exist in this country and, consequently, their enthusiasm is misdirected. This enthusiasm must be canalised towards the object. If it is not, I doubt whether a single seat will be won in 1935 or 1936.

The Defence Force must be limited to what it is intended for – the defence of free speech. It should be as inconspicuous as possible, whilst the mass of active and non-active members must be given a political outlook, and this out-look must dominate. So long as the Defence idea dominates, it is as if the police dominated the government. This is not dictatorship, but despotism. The Movement is sadly lacking in able men, and one reason for this is, that they are cold-shouldered out of it. Rothermere's support should have greatly benefited the Movement; in place it proved detrimental – why? First, because the organisation was not flexible enough to absorb a large number of recruits, and secondly, because the discipline was such that the more able recruits were not utilised; they joined up, became disgusted and then left.

There followed detailed plans for reorganising administration: these were mainly to do with ways in which the position of the Leader might be made less solitary and unapproachable – a Deputy Leader with more authority, or even a deputy 'triumvirate', were suggested – and ways in which 'political organisation' should be kept clear of 'general organisation'. Questions of policy, that is, should not be open to obstruction caused by fear of 'someone treading on someone else's toes'.

Fuller also sent to Mosley a letter in which he offered his own services for the job of getting 'the organisation pulled together' – presumably as one of the 'triumvirate'. Immediately at Headquarters there was the inevitable outcry that Fuller was plotting to take the whole movement over.

Mosley did not for the moment do much to implement Fuller's suggestions. He was occupied with matters such as the Worthing assault

charge, on account of which he seemed to feel it necessary to demonstrate loyalty to old comrades-in-arms; also with the libel action against
the *Star* which had finally come to court. The *Star* had reported, as
a result of his debate with James Maxton in 1933, that Mosley was
ready to take over the government with machine guns: in fact he had
said he would resist communists with machine guns if it was they who
tried to take over government illegally (see page 275). Here too in the
witness box he had a chance to demonstrate his contempt for conventionally cautious attitudes. The counsel against him was Norman
Birkett, who some five years later was to preside over the Tribunal
enquiring into his, Mosley's, imprisonment without trial. In November
1934 –

Counsel: If a Communist Government is called to power with the
           assent of the King, would you shoot them down?
Mosley: It is possible to put questions on ever increasing hypo-
           theses which lead at last to an absurdity. You might as well
           say that if His Majesty the King of England enacted the
           law of Herod that every first-born shall be slain, would
           you, in those circumstances, be a revolutionary?
Counsel: Who is to be the judge – you?
Mosley: When there is a condition of anarchy, it does not require
           much judgment. If you were shot in the streets it would
           not require any great condition of judgment to know you
           had been shot.

The Jury, still confident that words should mean roughly what they
say, awarded Mosley £5,000 damages. The Lord Chief Justice Hewart
in his summing up said of Mosley – 'Did he not appear to you to
be a public man of no little courage, no little candour and no little
ability?'

Within the movement however there was still the impression of
things being out of control. A. K. Chesterton was sent round provincial
branches to report on conditions: he found in Coventry 'a snug club
with separate bars marked "Officers" and "Blackshirts" '; in Stoke,
which had the largest branch membership in the country, there was
an organisation which was 'part thieves kitchen and part bawdy house'.
A woman member wrote to 'Ma' Mosley complaining of the behaviour
of members of the 'I' Squad; people were apt to feel they were at
the mercy of any 'whipper-snapper in big boots.' The problem of what
fascists, brought together to deal with a crisis, in fact did when there

was no crisis, was now seen unavoidably to be coming to its own climax.

Eventually early in 1935 Mosley announced his decisions about reform in an article in *Blackshirt* entitled 'The Next Stage in Fascism'. Discipline, especially at National Headquarters, was to be tightened up: the atmosphere of headquarters would be 'that of a workshop rather than of a clubhouse or playground'. The organisation of the movement would be even more specifically on army lines. Every blackshirt was to be a member of a unit of five or six; units were to be part of Sections; Sections were to be part of Companies; and so on in a hierarchical structure up to the single Leader at the top. Only those who gave to the movement at least two nights a week would be entitled to wear a blackshirt; in this way there would be no need for a special Defence Force, because any blackshirt would be trained to steward meetings. Also –

Distinctive badges and dress will be worn by units giving more service according to the amount of time they give and to the degree of efficiency attained by certain standard tests which will be laid down. Units giving five nights a week will be permitted to wear the dress now worn by 'I' Division N.H.Q. provided they reach the required high standard of efficiency. Blackshirts will in every way be graded according to their service, and will be honoured within the Movement by the degree of sacrifice they make for the cause.

The most vital work in the future would be door-to-door canvassing; the aim once more was to have a BUF branch in every parliamentary constituency. There were complex instructions about methods of selection and promotion of group leaders. But above all –

I am determined to preserve pure and immutable the fine flame of the original Blackshirt movement. In the present great growth of our movement this can only be done by confining Blackshirt membership to those who prove, by real Blackshirt service, that they are inspired by the true blackshirt spirit.

The processes of weeding out were not always happy. 'Ma' Mosley had been leader of the Women's Section of the BUF since 1933; she had an office in the Black House and was responsible for the women who acted as secretaries and paper-sellers and even stewardesses at meetings: she would travel round provincial branches dispensing good cheer

like a dowager queen. She had confronted danger: at Dumfries there
had been a communist poster which exhorted people to 'Give Maud
Some Bouquets', which referred to the throwing of stones. She was
sixty: she had done her job with courage and with dignity. But there
had always been something bizarre about her appointment by her
adored son and Leader.

In February 1935 she was writing to him:

My Darling Tom,
You succeeded in making me look a complete fool this afternoon –
and thereby justifying your shelving of me. You will always make
an idiot of me by being rude to me in public; but it was not necessary
to be quite so brutal. I would have 'gone quietly' and fully meant
what I said some time ago – that in the cause of Fascism I would
be ready to give way to a better woman at any time. It remains
to be seen if Miss Shore is superwoman enough to do all she has
undertaken. I hope so. So far I have shouldered all my officers'
mistakes and done the *whole* of the work of the country branches
since I came out of hospital six months ago. Lady Makgill did nothing
but use the premises for her own business and told her secretary
'If Lady Mosley were fool enough to sweat over country branches
she could'. Then came Miss R – with her dishonest inefficiency,
later backed by Miss S – and Miss A – in sullen opposition to me.
To them I was a stumbling block to collaring the machine and all
its resources.

And a few months later she was writing:

I do not think you have any idea of the difficulties I had to face
during the early months and when we moved to N.H.Q. Intrigue
the whole time. Insubordination from people whose word you preferred to take to mine and who have since disappeared from the
movement by your instructions.... No, Tom, it is not quite good
enough; there is a limit to one's endurance.

Intrigue and back-biting are a recognised part of political machines:
in the BUF they seem to have become exaggerated probably just on
account of people dedicated to dynamism having so little chance to
exercise real power. Regarding the Leader's handling of headquarter's
court intrigues A. K. Chesterton, after he had left the movement a
few years later, wrote of Mosley:

In order to back up his favourites there is no affront which he will refuse to offer to common sense and no specious excuse he will hesitate to advance. If a leader shows himself unable to maintain even the presence of a judicial attitude in dealing with his own organisation, he can plead with no convincing justification for the sacrifices which service to him imposes.

But then Chesterton had been writing of Mosley only a few months earlier:*

> Oswald Mosley is a very kind man, far and away the kindest man I know ... Mosley's kindness is born of strong, tense generous emotions; of a sense of the innate decency of mankind; of a natural inclination to think well of his fellow men and of a very profound insight into the mainsprings of human action which enables him to understand when they fail... He is also one of the most patient and approachable of men... His extraordinary intellectual power often enables him to synthesise what first appears to be conflicting opinions... his own views are almost invariably confirmed by events. That is part of Mosley's real greatness: he has no need to dictate, for the good reason that his spiritual quality precludes the necessity of 'laying down the law' to men who share so completely his own outlook and serve him with so large a pride.

These two descriptions of Mosley are concerned with the same set of events: it seems to have been part of the atmosphere that he engendered that the attitudes of his followers to him should have been often so adoring, and then sometimes suddenly so alarmed and hostile. He seemed to give people the vision of being in touch with great events; then perhaps there was a glimpse of the vacuum.

What Mosley seemed to be trying to do with his movement at this time was to keep in existence as many different strands as possible: he recognised that the bravado of cheap propaganda and of the Defence Force had been overdone; but he wanted to maintain something of it in existence while he looked at other possible channels for the movement's future. He had by now accepted many of Fuller's recommendations: the party was to turn from being a movement ready to deal with a crisis to one with the aim of winning a parliamentary election; for this there had to be more emphasis on explaining what fascists were

* *Portrait of a Leader.*

for, apart from the demonstration that they would be able to maintain law and order. In fact for some time there had been two strands running side by side in the pages of the *Blackshirt* and the *Fascist Week* – on the one hand the virulent tub-thumping of which the chief exponent was William Joyce, and on the other a calm and comparatively civilised effort to explain fascist ideologies and policies of which the chief representative was Raven Thomson.

Raven Thomson was a free-lance philosopher and sociologist who in 1932 had written a book called *Civilisation As Divine Superman* in which he had suggested that civilisation itself should be seen as the higher form of entity such as was symbolised by Nietzsche's image of the 'Superman': in 1933 he had written for the *Blackshirt* an article on Smuts's 'Holism' in which he had elaborated this idea. 'An atom is more than a mere system of circling electrons, a molecule more than a collection of atoms and... the civilised state as a "whole" must be something more than the mere collection of individuals each working for his own end.' In the early numbers of the *Fascist Week* he was applying these ideas specifically to fascism: 'The Fascist call for national unity and a patriotic purpose is fulfilling that divine urge to wider life and nobler consciousness which is inherent in the whole scheme of existence.' This could be brought down to earth in the practical vision of the Corporate State:*

The Corporate State is built up on the analogy of the human body which is composed of millions of cells all working harmoniously together and constituting the human personality... In order to enable the human individual to carry out his proper function in society, Fascism intends to reorganise the industrial life of this country under a system of discipline and control...

Existing industries would be placed under Corporations on which would sit representatives of the employers through their Federations, representatives of the workers through their Trade Unions, and representatives of the consumers. These corporations would fix fair prices, eliminating cut-throat competition; and fair wages, preventing exploitation.

All these Corporations would be under the control of a National Corporation whose duty it would be to direct the various industries to the best interests of the State and the Community.

* *Fascist Week.*

This was the vision of an ideal. The unasked question here was, as usual – who on earth would be these controlled and harmonious men, free from intrigue and back-biting, who would run such a Corporate State?

Next door to such articles in *Blackshirt* and *Fascist Week* William Joyce would be writing –

Miserable pedantic intellectuals, who skulked in lecture rooms throughout the war, have now discovered that the Germans can commit atrocities. They chose to ignore the execution of Nurse Cavell, yet they twitter with execration because 'at Worms a number of Jews were arrested, shut up in a pigsty, and beaten on the buttocks...' When the spoilt body of capitalism is put into the straightjacket of the Fascist State, these little by-products of the political system which Capitalism had made possible will of course be cleaned up too.

This was the style of that part of the movement represented by Joyce. He would write: 'Our purpose is to crush all compromise out of existence ... the concept of right admits of no pollution by wrong... Just as democracy is a psychopathic expression of inferiority, so tolerance is the habit of countenancing in others the faults which we ourselves desire to develop.' (In many of Joyce's utterances the sense seems to come out not as intended.) But what had this got to do with Raven Thomson's vision of 'Holism'?

Another writer in *Blackshirt* was E. de Burgh Wilmot who announced: 'Our first duty to Culture is to destroy it... the slow insidious advance of its hateful poison is comparable to the destroying terror of the plague.' There were attacks on particular aspects of 'culture': Proust was one of the writers 'overcome by the neurosis of an effortless megapolitical life and the fragrance of their own personalities': also – 'it is time that Mr Eliot was told that mankind has plenty of use for courage and sense of direction, none at all for defeatism and disease'. Then – 'Who is this Korda who comes to England to make comedies and monstrosities of our Kings and Queens? Under a fascist government he would not find himself at liberty to make fun of monarchy.' A subject of repeated attack was psychoanalysis – a 'black magical art' which 'dabbling with the mysteries of sex, has elaborated from them an occult science which undermines self-confidence ... and therefore strikes at morality and the family and so at the foundations of Christian Civilisation'.

Anti-semitism was of course never far beneath the surface in this
kind of writing. General Fuller had remained for the most part on the
reasonable side of the fence in fascist propaganda: in his report he had
warned –

The Jews cannot destroy fascism unless fascists create a fulcrum from
which Jews can operate their financial lever: this fulcrum is anti-
semitism in such forms as will lead to a popular outcry in their
favour. What the big Jews yearn for is that fascists will knock little
Jews on the head, so that non-Jewish popular opinion will be shocked.
Then they will spend millions to exploit the situation.

But then in January 1935 in the first number of the *Fascist Quarterly* –
a magazine in which a serious attempt was made to raise the tone of
fascist propaganda – Fuller wrote an article entitled *The Cancer of Europe*
in which he said:

For over a thousand years an obscure tragedy has been played on
the stage of European history by that outcast race – the Jews. Having
given Christianity to the world, this strange people have never ceased
in their efforts to destroy Christian culture...
    The predominant characteristic of the Jew is his materialism which
endows him with a destructive social force when he is placed in a
spiritually ordered society... By predilection a trader, a banker, a
dabbler in the occult, like a mole he works underground, silently
and hidden, and like a bat he flits through the night seeing things
unseen by creatures of day...
    He may be of diamond or of dirt, yet, whatever he is made of,
he is like the grit within the oyster: pearls of wealth form round
him, but only at the expense of the organism on which he feeds....
    Self-defence has compelled him to rely upon craft and cunning,
always the weapons of the weak, and to enter into alliance with
every subversive movement. In these Jews see power – power to
avenge their wrongs, and power to gain world domination under
an avenging messiah – as foretold by Talmud and Qabalah.

General Fuller turned out, in fact, to be a fervent exponent of conspiracy theory: it transpired from letters to my father of this time that
he had once been an admirer or even some sort of associate of Aleister
Crowley, the self-styled apocalyptic 'Beast'. He had once threatened

a libel action as a result of some suggestion concerning this relationship, but had been advised by lawyers to withdraw.

In the pages of *Blackshirt* there appeared a jingle which seemed to epitomise the split in fascist mentality concerning many things but especially Jews: on the one hand, how rational; on the other – did the left hand know at all what the right might be up to?

> There are Jews and Jews! and I refuse
> To condemn a man for his race.
> If he's born in this dear old land of ours
> If he loves her soil, her trees, her flowers
> And brings on her no disgrace
> That man is my brother!
> But not the other –
> The oily material swaggering Jew
> The pot-bellied, sneering, money-mad Jew
> Who sells his country and his soil for gain
> Who sweats his fellows, whose life's in vain. . .

In the summer of 1935 the BUF gave up the Black House in Chelsea and moved its headquarters to much smaller offices in Great Smith Street. This was partly for reasons of economy; also to put into effect the policy of running the headquarters 'as a workroom not as a club-house'. Then, in August, Italy began to threaten Abyssinia with invasion, and General Fuller wrote a front page article in *Blackshirt* entitled 'Britain Must Keep Out of War'. There was the question – had the BUF at last found a positive and worthy cause to fight for? Suddenly dozens of young men appeared in the streets wearing black shirts and carrying placards with a new slogan – Mind Britain's Business! Could a fascist movement appeal to a democratic electorate in the cause of peace?

CHAPTER 11

Holidays

For the summer holidays of 1935 my father took my sister Vivien and myself to a rented villa at Posillipo on the bay of Naples. We flew from Croydon Airport in an aeroplane that my Aunt Irene described as 'the Mail de Havilland'; we landed at Rome; there, my father and my sister and I were photographed and were in the papers the next day – my father with his chin up like Mussolini and my sister looking normal and myself under one of those soft grey felt school hats that made me look like a toadstool. We stayed in the Grand Hotel and were given boxes of chocolates by the management and the next day we were in the crowd at a march-past of innumerable fascists while my father was on the saluting base with Mussolini. There had been some talk of our being up on the platform too: it had probably been decided, after a look at the photograph, that we might not add to the glory.

The house at Posillipo belonged to Sir Rennell Rodd who had been British Ambassador in Rome; it was said to have been built as a result of a competition amongst the young men of the Embassy to see who could design the most hideous villa and Lady Rodd had come in and picked up the winning design and said it represented her perfect house. It was dark and cool with wide corridors and arches; it was on the top of a cliff and looked out across the bay to Vesuvius with the Isle of Capri lying like a Sphinx in the sea to the right. This seascape and landscape were quite different from those of the South of France or the Lido at Venice where we had been on previous summer holidays: there, people seemed to have been spilled on to rocks and beaches as if from some shipwreck: here everything was bright and mythical and exact.

It was during this holiday that I began to feel in some stronger relationship with my father: I was twelve; I loved the place; my father seemed to be at home in it with us. We spent much of the time as a family – first with my Aunt Baba and then, for the other fortnight as in the previous year, with Mrs Guinness. Baba did seem to be a mother-companion to us: she swam with us, played; she and my father seemed happy. I was able for the first time to take on my father at some sports. There was a dusty deck-tennis court at the side of the house where we played with a rubber quoit; I had become quite proficient at this game since the time of our cruise to the Canary Islands two years previously. My father played, as he played all games, with a vast histrionic exuberance: he would fling the quoit, spin it, lunge, shout; go hurtling across the court yet so delicately on his injured leg. I found that for once in a game I did not care if I won or lost; the enjoyment was in the cunning; the laughter.

My father had bought a 30ft motor yacht which was moored in an inlet at the bottom of hundreds of steps down the cliff. The boat was called the *Vivien:* it had cabins at the front and in the middle and one at the back where the two crew lived – the Capitano, and a sad sailor who raised and lowered the anchor. No one else, except occasionally, slept on the boat: what my father liked doing was to sail across the bay to Sorrento or Capri, to eat there in the marvellous restaurants, to swim off rocks where no one else was swimming. If we felt bold, we would venture for the day as far as Ischia. I remember my father's ability to make almost any excursion seem an adventure: speeding round the Sorrento peninsula would be like going round Cape Horn; my father would stand in the prow as if he were Odysseus; he laughed at himself creating an atmosphere like this; his laughter would be part of the adventure.

We would swim and explore grottos; we would sit on rocks and my father would quote Byron or Swinburne to us; he would do his extraordinary joke quotation – 'and bluer the sea-blue stream of the bay' – which meant that while in the sea he was peeing. He had a way of making ordinary things seem hilarious: his liking for teasing in this context even seemed fitting. There is something about this particular land and this sea that makes it seem anyway like a place where gods might have come down; this is an impression that has never wholly left me.

One of the ways in which our father made his teasing contacts with us children (was not this somewhat godlike?) was by offering us bets or bribes in the way of challenges – one lira for the first one into the sea; five lire for her or him who jumps or dives off the cliff. My sister Vivien was much better than myself at diving: I perfected a rather crab-like technique of slithering more quickly into the sea. My father would recline in his chair on the deck of the boat and laugh: what mortal children would do for money! My sister and I chalked up quite a lot of winnings in this way; my father was slow at paying. One day my sister and I went on strike. We would accept no more challenges nor bribes until he forked out. He was amused at this: he offered us higher and higher prizes in order to try to break our strike: we grimly sat it out around restaurants and grottos. Eventually, still laughingly, he paid.

Sometimes the teasing went wrong. The relationship which he had with my sister Vivien was, I had noticed, different from that which he had with me: it was often characterised by what my Aunt Irene had called 'his insensate silly slapping "boppy" chaff'. Viv, aged fourteen, was almost the only person who did not seem to be in awe of my father; she answered him back; often she even got in a bit of 'chaff' first. She would tell him how ridiculous he looked when even for family snapshots he posed like Mussolini on the prow of the boat; how he cared too much about food. In return he would goad her when she was reluctant to do her dives off high rocks; he would tell her that she was fat. My Aunt Irene wrote of the 'pertness' with which Vivien seemed to be copying her father: all this went on amongst the rocks where it seemed gods must have come down; there was something between my father and Vivien like that between Wotan and Brünnhilde. Once at about this time Aunt Irene was looking for a boarding school for Vivien and she told my father that she had found a school that was 'enchanting' and my father replied – 'She doesn't need an enchanting school, she needs a barracks.'

My own role in this was to watch, I suppose rather like one of the Nibelung dwarfs from under the cover of whatever were symbolically my toadstools. My sister and I were in heart-felt alliance together; but there was also it seemed some quite solitary fight for survival.

My own characteristics were the opposite of those of Viv: I admired her courage: sometimes I felt I could hardly speak at all. That spring I had spent a term away from school in order to go to a stammer specialist in London. He taught me to speak in cadences so that I could declaim like a politician in front of an audience: I could do this quite well: then, when I was not with him, I would stammer as before. How could I explain – but I do not want to be like someone declaiming in front of an audience! My Aunt Irene recorded – 'Nick's stammer is quite unbelievable, and curiously he has no idea of how awful he is. Nanny tries to make him see his contorted face in the mirror and how hard it is for us to listen.'

At Posillipo for the first part of the holidays there was Aunty Baba with whom my father seemed at home. Then one day we had a rare visitor: the Crown Princess of Italy came to spend the day – she had been Princess Marie José of Belgium before her marriage, and had been Baba's childhood friend at Hackwood in the first world war. We all went for a trip on the boat from Posillipo to Ischia. Then in the evening back at the villa and after we children had gone to bed there seemed to be strange comings-and-goings in the grown-up world; doors banged here and there; but what might one expect with Crown Princesses? But then the next morning when I was prowling about hitherto uninhabited parts of the house to try to find out what was happening I was stopped in the passage by Andrée, my mother's ex-lady's maid who was with us on the holiday as usual to 'look after us'; and Andrée said in the stage-French accent that she never lost after all her years in England – 'Do not go in there, eet ees Mrs Guinness.' So – was this or was it not a surprise? Was it not the sort of thing, after all, we knew went on in the grown-up world?

What in fact seems to have happened – people inevitably have slightly different memories of this story – was that Diana, who had been due to arrive somewhat later in the week when my Aunt Baba had moved on to continue her holiday in Tunisia, had arrived in Naples early. She had recently been injured in a car-crash in London and had had to have plastic surgery; she had so longed to get out of the nursing-home and into the sun that she had persuaded her father to help her to escape from the nursing-home and to get a place on an aeroplane; the telegram announcing her early arrival coincided with her actual arrival at the house at Posillipo in the middle of dinner. This was, of course, a social and a personal challenge worthy of the mettle of someone like my father – on his tightrope, as it were, juggling with his plates above Niagara! My sister Viv remembers a row in the middle of the night: but it was with Aunty Baba that we set off the same day on the boat on a three-day trip to Amalfi for the remaining days that had been planned of her holiday. I remember this occasion because it was the one time during those holidays when Viv and I slept on the boat: my father and Baba were in the hotel on the cliff. Mrs Guinness was left in charge of the house, being looked after by servants.

While Diana had been in the nursing-home my father had written to her:

Hurry up and get better as this place is lovely – no great horrors been revealed except the ancient truth that 'Rodds never wash' – also 1,000 steps down to the beach – soon get used to them – we run up them now – saying 'Won't they be fun when Diana arrives!'

I feel so badly about being away while you are so bad, why is it? .... You may think this place too picture-postcard – being so precious – but it is very enchanted.

It is in relation to this holiday that my memories properly begin of my future stepmother Diana. At first because of her injuries she did not venture far from the house; she would sit under a sunshade; there were faint scars on her face, like the trails of snails, which were healing. Viv and I would approach her cautiously like animals looking for food; after a time she was playing games with us; she taught us poker, and I think bridge. Then she was venturing down the hundreds of steps with us and coming on the trips to the islands. Her relationship with my father was different from that of other people; she did not argue with him, did not reply in kind to his teasing; she did not enter into any sort of contest really: either she seemed to like what he was saying or doing, or else she would close her eyes for a time with a look on her face that my father came to call 'tired' or 'patient'. And then he would laugh, and she would laugh; and when she opened her eyes whatever it was she had not liked had usually (but not always) disappeared. She would sit on the boat and there would be an air of stillness about her like that of the sphinxes and classical statues that looked out over the sea from the terraces of villas on Capri. My father's way of teasing her – I suppose he had his ways of teasing nearly everyone – was to tell funny stories that were in fact in praise of her. There was the story of a press reporter who had got into her room in the nursing-home just after the operation on her face; he had asked her what were the results of the plastic surgery; there was a headline in the papers the next day – 'Mrs Guinness says "I am more beautiful than ever."'' There was a story of how my father and she had been driving once on a mountain road in France and he had had to back the car to turn it and he had asked her to look out of the window to tell him when to stop; when the back wheels were half over the precipice she had murmured – 'Vaguely wo.' My father would tell such stories giving an exaggerated imitation of her *cor anglais* Mitford voice: Diana would listen with her 'tired' look and at the end would say, 'Oh you are silly!' Then she would smile at him with her huge blue eyes and he would do his strange clicking laugh behind his teeth.

There were the strange names that they each had for the other: my father always called Diana 'Percher' (pronounced persher) which was a reference to a breed of golden and heavy Flemish carthorses called Percherons; and she, for some reason, called him Kit. On the boat she would take photographs of him and would not object when he posed like Mussolini; she would sit on the prow like a mermaid, and indeed sometimes play a small piano accordion and sing sad German songs such as the *Lorelei*.

One conversation that I remember having at this time with Diana (I think this was the following summer, 1936, when we were all together again in a hotel in Sorrento) was concerning my schoolboy passion, cricket. There was a day when my hero, W. R. Hammond, scored 317 runs for Gloucestershire against Nottinghamshire; Diana asked me why I looked so pleased; I showed her a newspaper headline which said – 'Sublime Hammond'. I could not understand why she laughed so much. She reassured me – Yes, she was sure, Hammond had been sublime: it was only – well, what was it? I imagined I understood. I wondered if there would ever come a time when I might laugh at W. R. Hammond's being sublime.

Before this 1936 holiday at Sorrento there had as usual been a good deal of jockeying about who would be where and when and with whom: there had been some plan by which my father and we children would as in previous years be for a time with Baba; then at the last moment my father had to have an operation for appendicitis, so Vivien and I had gone to Cornwall with Irene and Micky, and then when we did get to Italy our father had been accompanied there by our grandmother, and it was Diana who was there with them, having come on from the Olympic Games in Berlin. I have a memory of Granny in the boiling heat always seeming to be equipped with her full complement of hat, scarf, frilly blouse, black suit and chain-mail bag – like the character of Grandma in Giles's cartoons. She was kind and gallant and did her best with us children; but she used to cheer herself up with phrases like 'It's a poor heart that never rejoices' which was apt to send at least my heart into my boots. Perhaps my father and Diana needed her as a sort of chaperone: these were the days in which it was still thought that if the two of them were seen together staying in a hotel, it might do him political harm.

Viv and I had some notable quarrels during these holidays: we would play chess, and she was liable to hit me over the head with the chess board. She was under a certain stress because she was waiting for a telegram which would tell her the results of her School Certificate

Examination: when the telegram came she opened it and rushed out of the room in tears. We got ready to commiserate with her; but of course the telegram had said that she had passed.

It was probably good of my father and Diana to have us children with them in these holidays; they could have left us with Nanny and Micky in Cornwall. They did not have many chances to have holidays on their own together; and we were now of an age to be staying up for dinner.

Some time during or just before the summer holidays of 1936 my father and Diana decided to get married. They wanted to keep the marriage secret because, my father explained later, his first wife Cimmie had suffered much public hostility due to his politics and he did not want Diana to be in an even more exposed position now that he was a notorious fascist. He and Diana worked out that the only place where they might be married and where there might be a chance of this remaining secret was Germany: there was an agreement between England and Germany by which the nationals of each country could be married in the other by a registrar and not – as was the rule in other countries – at the Embassy. And Hitler himself could be prevailed on, they thought, to ensure that news of the marriage did not get into the papers.

Diana's and Unity's relationship with Hitler had prospered since the time they had first met him early in 1935. In September of that year, after the summer holiday at Posillipo, Diana had joined Unity in Munich and they had gone for the third time to the Nuremberg Parteitag; they were known now as Hitler's friends; when they told Hitler of the difficulties that Putzi Hanfstaengl had made for them in previous years when they wanted to meet him – especially over his, Hitler's, reputed horror of lipstick – Hitler laughed, and said that Hanfstaengl usually bored him by introducing him to old American women. Diana and Unity were taken to a village rally by Unity's new friend Streicher; he asked them to stand up in front of the crowd and he announced 'They may be taller and more beautiful than we but they have the same blood'; and then in English – 'They are not Angles but angels.' In the autumn their mother visited Unity in Munich and was introduced to Hitler: she got the impression that Hitler had 'plenty of leisure.... in congenial company he would stay and talk for ever.... he gave the impression of doing always whatever he wanted at the moment, unhampered by any set time table or urgent work waiting to be done'.

In March 1936 when Hitler's troops entered the Rhineland Diana and Unity were in Cologne to greet him; he recognised them in the crowded foyer of a hotel and came over and asked them to tea; then he asked them to be his guests at the Olympic Games in Berlin. They stayed in the Goebbels' house and were driven to the games each day: they also went with Hitler to the Wagner Festival at Bayreuth. Diana found the latter 'an experience as heavenly as the Olympic Games were boring'. She told Hitler that *Parsifal* was the only opera of Wagner's that she did not like. Hitler told her that she would feel differently as she grew older.

Diana made friends with Goebbels' wife Magda: she told her of her and my father's hopes to get married. Magda suggested that the wedding should be in her and her husband's house, then secrecy could be ensured. She wrote to Diana at Sorrento after she had heard of my father's operation for appendicitis:

Schwanenwerder 14th August 1936

Dearest Diana,

A thousand thanks for your lovely letter, but how sorry I was to hear of your and the Leader's bad luck... I sincerely hope that you have now got over it all and that the Leader very quickly recovers.

Here the beautiful but exhausting days of the Olympics will soon be over. I shall be back on 1st September and we will then settle your problem. The date of the 17th is a good one and we will be able to do all the paperwork etc. in peace. Your stay in Germany will be a little longer and the whole business settled in Germany.

Have a good rest. You are taking on difficult tasks, and just as in the past, so even more in the future will you need your strength and health. Give my best wishes to the L [Leader]. A thousand best wishes and kisses to you too. I am so fond of you.

Your Magda.

My father and Diana were married on October 6th in the Goebbels' house in Berlin. Of their families only Unity was present. Diana told how* –

Unity and I, standing at the window of an upstairs room, saw Hitler walking through the trees of the park-like garden that separated the house and the *Reichskanzlei*; the leaves were turning yellow and there was bright sunshine. Behind him came an adjutant carrying a box and some flowers.

* *A Life of Contrasts.*

Inside the box was Hitler's wedding present – 'a photograph in a silver frame with A. H. and the German eagle'.

My father had travelled to Berlin on October 5th; this was the day after the traumatic event in East London that came to be known as the Battle of Cable Street, which is described in the next chapter. On the night of the wedding, October 6th; Diana recorded that in the Kaiserhof Hotel she and my father had 'a quarrel of which, try as I will, I cannot remember the reason: we went to bed in dudgeon'. Next day they flew back to England.

No one in England was told of the wedding except Diana's parents and her brother Tom. It was thought, probably correctly, that others could not be trusted with the secret.

One odd result of my father's links with Hitler through Diana was that his relationship with Mussolini was broken. For some time Mussolini had seemed to be rather aloof. There had in fact been Count Grandi's letter of the previous year advising Mussolini to reconsider the question of payments to my father: by now, in 1936, the payments had stopped. When my father was in Rome later that autumn and he tried to arrange his customary meeting with Mussolini he was interviewed instead by the Foreign Minister Ciano who asked him pointedly whether or not it was true that he had been just previously in Berlin. When my father said that he had, Ciano said that Mussolini was too ill to see him. Mussolini was at that time envious of Hitler. My father never saw Mussolini again: nor, for that matter, did he again see Hitler.

In his autobiography my father wrote:

Clearly, my normal relations with him [Mussolini] would easily have been restored if I had gone back to Rome a year or two later because he and Hitler were then on good terms. But for the last three years before the war I never left England at all; I was held fast by the growth of our movement and the ever increasing intensity of our campaign.

CHAPTER 12

The Battle of Cable Street

Towards the end of 1935 Oswald Mosley found himself with a movement somewhat pruned and reorganised: the Black House had been
given up, and attempts were being made to fit the style to the policy
of putting emphasis on the winning of elections rather than on
demonstrations of toughness. The Italian-Abyssinian war which had
begun in October 1935 had provided the movement with a slogan –
'Mind Britain's Business' – and this for a time had concentrated members'
energies. But then the Prime Minister Stanley Baldwin, who six months
earlier had taken over from MacDonald as head of the National Government, called for a general election in November, a year or so before
it might have been expected: the BUF found itself in a difficult position.
The election it had been working for was at hand, yet its electoral
organisation was clearly still inadequate – it was short of funds and
had few suitable potential candidates. Two years earlier the BUF had
boasted of putting up four hundred candidates at an election: now,
Mosley must have remembered the débâcle of the New Party in the
1931 election when all but two of the twenty-three candidates had lost
their £150 deposits. What should be done by a movement that had
so recently decided that its *raison d'être* was the putting up of candidates?

Mosley hit on the original idea of trying to make it seem a positive
move in the electoral game to put up no candidates at all: he announced –

My advice is not to waste a vote for a farce. Wait for the real battle.
This election is a sham battle, which at the next election will be
followed by the real battle: for not until Fascist candidates enter the
field as challengers for power will any reality be introduced into
British politics.

And indeed the 1935 election was rather vapid, because both the National and the Labour parties were adopting the same indecisive attitudes towards the crisis that mattered – that of the Italian-Abyssinian war. They were advocating sanctions against Italy but that these should not occasion any threat to European peace. Baldwin was restored to power as the head of a new so-called National but in effect Conservative Government. Mosley wrote in *Blackshirt*:

> It was the lowest poll of the last thirty years with the single exception of 1918 when the men had not returned from France... the old force and the old system are a dying force in Britain... Fascism alone emerges as the triumphant challenger... the future is with us.

Fascists were becoming adept at arguing that whatever happened was probably for the best. They were still searching, however, for some practical cause to harness their energies to.

During the course of 1935 there had sprung up in East London a movement which, almost uniquely in the history of the BUF, gained a large and spontaneous local following without direction from head-quarters or at first the impetus of the Leader as a speaker. Up till now the BUF's outgoing energies had been directed mainly at industrial parts of the country where unemployment was highest and at country districts where government agricultural policy might be felt to be ruinous: the fount of these energies was central London where it was felt that political influence resided. The East End had seemed to be a political backwater – a world of its own, a hive of small industries, a slum. A large proportion of the population were immigrants; a large proportion of these were Jewish.

In October 1934 at the Albert Hall Mosley had thrown down, or taken up, the challenge concerning the Jews; but the enemy had re-mained somewhat amorphous, mythical. In April 1935 he was reiterat-ing – 'I openly and publicly challenge the Jewish interest in this country commanding commerce, commanding the press, commanding the cinema, commanding the City of London, commanding sweatshops': in response to this he had received a telegram of congratulation from Streicher in Germany to which he had replied, 'I greatly esteem your message in the midst of our hard struggle: the forces of Jewish corrup-tion must be overcome in all great countries before the future of Europe can be made secure in justice and in peace'. (Mosley later explained that this was a sort of routine reply sent out by his office in response to congratulatory telegrams and he did not remember being personally responsible for it.) Then in September, as part of the run-up to his 'Mind Britain's Business' campaign, he was saying: 'Over the whole of this Abyssinian dispute rises the stink of oil; and stronger than even the stink of oil is the stink of the Jew.' (He later explained that unfortunately one did sometimes get carried away in the heat of speeches by phrases that one later regretted.) But not much of this rhetoric was directed against the sort of Jews that were in London's East End.

The first BUF branch there had been one at Bow, opened in the winter of 1934/5. Then a branch at Bethnal Green was opened by District Officer Mick Clarke. Clarke was a Cockney, a powerful and vituperative speaker; it was he who built up a political following almost independent of Mosley. Fascism in the East End became directed specifically against Jews. There were about 20,000 Jews in Bethnal Green; about three times as many in nearby Stepney; somewhat less in Hackney, Shoreditch and Bow. There were about 150,000 Jews altogether out of a total population of about half a million.

These Jews had come for the most part from the ghettos of Russia and Poland and Hungary as a result of the pogroms at the end of the last century. They had brought with them their distinctive clothes, their distinctive food and their distinctive language (Yiddish). They observed their day of rest on Saturdays instead of Sundays; they were opposed to intermarriage with non-Jews; and they kept themselves to themselves. There was no district of East London in which they were in an actual majority, but it seemed as if in many places they were in positions of power: they worked hard – mostly at the tailoring and furniture trades – and saved money. They often became landlords, and were apt indeed understandably to give preference to their people in matters both of accommodation and of jobs. Surrounding them were people of a more free-and-easy, almost anarchic tradition, often Irish; but who themselves were dependent on a feeling of group-solidarity if they were not to lose identity in their hard-pressed lives. This was a situation that would seem to have been only too ready for the introduction of a racialist type of fascism: what is of interest is the slowness of BUF headquarters to have taken any advantage of it.

At first there were the usual street-corner meetings with Mick Clarke's men on soap-boxes and a flag or two: there began to be phrases like 'hook-nosed unmentionables' and 'yiddish scum'. The accusations were mostly about conditions of employment in local businesses: there were sexual overtones too in the charges of non-Jewish girls being 'sweated' in back-street tailors' shops. Sometimes the style of this remained within the knock-about tradition of British street-corner politics:

there were protests for instance by non-Jewish ponces against Jews who had cornered the prostitution industry: slogans appeared on walls – *British Streets for British Cows.*

Mosley addressed his last huge meeting at the Albert Hall in March 1936: in it he repeated (according to *The Times*) that 'it was the intention of British Fascism to challenge and break for ever the power of the Jews in Britain'. He also went into one of his more rousing flights of peroration –

> We count it a privilege to live in an age when England demands that great things shall be done, a privilege which learns to be of the generation which learns to say: 'What can we give?' instead of 'What can we take?' For thus our generation learns that there are greater things than slothful ease; greater things than safety; more terrible things than death.

William Joyce and Raven Thomson had begun to go down to the East End and add their voices to those of Mick Clarke and his followers. Then, in June 1936 Mosley himself appeared on the scene. He marched at the head of what *Blackshirt* described as 'a half-mile column': he spoke in Victoria Park, Bow, to a crowd that was variously estimated at anything from 5,000 to 100,000. He announced that from now on fascist effort would be concentrated in the East End: the BUF would put up candidates for the municipal elections in 1937. This was a new departure for the movement: so far, there had only been talk of fighting parliamentary elections. To lead the march Mosley and other members of headquarters staff had appeared in a completely new uniform – jack-boots, breeches, military-style jacket, Sam Browne belt and officer-type hat. The uniform was seen by many to be in emulation of the Nazi SS. One caustic member of the BUF said that it seemed to him more like that of 'King Zog's Own Imperial Dismounted Hussars'.

Soon after this Mosley had his operation for appendicitis; then there was the holiday in Sorrento; he was out of the fray for nearly two months. But the campaign in East London had been given its impetus. From now on, and for the next nine months, the BUF seemed to have found a cause and an actual enemy to fight.

For night after night there were meetings often in the same streets; fascists would arrive with their drums and loudspeaker vans; the crash of fascist oratory would go on for hours; it would break up old patterns of social life. If protests were made there was the likelihood of a fight and broken windows: if protests were not made there were jeers about Jews being 'on the run'. All this, it was claimed, was being done in the name of 'free speech' as part of a run-up to democratic elections. Before he had temporarily left the arena Mosley had again laid down the rule – 'Mere abuse we forbid... it is bad propaganda and alienates public sympathy.' But there were always fascists who seemed to care little about alienating public sympathy. Gangs of youths went through the streets chanting 'The Yids, the Yids, we've got to get rid of the Yids'. William Joyce's favourite phrase for Jews at this time seems to have been 'sub-men with prehensile toes'.

BUF speakers played a game with the police to see how far they could go in the matter of abuse without breaking the law. The law at this time was that it was an offence to use threatening words with intent to provoke a breach of the peace, but it had to be shown that an actual audience was being provoked. This led to prevarications such as are loved by barrack-room lawyers: words like 'Oriental' and 'Simian' were defended as being geographically or physiognomically descriptive: a word 'Licean' was introduced as if it referred to a middle-eastern race; it was understood by those who used it and most of those who heard it to refer to lice. An animal called the 'She-Neelouse' was described which had 'a large hook-beaked protuberance and vile smell when it clusters'. The police would painstakingly write such stuff down and try to decide whether or not to instigate a prosecution. During the three years from the beginning of 1936 to the end of 1938 there were in fact brought by the police 39 cases of insult, 61 cases of insulting slogans chalked on walls, 60 cases of alleged assaults by fascists or fascist sympathisers on Jews, and 100 cases of damage to property – largely the breaking of windows. During this period there were 29 cases of alleged assault by Jews on fascists – but this statistic applied only to such cases in which there was evidence that the assailants were Jews. A reporter in the *Evening Standard* at the end of 1936 wrote that in fact 'most of the back-street assaults seem to have been directed against Blackshirts'. One part of the criminal gang life of East London seems to have been run at this time by Jews: they would have been skilled both at violence and, presumably, at the covering up of their traces.

One of the self-confessed leaders of the opposition to the BUF was Jack Comer (known also as Jack Spot for his propensity for being 'on the spot') who later became notorious as a leader of London's underworld and an expert (and victim) in razor fights. In 1937 he was sent to prison for six months for causing grievous bodily harm to a fascist. Another gangland leader sentenced in 1936 for assault was Barnet Becow of whom the magistrate said – 'He is a man trading in violence and is more likely to lead to the destruction of the Jewish community in the

East End than the fascists are'. But in all the carefully kept police records there is, again, no evidence of a crippling injury or death. It is understandable that the Jewish community, with its memories of eastern European pogroms, must have feared that it was about to be subjected to a persecution such as had already begun to be perpetrated by Hitler: it is also just possible that non-Jewish toughs might have seen the style of violence as not much more than that which had traditionally been perpetrated from time to time in the East End.

Very occasionally in fascist publications there was some discussion about where, if the 'Yids' were to be got rid of, they might go: Mosley in his last Albert Hall speech had made it clear that under a fascist regime Jews who did not 'put Britain first' would be deported. It was not suggested that they should go to Palestine because of the local Arab population. Sometimes Africa was mentioned; a writer in *Blackshirt* pointed out that there were 'many waste places of the earth possessing great potential fertility'. But for the most part it was recognised that the East London campaign was not concerned with such distant practical questions; it was a contest for local mastery. Virulence increased confusingly when Arnold Leese's Imperial Fascist League turned up in the area; Leese was explicit that all Jews should be sent to Madagascar and the world's navies should be assembled to see they did not get out – even that a more 'permanent way of disposing of the Jews' (this was in Arnold Leese's paper *The Fascist*) 'would be to exterminate them by some humane method such as the lethal chamber'. To the inhabitants of the East End, it must often have seemed not worth while to attempt to distinguish between one set of fascists and another.

Perhaps in order to try to remove from his movement the effects of the excesses of other fascists Mosley had decided early in 1936 that the word 'Fascist' should be demoted in the title and that the movement should be known from now on as 'The British Union of Fascists and National Socialists' or just 'British Union' for short. This was possibly in some deference to the National Socialism of Germany: but in the main the emphasis was from now on to be on the Britishness of British Union. And it was true that 'National Socialist' might have a patriotic ring: a slogan was coined – 'If you love your country you are national, if you love your people you are socialist'. The old emblem of the Roman or Italian fasces was dropped and in its place there was introduced a home-grown symbol of a flash-and-circle. This represented (in my father's words) 'the lightning of action based on the circle of comradeship'. To the enemies of the British Union it became known as 'the flash in the pan'.

In October 1936 when Mosley returned from the holiday at Sorrento there was planned for his re-appearance in the East End the biggest demonstration yet: a march would start by the Royal Mint near the Tower of London and would proceed through Shoreditch, Limehouse, Bow and Bethnal Green: in each district there would be a halt and a speech by Mosley. This was an occasion such as that of the meeting at Olympia two years earlier when the opposition also decided to make their biggest demonstration yet: as before, the technique would be to try to discredit British Union by making out that they were simply trouble-makers and thugs.

The march had been well publicised: both fascists and anti-fascists rallied their forces. The anti-fascists (this was shortly after the outbreak of the Spanish Civil War) coined for their slogan that of the defenders of Madrid – 'They Shall Not Pass'. On the day itself, October 4th, bus-loads of communist and left-wing militants arrived in the area from outside: the local leader was Jack Spot; he had armed himself (so he told a newspaper reporter) with a 'type of cosh shaped like the leg of a sofa but filled with lead at the end which had been made for him by a cabinet-maker in Aldgate'. Before Mosley's arrival there was chanting and stone-throwing by the anti-fascists; the fascists were in orderly ranks; there were 6,000 police to keep the protagonists apart. When Mosley arrived – with a motor-cycle escort and standing up in the open Bentley doing the fascist salute in his new uniform (Jack Spot called this 'the rummiest sight I've ever seen in the East End') – he walked up and down the columns of blackshirts inspecting them while the crowd, beyond the lines of police, tried to charge, were pushed back, but here and there broke through. There were some arrests. The Police Commissioner Sir Philip Game told Mosley not to start his march before the police had set about clearing the streets across which barricades had been erected. The largest barricade had been built across Cable Street, on the route of the intended march going east from the Mint towards Limehouse. A lorry had been used to construct a formidable defence work.

Sir Philip Game saw the whole occasion as primarily one concerning the police: he seemed determined to show that the streets would be controlled by his men and not by rival gangs. The police tried to push their way through Cable Street; they failed; they charged the barricade and captured it only after a battle with the defenders in which stones, bricks, truncheons and iron bars were used. The defenders, however, withdrew to further barricades, scattering broken glass in their wake to discourage the police on horses. After two hours of this sort of fighting

during which 83 anti-fascists were arrested and there were over 100
injuries including those to police – and during which time the fascists
remained out of the action lined up by the Royal Mint – Sir Philip
Game telephoned to the Home Secretary, Sir John Simon, who was
in the country for the weekend, and asked for his permission to give
orders for the march to be called off. Sir John Simon agreed. Sir Philip
Game came to Mosley and said, 'As you can see for yourself, if you
fellows go ahead there will be a shambles.' Oswald Mosley asked (this
was according to newspaper reports), 'Is that an order?' Sir Philip Game
said, 'Yes.' Then Mosley gave orders for his men to turn and to march
the other way – back down Great Tower Street and Queen Victoria
Street towards the Embankment. Newspapers reported that amongst
his ranks there were 'cries of disappointment'. Before Mosley dismissed
his men near Charing Cross Bridge he made a short speech:

> The Government surrenders to Red violence and Jewish corruption.
> We never surrender. We shall triumph over the parties of corruption
> because our faith is greater than their faith, our will is stronger than
> their will, and within us is the flame that shall light this country
> and shall later light this world.

The London District Committee of the Communist Party announced: 'This is the most humiliating defeat ever suffered by any
figure in English politics.'

In popular mythology it came to be thought that the Battle of Cable
Street was a battle between the fascists and anti-fascists – that fascist
thugs had tried to march through a Jewish area of the East End and
residents had heroically prevented them. In fact the battle was between
the police and left-wing militants to some extent brought in from outside: the fascists did not become involved in the fighting at all. They
had behaved obediently according to the law.

Two years previously at Olympia the BUF had taken on the left-
wing militants and had 'won' the physical battle but had been branded
as thugs and the meeting had been a propaganda disaster; now it seemed
that they were to suffer a similar fate by having remained passive. There
was something just in their style that made people imagine they had
been violent even when they had not: and when they were law-abiding,
there was the added impression that their violence had been defeated.

It is conceivable that Mosley might have instructed his followers
not to conform to police orders in such a way as to have brought
upon them neither ignominy nor a reputation for lawlessness – nor

indeed the chance of serious charges being laid against them. They might have marched – in some sort of formation or in none – along another route; they might, if this was the way things went, have got themselves fairly honourably arrested. It is doubtful what charges the police could in fact at that time have brought: but even if they had the BUF might at least have appeared as martyrs.

As it was, they appeared to be a revolutionary movement prepared for a crisis who in a crisis did exactly what they were told by the authorities. People wondered – what on earth then was Mosley doing in his jackboots? He was in fact due to be in Berlin the next day for his wedding: but then, hardly anyone knew this.

The next Sunday in the East End there was a 'victory' parade by anti-fascists; the police now had to make baton-charges to clear the way for them. While the police were thus occupied, a gang of about 200 pro-fascist and mostly teenage youths ran down Mile End Road smashing Jewish shop windows and attacking anyone who might be thought to look Jewish: a hairdresser and a four-year-old girl were reportedly thrown through a plate-glass window. British Union officials denied responsibility for this; they said as usual that such behaviour was strictly against orders.

Then during the following week British Union held a series of what it claimed to be its largest and most peaceful meetings ever held in East London. In Stepney, Shoreditch, Bethnal Green and Limehouse huge crowds listened attentively: the meetings were orderly, the speakers claimed, because no agitators had been brought in from outside. On Wednesday October 14th Mosley himself addressed a crowd of 12,000 at Bethnal Green and then marched to Limehouse: police reports noted that there was little or no opposition whereas 'in contrast, much opposition has been displayed at meetings held by the Communist movements' speakers'. Mosley said in his Limehouse speech – 'We make no appeal to violence because we have behind us the British people . . . I challenge and expose tonight the corrupt power in England of international Jewish finance.'

He might seem, as usual, to be winning the particular argument; but also, as usual, other impressions were what remained in the public mind. *The Times* referred to the activities of both fascists and anti-fascists in East London as 'a tedious and pitiable burlesque' which made the lives of East Enders 'unbearable'. Beverley Baxter MP wrote – 'Here is a picture of Sir Oswald Mosley surrounded by his bodyguard just like a dictator or a gangster: he is wearing riding breeches and riding boots though I cannot see any horse.'

There were arguments in the press about what was, or was not, the duty of the police in the matter of ensuring that citizens should be able to march through streets: it seemed to be generally accepted that it was the appearance of British Union in the uniforms of a private army that caused provocation.

The Government decided to push through a Public Order Act which would prohibit the wearing of military-style uniforms. Mosley protested that the British Union was being discriminated against while all the evidence showed that it was their opponents who were causing the disturbances. He also pointed out that without the uniforms it would be difficult for British Union to maintain the discipline that had enabled them to be law-abiding till now. In later years, however, he would admit that the wearing of military-type uniforms had resulted in a propaganda disaster.

The campaign for the municipal elections of 1937 continued. British Union were putting up candidates in three districts – Bethnal Green, Shoreditch and Limehouse. Fascist publications kept up their anti-semitic tone. The doggerel verses increased in unpleasantness –

> His hair was sleek and full of oil
> And so his manner too
> His hands were far too soft for toil
> The son of a son of a Jew –

and bands of drummers went through the streets singing to the tune of *Daisy Daisy* –

> Abie Abie now that we've tumbled you
> You'll go crazy before we have done with you.

The British Union election manifesto, however, tried to put it more reasonably:

We guarantee that, if elected, we will oppose all grants and donations for foreign causes of whatever kind. No more Basque children will be supported in luxury at 10/- per week while the children of the unemployed get only 3/-; nor will we give away facilities for collections for foreign wars while the war against poverty and bad conditions at home is neglected.

We ask you to return us as your watchdogs on the Council to keep a sharp look-out that no grafter of Right or Left takes advantage

of the present rotten system to fill his pockets pending the great
National Revolution for which we are all waiting.

HONESTY THE BEST POLICY

On 6th March 1937 the election results were announced. Mick Clarke
and Raven Thomson in Bethnal Green got 3,000 votes each or 23%
of the votes cast; Charles Wegg-Prosser and Anne Brock Griggs in
Limehouse about 2,000 or 19%; and in Shoreditch William Joyce and
Jim Bailey 2,500 votes or 14%. In other parts of the country where
British Union had put up candidates – Edinburgh, Leeds, Sheffield
and Southampton – their results were insignificant.

Immediately after the announcement of the East End results Mosley,
according to John Beckett, sat down with a pencil and paper and worked
out how British Union had done better than Hitler had done in Germany
a few years before he had come to power: in 1928 in a general election
Hitler had polled only 2.7% of votes cast and in 1930 18%. It could
also be pointed out that in the East End municipal elections only house-
holders had been eligible to vote, so much of the support for British
Union amongst the young had not been represented.

However two weeks after the poll Mosley summoned all his senior
staff to headquarters and told them that most of them would have
to be dismissed; salaried staff had to be cut from 143 to 30: there was
now just no money to pay any more, though he hoped that some might
carry on in an unpaid capacity. Two of those who did not choose
to stay were William Joyce and John Beckett – the Director of Propaganda and the Director of Publications – both leading anti-semites.
They were angry at having been dismissed, and started a movement
of their own – the National Socialist League – in which they were
heavily critical of their once so admired Leader. But it was while they
had been with him that they had done him much damage.

Years later my father was asked by a journalist whether it was true
'that your reason for dismissing Joyce was less a financial one than
a personal and political one'. My father replied: 'He gave no trouble
in our movement until he was dismissed... he resented that in financial
difficulties we dismissed the speakers and retained the organisers.' This
was long after Joyce – by then better-known by his war-time nickname
of 'Lord Haw-Haw' – had been executed as a traitor in 1945. My father
seldom noticed the damage that people on his own side did to him:
he seemed to float above such things: but then, what was it in the
clouds that he had his eyes and heart on?

CHAPTER 13

Wootton Lodge

In the autumn of 1936 my father and Diana rented a very beautiful
house, Wootton Lodge, in Staffordshire. It was an early seventeenth-
century house with an imposing front with huge windows. Some of
the back was said to have been knocked away by a bombardment by
Cromwell.

During 1937 my father was spending much time speaking in the
Midlands and in the North: it suited him to have somewhere within
driving distance where he could spend nights. Also now that he and
Diana were married they needed a home: but because their marriage
was secret, my father could also keep going to the family home at
Denham without anything much appearing to have changed.

At Wootton there was a long drive through beech trees and then
suddenly the house below with two lodges and a circular lawn in front,
very formal like the backdrop to a ballet. The ground fell away sharply
behind the house to a ravine with trees and a semi-circle of lakes; beyond
this again was a curve of green hills so that the house seemed both
to be high and solitary on a rock and yet protected. It was the most
beautiful house I have ever lived in: like a castle in storybooks.

You went up a wide flight of steps into a panelled hall; the drawing
room was to the left where there were Chippendale chairs and a settee
shaped curiously like sea-shells; here Diana would sit like someone in
a painting by Botticelli. There was a bow window full of light and
a round table on which would be set out tea. In a smaller room towards
the back there was a gramophone with an enormous horn, also like
a shell; you sharpened triangular wooden needles with an instrument
like a cigar-cutter; out of the horn came tiny pure music as if from
a homunculus. This was music I had never heard before – *Das Rheingold*;
Götterdämmerung; Marlene Dietrich singing two sad German songs called

Peter and *Johnny*. From this room you went out on to a terrace which looked down over descending gardens to the chasm at the bottom with woods and caves and lakes. On a platform at the back of the house, where the part knocked away by Cromwell had been, there was a deep lily pond or a shallow swimming pool – according to my father's mood. At the back of this, on the cliff-face, were paths slanting down between rocks and trees that were haunted by wild cats like those of witches. In the lakes there were a few old and very large trout that seemed too sophisticated to be interested in such things as flies. Beyond the lakes were the hills with huge warrens of rabbits; beyond these again wild woods of elm and beech and oak.

I was often at Wootton without my sister and brother; they remained for the most part at Savehay Farm. Because it was not known that my father and Diana were married there was some difficulty about us children going to Wootton: Irene wrote in her diary of my father: 'He has no right to put growing Vivien in such a position: oh dear God help us!' I do not remember any pressure being put on me. I loved being at Wootton; I liked splitting the holidays between it and Savehay Farm.

At Wootton there were the woods, the mysterious lakes, the disused shafts of lead mines going deep into the hills. These I could crawl along until I seemed to have found the ultimate hidey-hole from the grown-up world; yet I did not need this at Wootton because no one was now trying to stop me being alone. My father would return from his speaking tours; he taught me how to shoot rabbits with a .22 rifle; I would sit quietly at the edge of one of the lakes in the evenings while he fished. Then he would be away again, and I could carry on doing such things on my own. One had to stalk the fish as one stalked the rabbits, crawling to the shelter of a tree and casting a line as if threading a needle.

I would have meals quite often on my own with Diana, the two of us in the large panelled dining room to the right of the hall. There were servants of course – a cook and a housemaid and a footman – but I was old enough now (thirteen and fourteen) to feel myself as no longer part of the servants' world; and besides, my father and Diana treated me as if I were not. They, on holidays or at Wootton, were the first grown-ups I knew who treated human relationships straight-forwardly: others were liable to use words to attack or to defend or to complain; my father and Diana seemed to listen, and to reply to each question on its merits.

I do not remember talking much with my father at this time; perhaps

he was too often away; when he was with me in the woods or by
the lakes we liked to be quiet. But with Diana in the huge dining
room, in which I suppose we were like tiny figures at each end of
a table in one of those joke cartoons, I would ask about politics, about
Germany, about Hitler. I had fairly conventional English attitudes
towards Hitler: neither my father nor Diana had ever tried to influence
us children in our political views – much more vocal had been aunts,
schoolfriends, schoolmasters. I would say to Diana – But surely, I mean,
look – Hitler just can't be a good thing, can he? Diana would say
– But you see, there are all the things he has done for Germany. We
would go thus to and fro -- this is his style, but this is his achievement.
Then once she said – To understand, you would have to come to
Germany and look. I said – Would you take me to see Hitler? She
said she would ask my father, and write and see. But then this was
the year of the Munich crisis, and there was no chance of my going
to Germany.

One summer holiday (I think this must have been the year after
the news of my father's and Diana's marriage had been made public)
I had two schoolfriends to stay with me at Wootton: we camped out
on the green hills: in the evenings we would all take up the arguments
with Diana. This was a time when my father was reiterating his claim
that Jews were a dominating influence in advertising, in films, in the
press. When one of my friends, my future brother-in-law, came to
write his thank-you letter to Diana he ended his formal, schoolboy
phrases with – 'P.S. My father says the *Yorkshire Post* is not run by
Jews.'

I, returning to Savehay Farm, would write to Diana:

Thank you so much for having me to stay. I always enjoy myself
so much at Wootton. Everyone was very cold to me when I got
back as they were teased that I had stayed on till Wednesday. I told
them of the great Dramas in the fishing, and of the Wailing Woman
in the cave; but all they did was to say 'Oh' in a very bored voice.
By the way, I left Mummy's picture in my room so would you
be so kind as to send it on to me.

Life at Savehay Farm continued as before with my sister Vivien,
my brother Micky, Nanny and Andrée the housekeeper. Aunt Irene
would come down when my father was not there: Aunt Baba would
come down usually when he was – until she learned about his marriage.
My father would visit Savehay Farm when he was seeing to things

at his headquarters in London. This was the time when there was trouble
with the Courts about the provision of our – the children's – money
for Savehay Farm: a judge had reduced the payments on the grounds
that they would enable my father to spend more of his own money
on fascism. My father approached Irene to see if she would make up
the amount withheld; he suggested we children could pay her back when
we came of age. She agreed to this: she still complained that she was
not consulted about arrangements.

During Christmas 1936 all of the family for whom it might be thought
proper were at Savehay Farm – my father and Irene and Granny and
we three children: Baba and her family came over on Boxing Day.
Diana was not there: we did not yet know that she and my father
were married. On Boxing Day at dinner my father was rude to all
the grown-ups in turn; one by one they rushed out of the room in
tears or to give each other comfort. Irene recorded – 'Viv got more
and more scarlet, and tears ran down from behind Nick's spectacles
whilst Granny talked madly about any piffle.' I remember this scene
quite well – though not my own tears. We were fairly used to my
father's roaring off like this: he was like someone fighting against being
trapped. What he might feel himself trapped by, we did not know.

My grandmother wrote to him afterwards –

Dear lad, I know very well how hard Xmas is for you and how
you miss Cim – the very spirit of Xmas. I think the way you work
to make the children's Xmas as happy as she would wish is wonderfully brave and very like you.

The continuing feud between the one part of the family and the
other was still mainly due to what my aunts and grandmother had
felt about my father's relationship with Diana at the time of my mother's
death. But it was now kept going by a growing divergence of feelings
about Hitler; also by a divergence of attitude towards the conventional
upper-class world. My father kept up the house at Denham, he said,
because of us children; he himself showed less and less interest in the
traditional sort of arrangements that my Aunt Irene made about schools
or occupations for the holidays, and in particular he paid almost no
attention to his youngest son Micky. Irene, with her warm-hearted
but sometimes ponderous style, had for long been a butt to my father's
teasing (he used to refer to her as 'flying nose-heavy' – a reference
to a tendency of aeroplanes in the first world war). But now his impatience with things at Denham seemed to influence even his feelings

about the elaborate tomb that he had constructed for Cimmie: he did not often visit this, and his reluctance seemed to increase.

However, in the summer of 1936 it had been Irene who had been as an official guest of the German government at the Nazi Parteitag at Nuremberg: she had come home with stories of the occasion 'breathtaking in its splendour and its gaiety'. In her diary she had thanked God 'for bringing me here and guiding me through an evening of delirious enjoyment'. When she had been introduced to Hitler she had been struck, as Diana had been, by 'the freshness of his skin, the beauty of his smile, the frankness of his eyes'. She too had felt 'the aloneness of that man in his colossal undertaking'. Also – 'It is quite shattering and makes one gulp and say – What was the war all for? – with this tremendous, spiritually inspired people with one heart and mind – their Germany above everything'.

1937 was a difficult year for my father: there had been the financial crisis and the dismissals of headquarters staff at the BUF; the turning against him of people who previously had been almost sycophantically loyal. He had recently brought another libel action on much the same grounds as those on which he had won £5,000 from the *Star* two years earlier; now he was awarded damages of a farthing – such was the change in the public mood about him. He continued to get large audiences in his meetings up and down the country: sometimes the audiences were attentive and enthusiastic and sometimes they still became involved in the violence with which his movement had become associated in the public mind. But always after he had gone the local enthusiasm he generated seemed to wane, and there were left just groups of people wondering when he would return – as if he were a famous actor in the business of undertaking tours.

Inevitably it was still the meetings at which there was violence that were reported in newspaper headlines; meetings that were orderly were not recorded at all. Indoor halls were now almost all banned to him because the owners or trustees feared violence (or such was their excuse); and many public places such as parks were withheld for the same reason if local authorities had the power. And with the banning of the uniform it was true that discipline and thus also self-protection had become more difficult. In Southampton he was hit in the face by a stone and had to be rushed away by the police in a tram; at Hull a bullet was fired through the window of his car. Another march through East London was banned; then one through South London was so controlled by police that there were fights again simply between police and antifascists as there had been at Cable Street. And then in Liverpool, in

October, my father was hit on the head by a jagged brick and was quite dangerously injured; he was lifted down from his van and carried to hospital half conscious; a minor operation was performed on a 'punctured wound of the skull'. He remained in hospital for a week, then went to Wootton to recuperate. My grandmother professed herself outraged by this, in the light of her belief that he and Diana were not married.

While he was in hospital a libel case came to court against the British Union newspaper *Action*. *Action* had taken the place in 1936 of the now defunct *Fascist Week* as yet another attempt to run a paper which would have a more sophisticated appeal than that of *Blackshirt*. Its editor had been John Beckett: he had written an article in April 1936 in which he had suggested that Lord Camrose, the owner of the *Daily Telegraph*, was (in the words of the plaintiff's Counsel) 'a Jewish international financier with no loyalty to the Crown and no sense of patriotism, and that in his conduct of the *Daily Telegraph* he allowed his duty to the public to be subordinated to his own financial interests'. Lord Camrose sued for libel and the case came to court on 14th October 1937. For the defence it was argued that the words did not have the meaning implied by the complainant – for although Lord Camrose was not in fact a Jew it was no offence to be called Jewish. John Beckett was not called as a witness: but after he had heard the case for the defence he asked if he could make a statement from the witness box. He said, 'When I wrote that article I honestly believed it to be true because I had the information in it given me by people on whom, rightly or wrongly, I placed great reliance ... To me, to tell a man that he is a Jew and that his financial interests are far greater outside this country than in it are two of the greatest insults that can possibly be offered to any man ... When I discovered that so far from the information my titled friend gave me about Lord Camrose being a Jew being true – he was a Welshman and, if I may say so, an obvious Welshman – I did not want to go into the box to justify that.'

The 'titled friend' of Beckett's statement was evidently Mosley: Beckett suggested that the article had been approved by Mosley himself. In the course of the trial Mosley's secretary George Sutton said that he 'could not confirm this' and that he believed Mosley had been 'ill at the time'. Lord Camrose was awarded £20,000 damages and costs: John Beckett could not pay; *Action*, owned by a company with £100 capital, went bankrupt. Beckett made a statement to the press in which he referred scathingly to a man who would 'send his secretary into the witness box to say he had had influenza'; he announced that he envied the editor of the *Daily Telegraph* whose 'chief, at any rate, was man enough to say he was the chief and did not hide behind a £100 company'. British Union issued a statement – 'The company laws of this system were devised by capitalists for use against the people, and no one can complain if the people now use the company law for their own purposes'.

Several more of those who had been Mosley's most loyal and out-spoken supporters turned against him at this time. Charles Wegg-Prosser who had been the BUF candidate at Limehouse wrote to him:

> You are side-tracking the whole issue of social betterment by the anti-semitic campaign. Anti-Jewish propaganda, as you and Hitler use it, is a gigantic side-tracking stunt – a smoke-screen to cloud thought and divert action with regard to our real problems. Our people are fair, tolerant and humane. You introduce a movement imitating foreign dictators, you run it as a soulless despotism. You sidetrack the demand for social justice by attacking the Jew, you give the people a false answer and unloose lowest mob passion.

Jim Bailey who had been the BU candidate for Shoreditch also resigned but for somewhat opposite reasons: 'I am a disillusioned man, and have lost faith with our Leader ... from being a party with great ideals and a great future it has become a children's Sunday School outing: they have guyed a great ideal.'

Then early in 1938 A. K. Chesterton resigned. In 1936 he had published a hagiographical biography of Mosley called *Portrait of a Leader*. In it he had perorated –

> Now he moves forward to a still greater destiny, an implacable figure looming ever more immense against the background of his times: through his own eager spirit, so full of aspiration and boldness, symbolising the immortal spirit of his race ... Hail Mosley, patriot and revolutionary, and leader of men!

Now two years later he was writing –

> I have been amazed that a man so dynamic on the platform should prove so unimaginative, so timid, so lacking in initiative and resource ... the public aspect of this shows itself in his refusal to deal objectively with the movement's fortunes. 'Flops' are written up as triumphs, and enormous pains are taken to titivate reports so as to

give the impression of strength where there is weakness, growth where there is decline, of influence where there is only indifference. In a recent issue of his journal there were two major attacks on the veracity of the National Press and yet in this very issue, to my knowledge, there were several statements which were sheer lies. National Socialism should have some nobler inspiration than to oppose one kind of corruption with another still less pleasing to the nostrils.

One of the characteristics of my father's career had always been his trust that he could charm people and keep them loyal to him by his use of words: that if one made an argument sound convincing enough, then one need not be too anxious about the relationship of argument to events. This was, indeed, a general tendency of fascism and national socialism: Mussolini claimed that he had 150 front-line divisions when in fact he had 10; that he possessed the largest airforce in the world when in fact he had no idea how many planes it contained. Hitler did not boast like this; but he did use arguments as if words might dominate the people whom they concerned – Germany needed room for its population and for raw materials *therefore* it had to move into the Ukraine; a homogeneous nation must feel disturbed by its minorities *therefore* the solution was to get rid of them. All this happened at the one time in history when politics in fact was dominated by the disembodied voice – radios were in every home and loudspeakers blared on the street corners – there was as yet no television, on which the oddities of often uproarious human beings could be seen. But the efficacy of words being used like this depended on those who spoke them having power: people then wanted to believe the words, because they wanted to hand over their trust to leaders with power. Mussolini in Italy and Hitler in Germany, however, had come to power by more savage and even more subtle political means than simply the use of words: my father did not have power; but he still seemed to use just words to pin his faith on.

People adored him because of his fluency: but then some turned against him perhaps just because they felt he was more interested in words than in power. This was felt by people like William Joyce: in 1934 Joyce had said, referring to Mosley, 'There is no greater man that God has ever created!'; after his defection, he referred to 'the Mosley group ... who never dared to say boo to a goose except when coppers were in front of them'. It seemed to be the accusation of such people that Mosley would not in fact, in a crisis, be contemptuous enough to treat people as if they were just words.

My father was never in the same sort of business as Hitler: he would appear half to hypnotise people with his talk and flashing eyes; there seemed about to be thunderbolts; then he would switch off, become himself again, as if after all life was too precious for there to be time for more of the boring chicaneries of manipulation. He had an instinct perhaps about the way in which human beings who did obsessively act like this might destroy themselves: he had read, after all, poetry, tragedy. He did not often read novels (Hitler did not read novels) but he had read one or two which he loved such as Stendhal's *Le Rouge et le Noir* and he knew something of the ironies of human nature. If it gave my father pleasure often to be carried away by words he also had the wit sometimes to see himself being carried away: if he was Mephistopheles seeing that good can come out of evil, at least he knew Mephistopheles laughed at this.

When he became exhausted or ill – such as the time he had been hit by a brick at Liverpool – he would return to Wootton as if it were his fairy castle and Diana was his princess – as if after all this was his reality. Only a few of the old friends of either of them came to stay at Wootton: my father was apt to be jealous of Diana when he was away. Diana's sisters came – though her sister Nancy was in bad odour with my father as a result of her novel *Wigs on the Green* in which she had made mock of a fascist called Captain Jack the Leader of the Union Jackshirts. My father always liked to keep separate the different compartments of his life: perhaps this was one reason why he did not announce his marriage – he wanted somewhere to return to which could remain in some way mythical. Diana never had much money at Wootton; she paid for the house largely from what she got from her first husband: she once said that sometimes she had difficulty in paying the servants, and even in buying Christmas presents for her family. My father was often obstinate about handing out money; he thought that he needed all he had for politics. But Diana managed to create an atmosphere of extraordinary beauty and stillness at Wootton. There was an aura around her and my father such as there is around people who are in love.

While he was away she would write to him –

My beloved Darling: it is a long time since I wrote to tell you how much I love you because my letters are bad and stupidly written. But today as my heart is full of love I shall write what is always in my thoughts; and that is, that I love you more than all the world and more than life; that to be with you is paradise, and each parting from you a little tragedy which does not become less with the years. Thank you my precious wonderful darling for the loveliest days I could possibly imagine and for the happiest love. I wish I could write as I feel. God bless you and keep you safe.

And my father would write to her –

Darling Dimpler,
Tried to ring you late Saturday but told no answer – nothing special – just love!
Nothing like plump Percherons for pulling the loads of life....

Sometimes when he returned to Wootton Diana would suggest that he might give up – not exactly politics, but the apparently endless round of meetings at which crowds cheered or booed but at the end of which there was little to show except as it were the litter and flowers of a stage performance. At moments he would get dispirited and almost agree: then his energy would return – there were people who needed him after all – and what else should he do with his enormous talents and his idealism?

The one time in my childhood when I myself was taken from one to another quite frightening of the separate compartments of his world was when, in the summer holidays of 1937 (just after my first term at Eton) I was transported as if on some terrible magic carpet from the commodious double-compartment of life at Savehay Farm and Wootton to that of the British Union Holiday Camp at Selsey, in Sussex. I had heard of the plans for this with unutterable alarm: I was to spend a night or two incognito in a tent with four or five other boys; how could I be incognito! how could I not – or indeed how could I – open my mouth? What I remember about the fascist Holiday Camp at Selsey apart from the pots and pans and bugle calls and sad songs round camp fires at twilight was the way in which, in our tent at night, the other boys brought out photographs rather portentously as if they were indecent or of film-stars; they passed them round: this was so-and-so, this so-and-so: they were of my own family! – Granny, Viv, Aunty Baba – good heavens was there, or why was there not, one of me? A wrong name was attributed to one of the photographs: I thought – well, why not correct this? The boys observed me. I thought – I might either be, or not be, the son of the Leader?

The other instance I remember from this weekend was when my father made his spectacular entrance into the Camp the next day – he

had been staying in a near-by country house – and we all went off
to have a ceremonial swim in the sea. But there was a very low tide,
and the shallow water seemed to go on for ever; and it seemed to
be protocol, as it might be with royalty, that no one should immerse
themselves until my father had immersed himself first. But there was
not enough water to allow him to do this; we seemed to be proceeding
across the English Channel like the Children of Israel through the Red
Sea. Eventually my father flopped down in a foot or two of water;
we all flopped down; then he laughed; we all laughed; I think he caught
my eye. What a joke! Was not this the sort of thing he was good
at – laughing at himself laughing in a foot or two of water – and
was it not this that I was learning from him?

That week the *Blackshirt* reported –

Clustering round the Leader, chanting the songs of the National
Socialist struggle, the whole twelve hundred left the Blackshirt camp
and passed through the encampment of the general public in one
huge procession. The holiday makers tumbled out of their tents in
amazement and, apart from one or two offensive remarks by women
spectators, stood watching the proceedings very quietly.

Some of us discovered that a boy named 'Smith' who had slept
in one of the tents overnight was in fact Nicholas Mosley, the Leader's
eldest son. He showed himself to be a fine swimmer.

CHAPTER 14

'Tomorrow We Live'

In two months during the winter of 1937/38 while he was staying at Wootton to get his strength back after the wound to his head my father wrote *Tomorrow We Live* – a 35,000-word book which put a slightly different emphasis on his brand of British fascism.

In *Tomorrow We Live* the enemy is 'money power': it is the lure of money that drives financiers 'firstly to supply backward nations with the means to undercut us in the markets of the world and secondly to draw a high rate of usury from the transaction in the shape of cheap sweated goods which enter the British market to the complete displacement of British labour because they are balanced by no form of export . . . so in the final frenzy of the system finance drives the West to produce the means of its own destruction'. The remedy for this is, as before – 'to build a home market in which the British can consume what the British produce by the joint method of excluding sweated products from without and the prohibition of sweated products from within'. This can be done by an authoritative fascist government by the manipulation of high wages and reasonable prices, and by the keeping of the countries of the Empire as sources of raw materials without their being allowed to become producers of manufactured goods.

Under the present system of industrial investment abroad there 'may develop in the Dominions an economic self-sufficiency which may lead in time to the complete inability to accept our exports. Great Britain will then again be faced with the retribution of internationalism in dependence on foreign supply . . . We have to choose between Empire and Usury: British Union chooses Empire'.

But this concept of 'Empire' depended on Dominions and Colonies being kept as non-industrialised areas.

The question is sometimes asked whether we can rely on the co-operation of the self-governing Dominions with whose self-governing status we have no desire in any way to interfere. The question does not arise in the case of the Crown Colonies, because their control changes with the Government of Britain. In the case of the Dominions it surely follows that they will co-operate in the policy for which they have always asked. It is they who have demanded a market for their raw materials and for such foodstuffs as we could not produce in this country, and it is the Government of Britain who have refused in order to accept goods from foreign countries for reasons above stated. It is inconceivable, therefore, that the Dominions for any political reason should refuse a policy for which they have always asked and that offers to them such a great advantage. If any Dominion Government for any purpose of political spite adopted such a course, we would rely with complete confidence on the Dominion producer at an early election to sweep them from power; for he would not tolerate the sacrifice of his economic interest to any political prejudice. Our appeal for Dominion co-operation is based not only on kinship and on history, but on an over-riding mutual economic interest.

This was the appeal once more to human beings as if they were rational: but it was a statement of belief that the highest rationality would involve a yielding to money-power – which had previously been seen as the enemy. What if a Dominion, or Colony, were imbued with the same sort of non-materialistic, regenerative spirit such as was supposed to be at the heart of British Union?

In *Tomorrow We Live* British Union is spoken of as an 'instrument of steel' that will cut through old economic interests: 'the struggle of a National Socialist movement is a necessary preliminary to the exercise of power, because the bitter character of that struggle gives to the people an absolute guarantee that those who have passed through that test unbroken will not betray their people or their country'. The appeal is specifically to a sense of 'greatness' that is spiritual.

Are we really to believe that a great people cannot make up their mind that they do not like a Government and give a vote to that effect without a lot of little politicians bawling in their ears that they do not like it and asking them to vote for a dozen confused and contradictory policies? . . . In physics the influence of the external to matter, the unknown, in short the spiritual, provides phenomena for which the purely material can afford no explanation. In fact, every tendency of modern science assures us that in superb effort the human spirit can soar beyond the restraint of time and circumstance.

In *Tomorrow We Live* the only Jews who are mentioned as specific enemies are Marx and Freud: the one 'tells us that man has ever been moved by no higher instinct than the urge of his stomach' and the other 'supports this teaching of man's spiritual futility with the lesson that man can never escape from the squalid misadventures of childhood'. The characteristics of these enemies are materialism and determinism. Against these is projected a spirit given confidence by interpretations gleaned from modern science – such as that reality is composed of what might be called mind and will, rather than of matter.

One of the themes in *Tomorrow We Live* is an attack on concepts of 'class' – especially those held by the *nouveaux riches* who exercise power without a balancing sense of responsibility. 'The act of birth and the mere fact of being their "father's son" is held by these miserable specimens of modern degeneracy to elevate them without effort of their own above their fellow men'. What characterised these people as members of some spiritual lower order was simply the fact that they assumed for materialistic reasons they were higher. What was advocated in *Tomorrow We Live* was that 'the award of honour, as the award of money, may go to great service and may be transmitted to children, but will be liable to be removed if the children are unworthy'.

The arbiters of all this would be, of course, members of British Union as represented by their Leader. Much of what my father advocated at this time seems to have been the outcome of the position in which he found himself: he was gravely short of money but need not feel defeated if it was true that material circumstances were subservient to will; the people who felt they might have defeated him were themselves in fact the slaves of economic materialism. And it was during this time of the late 1930s that people in British Union, tempered by adversity, did apparently feel most confidently at home. Their aim had always been to take part in what seemed to them an almost religious crusade; the actual outcome, as with everything properly to do with religion, seemed a secondary consideration.

My father wrote in later life of the atmosphere within his movement at this time:*

* *My Life.*

We were a band of companions wholly given to the saving of our country for purposes in which we passionately believed and by methods which we became convinced were entirely necessary. In action all command depended on me, but in the common room of headquarters or in the local premises of something over four hundred branches throughout the country I was just one of them. I joined in the free discussion of politics which always prevailed among us, in the sports to which our spare time was largely given, in the simple club-room gatherings where we would drink beer together or cups of tea. This was the most complete companionship I have ever known, except in the old regular army in time of war.

In war the spirit of soldiers is maintained without too much emphasis being placed upon who wins and who loses; this attitude is necessary for the maintenance of spirit. All through my father's career he had the vision of politics being run as if by an army; the quality of this army would be judged by its heroism – as at Thermopylae, as in the valley at Balaclava – rather than by its immediate results. In this respect he was indeed not materialistic; and it is a fact that there is historically something effective in legend. Of those involved in the Charge of the Light Brigade, for instance, it is the cavalry who are remembered and not their killers behind the Russian guns.

What was extraordinary about British Union was that it kept up its martial spirit while at the same time reaffirming that its aim was to prevent war: it was a quality of my father's leadership that he was able to contain this sort of paradox. He was also able to maintain the impression that he and his men were getting somewhere when to outsiders they seemed beset by defeats. What they were getting – and this was what was provided by my father – was just the sense of belonging, of finding meaning, of being involved in 'greatness' just by having him at their head.

When my father talked about himself and his movement being 'classless' this did not mean that he deluded himself about the hierarchical nature of what he believed in: armies usually work best when distinctions are maintained between officers and men. What is aimed at is a style of camaraderie in which each man shall feel satisfied by his own place and thus shall not resent the places of others. My father continued to accept the social patterns of his time: a symptom of this was indeed his keeping separate his political and his private worlds. No members of the movement called my father by his Christian name unless they were on some sort of social terms: few of them came to stay at Wootton.

There is a story of how Neil Francis-Hawkins was once dining at Wootton and in the course of making conversation he asked one of Diana's Mitford sisters – 'What make of bus do you run?' After this remark had been interpreted, it duly passed into Mitford legend.

Some time during 1937 it struck my father that if indeed he was on some crusade rather than in the business of trimming ideals to catch the winds of political power – and if moreover one of his ideals was that he should not be corrupted by the strings attached conventionally to requirements about money – then either very soon he would be reduced to penury, so much money of his own was he now spending on his movement, or he had to find some fresh source of money over which he would have control and which thus would not be corrupting. In a piece dictated years later for his autobiography and typed out but then not used, he wrote of this time:

> The growing hostility of the capitalist, which had begun with my public refusal of Rothermere's suggestion to adopt a more conservative policy and to abandon anti-semitism, appeared to have resulted in the entire hostility of the money world and a practically complete boycott of our funds. Capitalism had discovered we were a genuine revolution and were not to be bought off or used for their own purposes. It was plain to them that our victory meant the end of the capitalist world; and for once the fools were right.
>
> I was therefore confronted with the classic problem of the revolutionary: lack of money. So far the problem had been solved in one of two ways. (1) The Socialist way: to take money from capitalism and stay bought. (2) The Fascist way: to take money from capitalism and to double cross the capitalists in the interests of the workers.
>
> Naturally of these two methods the latter was the only one open to me. It was no use (a) because I do not like double crossing anyone even a capitalist; (b) because the same trick had been worked twice before and could not be worked a third time – even the capitalists had woken up to it. I had, therefore, either to conceive a new method, or to witness the exhaustion of my own fortune before my object was achieved. I did not object to spending all my own fortune, but I did object to failure.

What he 'found fascinating', he said, was 'the possibility of leading a movement with a revolutionary idea to power while at the same time making the necessary money in business without financial dependence on anyone; this achievement would be unique in history; but what a labour to undertake!'

During 1937 one or two business schemes were bandied about. One that I remember – perhaps because it was not very serious and so it could be toyed with over the dinner table at Wootton – was to do with the manufacture and marketing of a pill that would take smells away from breath; this was before the days of mass deodorants. There was a young scientist who came to Wootton and I remember conversations between him and my father and for some reason my grandmother on the amazing fortune to be made by someone who found the magic touch of deodorising breaths – how many marriages might be saved, for instance, by the removal of the smell of whisky! I found all this very mysterious – was it really true about marriages – let alone the enormous fortune. Then there was another scheme – I don't think this got very far – about the concession for the organisation of football pools in France. But by far the most serious scheme, and one which indeed it seems might have come off if there had not been war, was one to do with the launching of radio advertising over Britain.

My father founded a company called Air Time Ltd which was financed largely by his own money but which was hedged around by legal and accountancy smokescreens so that in the early days at least his connection with the business should for obvious reasons not come to light. The person responsible for most of the front organisation was W. E. D. (Bill) Allen, who it seems likely had been involved in the handling – and in the keeping of the secret – of the Mussolini money: he was chairman of his family firm David Allen & Sons who were an advertising company based in Northern Ireland. By a system of loans and guarantees and agreements (including a document by which the signatories undertook not to divulge that my father was involved) Air Time Ltd was set up, and negotiations began in the matter of acquiring stations. The BBC of course had a monopoly of broadcasting stations in Great Britain: there were two foreign stations – Radio Normandie and Radio Luxembourg – who put out a mixture of entertainment and advertising from the Continent, but these were not aimed exclusively at Britain and in any case their range did not extend very far. My father's plan was to set up and run a network of radio stations which would cover much of Britain from the south and from the west and from the east; these would not only put out advertising but would (in his words) 'provide the people with an entertaining alternative to the dreary schoolmasters at the BBC'. One of these stations would be sited in the Channel Island of Sark, whose semi-autonomous ruler, the Dame of Sark, was an admirer of my father and with whom he had come to some preliminary understanding: it was thought that legally Sark could be shown to be outside the area of the BBC monopoly, though in fact later this proved not to be the case. Another station, it was hoped, might be set up in the Republic of Ireland, where my father was still a popular figure as a result of his stand fifteen years ago against the Black and Tans. But by far the most important location, because it was thought that if this station could be set up the others would follow, was planned to be in Germany, in Heligoland, from where most of the east of England could be covered. The Germans, if they came in, could provide much of the technical and constructional assistance.

My father had in partnership with him a radio expert called Peter Eckersley who was in charge of technical affairs: Eckersley was sympathetic to British Union, and had been a chief engineer at the BBC. In order to get the Germans interested in the scheme Diana began to travel to and fro between Wootton and Berlin; she would sometimes take with her a young barrister, Frederick Lawton, whom my father had had instructed by his solicitor to advise him on the legal side; he too was in some personal sympathy with my father. Diana had discussions in Berlin with officials in the Ministry of Propaganda.

From time to time Diana would see Hitler. The hope was that Hitler himself would give his blessing to the scheme. At first there were difficulties. Hitler's adjutant, Captain Wiedemann, wrote to Diana –

Obersalzberg b. Berchtesg.
Berghof Wachenfeld, den 9.10.1937

Dear Mrs Guinness,
I have today finally reported to the Führer the whole matter concernning the advertising transmissions. I had also in this connection to report to the Führer that apart from considerations of the technical matters and so on that the Ministry of Propaganda has raised – considerations which under some circumstances could have been disregarded – the greatest objection was raised from the side of the appropriate military authorities.

The Führer regrets that under these circumstances he is not able to agree to your proposal. I am very sorry that I cannot give you any other answer.

Diana however persevered. Because so very few people knew what in fact was going on, it might have appeared that Diana's frequent visits to Berlin and indeed to Hitler were due to the close relationship that the Nazis had with my father: this might have told against him (the security people must surely have known of the visits) in 1940 when he was locked up. In fact Diana's visits were aimed, even if optimistically, at trying to make my father independent of any sort of outside influence. During 1938 she saw Hitler several times in Berlin; she succeeded in re-awakening his interest in the plans; Wiedemann wrote to her in February – 'The Führer took the documents himself some time ago: whether in these last few stormy weeks he has got round to reading them, I don't know. I would advise you to come again to Germany when things have settled down and then get your decision from the Führer himself.' This was the time when Hitler was on the brink of annexing Austria. Frederick Lawton knew nothing of Diana's meetings with Hitler. But by 1939 the prospects for Air Time Ltd were from a legal point of view looking good.

Diana would try to time her visits to coincide with periods when Hitler was in Berlin; she would let him know of her arrival, and he would send a message to her hotel usually late in the evening asking her to come round to see him in the Chancellery after he had finished work. When he was in Berlin he saw officials and made speeches; in the evenings, he would find it difficult to rest. He suffered from insomnia and liked to stay up half the night talking; he liked talking to Diana. He and she would be left alone in his private room in the Chancellery by officials who were grateful that they themselves could get some rest. Years later I would say to Diana – But what did you talk about with Hitler? and she would say – Oh, we chatted: about what was going on in England, what was going on in Germany, your father, the state of the world. I would say – But what was his charm? What was his power? She would say – Can you describe charm? Then – Of course it has something to do with power.

By the summer of 1939 the arrangements for the launching of the radio station in Heligoland were almost complete: it seemed, my father wrote later, that he was on the edge of making 'an immense fortune'. The organisation was purely commercial; it had nothing to do with the German Government – except that it was they who gave permission, and provided the vital wavelength. Profits were to be split between the shareholders of Air Time Ltd and an independent German company in the same sort of proportion – 45% to 55% – as was in operation between Radio Normandie and the French Government. One reason why the German Government approved of the scheme was probably because they needed foreign currency. But above all, from his side, my father wrote – 'Our money would have been clean money, made by our own abilities and great exertions'. He would have achieved his ambition to be 'the first revolutionary in history to conduct a revolution and at the same time to make the fortune which assured its success'.

This attempt was defeated, he said, only by the 'accident' of war. I don't think my father ever quite believed there would be war. It would have been difficult for him to credit that human beings could be taken over by such patterns of self-destruction.

CHAPTER 15

Schoolboy Patterns 2

In the summer of 1937 I left my pleasantly anarchic school of Abinger Hill and went to Eton. This move from prep school to public school was traditionally held to be a release from infancy: one was supposed to find oneself on a training-ground for what life was actually like.

It seemed to me that I moved from a society in which people for the most part learned how to go their own ways and to keep out of the ways of others going theirs, into a society in which lip-service was paid to individuality and freedom but in practice this involved looking for means of imposing oneself that were glamorous; of making rules so customary that they hardly seemed to be there.

A new boy at Eton had to learn, during his first fortnight or so, a mass of local information such as the names of the twenty-five or so 'houses' and their 'colours'; he had to become versed in the peculiar jargon that it was imperative for Etonians to use ('half' rather than 'term'; 'sock' rather than 'food'; 'm'tutor' and 'm'dame' rather than 'housemaster' and 'matron'); he had to demonstrate his knowledge of tribal taboos such as those to do with which shops one could visit and which one could not, which side of the street it was permissible to walk on and which clothes were *de rigueur* at what places and at what times. One had not only to learn this information but to find out what it was that one had to learn: what was being inculcated was not just a list of rules, but a habit of knowing the areas in which such rules might have to be observed.

After I had been at Eton a week I wrote to my father – 'Darling Daddy' (my father and I addressed each other as 'Darling' in letters up to the end of the war) 'Eton is very nice and I like it, except that it is rather dull as nothing exciting ever happens. The boys are all awfully stupid and dull. I am very disappointed in the cricket here, as there is no master looking over us and there are one or two boys in our game who are very bad and hate cricket and who fool about the whole time and spoil the game'.

Every boy had a room to himself; this was one of the privileges of Eton. Curiously, I do not remember having much appreciation of this. Some boys hung up pictures and decorated their rooms to try to make themselves feel at home: I hung up two sporting prints that had been given to me by my Aunt Baba. I do not think I really wanted to feel at home; this might have seemed like setting up one's household gods in the camp of the enemy.

I wrote to my father: 'Fagging is rather a bore, but it is not very hard. The person shrieks "Boy!" and we all have to run to him, and whoever gets there last has to do the job. I am not often last as my room is in such a convenient position.'

I remember little of the academic work at Eton; I was quite clever; I worked hard when it seemed sensible to do so, which was just before exams. But there was anyway never the impression that one was at Eton mainly to do academic work: in so far as the accustoming of oneself to rules and jargon was aimed at making oneself feel part of a tribe, the superiority of one's own tribe over others would be demonstrated by the effortlessness by which one did not even have to work much to be superior.

In each house there were about forty boys of whom the top six or eight were known as 'the Library': this was with reference to their having a special sitting room of their own. It was usually from the door of this room that to summon fags they uttered their shouts of 'Boy!': it was here that new boys came, one by one, to be tested on what they had learned of the rules of the game. In the library there was a hot, languid atmosphere as if of men separated by plate glass from the girls of eastern brothels. It was in the library and by 'the Library' that boys were beaten when they failed to perform satisfactorily the tasks of fags, or to have discovered what were the areas of the game.

At Abinger Hill sensuality had been shameless and a bit of a joke: we had experimented languidly when we wished like pubescent Trobriand Islanders. At Eton it was like an enormous genie inside a bottle, liable to erupt portentously if rubbed. There was comparatively little about sexuality that boys at Eton seemed actually to do – even the eighteen-year-olds in 'the Library'. Running after girls was very much taboo; and the hankering after small boys seldom got beyond the accepted form of loitering romantically in passageways or on street corners. There were certain socially acceptable jockeyings for position concerning, for instance, who might sit opposite whom in school chapel: who might follow or precede whom in the house roster concerning baths. But for the most part the outlet for sexuality was in talk: the talk was bawdy-romantic as it must have been I suppose at the time of Boccaccio when girls were locked up in towers: there were dreams of what one might do in a world in which dreaming was not the convention. But one way in which sexuality came down to earth in a socially acceptable form was in the matter of beating.

Boys in the library would loll about in their wicker chairs as if on the verandahs of empires; would twiddle canes between their legs looking down on native populations. It was their very frustration, I suppose, that gave them their air of control – as it must have been over empires. Canes became the emblems of school rule like orbs or sceptres: there were three kinds of cane – an ordinary cane which was smooth, a sixth-form cane which was thicker, and something called a Pop cane which had knobs on. 'Pop' was the exclusive, self-electing-club of boys who were the arbiters of school conventions; they had a super-library in a building of their own. They were further distinguished from the populace by being able to wear coloured waistcoats and sponge-bag trousers (as opposed to dark ones with or without stripes); they could even put sealing-wax in their hats, as if they were cattle specially branded. The actual business of beating – performed by boys in House Libraries and by Pop – did not, as with sex, in fact too often occur; what was prevalent was the image of beating that seemed to hang over the place – a sort of soft bald genie looking down on small boys in what were known as their 'bum-freezer' Eton jackets.

My own feelings about sex at this time were romantic and comparatively straightforward: the boy with whom I had been in love at Abinger Hill had come on to Eton: we were in different houses – there was a suggestion of social indecency about being friends with a boy in a different house on the grounds that personal predilections should not take precedence over the social structure – but we would go out walking on Sunday afternoons: we were still very innocent; I see us even at Eton as some sort of illustration to *Winnie the Pooh*. (We would in fact spend part of our Sunday afternoons playing the game called Pooh-sticks which involves dropping bits of wood into a river by a bridge and seeing which comes out first on the other side). But the places where it was pleasant to walk on Sunday for the reason that in such places one would be apart from the crowd were those which, presumably for the same reason, were themselves considered somewhat improper. Known as 'Arches' and 'Butts', the former was the place where the railway viaduct of the Slough-Windsor line went over the meadows, and the latter was where there was the school shooting-range. And around these places there were apt to lurk the sort of gangs that often hang around, and take their toll from, whatever it is that society thinks is improper. My friend and I had made for ourselves a hidey-hole within a hedge by a stream; here we would recline for an hour or two like hares; we would talk – about the meaning of the world, I suppose; about how we would always be immune from absurd rules and temptations such as those to do with the putting of sealing-wax in hats. Then one day when we were walking back over the fields, I was shot in the face. The projectile, which felt like a stone, was a pellet fired from an air pistol by a boy from one of the gangs; the pellet had gone between the inside of my spectacles and my eye and had come to rest in the side of my nose, which bled profusely. The boy who had shot me and a companion came up; they explained that they had been aiming at my top hat, as if this of course was a valid pastime for a Sunday afternoon. They apologised for their bad marksmanship, and said they hoped no physical damage had been done. When it had been established that I was not blind, the question was – would or would not my friend and I tell? But of course, unless the physical damage proved to be too bad, the rules of the game were that we would not tell. We reassured them about this. Also – might it not be to our advantage to be in favour with a gang of toughs?

My 'dame' (house-matron) wrote to my father 'Nicholas had a very fortunate escape this afternoon. . . . the doctor can find nothing beyond a bruising on the eyelid . . . he is a dear boy and no trouble'.

My father asked me later whether or not I thought the incident might have been some sort of demonstration against fascism. I told him I did not think Etonians thought much about things like that.

One of the things that thirteen- and fourteen-year-old boys did think about (is not enough known about this now for it to be treated with amusement rather than with disgust?) was – apart from who sat opposite whom in the school chapel and so on – the question of lavatories. At Abinger Hill lavatories had been restful places where one could lock oneself away and read the *Wizard* or the *Modern Boy*: at Eton they were in a row and had no doors, and were apt to become like a bear-garden. It was probably thought that lavatories might be the sort of place where, behind locked doors, Etonians might at last get up to what was thought of as no good: with the doors removed, what was provided was an arena for concentrated ragging and badinage. There was only one lavatory in the house which had a door; this was set apart like a loose-box next door to stables, and was for the exclusive use of the Library. I thought some heroic stand on principle should be made about this: I determined to try not to use any lavatory except the secluded, discreet one of the Library. This of course, was very much taboo; it meant much spying-out-of-land; much use of odd hours. Perhaps because such sacrilege was almost unheard of, I was never caught.

There were other incidents in the guerrilla warfare that I felt for one reason or another should be carried out against the school. Some time during my first year – I still had the reputation of being a meek little boy – I took down, or altered, or played some joke upon (I cannot remember) one of the notices that were pinned on the notice-board at the head of the stairs of my house: this was of course also the breaking of some heavy taboo. All the tribe were gathered together and it was announced (no one had seen me do the deed) that either the perpetrator owned up, in which case nothing much would happen to him (such was the game), or else – some fearful punishment would descend on the whole tribe. I did not know what were the rules about this: I did not want to harm my innocent image; but was I not someone anyway who was beginning to be interested in what might be beyond accepted rules? This otherwise trivial incident has stuck in my mind with such clarity because, I think, it was the first time I was struck with the idea that if life was not to seem meaningless there had at moments to be a regard for something beyond either the conventions of games or self-interest; there had to be what might be called – for want of a better phrase – an effort at truth. We were told that the Captain of the House would come round to each boy's room that evening and would ask for a confession. The question seemed to be – was there, or was there not, any actual virtue in truth? Now it happened that this Captain of the House was in some sort of particular relationship with me: he, as part of the roundabout of things such as who sat opposite whom in college chapel, had taken to coming to my room in the evenings (this was the appointed time for Captains to deal with administrative matters) and would sit and watch me and chat; sometimes we would play chess. I had thought of myself as an unattractive little boy; now, amongst my own age-group it was suggested – Well, there's no accounting for tastes! This evening when the Captain of the House came round asking for confessions he stood in my room and said with heartfelt eyes – Of course I need not ask if it was you! I said – Well yes, it was, actually. I did not know quite why I said this. Perhaps it was because I wanted to confirm (I think I did) that, at such moments and perhaps in any such relationship, there was importance in truth.

In formal areas of school life the question of honesty seemed less pressing. One of the routines was that each week one had to show to one's 'tutor' something called an 'order card': this was a piece of cardboard on which were written one's marks and the comments of masters one was 'up to' (was being taught by). One's house tutor thus kept an overall eye on one's work; each week he signed his initials on one's order card. He did this in the evenings after supper; there would often be a queue outside his room. One wanted to go to bed oneself: he, very probably, wanted to get back to his dinner: it often seemed more sensible and even more charitable not to join the queue but to learn how to put his initials on one's order card oneself. Since the remarks on my card were usually favourable, it seemed to me that in no area of importance was I cheating. I became quite proficient at this forging of my tutor's initials: of course one had to join the queue from time to time or else one's behaviour would be noticed; so the previous forgeries had to be good enough to take in the tutor himself. I think he must sometimes have had an inkling of what was going on; but he was an intelligent man: he saw occasionally that I was getting good marks, so why should he not at other times have had a chance to get back to his dinner?

As for masters one was 'up to' – they used to sit behind desks on platforms in front of classes and life would drone like flies trapped between window panes. Myself and my cronies would sometimes liven up the time by playing paper games such as *Consequences* or a more highbrow version of this called *The Poetry Game*: this involved writing the first line of a rhyming couplet, passing it on, then the next person writing the second line, folding the paper over, writing a new line, passing it on, and so on – until at the end there would be unfolded like a Japanese flower a whole sonnet. The pleasure of this of course was in trying to make it funny; when we opened the bits of paper and read them – all this going on under the sleepy but ever-present buzzing of trigonometry or Latin construe – there would be the agonising and ecstatic business once more of suppressed laughter – the whiff of the beatific vision – the knowledge that even if trigonometry and Latin construe were the surfaces of life there was yet something that could break through, like a pin through a bubble, towards enormous and proper events elsewhere.

There was one master whom we were 'up to' for Greek and with whom we were 'doing' the *Medea* of Euripides: this master was a rather formidable man with steel spectacles and close-cropped hair: he announced one day that he was going to read aloud to us what was, in his opinion, one of the most beautiful speeches in all literature – that in which Medea says goodbye to her children just before she murders them on account of their father, Jason, having been unfaithful to her with another woman. The master read this speech to us in a soft voice standing in front of class; he swung his watch-chain to and fro like a water-diviner; he seemed to have found, at the end, the fount in himself of tears. Afterwards he asked for our comments. I said – I did not often have the courage to put such questions into words – how was it that he found this speech so beautiful, when it was about a mother on the point of murdering her children? He said – That is an interesting question. The class discussed it. It was agreed – But it's poetry, isn't it? I wondered – But what is poetry?

I got a terrible dislike for the *Iliad* at this time: all those ridiculous people bashing one another: the gods standing round like seconds with towels and buckets. One could see why people liked it; but was not the interesting question why people liked it?

About boys in my house bashing one another, I remember two instances. The first concerned almost the only boy of my generation who did not seem obsessed with the talk about sex: he declared one day he had never masturbated; he was laid on his back across a table – he appeared about to have a fit. The second concerned a boy who was held to be 'sucking up' to older boys: he was put in a bath, had oil poured over his head, and was beaten. There was the terrifying impression – was it going to be difficult not to be part of conventional bullying?

Violence, sexuality, at fifteen, sixteen – if they were to go anywhere decent, it seemed, had to go inwards. But what on earth did this mean? In the privacy of one's room there were – the bed that folded into a cube, a Dali-like chest of drawers, a padded object called an ottoman. Somewhere about this time I had come across amongst a pile of unshelved books in a back room at Wootton – amongst the Proust and the Henry James and other intimations of the vast complexities of the grown-up world – a book called the *Encyclopaedia of Sexual Practices*. This contained mostly of course stuff I already knew: but there were one or two stories of a kind I had not heard before. These concerned people in dire and solitary straits: the one that I remember was of a man who had got himself stuck in the overflow pipe of a bath. How amazing: and yet how apt! Were not human beings indeed like things helplessly propelled towards the overflow pipes of baths? But why were we not taught about this – rather than the *Iliad*?

The highest dignitaries that bobbed about like ships' figureheads on the ocean of the school's unconscious were, in ascending order, the Lower Master, the Headmaster and the Provost. The Lower Master was a huge, bony man who was in charge of Lower Chapel choir; I was for a time a member of this; his way of criticising choirboys (I used to sing sharp) was to give them such an enormous hug that they were lifted off their feet and pouched like a baby kangaroo in his cassock. The Headmaster was a stately, shiny man who walked up and down the aisle of College Chapel preceded by a man with a wand like a lamplighter. The Provost was a very old man who read the lessons in College Chapel and when he was at the lectern his hands used to shake so much that the pages of his Bible went off against the microphone like machine guns.

One day my father came down to take part in a fencing contest against the school: he was one of a team from the London Fencing Club. I wrote to him – 'I will be working all Tuesday morning till 1.45 and in the afternoon I will be playing cricket but I will try to come to the gym and see if you are there.' This is the only time that I remember my father visiting the school. For the most part I was visited by Nanny and my sister and my two loyal aunts.

In November 1938 the news suddenly broke that my father had, for the past two years, been married to Mrs Guinness: there were headlines in the papers – 'Mosley Secretly Married' and 'Hitler was Sir Oswald's Best Man'. The papers said that my father and Diana had been married in Munich a year ago: my father issued one of his categorical denials, saying that he had not been in Munich during the last two years. The papers also said that Diana had just given birth to a son. When I had been at Wootton in the summer I had noticed that Diana had seemed large, but this had aroused not much curiosity in the mind of a fifteen-year-old schoolboy. It made sense now however that Diana and my father should be having a baby; what did not make sense was that my father should not have told any of his family of his marriage even if he had wanted to keep it secret from the world. So after break-fast – what apprehension there had come to be about what might be seen in the papers about one's father after breakfast! – I explained to my school friends: Of course, it is rubbish that my father and Diana are married; you think it is shocking that they are having a baby? But then the next day (why the next day?) there was a message from

my father that, yes, he had indeed been married all the time to Diana.
To this letter I replied:

Darling Daddy,
I was naturally very surprised when I got your letter as I had gone
round telling everyone that it was not true. The only thing I really
felt was that it was a pity you had not told us, for although I had
no idea that you really were married I was always wondering if
you would be. You know that I have always liked Diana very much,
so I had no feelings on that part of it; but I am longing to have
a talk with you about what you feel about Mummy and Diana.
I have always loved Wootton and the life at Wootton, and I at any
rate would always love to come up there when you are there.

The last three days have been terrible here as everyone has been
asking me about it all, and they think I am mad as first of all I
said it was rot, and then said it was all true.

Granny told me that you had had a baby boy and apparently
it looks just like Grandfather Mosley with a bull neck and a great
red face. I am longing to see it.

I was confirmed yesterday and Granny, Nanny and Aunty B came
down for it plus a long confirmation letter from Aunty N all the
way from America. In the afternoon we went over to Denham.

Are you going to spend Christmas at Wootton or at Denham?
Do try and be at Denham just for that day.

Yesterday I had an awful puff with Aunty Baba about having
a dog at Christmas and also about Micky going to Abinger. She
was against both of them; but I think that Abinger is the nicest private
school I can imagine, and there is absolutely nothing against the
dog.
                    Much love from
                    Nicky.

In fact, I found a way of dealing with the mocking looks of friends;
I explained that of course I had known about the marriage all the time,
but I had had to keep up the secrecy until I was officially as it were
absolved.

My father put out to the press his own justifications: 'My first wife
was subject to the most blackguardly abuse from some sections of the
Press and it was my strong desire that no woman should again be
subject to such treatment merely because she happened to be married
to me.' Also – 'We [in British Union] believe in real sex equality,

and therefore both men and women perform their own service in their own way without reference to the purely private fact of marriage.'

My Aunt Baba read of my father's and Diana's marriage in the newspapers while in a train between London and Paris. Years later I said to her that I thought one of the reasons why my father had kept his marriage to Diana secret was because he could thus during these years maintain his relationship with her, Baba, whom he often saw in London while Diana was at Wootton. Baba said that she thought this interpretation was probably correct.

From this time on, occasionally and briefly, my father did in fact talk to me, as I had asked him to, about what he felt 'about Mummy and Diana'. He used to say – as if he were making a special point of this – Of course his second marriage was very good, but his first marriage had been perfect.

CHAPTER 16

The Fight for Peace

There were three stages in the history of British Union: the first was when there had been enthusiasm and genuine hope about being carried to power within a few years: the second had been characterised by the anti-semitic campaign in East London; and the third was when efforts came to be concentrated on the prevention of war.

Throughout his political career Mosley had made stands against war: in 1919 he had spoken against an expeditionary force being sent to Russia; during the twenties he had criticised signs of British imperialist expansion; then when Mussolini had invaded Corfu he had asked that the League of Nations should take positive action to prevent further aggression. In this sense it was a coincidence that now, in the late nineteen thirties, his demonstrations against war should be seen as moves in favour of Hitler or Mussolini: it was they who happened at the time to be driving other people to think of war. He had no faith now in action by the League of Nations; he simply wanted Britain to stay out of trouble. His slogans were – *Mind Britain's Business* and *Britain Fights for Britain Only*. He advocated the creation of a large navy, army and air force for the purpose of enabling Britain to defend herself if attacked. He was never a pacifist.

The first *Mind Britain's Business* campaign got under way when Mussolini invaded Abyssinia. Then in March 1936 when Hitler marched into the Rhineland, which had been demilitarised according to the provisions of the Treaty of Versailles, Mosley made a statement that such a reassertion of natural German rights was justified: however – 'Whether it proves in the result to be the best or the worst thing that has happened in European relationships since the war depends on whether or not the steady will to peace of the British people is maintained.' Then in 1938 there was the German occupation of Austria and Mosley wrote – 'What on earth does it matter to us if Germans unite with others of that race? If all Germans outside the Reich were added to Germany their population would only increase from seventy to eighty millions: has the British Empire sunk so low that we have to shut up shop if another ten million Germans enter their fatherland?' When later in the same year the crisis came to a head about the Germans in Czechoslovakia he praised Neville Chamberlain's peace-keeping efforts; he wrote: 'I don't care if 3½ million Germans from Czechoslovakia go back to Germany, I don't care if 10 million Germans go back to Germany, Britain will still be strong enough, brave enough, to hold her own.' British Union coined a more recondite slogan – 'Nineteen fourteen echo, we will not fight for Czecho'. Mosley never saw much in the argument that Hitler's moves should be resisted because they were immoral; the Treaty of Versailles had not been moral; the tensions in Europe were now largely the result of the Treaty of Versailles; people only talked about morality in international affairs when they lacked national power. And anyway, what could be more deeply immoral than moves towards the starting of another war between England and Germany – which Hitler said he did not want?

What had stayed in my father's mind was the senselessness and horror of the 1914 war: when he spoke of his companions who had been killed in the Royal Flying Corps, tears used to come into his eyes. In the 1930s he saw no logical reason for conflict between England and Germany. As early as 1936 he had written in the *Fascist Quarterly*:

More than any other European nation at present the objective of modern Germany is the wealth and happiness of its own people. It is true that in order to secure that happiness and wealth it is necessary for her to possess an adequate supply of raw materials and full outlet for expanding population. But less than any other great nation of today her philosophy leads her to think of limitless colonial Empire – which to the Nazi mind suggests loss of vital energy, dissipation of wealth and the fear of detrimental admixture of races. Her natural objective lies in the union of the Germanic peoples of Europe in a consolidated rather than a diffused economic system which permits her with security to pursue her racial ideals. In fact, in the profound difference of national objective between British Empire and the new Germany rests the main hope of peace between them. Our world mission is the maintenance and development of the heritage of Empire, in which our race has displayed peculiar genius and which in our vast experience we may pursue not only without fear of racial

detriment, but with the sure knowledge that in this arduous duty
the finest and toughest characteristics of the English are developed . . .
British power throughout the world and German power in Europe
can together become two of the main pillars of world order and
civilisation.

This was almost precisely the attitude that Hitler himself professed:
ever since he had written *Mein Kampf* in 1925 he had said that he did
not want war with England: he needed England as an ally to control
the world's trade-routes while he marched east to get access to raw
materials and more 'living-space' for Germans. There were no secrets
about this. To my father it seemed inconceivable that this would not
be the sort of programme that would appeal to serious English politicians: was not politics about power? and was there not the chance
here for politicians, English and German, hand in hand to wield a
uniquely far-reaching form of power? For English politicians suddenly
to be talking about morality seemed to my father so bizarre that it
could not be taken seriously; it seemed that it must be a cover for
some other form of power – that of the international financial conspiracy.

Then in November 1938 there was the *Kristallnacht* in Germany in
which, as retaliation for the murder by a Jew of a German Embassy
official in Paris, there was a widespread smashing of Jewish shops and
burning of synagogues throughout Germany; there was no effort to
disguise this activity nor to hide that it was encouraged by the authorities.
The argument that German anti-semitism was an attempt to deal
rationally with the 'Jewish Question' no longer made sense; it began
to seem to English people that what had to be faced in Germany was
the power of something irrational. Mosley, however, wrote in *Action*:

Supposing every allegation were true. . . . supposing it were a fact
that a minority in Germany were being treated as the papers allege;
is that any reason for millions in Britain to lose their lives in a war
with Germany? How many minorities have been badly treated in
how many countries since the war without any protest from the
Press or politicians? Why is it only when Jews are affected that we
have any demand for war with the country concerned?

Then in March 1939 Hitler moved his armies into the main part of
Czechoslovakia in contempt of the Munich Agreement which with
such difficulty and in the face of such criticism had been worked out

the year before. This made nonsense of Hitler's claim that he was only concerned with bringing de-nationalised Germans back into the national fold. Almost immediately he seemed to be making threats against Rumania and against Poland; his activities now seemed not only irrational but insatiable. But still, Mosley argued, what better could Britain do than to see that she herself was well armed so that she could defend her own interests against even what was irrational?

Years later he wrote in his autobiography:

Was this policy more immoral than a war which killed twenty-five million Europeans? Was it more immoral than a war which killed 286,000 Americans and 1,500,000 Japanese? Was it more immoral than Hiroshima? ... Was it more immoral than the cold-blooded killing of prisoners in German concentration camps on a vast scale? ... None of these things could have happened without the Second World War.

At the end of March the British Government gave a guarantee to Poland that, if its independence was threatened, 'His Majesty's Government and the French Government would at once lend them all the support in their power'. There was little pretence that this guarantee made practical sense: no efforts were made to prepare any material 'support' for Poland. What was being made was some gesture that might inform Hitler that if he went any further in the way he seemed to be going, there would be war. Hitler in fact made no further moves for a time. But from now on, Mosley wrote in *Action* – 'any frontier incident which excites the light-headed Poles can set the world ablaze: British Government places the lives of a million Britons in the pocket of a drunken Polish corporal'.

Few other politicians seemed to be thinking about what a European war would actually be like. But then – a vision of the horrors of war has seldom been a deterrent either to the bellicosity or to the nonchalance of politicians.

The run-up to war during 1939 coincided with what was known as the 'coming-out' of my sister Vivien: this was the complex of rituals by which eighteen-year-old girls were initiated into membership of the upper-class tribe. Vivien's relationship with her father had developed in its ding-dong style: as she grew older he liked at least the thought of visiting her at school: he initiated a 'tease' with her by which he suggested that all her fellow schoolgirls must be longing to have a glimpse of him as he drove up in his Bentley. (Vivien wrote: 'I loved going out with you on Sunday ... you must have had a great disappointment when there was nobody looking out of the End Room window'). She went to finishing schools in Munich ('It is Wagner that you like isn't it?') and in Paris where here he took her out once on the town: he behaved as if he felt again (as a French journalist had once described him) like 'the young Alcibiades ... trailing after him many entangled hearts .... a few confidences'. But when Vivien returned to England he made clear his aversion now to rituals of upper-class life: these were not in keeping with the image of classlessness that he was trying to inculcate with his fascism. Aunt Irene became Vivien's mentor in the round of cocktail parties, dinner parties and balls by which eligible neophytes could become acquainted with one another and those already in the tribe; there were Ascot, Henley, the Eton and Harrow match: as a climax to the 'season' was something called Queen Charlotte's Ball in which dozens of vestal virgins cut an enormous cake. Then in the middle of the summer there was a full-page piece of gossip about Vivien in the *Sunday Express* – it went on about her wealth and her grandfather having been called Levi Zebidee Leiter – and her father felt driven to reply to this in a statement published in *Action*.

It has ever been the American habit of the Beaverbrook Press to attack the Leader of the British Union through his relations, preferably female. His daughter, Miss Mosley, is the latest object of their chivalrous attention.

As Miss Mosley is a Ward in Chancery whose every arrangement is in the charge of her aunt, Lady Ravensdale, her father has nothing whatever to do with her present activities. Therefore, the Beaverbrook malice shoots very wide of the mark, as an attack on a man who has neither the time nor the inclination for any social life at all.

On the other hand, it should be stated in fairness to this pleasant but ordinary girl, whose appearance in the world would have attracted no extraordinary attention if the Press had not detested the person and politics of her father, that not one word written about her in the national Press should be believed without verification.

Our father was still at this time our legal guardian: his statement in *Action* was not true (only the income of our money was in the hands of the Chancery Court); nor indeed was it chivalrous.

One of the high points of my sister Vivien's (and indeed my own) social season occurred on July 15th when, in the Eton and Harrow cricket match at Lords, Harrow won for the first time for thirty-one years. My Aunt Irene recorded that thereupon –

A most disgusting riot and shambles took place. It was not mere 'top-hat bashing'; middle aged men rushed in and were bestial and savage in their onslaughts on boys and older youths alike; one small boy was badly hurt and was carried off; the savagery shown was sickening, even trying to debag people! Eyes teeth and noses risked being smashed.

The next day, Sunday 16th July, was the occasion of my father's last and greatest indoor meeting in London. He had been able to hire the vast and new auditorium at Earls Court – the management not having believed, it was said, that any political leader would be so rash as to try to fill it. On the night it was 95% full with an audience of more than 20,000. The family was there – myself, Viv, Irene, Granny – we listened to the fanfares and watched the parade of flags: there were the usual banners of *Britain First* and *Mind Britain's Business*: and then there was my father marching alone up the aisle and climbing to the top of a high rostrum like a rocket as if he were an astronaut. He spoke for two hours: as usual, without notes. He said:

We have shown over and over again in infinite detail how the money and credit of the British people, created by the exertions of the British people and by no other force on earth, has been used for their own destruction in the equipment of the Orient with its sweated labour to undercut and to destroy the West; in order that usury, international usury, may draw its dividends and its interest by destroying the country of its origin through the equipment of our world-wide competitors against us. We have shown again and again how the British Empire, as well as the British people, the British industrialist and the British worker, has been relentlessly sacrificed to this international power; how the whole of our international trading system, how our conflicting party system, and our foreign policy above all, is maintained for one reason and for one reason alone – that the money power of the world may rule the British people and through them may rule mankind.

It is almost impossible to recreate the effect of one of my father's speeches; there was such certainty and such passion; one felt one's mind being taken over – either this, or one had to be ready to turn away as if from a fire.

I am told that Hitler wants the whole world. In other words, I am told that Hitler is mad. What evidence have they got so far that this man, who has taken his country from the dust to the height in some twenty years of struggle – what evidence have they got to show that he has gone suddenly mad? Any man who wants to run the whole of the modern world with all its polyglot population and divers peoples and interests – such a man is undoubtedly mad, and I challenge my opponents to produce one shred of such evidence about that singularly shrewd and lucid intellect whom they venture so glibly to criticise. 'Oh,' they say 'any man who gets to such a supreme position must go mad.' Well, of course any democratic leader would; but we knew before they told us that they had got weak heads.

Somewhere about this point Randolph Churchill, the son of Winston, got up and walked out: he had been pointed out to us by Aunt Irene in a row in front, in the company of the dancer Tilly Losch. My father went on to describe an incident in which British citizens had been molested by Japanese troops in China about which the British Government had made no protest:

Why is it a moral duty to go to war if a German kicks a Jew across the Polish frontier but no moral duty to lift a finger if a Briton is kicked in Tsientsin? Is it only because English men and English women are being insulted that the Parties are indifferent? ... We are told that this is the policy of the Conservative Party which stood for security, for prestige and for Empire. The Empire is sold and war is bought in British money today, in British lives tomorrow ... My friends, can we conceive of a policy of greater insanity, heading more straight for suicide, than this: to be prepared to fight a world war over a few acres which do not belong to us, but to make a present to the whole of mankind of the land which was won by the sweat, blood and heroism of our forefathers?

One could tell when my father was arriving at his peroration; his voice and his personality seemed to change; it was as if the count-down was beginning; he was ready to take off into space. For his audience there was a tingling up and down the spine –

I ask the audience here tonight whether or not we are going to give everything we have within us, not only material resources but our moral and spiritual being, our very life and our very soul, in holy dedication to England that she shall not perish, but shall live in greatness. We are going, if the power lies within us – and it lies within us because within us is the spirit of the English – to say that our generation and our children shall not die like rats in Polish holes. They shall not die but they shall live to breathe the good English air, to love the fair English countryside, to see about them the English sky, to feel beneath their feet the English soil.

This heritage of England, by our struggle and our sacrifice, again we shall give to our children. And with that sacred gift, we tell them that they come from that stock of men who went out from this small island in frail craft across storm-tossed seas to take in their brave hands the greatest Empire that man has ever seen; in which tomorrow our people shall create the highest civilisation that man has ever known. Remember those who through the centuries have died that Britain might live in greatness, in beauty and in splendour. Remember too that in the spiritual values that our creed brings back to earth, these mighty spirits march beside you and you must be worthy of their company.

So we take by the hand these our children to whom our struggle shall give back our England; with them we dedicate ourselves again to the memory of those who have gone before, and to that radiant wonder of finer and nobler life that our victory shall bring to our country. To the dead heroes of Britain in sacred union we say – Like you we give ourselves to England: across the ages that divide us – across the glories of Britain that unite us – we gaze into your eyes and we give to you this holy vow: We will be true – today, tomorrow and for ever – England lives!

For some time before the end of this my Aunt Irene, on the seat beside me, had begun to sway as if she were a snake being lifted up out of a basket; she was murmuring half under her breath over and over – 'Oh this is very good!' People around us had begun to cry; there was a stir as if in undergrowth on the edge of a forest fire; we were sparks swirling up in the wake of my father's chariot-rocket to heaven. I can still, when I read this speech, get some tingling in my spine. We were most of us at the end standing on our seats and cheering.

Much of my father's argument against war with Germany was based on his assumption that human beings were rational: it was rational that Germans should want to re-join the main part of Germany to East Prussia that had been arbitrarily split from it by the Polish Corridor at the Treaty of Versailles; it was rational that Britons should not feel threatened if Hitler marched in the opposite direction to them – and in any case, what on earth did Britons think they could do to help Poland? What my father did not see – which he might have seen because it was so much part of his own technique to sway people as if they were hypnotised – was that human beings are not rational when they feel themselves either charmed or threatened by a force that is taking them over like flames.

Politicians talked about things like the guaranteeing of Poland's independence or the balance of political power because this was the way in which they were accustomed to talk: there was no tradition of talking about fear of a massive psychic invasion or paralysis. But in fact what people felt about Hitler at this time had little to do with rationality or even political self-interest: they felt that with the Nazi regime they were on the edge of being in the presence of things like devils and witches; these had to be fought, because tingling changed to shivers of alarm down the spine. And in fact, it is usually for this sort of reason that people go to war: there is always some excuse for war in terms of the breaking of a guarantee or an unbalancing of power; what makes people choose this instant rather than that to fight is best described in terms of the prevalence of evil – possibly the evil in oneself, of course, as well as that in others.

After the Earls Court meeting the family went back to Ma Mosley's flat for supper: we waited for my father. Suddenly he put his head round the door so that he was like a clown popping his head through curtains; he looked mock-penitent. Someone said 'You promised!' He came into the room and gave himself a pat on the behind and said 'Naughty!' This was a reference to a promise he had given to my Aunt Baba that in his speech he would say nothing unpleasant about her friend Lord Halifax: he had in fact said that it was Lord Halifax's 'particular genius' that 'when you are walking down in the street and someone comes up and gives you a hard kick behind you can pretend not to notice it'. At Ma Mosley's he then laughed; we all laughed. Diana arrived with her brother Tom and her mother Lady Redesdale.

Next month, August 1939, Diana went to Germany for the last time and saw Hitler. He was at Bayreuth. There he told her that he thought war between Britain and Germany was inevitable, because of the guarantee that Britain had given to Poland. He said that this guarantee made no sense rationally, except in terms that it was Britain who was determined to go to war.

CHAPTER 17

War

During the summer holidays of 1939, as war approached, most of the family went to Wootton: this was probably considered to be safer than Savehay Farm from the threat of bombing. My Aunt Irene and Nanny with my brother Micky arrived at Wootton treading warily: Irene recorded that she recoiled from a photograph of Hitler by Diana's bed: that she 'removed from the sitting-room mantelpiece photographs of Goering and his baby' (she probably meant Goebbels). Diana herself was in London with my father. My father was stepping up his campaign for peace.

The old spirit of British Union seemed to have come alive again: Mosley held large meetings up and down the country: the feeling of being on a crusade, always crucial to the movement, now seemed a reality. There was an appeal to members to give bits of jewellery to provide much-needed funds: a lady from Harrogate wrote: 'I am sending you my wedding ring to hasten the day when all Britain will hail Mosley!'

The Leader orated:

There are thousands of women living in East London today with their husbands, their brothers, their children who may be doomed by this war conspiracy to the bitterest tears that a woman can shed. What good does it do to such a woman to know that German women too are doomed by us striking back at a foreign city? War is a crime against the people of all lands.

For moments, it seemed that my father might attract more solid support than that which he usually inflamed by his oratory. After listening to the Earls Court speech Major Yeats Brown, a recent convert to the

British Union, wrote to Lord Elton, who was trying to form a group
dedicated to preserving peace:

> Personally I agreed with ¾ of what he said, but the other ¼ is the
> stumbling block. He declares that there can be no compromise nor
> conciliation with any of the old parties, and this is absurd in England
> . . . I listened in vain for any word that would have shown that if a
> crisis came suddenly he would be behind the government. I suppose
> he wouldn't be, and that he would use the opportunity for political
> ends.

This had been the stumbling block about much of my father's politics:
people could not understand how, if he saw himself as a politician, he
would not play the political game of manoeuvring for the successful
outcome of his policies by making use of such forces and alliances as
were available. People could not understand that he might not be
interested in power on such terms; that more important to him might
be just the announcing of his policies like some sky-sign – Listen to
what I say and take it or leave it – and then leaving the rest to fate. In fact
his peace campaign of 1938 and 1939 did often have an apocalyptic
ring about it. In April 1938 he had written in *Action* in a style that seemed
almost knowingly to be parodying the *Book of Revelations:*

> Facts will then be brought to light which are partly known to many
> already but are hidden from the people as a whole by the machinery
> of the system . . . Then all things will be known and at last will be
> revealed to the people. Mighty on that day will be their wrath, and
> justice shall be done.
>
> Let the rats of this system not think that any land will safely shelter
> them, nor any sewer of the world provide them with a refuge. For
> revolution sweeps across the earth and will overtake them in the
> furthest cranny that the fugitive criminal can reach. The victory of
> British Union will seal the doom of their world power.
>
> So to the jackals of putrescence we say today 'Beware!' Britain
> will have no mercy on you and the world will find you no refuge!
> The cleansing flame shall pursue you to the uttermost ends of the
> earth.

Hitler marched into Poland on 1st September 1939; Great Britain declared war on Germany on September 3rd. My father and Diana were
still in London: my Aunt Irene, Nanny, my brother and sister and I

heard Neville Chamberlain's sad, tired voice making his announcement over the radio in the nursery at Wootton. My aunt recorded that she 'expressed to Nanny my pain and horror if Diana turned up here with her adulation of Hitler, and that she and Unity were two of those who had so inflamed his vanity that in the end he thought he was invincible'. I remember going out on to the lawn to practise football. I explained to Nanny – You see, this war is all a game: there is something impregnable called the Maginot Line, and there is something impregnable called the Siegfried Line, so nothing can happen; and after a time the war will stop.

My father, in London, put out another of his apocalyptic calls containing echoes from the past –

Stand fast, my comrades and companions. Come what may, you have lit a flame in Britain which all the dark corruption of Jewish money-power cannot extinguish. Alone you stand undaunted in the face of the war conspiracy. Alone British Union marches to this decisive struggle, for all lesser things are gone.

However he also wrote and distributed a practical 'Message to All British Union Members' which is of vital importance in any assessment of his attitude to the war – and of the attitudes of others concerning him and the war.

The Government of Britain goes to war with the agreement of all the Parliamentary parties. British Union stands for peace. Neither Britain nor her Empire is threatened. Therefore Britain intervenes in an alien quarrel. In this situation we of British Union will do our utmost to persuade our British people to make peace.

Before war began, in our struggle for peace, our thousands of members had awakened great masses of the British people to demand peace. But sufficient of the people could not be awakened in time without the money which we did not possess. The dope machine of Jewish finance deceived the people until Britain was involved in a war in the interest of the Money Power which rules Britain through its Press and Parties. Now British Union will continue our work of awakening the people until peace be won, and until the People's State of British Union is born by the declared will of the British People.

To our members my message is plain and clear. Our country is involved in war. Therefore I ask you to do nothing to injure our country, or to help the other Power.

Our members should do what the law requires of them; and, if they are members of any of the Forces or Services of the Crown, they should obey their orders and, in every particular, obey the rules of the Service. *But I ask all members who are free to carry on our work to take every opportunity within your power to awaken the people and to demand peace.*

The italics are in the original. To my father, it would have been inconceivable that there need be any contradiction in being at the same time completely loyal to orders to fight, and occupied in work for peace.

A few days before the declaration of war, at a huge street meeting in Hackney, he had (according to *Action*) 'asked those to hold up their hands who wished to fight for Poland: in all those tens of thousands of closely packed people only two raised their hands to the derision of the crowd'.

At Wootton, my Aunt Irene continued to write in the strain of – 'I wonder what my brother-in-law and his wife and her sister Unity Mitford are thinking of their hero Hitler now?'

In Munich Unity Mitford, one hour after war had been declared, went to the office of Gauleiter Wagner, put a sealed envelope on his desk, then went out into a park called the English Garden and shot herself in the head. When after some time Wagner opened the envelope he found in it the signed photograph that Hitler had given to Unity the first time they had met, Unity's Nazi Party badge, and a letter to Hitler in which she said that since war between England and Germany would be the end of the hope to which she had dedicated her life – that of friendship between the two countries that she loved – she would kill herself. Wagner instituted a search, and his men found Unity in the hospital to which she had been taken from the English Garden. The bullet had entered her skull, but she was not dead. Hitler came to visit her three times in a clinic in Munich: she recovered partially. Once when the wife of one of Hitler's adjutants visited her and put on her bed her party badge and her photograph of Hitler, Unity frowned and placed them under the bedclothes. When she was well enough Hitler arranged for her to be moved to Switzerland where she was met by members of her family and brought home. At Folkestone there were hordes of reporters offering money for an interview. Unity lived for another eight years before the bullet moved in her skull and killed her. She remained something like a child.

During the first autumn of the war, after the defeat of Poland, nothing much happened: this was the time known as the Phoney War: Britain and France had gone to war to preserve the independence of Poland, but Poland had been very quickly overrun not only by Nazi Germany but also by Communist Russia which just before the war had entered into an alliance with Germany. Britain and France had done, and could do, nothing to prevent any of this. The situation seemed to my father so grotesque that he thought anyone reasonable must now want peace. Hitler in fact made peace proposals which, if accepted, would leave Britain and the Empire much as they had been before; these proposals were rejected. It seemed that people in England were feeling, without much obvious reason, quite cheerful about the war. In the press there were the usual fantasies – all Britain had to do was to sit tight and then Germany would mysteriously collapse because of internal dissent or because of the shortage of this or that vital material. My father wrote articles in *Action* pointing out that in such respects time was on the side of the Germans: war materials were now available to Germany from the east, whereas it was Britain, being an island, which was vulnerable to blockade by aeroplanes and submarines. So, if we refused to make peace now, what could be at the back of this except madness or conspiracy?

Then in November Russia invaded neutral Finland for not much reason other than that she might want a lump of border territory or training for her army; so if international morality was being talked about, should not Britain logically declare war on Russia? There were in fact some voices in Parliament that advocated this; ministers in France talked about an anti-bolshevik crusade; there were suggestions about turning the flank of the immobile western front by an attack through Norway and Finland and Russia into Germany; or perhaps the Germans might suddenly overthrow Hitler and come in on an anti-bolshevik crusade themselves. My father must have thought all this indeed evidence for his theory that the western democracies had gone mad: such fantasies were outside the range of what could even be explained by conspiracy. In fact during the winter of 1939-1940 an Anglo-French force was assembled to come to the help of the Finns against the Russians; but then in March 1940 Finland made peace with Russia. The British and French governments felt themselves under impetus however to go ahead with some sort of activity in the area; it was decided that Norwegian coastal waters, through which iron ore was brought to Germany, should be mined. Neville Chamberlain announced, apropos of nothing much in particular, that 'Hitler had missed the bus'. My father wrote – 'Can anyone pretend much longer that these men are fit to govern a great nation in a great age?'

During the winter he had announced that British Union would fight
two Parliamentary by-elections: he had been encouraged in this perhaps
by the large and apparently enthusiastic audiences that had been attend-
ing his meetings. But then at Silvertown in East London in February
1940 Tommy Moran, the British Union candidate, got 151 votes against
the Labour candidate's 14,343; and in North-East Leeds in March the
British Union candidate got 722 votes against the Conservative's 23,882.
About the Silvertown result *Action* made what was, for it, an almost
unique admission that the British Union vote had been 'very poor'.
About the North-East Leeds result it argued that since 1,000 people
had come to a meeting addressed by Oswald Mosley, this was evidence
that 72% of them had been won over by the British Union message.

On April 8th the British Government decided to mine Norwegian
waters: the same day Hitler set about taking over the whole of Norway.
This he did within a few days. The British planned landings in Norway
here and there; while they were carrying these out, and having to
withdraw them, Hitler, on 10th May invaded Holland and Belgium.
Neville Chamberlain resigned: Winston Churchill became Prime
Minister. My father reiterated the message which he had made to his
followers at the beginning of the war – 'I ask you to do nothing to
injure our country or to help any other power.'

By 19th May the Germans were approaching Paris; the British army
was retreating towards Dunkirk; Mosley went to Middleton, in
Lancashire, to speak on behalf of his third British Union parliamentary
candidate at a by-election. He was attacked by a mob when he tried
to speak from the top of a van and was escorted from the area by
police. The British Union candidate polled 418 votes and the Conservative 32,063.

On 23rd May Mosley wrote in *Action*:

The question has been put to me why I do not cease all political
activity in an hour of danger to our country. The answer is that
I intend to do my best to provide the people with an alternative
to the present government if, and when, they desire to make peace
with the British Empire intact and our people safe ... I can conceive
no greater tragedy than the British people desiring to make such
a British Peace and having no means to express their will.

The next day, May 24th, Hitler gave orders that the pursuit of the
British army in France should cease; the result was that much of that
army was able to get away at Dunkirk. There is evidence that this

order was given in the light of Hitler's genuine desire to make peace with Britain; he still hoped that Britain might look after the sea-routes of the world while he, Hitler, turned to the East. It seems that he thought this might be feasible if the British army was not humiliated. But there was no one in England both willing and in a position to make this sort of peace that was also envisaged by my father.

On May 22nd the British Government rushed through an Emergency Powers Act which gave them almost unlimited power over all British citizens and their property. Just before the outbreak of war there had in fact been an earlier Emergency Powers Bill which had empowered the government to make Regulations by Orders in Council for the Defence of the Realm; this had, ironically, given to government the sort of powers that my father had advocated in 1930 in order to deal with unemployment. One of the regulations suggested in 1939, however, had gone beyond anything ever advocated by my father: it was labelled 18B: it empowered the Home Secretary to detain in prison 'any particular person if satisfied that it is necessary to do so'. There had been parliamentary protests about the unparalleled scope of this: the regulation had been amended to the Home Secretary's being able to detain anyone whom he had 'reason to believe' to be 'of hostile origin or associations'; or to have been recently concerned in 'acts prejudicial to public safety or to the defence of the realm'. Now, in May 1940, the Home Secretary John Anderson reported to the Cabinet that under the existing Regulations he had no power to detain Oswald Mosley or other members of British Union. He admitted that Mosley had given explicit instructions to his members to obey the law and to do nothing to injure their country or to help foreign powers; but he also reported, according to Cabinet minutes – 'Two officers of MI5 have given it as their opinion that a certain proportion of the members [of British Union] ... say 25–30%, would be willing, if ordered, to go to any lengths': and that although he, the Home Secretary, was of the opinion that Oswald Mosley 'was too clever to put himself in the wrong by giving treasonable orders ... he [the Home Secretary] realised that the War Cabinet might take the view that, notwithstanding the absence of such evidence, we should not run any risk in the matter however small'.

Accordingly the Cabinet (consisting of just Chamberlain, Attlee, Halifax and Greenwood; Churchill was in France) authorised Anderson to have the Regulation 18B amended in such a manner that Mosley and his followers might be detained. It was this Emergency Powers amendment that was rushed through on the evening of May 22nd:

Regulation 18B (1A) now gave the Home Secretary power to detain any members of an organisation which in his view was 'subject to foreign influence or control' or whose leaders 'have or have had associations with persons concerned in the government of, or sympathetic with the system of government of, any power with which His Majesty is at war'. Thus my father became liable to arrest and imprisonment because he had met Hitler twice and Mussolini five or six times before 1937; and for this reason all his followers became liable to arrest too. The Regulation did state that the Home Secretary had to be satisfied 'that there is a danger of the utilisation of the organisation for purposes prejudicial to the public safety, the defence of the realm, the maintenance of public order, the efficient prosecution of any war in which His Majesty may be engaged, or the maintenance of supplies and services essential to the life of the community': but these considerations had only to be in the mind of the Home Secretary. The way in which the Regulation had been specifically amended was evidence of just what in fact was in his mind.

On May 23rd my father and Diana were at Savehay Farm: Wootton had been abandoned when the Phoney War came to an end because my father felt it was necessary to be near the centre of events. He and Diana drove in the afternoon to London to the flat at Dolphin Square which they had rented: (during the mid-thirties my father had moved from Ebury Street to a house on the river at 129 Grosvenor Road: this was too large for wartime, so in 1940 he and Diana moved to Dolphin Square). Outside the block of flats Diana noticed four or five men standing on the pavement 'aimlessly staring into space': my father recognised one or two of them as policemen who had been on duty at his meetings. They said they had a warrant for his arrest. He was allowed to go up to the flat to pick up some clothes. Then he was taken to Brixton Prison.

That evening Diana, back at Denham, was having dinner (I was at school) when the garden gate was pushed open and policemen poured across the lawn. They said they had come to search the house. They leafed through many of the books in the library; some of them began to dig up the garden looking for arms. After a time they left.

The British Union Headquarters was searched for three days: crates of papers were carried away. The last number of *Action* appeared on May 30th: it reported that between 70 and 80 members of British Union had been arrested including Francis-Hawkins and Raven Thomson. Some of those arrested had fought in the last war. *Action* made a statement that 'not a shred of evidence had been found to support any allegation that British Union was, or ever had been under foreign influence'; that there had been 'a clear violation of British justice, which is that a man (or for that matter a body of men) is deemed innocent until he had been proved guilty'. There was a biographical account of Mosley's career showing him to have been a steadfast and passionate patriot. During the following days British Union members were arrested as they came back from the beaches at Dunkirk; one was arrested as he returned from a bombing mission over Germany.

Up to the time of Hitler's invasion of the West, British Union's advocacy of peace had been tolerated if not electorally supported: now, with the threat of invasion, all had changed. Diana recorded – 'There was an indescribable air of panic, barely suppressed; and wherever I went I was met with glances not so much hostile as terrified.' After my father's arrest the Mosley family solicitor refused to help Diana with her enquiries: Diana's friend Gerald Berners, when he told some Oxford friends of his intention to visit her at Savehay Farm, was warned that if he did so he would be putting himself in the way of arrest. Nanny and my brother Micky left Denham and went to stay with Irene and Vivien in London; Diana remained at Savehay Farm with her one-and-a-half-year-old son Alexander and her six-week-old baby Max, and their Nanny. Diana received anonymous letters from people saying they were coming to murder her, and to pour vitriol over her babies.

People were afraid, and they needed scapegoats: they argued – Mosley has been arrested; does not this prove he is a traitor? The writer Henry Williamson, a friend of my father's and an outspoken supporter of British Union, wrote to Diana describing how he had been banned from the local Defence Corps for having 'blasphemed against King and Country': when he had protested that this was a 'damned lie' the local organiser had said, 'I don't care if it is a damned lie, I believe it.'

But Henry Williamson also wrote:

I thought of writing to the Times saying that as a non-active member I wanted to know if it had been discovered that funds had been received from any foreign country; for if so, thousands of people like myself would then immediately disclaim all connection with such a party; that there was a considerable and harmful amount of rumour going around and for the sake of public *morale* a Govt statement about the existence of such contributions to the funds, or non-contributions, should be made public. If such funds had been received,

then I and thousands like me were gulled fools and deserved imprisonment at once; if not, the air of Britain should be cleared of at least
that amount of enervating rumour.

Rumours about these funds were now rising up to haunt my father.
Vengeful passions were anyway running high. On May 16th, shortly
before my father's arrest, my Aunt Irene had recorded in her diary:

> I had to go on to Sir John Anderson: he wanted to ask me if I
> had any evidence that Tom Mosley would betray his country in
> its peril with the 5th column. I said I had no evidence of that, and
> Sir John told me *Action* had become milder. But I told him that
> if Tom thought such a thing was good for England in conjunction
> with Hitler's regime then he might do anything if he got angry
> and thought we were mucking the whole thing. I gave him bits
> of conversation from Tom and Diana and I said I had been useless
> as we had not met for weeks. He said I had given him all he wanted.

And then on May 25th, just after my father's arrest, Irene wrote in
her diary:

> I asked Vincent [Massey] if he did not think that Diana Mosley was
> as dangerous as Tom and I wanted to write that to Sir John, and
> he entirely agreed.

And then the next day:

> I wrote to Sir John Anderson on Diana Mosley.

Diana was arrested on June 29th: it was reported in the papers that
it had been intended from the first that she would be arrested, but
she had been left for a month on account of her baby. A gang of
police came to Savehay Farm: she was given the choice of either taking
or not taking with her eleven-week-old Max whom she was still breast-
feeding. She was told she would not in any case be able to take with
her one-and-a-half-year-old Alexander, so she decided not to separate
the children but to leave them with their Nanny. She arranged for
them to go to stay with her sister and brother-in-law Pamela and Derek
Jackson in Oxfordshire. On her way to Holloway Prison Diana asked
to be allowed to stop at a chemist in Wigmore Street in order to buy
a breast pump to get rid of the milk that should have been for her
baby.

On the evening of my father's arrest I was in my room at Eton; I was visited by my amiable and intelligent house tutor; he told me my father had been arrested – he had been telephoned by my stepmother Diana. I said – I see – or some such. Then my tutor hung about my room as if he wanted to say something more; I wondered what it was; eventually he said – Do you think there might be anything – I mean – in it? I could not make out what he was implying. Then I realised – He was asking me if I thought my father might in fact be some sort of traitor. I said – Oh good heavens no! Then – It is just, you see, that he doesn't think there's any sense in this war. My housemaster seemed to accept this. But it was as if he still felt there might be something more to be said. I wanted to ask him – Do you think it's wrong to wonder, then, whether there's any sense in this war?

CHAPTER 18

Background to Imprisonment

The story behind my father's detention in May 1940 and his imprisonment for the next three and a half years has remained obscure because
of the refusal by the authorities to release their papers about it. In July
1940 my father appeared before an Advisory Committee set up by
the Home Office to examine the validity of the reasons for people
being detained under Regulation 18B; my father was questioned for
sixteen hours over a period of five days; the chairman of this Advisory
Committee was his old adversary from the *Star* libel case – Norman
Birkett KC. The transcript of this cross-examination apparently exists:
it is in 'a category of Home Office records which are closed to public
inspection for a period of up to 100 years by order of the Lord
Chancellor'. This statement was made in a letter to myself, the author,
from the Departmental Record Officer of the Home Office when I
applied in July 1981 for permission to see the transcript. Normally
public records become available for inspection after thirty years. The
letter said that the Lord Chancellor has powers to impose a longer
ban under 'section 5(1) of the Public Records Act 1958'. This act
describes the circumstances under which such powers can properly be
exercised as those in which there might be a 'breach of good faith';
'distress or embarrassment to living persons might be caused'; or the
papers might be so 'exceptionally sensitive' that their disclosure would
be 'contrary to the public interest on security or other grounds'. Further
correspondence with the Departmental Record Officer established the
fact that the papers concerning my father's imprisonment were being
'retained by the Home Office on security grounds'.

The idea that publication of my father's cross-examination in July
1940 might be a danger to security in 1981 was so bizarre that further
representations were made to the Lord Chancellor himself, and a ques-

tion was asked in the House of Lords by my father's old friend Bob Boothby. Nothing further could be elucidated other than that, yes, the information was being withheld because it might be a threat to present security.

The question at stake in 1940 had been – what were the justifications for arresting and imprisoning people indefinitely without trial as a result of a regulation which was invented the evening before their arrest and of which they had never heard, and which rendered them liable to imprisonment on account of matters which at the time of their happening had been quite legal? This was an exceptional departure from traditions of English justice. Moreover the amended regulation was used mainly against people who had publicly reaffirmed their patriotism. But the added question at stake now is – what on earth happened in 1940 the disclosure of which even in 1981 might be a threat to public security?

On 9th May 1940 when Neville Chamberlain realised he might have to resign as Prime Minister the Labour leaders Attlee and Greenwood had been approached about whether or not they would serve under him in a coalition Government; they said they would have to consult their national executive at Bournemouth, where the party was assembled for its annual conference. At the Bournemouth Conference one of the delegates, Hugh Ross Williamson, remembered – 'One of the main subjects of conversation which I heard at unofficial talks was whether or not the Labour Leaders had made the arrest and imprisonment of Mosley a condition of their entering Government. The general feeling was that they had – or at least, that they ought to'. On May 10th Attlee and Greenwood, back in London, said that they would serve under Churchill but not under Chamberlain. They became members of Churchill's coalition Government. The amendment to 18B which enabled Mosley to be arrested was made on May 22nd on the orders of the four-man Cabinet group that included Attlee and Greenwood.

Labour politicians – perhaps because their feelings of loyalty are apt to be divided between party, nation, internationalism and class – sometimes seem vengefully to need the scalps of those who they feel have betrayed them. They had not forgiven Mosley for having been what they called a 'traitor' to their party in 1930; they now had a chance to suggest he might be a traitor to his country.

What members of British Union found objectionable in this was the fact that so many of them who were arrested had been members of the fighting services either in the first world war or indeed in the second – one officer in 1940 was arrested in front of his men on the parade ground – while many of those responsible for their arrest had chosen not to fight in the first world war (Greenwood; Morrison) and indeed many of those who were to be future Labour leaders remained out of the fighting services in the second.

It could of course be said that members of British Union just by dressing up in black shirts and making aggressive noises in the cause of peace had invited retaliation. But it seems likely in fact that there were more pertinent influences at work than any of these at the back of the decision to detain them.

My father kept a record of what he intended to say to the Advisory Committee: this was in the form of 'answers' to suggested 'reasons for detention' that his solicitor had put to him in anticipation of the sort of questions the Advisory Committee might ask. My father seems to have been at least partly aware of what might be at the back of decisions concerning regulation 18B – even possibly to have had an inkling about why these might be kept secret.

His statement began –

The police have raided my flat, my wife's flat, the London house we used to occupy and my children's house in the country. They have raided the offices of British Union. At the end of this process what shred of evidence can they produce to support the allegation that I would play traitor to my country?

I believe that I was one of the first two Cavalry officers who volunteered to go to the Royal Flying Corps in 1914. I served with the R.F.C. in France in the winter of 1914/15. The following winter I was back with my regiment in the trenches. I have since been a member of Parliament for some twelve years and am an ex-minister of the Crown.

It is apparently suggested that I want my country to be defeated. Yet for the last seven years I have spent much of my time demanding that Britain should properly be armed to resist attack, and have violently attacked the old parties in and out of season for neglecting our defences. In particular I have demanded air parity with the strongest other country – which was Germany.

I opposed this war on two grounds: (a) the members of my movement are ever prepared to fight in defence of Britain but do not think that Britain should go to war for the sake of Poland or any Eastern European question: (b) they were more than ever opposed to intervention in a foreign war when Britain was not properly armed for war.

I admit quite frankly and have always admitted that I hold the high ambition to make a great country even greater. I cite my whole record and whole career in refutation of the charge – as absurd as it is vile – that any aim which I have ever held can be achieved through disaster to my country.

I desire to advance one concrete argument and one constructive suggestion. If it is considered that we were wrong to state our opinions in time of war and openly to advocate Peace why were we not told to shut up? The Government had ample power at any time to close our mouths. The Home Secretary possessed powers to give publications such as *Action* a warning and after the warning those responsible would be liable to prosecution with heavy penalties. A warning was never given.

I make the suggestion that we be told to live in any place or to act in any way that the Government may specify and that we shall be forbidden to speak, write or communicate with anyone without permission. I further suggest that if possible we shall be permitted whether on the land or elsewhere to do useful work instead of being an incumbrance to the nation in gaol. I offered again and again in public speeches to fight if the nation was invaded. Now this situation appears to be imminent, I ask to be permitted to do something useful for my country rather than be a nuisance to it, even if I am not to be trusted with the weapons with which in my early life I was brought up.

The statement went on to deny the charges that the names 'Fascist' and 'National Socialist' implied that British Union was under foreign influence; that what might be called its brand of anti-semitism had anything to do with German anti-semitism; that its officials ever made official contacts with members of foreign governments. But then – the possible charge that my father was at most pains to be ready to refute was that concerning funds. He seems to have expected that he might be faced with the charge that British Union had received funds from Italy during 1932–1935: the Committee might even have got hold of some evidence about this. He was ready to reply –

I personally had nothing whatever to do with the finances of the organisation during that period because I had divorced myself from that side in our original constitution on the grounds that it was improper for the Leader of the Movement to be familiar with those who subscribed. My general directions were that no money should

be accepted except from British subjects and that no conditions should
be attached.

The allegation is denied: but even if it were true, I ask why it
should be a reason for holding me or my colleagues in gaol? It was
stated in Lord Snowden's biography that the *Daily Herald* was started
by money from Russia and that the late and highly respected Mr
George Lansbury was the principal figure in the transaction. He was
afterwards Leader of the Labour Party in the House of Commons.

Then my father described how after support by British capitalists had
been withdrawn and he himself had subscribed £100,000 of his own
money, he had become involved in the radio advertising business in
which agreements had been under negotiation with Sark, Ireland and
Germany. He emphasised that the dealing with Germany had been
purely commercial:

> I finally got the German concession some fifteen months after
> the Sark concession: I eventually secured an interest of over 90%.
> The terms were much less favourable than in the case of Sark; they
> were roughly the same as I have always understood the French
> government gives in the case of Normandie. The German company
> got 55% of the profit and the British company 45%. The Directors
> of the German company are businessmen and are not in the govern-
> ment of Germany.... If we get radio advertising in Sark, all this
> money will stay within the Empire; why oppose it?

At the end of the actual hearing, the details of which are still taboo
on the grounds that their publication would present a threat to present
security, my father asked the chairman Norman Birkett (this is my
father's publicly stated recollection which has never been challenged),
'Is it suggested that we are traitors who would take up arms and fight
with the Germans if they landed?' and Norman Birkett replied 'Speaking for myself, you can entirely dismiss that suggestion.' My father
then said, 'I can only assume that we have been detained because of
our campaign in favour of a negotiated peace?' and Norman Birkett
replied 'Yes, Sir Oswald, that is the case'.

It seems possible that this Advisory Committee recommended that,
once it had been effectively decreed that all further political activity
by British Union must stop, there would no longer be a sensible or
legal case for British Union members such as Oswald Mosley to continue in gaol. If so, such a recommendation was overruled. Such an

Oswald Mosley

B.U.F. hierarchy in 1935; Back row: J. H. Hone, E. Atherley, J. Thompson, R. Platten, R. Gordon-Canning, J. Beckett, B. Donovan, C. S. Sharp, W. J. Leaper; Front row: A. Raven Thomson, E. Piercy, I. Dundas, Oswald Mosley, N. Francis-Hawkins, W. Risdon, W. Joyce

Micky by Cimmie's tomb

The Leader speaking (*Fox Photos Ltd*)

Vivien, Micky, Baba and Oswald Mosley at Savehay Farm

Diana Guinness

Alexandra ('Baba') Metcalfe

Vivien, Florence the nursery maid, Nanny, Micky, Nicholas, Andrée – summer 1933

Fascists marching to Euston Station – 1933 (*BBC Hulton Picture Library*)

The Black House – Entrance (*BBC Hulton Picture Library*)

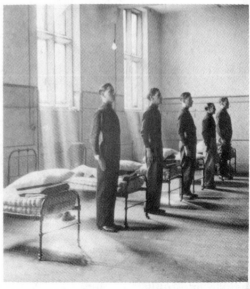

The Black House – Interior (*BBC Hulton Picture Library*)

Oswald Mosley with the 'I' Squad – Hyde Park 1934 (*A BUFPA copyright photograph*)

Crowds held back by police – Hyde Park 1934 (*BBC Hulton Picture Library*)

Lady Mosley (Oswald Mosley's mother) – Hyde Park 1934 (*A BUFPA copyright photograph*)

Diana – Capri 1935

Oswald Mosley and Nicholas – Capri 1935

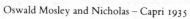

Nicholas, Oswald Mosley, Baba – South of
France 1934

Baba, Oswald Mosley – South of France
1934

Mussolini and Oswald Mosley – Saluting base, Rome
1935 (*Keystone Press Agency Ltd*)

Unity Mitford and Diana – Nuremberg 1934

Irene Ravensdale and Micky – Eton 1936
Right: Nicholas and Micky – Eton 1938

The Battle of Cable Street – Crowds running (*BBC Hulton Picture Library*)

The Battle of Cable Street – Police chasing (*BBC Hulton Picture Library*)

Wootton Lodge

Oswald Mosley at Wootton

Diana

Oswald Mosley and Diana at Wootton

Nicholas, Diana, Jonathan Guinness

Right: Oswald Mosley and Diana

Earl's Court meeting – 1939 (*C. A. Daniels*)

Street meeting in Bermondsey – 1938

Oswald Mosley on way to court from Brixton Prison as plaintiff in libel action – 1940
(*S & G Press Agency Ltd*)

The author's platoon in troop carriers – Northern Italy, April 1945

Mervyn Davies and Nicholas

Nicholas

Alexander, Diana, Max, Oswald Mosley – Crowood 1946

Oswald Mosley speaking at inaugural meeting of Union Movement, 1948

Oswald Mosley in pub with followers, 1954 (*BBC Hulton Picture Library*)

Rosemary – North Wales, 1950   Nicholas – 1950

Alexander, Max, Diana, Oswald Mosley – Venice, late fifties

Oswald Mosley in Trafalgar Square – early sixties

overruling might itself be a reason for the papers continuing to be withheld. There is evidence that the Advisory Committee did in certain cases make such recommendations which were indeed overruled on the authority of a more powerful and secret body; and it may be in order not to divulge anything about this body that the papers are still banned.

In May of 1940 there was set up a Defence Security Executive whose job it was to investigate 'suspicious political activities' and report directly to the Prime Minister. Winston Churchill said in the House of Commons in July 1940 – 'I take full responsibility for the control, character and composition of this committee'. This 'Executive' was the effective power behind the legalistic façade of Birkett's Advisory Committee. It consisted for the most part of men to do with 'security' – with MI5 and MI6 – who by the nature of their trade are concerned to keep their activities secret.

The chairman of this Defence Security Executive was Lord Swinton, a Conservative politician and ex-minister and a director of multi-national corporations. Other members included Sir Joseph Ball, known to be a high-ranking officer in British Intelligence, and Alfred Wall, a leading trades unionist and a communist activist in South London. The Executive was formed at a time when the Hitler-Stalin pact was still in force: security people, again by the nature of their jobs, are sometimes arbitrary about matters of loyalty. One thing they could all agree on perhaps in 1940 was their dislike of British Union. My father would have been anathema to such men – if for no other reason than that they, in their respectably treacherous world, would have been anathema to him.

Questions were asked by Aneurin Bevan and Richard Stokes in the House of Commons about the composition of this Executive; and whether it was true that there was a government directive prohibiting newspapers referring to it. Churchill replied that it was accepted 'that it was not in the public interest that questions should be asked and answered about..... Secret Service work'. In November 1941 Conservative MPs were bringing the subject up again. Sir Irving Albery asked – 'Has not the Home Secretary some advisor other than the independent Advisory Committee? And was not the advice on which the Home Secretary relied that of the Security Department, the body which originally advised the detention?' Sir Archibald Southby said that it seemed –

There was no obligation on the Home Secretary to accept the advice of the Advisory Committee, and in numerous cases he had rejected their advice. The only reason could be that the Home Secretary had not disclosed all the facts and suspicions in regard to the detained person to the Advisory Committee. Undue state control on the individual, if allowed to go unchecked, must inevitably lead to something approaching the tyranny of Nazism.

It is inevitable perhaps that security people should have the last word in war – even if it means that people are innocently at the mercy of such men. In 1940 it might have been the case that the Home Secretary had 'suspicions in regard to the detained person' fed to him by the Defence Security Executive which were not divulged to the Advisory Committee let alone to the House of Commons. In particular, there were the continuing rumours about the money from Mussolini. My father had taken great care that no hard evidence concerning this money should be procurable (it was stated in the House of Commons on 11th December 1940 that 'the Advisory Committee and the solicitors had had to admit that there was no foreign money coming into the British Union') but he must have known that security people do not work in areas to do with hard evidence.

As early as 1935 Robert Forgan had written to my father: 'I wonder if you realise that one source of income is known to a number of people who are not in our confidence – I mention this merely so that you may be on your guard'. Even earlier a BUF member in Rome trying to get an increased expense allowance had written 'I am sure that the powers that are here will thoroughly approve of this payment as the sums being transmitted to you are for the general expenses of the BUF'. My father had replied – 'I am at a loss to understand the reference in your letter' and had 'forthwith suspended' the member from his duties. But the most bizarre fact that has come to light concerning the possible ways in which such information might have come to the notice of the security people is to do with W. E. D. Allen, who was not only likely to have been my father's go-between in the matter of the Mussolini payments but was certainly his front-man in the radio advertising deal: Allen himself, my father divulged later, worked for MI5 in the 1930s – and my father even knew of this at the time. In a statement he recorded in later life he said of Bill Allen – 'Very much involved with MI5, made no bones about it, that is why he wasn't imprisoned in the war, of course, because he had done so much for them.' Also, when asked whether he thought MI5 had used Allen to find out what was going on in the movement my father replied – 'To some extent: probably reporting conversations with me which were probably largely fictitious: he was a tremendously boastful man ... one of those men who simply lived in a dream world – a Walter Mitty world, as we would call it now'. In addition, my father had quarrelled with Allen in 1938 on the subject of loans that the latter had made to Air Time Ltd, and Allen had told him he was in danger of losing his 'one surviving friend'. In the light of all this, it seems more than likely that the Defence Security Executive must have been fed some information about the links with Mussolini; and then they could, owing to my father's intransigent denials of the whole affair, make from it whatever they liked. And they might according to their custom have wanted to keep their sources secret: it might even conceivably be considered advisable on 'security grounds' not to have the nature of these sources, and such elaborations as were made from them, spelled out now.

Whatever the nuances of the truth about this, it seems probable that the very skill with which my father had operated in the business of keeping the payments secret worked in 1940 to his grave disadvantage: it could be argued by his opponents that if he had gone to such lengths in the matter of this form of secrecy, what other kinds of contact with foreign governments might he have covered up? There were of course Diana's visits to Berlin on the radio advertising business: my father had been at pains to keep his own connections with this secret. He had been ready later to give an account of this to the Advisory Committee; but still, what he had been involved in was the setting up of a radio business of which a German company would own over 50%; and more than this, Diana's visits to Hitler's Chancellery late at night were probably known to British Intelligence. Such information would have reached the Defence Security Executive; and how were they to know that what was talked about was no more than charming gossip about the state of the world? Or rather – what more evidence might such men as those who worked on the Executive require, when it was probably in their minds to find reasons to imprison my father anyway? My father, by entering himself so deeply and yet apparently so carelessly into the world of secrecy and cover-ups, laid himself open to the revenges of those who played such games professionally.

My father's amazing *insouciance* about all this was in keeping with his image of himself as a gambler going for very high stakes: he took risks about money for the sake of what he believed about the fate of Britain and of Europe; he had always known he might lose; of course, he would have had no problems if he had won. As things were, he prepared his defences for the Advisory Committee; but he did not complain much when he was imprisoned, nor did he complain very much afterwards. It was not in his nature to complain; but his continued denials make it seem as if he knew of the dangers he had run with the Mussolini payments. Curiously, in later life he did not seem to see the risks that had been attendant on the radio deal involving Hitler. But there would have been no personal disaster if there had not been war; and were not risks worth running to prevent the huge disaster of war? With regard to his imprisonment he must have felt that he had struggled to the best of his ability to prevent a war that he considered catastrophic: perhaps it even seemed fitting to him that he should be imprisoned by men who he thought were dragging the country to perdition.

When Diana came up in front of the Advisory Committee in the autumn of 1940 she made no pretence of being anything other than contemptuous. She said in her autobiography that later she regretted that she had not prepared 'a devastating indictment of the unprincipled politicians and their disgraceful behaviour': but she felt herself helpless in the face of the 'triumph of rumour, gossip, spite, and lying tongues'. She found Norman Birkett's questions simply silly: 'Why had we been married in Berlin?' 'Because we wished to keep the marriage secret for a while.' 'Why had Hitler arranged this for us?' 'Because I asked him to.' Then* –

Birkett pounced: 'This friend of yours is now bombing London!' I said that since Britain had declared war on Germany and we had bombed Berlin it was rather obvious that the Germans would bomb London. Birkett asked me when I had last seen Hitler. In Bayreuth in 1939, I replied. And what had I said to him about Britain? Had I said that Britain would not fight? I replied that Hitler had told me he was certain Britain would declare war; he was convinced of it.

Diana recognised on the committee an old acquaintance, Sir George Clerk, who had been Ambassador in Istanbul in 1931, when Diana had had lunch with him (my mother Cimmie had stayed with him the year before when she had paid her visit to Trotsky). The Committee was holding court in a requisitioned hotel in Ascot: one of the members sent Diana a bottle of claret for lunch: she shared this with her wardress in the stables.

* *A Life of Contrasts.*

In July it had seemed to my father that once the panic about invasion had died down, reason would prevail and he would be released; after all, many people in government knew him; whatever risks he had taken, they would know his true character. But such people did not have the effective power in the matter of letting him out; he was in the hands of people for whom there was probably little meaning in truth of character.

To myself it is inconceivable that my father would in any way have aided the Germans in 1940. He would have fought the Germans if they had invaded Britain and he had a chance to fight – this was in keeping with his whole character and tradition. It also seems inconceivable that in the event of a German victory in 1940 he would have played a part as a national leader installed by the Germans: this would not have been in keeping with his hope and determination to lead Britain back to a position of national and imperial 'greatness'. Whether or not, or in what way, he might have accepted any turning of British people to him as someone who, after a period of German domination, might restore national honour – this would have depended on the circumstances at the time. There would have been nothing dishonourable in his holding himself ready to try to retrieve something from a disaster to his country which he had always said others would cause.

It remains a fact that in 1940 the majority of people in the country seemed to want him locked up: evidence for this can be seen in the violent reactions of people when the news broke three and a half years later that he was to be released – and this was when the winning of the war was in sight. In 1940 Hitler had gained such an easy victory in France that people were confused and afraid: when people are afraid they need scapegoats on which to vent in simple form their rages: members of British Union, and especially my father, had set themselves up as obvious Hitler substitutes. My father seemed to accept responsibility for the risks he ran; but of course he had been gambling with lives other than his own. As Henry Williamson had written – 'If such funds had been received, [from a foreign country] then I and thousands like me were gulled fools and deserved imprisonment at once'. The cost to others was sometimes great.

Over 700 British Union sympathisers were arrested and thrown into jail: some were taken on the mere gossip of neighbours; their families were persecuted and their homes sometimes pillaged; they lost their jobs and the businesses they had built up; they were spat on and reviled. In jail they had to suffer sometimes from solitary confinement and from hunger. They had genuinely seen themselves as patriots banding together to defend the honour of their country: they were suddenly branded as traitors in a way that seemed likely to scar the rest of their lives. Such a gigantic disparity of vision implies a terrifying naivety on both sides: it was not only the fascists who, in Jung's phrase, failed 'to see their own shadow, their own worst danger'.

My father's one-time henchman William Joyce was someone who did in fact act according to the popular view of fascists: he had gone to Germany just before the war and he now became involved in the broadcasting of German propaganda in English. After the war he was captured and executed as a traitor to England – on doubtful legal grounds, since he was an Irish-American. But in the meantime he had become known to the English jokingly – in keeping with the style of the British in wartime – as Lord Haw-Haw. One evening in the winter of 1939/40 our family was listening to him on the radio at Savehay Farm, and my Aunt Irene recorded: 'I told Nick that for weeks now it has been known that it was Tom's man Joyce: the War Office knew it and Mrs Joyce had written it to the papers.' Irene added, 'Curiously the children, perhaps feeling ashamed, always seem angrily to stand up for these awful statements; and to argue violently with me on the defensive.'

CHAPTER 19

Parental Attitudes

During the winter of 1939/40 my father, who had seemed close at least to me of his children at Wootton, had increasingly moved out of sight; he was in London intent on his drive for peace. We would visit him sometimes in his house in Grosvenor Road which had once been (and was to be again) a night club – it had a huge pale-blue sitting room with mock marble pillars and a dark purple bedroom like a stage set. Here he would be preoccupied, stride about, make up his speeches; shout at his large gloomy manservant who was called Littleberry, and was like Don Giovanni's Leporello.

Shortly after the outbreak of war and the summer holidays in which members of the family, some reluctantly, had been inveigled up to Wootton, there was a big family uproar because my Aunt Irene, who said she would continue to put up money for the children's expenses even when they were based at Wootton, now rebelled – perhaps because there was no need to stay at Wootton because there was no bombing of the home counties; perhaps because of the photographs of Goebbels and Hitler on Diana's tables. Irene told my father she would put up no money except for the old family home at Denham; whereupon in Grosvenor Road my father (Irene recorded) –

was so wild with rage he tore up and down the room in a filthy blasphemous state with dear Ma trying to calm him. I gave out some pretty stiff heated rejoinders while Diana never uttered. The arguments were that it was due to me that the children must live like workmen, Wootton was lost, Eton might go, and Micky thanks to me must go to Baba and in the spring must go to school. I repeated my Denham offer, which was actually listened to politely, but he continued to say he was through with me. The real truth is I have crashed their castle and brought Wootton to ruins and the funds they wanted to give to fascism cannot now be safe unless they live in a cottage.

My father, it was true, was now giving all his income to British Union. It seemed to me, aged sixteen, that his commitment to the cause of peace was admirable. I wrote from Eton:

> Darling Daddy,
> I have just heard about the bust-up with Aunty Nina. Of course it is a pity we will have to give up Wootton after all, but I am sure it will make no difference to Viv or I if we have to live in a much smaller house. I do hope you manage to let Denham, as the money from that will make all the difference.
> I am in all the top divisions as usual and doing much the same. Eton is incredibly dull in war time. The people are so terribly stupid here. They think the Germans will revolt at any moment, and that everything is going to be perfectly easy for us. I must say that from reading the papers you find it hard to believe that the French troops are not on the outskirts of Berlin. Of course all the boys believe every word the papers say, and worship that fool Mr Churchill. I have found it does not pay to try and tell them how wrong they are. The sensible ones, including me, are just waiting for Eton to be bombed so we can all go home.

I had developed a sort of patter by which I could defend my father's points of view: I had also developed an arrogance which was at least in part, I suppose, a mechanism by which to protect myself and show sympathy with my father. I had for some time been echoing his arguments – what is the point of a Parliamentary system that pays a Prime Minister £10,000 a year to run the country and a Leader of the Opposition £2,000 to stop him?; and now I would say – why should not the Germans march East and then they and the Russians can just bash one another? People seemed able to give me no reasonable answers to such questions. I did not, of course, expect people at Eton to be reasonable.

I followed my father's analyses of strategy in *Action* during the period of the Phoney War. These explained how we could not win the war, how we could prevent the Germans from winning, how with such a stalemate it was only reasonable to make peace. I could not imagine how people did not accept this: even people who did not agree with my father, such as my aunts, continued to say he had the most marvellous brain. My aunts insisted – What a tragedy, and especially in wartime, that England was not getting the benefit of such a brain!

At Eton there were supposed to be masters with good brains, but what was striking was that no one discussed the war with us; no one seemed to wonder why we were fighting or what we were hoping for; why it was that we did not, for instance, just let the Germans and Russians bash one another up. Certainly no one seemed any longer to be under the illusion that we could help Poland. There were certain 'War Aims' officially published, but these did not seem to make much sense beyond the impression of vague sentiments. My Aunt Baba's friend Lord Halifax, for instance, announced – 'We want, I suppose, that every man and woman in Europe should have a chance of leading a decent and orderly life and of developing his or her personality according to opportunity.' This was all very well – but how was it thought that this might be achieved through a European war? (I learned likely answers to such questions so many years, and so many travails, later.) In the meantime it appeared absurd that our teachers at Eton just accepted the occurrence of a European war in the same style that they accepted, and so unquestioningly taught us, the history of the Trojan or the Peloponnesian Wars; or indeed the story of Medea so beautifully murdering her children.

There was a time early in 1940 when my father had wanted to take me away from Eton; he had a plan whereby I should study science under Diana's brother-in-law Derek Jackson, who was a physicist. I wrote to my father: 'If you have been able to arrange anything definite with Derek Jackson I still think it would be best to leave at the end of the summer but if nothing satisfactory can be fixed perhaps it is not worth it.' Part of my protection was nonchalance. In the same letter I described how: 'We had the house sports the other day and amidst great excitement I proceeded to win the Senior High Jump and come second in the Half Mile: I jumped 4ft 10ins in an enormous pair of walking shoes as I had lost my running shoes as usual.' At the end of the letter I put a PS. 'I was so sorry about the Silvertown election [in which there had been a BU candidate] but I think very few people would have got even 150 votes in such a short time.'

When my father was imprisoned there was the business again of running the gauntlet of people's polite, not-quite-observing eyes: more painful this time than that of the publicity concerning my father's and Diana's secret marriage eighteen months earlier, but still not the sort of occasion at which Etonians showed any venom. Eton is good about this sort of thing: it is almost the one place on earth, I suppose, that has such a built-in confidence in itself – in the virtue just of Etonians being Etonians – that this is stronger than any stray occurrence such as that of some Etonian's father being locked up in jail. For this I was, and still am, very grateful. There was no more talk of my leaving Eton.

My Aunt Irene visited me during this summer; she wrote:

I heard Mr Elliott [the headmaster] preach and he gave an admirable sermon on the burden of being an Etonian because those boys had wealth and privilege and theirs must be the future to lead and be worthy of it. Nicky all the time held his head and I felt he was not happy. Later walking me to the station he said he thought Mr Elliott was right but they were all bored with him.

The problem for me was – however much I might be grateful to Eton with its crazy self-confidence, what on earth had this got to do with what was happening in the world outside? School work went on with its strange intensities as if we were learning tribal dialects in New Guinea. I continued to be good at passing exams: I worked at night when necessary: I won prizes. The only sport I was good at was athletics: I had given up trying at cricket. On summer afternoons I would wander off to the cinema at Slough: this, of course, was strictly against the rules. I became fascinated by sophisticated, witty comedies such as those of Lubitsch and Preston Sturges. Was this the 'decent and orderly life' that the grown-up world was aiming at? But why was such honour given to the people in the *Iliad?*

For the summer holidays of 1940 myself and my sister Vivien and my brother Micky and almost everyone in the family who were not in jail went to Loch Awe, in Scotland. I wrote to my father in jail in a style that I must have thought was sophisticated:

I wish I had known earlier that we are allowed to write as many letters to you as we like. We all thought for some unknown reason that you were only allowed to have two a week and therefore our letters would never reach you. But Granny says that all our letters will reach you after censorship, so I can write often now.

We are having great fun up in Scotland. Viv and I with Andrée and Aunty N live in the hotel, while Nanny and Mick live in a cottage three miles off with Aunty B and family. It has never stopped raining for a minute since we got here. The hotel has not a person under 42 in the place. I have been salmon fishing once or twice in the river Awe but I never catch a thing. The shooting is really pathetic. There are supposed to be hundreds of rabbits round about and David [Metcalfe] and I walk for miles every evening only seeing one or two. David has got a retriever which he and Aunty B are very proud of: they have sent him to all the best trainers and he is supposed to be the world's best shooting dog. But because he is a very stupid animal to begin with and because the Metcalfe nursery world is enough to drive any dog dippy he runs about in every direction, never comes when he is called, and has to be lifted over every fence.

Thank you so much for your letters. I want to come and see you very badly, but I don't think I am going to be in London at the moment.

We shall all be together again some day, but in the meantime don't worry about us, we will be all right.

Concerning this letter my father wrote to Diana who was in Holloway Jail – 'A long letter came from Nicky – wonderfully catty about his stay in Scotland with his relations.'

I have only one clear memory of visiting my father during his year-and-a-half in Brixton, though it is evident from my Aunt Irene's diaries that I visited him at least four times. I suppose the visit that has stuck in my mind is the first: they were probably all somewhat traumatic. I remember the prison visiting room like something in a railway station: Vivien and I waited like displaced persons. When my father bounded in he was, as he always was, full of energy and ebullience and light. He wore something like a boiler suit and had grown a reddish beard. He carried the whole social occasion splendidly. What do children say to a father in jail?

After one of Vivien's and my visits, he wrote to Diana:

Viv and Nick came to see me on Monday – very much themselves, Nick had won the High Jump at Eton – isn't it extraordinary. Only other news of note is that Micky had fallen off a tree and broken his wrist. The luckless Nick seems doomed apparently to stay at Eton in perpetuity. However one can do no more, and I imagine his particular gift has already and finally been destroyed.

Before this – not long after my father had been imprisoned – things had come to a head in the dispute he had been having with the Courts

about his children's money. He had been brought from jail to appear
before the Chancery Court to be questioned about what arrangements
should be made concerning the children's livelihood: the lease of
Wootton had been given up and, at the same time as Diana's
arrest in June 1940, Savehay Farm had been requisitioned by the
Ministry of Supply (it became a centre of research into Chemical
Warfare). In anger against what my father saw as the Judge's right
to question his authority in any matters concerning his children – and
after questions concerning the role played in all this by Aunt Irene
Ravensdale – my father renounced all further responsibility for his
three children by his first marriage. His account of this in a letter to
Diana was –

> The children today were duly removed – the Judge took the line
> that I should remain guardian in name, but as it was clear that I
> should have no direction in their education or anything else, I declined
> responsibility without authority and Lady R was made guardian.
> I informed the Official Solicitor that this was finality as far as I was
> concerned. It was suggested that Micky should go with Abinger
> School to Canada where his cousins were also going: I stoutly op-
> posed this on the grounds that it was disgraceful for well-to-do
> children to run away to Canada leaving nearly all the rest of the
> nation's children to whatever is coming. The Judge warmly agreed
> with this and decided in my favour. So that is something. I am afraid
> they will keep Nicky at Eton till he is 18 and try to make him
> as big an ass as most of that class: however I think he will survive
> it.

My Aunt Irene's version of this story was that since the children's money
had anyway been for years under the jurisdiction of the Court, and
since she recently and with my father's blessing had been responsible
for a large part of the day-to-day planning for the children as well
as for the financial loans which kept our old home going, the Court
had suggested to her and my father that now he was in jail they might
share some joint form of guardianship: they had both said, however,
that they thought this would be unworkable. Then when my father
was brought from prison to appear before the Court (this is still Irene's
version),

> he inferred he never knew the judges had any control over his chil-
> dren. The judge was willing to waive all questions of guardianship

and cooperate with him on important issues but he flatly refused and wanted entire control for the boys – he was not interested in the girl. After discussion and deliberation the Judge could only ask for outside guardianship as he had refused to have any assistance. My name was put up. He [my father] sent me a lamentable message saying that I must understand he would never later have anything to do with the care or guardianship of any of his children, he was through with them. God in his inimitable way has handed me Cim's children.

When the Official Solicitor, Mr Gilchrist, came to Irene's house to break the news to the two older children that their father was no longer their guardian Irene recorded:

Viv seemed very unmoved and unsurprised, and said Daddy had always disliked butting in on Gilchrist. Nick seemed a bit silent and sad, so I left him and Viv to talk and when I got back Viv reported Nick was not so upset as his father even at Xmas had said – Things may happen to me, and with those judges I will not work, I would rather resign.

When Irene told Nanny that she, Irene, was now the children's guardian, Nanny said – with perhaps one of her startling shafts of wisdom if not tact – 'The judges might have suggested some man to look after Micky instead of all this petticoat government.' Irene commented, 'This was not very helpful for me.'

At Eton I moved with as much detachment as I could up the rungs of destined ladders: I became myself a member of the Library; eventually Captain of my House. I never became a member of Pop – that self-electing society dependent upon fashion. But I was now myself one of the lugubrious, cumbersome boys who moved round small boys' bedrooms after supper; sat in wicker chairs impassive and observant; occasionally played chess. Once or twice after some offence it was mandatory that as Captain of the House I should beat someone; I wondered if, after all the talk, I might enjoy this. I found I did not. I wrote cryptically to my sister – 'What would you do if you had to beat two boys for throwing mud at a policeman? Split your sides – so I am all right, as I balance out.' During my last year at Eton I used to go up once a week to London to see a stammer specialist: he was a new one but he practised the same techniques; I learned to swoop

and throb like a public speaker. I could still do this quite easily; but
it still seemed to me afterwards that I would rather stammer. On my
way back from Harley Street to Paddington Station I would sometimes
call in on the pornographic bookshops which were at that time concentrated in Praed Street: I might thus fill up one or two gaps in the
Library shelves. Or I would make a detour to the non-stop revue at
the Windmill Theatre and join the rows of men ready to steeplechase
over the backs of chairs when seats became vacant closer to the stage
where girls stood from time to time absolutely motionless with no
clothes on. I loved the girls: I thought the steeplechasing not quite
part of the game.

There was only one local girl at Eton whom I remember anyone
ever showing any interest in: she was called, literally, Nina Birch.
She would ride past our house each day at the same time on her bicycle:
we would all rush to our windows like American sailors are supposed
to do in films about the Pacific. Once a boy was caught with her in
a pub in Windsor and was duly expelled.

In 1941 older boys had to partake in Air Raid Precautions during
term time and in Home Guard duties during the holidays. When in-
cendiary bombs were dropped we had 'terrific sport' (I wrote to my
sister) putting them out with stirrup pumps. When a large bomb
dropped on one of the main school buildings I and others were having
a tutorial next door: what was interesting was to see who dived, and
how far, to get underneath furniture.

I described the atmosphere:

> The siren still goes continually: we pile down into the shelter and
> play endless games of Vingt-et-un at a *penny a counter* which as you
> know means you can lose ten bob in five minutes. I am terrified
> all the time, but so far have lost nothing greater than five bob.

The style of most of us at Eton was, of course, to be nonchalant about
practical matters concerning the war: I approved of this: it was the
sensible counterpart to the lack of speculation about what the war was
actually for. It was taken for granted that all of us when we were
eighteen were going to train to fight with a likelihood of being killed:
this was just one of the 'privileges' (as the headmaster had seemed to
suggest) that Etonians had to be 'worthy of'.

In the meantime this gave one a sense of freedom from constraint;
but also the arrogance that I suppose is a characteristic of soldiers in
wartime. I wrote to my sister –

The Home Guard fortnight was good stuff – two cinemas a day, all quite illegal; bicycling into Bray and Maidenhead to booze and rolling home at night; climbing in through bedroom windows, etc. Many a practical joke. Have you ever realised that you can loosen the springs of a bed so that it collapses when lain on? Good thing to know.

But then when during my last year at Eton I went up to Oxford to try for a history scholarship at Balliol for which I had done hardly any work, I wrote to my father:

The history scholarship was not a success, as I expected, but it was interesting to have tried. I spent 4 days in Oxford while I was doing the exam, and that short time was sufficient to convince me that I was right in choosing to stay on at Eton. The people, especially at Balliol, are ghastly; stiff with Jews. I never saw one person who could have been considered respectable. The atmosphere was rather like that of a girl's school. So I came away with a profound horror of Oxford. I don't think I shall be able to face going back there after the war.

My letters of this time sometimes make painful reading. I have tried in this book to quote what seems representative of other people; I shall try to quote what seems to have been representative, even if unpleasantly, of myself. I suppose at this time I was trying to make myself acceptable to my father. With him in jail, I must have thought one of the ways to do this was to show contempt for the outside world.

Sixth-formers at Eton had to partake of a ritual each 'half' in which they stood on a platform in front of an assembly of boys and parents and declaimed a piece of poetry or prose of their choice. I had the chance of getting out of this because of my stammer: but I wanted to do it – was not the piece I wished to choose to do with heroics? It was a chorus from Swinburne's *Atalanta in Calydon* which had been one of my father's favourite pieces; he used to recite it to us as children. But how would I fare as I climbed up on to my platform? For a time nothing came out. But then fluently, as if with flags and banners –

> Before the beginning of years
> There came to the making of man
> Time with a gift of tears
> Grief with a glass that ran

Pleasure with pain for leaven
Summer with flowers that fell
Remembrance fallen from heaven
And madness risen from hell

And so on. I think stammering is something to do with one's realisation that what is likely to come out, for all its lovely cadences (perhaps because of them?) has little after all to do with what is going on in one's head. This knowledge is like that of someone standing at the top of the Tower of Babel and being struck by the thought – what must things have been like before?

On my last day at Eton I walked round the playing fields where I and my friends had been happy: there were the hedgerows where we had reclined and talked: the cricket pavilion with its sloping roof against which we played a game of our own invention like real tennis. I felt that Eton had been good to me because it had taught me to be both part of and yet not part of its odd, self-confident world: some such balancing act seemed to be necessary if life was not to become too savage or too blind. But as I walked round the playing fields I swore that I would never send any of my own children to Eton: I would hope for somewhere more steady than the tightrope between rebelliousness and charm. Eton had been good to me because it had oiled wheels with regard to my father; but perhaps the same oil might be making smooth the slope down which people seemed to be sliding to perdition. I had written to my sister about my last year at Eton – 'Vice, sordidity and sloth have come into their proper place at the head of things': this was a joke, of course, but then – what was not a joke? What had happened, what would happen, to the things that my friends and I had tried to talk about as we hid away in our by-ways and hedgerows – God, truth, love?

One of the last essays I wrote at Eton was on the subject of *Words Words Words*. A stammerer is someone who is cryptic perhaps in some effort to get back to that state before the confusion of languages.

Perhaps the world would be a happier place today if God had gone further when he decided to destroy the Tower of Babel. By making men of the world speak different languages, he was only putting a temporary obstacle in their way. But even if he had destroyed their power of speech, they would soon have learned to make their pompous speeches and spread their scandals in another way.

CHAPTER 20

Love Letters

It had seemed to both Diana and my father that they would be let out of prison once the immediate invasion scare was over; there might have had to be some temporary concessions to public panic, but now that their premises had been searched and nothing incriminating had been found – what on earth would be the point of keeping them in? Diana wrote later, 'I imagined there would be a rule against free speech for the rest of the war.' As months went on in fact a great many of the 700 British Union members detained under Regulation 18B were released on the advice of the Advisory Committee; but there was always the Security Executive to have the last word about those whom they did not want to let out.

When my father was locked up in Brixton he was at first put into a cell with a black man; he wrote later – 'some whimsical jackass in office probably thought this would annoy me, but on the contrary, I found him a charming and cultured man: I understand that he was alleged to have played in the Berlin Philharmonic Orchestra before the war, and was arrested on account of the peculiarity of that occupation at that time for a coloured man'.

The detainees were locked in their cells from 4 pm to 7 am; at first they were let out for exercise for only two one-hour periods each day to walk in pairs round the yard. One of the chief afflictions was that of bed-bugs. An ex-BUF inmate wrote:

We used to have bug-hunts every night. They would lodge in the cracks in the bed-boards and tables. Night after night one could hear hammering from cells all over the hall. This was caused by the bed-boards being knocked against the floor to dislodge the inhabitants, which could then be dealt with.

This inmate had a memory of my father:

> I went into O.M.'s cell one morning just after he had finished wash-
> ing. I happened to catch sight of his arms as he was in the act of
> rolling up his sleeves. His arms were covered in bites, by far the
> worst I had seen. I asked him if he had made any complaint about
> it. Not he! He would have let himself be eaten alive before complain-
> ing. 'If the boys can take it so can I' was his answer.

Diana wrote later of the time she was locked up in Holloway –*

> The cells were six feet by nine; each contained a hard bed, a hard
> chair, and a small heavy table. Under the bed was a chipped enamel
> chamber pot with a lid upon which in dark blue was a crown and
> the royal cipher. There was a battered jug and basin and a small
> three-cornered shelf. The sheets were made of canvas, painful if it
> touched one's chin.

> The cold weather came and the prison was icier than ever. A wardress
> appeared with a convict carrying a pile of blankets. I went to get
> one. Never have I seen a more disgusting sight than these old hard
> blankets; every variety of human filth had left its unmistakable marks
> upon them.

> One night a bomb fell near the prison. It broke the water mains.
> In the dark early morning there was the sound of lavatory plugs
> being pulled in vain. The lavatories, always foul, became frightful
> – floors awash with urine, everything choked, an appalling smell.
> We were all grey with grime because the bomb had shaken the
> old prison and a thick layer of dust and soot covered everything.
> We were given half a pint of water each. I drank a sip and tried
> to wash in the remainder.

Diana spent much of the time reading. The wardress told her that most
of the women chose books with red covers from the tray that came
round because they could then lick their fingers and get a bit of red
dye to put on their lips.

My father said that it suited him when the prisoners were locked
up for 'twenty one hours out of twenty four'; he too could get on

* *A Life of Contrasts.*

with reading. But it was misery to other prisoners, especially to the Italians who had been indiscriminately thrown in jail. So my father headed a deputation of protest to the governor, and after this cell doors were kept unlocked during the day. But then, my father wrote – 'the echoing sea-shell of the building resounded to the music of ping-pong and Latin laughter: the subsequent discomfort of being in locked cells when bombs were falling was nothing to it'. He told a story of how a group of warders used to congregate in a cell directly underneath his when bombs were falling, on the grounds that they thought Hitler could pin-point his bombs with great accuracy and he would be sure to spare my father.

Diana found she could not eat the prison food except 'the delicious bully beef' and the prison bread; she lived on these and Stilton cheese which was ordered and sent in for her by my father. Parcels of food were allowed; but it was expected they would be shared amongst fellow prisoners. Half a bottle of wine was permitted; Diana ordered port: 'a glass of grocer's port and a bit of Stilton cheese helped me through many a sad evening'.

The *Daily Mirror* and the *Sunday Pictorial* ran stories about how she and my father were enjoying luxury in prison (my father had in fact given up alcohol) –

Every morning his paid batman delivers three newspapers at the door of his master's cell. Breakfast, dinner and tea arrive by car. After his mid-day meal Mosley fortifies himself with alternative bottles of red and white wine daily. He occasionally asks for a bottle of champagne. He still takes great pride in his appearance. He selects a different smartly cut lounge suit every week. His shirts and silk underwear are laundered in Mayfair. . . .

My father and Diana brought a libel action against the *Mirror* and *Pictorial*: they were awarded damages with costs. The papers admitted they had invented these stories. Diana used her share of the damages to buy a 'huge fur coat' in which she said she looked like 'Fafner and Fasolt rolled into one'.

I wrote to my father from Eton: 'We thought the stories of you playing bridge the whole time were very funny: you know how you used to grunt when anyone played at Denham. Also the champagne.'

They were each allowed one visit a week: my father saw his mother and sometimes his ex-sister-in-law Baba. He told his mother that he would not ask to see his children, they could ask to see him if they wished. Diana was visited by her mother who brought her two older children up from the country – 'I shall never forget their dear anxious faces as they stared at me, and the relief when they saw I had not much changed and that I laughed as usual' – also her babies Alexander and Max. 'Alexander looked beautiful beyond words with huge dark eyes. Max was completely changed from the little baby I had left, he sat up and gazed about him with a solemn expression.'

My father and Diana were at first allowed to receive only two letters a week; they each wrote once a week to the other. Then, when these regulations were relaxed, they each wrote to the other twice a week. My father's letters to Diana have survived. They are written on the small four-page lined prison writing paper and are like the letters that men write from the front in war. They bear the marks of the censors at both Brixton and Holloway. He had been told not to write about anything political. In prison, his life in ruins, separated from Diana whom he loved, there was still an ebullience such as there usually was about my father. But now – how gentle he was, when he could not be concerned with anything about politics!

Extracts from these letters can show, better than anything else can, the side of my father that was caring and enduring. The first letter was written on the day after Diana's arrest.

July 1st 1940
My Beloved Darling,
I have just seen the news, and you know what I feel about it. I write this quickly to say that I am worried about the milk condition and that something must be done at once. If you are at all ill you are to telegraph for Dr Gilliatt – in any case you are to see him as soon as possible. If it is better for you to have the baby in do get him in at once – I will not have any chances taken with you in a delicate condition. All my fondest love my darling.
Telegraph Gilliatt. X K.

July 8th
The Official Solicitor had the impudence to write and enquire in what manner I would like to pay the school fees of the two boys he had just removed – the answer was a raspberry the results of which I have not yet heard ... Nearly a year since the Earl's Court meeting – Do you remember it? What a lot has happened since ... Darling Percher, I do miss you so – you are such a brave and wonderful Percher – I do hope you are not too depressed. Above all do

not worry – take things as easily as you possibly can and do not notice the unpleasant. Make the latest affectation – Gaol's the place! We live in a great and changeful age. The present hysteria must pass quite quickly, and we might soon be together again. Poor Percher will have a job not to see the moon through glass!

July 12th
What a gay life the girls have with a gas cooker – you are lucky! – when I talk about cooking here they all 'simply shriek' and obviously do not believe I can really do it. Is £2 a week arriving for you from Barclay's Bank? ... She must keep herself fit. I do P.T. twice a day morning and evening in my cell and it makes a very great difference. Start by touching the toes a lot – a very good chop exercise ... I am re-reading Anatole France's Penguin Island....

July 25th
Am now resuming my language studies after an interval of five weeks – Wie war das Percheron? Is it correct that all virgins are neuter? Isn't it? Silly Mr Kit!

July 27th
I have started growing a beard. It is to be the Old Brixtonian tie. And guess what colour it is – red!! At least quite a lot of it – silver threads among the gold ... Darling one, I must stop now, it is this incessant social round, quite like you before the shadow fell.

August 18th
Here I am outside, still reflecting with bewilderment that eating is the difficulty with this beard business; it is even more liable than eyebrows to get blown into the soup. What a difference sun does make in this place – it makes me almost feel as if we were again on the magic road just beyond Lyons – we must do that as soon as ever we can when all this is over ...

August 28th
My Darling Beloved,
I hope you are not kept awake all night nowadays by having to go to a cell lower down; but at the same time I would rather you went down than stayed upstairs. Personally I sleep blissfully through them all [the bombs] – retiring to bed soon after the first sirens usually around 9 p.m. and not waking up till next morning. Today seems to have been the liveliest so far ...

December 8th

The noise about prison is certainly much the worst thing ... My precious one I do so long to be with you and hope so much it may soon be arranged – it would be such a joy to me, and I think she would 'do' better. She must not have bad dreams – that one was due to your feeling you were wasting your youth in prison, probably coupled with old memories of the motor smash: but she must always say to herself it is not for long.

December 16th

Always remember that nothing great is ever done without the most agonising experiences: it is sad, but it always seems to be one of the invariable rules of this world. I know no single case without it. Our capacity to endure is the passport without which all our other qualities take us nowhere: courage, constancy, character. In the last is comprised the power to endure. I am immersed in *Wahlver-wandtschaften* – to spend this time in the company of Goethe is in a sense 'such a tease' on everything as a Percher would say. But I do so miss my Darlingest one, and long again to be with her so.

December 19th

I have read 100 pages of the Goethe and much of it does remind me all so much of Wootton – I like reading it so much that I cannot bear to stop and look up words – does the title mean 'by choice' or 'alternative relationships'? *Wahl* can mean either ... It is a curious reflection of his genius that, if I did not know the age at which both books were written, I should say *Werther* was the more mature book of the two: he certainly fulfils the definition – outside time, outside class – the Eternal Contemporary. He could never have had any 'age' – although he is supposed to sense this when Faust goes blind: 'Thou shalt know care at last!'

December 27th

It was a sad Christmas without my darling one – I thought so much of her last year in lovely Wootton looking so beautiful when she was doing the tree ... I feel in a grey mood, but I truly do not believe our present circumstances will last much longer and my mind is full of so many things for the future.... Have sent you a copy of *Zarathustra*: the 3 metamorphoses are at the very beginning; and the Night Song, even translated, is one of the loveliest things in all literature.

January 3rd 1941

I am glad A.F. has written to that man: [A.F. stood for Arabia Felix which was my father's and Diana's name for her mother Lady Redesdale: 'that man' was probably Walter Monckton]; he is a good man, and could help a lot to get us together if he tried. With so few couples left [many of the original 700 BUF detainees had by now been released] it is perfectly easy for them to arrange if they liked – and I think it could be done if enough pressed for it in the H of C ... I have been lazy and have hardly read at all for a day or two – reflecting much on the coming year and the future – how interesting everything is! This time certainly gives an opportunity to think things out. That precious one must not go and alter herself too much and lose her pretty ways and paces – he would hate that – he would like just his same darling Percher – not all hogged and pulled to look quite different.

January 9th

I shall see Vivien on Monday and will tell her myself ... control of them [the children] now is absolutely nothing to do with me – I am not even nominally their guardian – I think, in the circumstances, it is a good thing for that to be made quite clear to everyone. As you know I would not be associated in any way with the handling of Vivien before the war and I could not more disapprove of the way they are now being handled – Nick was left at that idiot school by order of the court against my express wishes. I feel very strongly about the whole thing. Miss Ottolie [a character in Goethe's novel *Die Wahlverwandtschaften*] in poignant contrast, goes from strength to strength, her tagebuch yielding a rich store of accumulated wisdom. Some of his remarks have an amazingly modern application: I have just got to the part where the English Lord decides to cheer the party up with the result that everyone is in tears ...

January 17th

The children came and were very much themselves. Nick was pro beard and Viv said it was not nearly so bad as she had expected – ecstatic for her! It is twice the beard since you saw it ... Nick has been studying German at Eton for exactly the same time as I have been studying it at Brixton – but a brief examination revealed that he knew little or nothing of it. So I am telling Miss M to send him my books with the remark that I regret to observe that six months study of a subject in Brixton Prison yields such much greater result than a study of the same subject over a corresponding period at

Eton College.... I hear Schiller always entirely re-writes history, and never permitted Mary Queen of Scots to be beheaded – I always feel, too, that so many things could have been much better arranged ... This has been a long and dreary time and such a waste of life. But I feel now things are beginning to move a bit and much of the long and dreary time may be behind us.

January 30th
Wonderful news appears in answer to a parliamentary question that we are to see each other once a fortnight ... In the same answer it was said that it had not been found possible to put us in the same establishment; but again, a good many other enquiries are likely to be made about why it is possible to clear out a whole village to make room for the purpose of having alien husbands and wives together in the Isle of Man but not possible to put us together in one house in England which is all that is necessary and is offered free – the disparity in treatment is becoming grotesque.

February 8th
Bores are the affliction – we have a few – I fear I have been rather rough with them. My latest device is to put a notice 'Busy' on my door: try it, and say I do it: then I don't think it could offend any of our friends. When the notice is down anyone can come in – it is really the only way to have any peace for thought or reading. I find the poetic form of Schiller a little difficult ...

February 10th
My Darlingest Beloved,
I am writing this on getting back to Brixton [he had been driven to Holloway briefly] to say how wonderful it was to see my most precious one in all the world today and what a relief it was to find her the same darlingest one – if possible more beautiful and sweet than ever – but it made me long more than ever to be with you. The time was so short and I had so much that I wanted to say and especially how much I love you ... I think so much of Wootton and all her loveliness and sweetness there – we will do beautiful things again.

February 24th
I have started on Egmont and find it much easier than Schiller; though the latter I was reading quite easily towards the end. I gather from the notes in this volume that the conversation of the locals with which they always appear to prelude their plays consists largely of

obsolete slang – so no wonder I find it rather heavy going. But
I also always found the corresponding parts of Shakespeare a trifle
tedious. But directly they introduce the great characters they are
superb. So far I prefer Goethe on the whole to Schiller ... Now
it is only four days before I see my own Beloved Sonnenpferd again;
I just live now from fortnight to fortnight ...

March 8th
It is such good news that Weedoms [Max aged 11 months] is coming
up next week, I will leave a V O [Visiting Order] for Pam [his sister-
in-law Mrs Derek Jackson] as I did when Stodge [Alexander aged
2 years] came. I am so excited to see him and do hope he will be
wearing his well-brought-up face as in the photograph. From his
demeanour there I feel I should at once discuss with him the word-
meanings of Goethe and Schiller, but expect it will turn out a little
different ... By the way, why have *I* got a well-brought-up face?
Because I am listening to Chamber Music!! There is a man here
who is a distinguished musician – English or rather Welsh – and
he plays for me in the chapel – a new treat. Have you ever heard
our Elizabethan music? I never had – it is terrific – explains them –
gay and heroic.

March 9th
I have just finished the last of the wonderful food you have done
for me – the salad dressing was a poem – she is the cleverest of
Perchers and a reine de Gastronome! It really was so good and I
was enthused by the sauce – how does she do it with scanty material ...
I have also been reading Nietzsche's Zarathustra: the great passage
which I love so much – anyone if interested can find it on page
35 of the Zarathustra in my cell. It describes the 'child' in the third
of the metamorphoses which you have often heard me discuss: you
remember – Camel, Lion, Child. It is good enough in English but
in the original is colossal and really untranslatable without losing
much: for instance how can one do justice in English to the tremendous 'bedarf es eines heiligen Ja-sagens'? 'We require a Holy Yes'
isn't quite the same thing!

March 16th
Have not yet been all through Zarathustra in the original, but I
think it is in this book that occur the great lines I like so much
on the relationship of cynicism and idealism that you mentioned
in your last letter – 'Man is the rope over the abyss that divides

the animal from the superman.' He is referring to the incompleteness of contemporary humanity that must 'go beyond' itself. And, again, one of his greatest and most misunderstood lines – 'I love the great Despisers, for their souls are the arrows that are yearning for the farther shore.' He means that if man is really an idealist he cannot be content with 'contemporary' humanity; this must 'surpass' itself... It is indeed difficult to believe in the 'essential goodness' of contemporary mankind; but it is not too difficult to believe in the Purpose which works through present humanity to the attainment of something higher. Without the Purpose it is all just nonsense – merely silly – an accident – too complex to be easily believed an accident – a confusion made up of a myriad of seemingly related chances. With the Purpose it has sense only if it works through the present to something beyond. The complete realist, therefore, will combine complete cynicism toward contemporary humanity with complete idealism towards posterity. But to be the entire idealist would be a little tedious – so it is possible to embrace a compassion for contemporaries with a thorough understanding of our undeveloped state ... Too often in recent philosophy you see the idealist turned cynic – he begins by swallowing the goodness of everything and ends by vomiting the badness of everything ... in fact typically unbalanced and hysterical and lacking in all historical and biological perspective. The child is father to the man – but not yet the man – so watch out while it is near to the fire, while you work for its future.

March 24th
How I hope to be on the long road to Arles with stops at Pyramides [a restaurant at Vienne] and Avignon – what beautiful times we have had and how I long for them with you again. How quickly we could recover from all this with such a little sun and life. I would like to sit with you on that fallen log among the bluebells till we felt better – my memories of you at Wootton are so beautiful and my hopes for the future with you – how the wheel swings! This is not an age built for happiness – it is too great. But we have had some. We have not suffered entirely from the Siegmund compulsion – 'to whom the gods gave but one gift – the art of loving without happiness'. We have known a little of Siegfried and the hours where ends the 'aus sich rollendes Rad' [self-rolling wheel] of which element we too have a little ...

April 4th
I have sent many quotations because I felt in too savage a temper

really to write – no particular reason at all – just internal combustion. But whatever my mood or humour I always love that Darlingest Percher just the same ...

April 18th
I cannot tell you how precious Stodge [Alexander] was. He sat on my knee as good as gold the whole time and talked – in a proud Oxfordshire accent I thought. When he first came in he stroked my beard and said 'Funny Man'. Finally when they had reached the main gate and I was a long way off I waved to him and he broke loose from trainer and ran all the way over to me – so I was very proud! ... She is such a Beloved one to have given me two such precious sons.... I expect you know that Egmont was really married and had 11 children – Goethe kept it dark for romantic reasons – I take rather hard the view that a man becomes less romantic because he has a lot of children.

April 21st
Am mad about Stravinsky – shrieks or not? – it is my latest affectation ... I thought always he was just a Ballet Boy tho' a very good one – but of course he is much more – has the future within him. He seems to me strangely related to Wagner; this comment I made with trepidation – but was assured it was perspicacious – so was fortified in my well-brought-up face ...

April 27th
My phlebitis so far does not appear to have spread – I expect it is bound to appear in other places as it always does once it starts – but that is nothing to worry about as I can always get the specialist to bind it up as before if it goes much higher up the leg. After all I am an old boy at that business, and know it is all right if it is carefully handled.

May 17th
For me it is a year in prison next week and for you so very soon after. We were trying to think of any examples in which what are called civilized countries had kept political prisoners in gaol for a year under an order of this kind and we could think of none. Plenty of examples of course of keeping political prisoners in other places but not in prison. Furthermore the keeping the woman in prison for such a period finds no precedent or parallel anywhere.... Rather a good aphorism in relation to the present world someone has sent in to a competition in 'Cissy's Weekly' [*The New Statesman and*

Nation] – 'Progress is a convenient term for describing our journey from the golden ages' ...

May 19th

You too might study the subject on which I am thinking of embarking – the study of all societies which have attained or striven to attain strength and beauty in union with – or even through – simplicity of life: eg Sparta, the whole great Hellenic Epic, the Christian attempts – Knightly and Monastic Templars etc – mostly flops in the end, being set up in opposition to instead of in unison with women; the latter necessity being understood by the Samurai who probably created the most enduring and influential aristocracy in the world. As you know, these ideas have always fascinated me.

June 2nd

Curious that in this strange place I am still always short of time – the sole occupation of course is in the mind – that is why, no doubt, some inmates can find nothing at all to do ... The things to which you object in current art are plutocratic values and the demand they create: whatever the character of the labour it merely supplies the demand – to some extent this is true even of genius in art. Have first in all things the transformation of values. When the market is the 'appreciative' artist – whether it be Lorenzo de Medici or a modern world of different values – instead of a successful speculation, the 'creative' artist has his opportunity.

June 30th

I have had a letter from Nick; he is going in for a Balliol history scholarship but does not think he will get it. His letters have suddenly become strangely adult – rather affected. He has evidently benefited from his last visits to the 'great school' – not Eton of course: the real one! [a reference to a visit to Brixton]

July 6th

Lately I have been reading so little that it is really terrible. Sometimes I feel that reading is only useful to start up one's own mind – it is like putting a little petrol in the carburettor of an engine – one just reads a few pages and then starts thinking – it is really the answer to the question one asks so often – what did that book give me for the trouble of reading it? Such however is never true of the immortals – Faust, and Plato. How beautiful is the answer of Achilles when told by the gods that if he avenges Patroclus he too must die – the words of the eternal hero. They were the most exquisite people,

those Hellenes ... I was thinking the other day of how modest I
am in comparison with most in this establishment in that their idea
is always to collect a small circle of others whom they can instruct,
while my one idea in conversation with anyone is not to tell him
anything but to ask him questions in order to acquire from him
any knowledge he possesses – if, by any strange chance, that amounts
to anything at all. Flattering myself therefore on this relative simplicity and humility of spirit, I suddenly realised it was really exactly
the opposite – for the habit of interrogating rather than informing
really arises from my almost sub-conscious feeling that a new fact
reposed in my head is so much more important – as it becomes
so much more useful – than any new fact lodged in his!

July 17th
The other day I heard the second American joke in my life that
made me laugh: 'Do you know where bugs go in winter time?'
'Search me.' The other I think you know – 'How are you feeling
this morning?' 'Not quite myself.' 'Congratulations.' Simple, aren't
they?

August 4th
I suspected that Nick was reaching a precious stage but did not know
it had developed so far as a book by Gerald [Lord Berners' novel
The Girls of Radcliffe Hall]: he has come on so much that I would
quite like you to see him – quite grown up – 6ft 3″ – he is in their
top division now with 20 oppidans and 20 scholars. They asked a
lot about you and sent love.

August 25th
My Darlingest Beloved,
Oh the Foals! [Alexander and Max] – they are such heaven. They
arrived in state escorted by kind Tom [Diana's brother] and the
proudest of trainers – they could not be more fascinating and made
me long more than ever to be with you and them. Stodge [Alexander]
was enchanting and asked repeatedly to be thrown up in the air
which was greeted with delighted shrieks – not so the Entschlossener
[Max: 'the determined one'] who shouted Go away! when approached
and reared back fiercely striking out with both forefeet. However,
great was the triumph when the clever finger of the experienced
stud-groom melted him to the most charming plump chuckles by
the simple expedient of tickling him in the ribs ...

August 28th
She is so clever with her cooking now – what fun we could have

with it if we were together – you doing it and me admiring – so lovely to do all those things in a leisurely way when there would be no time pressure. I have lost the latter sense now – it stayed with me for some months after I had got here – it was such a busy time before – always with too much to do and too little time. I think that sense is the greatest disadvantage of the kind of life I used to lead – it takes away too much from life. The dullness of most people's lives which you mention is of course entirely due to themselves: as I always used to say to my revered relation – He suffered under a terrible life sentence – his own company.

September 25th
On Saturday B [Baba] came with Nick ... no real news yet of the matter in hand but I am hopeful [Baba was putting pressure on her political friends to try to get my father and Diana imprisoned together]. More than anything in the black existence I long to be with my Darlingest which would turn everything into gold ...

September 26th
That awful Mr Fowler [author of *Modern English Usage*] in a disquisition on the use of French words in English sentences said it was intolerably affected for English people to use such expressions as 'A merveille'. The beast! ... I remember reading Quintillian when very young and coming to the conclusion that it was obviously impossible ever to make a speech: years later I read him again and realised that every night I was using the methods which he described so tediously and with such unnecessary complication: which proves again the truth of my ancient adage – 'Tell me where is knowledge bred, Twixt the chops or in the head?' Emphatically the former, as my Percher has always maintained with her usual insight. My darlingest one has a great natural gift for style and should develop it in all languages. I am indescribably sloppy and bad except when performing; but that is always so with me – the engines are either switched on or off. I flatter myself that they are too big to warm up except for an ocean voyage – really of course it is just lazy – but perhaps on the way energy is conserved.

October 25th
I can see no harm in Tom [Diana's brother] writing a letter on the following lines which were the same as those given to Baba – 'Whether it is the final decision of the government that they should be imprisoned separately, if it is determined to keep them in prison

at all. They have now been in separate prisons for nearly 18 months despite repeated requests that they be imprisoned together. There are several prisons outside London which are used for both men and women and could in part be used for this purpose by a slight rearrangement of prisoners. I will not raise the question of the justice of the detention nor the conditions of their imprisonments as, apart from recording their strong protest, they have throughout refused to make any personal appeal for consideration. But the decision to treat some 25 married couples of British nationality so very differently from alien internees who are detained together, appears so remarkable a principle that it may be legitimate for me to enquire whether this is the deliberate and final decision of the government.'

November 7th

My Darlingest Beloved

No Monday letter again today ... It annoys me so much because they are the only things I look forward to in this hole ... If again it has gone to Liverpool I shall put in a formal complaint. Today is cold but I have been playing my heavy ball game and feel warmer – most of the best players have gone, and I am trying to teach it to new boys. If we are together I will hardly ever play my silly games and not be so ernst over languages but just concentrate on that Darling Percheron ... Do tell if the tone of the gram is all right, and please do change it if not; because what is a gram without *tone* – in fact what is life without *tone* – what is it without a Percheron – all grey and dull and sad.

December 7th

I have really no news at all – so sorry to hear of Decca's sorrow [Diana's sister Jessica's husband Esmond Romilly had been killed in the RAF] – this age is very sad – there is nothing one can say. We heard more from another expert about the world destruction of the soil – soil erosion – I have studied it lately – it is appalling – I feel all those things so much nowadays – more even than in the past. The old tree throwing out roots, and becoming dull – but still beautiful! Today, Monday [December 8th] I have had a communication which, it said, was also to go to you – made me very happy! I am saying nothing about it to anyone else at present – the rest when I see you. Would not do *too* much about *meubles* at first, because I know what Perchers are when they start galloping. The air anyhow will be pink and blue and gold!

There is just one letter from Diana amongst all the ones from my father. This says:

17th December 1941 Letter 145
My Precious Darling, I got your sweet letter and now I am writing to you for the LAST TIME – imagine it, next time I would have written I shall have the exquisite joy of your beloved self near me with all that means in happiness and bliss ... Today Muv came and the two boys [Jonathan and Desmond] straight from school. They were very sweet and excited but a little bit sad to go off to yet another Christmas without me. I do hope it will be the last. I felt very selfish because my Xmas will be so happy especially compared with last. Muv looked sad I am afraid but was delighted of course we are to be together at long last ... These last days seem more like weeks to me. There is no need for you to bring anything but your eider-down and the little brown Marmite (which is my favourite cooking pot) because I have everything for you even a hot water bottle. I am so longing for you that I walk about in a dream and am not good company at the many farewell parties I spend my time going to. Goodbye my precious beloved for a little while. I will make it rush over – the time that remains to separate us. Come quickly because I love you so much more than all the world. From your very own Percher. X

In early December Diana's brother Tom had been to visit my father in Brixton and then he had gone to Diana in Holloway: he was in the army, on leave, before being sent to the Middle East. He had told Diana that he was having dinner that night in Downing Street with their cousin-by-marriage Winston Churchill; that he would try again to bring the subject up about my father and Diana being imprisoned together. Other friends including Walter Monckton and above all Baba had been working for months to achieve this. That night Tom Mitford managed to get Churchill into a corner: this, in addition to the pressure built up by Baba, resulted in what had previously been called 'an administrative impossibility' being put into effect almost immediately. My father was transferred to Holloway Prison where he and Diana had two rooms in what was called The Preventive Detention Block. My father could now make jokes about being the patriarch of a women's prison: Diana could write that when he arrived their joy was such that 'one of the happiest days of my life was spent in Holloway Prison!'

CHAPTER 21

One Kind of War

The focus of the last third of this volume has necessarily to emanate from a somewhat different direction: my father is locked up: he is out of politics for seven years. He was in Brixton Prison from May 1940 to December 1941; he was with Diana in Holloway till November 1943; he was then under house arrest until the end of the war in Europe in May 1945. Then for two and a half years he lived the life of a gentleman farmer in Wiltshire, and wrote two books. He was drawn back into politics at the end of 1947. From then on his life was some repetition of the 1930s, but (or so it seems to me) on a circuit of the spiral that was only like an echo.

He himself saw the seven years of political inactivity at the very centre of his life – from the age of forty-three to fifty – as providing him with an opportunity for reflection and reappraisal. He was grateful for the chance to learn. He wrote in his autobiography: 'Plato's requirement of withdrawal from life for a considerable period of study and reflection before entering on the final phase of action was fulfilled in my case, though not by my own volition.'

During the 1930s he had not only created his own political movement but had demonstrated his peculiar conception of what a political movement might be: he had formed a fascist movement dedicated to peace, a revolutionary movement whose members were instructed at all times to obey the law. This meant that in practical politics he had often seemed to get the worst of both worlds; he was reviled by those who feared a fascist revolution; he was treated with no great seriousness by those fascists who saw revolution in terms of the manipulation of violence. But none of this sort of criticism seemed to him to be of much importance. What mattered to him was not so much that a political movement should succeed as that any success should be on his own terms, and these included at least the intention of orderliness and rationality. If, in the hard light of what human beings were actually like, this attempt failed, then he did not seem to mind too much if the rest of his activity failed. His business was to promulgate his ideas – and then people could either follow him or try to destroy him as they liked.

There is a sense in which – for all the hardship and frustration which eventually made him ill – he did not feel imprisonment as a disaster: he had done his best to prevent a European war – to argue rationally against what he saw as the real disaster. If other people chose to defeat him, at least, there was beginning to be the evidence of the appalling cost of any victory. His imprisonment would be evidence of how strongly he had fought in the cause of peace.

The first world war had been a decisive experience for my father: he had come to see his subsequent political movement as an army that would march to prevent further wars. In this the direction of his aim had been the opposite of Hitler's (how much simpler to follow was Hitler's!) but how did my father come to hold such paradoxical ideas?

A largely unknown part of my father's life is that to do with his experiences in the first world war: it is upon this that light would presumably have been shed by his mother's diaries – which he himself in later life went to such lengths to destroy. During the first world war it seems there must have formed in him the patterns of mind that later tried to impose themselves on politics: in his auto-biography he gives the impression that he emerged on the social and political scene after the war almost as if he had discovered he were a changeling: he felt free from conventions of his past: a controlling pattern was simply his horror of war. And yet he wished to continue to act in the manner of a soldier.

My father, as with most of his generation, had been starry-eyed in 1914: he had been anxious to get into the fighting before it might be over. He had left the Cavalry when it seemed that there was no prospect of its being used and had joined the Royal Flying Corps as an observer: he had been flying over the enemy lines in flimsy machines at a time where there was a high likelihood of their being shot down by machine guns. He had trained for his pilot's licence, but then during training he had crashed. As a result of injuries sustained in the crash, and after a winter with his regiment acting as infantry in the trenches defending Ypres, he had been invalided out of active service in March 1916. It was perhaps his initial enthusiasm for war that made his sub-

sequent horror of it so profound: he was also perhaps influenced by
the fact that the considerable courage he had originally shown and
had hoped to continue to show had been thwarted by injuries sustained
as a result of misfortune or misjudgment. From his own descriptions
of war he seems to have played peculiarly passive roles: he does not
seem to have found himself involved in circumstances calling for the
sort of responsibility and dash – even the jokes – that in later life he
saw as being characteristic of soldiers and which he said he so much
admired.

It so happens that just at the time when my father was forcibly
removed from the political arena as a result of his efforts to stop war –
and was given a chance to reflect upon both his own failure and what he
saw as other people's ruinous stupidity – at just this time I, his eldest son,
was preparing to go off to war: I joined the army a few months after my
father and Diana were reunited in Holloway. My attitude was almost
the opposite of what my father's had been in 1914: I was, after all, the
child of what he had learned and what he had become. In 1942 I saw the
war as something of an absurdity; but nevertheless I accepted it was
something that had to be undergone; there did not seem to me, as there
did not seem to my father, any contradiction in the idea that one could
properly both fight for one's country and yet be outraged that there was
not peace. In some sense in 1942 I was behaving with regard to the war as
my father said he would have behaved if he had not been imprisoned.
Such paradoxical attitudes did indeed, for myself too, result in some
hostility to conventional passions: it was perhaps the defence of myself
against the inroads of these that resulted in my sometimes unpleasant
intellectual arrogance.

The years when my father was in prison and I was going and had gone
off to war were the years of my closest relationship with him. He looked
from a distance on, and wrote his instructive letters to, someone who
might have been, who might be, something like himself. To me, and in
my correspondence with him, he seemed the person from whom I could
learn. In writing about myself in war I have felt I might in some sense
still be giving information about my father: there were multiple reflections here: for both of us there was the question of what we had learned
and might still learn.

I have tried to write of myself, as I have said, in something of
the same style in which I have written of other people: this is not
easy: admissions about oneself are apt to move, if not towards self-
defence, towards self-flagellation. But one of the points of this book –
biography or autobiography – has been the attempt to create an attitude

by which the darkness in people (there is always darkness) might be
made to seem not so much evil as somewhat ridiculous: evil may thus
be exorcised: ridiculousness becomes life-giving.

This sort of attitude, I think, was representative of some characteristic
of my father's: he could go roaring off; but then he could sometimes
laugh at himself. At the end of his life he could even be kindly about
what previously he would have railed against in others. Of course he
continued to let himself be surrounded by people who could not.

In 1942 what I had in common with my father was this contempt
for people who so senselessly and trivially seemed to glory in war:
who seemed so complacent about the holocaust they were accepting
if not causing. This contempt was I suppose one of the things that
my father had learned from war: this is what I, his son, felt even before
I went into it.

From then on, it seems to me, the way one goes is partly luck; partly
a matter of everything one has ever learned from oneself and from
those close to one.

Both in war, and in the battles one has with what one is and what
one becomes, the questions are – how does one survive? but also and
perhaps more practically – what are the parts of one that one comes
to feel are worthy of survival?

It was taken for granted, as I have said, that from Eton one went
as reasonably quickly as one could into some front line in war; this
was one of the duties, or privileges, of being an Etonian. One usually
joined the army: there was likely to be some family reason for joining
the navy, and the air force was definitely *outré*. In the army one went
into either the Guards or a Cavalry regiment; or – if one wished to
be slightly dashing but still well within the pale – one joined the Rifle
Brigade or the King's Royal Rifle Corps. These regiments had the
reputation of being more intellectual and even artistic than the more
solidly snobbish Guards. For this sort of reason – and because I think
my Aunt Irene was on good terms with one of the senior colonels
– I decided to let myself be put forward as a potential officer in the
Rifle Brigade.

There were questions, of course, about whether or not I would be
accepted. There was my stammer: there was the more ominous question
of my father. In 1940 there had been doubts about whether or not
my brother Micky would even be accepted into a prep school; there
had been an occasion when my Aunt Irene, applying for a job in the
Women's Voluntary Service, had herself apparently been the subject
of a security check on account of her being related to my father. By

1942 it was true that the atmosphere was less conducive to panic. But apart from any of this I still had the confidence generally felt amongst Etonians that the very fact of being an Etonian would be of more weight, even in army terms, than the fact of something like one's father being in gaol. I went for an interview early in 1942. I was accepted – it seemed without too much difficulty. I was to report to the Rifle Brigade depot at Winchester in April.

I went with a group of ex-public schoolboys who were earmarked as potential officers: it had been explained to us that for two months we would be treated no differently from other private soldiers. I wrote to my sister of our arrival at Winchester Station:

> At once of course we split up into our school cliques – Etonians rather aloof and bored and hands in pockets: the rest alternating between Rugby raucosity and grammar-school timidity. We walked crocodile-wise, Etonians drifting at least 100 yards in the rear, until we arrived at a place which reminded one of Brixton ... We were herded to our quarters, the basement of a morgue, with rows of beds constructed of steel bars, many vertical, and a few bent horizontal and arranged neatly so that the bars coincided with one's hips and chest and the gaps with one's head and waist ...

A week or two later I was writing to my father:

> The routine is as intense as expected: non-stop from 6.30 to 6 and very often extra fatigue after that. But there is barely time to stay depressed, and the evenings are made happy by the mere fact that we can get outside the barrack gates. We are all mixed up with the conscripts – men of 35–40 – better than younger ones who would be more aggressively hostile to us future (we hope) officers. But these are bad enough. They fuss around swearing (*always* the same drab monosyllable) spitting and interfering with everyone else with hoarse belches of amusement. The sergeants are wonderful men, who give us hell on the parade ground call us such names that make us laugh and wonder at the power to conceive such obscenities. Off duty they do quite a lot to help us.

What I remember now about the Rifle Brigade Depot at Winchester is the strange mixture of bonhomie and misery – the former mostly to do with the drinking of beer and the bandying of insults; the latter often to do with my stammer. We potential officers would be taken

out of our squad one by one on the parade ground and made responsible
for the drilling: it sometimes seemed that I, standing with my mouth
open like an Aunt Sally at a fairground, might unwittingly become
like the Emperor Christophe of Haiti who used for his amusement
to march his crack troops over a cliff. However once when my squad
was proceeding at the fast trot that was the customary style in the
Rifle Brigade straight towards the doorway that led from the parade
ground into the NAAFI canteen I thought I might after all take some
advantage of my odd situation: I relaxed: my squad were half way
in towards cups of tea before the sergeant-instructor beside me started
bellowing – About Turn! Left Turn! Right Turn! Knees Up! At The
Double! and so on. The insults that the sergeants were so proficient
at hurling at us pleased us, I suppose, because as at school we wanted
to laugh but ecstatically could not: there was a friend of mine called
Pollock who became something of the platoon butt; the sergeant would
stand very close to him and yell – 'Pollock! Spell it with a P do you?
You sack of shit!'

From Winchester we moved on, in our ex-public school *bloc*, to
Tidworth on Salisbury Plain; then on to an Officer Cadet Training
Unit in the outskirts of York. At each new place there were forms
to be filled up which included questions about 'father' and 'next of
kin'. There was the weird feeling of ground being apt to fall away
as I wrote 'Oswald Mosley, Holloway Prison, London N7'.

I wrote to Diana:

I do hope that Daddy and you will find life more bearable now
that you are together. I am longing to come and see you and will
do so at the first opportunity. Are you allowed to cook? I pity any
poor third person who has to listen to you talking about food all
day like Viv and I had to at Wootton. Although I am actually
sympathising more and more with this.

To my father I wrote:

I will visit you as soon as they let us animals out of the zoo. Till
then I am sure you are having a much happier and more comfortable
time than me, which is peeving. I wonder if I might get arrested?

Into these letters of mine to my father there returned, at intervals, the
phrases to do with the rhetoric of contempt. At Winchester there were
the men whose 'humour is the humour of the over-sexed schoolgirl

and their habits the habits of verminous bluebottles'. At York – 'It is unfortunate that even the OCTU is capable of procuring little else than these baboons, several diseased debauchees, and many pleasant nonentities.' My letters continued – as the one after my trip to Balliol the year before – from time to time to sound fearfully like an article in my father's old newspaper *Blackshirt*: I still hoped, I suppose, thus to show solidarity with him. I was however (or so I boasted) reported by those responsible for my training to be 'a popular and successful leader' and 'an excellent cadet'. It seems to me now that what was going on was an example of the way in which humans do indeed get carried away by words in their needs for defence or attack: the fact that they hardly see themselves doing this (and only with such difficulty learn!) is one of the tragedies (not excuses) described in this book.

I wrote to my sister of my 'idle pansy pose' with which I was apt to 'baffle people' because alongside it I had, for instance, just won some regimental athletic contest. This attitude was a more conventinal one for ex-public schoolboys to adopt when faced with the problems of dealing with an alien world. From the OCTU at York I wrote to my father:

The training thank God has become more interesting, and we play around with theories of defence and attack for armoured divisions rather than with our drab rifles and Bren guns. The officer, too, is charming; and one can afford to be rude to the sergeant, a flea of a man, with a certain impunity. The physical exertion demanded is extreme: we frequently do 10 miles across country with packs, rifles, equipment, etc. in under 2 hrs, which is heavy going.

We have now finished our mechanical course from which I passed as a 1st class driver mechanic which is really very bogus and was granted only through systematic flattery of the instructor; also our wireless course, which was not so successful, as I was rather over-confident and spent most of the time listening to the BBC and trying to wreck wireless schemes by sending out false messages which displeased people and I am afraid I got rather a low mark.

But we are embarking on the most important part of our training now – endless tactics and toughening courses; horrible 5-day man-oeuvres in Northumberland sleeping open-air with one blanket and being harassed by live ammunition and artillery barrages. Then on December 18th we pass out, complete with natty suiting and prominent chest, and are allowed to show off to families for a week

or two. I will come and see you just before Christmas. Love to
Diana.

The world outside went on in what seemed to be its own senseless
way; few of my father's prognostications about the reasonable behaviour of men in war had turned out to be true. Hitler had not tried
to destroy the British army at Dunkirk; he had chosen not to try
to invade England when it was the only country left facing him; then
in 1941 he had turned his back and invaded Russia, thus putting himself
in the one position that he had declared previously would be disastrous –
that of having to fight a war on two fronts. My father's arguments
for not standing out against Hitler in 1938 and 1939 had been based
on the supposition that Hitler was not mad: now Hitler seemed to
be aiming at some grandiose self-destruction. However the British did
not seem to be adopting any very rational attitude to the war themselves:
we were now fighting side by side with Russians with whom we had
considered declaring war on two years before; it did not seem likely
that even after victory the Russians would help us to carry out what
were our stated war aims – to do with the providing of a decent and
independent life for people in Eastern Europe.

   During 1941 and 1942 my sister Vivien and I during holidays or
periods of leave (my sister, after a time of working as a nurse and
in a mobile canteen, settled for doing war-work as a machine-tool
operator in a factory making nuts and bolts for armaments just off
Curzon Street) found our lives now revolving around the London world
inhabited by my Aunt Irene. Irene's house on the edge of Regent's
Park had been bombed; she moved in 1941 to the Dorchester Hotel,
where she stayed on and off for the rest of the war. The Dorchester
Hotel had become a rallying-place for many of the influential and once-
beautiful people of the kind who had used to gravitate around my
father and mother; they were now in the entourage of the people who
were running, or were letting run, the war. Irene spent much of her
time doing relief work in the air-raid shelters of London's East End
('under the LMS railway was sheer animal life in all its nakedness and
horror'): then –*

   when I went back as I sometimes did to the Dorchester Hotel to
   get away from the filth, fear and hideous suffering, and to get a
   quiet night and bath, it always seemed a grotesque contrast to see

* *In Many Rhythms.*

a whole roomful of well-known men and women dining and supping in evening dress whilst the nerve-racking detonations went on all the time and the Hyde Park barrage shook our very foundations ... The air-raid shelter in the Dorchester, which Lord and Lady Halifax showed me with Mr and Mrs Maisky [the Russian Ambassador and his wife] with rows of chairs with their occupants' names, made me feel I would be happier with my gallant East Enders.

In London on a weekend leave, I myself was sometimes given what had once been a servant's room at the top and back of the Dorchester Hotel; I would drift between here and where my sister shared rooms at the top of the Park Lane Hotel with two other girls working in her factory. Irene described how the American Presidential Candidate Wendell Wilkie came to dinner at the Dorchester and was 'violently critical' of women 'in furs and jewels': he said he 'could not make them out, as if the war were not on'. Passing through, I did not see anything so very odd in this: was it not what I had always imagined of the grown-up world? And, since it was quite likely that one might soon die, might one not take advantage of whatever the grown-up world had to offer?

One of the only good (but it seems to me truly good) side-effects of war is that it breaks down some of the social conventions which in normal times are to do with the power of money and it gives genuine social prestige to people who are about to go and risk themselves in battle. In London at this time to be in the uniform of a front-line infantry regiment meant that – however young – one got things like – well – the best tables in the best restaurants. Some money of course was needed but not much: there had been imposed, as if miraculously, limits on things like the cost of meals. So when one was not frozen on manoeuvres in Northumberland or beleaguered in raucous barrack-rooms one could be – as soldiers are apt to be – on the town. Even behaviour that is absurd is smiled upon in wartime: society can be generous to its sacrificial victims.

The peculiar circumstances in which my sister Vivien and I found ourselves – with no family home and our parent in jail – meant that we had surrounded ourselves each with a surrogate family-circle of friends; these would come together at moments when I and my friends were on leave (Viv worked a ten-hour day on weekdays and seven hours on Saturdays). We formed a self-professed 'gang' or 'clique': we enjoyed the oddities of what was offered by war-time London. There was a fashionable (but not too fashionable) night-club of the time called The Nut House: here presided the comedian Al Burnett: habitués would squeeze into a cellar and would become stupefied and at home while Al Burnett sang songs like *The Sheik of Araby* (the required response was – 'With no pants on!'); there was a song which began 'Bell bottom trousers coats of navy blue' and we would intone the mysteriously significant antiphon – 'He'll climb the rigging like his father used to do.' There were girls called hostesses who would come and sit at our table when my friends and I were on our own; but they were only there, they would explain laboriously, to encourage us to order champagne. This suited me, who was still obviously, from Eton and after, massively mixed up about sex. The style of going 'on the town' seemed to most of us still to do with elaborations of the games we had learnt in childhood: there were ritualistic drinking games to see who would or who would not pass out; races round Berkeley Square; waltzing on empty bandstands. Once we got hold of a boat on the Serpentine and sank with it gallantly at midnight.

I had one rare Etonian friend however who was normally and aggressively sexual: he was determined – I think this was during our last holiday from Eton – to do what young men sooner or later traditionally are supposed to do – which is to pick up a tart. It was assumed that I was to be his companion in this; I was flattered rather than enthused. I had been somewhat emboldened recently, however, by the proprietress of The Nut House – a middle-aged lady who had told me, inevitably, that she had known my father – asking me also, did I know how like him I was? My friend and I set off once more for The Nut House. The hostesses explained as usual that they could not help us; however the doorman might. While we waited for the doorman to summon a taxi with two tarts in it I remembered how my father had told me many years ago when he had given me his pre-school talk about sex – If you ever want a woman, don't pick up just anyone, come to me. I had thought this uncommonly nice of him – though always unlikely, in the event, to be practical. The taxi arrived. My friend and I piled in. In the black-out, but unerringly, my friend got hold of the one of the tarts who turned out later to be quite pretty: I had got someone who, as we struck matches to light cigarettes, seemed to have the appearance of my grandmother. The taxi took us to one room where there was a bed and a sofa: my friend settled quite at home on the sofa; Granny and I got nowhere on the bed. I remember her playing with me a variation of 'This little piggy went to market': if I had been feeling witty I might have riposted – 'It looks more as if this little piggy's staying at home'. But one of the morals of this story was –

it was my friend, and not I, who had to worry about the clap.

When a year or so later I turned up in the hall of the Dorchester Hotel – 'looking grand' my Aunt Irene said 'in his new officer's uniform' – I was about to be put in charge of men to train them for, and then lead them in, matters of life and death. I was aged nineteen. For Christmas that year the family went off to our Aunt Baba's house in Gloucestershire. There, on the evening of Christmas Day, we were joined by some of our gang of friends and we played our games – word games, acting games, paper games, hiding-and-catching games. Irene reported – 'Viv and Nick were furious because at midnight Baba rushed down and stopped them dancing a ballet to Tannhäuser.'

CHAPTER 22

Conversations in Holloway

Some time after I had joined the army my father seems to have felt that although (or because?) he had no more responsibility for me in matters of guardianship, he might yet become some sort of mentor to me in intellectual affairs: he had few outlets for his restless energy in prison: I think also he liked to feel that he was in some sort of liaison with me as I went off to war.

He wrote to me from Holloway:

11th January 1943
Darling Nick. I am so glad to get your letter: the blankets, I heard, will be being supplied by family. Have you got a 'flea-bag?' – the only comfort in the last war. I nearly got one for prison and will send you one if you like. It is a jumble of blankets stitched together like a sack: once inside – Nirvana! You will anyhow have a chance to read at your new place – would you like me to send you some moderns – simply selected for Prose Style? I have here for instance an odd job lot such as Trevelyan and Heard – former on Hellenism and the latter on what N S & N [*New Statesman and Nation*] calls 'Back to Mumbo-Jumbo' – you should take in the latter journal – 'Cissy's Weekly' as we always call it – to be diverted by a prettily precious intellectualism. It is very well done from its standpoint. Both T and H are good exponents of a limpid modern style. Ditto Ross Williamson in *AD 33* – Christianity extolled and churches assailed: to signalise publication he has just been ordained! He was here the other day and promised to do anything he could to help you in early literary efforts. Then I have the other Williamson, Henry, also a friend of mine as you will see from beginning [Henry Williamson had dedicated his *The Story of a Norfolk Farm* to my

father]. He is much the best seller of the lot. But I do not advise following his style, which is idiosyncratic – something of Lawrence who
was his great friend. Have you ever looked at the latter's *Seven Pillars
of Wisdom?* Will send you Lytton Strachey's *Books and Characters* if you
have not got it; he is really the father of contemporary style – you will
enjoy him – also J. B. Stephens' *Crock of Gold* if you have not read it – I
guess you would particularly like this from what you said you were
reading when here. It made a great impression on me when I first read
it and again later. You should of course read the classics, Gibbon and
Macaulay – *not* in order to write like them but to absorb a sense of
rhythm and thought-sequence – just gymnasium work – one does not
do the exercises in the street but walks better down the street for
having done them. Liddell Hart and Fuller are both good stylists and
write on your job: I can send them also if you like. I loved D'Annunzio
at your stage – in pessimistic romantic vein – but am not sure he would
be good for you! He is translated into beautiful English. My favourite
work at *this* stage is Simon's (André, not St) 'Soups, Salads and Sauces'
– wartime fare for the fastidious.

My father had said that he had selected these books for their prose style;
however half the contemporary authors he mentioned were friends or
acquaintances who admired him or who had worked with him at some
time; he would not have seen anything odd in this. He did manage to
send to me many of these books. I had been posted to the Rifle Brigade's
Holding Battalion at Retford, in Nottinghamshire. I wrote to him:

We stay here for three months anyway, and then the first batch are
sent abroad. I don't really mind whether I stay or go very much. The
great hope is to get out to Africa just as everything is clearing up
there. I think I would be good at reorganising Arabs. But I shall want
a little fighting to impress my grandchildren if nothing else.

Because I was now an officer and thus considered fit to be responsible
for the lives of men in battle, my father asked the authorities if, when I
visited Holloway, I might be allowed to spend the whole day with him
and Diana in their room in the Preventive Detention Block rather than
just the regulation short time in one of the visiting rooms. This application was granted. This was the beginning of my close relationship with
my father. The circumstances were propitious: it was as if we were
outside normal categories of space and time: we were like revolu-
tionaries meeting to discuss our plans for the world in Siberia.

February 1943, Holloway.

Darling Nick,

The Governor has been so good as to apply for you to lunch over here and now awaits the reply: if affirmative, Sunday would be the perfect day ... Trevelyan book on *Hellenism*, such are the pitfalls of my writing [I had mis-read 'Hellenism' as 'Hitlerism'.] Heard was a very good semi-popular writer of philosophic-scientific stuff and was used for this every week in *Action* when Harold Nicolson was editor. Sachy [Sitwell]'s *All Summer in a Day* I would recommend – one of the best titles I think – next to old Watts Dunton's *Revival of Wonder*. Also of course Sachy on Baroque: he is, perhaps, the most gifted of the S trio; but for purposes of forming style try Osbert – either of them you would find enchanting as guides to literature. I was going to suggest Virginia Woolf, whom you have found already; also, in something of the same category, David Garnett and E. M. Forster. How strange and interesting about *Crock of Gold* [I had known and loved this since childhood] – a great favourite with Mummy too. And what about English poetry? I will try to get together a mixed collection for you. Have you read Shaw's *The Perfect Wagnerite*?

February 10th 1943 Ranby Camp. Retford. Notts.

Darling Daddy,

Wonderful news that I will be able to stay for lunch and sample the choice vegetables and gourmet dishes ... I am beginning to enjoy the duties of officering a little bit more now that I know the men in my platoon and can take an interest in them as human beings rather than as particles of a military machine. I don't think I shall ever like the work – perhaps I am too lazy or perhaps because it seems such an appalling waste of time for everyone; but I get on well enough with the men and we manage to have quite a merry time whenever circumstances permit. Since I last wrote I have sampled E. M. Forster (*A Room with a View*) and found him very entertaining; together with Maurice Baring, Aldous Huxley, and still more Virginia Woolf who never ceases to please. Of poetry I am disgracefully ignorant. I went through the stage of Swinburne-worship while I was at Eton, but I suppose I want something more than that now and the truth is I have found nothing to take its place. Keats, Shelley – the old worthies – mean very little. I think perhaps Milton is the man for me.

I was first allowed to spend the day with my father and Diana in Holloway on February 21st 1943. I got off the bus in the Caledonian

Road and turned up a side road towards the prison: there were huge gates like the porter's lodge of an Oxford college. My credentials were checked; there was a clanking of keys; a slow walk beneath high walls across cobbled courtyards. This first time I did not know what to expect; later, I would prepare for these visits and would smuggle in under my huge army overcoat – worn even at the height of summer – food (one could still buy odd luxuries at Fortnum and Mason), drink (a bottle of brandy or champagne), gramophone records (Kirsten Flagstad singing Isolde), books (the second volume of Spengler's *The Decline of the West* which no one else had been able to find for my father and which with much pride I had hunted down in the Charing Cross Road). The wardress would lead me to a door in a high inner wall; the scene was like an illustration to some fairy story gone damp and burnt at the edges. Beyond the wall my father would be waiting. We went past his kitchen garden of which we had heard so much – on a piece of ground like a railway embankment he was growing aubergines and *fraises-de-bois* as well as cabbages and onions – up an echoing stone staircase in a building like a deserted cotton mill to the room where he and Diana lived. This was high and austere and dingy and yet contained bits of Diana's furniture which gave it an elegance like that of some provincial museum for shells: there was Diana's old gramophone with its enormous horn that had contained tiny sounds like those of the sea. My father and Diana seemed trapped by a sort of ring of dampened fire: within, there was as there usually was with them some demonstration of order and light.

The days that I spent in Holloway were always days of celebration: for my father and Diana, I suppose, they were breaks in the monotony of their lives; for myself they were times cut off from the crazed projections of the outside world. Diana would prepare one of her legendary dishes from, later, my father's legendary vegetables: I would produce my tinned ham or my bottle of champagne; on the gramophone there might be the *Liebestod* or *The Entry of the Gods into Valhalla*. Afterwards my father and I would go out into the garden to talk. Of course I myself may have made something of a legend about all this: but this was what it seemed like – we were conspirators believing that we might alter the world: shadows coming together beneath high walls with spikes on top like crowns of thorns.

March 14th Ranby Camp. Retford. Notts.
Darling Daddy,
I am at the moment most violently in the throes of Ross Williamsonism.

You remember that book of his that you sent me – *A.D. 33*? He answers the perpetual question of how to reconcile God-all-good with God-all-powerful by the simple assumption that God is not good (in our sense of the word) to everyone, which is a far more satisfactory answer than 'God is not all powerful': it is easier to have faith in a capricious God than in a weak god continually harassed by the sharp tail of a powerful Devil. And equally logically he shows that all our worldly conventional standards of good and evil are entirely contradicted by Jesus's (and God's) standards of good and evil (a conclusion to which one might come, I think, merely by a glance at the horrors of worldly conventions). The only thing which leaves me rather doubtful is the way in which he accepts Humility as a cardinal and essential virtue. Perhaps I have the wrong conception of humility but I do not see how he reconciles it with his horror of any signs of passive indifference. Can one be actively, vitally, and effectively humble? Humble towards God, yes: as he says, if you recognise yourself to be one of God's elect your gratitude and devotion to him will take the form of humility; but surely the doctrine of Humility implies it as a general form of behaviour toward one's fellow men; and as one's fellow men are 90% the dull indifferent baboons whom R. W. detests, what place has Humility in his relations with them? But perhaps I have got the wrong end of the stick.

I don't know why I am bubbling on like this; it will do me good to put on paper some of these ideas which seem to me so momentous; I expect they will all seem very commonplace to you.

I am known amongst my men as 'Mad Mr Mosley' which I take to be a well-merited compliment but I feel it would be frowned on by authority. I feel I am a very bad soldier, but I am able by my wits to keep pace with the dimly serious militarists who seem to haunt this morgue. But there are times when circumstances are too much for me, and I weep for the waste of it all.

Give my love to Diana. I sometimes very seriously wish I could be with you in Holloway, to sit and read and listen to Wagner on the gram and sample the excellence of Diana's cooking. I know I should find it more congenial than army life. And I could learn more from you than from all the books I have time to read now.

25th March 1943 Holloway
Darling Nick,

I was so glad to hear that you liked the books. R. W. says he would like to see you some time when you are in London. His theme, which you mention, has something of Spinoza – 'Because you love God, you have no reason to demand that God should love you'. He might have added – 'Particularly when we compare the attributes usually ascribed to God with those which we can observe in mankind'. But the idea of a God who likes and dislikes – however well founded on some cases – does not seem entirely to answer the old 'God-all-good and God-all-powerful dilemma': for clearly the buffets of fate are directed not only at the nasty but also at the very highest types – not only the tragic romantic of Byron vintage but also real and obvious good men – saints and martyrs etc. In fact it may also be said that not only the capacity for suffering but also the experience of suffering often culminate in some of the finest types the world has seen. Unless therefore the God standard deviates entirely from anything we can conceive it would appear that an all-powerful God afflicts these because he capriciously dislikes them. We are therefore driven back towards a conception of suffering – of all the phenomena which are shortly called evil in the experience of man – as fulfilling some creative purpose in the design of existence: back in fact to the Faustian Riddle, usually stated with the utmost complexity but for once with curious crudity in the 'Prologue in Heaven' [in Goethe's *Faust*] when The Lord says to Mephistopheles – 'The activity of man can all. too lightly slumber; therefore I give him a companion who stimulates and works and must, as Devil, create'. *Faust* is meant to cover the whole panorama of human experience; but I believe this to be, on the whole the main thesis of all its innumerable pro-fundities. Many commentators would disagree; and, as more books have been written about it than any play in the world except Hamlet, we had better leave it there for the moment!

But Goethe does not attempt to answer, within my knowledge, the still underlying question – 'Why then the agonising process of creation at all?' Why did not perfect and powerful God forthwith create perfect beings without the long process of evolution lashed forward by suffering? To that I know no adequate answer in any of the philosophies or religions of the world: here we approach the mysteries. It is a sobering thought that the foremost minds of mankind have striven with these things for 3,000 years and that the greatest among them have admitted to mysteries which cannot be pierced: many, like the Greeks and German neo-Hellenists, even go so far as to say it is fatal to attempt to do so. Can one say more than that the dominant phenomenon of life as we see it is the organic processes of nature – beginning with such small and crude material and working under the impulse of struggle and suffering to every higher form and beauty – 'recurrently' perhaps but also 'spirally'. Here, as so often, the poets and prophets (I mean the real ones!) serve us better than the philosophers. Can we go much further than Schiller in *Die Künstler* with the lines which he repeated in the moment of his death – 'That which on earth appeared to me as Beauty will meet me on the other side as Truth.' The consideration is also often present in my mind that the purpose of existence might well be frustrated through a complete solution of the mystery of life by mankind: we are plainly here to live this life: how much interest would the purposes of this life retain if we saw the whole purpose? Nietzsche, here at any rate, plays his part in his triumphant affirmation of this life and his furious denunciation of the flight from it.

I am sending you under a separate cover a commentary on his doctrine by a Cambridge don [A. H. J. Knight] who sets out much of it quite well but is so opposed to him that he finally produces a feeble travesty of what N meant which is refuted by quotations kindly supplied in his own book. Oh these dons and commentators! the depths of their intellectual dishonesty are unfathomable! But let them by all means direct you to great subjects with the vast store of their erudition. But then always go to the original – in the end even genius should be allowed to speak for itself! I pondered long before sending you any Nietzsche, but think you now are intellectually strong enough to take it. The real thing is not to swallow him whole but *to see him in relation to the whole*. To be lightly repelled by the unbridled violence of his mind and exposition is as great an error as to become obsessed by the power of it – as many have been.

In Christianity you have the thesis: in Nietzsche the antithesis. There remains synthesis, eternal synthesis, which is the task and hallmark of all supreme minds. I mean not merely the narrower terms of the Hegelian dialectic which you should one day study – thesis, antithesis, synthesis – the statement of the idea, its refutation by its opposite, the synthesis of both which approaches truth – but the wide clashes of the great spiritual movements whose fiery collisions can fuse into a higher unity. You might attempt the Christian – Nietzsche synthesis one day, and would be helped in the attempt by the 'child' of the third metamorphosis – 'Unschuld ist das Kind und Vergessen, ein Neubeginnen, ein Spiel, ein aus sich rollendes Rad, eine erste Bewegung, ein heiliges Ja-sagen. Ja, zum Spiele des

Schaffens, meine Brüder, bedarf es eines heiligen Ja-sagens: *seinen* Willen will nun der Geist, *seine* Welt gewinnt sich der Weltverlorene'. ['The child is innocence and forgetfulness, a new beginning, a sport, a self-propelling wheel, a first motion, a sacred Yes. Yes, a sacred Yes is needed, my brothers, for the sport of creation: the spirit now wills *its own* will, the spirit sundered from the world now wins *its own* world']. Perhaps not so remote as N thought from a conception of Christ which, however, is not quite accepted by the churches! You will find a vehement reflection of some of your feelings on humility in his 'trans-valuation of values': pride is among his cardinal virtues: though here again, was Christ humble? Not with the money-changers in the temple at any rate; though the feet-washing etc would seem to indicate the con-trary. In genius, or the inspired, or whatever we call it, superficial con-tradictions however so often cover an underlying unity. Is this seeming contradiction more than an inspired extension of the old Roman 'Parcere subjectis; debellare superbos' [Spare the humbled; make war on the proud] carried to the extent of an overwhelming pity and tenderness towards the poor and afflicted, compared with an arrogant combativeness towards the corruptly affluent? Synthesis, ever synthesis!

There was a day in April when I went to visit my father and I had a bottle of brandy amongst other offerings festooned beneath my greatcoat; we sat late around the table where we had had lunch – talking of Nietzsche, I suppose: about the problem of pity possibly being a mechanism by which nothing might be allowed to change; might not arrogance then in some way be a love because thus humanity might evolve? We were getting no doubt towards the end of the bottle of brandy; there was the sound of footsteps coming up the echoing stairs. We listened; we were in gaol after all; like schoolboys, we hid our glasses and the bottle beneath the table. There was a knock on the door. My father said, 'Who is it?' A voice said, 'The Governor.' My father said, 'Oh, do come in!' The Governor was a pleasant, sandy-haired man: he said that he had come to tell me that I had long over-stayed the time allowed for my visit; but he had not come to complain, he had just come to tell me how now to get out of the prison. My father said, 'I wonder if you would like a glass of brandy?' He produced the bottle from under the table. The Governor said, 'Ah, you don't often see brandy like this nowadays!' And so we all had some celebra-tion – perhaps, as my father might have said, some synthesis; perhaps even a move towards the metamorphosis of the child.

I remember going back after this day in Holloway (I was smuggled out through a side gate by a smiling wardress) all the way on foot through blacked-out streets to the Dorchester Hotel: I had made some plan to meet my sister and a friend there and go to a play. I was hours late: I had missed the play: I did not mind. I was pulled along on some tightrope as if by strings from the sky. I was thinking of all that my father had said – about Nietzsche's theory of Eternal Recurrence, perhaps, by which Nietzsche seemed to be throwing down a challenge to life by saying that one should be brave enough to live every moment as if one knew it might endlessly recur (had my father got this right? might he not think Nietzsche was talking about a fact rather than a state of mind?); or about the way in which Nietzsche distinguished between what he called master-morality and slave-morality – which distinction was not a technique for domination (was it?) but rather a means of assuring that each person could choose only such freedom as he was able to bear. I was thinking also of the jokes, the laughter – the story my father had told in his best Mitford-copying voice about the time when the compost heap that he had so lovingly prepared in his garden had been cleared away and he had overheard Diana crying out to the wardress – 'But it was the *breath of life* to Sir Oswald!' I was being pulled along by all this – and by the question: does not the ridiculousness of things become not ridiculous by the virtue of your knowing it? – so that when eventually I arrived at the Dorchester Hotel and found that my sister and our friend had waited for me and had missed the play (*Hedda Gabler* of all things!) and were understandably annoyed (they had been anxious about me and had even thought of ringing up the police to ask – Is he still in prison?) I remember walking away across Park Lane and sitting on the plinth of the enormous statue of a naked man with a drawn sword and a shield raised to the sky. My Aunt Irene, also at the hotel, recorded – 'I suddenly saw Nick on the edge of tears.' I wondered beneath my statue – What does one do with all these images that come down like bombs, like lightning flashes, like doves or manna from heaven?

May 29th Ranby Camp. Retford. Notts.
Darling Daddy,
I do not see that Eternal Recurrence is incompatible with the Superman theory so long as the circle begins to recur only after the Superman stage has been reached: the Superman stands at the summit of each circle and the Superman himself is endlessly repeated: this has nothing to do with Goethe's spiral, which is altogether a smaller

and more limited thing in time. If one accepts Nietzsche's contention (I don't see why one should) that time is endless and energy is limited, I suppose some theory of Recurrence must follow naturally.

I really have no opinion here. I see everything as a possibility, and have not the conviction to decide what is a Truth and what is Right. I do not see how one can ever have this conviction, and even if one has it, why one should presume that one's convictions are right. My reason tells me what theories are the most possible, the most likely, the most desirable; but it needs more than Reason to put any theory across; it needs a great Faith. And my Reason tells me that it is dangerous to trust in Faith, for how does one know that one's Faith is Right? And so I am stuck; and am likely to remain so, I feel, until I am old and wise enough to have Faith in my Reason.

Nietzsche's contention that the Übermensch [Superman] is 'beyond good and evil' is of far deeper significance than 'above morality'. To be above morality is merely to be sufficiently civilised to be able to do without a conventional code of behaviour to control one's filthy impulses: to be 'beyond good and evil' I think implies that one does not recognise good and evil as such, but one does have values (both ethical and religious) that are based on entirely different standards.

With Nietzsche's values I have very little sympathy: 'Heiterkeit' [serenity] – yes, that is perhaps the most desirable quality that any mortal can possess. But 'Härte' [hardness] – why always the emphasis on domination and power through 'Härte'? With the principles of Herrenmoral [mastermorality] I agree entirely – duties towards one's equals; a belief that 'what is harmful to me is harmful in itself etc' – but is it necessary for the Herrenmoral to take Härte as its primary value? There is no beauty, and I would say very little nobility, in Härte.

I am just back from the most perfect fortnight spent camping out with my platoon in Derbyshire. We wandered through many of the old haunts – the upper reaches of Dovedale and the valley of the Wye; we spent two nights in a lovely valley called Ravensdale, which was fascinating, and once we passed close to Wootton but I was afraid that the sight of it again would make me sad, and so we swept past. Now the boredom of barrack routine has set in again.

I have become involved in a correspondence upon the Church with Aunty Irene. One of her East End priests to whom she sent on my letters wrote me the most half-witted reply; I really do believe that these men do not understand what they say: which perhaps is best, for it is happier for them to be charged with ignorance and stupidity than with gross perversion and distortion.

I wish I could talk with more energy and conviction when I come to visit you. I think you stuff me so heavily with delicious food, and drench me so plentifully with great flagons of Bristol Milk, that it is all I can do to hold myself together. I do enjoy those visits so very much, and I learn more and am more stimulated in those few hours with you than I would ever be in a lifetime with any of my pseudo-intellectual friends. We (my friends and I) do have the most fiercely profound arguments, but I always feel that they are somehow entirely irrelevant. So I yearn for more conversation à la Holloway.

1st June Holloway Prison.
Darling Nick,

I was delighted by your letter – in fact I turned to the Percheron and said 'It is odd, the lad really is brilliant!' She observed that she did not see why it was odd: and there, as Beachcomber says, the matter rests at present. I will write you at greater length later – unless, by any luck, you come here in the interval: but herewith a few preliminary grunts.

I agree that one of the prime needs of the world today is a Faith in the shadowy realms of metaphysics which can be believed by the modern and educated mind: further agree that it is impossible for finite reason to elucidate all the mysteries; but I come more and more to the conclusion that it would be possible to formulate a Faith (now largely felt but inarticulate) which draws the spiritual in life from the best of the thought, creeds and civilisations that the world has so far produced; weaves it into a coherent whole of conduct and attitude to human existence, and attunes it to the main tendencies of modern science which, in turn, can defend its novelties from the usual reception of new ideas by a hard analysis of those motives in human conduct and belief that have preceded it. As I am probably too old, and in these circumstances anyhow in no fit state to undertake anything of the kind, you had better get busy!

Incidentally and disjointedly there is all too much Härte in nature and in all evidential 'Purpose' in life: the problem of the extent to which this 'Härte' can or should be modified or sublimated in higher developments of communal organisation is one of the profoundest of all – we want to fulfil and not to frustrate the Purpose as revealed in nature, but in ever higher forms. I am glad you don't swallow

N whole; but, re Härte, the old boy would probably reply – 'No beauty nor nobility in Härte, agreed: but what have men (majority) done to Beauty and Nobility – destroyed the one and persecuted the other. What then is the answer of the emerging Übermensch to this situation except Härte?'

One must always remember that to the lonely N the higher men appeared almost as a persecuted sect struggling for survival. I always found his attitude to Mitleid [pity] repulsive: but believe that 'compassion' will come again in a higher form one day when the higher men are not underneath but on top. How in fact can they express their destiny except through the constructive equivalent of pity – which is a high design to lift mankind? That is the will to achievement which is as far beyond N's will to power – isolated self-development and self-assertion – as his Will to Power is beyond the Will to Comfort – disguised as self-sacrifice by those who cannot achieve. I sometimes think that my initial error which lasted too long was the belief that reason and goodwill were enough – Love is still the end, I believe, but, in the world as it is, Love is not enough – so perhaps I should say with Swinburne – 'I have lived long enough having seen one thing that love hath an end'. You are right, I think, that N really means 'Beyond Morality' rather than 'Beyond Good and Evil' – eg he would say that Pride as evil and Humility as good should be reversed; but that is really a moral question; he would not say he was in favour of cancer, where we really enter the realm of evil – natural catastrophe which is not man-made. But as you say, in Divine Purpose – what of the phrases Good and Evil? What is the place of the latter in the scheme of things? I should think it can be discerned – Goethe had a glimmer – but it can be taken much further: it is the basic problem before which all churches have relapsed into the childish. The natural non-man-made-horror – that is the fundamental question. Every Greek tragedy was largely man-made for all their passion for life – quarrelling and murdering each other about matters of small consequence in any world ruled by reason and beauty. But when man has done his worst, remain the things that God has done. Why? The riddle of existence. Some reply should be attempted.

Love Daddy.

CHAPTER 23

'Any Relation – ?'

With myself in the army and my father in prison I continued to want to strike some attitudes as if with him against the world. I wrote to him that I had found hitherto 'no true kindred spirit with whom either to disregard or to shock this pallid society'. He seemed to become this kindred spirit.

Surrounding my growing relationship with my father was my day-to-day life in the army. I began to keep a diary of this: in the diary is shown something of the obverse side to what was arrogant – of the language of contempt perhaps being turned back against oneself. I wrote fairly often of my stammer: a stammer is the indeed often ludicrous outward sign of an inward contradiction; it is as if the sufferer were half conscious of having swallowed paradoxes as if they were some snake. I wrote at this time (of course there is nothing less conducive to sympathy than self-pity) – 'How despairing I am become! my thoughts are all of death this week: it is all due to stammer: I cannot remember it so bad. It is obvious I have no idea where it comes from, and no control over it whatsoever.'

I had got fairly used to the yelling out of orders; but as an officer in charge of a platoon I also had now to give lectures – on subjects such as Chemical Warfare or Current Affairs. I would find myself once more on a platform like a scaffold; my sergeant would shout for silence; amongst the thirty or so assembled men there would be an air of appalled expectancy. After a time in which nothing much happened one or two of the more sensitive of my audience began to roll about in the aisles: how well I myself remembered this! – the agonies and ecstasies of half-suppressed laughter. My sergeant would yell – 'Don't laugh at the officer!' There was, I suppose, something healthily inimical to illusions about 'master-morality' in this. Oddly, I think my platoon

did get to know quite a lot about Current Affairs and Chemical Warfare: perhaps people learn when there is the opposite of an imposition
on them.

I am going on about this because in so far as fascism is a subservience,
as I have intimated, to the despotism of words, then the stammerer
is an archetype of that within which the battle of the fascist versus
the anti-fascist is fought. It is not that he renounces the use of words:
he recognises their terrible power by which he himself might be taken
over; yet there is a part fluttering inside him that cannot, or will not,
have this. Stammering is the protection of oneself both from other
people's aggression and from one's own aggression against others; but
then the question of interest is – in what ways might this be or not
be beneficent? If there is something destructive in the take-over power
of words – in the illusion that one can deal with people as if they
were words – then might there not be some efficient virtue in the
rebellion, however tawdry, against this? At Ranby Camp it was a fact
that I did manage to have a good platoon – perhaps simply as a result
of some sympathy. I wrote in my diary: 'Maybe it is true to say that
lack of means of slick expression has made me rely on "charm" and
given me cause to understand – both of which I would not have
cultivated were I let loose among the flurry of words.'

Discipline in the army was conventionally maintained by men being
shouted at by junior officers and NCOs or, for more serious offences,
by these putting a man on what was called 'a charge'. This meant
that the offender came up before the Company Commander who was
a Major or the Battalion Commander who was a Lieutenant-Colonel;
they were empowered to dole out punishments such as loss of pay
or confinement to barracks. I found myself with a deep reluctance ever
to put anyone 'on a charge': all the time I was in the army I think
I did this only once – when I was sharing command of a platoon with
another officer and thus had to go along with convention. For the
rest – it seemed to me that the point of an officer was that he should
be superior to convention – necessarily, perhaps, if he himself from
time to time was apt to find himself marooned in front of his men
like an Aunt Sally. Of course, in this attitude I was protected by the
whole traditional weight of army discipline.

Ranby Camp, Retford, was a lot of huts in flat fields with the officers'
quarters on one side of a road and everything else on the other. I wrote
to my sister: 'In the ranks one was restricted physically by petty regulations and intellectually by the insensitivity of one's comrades; but as
an officer one is up against these two body-belts to just the same degree

and combined with them is the appalling tyranny of etiquette and good manners.' But it is not of this that I now remember very much. I remember the ways in which we were able to get away from the rituals and rigours of the officers' mess into the training schemes, for instance, in the hills and vales of Derbyshire; into the war-games which were extensions of the games of hide-and-seek and 'lions' which we continued to play as grown-up children. My friend and rival platoon commander in this was often Raleigh Trevelyan – who later wrote *The Fortress*, one of the best books about the Second World War. Raleigh and I would set up camps in the Peak District with our platoons on different hills; we would meet to carouse at night, then separate in order at dawn – surprise surprise! – to attack each other with whoops and blank cartridges and things called thunder-flashes. Then we would drive to picnic at some beauty spot: this was called training in embussing and de-bussing.

With regard to what I described to my sister in my niggardly manner as 'the simpering solemnity of this miserable mess' – what I now remember of life in the officers' quarters was the way in which, when we got drunk at night, some of us would congregate in one of the junior officer's rooms which had been turned into a night-club called *The Juke Box*: here we would indulge in some of the fantasies that seem often to be on the periphery of the consciousness of soldiers – among Greeks and Trojans, Shakespeare seems to suggest; apparently among – ah! – the Nazi SA. We would put music on and dance; one or two of us would dress up; we were Narcissi paddling amongst our own murky reflections. How innocent this was! – or is it innocent if soldiers thus manage the dirty business of war?

As Narcissus I tried to explain myself to myself. I wrote in my diary: 'Theory – damn the world if you feel like it: practice – don't be rude to anybody except those who cannot hurt back'. I became obsessed with the matter of what was and what was not hypocrisy. One had to present some façade to the world to stay alive: when one became conscious of doing this, did this or did it not provide a centre from which one could balance the demands of the outside world with what was going on inside?

It seemed to me the worst danger of all was not to be conscious of the predicament – to be taken over, helplessly, by the demands of one or the other of the outside or the inside world. Everyone was engaged on some wheeler-dealing with those around them; they lashed out in the struggle to be on top; they lay down in surrender in order not to be destroyed. But regarding the inside – how seldom people saw what puppets they were: how little they knew of the strings! It was people like this who blindly caused destruction – and were destroyed. A creative sort of arrogance might be a characteristic of those who were conscious of their helplessness; who would thus have a freedom of vision not available to those who were not.

I wrote in my diary – 'I am completely selfish re the myth-picture I have imagined of me: fortunately, one of the virtues of this picture is unselfishness'.

One of the ways by which I tried to escape from a self-reflecting solipsism was through my relationship with my father: he seemed to me an oracle of which I could ask the answers to things; it was with him I shared hopes about finding meanings in the world. I could, by getting drunk with friends, imagine at moments I glimpsed the beatific vision; I also dreamed of some girl with whom one day, hand in hand, I might look down on the maze of common myth-making. But my father seemed to do with what was sober.

Another way of hoping to get some hand-hold on 'reality' was through religion. I was trying to take Christianity seriously: I carried on a correspondence with priests through my aunts Irene and Baba. I could not make any sense of the words of Christianity: it seemed that they made out God to be some fearful kind of moneylender who laid out loans of life and then demanded from humans heavy interest; when humans could not redeem their pledges God then sold his own son as a sacrifice. The priests who wrote to me insisted this imagery was a travesty; then they just seemed to repeat it in different words. So in what manner was it that they heard their words? I began to make up what I thought was my own hugely original religion – in fact obviously influenced by my father. I suggested that there were four stages at which humans could be in their relationship with God (I assumed the existence of God: so did my father). The lowest stage was that in which humans were unaware that such a relationship with God could exist; the next was that in which humans were aware of being in some relationship with the universe but did not know what to do about it (I put myself in this category); the next was that of people who seemed to know what to do even if they could not clearly put this into words (saints and mystics); and the fourth stage was Christ or what might indeed be called God himself – God both found, and made of oneself, as a result of a process. God the Holy Ghost was demonstrated by the fact that humans were able to glimpse all this; they could launch themselves on, even be guided in, this process if they chose. This was some version of what my father came to call his 'doctrine of higher forms'. But within all this there was a recognition of the limitation of words; words were not ultimate; they were tools that could be used, understood, for good or evil.

Such things went on in my mind as we jogged along the road between Retford and Worksop carrying what seemed like half a hundredweight on our backs; as we drank ourselves at night into the imagined company of Erich von Stroheim or Marlene Dietrich. There were always rumours about when, and where, we might be sent abroad: I wrote to my sister: 'One is being made pretty for the slaughter'. But also – 'I want to go abroad because there at least something definite will happen: here one is entirely negative, everything one does is exactly the opposite of what one feels one should do, and what time one has free is spent bolstering energy for further self-repression. Oh dear!'

By the summer of 1943 the war in North Africa had ended; there was the invasion of Sicily; then the start of the long, slow crawl up Italy. There seemed no doubt that the Allies would win the war: the Russians were advancing from Stalingrad; Hitler was beginning to put into effect his plan of taking transport away from his hard-pressed armies and using it to promote the murder of millions of harmless Jews – thus spurring on his own self-destruction. The Allies had just announced their policy of unconditional surrender – thus making things more difficult for themselves by stiffening the resolve of the forces around Hitler. Things did indeed seem to be happening the opposite of the way people intended. For myself – I felt I had to fight; but what on earth was the style in which to fight sensibly?

Some time in August I was sent on embarkation leave; I visited my Aunt Irene and Micky and Nanny in Cornwall. Irene made three comments about me in her diary: 'Nicky is in a curiously aloof and pondering attitude and was shatteringly crude and offensive about Christ'; 'Nicky told me he and his father were now in perfect accord in their outlook'; and 'Nicky owned that he thought his father had gone so wrong in his views that he had had to be arrested'.

I have a strangely luminous vision of my last visit to Holloway: my father and I had gone as usual into the garden to talk; we were by the cabbage patch once more like conspirators beneath the high walls that might have ears. He said – If anything should happen to you (I do not think I can have dreamed this) anything such as if you got stuck, I mean, in a foreign country – then he gave me some sort of password. I have forgotten exactly what – some code-phrase – something about the poplar trees I think at Denham. I was to re-member and if necessary use this code-phrase, if ever one of us were in a position in which the other wanted to get in touch with him secretly. I thought – But the Germans cannot now win the war: so you mean – I might be taken prisoner? It was true I had sometimes wondered about being taken prisoner: how I might spend the rest of the war sensibly reading Goethe, Nietzsche – as if beneath the high walls of Holloway prison. My father had often had a conspiracy view of history. When I said goodbye to him he looked very thin and ill and tired.

One of the last acts I performed before I went abroad was to go with my grandmother on a deputation to the Home Office in order to put to a high-up official a plea for my father's release. My father was truly ill now, his phlebitis was getting worse, doctors had even said that without freedom to exercise he might die. He had been three and a half years in prison; he had been charged with no offence; it was inconceivable in the present state of the war that he could be any threat to security. We said all this in the Home Office; my grandmother did most of the talking. The high-up official sat behind his desk with the tips of his fingers together: he seemed to be listening and yet not really penetrable; like some sort of portcullis. He said – He would take note of our arguments and would pass them on to the Minister. My grandmother said – This is his son going off to war. I thought – Yes, you bugger, I'm going off to war.

I sailed on a troopship with one of my old Etonian friends called Anthony and we went far out into the Atlantic to pick up a convoy and then turned down through the Bay of Biscay; it became very rough and gradually the officers' dining room emptied and I and one or two others were on our own eating mountains of eggs and steaks and oranges because the ship had stocked up recently in South Africa. We did not know where we were going; we looked out vaguely for the Rock of Gibraltar or the Cape of Good Hope. I had arranged my own code with my sister whereby I should be able to get news of our whereabouts past the censors of our air-mail letters. We landed at Philipville in North Africa not far from Algiers: I wrote to my sister (we were both cinema fans) – 'We might be able to visit Jean Gabin or Charles Boyer'. At Philipville we stayed for two months in a tented camp amongst sand-dunes: we bathed, we drank red wine, we played bridge. I wrote to my sister:

Yesterday we played football in a temperature equivalent to the melt-ing point of flesh: ten effete and flabby young officers beat eleven horny old Scotsmen, who have sulked most ungraciously ever since.

To my father I wrote:

> We went out on a little manoeuvre last week and toured round
> in armoured cars miles into the interior. During one scrimmage with
> the 'enemy' I captured an enormous Captain in some rather hush-
> hush job whose face seemed vaguely familiar. Unfortunately I treated
> him with great respect, for it later turned out to be Randolph
> Churchill. If I had known earlier, I would have hurled him into
> a dungeon full of syphilitic Arabs. I am sure he would have enjoyed
> a taste of the Brixton atmosphere.

The attitude of myself and indeed to some extent of my friends towards
the war continued to be enigmatic. Becoming fed up with the hanging
about in Algeria, I and some others volunteered for the Parachute
Regiment; I was told I was too tall and too myopic. Then I was having
renewed fantasies about being taken prisoner – having made my gesture
to dutiful behaviour, I might thus spend the rest of the war profitably
studying and practising writing in a camp. This was again of course
a joke – yet not quite a joke. The war was as good as won after all:
what was the point of being killed in what seemed to be everyone's
long haul towards self-destruction? And part of me still wondered –
what on earth were we doing in a war in which in practical terms
(as my father had so often said) the only real winners in an allied victory
would be America and Russia? Britain would find herself as a second-
rate power without her Empire. I wrote to my sister, 'The whole
business is so obviously absurd: so tremendously ridiculous.'

On 16th November 1943 I was on a boat again to Taranto in the
heel of Italy (my code-phrase for this to my sister was – 'In whose
beginning is the home of Scarlett O'Hara'). The fighting in Italy had
got stuck in the mud and mountains somewhere half way between
Naples and Rome. My friends and myself had been destined as reinforcements for a Rifle Brigade battalion; when we arrived, there was
no Rifle Brigade battalion left in Italy. We were told we were to be
parcelled out as reinforcements to other regiments which were in need
of officers. One of my friends had a brother who was in Army Group
Headquarters; we went to see him and he arranged that we should
be sent to a battalion of the London Irish Rifles which was a 'black-
button' (rifle) regiment, and thus we would be spared what we made
out we saw as the indignity of having to join a 'brass-button' regiment
of the line. This arrangement was to have important consequences for
me: I remained with the 2nd Battalion of the London Irish Rifles for

the rest of the war: I moved out of the somewhat snobbish confines represented even by the Rifle Brigade, and was from now on – at first by chance but later by determined and happy choice – beyond some sort of pale within which I had been brought up.

On my way up to the front line, in a Transit Camp called 3 C R U, I read in the local army newspaper that my father and Diana had been released on health grounds from Holloway Prison; there were enormous crowds in Parliament Square demanding that they should be put back. Headlines continued for days: there was a photograph of a placard saying 'Hang Mosley!'; a re-print of a *Daily Herald* article which declared 'Mosley is not merely a man whom the Government considered potentially dangerous and therefore not fit to be left at large, he was a symbol of the evil against which this country is fighting to the death.' I wrote in my diary: 'O frabjous day calloo callay! God am I glad and relieved! It is now imperative to get home as soon as possible.'

In transit camps, and away from my sophisticated friends of the Rifle Brigade, the name of Mosley suddenly became a difficulty such as I had not known it to be before; people to whom I had to introduce myself, perhaps with some newspaper open on their desks, were apt to say – 'Not any relation of that bastard?' – not imagining that the answer could be Yes. When I would say just 'Yes' (what more does one say?) for the most part my questioners would apologise profusely. Sometimes their embarrassment became so drawn-out that I wondered – Might there not be some style, some look in the eye perhaps, by which for the sake of all concerned one could say Yes without the rigmarole attendant on saying it?

I wrote in my diary:

It seems obvious that I am to make my base with Daddy and Diana after the war. I hope to God Daddy never does anything rash politically again. It is terrible to think how he bungled things earlier – how a wee bit of hypocrisy and political licence would have made all the difference ... They are obviously still very frightened of him. But perhaps after all this screaming is preferable to apathy; he is still a force to be reckoned with in the political world. With a little shrewd propaganda I have no doubt he would be most urgently reckonable. But where is the propaganda to come from? If only he had friends worth tuppence! ... Me?

CHAPTER 24

Another Kind of War

On the 1st of October 1943 my father, from prison, had written to his mother:

> My darling mother,
> You asked me to write to you my views on my physical condition which has worried you and other relations. I need not enlarge on the medical reports which you have in your possession. The condition is ascribed to confinement; and freedom, fresh air and contact with friends is prescribed. On the other hand I understand that the Home Office medical opinion ascribes my state of health more to psychological circumstance than to the physical conditions of my confinement. How phlebitis in the thigh is psychologically produced the text books do not describe. In short, I believe the Home Office views to be not only nonsense but dishonest nonsense. The purpose is perfectly clear and is two-fold: 1. to suggest that nobody could become so ill in their pretty prisons for physical reasons; 2. to suggest that, the condition being psychological rather than physical, it does not matter so much whether I am in prison or outside – in fact, that release is not essential to recovery.
>
> I have some little advantage in this matter having read at least as much psychology as most practitioners in the subject. But in this case, no very specialised knowledge is required to psycho-analyse the psycho-analysts! The medical facts seem to be perfectly plain: 1. I come of country stock which is naturally and severely afflicted by close confinement; 2. I was warned years ago, and correctly, that I had a physique well constituted to endure exceptional strain and fatigue but, conversely, particularly and adversely affected by inactivity. The outward symptoms were slow pulse and the necessity

to take violent exercise such as fencing to ward off diseases of a sluggish bloodstream such as phlebitis. On the other hand, as all my intimates know, psychological matters do not and never have affected me one jot. It is suggested that I feel a great sense of injustice at my imprisonment, and that the necessity to repress this feeling has psychologically and therefore physically affected me. It is true that I think our treatment is a disgraceful and disgusting business but I never worry about something that I can do nothing about. It is further suggested to me that I am oppressed for the time being by the thought of one day having a great public struggle to justify myself, etc. It is incredible that anyone should think I could be worried by anything so remote. Such a struggle cannot, anyhow, arise till after the war. My organisation is banned; I cannot speak as a member of British Union. Therefore, in or out of prison, I will not speak at all. It is further suggested that I may be worried by public opinion concerning me. When have I ever been? Twenty years ago I joined the Labour Party. Since that moment I have never lived a day when some section of the public did not think me a double-dyed villain; sometimes more, sometimes less; all depends on circumstances! No one has ever been more abused than I have been throughout my political life. The only difference is that now I cannot reply. But my reply can keep till after the war: like whisky, it will improve with keeping! I withdraw not a word I have ever uttered, nor ever will, whether I live or die in prison or outside. But I remain silent so long as British Union is banned. That is all the law requires of me, or can require. Let me sum up this pyschological nonsense with a little analogy. If you put a wild animal in a cage of course it affects his health and, before very long, probably kills him. Furthermore, it probably annoys him if people rattle their sticks along the bars of the cage. Once back in his natural jungle, every mandarin in Fleet Street can rattle a bit of iron or a bit of wood till he is blue in the face without that animal suffering any pyschological disturbance whatever.

People closest to my father at this time thought that psychologically he probably did encourage the worsening of his phlebitis – and why should he not? – there was little chance of his being released except on health grounds from the imprisonment in which he was now being kept largely for reasons of spite. He passionately wanted to get out; he really did become ill: he would have to protest in words that this was nothing to do with his own volition.

He was examined by three prison doctors and two eminent consultants brought in by the family – Lord Dawson of Penn and Dr Geoffrey Evans. In the opinion of all five (in the words of the Home Secretary when reporting to Parliament) – 'If the patient remained under conditions that were inseparable from detention there would be substantial risk of the thrombo-phlebitis from which he is suffering extending and producing permanent danger to health and even to life.' This weight of doctors' opinions was added to the efforts of people who had been working for his release behind the scenes: my Aunt Baba had unceasingly been getting her friends Lord Halifax and Walter Monckton to put pressure on the Home Secretary; Diana's mother Lady Redesdale had gone to Winston Churchill's wife Clementine, who had been a bridesmaid at her wedding forty years before, and had asked her to ensure at least that the facts of my father's illness were known to her husband. (Diana wrote that Clementine Churchill had 'infuriated' her mother by remarking – 'Winston has always been so fond of Diana'; also for suggesting that prison was at least protecting my father and Diana from the fury of mobs outside.) The Home Secretary Herbert Morrison took the decision to release my father and Diana in November 1943; there was immediate uproar from the press and from Labour MPs and trades unions.

Herbert Morrison explained to Parliament that he had chosen not to run the risk of 'making martyrs of persons undeserving of the honour' and so had 'substituted for detention some system of control approximating to house arrest'. He had done this because 'at this stage of the war.... I was satisfied that no undue risk to national security would be incurred'; also 'on the general principle that the extraordinary powers of detention without trial must not be used except in so far as they are essential for national security'. None of this meant much to some Labour MPs: one insisted that 'Mosley had been let out because of his social position'; another that 'this man used to go to Bethnal Green in an armoured car with a chauffeur ready to hit anybody on the head with a steel bar'. Ellen Wilkinson, loyally defending Herbert Morrison against what she called such 'mob-hysteria', was herself accused by the Distributive and Allied Workers' Union of being thus responsible for 'one of the greatest crimes ever perpetrated by an individual against the working class'. The *Daily Mail* commented that the Labour Party seemed to be 'struggling with its own confused complexes'. Arthur Greenwood was one critic of Herbert Morrison who made partial sense even if it was irrelevant: he said – 'Mosley has tried to destroy every kind of democratic institution.... and has made no public statement saying he has renounced his views'.

When my father and Diana were released they had to be smuggled out of the 'murderer's gate' of Holloway because press photographers had constructed a sort of grandstand outside the front gate. They went to stay in Oxfordshire at the house of Diana's sister and brother-in-law Pamela and Derek Jackson. The house was besieged by reporters: in London booths were set up on street corners in order to obtain thousands of signatures to advocate the Mosleys' reimprisonment. Various eminent people were lobbied for their opinions: Bernard Shaw was asked – 'Do you think it is too strong to say that the Home Secretary's decision is calculated to cause alarm and despondency among the masses?' He replied – 'I do not think your proposition is strong at all, it makes me suspect you are mentally defective.' Diana's sister Nancy wrote that she had only been able to squeeze through the crowds and get into her local underground station by joining a column of demonstrators chanting 'Put him back!' Diana's sister Decca, who was a communist, wrote an 'open letter' from America to their cousin-by-marriage Winston Churchill demanding that 'they should be kept in jail where they belong'.

The Home Office realised suddenly that Derek Jackson was a notable physicist as well as having been an RAF rear-gunner; he was at the moment doing secret research work for the Air Ministry. It was decided that thus he was not a suitable host for my father and Diana; they had to move; they went to a half-deserted pub in the Cotswolds, *The Shaven Crown* at Shipton-under-Wychwood. Here the siege by the press went on. It was reported that the Mosleys could not find domestic help because of the hostility of local people towards them; offers of help then poured in, causing my father to remark that they had been given '£50,000 worth of free advertising'. After a month or two my father bought a house at Crux Easton, near Newbury (Savehay Farm was still requisitioned). At Crux Easton the conditions of house arrest were quite stringent: my father and Diana could not move more than seven miles from the house, every month they had to report to the police in person, they were not allowed to communicate with any former member of the British Union, and all speeches, publications and indeed any form of political activity was banned. These restrictions remained in force until the end of the war in Europe in May 1945.

I wrote to my father:

November 22nd.   3CRU   CMF
What exultation there was this morning when I read in an old news bulletin 'Sir O.M. was to be released for reasons of health'. I have

gone about ever since with grapes and vine-leaves in my hair ...

What are your plans? I long to know everything. I do so wish I could be with you to enjoy the first fruits. We have been deprived of so much time together, and it seems it will be further ages now before we can finally escape the evils of this bloody war.

I have been plunging here and there into Plato with whom I am very disappointed. He seems to spend his time in arguments to prove that the Good is not the same as the Bad, and that the immortal differs in many respects from the mortal ...

Meanwhile my programme is Rome by Christmas and Venice by the Spring, where you must join me and we will revive the glories of the Renaissance.

December 5th

The news out here arrives in the most unsatisfactory and unreliable gusts so I am in ignorance about the latest developments in the great public squealing-match. Yesterday I was visiting a friend in Army Group HQ and thank God he had a very recent Hansard: but since then there has been uncomfortable silence punctuated by rude letters in the local papers from repressed corporals ...

In the meantime I am most fiercely engaged in a prolonged discussion upon eternal verities and practical politics with two refreshingly intelligent people who, although they were inclined once to think of you as the most horrible of ogres, and even now fight most stubbornly against the penetration of my logic, have yielded enough to give one hope that there are still sane people in the world. The trouble is that they would really prefer absurd chaos in government to organised system because they consider the one 'english' and the other 'unenglish'. At which I give up. What is the answer?

I have read most of Zarathustra. There are bits of it that might have come straight out of the New Testament ...

My father's release meant that now more than ever I wished to get home: the reaction of people to his release had been so venomous that it suddenly seemed difficult – with the war largely won – to put one's heart into the triumph of this society. I continued my spasmodic journey towards the front line: I reached the 2nd Battalion of the London Irish Rifles just before Christmas: their headquarters were in a village called Pietra Montecorvino at the foot of some of the highest mountains in central Italy. While I was reporting to the battalion orderly room my kitbag with all my clothes and bits and pieces was stolen, presumably by villagers: I had left it in the street outside. This was a disaster of unimaginable proportions! we were already high up in snow and ice: now – good heavens – I would have no more comforts than anyone else! I joked to my sister: 'Oh would that we could take 50 hostages from the village and shoot them if the kitbag was not produced in 5 minutes!' My tin box full of books had survived. Literature suddenly seemed of less importance than clothes.

On my way up through southern Italy I had depended on books: I had been reading T. S. Eliot: I wrote in my diary: 'He casts spells with words but with meanings as well as with sounds.' I had found a few people with whom to discuss such things; but for the most part I had been on my own. Then suddenly with the London Irish Rifles I was writing – 'My Company Commander has actually read *The Mill on the Floss*!' and a day or two later – 'He began to quote "Footfalls echo in the memory ..." and with what delight did I carry on (not without error) towards "the door we never opened into the rose-garden"!' My Company Commander was a calm, authoritative Welsh-man called Mervyn Davies. He was some five years older than I. He became my friend, and in many ways my new mentor, until the end of the fighting in Italy. I wrote then of my relationship with the 2nd Battalion of the London Irish Rifles – 'My posting to this Bn in 1943 was a true miracle.'

With the London Irish Rifles I was with men who had fought in North Africa, Sicily, up through the calf of Italy: many of them were exhausted: I knew nothing about war. In front of us there were mountains nine thousand feet high; the Germans were entrenched some-where on the range in front; the immediate enemy seemed to be the weather. Our own front-line companies had been withdrawn because of snowdrifts and bitter cold; supplies had not got through, and men were suffering from frostbite. They for the most part had no special winter clothing – and I now had none either, with the loss of my kitbag. But, as is the way with armies, it was thought that morale could best be kept up by the sending out of patrols. Early in 1944 I wrote in my diary:

Jan 2: Big moment when I take out my first patrol; sweat up a snow-laden hill in the most brazen manner and slither down again à la Duke of York. Jan 3: Bigger moment when given baptism of fire by desultory shells and mortar bombs not close but a horrible whine as they drop overhead. Jan 4: Hellish day standing on top of a frozen hill covering G Coy while they dilly-dally with mules and two buriable bodies. Jan 5: Platoon and I on our own gibber in the face of blizzard for 4 hrs and I have seldom been in such desperate straits – except perhaps on Jan 6; which was a repetition of the day before, from 8–2.30.

There is a break in my diary for a fortnight. Then there is an entry – 'It is difficult to write retrospectively of an experience so horrifying and unreal and yet every minute of which I suppose I shall never forget.'

Some events do take on a portentous significance. For months now I had made my jokes – or were they jokes? – that the most sensible thing at this stage in the war would be to get myself taken prisoner: I felt this partly presumably because of what were obviously my split attitudes about my father and my father's own complex attitudes to the war, but I had myself felt some despair at the people who seemed to get excitement out of war without being involved in the fighting – and indeed without stopping much to enquire what on earth the war was for. And so – why should one die for their stimulation and enjoyment? But as I got nearer to the front line it did seem that people had perhaps here some feel of what war was actually about: this was nothing to do with what was put out by politicians: in fact front-line soldiers seemed to have a contempt for nearly all politicians, and indeed for all those at any base who talked in bellicose terms. Front-line soldiers showed very little approval of the killing of the enemy: the front-line enemy in fact were held to be in much the same sort of predicament as they: what war was about to these people seemed to be some almost personal even if appalling test of endurance put upon all front-line soldiers just by the near-lunatics at home and at the base. This test had to be undergone, and some sort of personal victory achieved – why? but of course, this could not be put into words. If one began to try, then one would end up sounding like people at the base. Among the London Irish Rifles within a few days I got some feel of this: of course the war was bloody ridiculous! Who ever thought it wasn't! And of course all politicians and base-wallahs were power-maniacs and parasites – so what? There was some revelation to me in this 'so what!' If war was really an endurance test for some people to undergo and learn from, and about, with bravery and cunning and honour – indeed, yes, so what?

The platoon I had taken over was composed of Irishmen and Englishmen and Welshmen: many of them had been fighting for a year: they had been told repeatedly they might be going home; they found themselves in arctic conditions among some of the highest mountains of

Italy. I was ten years younger than most of them; I was recently out from England and was not even from their regiment; there had been no time for them to get to know me nor I to know them. When we got back from our patrols to the village the officers retired to an upstairs room. There was too much tiredness for any effort that did not seem essential.

Then there was a day when the blizzard lifted and we were told we were to return to the positions in the hills. There was a two-hour trudge through snow-drifts: then the ruins of a dug-in tent with some shallow slit-trenches on a wooded slope. This was the foremost platoon position of the Company and indeed of the Battalion. The Germans were said to be across a valley half a mile or so away. We settled in – two men to a trench – the trenches three foot by six foot and about three foot deep; the ground was too hard to make them deeper. We could not move much by day or the Germans saw us and started shelling; mule-trains came up with provisions at night; food was carried to and fro in containers. Within the eight-foot-by-six dug-in tent which was platoon headquarters there lived and slept, as if in an igloo, myself, my sergeant, a wireless operator and a runner.

Every morning the section-leader corporals would come in from their outlying trenches for their orders. There was not much to say – Watch out for German patrols, keep your heads down, do not let your weapons freeze, do not let yourselves freeze, this cannot go on for ever. One or two men went back with frostbite. One wondered – would anyone be able to fire his rifle? But then – would the Germans be able to fire theirs?

One morning I was giving out orders to my three corporals and my sergeant all squeezed into the tent when the air went in and out suddenly as if an enormous noise had gone off in the sound-box of my head: it became apparent at once that almost everyone in the tent was wounded; I myself was covered with blood; I found out later that this blood was from my sergeant. It appeared that a German mortar-bomb had gone off either in or just outside the tent; there were other bombs going off; there were the sounds of machine-guns through the pine-trees. We knew the drill for this: we scrambled – we found we could move – to our action trenches; my sergeant tumbled into our trench in front of me; he crouched in the bottom face down, clutching his chest, saying over and over 'God have mercy!' There were noises, now, of men coming down through the trees on the left; more rifle and machine-gun fire; then a strange howling like that of wolves. White shapes flitted on the slope like ghosts. We knew the drill for this: I yelled – 'Enemy through the trees, one hundred yards, open fire!' Nothing happened. There had been no drill for this. I thought – Of course, we have been taught how to give orders; we have never been taught what to do when orders are not obeyed; such an event could not be thought of; yet it is the one that most matters. More mortar bombs and grenades were landing: I had a machine-gunner out at the front and on the left. I yelled my orders again; my sergeant, beneath me in the trench, said – 'Don't tell them to shoot, sir, or we'll all be killed!' I thought – Well, that's what we're here for, isn't it? Then – But this is ridiculous! I began to crawl out of my trench towards the machine-gunner on the left; there had not been much room in the trench anyway with my sergeant; I thought I might get the machine-gun firing. I myself carried only a pistol: this again was what we had been taught – officers only carry pistols, because it is their job to give orders to men who have rifles and machine-guns and will fire them. I thought – But did not the people who taught us this at the base in fact know that it is ridiculous?

I had got about half way towards the machine-gunner on the left; I was on my hands and knees like a St Bernard, my pistol hanging from its lanyard round my neck. Then a grenade landed on the snow somewhere beside me: it seemed to smoke: I went head first into a snow drift. There was the air going in and out again; the ringing of the bells in the head and in the heart. I used in later life to try to think I fired at least one shot from my pistol: I do not think I did. It was true, probably, that if I had, quite a few of us might have been killed. As it was I found myself being yanked out of my snowdrift by the lanyard of my pistol; there was a German in a white camouflage-smock above me; I helped him to pull the cord of the pistol over my head. I thought – This is really very shaming. Then – But all this that is happening is just what I wanted to happen, isn't it? I am being taken prisoner: I am apparently not wounded: I can spend the rest of the war in a prison camp thinking about Goethe and Nietzsche. Then – But of course I know, don't I, that I must try to escape.

The Germans were huge red-faced men in white uniforms some of them wearing snow-shoes and carrying snow-sticks. They were still making their strange wolf-like noises – I remember wondering afterwards if they had been drugged. They were prodding at us with bayonets; we were being herded into a column to be marched off over the hill. There were five or six of us wounded; most of these could walk. I began to complain to my men about why they had not fired a shot. The Germans told me to shut up. I said, as if to no one in particular – Well, we must get away.

I had had the idea that I wanted to be taken prisoner because this made sense if the war made no sense: but what was happening now was deeper than any sense: there was some impossibility in the soul. I had always known, hadn't I, that if one could bring oneself to look, there were forces deeper than sense.

We were being led off in a long line over the snow-covered hills. If I did not quite know why I had to escape, certainly I did not know how. The Germans were authoritative men like ski-instructors. There was still quite a lot of firing going on – from our own people somewhere back on the right; from the Germans giving covering fire from the left and front. But this was quite like one of the adolescent games I still liked to play; shouldn't I be quite good at it? I thought my best chance might be to wait till there were bullets or a bomb going off quite close, and then I would pretend I had been hit and roll dramatically down the hill. I lurked at the back of the column making out I was seeing to the wounded; then I put a hand to my heart, and fell. A German almost immediately came up and prodded me hard with a bayonet; I got up quickly. But I was still very ashamed: what had I been doing all this time thinking such things were a matter of words – war, and being taken prisoner?

I determined to make one more effort – to improve, perhaps, on my performance. I should hurl myself into my part like Macbeth; like Hamlet. When the next mortar-bomb landed close I took off, rolled over and over, I came to rest at the side of a rock some distance down the hill. I determined to try to stay there whatever happened. There were snowflakes in front of my eyes; their formations were so beautiful! There were the clear-cut mountains beyond. Some way ahead of me was one of our men who had in fact just been wounded: he was calling to me for help; I wanted to tell him – You fool, can't you see I'm dead? The German with the bayonet was coming down towards me: I thought – This time of course he will shoot me: it was good of him not to have done so the first time. There were lines from T. S. Eliot going through my head – 'And I have seen the eternal Footman hold my coat, and snicker, and in short, I was afraid.' Then the German was close to me and had the muzzle of his rifle pointing at me – he was a large, ruddy-faced man like a gamekeeper – and there was a thump – this was the first time I heard this thump – and the German put an arm out as if he were holding a flag and went down on his knees on the snow. What had happened, I learned later, was that my friend Mervyn Davies had been coming up in a counter-attack on the hills behind and he had shot the German at long range – an extraordinary shot, some two hundred yards. The German died a few feet away from me: he groaned, and then stopped. After a time I stood up. Most of my platoon and the Germans had gone over the hill: there were three or four wounded left behind. I saw Mervyn Davies in the trees: I waved at him: the mountains were very beautiful. Mervyn told me later that he had nearly shot me too, thinking I was a German. He had refrained from doing so only because he had not wanted to be involved in any more killing.

Some stage of my life ended here. Up till now there had been all the words – the idea that if human beings were ridiculous, oneself might not be. Now – what was more ridiculous than this idea! But some got away.

I greeted Mervyn: I helped with the wounded: I prepared my report for the Commanding Officer. Of course it was a bad performance that a young officer had lost the best part of his platoon at his first sight of the enemy: thirteen had been taken prisoner; three or four had not been rounded up at the beginning of the action. But still – I had been with them for only a few days; I had not trained with them; and I had myself got away. Beyond this – What I had felt, what had happened to me, how could this be put into words?

Some five years later when I came to write my first novel I tried to put something of it into words – in quite a different story, but trying to describe the same sort of thing. And of course the words are ridiculous! but what is it that happens when you know this?

War is too big a thing to think about from the outside when you are in it – you have got to accept it on its own terms, like the world, and not attempt to value it by some personal idea. To us it was a killing dying silliness but then the world was silly too; and we were part of it, the silly world, the dying people of Europe killing themselves and us killing them too – and we accepted it, the whole of it, and what thereby it entailed – you've got to fight so you might as well fight prettily, you've go to die so you might as well die prettily, you've only got yourselves to think about because the thing beyond you is entirely unthinkable so you might as well think yourselves pretty: that was all it was, and pride of course too; pride of the right kind, pride in pity, pride in pretty things.

CHAPTER 25

What Do We Learn?

I got a letter from my father written at the end of 1943:

> The Shaven Crown, Shipton-under-Wychwood.
> It is Christmas Day, and how I wish you were here – nothing was sadder than your absence on the first Christmas for 4 years. I have made a beginning with getting better, it will be a long job, wonderful the difference it makes getting out of that place. I hope soon to resume reading and thought with more capacity ...

> Darlingest Nick, I can never tell you what a joy to me it was to know you as an adult and to find what a perfect community of mind and spirit we had – to search together through all the higher and lovelier things of life – may the time come soon when we may be together again – in some happiness.

I wrote to my father (these letters were subject to military censorship):

> January 27th
> Your letters did much to save my life in the past month which has been something of a nightmare. The frightened 'porker' nearly fell a victim to the butcher's relentless axe; was actually being led away to cold storage when with many a grunt and shrill squeal he tucked his tail between his legs and ran. This is horribly obscure I'm afraid, but Viv may have been able to elucidate ...

> Ever since I began to live – since I surmounted the adolescent stage – I have been wandering like Shaw's Caesar 'seeking the lost regions from which my birth into this world exiled me'. I have found many

islands . . . but was always without a home, until one day I went
to Holloway to visit a stranger and then I knew that I had found
the 'lost region' – and now I do not believe I can ever be entirely
unhappy again.

My father, it seemed, had exemplified to me (as he perhaps had to
himself?) the feeling that war was a senseless game in which it might
have been rational for me to have been taken prisoner; but now – arising
perhaps from the ashes of this recognition – there was also, for me at
least, a knowledge that there had to be an effort at commitment to
deeper rules if one was not to be trapped.

Some time during the winter my battalion left the mountains and
moved down towards Naples and the plain. I had been given a new
platoon largely of reinforcements like myself: I trained with them;
began to know them. I wrote to my father, 'I even have a corporal who
lends me his complete Shakespeare!' At first we were not allowed much
beyond the limits of the camp: there were rumours of the big push
towards Rome in the early spring. Then –

March 13th 1944
The other day I managed to wangle a trip into the city of the 'Vivien'.
Having slipped away from my fellow visitors whose one desire it was
to drink the greatest possible amount of synthetic spirits in the
shortest possible time I wandered down upon the front below the
hotel in which we used to stay and on to the quay from which we used
to board the Vivien and sail happily across the sea-blue waters of the
bay. It was all much the same: Capri arose dreamily out of the mist:
I thought I could make out the cliff of Sorrento on the opposite shore.
The little restaurant on the quay where we used to eat those delicious
fish dishes was sadly battered, and there was none of the old noise and
gaiety; but I felt very sentimental and rose-blown as I ruminated on
the absurdity of our position in such serene surroundings, and the
futility of all worldly things.

This was the first of my sorties on leave or from hospital which were the
counterparts of the rigours of war. If wars had to be fought, Italy seemed
the place to fight in: there were enchanted gardens just beyond the act-
drops of squalor and fear.

The big push in the spring was held up because of bad weather:
at the end of March our battalion took up defensive positions on top
of Monte Castellone to the north of Monte Cassino. We climbed at

night in violent rain up a narrow rocky track that seemed at an angle of 45 degrees; mule-trains both came down against us and tried to overtake us from behind; war seemed, as so often, not against a human enemy but against forces of nature. At the summit we took over from Frenchmen who had constructed small stone shelters like hollow cairns; they shook hands quickly and disappeared. When the light came up there was the enormous and beautiful 14th-century monastery of Monte Cassino on top of its smaller mountain below: it was like some half-squashed slug. It had already suffered the most destructive of the bombing attacks made on it: every now and then as we watched more bombers would float over: they dived down like seagulls above flotsam.

There had been the arguments – should it or should it not have been bombed: what did one think about the bombing of any of the marvellous buildings of Italy? Monte Cassino dominated the road to Rome: Germans were said to be inside; later, there were said to have been none. But there were Germans dug into the slope of the mountain so what did it matter if there were none at the top? The point at issue was – what did a regard for one of the great art-monuments of history matter when put in the balance against the risk to even a single human life? From our stone igloos on our mountain it did not seem to us, looking down, that there was anything much to be discussed: of course to us and to those like us our lives seemed more important; of course to others, and in the future, they would not. Politicians and generals would, as always, fit their arguments to suit their own fears and ambitions.

Shells whizzed over the top of our mountain from the German guns in the valley beyond; sometimes they landed just short of the crest; sometimes they skimmed just over and down to the valley behind. Once there was the sudden collapse of air again as if in a soundbox, and it seemed that a shell had hit the stone roof of my igloo and had bounced off and on like a flat stone on water. My sergeant and I sat facing each other in our rocky hole with our knees almost touching; we scooped cold stew out of tins and used the empty tins to shit in; there were the jokes – could you tell the difference? At night we sometimes had to go out on patrol: there was this terrible army fantasy about the moral virtue of patrols: we would go just over the crest of our mountain and squat among the dead bodies and tins of shit; we could go no further because of a precipice. We were like targets for the shells that failed to go over towards the valley.

Then I was writing to my father:

April 17th

I am at this moment sitting on the beach 4 miles east of Amalfi
trying to decide whether or not to bathe. I think perhaps I shall
'milk it' for in April the sea-blue stream does not look too inviting
... I have been for the past 3 weeks on a bleak mountain until
yesterday when I tottered down in the small hours of the morning
and was the same day having lunch in Naples en route for four days
at this lovely village [Maori]. We stayed last night to hear the opera
in Naples – Bohème – which was on a grander scale than one would
find almost anywhere else in Europe. The transition from my bare
mountain to the bedside of the dying Mimi was almost too sudden
and I was near to tears with the poor Rodolfo.

I thought Ravello extraordinarily beautiful. Unfortunately we
were not allowed into the Rufolo Gardens – Wagner's enchanted
gardens in Parsifal.

Tomorrow I want to try to get to Paestum. Isn't it there that
there are the loveliest Greek temples outside Greece?

Then we were back training for the big push in the spring. Throughout the winter, troops had been slaughtered half-way up Monte
Cassino: there had been the landing behind the German lines at Anzio,
but this had been contained. It was decided now to try to block out
Monte Cassino with smoke and to attack straight up the valley underneath towards Rome. Why had this not been thought of before? My
father's old friend General Fuller wrote later that the winter battle for
Monte Cassino was 'tactically the most absurd and strategically the
most senseless campaign of the whole war'.

We were doing our training (I wrote to my father) 'in a beautiful
valley full of fruit trees in full blossom and lovely winding streams';
we were billeted on a farmer 'who was obviously a one-time gourmet
and he feeds us with eggs and bottles of red wine which we drink
solemnly from morn to night'. In training there was the problem which
had confronted me earlier so startlingly and which could now be studied
– that not of just how to give orders, but of how to ensure that they
would be obeyed. This seemed to be in the area of what could not
easily be put into words; it was to do with camaraderie; perhaps with
something like love. I now lived with my men in the stables of the
farmhouse: my officerly status was indicated by my sleeping-bag being
elevated to a manger. We went out on mountain-climbing schemes,
river-crossing schemes; we turned these into competitions with other
platoons like children's games. I taught them the actual children's games

I had played and we played these in the evenings – 'Lions in the Dark' was good training for night patrols. We spurred ourselves on in the river races by bellowing Paul Robeson's song from *Sanders of the River*: we made up a battle cry which was – for no known reason – Woo hoo Mahommet! We even evolved some private language by which, as at prep-school, our solidarity might be shown: in place of the ubiquitous word 'fuck' (I once questioned the driver of a broken-down truck, and he informed me 'The fucking fucker's fucked') we substituted the word 'waggle', with what seemed to be the appropriate attendant style – 'I say, just waggle over that hill, will you, and see if there are any wagglers on the other side.' We became a good platoon. I wrote to my father:

> The other day I heard two riflemen in my platoon bellowing at the tops of their voices the tune of the *'Horst Wessel'* with all the old words in English including the line – 'We'll fight for Mosley!' I was covered with confusion and have not yet dared ask them where they learned the words. They are very probably old members of the B.U., being extraordinarily pleasant and sensible men.

When the push began in May the 2nd Battalion of the London Irish Rifles were to be in the second wave as it was called to cross the River Rapido and to move up the Liri Valley. On the roads there were tanks with giant flails on cylinders at the front for exploding mines; iron rolls like bandages for laying across ditches. We were pushed off the road, we lay in fields, we waded across the Rapido River hanging on to ropes. There were shells whooshing overhead and a terrible sound we had not heard before – a vast moaning and shrieking in the sky as if from witches. This was caused by a multi-barrelled mortar said to have been invented by the Germans specifically to instil ghostly terror. We waited, as one so often waits in war, in hedgerows, in hollows; while people went to and fro trying to find out what was happening. I began to compose a poem. Was not this what people did in time of war? manipulating words, to try to make things orderly, to bring down witches.

> The cornfields wave towards the sky
> And from above the clouds reply
> With smiles of gentle sleepiness.
> Below the summer sun's caress
> Lies softly on the silent plains

> And deep within the sunken lanes
> The trailing thorns hang down to dream
> And slowly in the silver stream
> The leaves of weary willows drift
> And sway to lazy winds that lift
> The heavy heads of drooping trees . . .

And so on. Casualties were coming back from the battalions in front. We heard that our Colonel had been killed, when he had gone forward on reconnaissance. The Monastery on top of its hill, on our right, suddenly loomed up out of the smoke: it hung over us, decomposed, a dead genie out of its bottle. Mortar bombs came down. There was machine-gun fire. Nothing much seemed to be happening.

> But Stranger, Stranger, don't you see
> Behind each crimson-tinted tree
> Within these hollow haunted walls
> And torn upon each thorn that falls
> So gently, gently, groping down;
> Beside the shining fields that crown
> The sleeping summer's brittle glare
> With ripples in the sun-swept air . . .

I didn't like that line. I crossed it out. You could do this with poetry. Somewhere close to me there was a wounded German shouting – he had been hit in one of the first attacks – I was supposed to be able to speak some German, so I went to him in his ruined dug-out and held his hand. He poured out words to me; he was terribly anxious about 'das Brief'; I looked around and found what seemed to be a letter to his wife or sweetheart. I did not know what to do with this, he seemed to want me to read it to him. I tried to, but before long he died.

> That here one summer long ago
> The silent lanes did slowly flow
> With drops of dying hearts that bled
> And drained the dying to the dead.
> That here vain tears of frozen grief
> Once trembled on each withered leaf
> And hung from every tearing thorn;
> And out amongst the golden corn

> Blind eyes did strain in vain to see
> The light that mocked their agony.

Words, damned words: what were people doing with their poetry, their fine rhetoric? Did one think one could make war pretty? Would it not be better to shit on war?

During the night there were thousands of fireflies that got mixed with tracer bullets so that there were patterns in the sky like atoms and shooting stars: the mortars groaned as if the sky were protesting at having to receive back so many dead.

At dawn the next morning I was doling out food from a huge cauldron that had been carried to the edge of my hastily-dug trench; there were still stray bullets and bits of bombs dropping like dead flies; then as I stretched out my hand to take a second helping of food – I had apportioned it out to my platoon: there was a small amount left over: I thought, why not? – something struck me, very hard, on the wrist. I wondered – a bullet? shrapnel? nanny? I had in fact been wounded, it appeared, quite deeply in the wrist. It did not hurt much. I thought – I cannot be so lucky! Then – But is it quite bad enough? People gathered round to give an opinion. A bandage was put on; taken off; it was decided that I should go back and at least show my wound to someone at Company Headquarters. I found Mervyn Davies: I said to him – Do you think I should be one of those legendary heroes who are wounded but who carry on in war? He said – I don't know, should you? The doctor saw me and placed me, rather ostentatiously, on a stretcher. I was carried back to hospital.

On the afternoon of that day when our battalion at last made the attack for which we had prepared a German shell made a direct hit on the headquarters of my platoon where I would presumably have been had I not been wounded; the sergeant who had taken over from me and most of those with him were killed.

In hospital I thought – But one day I should try to put into words what cannot be put into words: what is chance, all right, you can look at it; but what is it that makes it work for you (is it just this looking?) or not?

Some three weeks later I was writing to my father –

June 9th
My wanderings have taken me into what I think is the most ex-hilaratingly beautiful place I have ever seen. You remember Ischia? – the lovely island opposite Capri which we visited in the 'Vivien'

and where the peasants welcomed us on the beach with smiles and bottles of sweet white wine. How I got here I hardly know. Sufficient to say that my way from the hospital back to the battalion seemed about to be so tedious that faced with a delay of ten days at some dreary reinforcement centre I stormed up to the C.O. and demanded leave. He complied with surprising readiness, only stipulating that I would have to find my own accommodation. From then on fate took charge. I arrived here yesterday evening from the preposterous barrel of a steamer ... I was met by a smiling old man who took me to a clean white room with a balcony that looks over the sea ... the dinner I ate that night was such as I have not dreamed of for years except perhaps in the noble precincts of Holloway. Today I strode over the high hills that run along the centre of this island; in Forio a crowd of children and old men gathered round me at the café begging for cigarettes and hoping to humour me by saying how wonderful they thought the English were and how they hated Mussolini. I told them that I was a fanatical admirer of Mussolini and a hundred per cent fascist, at which they at least stopped plaguing me for money. One little boy broke into the lusty strains of *Giovinezza* until he was hustled away by an outraged policeman. I wish you were here to enjoy it with me.

In Naples I met up with some old Rifle Brigade friends and there were, I rhapsodized to my sister – 'exotic bathing parties in the gardens of the Winter Palace of the Kings of Naples at Caserta; parties in limpid rock-bound pools surrounded by classical statues and pink champagne'. We went sailing from the harbour at Posillipo; each night there was the Opera. For my twenty-first birthday on June 25th we planned 'the Borgia of all orgies'. Then as it turned out I spent the day in a train in a railway siding on my way back to my battalion. I wrote to my father – 'But I am not sorry ... I need a little quiet rest at the front after the bewildering hilarity of transit life.'

I told him how the day before I had at last managed to get to Paestum.

I determined to make the pilgrimage thither from Naples, some 60 miles hitch-hiking over comparatively unfrequented roads, which meant that I arrived on the scene having walked the last 3 miles in the heat of the day. I came across the first temple quite unexpectedly rising rather bleakly from the bushes and long grass by the side of the road. In the suddenness of the discovery I think I was a little disappointed: it was such a cold and desolate ruin; the pillars looking rather thin and forlorn under the golden heat of an Italian midday sun. But then as I wandered up beneath the grey portico I caught a glimpse of the second temple – the only temple that really matters at Paestum – a glimpse of gold more golden than the corn which shone about it, more serene and beautiful than any concentration of Italian sun. I rushed towards it in an ecstasy of wonder.

I had expected to rejoin my battalion somewhere near Lake Trasimene and to continue with them fighting up through Italy. Instead, in my railway siding, I heard rumours that they were on their way back and I was advised to wait for them in Rome. Rome had been taken by the Allies some three weeks before: there was still an air of celebration. Myself and a South African officer who was also waiting for my battalion went sightseeing. I thought – All this haphazardness goes on like particles in the brain: they rush hither and thither: then suddenly the shape, the thing, is there; you know it exactly. My friend and I managed to attach ourselves to a party of American Roman Catholic padres who were on their way into the Vatican to have an audience with the Pope: we veered off down a side passage before our credentials could be checked; we found our way to the Sistine Chapel. There we had been lying on our backs looking at Michelangelo's ceiling for some time before the Swiss Guards came to chuck us out.

CHAPTER 26

A Fairly Ordinary Kind of War

The letters that my father wrote to me during 1944 have become lost: I carried them with me all through Italy; after the war he asked me if he could have them back because he wanted to use them as material for the philosophical chapters of the book he was then writing – *The Alternative*. He said he would return them to me later: he never did. The relevant chapters in *The Alternative* however give some distillation of these letters.

The questions left somewhat up in the air after our talks in Holloway were – can one look upon life as something that humans can push into shape by efforts of will, or does life in fact very largely go its own way and efforts to push it are counter-productive? And if this is the case, is not the best a human being can do to try to understand it and only by this (but in no certain way) influence it?

In one of his last letters to me of 1943 my father had quoted the passage in Eckermann's *Conversations with Goethe* in which Goethe is recorded as saying – 'It would have been a poor joke for God to have brought together this coarse world from simple elements and to have launched it rolling through the sun-rays of the centuries if he had not had the plan to found on this material basis a plant-school for spirits.' This, in later life, became something of a motto for my father: it was a basis for what he referred to as his 'doctrine of higher forms'.

At the very end of his life (1979) my father said in a letter to his biographer Robert Skidelsky that he had 'come more and more to believe that my main contribution to thought will be the "doctrine of higher forms". In *The Alternative* (as in the lost letter of 1944) he wrote of this doctrine and of what he saw as man's function as a result of it:

We believe that it is now possible to derive from the actual evidence available in the world some idea of the pattern of God. It is possible not only to discern his presence in the elaborate laws which govern the mechanistic universe, but also to perceive something of his purpose and method in the assisted evolution of striving man against that causal background. The very factors which appeared in earlier knowledge to deny that purpose, now confirm design and reveal method. The brutal ways of nature 'red in tooth and claw' are, in fact, necessary to stimulate into activity any elementary form of existence; and they persist, in some degree, in the great catastrophes of humanity which is not yet ready to advance in harmony with the natural purpose by strength of the spirit ...

To what end is the whole great purpose directed? *Ex hypothesi* it must be impossible for finite mind to comprehend the infinite: it is enough to discern sufficient of the purpose of God on earth to be able to place ourselves at the service of that aim. It is certainly clear that the purpose, and the proved achievement, of this will on earth is a progressive movement from lower to higher forms. When we assist that process we serve the process of God; when we oppose it, or seek to reverse it, we deny the purpose of God ...

We must deliberately accelerate evolution: it is no longer a matter of volition but of necessity. Is it a sin to strive in union with the revealed purpose of God? Is it a crime to hasten the coming in time of the force which in the long, slow term of unassisted nature may come too late? We go with nature: but we aid her: is not that nearer the purpose of God than the instinct to frustrate?

My own letters of this time left philosophy somewhat in abeyance: there were too many impressions coming in; of terror, wonder, uproariousness: whether or not one stayed alive – what luck! In order to put oneself in the way of luck, was there anything better that one could do than to be receptive to impressions through one's eyes, ears, mind; to impose plans, would be a distortion of reality.

When eventually I joined up with my 2nd Battalion of the London Irish Rifles I found that they were on their way back to Taranto in order to embark for the Middle East for a period of re-equipment and – for them – well-earned rest. It seemed to me that I was indeed having a miraculous war. I wrote in code to my sister about our probable destination – 'I have got Gippy Tummy'; or, more obscurely – 'Do you know a woman called Maugham?' (see page 241 of *Rules of the Game*).

We landed in Egypt and went to a camp between Cairo and Ismailia on the Suez Canal. Here a life of sailing, sightseeing and cricket continued. I wrote to my sister: 'The Sphinx has a pile of sandbags under her chin which gives her the appearance of suffering from tooth-ache.' To my father:

There is an interesting officer in my company who before the war was an active communist. He is intelligent and very reasonable, and when we feel earnest enough we talk of this and that, and the more we talk the less is the difference that I can see between the conceptions of the communist and the fascist corporate states. But then the only training I have had in the theory of fascism has been the pamphlets that you sent me when I was to debate upon the subject at Abinger Hill.

Also:

I think the Hellenists of the 18th and 19th centuries shrank from the acceptance of 'horror' in nature because they did not realise what far greater potentialities for horror there are in the *un*natural man. To a sensitive spirit of this generation the ruthless sense of doom in nature is not a quarter so horrifying as the miserable sense of futility when in contact with the 'unnatural' man of the present day. Anyone who has fought in the last 2 wars must realise this. It is incredible that there are sane men who believe that by renouncing natural life they can alter it or be immune from it.

When front-line troops were 'resting' it was the custom that they should be given a certain amount of licence: this was their recompense for having been in, and being about to return to, active war. During the summer several of my Rifle Brigade friends had been killed: survivors felt their turn might soon come; junior officers were especially vulnerable in a comparatively small-scale war like that in Italy. What I remember about our six weeks' rest in Egypt were dinners under fairy lights in the garden of Shepheard's Hotel; a nightclub on the Cairo race course round and round which I walked holding hands with a girl called Kitty and talking, I suppose, about the metamorphosis of the natural man from the camel to the child. In Alexandria one was apt to come across King Farouk in a nightclub and one would sing in chorus 'King Farouk King Farouk hang your bollocks on a hook' until there was trouble with either the Egyptian or the military police.

Towards the end of our stay tempers between soldiers and the local populace became so inflamed that there was a small riot in Cairo in which windows were broken and trams were overturned. It was said that men of the 78th Division (of which the London Irish Rifles were part) were to be sent back to Italy as some sort of punishment; but there are always such conspiracy theories in war.

I had been kept in touch by my sister with events at home: Vivien and Micky had been to stay with my father and Diana at Crux Easton: 'we all went for a vast picknicking bicycling expedition: Daddy looks quite wonderful with a pair of clips on his trousers and an ancient degraded cap turned back to front like a butcher boy'. The feud rumbled on between my father and my Aunt Irene – 'Daddy is terribly bitter about Aunty Ni ... he says he offered to have her as joint guardian but her reply was she could not be joint guardian with a person whose political views she so heartily disapproves of and for this he will never forgive her ... I think Daddy is a trifle unfair because I do happen to know for a fact that it was the Wards in Chancery people who approached her first with the project though she as usual did not do things too tactfully.' There was a weekend at which Vivien took down to Crux Easton my two great Eton friends who were both back in England with wounds: 'We all sat around till 3.30 a.m. listening to Poppa discoursing fascinatingly upon the theme of Wills to (a) Comfort (b) Power (c) Achievement – Superman to the Child and so on – with a spot of Democracy v. Fascism thrown in.'

When I landed at Taranto again at the end of September I wrote to my father: 'I am not really sorry to be back ... I hope soon to be able to visit Florence and Pisa and Siena and perhaps in a little while there will be Venice or Nice.'

There were now Rifle Brigade battalions in Italy and there was some demand that I should return to them: I made a formal request to stay with the London Irish Rifles, which was granted.

The front line had got stuck in almost as high mountains as those of the previous winter, this time between Florence and the northern plain. We were once more in trenches three-foot by six with rain filling them up and the sides falling in and ourselves not being able to move out of them by day: by night we slid about on patrols and sheltered behind haystacks and the rotting bodies of cattle. There were outbreaks of dysentery and malaria: this was a time when both men and officers were apt to go to their superiors and say that they could not go on. There was not much anyone could do about this; we were in the last winter of the war; such people were just sent back to some job or

other with which they felt they could deal. There was no evidence
that if some people were allowed to do this, everyone would: front-line
war was a battle with personal pride anyway. Every two weeks or
so we went back for a few days rest in a camp of tiny bivouac-tents
in the valley. I wrote to my father:

> I have been reading with a certain amount of concentration lately
> – quite a lot of Shakespeare and Ibsen – it seems to me that their
> greatness as artists depends upon the fact that they were neither of
> them ardent philosophers, thus they produce art for art's sake, even
> Ibsen, who is careful in his plays never to solve the problems he
> creates – or if he does, to contradict his first solution in a later play
> – using social and moral-spiritual problems merely as a framework
> for his art. This leads me to wonder if philosophy and art can ever
> be reconciled – in Goethe, perhaps, you would say? But I've also
> read Shaw's *Back to Methuselah* and his theory of creative evolution
> fascinates me: he proposes that man can surpass himself when once
> his desire and his will are strong enough ... but this is really too
> facile a proposition ... man will need vast painfully-acquired wisdom
> before the 'transvaluation of all values' can be achieved.

The situation in the mountains was that the allied armies had nearly
broken through to the northern plain before the onset of the autumn
rains; but now, largely because of the diversion of forces to the rather
unnecessary landing in the South of France, we were suspended once
more in country where armoured vehicles were unusable and even
infantry could move up and down the precipitous escarpments only
with the greatest difficulty and at night. Sometimes on a fine day we
got a glimpse through to the flat ground somewhere around Imola:
this was our promised land: when we got there, we felt, the war would
be over.

There was a day in October when the army commander thought
that a last effort should be made to get through to the plain before
the onset of total winter: following the belief that no one could move
by day, a divisional attack was planned for night. For two nights the
London Irish Rifles were part of a diversion within this attack; we
slid down chasms in driving rain and could not get up the other side;
we were shot at by machine-guns firing on fixed lines from the flanks.
We did not know where the enemy were, we did not know where
we were ourselves, we did not know who was being shot at by whom.
Several of our officers were killed; one, the South African with whom

I had gone sight seeing in Rome. When we retired we learned that the larger attack had failed because there was a ruined farmhouse on the spur of a hill occupied by the Germans from which with their machine-guns they could dominate two or three valleys.

It seemed that either this plan to break through to the plain had to be abandoned or there had to be a change from the convention that one could not move by day: in darkness, people simply gave up. There were conferences at Brigade and Divisional level: it was seen that in any case nothing further could be done until the ruined farm-house, which was called Casa Spinello, was taken. The Brigadier sent for the Colonel commanding the London Irish Rifles: the Colonel sent for Mervyn Davies. In a letter that I wrote shortly afterwards to my sister I said – 'They conferred: and Mervyn, to his everlasting credit, declared that he would take Spinello with his company alone, that he could do it in daylight, and that moreover he could do it that very afternoon.'

That day the rain had stopped. We had moved to trenches slightly on the reverse slope of our hill. We were standing up and trying to clean our weapons when Mervyn came along with a look both grim and apologetic and said to me, 'I've got an MC job for you.' This was a phrase used to describe a task for which, if it succeeded, one would probably be decorated; and if it failed, one would probably be dead.

The plan was that first my communist friend who was called Desmond Fay should go out on a patrol with just his sergeant and try to capture a prisoner at Casa Spinello in order to find out how many Germans were there: then my platoon would attack and try to take the farmhouse at 4 o'clock in the afternoon. Then the rest of the company would come up and consolidate.

Desmond carried out his part of the plan brilliantly: he got to the outbuildings of the farmhouse without being seen, grabbed a sleeping German out of a trench, and ran back before anyone knew much what was happening. The captured German said that by day the farmhouse was held by about thirty men.

My platoon was now down to about fifteen men; the rest were sick. When I gave out orders the plan did seem crazy: we were to try to do on our own by day what a whole division had failed to do by night; we were just to walk out into the open, and then run, and hope – what? – that the Germans would not believe that anyone would do anything so crazy? It was true that many of them would be sleeping by day; but after Desmond's patrol, would not they be alerted?

Some time before the attack one of my corporals began to cry in the bottom of his trench and said he could not go on: I was put out by this for a time: then I said it did not matter.

When four o'clock came Desmond Fay led us out along the route he had reconnoitred that would enable us to get to within about a hundred yards of Spinello without being seen from the farmhouse: we could, of course, be seen by the Germans on the hills beyond. Desmond was a short sturdy man with close-cropped hair who usually had a cigarette dangling from his mouth; he led us along the side of a steep slope of shale; one walked by putting one foot in front of the other; one kept going. We knew there were also our own people watching from a hill behind – the Brigadier and the Colonel, like Napoleon with his marshals. I suppose I had worked out that something like this sooner or later had to happen: I had been very lucky so far in war: perhaps I was lucky even now (I was becoming expert in working out how all was for the best in the best of all possible worlds) to have this chance to balance the rather inglorious events of my being captured at my first sight of a German and then being wounded just before the big attack in the spring. After a few hundred yards Desmond indicated the brow of the hill on the left beyond which was Casa Spinello. I crawled with my men to just beneath the top. So far, no one had reacted to us.

I remember fear quite well: it is quite different from pain, which one cannot remember. Fear is the feeling that there is something that may not be able to be borne.

When I gave the order to start running – I had been a good quarter miler at school – it was obviously in my interest to get across the open ground as quickly as possible. I was pleased to see how close the farm buildings were – not more than a hundred yards – they were mostly rubble; there were holes in this into what might be dugouts. I was carrying a Thompson sub-machine-gun (the days were long past when I felt properly armed with an officer's pistol); I could not see any Germans; when I looked back my platoon seemed unnervingly far behind. I yelled to one of my corporals, 'Come on, McClarnon!' He – a short-legged man – yelled back, 'I'm coming as fast as I can!' I reached the rubble of some farm buildings. The main farmhouse seemed to be one of those constructions on a slope where the ground floor at the back turns out to be the first floor on the far side. I was moving towards this first floor rubble when grenades started landing all around; a German popped out of one of the holes; I shot and missed; my other corporal, Corporal Tomkinson, shot and hit him. There was a voice which started shouting, 'Don't shoot Johnny! Play the game Johnny!' I called to McClarnon to look after the people in the farm buildings: Tomkinson and I ran on. We arrived at the first floor of the farmhouse and now there did begin something indeed like one of the catching games I had played as a child; the Germans were apparently on the ground floor below us with their entrance on the far side; when Tomkinson and I tried to get round on the right we were shot at; but if we did not get round, they could throw grenades at us continually from the far side. We tried to get round to the left where there was a hole through to the ground floor; when I peered down this there were three Germans peering up at me. I was very frightened and fired first and wounded one or two but then I ran out of ammunition (afterwards I was glad) and I watched them run or crawl slowly out of an opening at the far side while I changed my magazine. Tomkinson and I tried to get round on the right again and we threw one or two grenades at what seemed to be the entrance to the main dug-out on the ground floor; but there were bullets flying off the stonework from the hills behind and my magazine was once more empty; and then a German came out of the dug-out and fired at me at what seemed to be point-blank range; I disappeared round the corner of the house with a leap, as I described it in a letter to my sister later, 'like that of Nijinsky in *Le Spectre de la Rose*'. Tomkinson stayed for a while shooting back; then I gave orders that there were to be no more sorties to the far side.

We stayed on our first floor, crouched behind the skeletons of walls, and wondered what the Germans would do in their ground floor below. Once they started firing up through floorboards and we were all leaping about like people in the red-hot bull of Phalaris: then we fired back and there were cries again of – 'Don't shoot Johnny!' I tried to explain in my bad German (why does one insist on trying to use one's foreign languages?) that we would not shoot at them if they did not shoot at us (what were the conditional or subjunctive tenses?).

By this time Mervyn had arrived with the rest of the company; he tried to get round to the far side; he was wounded; he lay on the rubble. I tried to get him on to a stretcher; he said he would go back on his own. It was vital that he should arrange for reinforcements. I watched him hop away on one leg like a bird – straight through what later turned out to be a minefield. Reinforcements coming up later walked into it, and did not get through.

There was one German who from the beginning had been trying to get himself taken prisoner: he was going round smiling and nodding to everyone and people were telling him for goodness sake to shut up.

It was now becoming dark. We had settled down on our first floor; we suddenly felt confidence, even exhilaration. During the night I think two or three counter-attacks came in: once the Germans crept right up to the walls of the farmhouse and shot one of our men through a window: then grenades were flying about like crockery again and everyone was firing – I now had ten machine-guns in the small building and it seemed there was no question of anyone finding enough room to break in – one man had lost his spectacles and was firing straight up into the air with his machine gun – we were all yelling our war-cry – Woo hoo Mahommet! After a time, everything became quiet again. I counted our men. Out of the whole company we seemed to have only twenty fit men and ten wounded who could not be moved. But no one seemed to have been killed. There was some exhilaration in this.

The question remained about what would we find on the hills beyond in the morning. If we were successful in our attack, another large-scale divisional night attack was supposed to have gone in which, it was hoped, could now succeed because there would be no cross-fire from Spinello. But if this large-scale attack had not succeeded, we would ourselves of course be hopelessly exposed to counter-attacks in the morning. During the night we heard noises – comings and goings – but we did not know of whom. When light came up we were standing at our windows like lonely pioneers in Western films waiting for the view of Indians – or cavalry. As our paper-white faces became visible there were, yes, figures on the hills beyond: they were moving too openly, surely, for them to be enemy: we were confident enough to try a small cheer. And then we stepped out into the thin morning air. Around the right side of the house where so many of our men had been wounded there was the entrance to the main German dug-out; the body of the German who had shot at me at point-blank range was lying blocking it; we pulled him clear. I called to anyone left in the ground floor to come out. There emerged twelve men one by one like wasps out of their hole; they were most of them wounded. We sent them back with our own wounded. Then we stood about, not really doing much, in the cold bright air. We were told to dig trenches, to consolidate the attack which had so well succeeded; but we could not be bothered to do much about this. That evening we did the long march back to the valley where there were our bivouac tents. I remember resting half way with my seven or eight remaining men and being told by some senior officer to get up and get on. I told him to fuck off. There was this sort of aloofness now from both fear and exhilaration; but what had been the style of our achievement? In my account of this battle to my sister a month or so later I wrote: 'I find it hard to believe it was I who did all these peculiar things ... I have yet to meet a man who fought well because he believed in the cause for which he was fighting ... it is always pride that incites and succeeds in war.'

CHAPTER 27

Peace

The war in Europe lasted another seven months: I did not get home for nearly another year. After the battle of Casa Spinello the war became a matter of endurance – could one or not, and in what way, hold on. Nothing much in terms of the war was achieved by the battle of Spinello; we took one more ridge; we did not get through to the plain.

The Battalion stayed in the mountains until the new year: we were sometimes in tents; sometimes in the trenches filling with water and surrounded by the rotting bodies of cattle. I had one four-day leave in Florence when I bribed my way into the barred and bolted Museo Nazionale and stood gazing at the outside of the crates which contained, I was told, sculptures by Donatello. I wrote to my father: 'My Rifle Brigade friends live in a lovely villa on the outskirts of the town whither they invite the decaying remnants of the Italian nobility who are amusing for a while but eventually become horribly tedious.' Then I was in the mountains again where I 'constructed for myself a pleasantly secluded little dungeon about 7ft by 5ft and 3ft high where I hibernate for 24 hrs a day communing with the muses and concocting grotesque dishes of tinned food over a tiny petrol fire and beating off the savage assaults of rats'. What was terrible about this time were the continuing night patrols: a game was played with the higher levels of command about these: absurd orders were given – that one should penetrate miles behind the enemy lines over ravines and rivers and so on. What one in fact did was to tip-toe down paths which were likely to be mined and festooned with trip-wires, just as far as where one might reasonably say one had been 'held-up' – 'reasonably' being what one knew would seem acceptable to higher command. I remember one flat stretch of road in a mountain valley where there was a bridge over a stream almost exactly half way between the German positions and ours:

typically, each side was convinced that this bridge had to be in its hands by nightfall though it was abandoned by day; so when evening came each side would prepare a patrol for a complex sort of race to the bridge: if you started too early it was still light and you got shot up; if you started too late the other side would be there first and you got shot up. I remember becoming increasingly demented about this bridge: when the nights came round for it to be my turn to do the race I began to think again – For God's sake, is it not possible to find some way by which to give up?

There was an interval just before Christmas when we were in another part of the mountains and the days became clear and bright and in the valley in front, somewhere in no-man's-land, there was a farmhouse apparently deserted by human beings but which seemed to teem with turkeys and chickens and pigs: they could be watched through binoculars; we were hungry. There was a man in my platoon who claimed to be a butcher; he suggested – why not take down a small patrol – he would do the job quite silently – and there was our Christmas dinner! After a time (such is gluttony) I agreed to this: myself and five or six volunteers set off with the self-professed butcher; we arrived at the farm; our expert crept into the turkey house; after a time the turkey house exploded as if with shrapnel: birds came out in every direction pursued by the butcher with a bayonet: someone suggested – Shoot them! I yelled – No! Eventually we got two or three birds with rugby tackles. They were enough for a Christmas dinner.

There was one man in my platoon who was an ex-jail-bird from Belfast whom I had thought it best to try to keep under some slight supervision by making him my personal runner: we got on well together: he would procure for me mysterious perks. Once when we were about to move off from our tented camp to the front line and we were being inspected by the Brigadier he, the Brigadier, stopped in front of my runner and said, 'And what's wrong with you my good man?' and my runner said simply, 'I'm drunk!' Another time in the front line and in a fairly perilous predicament I told him to take some message and he refused: I said, 'Obey my orders or I shall shoot you!' – He tore open the front of his battledress and said, 'Shoot me sir!' I said, 'Oh, all right!'

Then there was a day when we were on our mountain and I watched our Colonel coming slowly up the path with his adjutant behind him and they were like some religious procession and I thought – Oh well, I think this is all right. The Colonel told me I had got the Military Cross for the battle of Casa Spinello, and so had Mervyn Davies and

Desmond Fay had got a bar to the MC he already had, and Corporal
Tomkinson had got the Military Medal and Corporal McClarnon had
been specially mentioned. I thought – Now, will it not be easier to
give that shutting-up look to people who inadvertently make remarks
about my father?

Then in the new year we were back at our road with the bridge
in the middle and I was thinking – This is all very well, but what
does happen if one cannot bear it? There was a hayloft in which I
sometimes slept and I remember wondering if I could fall from this
with one leg carefully placed under the other so that it would break:
this would be more aesthetic than the traditional shooting off of a
toe or a finger. Then one morning I found I was shaking; this seemed
too pleasurable to be with fear; I thought – Can I again be so lucky?
I went to the Medical Officer and he said I had either malaria, or
jaundice, or both. So I was in a luxurious ambulance once more,
bouncing back over mountain roads with a temperature of a hundred
and three, and so happy to be off again on one of my Grand Tours.

From a convalescent home at Sorrento which was in the very hotel
where I had stayed with my father and Diana and my sister in 1936
I wrote a 21-page letter to my sister on what I thought or hoped
I had learned from the war:

> I went into it with certain pompous opinions about my virtues and
> capabilities but amongst them were absolutely no pretensions that
> I would make a good soldier. I thought that all business-minded
> men would be 100 times better at organisation than myself, and I
> thought that all the eager hearties who seriously believed in the
> righteousness of this war would be 100 times more brave. After
> twelve months in Italy I realised that I was wrong: I did not under-
> estimate my own abilities, I overestimated everyone else's. And this
> startles me considerably; for I, as you know, consider this war a
> blasphemous stupidity, and yet in a spirit of unwilling desperation
> I have put more into the winning of it than most of those who
> say they consider it a holy crusade against the powers of the Devil.
>
> I still do not think I have any pretensions about myself as a soldier.
> When things are not dangerously active I am intensely and professedly
> idle. Every minute I have to give to this war I grudge angrily. Even
> when things are dangerously active I go about my business in a spirit
> of complete misery. And yet I have the reputation of being in action
> a model subaltern ...
>
> It is interesting to note that after 12 months of fighting I will

forgive anyone the old failings, the boorishness, the stupidity, the dullness, if he does not possess the failings of a bad soldier. That boils down to the realisation that out here the only thing that matters tuppence in a man is his ability to be brave. That is the only standard by which one judges anyone. For if they are not brave, it is 10 to 1 that they are miserably hypocritical as well.

Now there are incredibly few people who do possess this virtue. Those who possess it at least are those who preach most lustily about the holiness of the war crusade. Fortunately in my Battalion nearly all the officers do possess it: they do not remain long if they don't; and that is why I am able to get along very well with them whereas before I would have been driven into my frenzy of petulance by their shortcomings. But this breeds tolerance for people who are fundamentally worthy: the war is a great head-sweller to the few who fight it but it produces a lofty, cynical, benign swollen head – which does not rant or strut and still maintains an almost reverent humility towards anyone who knows why and whereof it is swollen. So although you may find me complacent I hope it does not take too odious a form. On the whole I think the tolerance and humility with those who understand will be far more prominent than the other feelings. But you will find out!

After Sorrento, I found myself once more in what I described to my sister as 'the full gaiety of the Naples winter season'. The Transit Camp seemed to have mislaid my papers; I came across my friend Anthony who was back in Italy after his time in England recovering from a wound; I rented a flat in Naples where we stayed high up in one of the tall narrow streets with the washing festooned across it like flags. There were expeditions to Pompeii and Herculaneum by day; Gigli and Caniglia were said to be coming to the Opera at night: if there were no seats one could usually squeeze into the orchestra pit or the Royal Box. My old friend from Retford days, Raleigh Trevelyan, also recovering from wounds, wrote from Rome that now there was even better social life there: 'I exchange pleasantries with Marchesas and dance on polished floors to the gramophone with Ambassadors' daughters: every Friday I partake of tea and scones with the Princess Doria . . . The Vestal Virgins are preparing a new bullock, snow-white, to sacrifice in your honour; the priests of Dionysus are already weaving garlands to adorn the pillars of the temple.' He added – 'How unfashionable you are supporting Gigli: you'll be a social failure in Rome.'

In Rome I missed Raleigh who had moved on to Florence. I caught up with the London Irish Rifles on the eastern edge of the northern plain at Forli. It was by now the end of March 1945. My return coincided with a delayed St Patrick's Day celebration and everyone got very drunk. I wrote to my father:

> I still wonder at my good fortune at finding my way into this Battalion ... The Rifle Brigade was all very jolly in the insouciant days of Winchester and York, but out here I think I would have been stifled by their so carefully posed artificiality of decency. Here the atmosphere is almost Dionysian ...
>
> When I went away in January I left behind my little translation of Zarathustra with earnest instructions to one and all that they should read it before I came back. To my surprise I find that they have followed my instructions to such good effect that the talk which floats around the Mess at dinner time is no longer of the obscenities or military pomposities to which one had become resigned, but is full of erudite allusions to Will and Power, Superman, Feasts of the Ass, etc; which, although no one knows very well what he is talking about, I find most comforting. It is surely unique to find the Mess of an Infantry Battalion that discusses Zarathustra?

From Forli we set off to play our part in the big last offensive of the war in Italy. A toe-hold had been established on the east of the plain: the London Irish Rifles were to work with a regiment of tanks and push west through something called the Argenta Gap. The people we were to work with were the fashionable 9th Lancers; in them were some old Etonians I knew; we eyed each other warily. The infantry were to be carried in armoured personnel carriers – a platoon of infantry to each troop of tanks. When the going was straightforward the tanks were to be in charge and go ahead, and then when they came up against anti-tank opposition they were to stop and give covering fire while the infantry took over and went round a flank and wiped out the opposition. This was my one experience of comparatively large-scale war such as it must have been in France or Russia; tanks drove fast over flat ground with dive-bombers overhead; these latter could be called up on the radio and would swoop down like hawks on recalcitrant opposition. It was not all easy: once one of the neighbouring troop-carriers was hit by an anti-tank shell and there was a sort of thin shower of flesh and bone: there were the times when we were out on foot again and stumbling along ditches with the vision of trip-wires and mines. But what I remember best is the awful, heroic feeling of being a conqueror – the Italians coming out from their farmhouses cheering and with bottles of wine; the Germans in columns with their hands up. Of course, there must be some reason why young men have so often liked going off to war.

The business of prisoners became difficult: the advance was often held up by the problem of finding anyone to escort them back. On the second or third day the Tank Major who was in command of our Infantry Company at the time told us that we were taking too many prisoners: did we understand? this was an order – we were taking too many prisoners. I think one of us – probably Desmond Fay – quietly spat. And of course, we went on taking too many prisoners.

I wrote to my father:

It is a happier form of warfare than any we have done before but I find it exhibits the most unfortunate characteristics of one's nature. I actually find this conquest and pursuit faintly enjoyable – and at last understand the fatal temptation of aggression. But nevertheless it is for the most part tedious, and I am irked by the feeling that the end ever remains the same distance from us even as we advance.

There was a day, however, on the edge of Ferrara when more than ever there were crowds coming out with garlands of flowers; bombers remained circling overhead as if satiated: the German dug-outs were empty except for the litter of old love-letters and the smell of stale bread. And on the wireless from Germany there was perpetual music by Wagner. The war was over.

I wrote to my sister:

Kennen Sie what victory means? It means at the moment I am the tempestuous possessor of three cars – a Mercedes which goes at such horrific speed that I am terrified to take it beyond second gear, an Adler saloon that cruises at 60 without the slightest indication it is moving, an open Opel which streaks hither and thither to the desperate confusion of all stray pedestrians. It means that we dine on champagne each night except when we feel leerish enough to start on the brandy with the soup. It means – oh well, so much really beyond cars and wine that I suppose that they are of an infinitesimal insignificance.

But then almost immediately it seemed that another war might break out; we suddenly journeyed (with our fleet of cars) to Udine, Tarvisio,

Villach – to the borders of Italy and Austria and Yugoslavia where there were Italian partisans fighting Yugoslavian partisans, Tito partisans fighting Mihailovic partisans, and the vast Russian army looming somewhere in the background and rumoured to be considering – dear God! – continuing its march westward. There was a night when we drove for miles to somewhere I think near Graz and came face to face with some Russians; they were solid-faced men in uniforms that seemed always a size too small for them; they had the ability to show absolutely no emotion whatsoever. Then we were removed from Graz as suddenly as we had come. We came to rest by a beautiful lake in Austria called the Ossiachersee. One of the buildings in our occupation was a warehouse full of the liqueur called Schnapps: a neighbouring battalion was rumoured to have captured a mobile mint which printed money. I wrote to my father:

> The end of the war seems to have been the occasion for Chaos to reign ... We are in Austria – in some of the most beautiful country I have ever seen (and with some of the most beautiful inhabitants) and although we have little or no trouble with the local people who receive us with bountiful grace and charm, we continually find ourselves surrounded by such a rabble of Serbs, Slavs, Croats, Creoles, Czechs, Chetniks, Chindits etc. as resembles the Tower of Babel on a sweaty afternoon. It has been a situation of extraordinary interest; too complex to allow me to scribble down my impression of it in this hasty fashion; but some day I might be able to tell in suitable words of the consummation of the great Tragedy.

We were close, in fact, to the area where there were being rounded up those Russians and their dependants who had fought on the side of the Germans and who became known in later years as the Victims of Yalta: they were to be returned to Russia according to an agreement at the Yalta Conference; in Russia, there was the likelihood that they would be shot. The London Irish Rifles were not involved directly in any of this; some neighbouring battalions were: soldiers were ordered to push protesting women and children into cattle trucks – some did; some simply did not. There was at least one commanding officer in the 6th Armoured Division who went up to his assembled prisoners and told them for goodness sake to bugger off. The orders from the top were terrible and daft; but then so many orders from the top in wartime are terrible and daft, and it is up to people on the spot to pay such attention to them as they think proper. This principle was established later at the trials at Nuremberg. The situation in Austria at this time was not easy for people at the top; some efforts presumably had to be made on paper to sort out chaos. The London Irish Rifles were engaged in trying to dig out high-up Nazi officials and members of the SS. I wrote to my father:

> I am acting second-in-command of the Company which entails end-less flap and fuss and as I am the only officer who can speak a smatter-ing of German I am continually handed out to be jabbered at by some miserable suspect. We have had some quite melodramatic scenes in the rounding up of such political and military personnel as are wanted by the authorities. Also much amusement. The local chaw-bacons are amazed at the way in which the British Soldier tends to dissolve in laughter during situations of the utmost gravity.

There was something life-giving in this laughter: there was also the memory of my father's prophecy that even if we won the war there would occur precisely what we said we had begun the war to prevent – the overrunning of Eastern Europe by a potentially hostile and an aggressive power. This prophecy was now coming true: so was this an occasion for laughter? I sometimes began to think it was. Human beings seemed to involve themselves almost inevitably with catastrophe: there was still the question of in what ways catastrophes must be learned from – even in what particularly profitable ways, just by their being catastrophes.

I wrote to my father:

> My admiration for the German forbids me to believe that they will ever rest so long as we are in their midst. Will we then have to resort to such savagery as they were driven to in the countries they occupied? The folly of it all! Are not pride and honour the Dionysian curses on mankind?

But I was wrong: out of the catastrophe something in fact had been, could be, learned.

All through this time my father had written to me his encouraging, discursive letters: he had followed my fortunes in the war: he had been pleased at my MC. I had few doubts that when I got home I would feel myself still close to him. I had felt myself changed by the war of course: there was something that I had learned about the life-giving qualities of ordinary virtues. But then – would not he too have been changed? He had said he had wanted to have a period of learning.

CHAPTER 28

Homecoming

House arrest ended for my father with the end of the war in Europe: my sister wrote to me: 'I arrived home from work one day to find Daddy squatting in the sitting-room – his first visit as a free citizen to London for 5 years! It was a lovely surprise.'

In a letter to me of 11th May 1945 (the first one preserved after the batch that has been lost) my father said, 'I have been suffering early stirrings of a book: what are the pains of women in childbirth compared to such a moment! I thought of including in it some of our themes, which might indeed be a book in themselves.' He added, 'It is my silver wedding day today – 25 years from first marriage. I thought so much of you all.'

The first book that my father wrote at the end of the war was called *My Answer:* its purpose was 'to justify our position in the past', not to 'provide a policy for the present or the future'. It consisted of a 20,000-word *Essay in Foreword* and then a reprint of the 1938 *Tomorrow We Live.* His aim was to show that he did not need to retract anything he had said before the war (he was reported in the press as saying somewhat cryptically, 'My opinions have not changed: indeed, they have developed'): he claimed that what he had written in 1938 had been justified by events. And indeed a year after the end of the war in Europe Winston Churchill was saying, 'This is certainly not the liberated Europe we fought to build up,' and my father was commenting that to such remarks he himself 'should merely write Q.E.D.' In *My Answer* he went back over other old ground: he quoted a speech by Lloyd George in 1900 – 'Is every politician who opposed a war during its progress necessarily a traitor? If so, Chatham was a traitor, and Burke and Fox especially; and in later times Cobden and Bright and even Mr (Joseph) Chamberlain.' My father described the activities of himself and other members of British Union at the time of the outbreak of war as those of a man 'whose old mother expresses her firm intention to go down in a fighting mood to the "local" where a number of tough characters are wont to assemble: he will be alarmed ... his disquiet will in no way be lessened by the fact that his old mother has seen fit to arm herself for the occasion with nothing more formidable than an umbrella and a shrill tongue. He will do his utmost to dissuade her ...(but) when the inevitable row begins he will do his utmost 1. to protect her; 2. to extricate her as soon as possible with the minimum possible hurt ... What an appalling conception that the son should be the first, when trouble begins, to stab his old mother in the back!'

My father suggested, following on from the study of psychoanalysis that he said he had been able to make in prison, that the reason why the charge of treachery was foisted on the British Union was because the Labour Party suffered guilt from the early days of their own movement – this guilt was to do with their 'early associations with Russian interests'. What had been objected to about British Union was not so much its attitude to the war, as its National Socialism. This* –

> could be suppressed, and its protagonists silenced in prison, by the whispered suggestion that they must be traitors to their country because they thought the war was unnecessary. We were at war and this was the excuse for everything. Any little man who had ever failed to answer our argument and never dared to meet us in public debate could stand with 'security' the other side of prison bars grimacing his defiance and jabbering his insults. Every little man with a 'hush–hush' job could flatulate his innuendos over the cocktails which he could never afford in such inspiring quantities when his own abilities in business had to pay for them instead of a salary provided by the tax-payer. What a chance for every mediocrity and dunce on the fringe of politics; for every little 'Tadpole' and 'Taper' to strut his little hour! ... Fine was that evening and deep the heady draughts of 'democratic' wine – when Stalin was so matey and the supplies were getting through to Archangel!

This was the style of my father's feelings; it represented something of what I had felt myself about people who flourished in the politics of war. But there was something numbing in the idea that he might have nothing to retract. In Italy and then in Austria I had continued

* *My Answer.*

to write my letters to my father about the things which, when he was in a benign and non-political mood, he would say mattered to him more than anything else in the world.

I am vastly interested in this physicist/philosopher controversy ... I agree with you that surely there can be no reason to suppose that human will is subject to physical laws; but do the physicists allow such a thing as luck? I feel one can bait a physical determinist by such a homely example as the toss of a coin – many vital decisions have been made through the toss of a coin: can the force of a thumb-flick be foretold by the knowledge of the background of the flicker?

It appears that the physicists have indeed done away with the old theories of matter and energy and have arrived by scientific means at much the same conclusions as Berkeley and Co hazarded in the 18th century ... The point I find fascinating is that the universe as we know it cannot be composed of ultimate matter and energy but only as the reflections of ultimate reality in some Universal Mind; and that we are only able to see these reflections as reflections again in our own minds. Now this is a very acceptable conclusion ... it does at least suggest that the Universal Mind has some affinity to our own feeble minds; thus giving us an enormous significance in the universe, when before it seemed as if we were of no account.

I think that if I get out of the army before I am 23 I shall go to a university and read philosophy for a year or so. I think it will be necessary to study quietly in some erudite backwater in order to reorganise one's thoughts after the chaos that war has produced. Or do you think the process of reorganisation could be more profitably performed in the octagonal room at Crux Easton?

In Austria we lived on the fringes of our beautiful tree-encircled lake: we had had to give up our cars but – 'riding is now the thing: I love galloping feverishly along straight tracks in woods'. I continued my conversations with my communist friend Desmond Fay. When he had entered Austria he had expected to find a people brutalised by Nazism; what in fact was there was an atmosphere like that of an idealised socialist state. We were billeted next door to an orphanage: the children were the most beautiful anyone had seen; the place was run by women of such calm, clear-eyed dignity that we, the conquerors, found ourselves behaving as if bowing and clicking our heels. Desmond Fay of course knew I was the son of Oswald Mosley; we had not talked of this directly until we reached Austria: then Desmond said – 'Ah yes, but Mosley, he was after all a serious politician!' Some time later I let slip the news that I was an Old Etonian: I don't think Desmond ever quite forgave me for this. To him a fascist, however much an enemy, was still within some recognised pale: but an Old Etonian!

From the Ossiachersee I went on leave to Venice; I stayed on the Lido where we had been as children in 1930 – in the summer holidays with Bob Boothby and Randolph Churchill and Mrs Guinness. I found it suddenly impossible, I wrote to my father, to do any more sightseeing: all I wanted was to come home.

I wonder if Nietzsche's final madness was really the decadent desperation that people suppose – if it was not perhaps 'tragic' in the ultimate sense – the culmination of a tragedy in the true Greek style – and therefore something to be greeted and accepted with a 'holy yea-saying'? Is anything much known of Nietzsche's final madness? It is a theory that entrances me – that perhaps it is the ultimate culmination of all 'great spirits' that they should appear to be what the rest of the world calls 'mad': that perhaps this one form of madness – the Dionysian madness – is really an escape into the 'eternity behind reality': neither an advance nor a regression in life but just a side-step into something that is always beside life. Or am I slightly mad?

It seems to me that the physicists have argued themselves out of their original premises and are floating blindly ... If all our sense-perceptions, measures, observations etc are unreliable, indeed misleading, when it comes to interpreting the 'real' world, why do they presume that any experiment they make has any bearing on reality at all? The only thing they can be certain about is that they can never be certain of anything ...

It seems that the Infinite only makes itself known to the finite by means of selected symbols or 'emotions' (which are really perhaps only the result of symbol-action): it is beyond the comprehension of the finite (human?) mind to understand the reality behind these symbols. But this does not exclude the possibility of creating – through a fuller understanding of the symbols – a higher form of consciousness which might ultimately glimpse the reality that lay behind.

At Ossiachersee there were rules about non-fraternisation. There was one very pretty Austrian girl who used these rules to play an expert fraternisation/non-fraternisation game: most of the young officers were a bit in love with her. Perhaps I was myself: but there were the hang-ups from Eton, from the tart who had been like my grandmother, even perhaps from the travelling exhibition about the dangers of venereal disease which followed us up through Italy like the Eumenides with huge warning photographs. There was a night in Naples when a friend and I went with two nurses on to the beach; but I still did not seem to have a proper hold on this game: did or did not No No really mean Yes Yes? Life was more simple as Narcissus.

I became Battalion Sports Officer, which meant that I could pick myself for any team: I could open the bowling at cricket and go in second wicket down: I could make out I was at home in basket-ball and hockey. The one game in which I could get away with none of this was soccer, which was taken seriously; I picked myself for the opening match and had to substitute myself after ten minutes. I was still able to justify myself in the job occasionally by my prowess at athletics; but then I entered myself for the 400 yards at Army Games at Klagenfurt; I was in a heat with the champion of the Jewish Brigade who had once run at the White City; I kept up with him for about three hundred yards, then retired from athletics altogether.

During the spring I was in correspondence with my father and sister about what would happen to the family after the war – where would we live, who would live with whom according to who were and who were not speaking to one another. My sister now had a flat in London; my brother Micky was at prep school and spent the holidays with Aunt Baba or in houses rented by Aunt Irene; my father said he did not want to go back to Savehay Farm, he wanted to buy a proper working farm and had his eye on one at Crowood near Ramsbury in Wiltshire. But he was adamant (my sister wrote) that he would not take up again any responsibility for my brother Micky. This was a mystery: did Micky remind him of my mother? or was it just that responsibilities for children, as opposed to dreams of being responsible for the world, were for him too close to reality's blood and bone? This seemed more likely as time went on and his attitude to his children became clearer: it was a measure of the peculiarity perhaps of his children's vision of him that they took it for granted he was too removed from mundane matters to take much responsibility for them. And so – was it not up to my sister and myself to make some sort of home with Micky, together with Nanny and my mother's old lady's maid Andrée who had been waiting loyally in the wings during the war and who previously had done so much to make life bearable for us? But it seemed vital to me that I should be with my father. In the spring of 1945 he bought the

1,000 acre farm at Crowood and planned to manage it temporarily at least by coming over each day from Crux Easton: it was arranged that for that summer Vivien and Micky and Nanny and Andrée would all move into a part of the house at Crowood that was empty and thus would have some contact with my father. On the periphery of all this were my Aunt Irene, still not on speaking terms with my father, and my grandmother 'Ma', as usual brought in to try to keep the peace. But there was some story now about Aunt Irene and Aunt Baba not being on speaking terms: I could not make out much of this from my lakes and woods in Austria: there apparently had been some dramatic confrontation in the corridors of the Dorchester Hotel, and my Aunt Irene had gone to recuperate with the wife of the Dean of St Paul's. My sister Vivien and I were apt now to see ourselves as arbiters amongst people who seemed sometimes slightly possessed: she wrote to me, 'You and I are what might be deemed the body of the octopus with all these tentacles stretching out'. I wrote to my father, 'I wish furiously that I could be home to organise the various family divergencies.'

Then on July 24th –

I shall after all see Crux Easton before you go. I leave the Battalion on July 30th en route for home and 4–6 weeks leave in England; after which I shall, unhappily, have to go to the Far East; but that at the moment seems such a remote contingency that it does not worry me a jot. The authorities declared that I was eligible for Burma – just, by three weeks – having been slightly under the prescribed limit of two years abroad; and as such I have to go, and nothing that any kindly C.O., Brigadier etc. out here can do can stop me.

As it happened I received the news with something like relief and would not now alter the arrangement even if it were possible. I have been growing moribund in Austria, with the harassing job of organising sports from the confines of a stuffy office. Leave I am sure will miraculously revive me.

So fatten the calf and assemble the chawbacons in preparation. I certainly could have been given no better time for leave. I should arrive about the middle of August and will have all the end of the summer holidays to play with. And with Nursery World settled at Crowood, the family can be combined without the tiresome need of splitting the leave between two camps. It will indeed be a heroic month.

The idea of seeing you all once again is really too great for me yet to assimilate.

I am saddest about leaving the Battalion, which is unique, and
had for me achieved the almost impossible of making war tolerable
in any circumstances.

I set out on the long and now familiar road through Florence and Rome
to Naples: at Naples I and my companions waited for a ship. We were
sitting one day on a terrace overlooking the bay when we read in the
local army paper that a bomb had gone off in Japan which was a new
sort of bomb – something to do with what goes on in the heart of
matter. It might indeed be so fearful that future wars would be impossible. The Japanese were already talking of surrender: so millions
of lives, including our own, might be saved. Of course, the cost was
the tens of thousands dead at Hiroshima. But was it not about just
this sort of thing that it was impossible to talk?

We sailed for home on August 22nd and arrived at the end of the
month. I caught a train from Liverpool and arrived at my sister's flat
in the evening. There was a message for me to come on to Crux Easton
– 'The room over the octagonal awaits you.'

I do not remember much about the first few days of my home-
coming: perhaps, as I had said, there was something too great for me
to assimilate. I arrived in the middle of the night: I have a memory
of everyone – my sister was there too – in the kitchen in their dressing-
gowns giving me eggs and coffee. My father and Diana looked absurdly
young: they were in their pretty, rather bourgeois house: we were
behaving as a family! Everything was so correct: I hardly knew how
to deal with this. I could not talk about anything much that had
happened to myself. I would say – I'll tell you one day.

We spent much of that summer holidays getting the harvest in at
Crowood; this was before the days of combine harvesters (a year or
two later my father was proudly one of the first possessors of one in
Wiltshire); we would follow the cutter round the large fields and pile
up stooks; throw them up later on to the cart for the thresher. It was
a fine summer and we worked in trickling heat; we rested against dusty
sheaves for picnics. All the children were there – myself and Vivien
and Micky and Alexander and Max and Diana's two elder children
Jonathan and Desmond. We were like Bacchanals and Cherubs: my
father and Diana were Zeus and Demeter.

We would shoot the rabbits as they came out from the last circles
of corn; we would later in the year embark on more formal shoots
– my father must have been the only landowner in England at that
time who had a black gamekeeper. I do not know how this occurred

– perhaps he had come with the estate. He was a West Indian: he organised pheasant and partridge shoots as if they were something like a carnival. He would say that my father was almost the only white Englishman he knew who did not seem to notice his colour. My father of course inevitably was still something of a taboo figure locally: not many people would come to shoot. There were one or two ex-military neighbours; and my friends, and friends of Diana who had not been involved in politics. There was a Swedish painter called Mogens who once wandered up on the wrong side of a hedge (the gamekeeper – 'Keep back dere on de right!') and was shot, somewhat harmlessly, in the thigh by one of my friends. Mogens went to the local doctor to have the pellets removed; he returned and announced, referring to the pellets (this was one of my father's favourite stories) – 'I still have one ball left!'

There would be the meals at which my father would hold forth as he loved to hold forth on his favourite themes – the world as a training-ground for spirits: the difficulties attendant on the vision that good can come out of evil. There was something so bright and assured about him that he held people entranced: the shooting-colonels and Swedish painters were entranced: my friends, who had expected – what? – stayed on and on to listen. He was like a dynamo switching lights on in people. Occasionally there was a brief fuse: a neighbour would ask a question about Hitler or Streicher perhaps: then what, in such circumstances, could be done? This was a time when the worst stories of German atrocities had not yet come out: there was not much news about the extermination camps, which were in territory overrun by Russia: the news was of Belsen and Dachau, the horrors of which could just conceivably and to some extent be explained by the disease and starvation resulting from the chaos and bombing of the last stages of war. There would be just a flash from my father's eyes; a guillotine look from Diana's bright blue ones. The people who came to dine at Crux Easton and Crowood during these months were mostly friends of Diana's and my father's from very old days – John Betjeman, Gerald Berners, Daisy Fellowes. With them the talk would go off into fire-works of laughter. Sometimes these friends would bring friends of theirs who did not know quite what to expect: there would then be some wariness again; people sat on the edges of chairs as if my father might swoop like Dracula.

From Crux Easton or Crowood I would go to London where parties were starting up after the war: I suddenly became aware – what on earth had I been aware of before? – of girls, of the ubiquitousness of girls, of girls pink and white and massed like flamingoes. A year before I had been writing to my sister – 'Can it be true that you and I are really immune?': now it seemed not only that of course one fell in love but how was it possible to fall in love with only one girl at once? Love was a condition, surely, of either nothing or almost all. At these parties I was like a donkey dashing between dozens of equidistant bundles of hay: not like my father – the excitement was not in conquest; it was more like some stumbling egg-and-spoon race. But I began more earnestly now to want to stay in England: there could be no delights equivalent to this even in the Far East. But also what had happened, what was to happen, to my determination to set up in some alliance with my father? My feelings towards him had not exactly changed: it was just that they seemed to have moved into an area in which there were no prospects.

One night in London in the ballroom of some enormous hotel I met, at the bar, a man who looked and indeed behaved like someone in an Evelyn Waugh novel: he was a Major in a fashionable Scottish regiment: he asked me what I was doing nowadays: I said I was about to be sent to the Far East. He said – What on earth do you want to do that for? I said – I don't. He said – Then come and see me tomorrow at the War Office. In the morning I did not know if he would remember me – we had both of us been quite drunk – he was in a not-very-grand office behind a desk. He said – I don't think I can get you anything in the War Office, but would Eastern Command, Hounslow, do? I said that Eastern Command, Hounslow, would do very well. So some days later I got a notice saying I had been taken off my draft for the Far East and I was to report to Hounslow where I would become a Staff Officer. I could travel out each day like a commuter on the underground.

In the Far East my friend Hugo Charteris was editing an English newspaper and was trying out his short stories on the Javanese; my friends Timmy and John were running a radio station and were filling in time by reading their own poems to Sumatrans. At Hounslow of course no one had expected me ('I suppose we can find you a desk') and at first I had nothing to do so I thought I would try to write about the war; but I found I could not write; there seemed to be no traditional way to make sense about the war, people wrote about it as if it were comedy or tragedy but it was neither (or was it both?); some sort of style had to be found by which absurdity might yet howl; horror might deflate by being ridiculous. After a time I was given a job which was to do with officers' pay and courts-martial: what I remember about this was the filing cabinet marked *Confidential* of which I sometimes had the key: in this were the files and the photographs (who on earth had taken them?) of officers who had been caught as transvestites. There were so many of these! I wondered – if there were more, might wars be fewer? people might thus work out their fantasies? But for the most part I sat and dreamed of girls: there was the terrible anarchy of these images: when let loose (or not let loose) what powers they had! did not victims end up bemused and dazzled somewhat like the transvestite officers? And what tenuous connections these images had with the forces of clarity and will that my father so rationally went on about: did he really think he had been immune personally from anarchy?

CHAPTER 29

'The Alternative'

The book that my father wrote after his apologia *My Answer* was called
The Alternative: it was his statement about the future. He took care
to emphasise that it was not a programme for a political party. 'This
book is written by a man without a Party as an offering to the thought
of a new Europe. Deliberately, I refrain from forming again a political
movement in Great Britain in order to serve a new European idea ...
All such ideas have originally been stated by individuals with nothing
to sustain them except the power of the spirit.' This idea was to be
'beyond both Fascism and Democracy'. The book is written sometimes
in the apocalyptic style my father had been using just before the war,
but which had been in abeyance while he had been in prison.

> At this time no other is in a position to state any real alternative
> to the present condition of Europe. The existing rulers of the earth
> are responsible for this darkness of humanity; they stand on the graves
> of their opponents to confront the Communist power of their own
> creation ... So I must give myself to this task. My life striving in
> the politics of Britain made known my name and character: my voice
> can now reach beyond the confines of one country because it
> has been heard before. The past has imposed the duty of the future.
> I must do this thing because no other can.

The idea was that Europe should be formed into one Nation and that
this Nation should regard, and use, Africa as its 'estate'. Africa should
provide the raw materials for a Euro-African closed economic system:
'trusteeship' of Africa should be 'on behalf of white civilisation and
not on behalf of a nominal stability of Barbarism'. But in order to
run this vast estate without the sort of barbarism which, it was admitted,

white men had been apt to practise before, a 'new' type of white man was required; this was a concept similar to that of the 'new' man seen previously as necessary for the proper working of the corporate state; but in *The Alternative* the need for such a man is stressed even more clearly. 'The mass of the people can only share in the benefits which modern science can bring through the devoted service of those whom they entrust with the task of government ... to secure that system they must not only create a system of state, but must also produce an altogether new and higher type of man who is dedicated in whole life and purpose to the service of the people and the State. The latter is by far the harder task'.

This higher type of man might be produced, my father suggested, by a programme of 'breeding, selection and environment' such as can be imposed on a species of animals: also – 'to these three factors a voluntary movement to evolve a higher human species would add the great fourth factor of training, or education, which, for all practical purposes, is not present in the animal sphere'. No details of the sort of training envisaged are given: in general – 'We require the union of intellect and will ... we must give robustness to the intellect and reflection to the will ... the genius of Greek civilisation consciously sought that balance and harmony'. Then there might emerge 'a Thought-Deed man who will be capable of high service to the people in the conception and execution of great design ... The future is with the Thought-Deed man because, without him, the future will not be. He is the hope of the peoples of the world. His form already emerges from his thought, in an idea which has been derived from theory and practice.'

My father saw the prototype of this Thought-Deed man as himself:

In the long years of prison and arrest opportunity was given to read what the psychologists have to say ... In an earlier period I had opportunity to study most leading statesmen of the world at first hand which is an advantage lacking to most psychologists and men of science ... In our system of ideas a Leader is appointed not by a committee as in 'Democracy' but by the test of nature which is his capacity to attract a following and to achieve ... My life is now dedicated to an Idea which transcends the diurnal politics of normality ... I have very many friends in many places who will be ready to listen.

What had prevented the 'Thought-Deed man' coming to the front before, he suggested, was 'the curse of the English' – a mixture of Puritanism and the Oedipus Complex. Puritanism was 'that cold, dark sickness of mind and soul' which had 'bent, twisted and deformed for generations the gay, vigorous and manly spirit of the English'. The Oedipus Complex of the English was exemplified by the desire of 'sons' to drag down anyone who might be a 'father' to them: Englishmen turned to leaders such as Lloyd George and Churchill in times of crisis, but afterwards 'the desire becomes overwhelming to destroy the strength to which they so recently looked for protection'. All this was due to the fact that the English, living on an island, had been protected by water from the necessity of choosing strong leadership: they had become tools in the hands of 'Mob' and 'Money' – 'Mob' being people such as communists who wish to drag down 'higher things' in order that in the resulting chaos they themselves might exercise power; 'Money' being those international financiers whose usury flourishes also in conditions of social disorder. Thus communism and capitalism, super-ficially at loggerheads, in fact go hand in hand to defeat the forces striving for a higher order.

In the last war the forces of order that Mob and Money defeated, my father suggested, were those of Nazi Germany. Nazi leadership had wanted an orderly Europe run by Germans and an orderly British Empire running world trade: if British leadership had wanted this too, then Mob and Money would not have been able to defeat them. Of course there had been roughnesses in the initial stages of the Nazi attempt to impose order; but these would not have come to such a head if there had not been a war in which the development of orderliness was lost. There was no evidence that Hitler had wanted world domination: how could anyone want this unless they were mad? And how could Hitler have been mad, when he had achieved so much in so short a time? For do not mad people destroy themselves?

The part of *The Alternative* where self-contradictions are most evident is where my father, having said all this, then describes graphically how Hitler did in fact seem to be mad; how there was something in him that seemed to set about destroying himself.

> The German leadership during the war ... appeared to violate every principle of realist policy ... History presents no more extraordinary phenomenon than the attitude of the German leadership towards the forcing of a quick decision with Great Britain ... All the evidence seems to suggest that the problem of invading Britain was never seriously faced and in requisite detail was vetoed by higher political direction ... The mystery deepens to the point of the inexplicable ... Did some extraordinary sentimental consideration traverse the

mind of German leadership to the destruction of every realistic consideration? . . . It is one of the tear-laden paradoxes of history that the man whom the mass of the English learnt to regard as their greatest enemy cherished a sentimental feeling towards a 'sister nation' which, in the eyes of historic realism, must border on the irrational and, in the test of fact, was pregnant with the doom of all he loved. This view seems too fantastic in such circumstances of life-or-death decision to permit any credence; but it appears to be supported in large measure by the sober testimony of diverse German General Staff Officers.

But if my father saw that this sort of pattern was apt to be the case – that forces dedicated to the promulgation of power by rationality seemed almost blindly to fall prey to even stronger forces of irrationality and self-destruction – what on earth was he himself doing in continuing to advocate the need for power to be exercised just by such rationality?: might this not be his own form of wilful self-destruction? He said that he had made a study of psychoanalysis in prison and indeed he used Freud's image of the Oedipus Complex to castigate others; but he refused to admit that such insights could be turned towards himself, and indeed for the most part he was dismissive of Freud as being exaggeratedly materialistic. In *The Alternative* he was more appreciative of Jung – 'the most outstanding and comprehensive intellect that the new science has yet produced': but he was wary of Jung's more recent work – 'the weight of years and pressure of current circumstances later dimmed that great contribution'. Perhaps he had come across Jung's lecture on Hitler and the Germans (quoted on p. 336) which had recently (November 1946) been published in *The Listener,* in which Jung talks of the probable appalling consequences of the inability of people to learn how to deal with their own shadow.

I myself now could not make much of this: my father's apocalyptic style was sometimes as evocative of strange stirrings as had been his speeches: but it seemed to have less and less to do with what human beings were actually like; it did not seem to have much indeed even to do with the day-to-day manipulation of power. In *The Alternative* my father said that he thought he and his ideas would win simply because 'the power of God in nature is now with us'. (There is a lot about God at the end of *The Alternative.*) But had my father not learned from the war, and from everything that he and I had been talking about for years, that the power of God in nature is not only to do with order and rationality and light?

My father was of a generation that was perhaps instinctively dismissive of psychoanalysis. But one of the intellectual and imaginative interests he had in a heartfelt way at this time was concerning Greek literature. A favourite play of his was *The Bacchae* of Euripides: he would tell the story of the play in his best epic-narrator style. Pentheus, King of Thebes, and Agave, his mother, have denied the divinity of Dionysus the God of darkness and of passion and have insisted on the rule of order and light. As a result Agave becomes a wild and unconscious devotee of the dark god: Pentheus too is drawn to watch his mother in her savage and secret rites; she and her followers catch him, and tear him to pieces. There is a speech in the last scene in the play where the script has been lost: this is where Dionysus himself seems to be trying to bring reconciliation between darkness and light. My father loved to speculate on what this speech might have contained: he would say – Synthesis; eternal synthesis! But then – why was there no feel in *The Alternative* of a person's own darkness being faced; of the vital need for the bringing of this to light? It is as if my father felt the force and beauty of such terrors and efforts in literature: he imagined that politics could be swaddled in some sort of cocoon.

He continued to lead his life of a country gentleman farmer. The house at Crux Easton was given up; he moved to Crowood. He was proud, as his grandfather had been, of his herd of shorthorn cattle; he studied the latest techniques of undersowing corn for grass. There was an air of extraordinary elegance and benignity about surface life at Crowood: my father had spent £100,000 of his money on his fascist party in the thirties; he used to say he made up this amount by speculations on stock markets during and just after the war. The house at Crowood had an eighteenth-century front and a later drawing room with high windows at the back; here were Diana's pale blue wallpaper and French Empire furniture; a huge and very beautiful Aubusson carpet. There were a cook-and-housekeeper couple and a housemaid who did the chores of the house from a servants' wing; outside, were a gardener and the gamekeeper. I remember a ritual of going down with my father to the cellar to decant very old claret; we would carry candles and a bit of muslin; we were conspirators again, like Guy Fawkes. I could still talk with my father and Diana about literature more profitably than with others of their generation; Diana introduced me to Proust; she would tell the story of how she had tried to get my father to read Proust but had given up when, after he had dipped into the first volume, he said he didn't see much in a story about a young man having an affair with his servant Françoise. What I remember my father reading at this time was Karl Popper's *The Open Society and Its Enemies* which was just coming out: my father took delight in the fact that academic recognition seemed to be being given to what he had for so long proclaimed – that Plato's *Republic*, for instance, was some sort of blue-print for the fascist Corporate State.

But by force of circumstance there was something cut off, marooned, about my father and Diana: it was mainly friends of a somewhat bizarre sophistication who visited them; my father came across little serious intellectual challenge to his flights of oratory at the dinner table. Certainly I myself at this time was too tongue-tied and between two worlds. Such intellectuals as did meet him seemed not to know quite where to start; his mental defence works were so idiosyncratic, so powerfully self-contained. Also, perhaps it suited people to see him like this – not to have to take him on at the verbal sword-play at which he excelled.

Once two airmen from a local RAF station came and knocked on the door at Crowood; when Diana answered the knock she found the airmen backing away; they explained that they had done it as a dare – they had expected to find thugs in jackboots.

My father showed little bitterness about what had happened to him in the war: he sometimes became depressed about the future. Diana cherished him and protected him from both past and future: she created a garden with him in the present. They would seem very loving together: they had their rituals: when my father was disappointed he would sometimes put on a mock baby face and Diana would run to him and put her arms around him and he would pat her, laughing over her shoulder. This might have been in some sense babyish; it was also some recognition of what human beings were actually like.

But there had always been the mystery of how someone instinctively sophisticated in areas of personal life could become so unsubtle and unstable in those to do with oratory and politics. My father had said that he did not intend to return to everyday politics; that if he did, this might damage the promulgation of his idea. But then – he could find no publisher to print and distribute his books; he decided he would have to publish them himself. And so – it was natural that he should turn for help to some of his old and trusted political followers; and it was natural that they, in spite of (or rather because of) their years in gaol, should wish to work for him. When his plans to publish his own books received publicity he had offers of help from all over the country: 'I have been reading of your new venture in the *Sunday Pictorial*; my own sympathies have always been with National

Socialism'; 'I have always admired you and what you stood for, it has always been an ambition of mine to belong to your Society'. At the same time others of his old followers had started up again on their own; they were holding meetings on street corners in London; headlines appeared in the press – 'Fascists Crawl Out': 'Our Impudent Fascists': 'Anti-Jew Chant Alleged'. Jeffrey Hamm, a member of the pre-war British Union, started a 'British League of Ex-Servicemen' (Jeffrey Hamm had been interned during the war first in the Falkland Islands where he had been a school teacher and then in South Africa); members of the League told the press that they were hoping that Oswald Mosley would come back as their political leader once he had finished his book – 'The Leader is a fast worker, and the book will be finished within the next two months.' There was a story headlined 'Mosley Records at Garden Fete' which told of complaints by local residents in a village in Essex about a recording of a 1934 Albert Hall speech which had boomed out from loudspeakers and had been heard 'over a quarter of a mile away'. When questioned about all this my father would repeat: 'I am not interested in active politics: my only interests are in books and farming.'

When I talked to my father about politics at this time and would try to encourage him to delve deeper into some of the ideas raised by *The Alternative* he would say, with a half frown – But I am a speaker, not a writer. But then, since so many of the things he said he was interested in were complex, could he not learn to be a writer? Speakers had to be so simplistic by the nature of their trade; and had he not recognised that involvement in practical politics would be harmful? But he seemed to see complexity as a matter for wit at the dinner table; it was difficult for him for long to imagine seriousness apart from politics. He wrote to his friend Henry Williamson who had made some criticisms of a proof copy my father had sent him of *The Alternative* – 'The ultimate life of my book will not be determined by any question of style, but by its thought-content. To me, only two things matter in style – clarity and power.' He was in fact to get a good deal of admiration for the style and content of *The Alternative* from members of a younger generation of writers: Desmond Stewart wrote to him – 'Without doubt it is the most important book on the future of Europe since – but it is hard to think of a parallel!'

Before long there were disturbances at the meetings in London of the British League of Ex-Servicemen. Rebecca West reported in the *Evening Standard* that the content of the speeches was 'anti-semitism and economic nationalism': however – 'contrary to popular belief' the speakers devoted 'far more time to their economic doctrine than to their anti-Jewish campaign. Their attacks on the Jews consist usually of vague references to international finance, abstract malignity about Palestine, and the disclosure of such weighty scandals as that Mr Litvinoff was born a Finkelstein and Mr Zinoviev an Apfelbaum'. Rebecca West observed that it was not, also as might have been expected, Jews who were causing the disturbances at the League's meetings but the communists who 'heartlessly exploited the grievances of the Jews against the Fascists in order to create disorder under the Labour government and to capture the Jewish vote in the forthcoming municipal and parliamentary elections'; and it was as if in reply to this that the 'fascists' were joined by the 'curious mob which attaches itself to them at such moments, though they never seem to listen to a speech'. The mob consisted of 'boys and girls between 16 and 20, adolescents who were children during the war and spent every night in the underground and now miss the excitement. These, singing and shouting about a Mosley whom none of them has ever seen, marched on a communist meeting and tried to break it up.'

Rebecca West saw that the aim of the 'fascists' in these meetings was to act as bait to lure my father back into politics. But she found it hard to believe (as he said he did) that he would fall for this: it would be 'indeed as if the proposition that Queen Anne is dead were disputed by Queen Anne herself'.

I went down to one of these East End meetings in 1946 or 1947: there was a man on top of a van shouting and waiting for the responses of the crowd: it was like some revivalist prayer-meeting. I remember one small man in a raincoat who put his head down at the edge of the crowd and dashed into the restraining arms of policemen; he bounced back as if from the ropes of a boxing ring; he seemed satisfied. After the meeting a paper-seller was set upon by a crowd and he crouched by a wall with his arms over his head and was kicked and pummelled. It was all, once more, quite like a crowd at a present-day football match.

My father was now publishing a monthly pamphlet called the *Mosley Newsletter* which was largely subscribed to by his old followers. It consisted of articles by him on current topics. Its tone became more overtly political.

One day I was driving my father up from Crowood to London – I had a small car in which I now commuted to and from Hounslow – and my father said that he was going that evening to some re-union of the old BU members in an East End pub and would I like to take

him there, and join them. He said he did not think there would be
many people. So I drove him and Diana to a street-corner rendezvous
– they had arranged to be picked up by a guide – and then suddenly
there were two motor bikes in front of us and we were being escorted
through streets like VIPs. We arrived outside some enormous East End
pub; there were men on the pavement in two lines as if at a wedding,
with their arms raised. My father had been the joking family father
in the back of the car; now he became urgent, with his chin up, striding.
What else could he be? As he entered the pub people clapped and
cheered; there were hundreds of them; as he walked between them
from the door to the bar they touched him, just touched the hem of
his garment, they wanted to get some magic from him. I could see
this because I was walking just behind him. And he was acknowledging
them, slightly lifted, glowing; his hand moving up no higher than his
shoulder, perhaps, in some not quite fascist salute. And then when he
reached the bar and we were being stood pints of beer he was called
on to make a speech of course – but no, he had given up speeches.
But he was called on again – and he was so modest, and wise, and
flashing. I suppose he was some sort of life to these people: they had
many of them been five years in jail; they had given up their lives
for him. So in the end he did make a speech: he did not say much
– just how glad he was to be amongst them again. And they were
all getting a glow from him. This was what he was so good at after
all – making people adore him – even if it might be the ruination
of his ideas. At the end of his short speech there were the hands coming
out again to clap him on the back, to shake his hand, just to come
to rest on him; and it was as if he were King Pentheus of *The Bacchae*
being fêted or about to be torn to pieces.

CHAPTER 30

Where Do We Go From Here?

For the two years after the war I remained close to my father: I would go to him on leave, for holidays, at weekends: I would bring my friends to stay. My sister and brother and their entourage had moved to a cottage near Wantage some fifteen miles away: I alternated between this 'nursery world' as I had called it and my father and Diana's home as I had done when I was a child. I had a girl friend at this time who got on well with my father; she said in later years that life at Crowood had given her a first glimpse, after war-time austerity, of what peace-time elegance might be. When her family saw that there might be some seriousness in her relationship with me her father said to her – 'But I would rather shake hands with Oscar Wilde than with Oswald Mosley!' I told my father this story: I imagined, somewhat naively, that he would laugh, as he laughed about so many of the attitudes struck against him by a crazy world. But he said – 'Does her father think I'm a bugger?' I tried to explain – 'No, Dad, it's not that he thinks you're a bugger'. But my father sometimes did not seem to see the sort of feelings there were against him.

One day there was a burglary at Crowood and six beautiful pistols I had brought back from the war as loot were stolen (my one other item of loot was a concertina): the thief, when caught, tried to ingratiate himself with the authorities by claiming to have discovered an 'arms cache' in Oswald Mosley's house. There were questions asked in Parliament about this: ones of the expected kind from Labour; then a Conservative – 'Can we have an assurance that these revolvers were not issued to Sir Oswald Mosley when he was Chancellor of the Duchy in the Socialist Government?' (cheers and laughter). Although I was still a serving officer I was charged in the civil courts with the illegal possession of firearms; my father was good about this: he hired a lawyer to make a passionate and embarrassing speech in my defence – 'Is this the gratitude society shows to a young man just back from war?' and so on. I was acquitted.

I went out to my staff job each day: I stayed up much of the night, talking and dancing. I chatted with my father about my party-going activities: he seemed anxious lest what seemed to be my lack of a steady physical relationship might be injurious to health. I half agreed with him about this; but then, were there not other and possibly worse dangers in being either a conqueror, or trapped?

From Hounslow I went two or three times a week to a stammer-man who worked under the auspices of the army authorities: he was the best stammer-man I ever went to. He spoke not of elocutionary techniques but of states of mind: stammering was some failure of relationship with oneself. One was too close: if one could stand back from one's words as it were, then words might be freed; by watching them one might deal with them. He would say – But perhaps you don't want to get rid of your stammer. I thought – Me not want to get rid of my stammer? But then, when I was with him, I was sometimes so tired I fell asleep. It was true there were simply too many impressions coming in: and I did not want to stop these.

My father wrote to me: 'I had probably not realised adequately your feelings on the matter, for the reason that your stammer never bothers me when we are talking and never seems to worry you. In fact psychologically it occurred to me that, by the strange law of compensations, it might in part account for your great gift for writing.'

There was a day when my father, Vivien and myself went down to pack up what remained at Savehay Farm; we had not lived there for five years; the civil servants and scientists had moved out; my father wanted to be rid of the place. There were my mother's glass walking sticks on the walls; the locked chest in my father's bedroom where I had imagined he kept her letters. My father told me that I could pick out any books from the shelves I liked; I found there were surprisingly few of these, and most of them had been given to her by her literary friends. There were no Proust, Joyce, Lawrence, Henry James. In the huge barns where my sister and I had climbed as children there were stored the old fascist 'armoured cars' from the 1930s. In the wood by the river there was my mother's marble tomb; it had a tarpaulin over it, as if someone had been trying to snuff it out.

At the house near Wantage my sister and I, with Nanny and Andrée, carried on with our friends playing the games we had played years ago. My brother Micky, aged fourteen, was in some state of rebellion at this time: from Eton he took to making anonymous telephone calls to my father: this was discovered when my father got in touch with the police. I remember admiring my brother's dash and courage. My father wrote a memorandum:

> It is difficult for me to be helpful in this matter because I have never succeeded in establishing any real contact with the boy ... my experience with him has been as difficult as my relationship with my eldest son has been ideal ... I have never had occasion to speak to him any word of reproof, or to experience with him any occasion ever approaching the unpleasant.

There were other manifestations of tension amongst the children – some probably arising from the separations enforced by war. When Alexander was young he had a fantasy in which he was called 'Mr Russian' and he would say – 'I have my home there: I have been dragged away.' Now, aged seven or eight, he would argue cogently the case for there being no good reason to stay alive.

I myself became invaded by feelings of futility. In war one had been told what to do and one's identity had been shaped by the style in which one either did or did not do it. Now, in the mornings, there did not indeed seem much reason to get out of bed. This nothingness – was it not a reason why people liked wars? but was not this realisation in turn a cause of nothingness?

My girl friend had a job in the Foreign Office. She worked for an official involved in the setting up of the United Nations. I would visit her in offices in Westminster and would lurk behind filing cabinets containing plans for re-ordering the world. But even concerning this effort people seemed best able to pass the time by threatening to fight one another. My girl friend wrote to me, 'Perhaps you can rescue me from this ghastly void; and perhaps I, at intervals, can rescue you from madness.'

I had earlier tried to get out of the army on the grounds of being needed as a farm worker on my father's estate; this had failed. Then there was a ruling that people would be demobilised early if they had a place assured them at a university. The scholarship exam I had taken at Balliol five years previously made me eligible for this: I got out of the army and was given a grey pin-stripe suit and a brown felt hat. I went up to Oxford in the autumn of 1946.

I did not expect much from Oxford: I had not liked Balliol when I had been there for the few days in 1941; now there were the people of the usual age-group of eighteen to twenty-one but also the older people such as myself (I was twenty-three) who had come back from the war. Balliol was crowded: rooms had to be shared: it was a cold winter. I remember writing my essays at one end of the room with a paraffin pressure-stove on the table beside me; at the other end my room-mate worked in a balaclava helmet and gloves. I was reading Philosophy, Politics and Economics – specialising in Philosophy. I would try to keep myself as it were like Odysseus strapped to my mast, while down the road in coffee-bars were the girls like sirens combing their hair.

Descartes, in his search for a certainty of which he could be sure beyond his doubt, had come across the statement 'I think therefore I am'. From this he attempted to create a whole system of philosophy. But this statement is indubitably valid only if it is taken to mean exactly what it says and no more.

Hume denied that the Self had any existence as a substance possessing endurance and identity. To him the self was no more than a collection of mental facts, experiences and ideas – we find ourselves thinking, hoping, desiring, fearing: but we never have an impression, either immediate or continued, of the Self that thinks, hopes, desires or fears. In fact there is no impression that is constant and invariable.

These arguments, however, fail to take into account one very important consideration. Hume talks about the 'I' – that is, the Self that is able to look into itself in order to take note of its impressions. He says – When I enter most intimately into what I call myself, I always stumble upon some particular perception. But what is this 'I' that possesses the faculty of entering into itself? It must be something, because Hume treats it as if it were; and moreover it is evident from experience that we do possess the faculty, in some way or other, of observing ourselves. And yet this cannot itself be one of the perceptions that it is endeavouring to perceive. What then is this primary Self?

The first time I read out an essay to my tutor the person who was sharing the tutorial with me asked – 'But is this the sort of stuff you want us to write?'

When I talked to my father about these things he seemed to have moved away from the interest in speculation that he had shown in the war: he would now talk about philosophy more in catch-phrases such as might be used by a politician. He would say – 'Descartes said,

"I think therefore I am"; then along came Bertie Russell and said, "How do you know it's you thinking?" ' And then my father would laugh, as if the scoring of such a point had ended the discussion.

I did not quite agree with my father about this: of course philosophy was absurd; but by knowing this, might there not still be good philosophy?

I continued to write my not-good poems now in imitation of T. S. Eliot –

> . . . And so to tea.
> The cups reflect
> The images of you and me
> Reserved, correct.
> I pass you silence on a plate
> And wonder if my feelings show;
> You mention that it's getting late
> And rise to go . . .

And so on. My girl friend went to America to continue with the business of disputing how to bring peace to the world. I thought – This is all very well, but what people are drawn back to are the sounds of cheering; the crowds coming out with their hands up.

It began to seem essential that I should get away and try to write my first novel. My relationship with my father had got as far as it could; now there seemed to be nothing happening, and he seemed set on going back to the battlegrounds of his old wars. If words were ever to mean anything, there had to be some effort by which victories could be held in my head.

There was a morning at Oxford when I knocked off work and went down for elevenses at the Playhouse Bar. Here there was the usual chatter like bullets, like fireflies; but there was one girl, a blonde, who did not seem part of this at all. When I spoke to her she did not appear to register what I was saying – Da da di dum dum, da da di da – we both seemed to be listening for something quite different. Later that day, in a pub, she said, 'Do you play darts?' and she threw a dart so wildly that it went into the next compartment right out of the gravitational orbit as it were of the bar. When I took her to lunch at Crowood with my father it was as if she did not hear him talking; his words seemed to be contained within some sphere like that of a homunculus.

After some time Rosemary (that was her name) and I became engaged (we did not use the word engaged: we had an agreement, for some reason, to elope to Hemel Hempstead). I wanted to get out from my past; Rosemary wanted to get out from hers: we planned, after our honeymoon, to buy a mountain farm in North Wales. Our parents met rather formally for lunch. Rosemary's mother told a funny story about how Lady So-and-so had gone to a seance to try to get through to her dead husband and all she got through to was her chauffeur who told her her car was at the door. Everybody laughed. Rosemary wrote to me: 'It seems to me that you and I are like your dream of standing on the world and everything whirling around in chaos. You do promise you will always tell me the truth, which is always less hard in the end.'

I wrote a poem to Rosemary which was the only good poem I ever wrote:

> You pause upon a sofa where
> A trembling shadow lends your hair
> The urgency of sunlight; there
> A sudden attitude betrays
> The cautious reticence of days
> And fracturing confusion lays
> Its finger on your meaning. Now
> A formal tension turns your brow
> And murmurs to the moment how
> Its policy has been decreed.
> The knowledge formulates the need
> Presenting each intended deed
> In glittering precision dipped
> And silhouetting that and this
> Like silver limbs of statues gripped
> Beneath a sunset's emphasis.

Rosemary and I were married on 14th November 1947.

The next day my father attended a conference of Mosley Book Club fans at the Memorial Hall in Farringdon Street – the site of the New Party's inaugural meeting eighteen years before and the site of the early meeting of the BUF at which my father had referred to 'three warriors of the class war all from Jerusalem'. Here, just a month after the publication of *The Alternative* in which he had said it was not his intention to found a new political party because this would not be helpful to his ideas, he announced it was his intention to found a new political party.

Rosemary and I did not, I think, want to get away from our pasts because we felt they had been bad, but because we had learned from them all we could: it is if things have gone to some purpose that children feel free to move on. I had had a dream of being with my father after the war but it had been this that had got me through the war; it had not much to do with what came after. What I had learned from my father was how to be passionate and serious and amused in circumstances that seemed daft: there was still the question of what proper circumstances one might make for oneself. I wanted to be a writer: Rosemary wanted to be a painter: we were lucky enough to be able to try to make of these desires what we could. It seemed to me that novels might be a way of using words by which one could not only set out what one saw of life but by this see the way in which one saw; and through this, because it was to do with not being trapped by life, something might change. What usually happened with words was that people argued in a straight line; and then it was as if after all the curve of space brought them back to the beginning, and nothing changed.

My father stepped back on to some wheel of repetitions: he never lost, within himself, his capacity for seriousness or laughter. He continued to say when I encouraged him to write books – But I'm not a writer, I'm a speaker. A writer sets out words to look at them as if they were the plumes of ridiculous armies: a speaker gets carried away by the crowds with their arms up cheering.

Rosemary and I had obtained two rare seats on an aeroplane going to the West Indies. There was a new type of plane doing this trip, and one had just disappeared in the mysterious area known as the Bermuda Triangle. Here ships and planes became lost and no wreckage was found: there were fantasies about their reappearing in some quite different dimension.

I had become confronted by a present nothingness: I had learned from my past that it was possible to move on. One thing we could always agree on, my father and I, was that there were the virtues of a possible freedom in being beyond the pale.

Epilogue

Oswald Mosley officially launched his post-war political party, which he called Union Movement, in February 1948. It was composed largely of pre-war members of British Union. In policy, it expanded the area of patriotism from Great Britain to Europe-with-Africa.

In 1951 my father gave up his farm at Crowood and went to live in Ireland and at Orsay on the outskirts of Paris. In answer to questions about how he thought he could lead a British political party from abroad he replied that he was now dedicated to achieving a united Europe. He made political contacts with right-wing forces in Germany, Italy, Spain and South Africa: he made only social contacts in France because, he said, he did not want to abuse the hospitality of the country in which he lived. He was the British representative at a congress of extremist right-wing groups in Venice in 1962; he made speeches (in German) to enthusiastic admirers in Germany where the translation of *The Alternative* had been a success; but nothing much came of his efforts at European organisation.

In South Africa he formed a relationship with Oswald Pirow, a pro-Nazi Afrikaner ex-cabinet minister. They produced a plan by which Africa would be clearly divided between whites and blacks – whites would take South Africa and the 'high central plateau'; blacks would have autonomy in the rest. This, it was claimed, would be a more reasonable form of apartheid than the present system in which blacks were kept in white areas as second class citizens. My father argued in his usual style that it would be possible to uproot millions of people and to transport them to new areas without there being too much fuss once the advantages of the scheme had been rationally and clearly explained.

From 1953 to 1959 he and Diana edited and published a monthly

magazine called *The European* which contained literary articles as well
as my father's political commentary and Diana's *Diary*. I myself sometimes contributed: I was warned by literary friends – did I not realise
that if one wrote anti-fascist articles for a fascist magazine this made
one a fascist? My father produced his best non-political essays for *The
European*. There was one in particular called *Wagner and Shaw: A
Synthesis* in which he argued against Shaw's interpretation in *The Perfect
Wagnerite* of Wagner's *The Ring*. Shaw had claimed that *Götterdämmerung* was a superfluous addition to an otherwise admirable mytho-
logical construction: the fall of Siegfried as a victim to the temptations
of ordinary human passion was senseless after all the hopes of super-
human achievement offered by the earlier operas. My father suggested
that in this respect Wagner had seen further than Shaw: it was inevitable
that Siegfried who sought 'adventures' as a conqueror rather than
'supreme creation' as someone dedicated to the task in hand should
fall a victim to humdrum passion; what was required before there could
be super-human achievement was the emergence of the being 'who
weeps because he has killed a swan rather than exults because he can
kill a dragon; who holds the all-powerful spear on condition that he
does not use it'. And my father claimed that Wagner had in fact outlined
such a being in *Parsifal*. Parsifal was not only Wagner's vision of
a Christian knight who was superior to Siegfried; he was also a prototype
of Nietzsche's third metamorphosis of the Child – though neither Shaw
nor indeed Nietzsche saw this.

In 1958 my father published a book *Europe: Faith and Plan* in which
there are elaborated many of the ideals, and reiterated many of the
begged questions, that had characterised most of his political life. The
ideals were – a united Europe running a large part of Africa and
governed by a democratically elected parliament and executive; this
Euro-African power-block would be independent of, and indeed
stronger than, the blocks of America on one side and Russia, to whom
control of Asia would be left, on the other. The begged questions were
– the assumption that all this could be done if Europeans just had 'will'
to 'greatness'; that it would even be possible to come to reasonable
agreements with leaders of the other power-blocks because they, having
got to such positions of power, must be rational men themselves –
and would not want to destroy the world by conflict. This left out
of account what my father had learned so painfully of the irrationality
and even will-to-destruction of someone like Hitler and indeed of other
politicians; it ignored what he himself had experienced of the absurdities
of political leadership during the one year when he had had govern-

mental power. He still had the conviction, against all the evidence, that human beings liked things to be neat and orderly.

During the early years of Union Movement my father held meetings at Ridley Road in North London and at Kensington Town Hall: later he spent much of the time in his houses in France and in Ireland promulgating his ideas in *The European*. Life at Clonfert, in County Galway, was something like pre-war Wootton; there was fishing and rough shooting; the house was a fine old Protestant bishop's palace at the end of a long avenue of yew trees. Then in 1955 my father was writing to me – 'I have a feeling that before long the rush may begin again, though I am as usual premature. But when it does, all charm of life flies, as well as all sense, for a long season!'

What brought him back to London to local day-to-day politics was, as it had been twenty years earlier, a particular issue – that to do with 'alien' immigration. In 1936 the issue had been that concerning Jews in the East End: in 1956 it was the coloured immigration into the area of Kensington north of Notting Hill. At this time there was no restriction on immigration from the Commonwealth: there was unemployment in the West Indies owing to the pact which the English Labour Government had made to buy sugar from Cuba; workers came from the West Indies to Britain where there was still the promise of jobs. In North Kensington after a time there began to be street fights between blacks and gangs of white youths who were at that time known as Teddy Boys: these fights came to a head in the summer of 1958 when there were what the press referred to as race riots in Notting Hill. Union Movement announced it would launch its largest campaign in the area; it professed to aim at trying to bring order to a troubled situation. Its stated policy was reasonable; a pamphlet was distributed which proclaimed, 'Most coloured immigrants are decent folk: they are victims of a vicious system which they do not understand.' My father wrote articles advocating forcible repatriation for recent immigrants but 'with fares paid ... and to good jobs with good wages'. What was required was capital investment in the West Indies: 'I say – Let the Jamaicans have their country back, and let us have ours.'

This was the policy: but – as had happened so many years ago – some quite different picture became lodged in people's minds. For the most part the Union Movement's weekly newspaper (at first called *Union* and then as in the old days *Action*) maintained a disciplined tone with little of the racialist jargon that had bedevilled the old *Action*: occasional lapses were noted: Diana wrote a memo to my father pointing out a bad example of *Action*'s fussy, indignant style, 'so repugnant to intelligent people who might otherwise heed our economic argument: "Fuzzie Wuzzies" "Hottentots" . . . Do not play into the hands of those who imagine our policy is based on hatred of the blacks'. But more important than any of this were the questions people asked about what was Union Movement doing in the area anyway: why had they chosen this area rather than any other to concentrate their attention on? what did they think would be the effect of a statement such as 'blacks should be sent home' on a volatile population? In September 1958 the Trades Unions' Council put out a statement that Union Movement was 'fanning the flames of racial violence' in Notting Hill. Union Movement replied with reiterations of its policy which it said was aimed at being helpful to blacks; it also claimed that it was serving the community by providing a means of keeping so-called Teddy Boys under control. In September 1958 *The Times* sent a reporter to the area to try to find out what was in fact happening:

The Movement is exploiting rather than creating the disturbances. It will not condemn the violence, but is rather pointing to a target behind the one that is now being attacked. At least a part of those responsible for the clashes hold a certain sympathy for the Movement. 'We both want the same thing; we're just going about it in different ways,' one demonstrator commented.

A clear distinction must be drawn between official Union Movement policy which has been formulated by Sir Oswald Mosley and the reasons most members have had for joining. Those immediately below the Leader look to him for political guidance and seem to have a genuine desire to see his policies instituted . . .

All this is incomprehensible to the majority of his followers, who understand the clichés in which the ideas are expressed rather than the ideas themselves. They have joined the movement for a variety of reasons; some, because they are anti-semitic, but the largest number, it seems, because they like fighting Communists and painting slogans on railway bridges. They fight because they have an instinctive desire to do so.

It is admitted by the leaders that these elements are out of the control of the party, and probably would not have joined if it was not for the sinister evocation of the word 'movement', the dramatic salute, the hero-worship implied in the word 'leader' and the fanatical hatred of the word 'Communism'. This element would riot whatever organisation they belonged to, or if they belonged to none at all.

The problem for someone close to my father was – how was it that he did not see (or did he?) the dangers inherent in becoming involved politically in such an area and in such a predicament no matter what the virtues of his policy and his stated insistence on discipline? Did he not remember the thirties? I myself had been too young to be an outspoken witness of events then: but over the years (as I had listened to my father's so rational explanations) I had wondered about what seemed to be the two sides to his character – the reasonable, and that which nevertheless seemed to go headlong looking for trouble: how much had his left hand known what his right hand was doing?

There was an incident from the early days of Union Movement just after the war that stuck in my memory. My father had summoned to him one of his lieutenants who had disobeyed orders that members should not become involved in the breaking-up of opponents' meetings: my father reprimanded the man in a room next door to where Rosemary and Diana and I were having dinner. My father shouted at him for a time; the man was saying, 'Yes sir, sorry sir'; then my father said quietly, 'Well don't do it again'. And as he showed the man out into the passage some sort of wink seemed to pass between the man and my father – some touch on the arm perhaps – a recognition of comradeship or complicity beyond the demands of discipline. And it was as if we all knew that the man of course would do whatever he had done again; my father knew this; the man knew that my father knew this – it was as if the reprimand was just some ritual by which my father might effectively not quite let his left hand know what his right hand was doing. And it must have been something like this, I supposed, that had happened in the thirties – both with my father, and with other national socialist leaders.

When I talked to my father about such incidents he would say – with his half-self-mocking half-smile-half-frown – 'It's a rough game' – or – 'One must keep the boys happy'.

During the fifties I had become involved in increasingly passionate arguments with my father about the kind of style that I now felt was characteristic of his politics. Rosemary and I in the early years of our marriage had spent summer holidays with him and Diana: we had come down from our Welsh mountain and had dallied happily in old haunts in the south of France: he and Diana moved from time to time into the powerful vacuum of social life in Antibes and Monte Carlo and Rosemary and I had not been much part of this; but when we were on our own with him and Diana there was, as there could always be, the gentleness, the funniness, his way of making quite ordinary things seem luminous. But as time went on I became involved in my own struggles to deal with or get beyond, areas and threats of double-think and nothingness. I had long since become convinced of the justness of the second world war; I had become something of a Christian, and an anti-racialist; I was a friend of Father Raynes and Father Huddleston who had been deeply involved in political and missionary work on behalf of blacks in South Africa. My father more and more professed himself scathingly anti-christian. As he entered into the politics of Notting Hill so I tried to take him on in argument head on, in a way I had not felt able or inclined to do before; I wrote him letters; discussions became less of a game and more belligerent at the end of dinner. The argument which I came to see with increasing passion as an area for battle was on the grounds not only that I thought his apartheid racialism ethically wrong (it seemed to me that simplification by separation was to do with death: evolution of life depended on the acceptance of ever greater connections and complexities) but that I thought his present attitudes and activities were evidence of his, and perhaps all fascists', tendencies to self-destruction. Whatever good ideas he had had in the 1930s had been destroyed by his laying himself open to charges of anti-semitism; now, any reasonable ideas of his were being treated with contempt because of his deliberately exposing himself to the charge of anti-black racialism; and if he had not learned how such exposure could defeat even the best ideas, what on earth had he learned? Of course he had the answers to this: there were real problems about the unlimited immigration from the Commonwealth; local people had asked him to come to Notting Hill as their champion; there was a chance at least in theory that he might be able to harness and discipline the gangs of white toughs. I would say – But did he not see that the point at issue was not so much what he himself said or did, but what people made of what he said and did, and especially his opponents? He would say – But were not all movements advocating new ideas at first unpopular? And should he yield to misrepresentation by the press?

It was difficult to make headway in arguments with my father because as always there was the deployment of words as if they were inexhaustible armies. I tried, as other people had done, to go into the attack. In October 1958 I wrote to him:

Your policy regarding black men is to provide jobs for them in their own homelands by providing capital for backward areas. This is admirable. Your intention in general is to have a movement which is 'manly, disciplined, restrained and self-controlled, which never begins trouble and never exults in it: just is prepared to meet it if others absolutely insist'. Again, this is unexceptionable. But what in practice happens is that your movement holds a meeting in Notting Hill, which is followed by violence.

To say that the speakers never wanted nor intended violence is meaningless. To believe this would be an opinion of such astonishing political naivety that it were surely better to be hushed up – it must still be better for a politician to be thought something of a villain rather than an idiot. If anyone does believe this then you've handed the game to your opponents without a struggle: for the explanation can only be pathological. It must always be remembered that this is what the struggle is – not one of policy versus policy, because no one is fighting you on this level; but one of your opponents accusing you of madness through the evidence of your actions and you, presumably, concerned with producing evidence that they are wrong. If you hand this game to your opponents so easily, you cannot blame them for not bothering to take you on in the further battle about policy ...

I've written at length because I care about it all perhaps more than you think ... I cannot bear to see the whole structure of thought and prophecy seeming to be led towards the ditch by exactly the same blind forces that ruined and destroyed it before the war. I sometimes complain that history repeats itself; yet I am bewildered that it can do so in this immediate and despairing way.

To sum up – Fascism, and therefore Union Movement, has got the general reputation, whether fairly or unfairly, of having to depend upon racial hatred in order to maintain its appeal and impetus. It was this reputation that made fascism so hated years ago.

Now you and your followers say that this reputation is unfair: but it is still in people's minds. Your obvious intention therefore, since it is so harming your cause, would be to take steps to eradicate it.

One would have thought these steps would have included instructions to avoid, in speech and writing and action, all controversial racial issues like the plague: there would be orders, surely, to hold meetings anywhere in London rather than Notting Hill: to keep all sneering references to colour out of *Action*: and when any unfortunate incidents did occur through the stupidity or indiscipline of subordinates, then immediately to take disciplinary steps against the subordinate and to publicise these steps fully, and with apologies to those concerned, in the national press.

Failure to take this sort of action seems only to mean that in spite of your words on paper, your intention is not seriously to eradicate from people's minds the impression of your need for racial hatred.

Your reasons for not wanting to do this are beyond my competence to guess. But the results of it are that your words seem destined only to bluff yourselves, and not to influence responsible people who will go only by your actions.

To this my father replied briefly that in fact no Union Movement meeting in Notting Hill had resulted in violence; and he challenged anyone to produce concrete evidence that it had.

In 1959 he stood as the Union Movement candidate for North Kensington in the general election. I went up to hear him speak: I stood on the edge of the crowd without his knowing I was there. There was Dad on top of a van again and bellowing; so much older now with his grey hair and grey suit; it was true that the crowd around him was large and quiet and respectful. I had expected that he at least would be putting over the aspect of his case that was reasonable; but instead – I still find it difficult to believe this but other witnesses have confirmed it – there he was roaring on about such things as black men being able to live on tins of cat food, and teenage girls being kept by gangs of blacks in attics. And there were all the clean-faced young men round his van guarding him; and somewhere, I suppose, the fingers of the devotees of the dark god tearing at him.

Shortly before the election I said that I must see him and talk to him; he said he was too busy to see me; I said I would come to his office and sit outside it and wait. At this time in addition to my feelings about his politics I was involved in a passionate struggle with him about the welfare of my half-brother Alexander. At the time of the race riots the year before, Alexander and Max, aged nineteen and eighteen, had been photographed in Notting Hill: they had said they were there to help Union Movement. Since this time Alexander had tried to get out: he was a brilliant boy; my father was refusing to let him go to a university. He had become (so Diana informed me) somewhat ill. In the waiting room outside my father's office I suddenly realised that I was frightened in a way that I had not been since the battle of Casa Spinello. When I finally got into my father's tiny office he and Diana and his lawyer were in a row behind a desk; I stood as if to attention like some private soldier; then I spewed it all out, in some frail rage, both the politics and the personal stuff – my father was not only a racialist but was using racialism to destroy himself;

what he was doing was not only wrong it was squalid; he had done this before, he was doing it again, was he so crazy as not to know what he was doing? And he was a lousy father – I might as well tell him everything now – he had never cared a damn about any of his children, he got rid of responsibility for them as soon as he could; when they tried to go their own way, when anything went against him, he was just contemptuous of them. I carried on like this for some time; then I stopped. I had thought perhaps some great thunderbolt would come down on me. But instead he said very quietly – 'I will never speak to you again!' He turned to Diana as if haunted. I had not expected this. I said something like – Well, I'll always speak to you. Then I left.

A day or two later I wrote to him saying that I took back just the thing about his having been a lousy father to me because I did not think he had been. He did not answer this letter. When I talked about this to my brother Alexander he said – 'Well, he wouldn't, would he?' Alexander did get away – eventually to a university in America.

In the election of 1959 at North Kensington my father got 2,821 votes out of a total of 34,912: he came bottom of the poll, and lost his deposit. This had never happened to him before. He had been confident almost of winning. His canvassers had taken unofficial polls just before and just after the voting and they had told him they had been assured of such support as to justify this confidence. When the result was known they would not believe it: they said that the ballot boxes must have been tampered with. My father went so far as to bring a court action about some irregularities that had been observed in the procedures; he planned to call witnesses to give evidence about how they had told his canvassers that they had voted for Mosley and now it seemed that they had not: how could this be explained? But when it came to the matter of appearance in court witnesses could not be found, or said they had changed their minds, or had forgotten. Nothing came of the case. What seemed to have happened was what had happened so often before to my father – he had charmed people with words; he had charmed himself into confidence by his ability to charm others with words; then when it came to a vote, to assurances being made effective, people behaved quite differently.

After 1959 there were renewed outbreaks of organised communist hostility against him: meetings were broken up; for a time he held meetings in Trafalgar Square, but then these were banned. In 1962 he was knocked down on his way to address a meeting in Ridley Road and was rescued from possible serious injury by the brave intervention of my half-brother Max. Max was acting as one of his right-hand men at this time. When I saw photographs of my father on the ground with demonstrators putting the boot in I had atavistic feelings – should not I, his eldest son, have been there to defend him? But then – what on earth were the people around him doing wheeling him out like an old Aunt Sally?

Max assisted my father loyally for a time; then moved on, with great success, into the motor-racing business.

The last time my father stood for parliament was for Shoreditch in 1966; he polled 1,600 or 4.6% of the votes. After this he gave up the leadership of Union Movement, and retired from active politics.

During this time I had been fighting the battles to do with myself: the problems were, as always – what happens when you realise that orderliness cannot be imposed by will? how do you get out of nothingness without finding yourself in a commitment which part of you knows is not to do with truth? The novels I had written soon after the war had been to do with doom and damnation: this had been a way of expressing perhaps something I had felt about the war: but in fact what I had also learned was that there was something in war's absurdity that was not a lie – though this, I had realised, could perhaps not quite be put into words. So what was I doing writing novels? Into this impasse there had emanated the hollowed-out, piercing figure of Father Raynes CR – a monk. Through the door that opened to Christianity there seemed to be a hope of impossibilities being made possible. But hope still seemed to lead if not to damnation still through doom – you did what you had to do, but the world crucified you: it was through this there was redemption. I gave up writing novels for a time; there seemed to be more obvious immolation in good works. But then if one read the Bible, as one was told to do, did it not in fact say something quite different from what people seemed to think it said? Had I not found this so many years ago? People thought it was talking about salvation-through-sacrifice but in fact it suggested that this sort of thing had been done; and now there was in operation some chance to trust life that indeed could not quite simply be put into words but which was to do with the Holy Ghost. And so – might it not be about this that one could write novels?

After a few years my two older sons, aged twelve and thirteen, said to me – Why do you never take us to see our grandfather? Is it that you are afraid he might influence us? I thought about this: I said – Perhaps it is. So it had to be arranged that Rosemary and I should take our two older sons to stay with my father and Diana in their house at Orsay. There had already been one or two moves towards reconciliation: there had also been jokes relayed to me from my father that indeed, yes, it would be some fitting recompense to him in our dispute about Alexander if he could now influence my older sons away from the shadowy world of Christians. And so we went over and sat in my father's and Diana's elegant dining room with its Empire furniture and marvellous food and I was at one end of the table and my two sons were on either side of my father at the other and he poured out his lava-flow of words – was not the present political predicament like that of people in an aeroplane who suddenly find themselves without a pilot; they are about to crash; is it not the first essential to give authority to a competent pilot and then later the debates concerning methods of selection and safeguards can continue. My sons listened to him gravely. I thought – Is not twelve or thirteen the sort of age at which it is proper to be fascists? to believe that life should be rational? Then – Ah yes, but I trust, do I not, that enough caring has been built up for them to know that these words go round and round like tigers trapped in cages. And later my sons said – You did not really think, did you, that we would be influenced by your father?

For the last thirteen years of his life my father became more as he had been in prison; in his seventies and eighties he liked to talk about ideas; he went for walks and ruminated on his own; he entertained his and Diana's old friends; he liked things to be funny. Occasionally he would roar off on one of his runaway slides with words – about the folly of war, the ruination of Europe, the hypocrisies of democratic politicians. He never ceased to be amazed that the communist world had fallen out within itself – Russia and China, for instance, had become enemies when just by being rational what power together they might have wielded! He did come more to accept the horror of things that had been done under the Nazis: when Hitler's name was mentioned his eyes would cloud over and he would sometimes murmur – Terrible little man! In certain moods he seemed to be waiting for the crisis in Britain and in Europe to materialise which he had for so long expected and which, he still believed, might cause people to turn to him as the one man who had foreseen it and which might be a means at least of his at last being called to power; but then with part of him he seemed to accept that this was a fantasy. For the most part when one was staying with my father during these years there was an air of celebration: the celebration was just for having come through.

The house outside Paris where he and Diana lived was called, of all things, Le Temple de la Gloire – it had been built for one of Napoleon's generals to celebrate his victory at Hohenlinden in 1800. There was a central block of just a dining room on the ground floor and a drawing room on the first floor and, on either side of these, two small wings containing my father's bedroom and sitting room and bathroom and Diana's bedroom and sitting room and bathroom; underneath these were the kitchen and servants' rooms, and two guest rooms and a bathroom. There was a portico like that of a Roman temple at the front; a lawn led down from this to a lake on which there floated one or two swans. There was a suburban road to one side of the lake and the municipal sports stadium on the other. The whole scene was like one of those microcosms of a grand world you look at through a peep-hole in a box: it was immensely elegant, yet almost on the edge of a parody. My father liked to see it like this; he called it 'our funny little house'. It seemed a perfect setting for him and Diana; they grew old there happily; they gave happiness to people around them.

The last time I saw my father was in November 1980, ten days before he died. I had gone over with my second wife to spend a weekend with him and Diana; now more than ever he seemed anxious to talk. He would be up in the mornings long before his usual time, and when I appeared in the drawing room he would say – Have some pink champagne! I would say – Now Dad? and then – Yes! It was quite like, after all, the times I had visited him in Holloway. Then we would talk for most of the day – of the past, of life before the war, of my mother, of her sisters. He wanted, I think, to make something clear about the past: he told me – as he had used to tell me so many years ago – how good his first marriage had been; how now of course his second marriage was very good, but what he wanted now, with and for everyone, was reconciliation. He said – Throughout the thirties, you know, it was as if I had two wives: do you think that was immoral? I said – Ah, Dad, immoral! He was this very old man who had Parkinson's disease; he took pills to make himself stop shaking. Sometimes when standing he would lose his balance and topple over like an enormous tree; from the floor he would explain, laughingly – 'It's these pills, you know; it's a wonder what can be done by modern science!' I told him that I wanted to write something about his life; that I wanted to try to write the truth; that no one of course ever quite caught the truth, but if one made efforts then these could stand for it. I said that I thought however peculiar his life had been – or just because of this – the story of it would be best served by truth; there had had to be prevarications in the past perhaps, but his life had been passionate enough and a struggle enough and concerned with real things enough for it to be proper that there should now be efforts at truth: and anyway, what other forms of reconciliation were there? And he watched me with the small rather distant eyes that I suppose had never trusted anyone very much – he had felt he had such reason to trust himself! – and there had always been people round him, as indeed there were now, to encourage him in this; who were not much interested in ways of reconciliation. And then my father said in a loud voice – my stepmother Diana was getting rather deaf – that he wanted me to have all his papers.

Notes on Sources and Acknowledgements

Material for this book was for the most part provided by my father's papers which, after his death, were put at my disposal by my stepmother, Diana Mosley. She has asked that it should be made clear that she is not associated with these memoirs, and that she disapproves of many of my interpretations and of the publication of private letters.

Of published works I owe most to my father's autobiography *My Life* (Nelson, 1968) and my stepmother's autobiography *A Life of Contrasts* (Hamish Hamilton, 1977), from both of which I quote. My other chief debt is to Robert Skidelsky's admirable biography, *Oswald Mosley* (Macmillan, 1975). I have quoted also from *The Fascists in Britain* by Colin Cross (Barrie & Rockliff, 1961); *Portrait of a Leader* by A. K. Chesterton (Action Press, 1936); *Portrait of the Labour Party* by Egon Wertheimer (Putnam, 1936); *Decline and Fall of the Labour Party* by John Scanlon (Peter Davis, 1932); volumes 1 and 2 of *The Diaries of Beatrice Webb* (1952 and 1956); *I Fight to Live* by Robert Boothby (Gollancz, 1947); *Tomorrow Is a New Day* by Jennie Lee (Penguin, 1947); *Unfinished Journey* by Jack Jones (Hamish Hamilton, 1938); *J. H. Thomas: A Life for Unity* by Gregory Blaxland (Muller, 1964); *Diary in Exile, 1935* by Leon Trotsky (Harvard University Press, 1976); *In Many Rhythms* by Baroness Ravensdale (Weidenfeld & Nicolson, 1953); and from *The Collected Works of C. J. Jung* (Routledge & Kegan Paul, 1978).

Other works by Oswald Mosley that I have quoted from (in addition to *My Life*) are *The Greater Britain* (BUF Publications, 1932), *Tomorrow We Live* (Greater Britain Publications, 1938), *My Answer* (Mosley Publications, 1946), *The Alternative* (Mosley Publications, 1947), and *Europe: Faith and Plan* (Euphorion Books, 1958).

Other helpful books about fascism in Britain in the thirties have been

Political Violence and Public Order by Robert Benewick (Allen Lane, 1969) and *Anti-Semitism and the British Union of Fascists* by W. F. Mandle (Longmans, 1968).

I have quoted from Harold Nicolson's *Diaries and Letters: 1930-39* (Collins, 1966) and was helped by being allowed to read Harold Nicolson's unpublished diaries in Balliol College Library. I have also quoted from Albert Speer's *Inside the Third Reich* (Weidenfeld & Nicolson, 1970), and have quoted extensively from the unpublished diaries of my aunt, Irene Ravensdale, which are in my possession.

I am grateful to Lord Boothby for permission to quote at length from the three letters he wrote to my father in the early thirties; also the letter he wrote to my mother in 1925.

I am grateful to Zita James for permission to quote from her unpublished diary of 1930.

For my chapter entitled "The Riddle of the Sphinx" I am indebted to Charles Hampden-Turner's admirable *Maps of the Mind* (Mitchell Beazeley, 1981).

My thanks are due to Mr David Irving for most generously allowing me to see the documents relating to the Mussolini payments and for allowing me to quote from them and to reproduce one in this book. I am grateful to Mr Dennis Mack Smith for his advice about the chapter on Mussolini.

My thanks are due to the Rt. Hon. Sir Frederick Lawton for giving me valuable help with chapter 14 of volume 2 regarding Air Time Ltd.

My thanks are due to Mr Richard Bellamy, who most generously made available to me his unpublished typescript of his years with the BUF.

My thanks are due to Sir Mervyn Davies for checking the wartime chapters.

Last, but not least, I am grateful to my sister Vivien (who has allowed me to use some of her photographs) and to my brother Michael, both of whom have generously assisted with what is to them the unearthing of old stories.

Index

Sir Oswald and Lady Cynthia Mosley are referred to as Tom and Cimmie in entries pertaining to volume one; for these nicknames, see pp. 3, 10.

British Union of Fascists—*cont.*
  Rothermere and, 306-10, 322, 328-29
  newspapers and magazines, *see Action;*
    Blackshirt; Fascist Quarterly; Fascist
    Week
  Tithe War, 312-13
  parliamentry and local elections, 352,
    357, 371-72, 374, 380-81, 426
  HQ moved to Great Smith Street, 361
  in East End, 372-81, 555-56
  new name and symbol for, 376
  uniforms, 380
  loses support (1937), 388-89
  Holiday Camp, 391-92
  attitude to Second World War, 412,
    418-20, 421-24, 426, 539
  HQ searched, arrests, 428-29, 433-34,
    441-42, 453
  National Socialism, 539
  members join Union Movement (*q.v.*),
    564
Brittain, Vera, 325
Brockway, Fenner, 168
Brown, Major Yeats, 421-22
Brown, W. J., 149, 169, 172, 173, 183
B U F, *see* British Union of Fascists
Butler, R. A. (later Lord Butler), 147-48
by-elections, fascist candidates at, 426
Byron, Lord, 363

Cable Street, Battle of, 377-79
Calder, Ritchie, 327
Campbell, B. A., 47, 87, 100
Camrose, William Ewert Berry, 1st
  Viscount, 387-88
Carlton House Terrace, Curzon residence
  at No. 1, 16
Carrington, Dora, 217
Casa Maury, Bobby, 132
Casa Maury, Paula, *see* Allen, Paula
Cecil, Lord Robert, 26, 27, 28, 29, 38, 47
Centre Party, projected, 28-29; 'alliance',
  149-53; *see also* New Labour Group
Chamberlain, Joseph, 60
Chamberlain, Neville, 58, 203, 413, 423,
  425, 426, 427, 433
Chamberlayne, A. R., 9
Chapel Royal, St James's, 24

Charteris, Hugo, 546
Chesterton, A. K., 346-47, 354, 356-57,
  388-89
Cheyney, Peter, 201
Chicago, 61, 62
Christianity, 300-301, 486-87, 495, 573
Churchill, Clementine, 502
Churchill, Lord Randolph, 55, 144
Churchill, Randolph (son of Sir Winston),
  203, 219, 242, 418, 498
Churchill, Sir Winston, 8, 28, 51, 120,
  150-51, 188, 203, 216, 227, 426, 427,
  433, 437, 468, 538
Ciano, Galeazzo, 370
City of London, 125, 170-71
Claire, Ina, 132, 133-34
Clarke, Mick, 373, 381
class, 395, 396
Clerk, Sir George, 158, 440
Cliveden, 94, 253, 280, 282
Clonfert, 566
Clynes, J. R., 158, 297
Cockburn, Claud, 324
Colonial Development Bill, 122
colonies, 60, 64
Comer, Jack ('Jack Spot'), 375, 377
communists, communism, 87, 94, 274,
  275, 276, 322-27, 378, 555; *see also*
  Marxism; socialism
Conservative Party
  Tom approached by, 8
  Tom leaves benches in Commons, 27,
    266
  Tom opposed by, at Harrow, 47-48, 49
  scorned by Tom, 50, 89
  in 1929 election, 120
conspiracy theory, 348
Contrexeville, Cimmie's visit to, 224, 225
Cook, Arthur J., 90-91, 168, 169
Corfu, invaded by Italy, 27, 47
corporate state, 314, 350, 358-59, 553
Coventry, B U F branch at, 354
Cowdray, Lord, 29
Cox, Mr (butler), 283
Crellin, George ('Captain Thornton',
  'Captain Latch'), 311
Crowley, Aleister, 360-61
Crowood, 542, 543, 544-45, 552, 556, 564

rapher), 331

House of Commons, *see* Parliament

Houston, Lady, 341

Howard, Brian, 223

Howard, Peter, 186, 199, 210

Hull, B U F meeting at, 386

human nature, 67-69; *see also* power

Hutchinson, Barbara, 217

Huxley, Aldous, 320, 327

Hyde Park, B U F meeting in, 284-86, 345-46

Hyslop, Nanny, 34, 45-46, 71-78, 91, 99, 102-3, 219, 244, 252, 260, 261, 279, 280, 281, 282, 284, 384, 409, 410, 421, 422-23, 429, 446, 447, 496, 542-43, 558

idealism, and practical politics, 141-42, 223; *see also* power

immigration, black immigrants, 566-67, 569-71

Imperial Fascist League, 272, 276, 376

Independent Labour Party (ILP), 61, 81-82, 91, 113

India, 13-16, 26, 343-45

Tom and Cimmie in, 59, 60-61, 79

inflation, 65, 66

International Court of Justice, The Hague, 154

Invergordan mutiny, 201

IRA, 27, 28

Ireland, 21, 27-28, 399

Irene, Aunt, *see* Curzon, Lady Irene

Irving, David, 294-95

Irwin, Lord, 344

Isherwood, Christopher, 201

'I' Squad, *see* Fascist Defence Force

Italy, war in, 496, 498-99, 504-10, 512-19, 523-36; *see also under* fascism, in Italy; Mussolini

Jackson, Derek, 430, 445, 503

Jackson, Pamela, 430, 461, 503

James (footman), 283

James, B. S., 343

James, Zita (née Jungman), 94-95, 157, 159, 160, 162, 163-64, 165, 257

Jameson, Storm, 327

Jane di San Faustino, Princess, 32, 208, 210

Jebb, Gladwyn, 209

Jewish World, 292, 310

Jews

Tom's attitude to, 222-23, 229, 230

fascists attacked by, 291-92, 329, 375

pressure on Rothermere, 328-29

conspiracy of, supposed, 347-49, 372-73

in East End, 373

see also anti-semitism

Joad, C. E. M., 150, 187-88, 191

John, Augustus, 216

John Bull, 330

Johnston, Tom, 121, 123, 143, 146

Jones, J., 39

Jones, Jack, 185, 187

Jones, Mr (fascist), 311

Joyce, James, 281

Joyce, William ('Lord Haw-Haw'), 290-91, 310, 340-46, 358, 359, 374, 375, 381, 389, 442

Jung, C. G., 304, 336, 551

Jungman, Theresa, 157

Jungman, Zita, *see* James, Zita

Kedleston, 13, 16, 30

Keynes, Maynard, 59-60, 127, 196

Kirkwood, Dr, 250, 251, 252

Kitchener, Lord, 16

Knight, A. H. J., 486

Korda, Sir Alexander, 359

Krane, Francis Peabody, 157

Labour Party

Tom joins, 49-53, 266

strongest party (1923), 49

Tom and Cimmie popular in, 54-56, 57-58, 80, 81-83

Tom on National Executive Council, 91

party workers at Savehay Farm, 99-100

puritanism in, 112-13

Tom's growing disillusionment with, 112-14, 266

in 1929 general election, 113, 120

Tom and PLP, 146-47, 149

Tom at Llandudno Conference, 166, 167-69